THE
SWORD
OF
KAIGEN

A Theonite War Story

M. L. WANG

www.mlwangbooks.com

ISBN: 1720193869
ISBN-13: 9781720193869

For Grandma Wang
whose grave is marked by trees

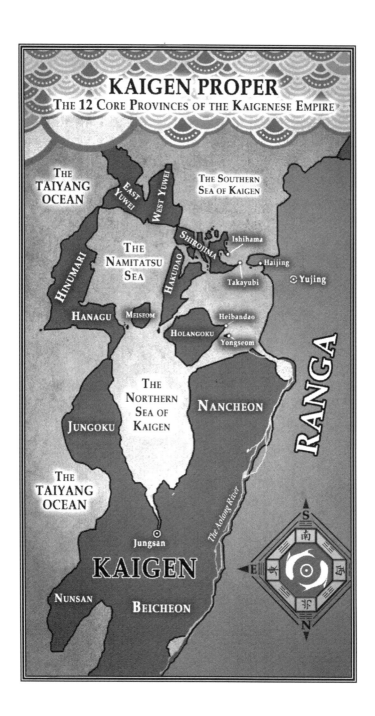

THEOTYPES

THEONITES are Duna's original elemental superhumans, who acquired their abilities toward the beginning of the human race

SUB-THEONITES acquired their abilities later in human history

TAJAKA

a theonite with the ability to control FIRE

FONYAKA

a theonite with the ability to control AIR

JIJAKA

a theonite with the ability to control WATER

FANKATIGI

a sub-theonite with enhanced STRENGTH

LITTIGI

a sub-theonite with the ability to control LIGHT

SONDATIGI

a sub-theonite with the ability to control SOUND

ADYN

a human with no enhanced strength or abilities

KAFONU

JASELI

The Kafo of Voices

Historians, musicians, singers, mediators, storytellers, political advisors

FINA

The Falleke's Kafo

Religious leaders

MANGA KORO

The Kafo of Queens & Kings

Political & military leaders

KELE KORO

The Common Kafo

Farmers, soldiers, merchants, hunters, doctors, anyone not tied by blood to another kafo

SENKULI

The Kafo of Glass

Artisans & craftsmen specializing in glasswork

NUMU

The Smith's Kafo

Craftsmen, architects, artists, artisans, engineers, traditionally specializing in metal-working

BOOKS FROM THE WORLD OF DUNA

Theonite: Planet Adyn

Theonite: Orbit

Theonite: City of Ghosts

The Sword of Kaigen

CONTENTS

1. THE NORTHERNER 1

2. THE MIST 22

3. THE ROOF 47

4. THE WARRIOR 62

5. THE FORGE 79

6. THE PAST 98

7. THE SUN 138

8. THE LETTER 164

9. THE FIGHT 179

10. THE REASON 190

11. THE PATRIARCH 203

12. THE RANGANESE 229

13. THE DRAGON 249

14. THE SWORD 274

15. THE KILLERS 292

16. THE SOUL 306

17. THE END   321

18. THE SHELTER   328

19. THE LANTERN   341

20. THE LAST TIME   362

21. THE STORMLORD   382

22. THE SOLDIERS   407

23. THE RIPTIDE   414

24. THE EMPIRE   433

25. THE GODS   443

26. THE SPIRIT   451

27. THE DUEL   470

28. THE STRANGER   495

29. THE APPRENTICE   521

30. THE FUTURE   538

31. ROBIN   553

    CAST OF CHARACTERS   602

    GLOSSARY   610

THE
SWORD
OF
KAIGEN

A Theonite War Story

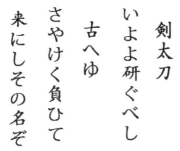

剣太刀
いよよ研ぐべし
古へゆ
さやけく負ひて
来にしその名ぞ

Now the name you bear
*   must be honed to a bright edge—*
for like a great sword
*   it has come to us in splendor*
*   from an age long ago.*

— Ōtomo no Yakamochi, *The Manyōshū*
(translation by Steven D. Carter)

1

THE NORTHERNER

Mt. Takayubi, Kusanagi Peninsula
Shirojima Province
The Kaigenese Empire
Planet Duna
5369 y. s. p.

It was a harrowing climb to the high school. Eight hundred twenty-one steps. Mamoru had counted one time on his way up—no easy feat while focusing on not toppling off the side of a mountain. For most fourteen-year-old fighters, the winding way up to the school was a true test of nerve and agility, but Mamoru, with his springy legs and boundless energy, woke each morning looking forward to the challenge.

"Mamoru!" his friends panted from the steps far below him. "Not so fast!"

Itsuki and Yuuta had no choice but to take the steep path to the school because they lived in the western village, further down the mountain. Mamoru's family compound was built high enough that he could have taken an easier way if he chose, but Matsudas weren't known for taking the easy way to anything. He rose every day before dawn, amid the chanting of crickets, so he could make the loop down the mountain toward the western village and tackle the steep climb with his friends.

"You two are too slow!" Mamoru called back. "We don't want to be late!"

"We're not going to be late," Itsuki heaved in exasperation from the mist below. "Just wait up! Please!"

"Fine, fine." Mamoru lowered himself to the rock ledge and sat, letting his feet hang over the edge.

It had still been dark when the three boys began their climb, but by now, morning had seeped through the veil of fog to touch the rock face with its pale brushstrokes. It was rarely possible to see the base of the mountain from the Kumono steps. Beneath Mamoru's dangling legs, there was only mist, rolling in slow waves against the cliff side, growing gradually lighter with the sunrise.

The moment Itsuki and Yuuta dragged themselves over the ridge where Mamoru was perched, he grinned and bounced to his feet.

"Finally!" he said. "Are you two ready to keep up now?"

"Are you kidding?" Yuuta gasped, doubling over to catch his breath.

"You're a monster!" Itsuki groaned.

Mamoru slapped each of them on the back. "I'll wait for you at the school," he said cheerfully and took off up the mountain.

His toes knew each crevice, each jutting rock, and he took the steepest part of the path in swift, confident bounds, skipping six steps at a time. He had just rounded the last curve when his feet slowed. There was a figure hunched over in the fog up ahead, a boy clinging hard to the rock wall as he gasped for breath. Mamoru wouldn't have thought much of it—there were dozens of students who climbed these steps each morning—but this boy's clothing wasn't right. Instead of Kumono blue, he wore a modern-looking black uniform Mamoru had never seen before.

"Good morning," Mamoru said, approaching slowly, so as not to startle the newcomer off the edge.

"Morning." The boy raised a hand in greeting before putting it to his chest, still breathing hard. He had a heavy accent.

"Are you…" Mamoru started and then switched to Kaigengua, the imperial standard. *"Are you a transfer student?"*

The boy nodded. *"I'm Kwang Chul-hee. Nice to meet you."*

A northern name. This boy hadn't just transferred from a neighboring province; he had come from a long way away. His uniform was the kind worn in the big cities on the Jungsan Peninsula, with its Yammanka-style cut and military bogolan patterns.

"Matsuda Mamoru," Mamoru introduced himself, bowing.

"Matsuda Mamoru…" the boy repeated. *"How much farther is it to your damn school?"*

"You're almost there," Mamoru laughed. "I can walk with you the rest of the way."

"I'm not afraid I'll get lost." Kwang looked vaguely exasperated. *"I'm afraid I'll fall off the edge."*

"No one's ever died falling from the steps." Below the mist, there was a spring-fed lake that never froze waiting to catch clumsy students who lost their footing.

"That's what I heard," Kwang said, *"but I bet it still hurts."*

"It does." One time, in his first year, Mamoru had jumped from the steps to see what it felt like to fly. He had regretted the decision deeply when he hit the surface tension of the lake, but he would never forget the feeling of the wind roaring around him, so ferocious it started to feel like ocean.

"But don't worry," Mamoru reassured the boy. *"I've climbed these steps a hundred times. I know where the rough places are, so if you miss a step, I'll catch you."*

"You're that fast?" Kwang didn't look convinced. Mamoru didn't mind. Let him think what he wanted.

"Speed is valued in this village," Mamoru said by way of explanation. *"We're all swordsmen here."*

"I see that." Kwang nodded at the wooden practice sword sticking out of Mamoru's schoolbag.

"We can fight empty-handed too," Mamoru assured him, *"but traditional swordplay is the preferred fighting style."*

"You any good at it?"

"I'm a Matsuda."

"I don't know what that means."

"It means 'yes,'" Mamoru said. *"And what fighting style is popular in your region?"* he asked, curious about what kind of warrior this boy was.

"What fighting style?" Kwang raised his eyebrows. *"Video games."*

Mamoru laughed. *"We don't play many of those here."*

"Why not? You do have info-com devices, don't you?"

Mamoru shook his head.

"What?" Kwang looked stunned.

"Well, the mayor has one, I think. We're a fairly traditional village."

"Yeah, I noticed."

Itsuki and Yuuta caught up to the pair on the last stretch of stairs, and the western village boys introduced themselves.

"I'm Mizumaki Itsuki," Itsuki said, unthinkingly using the Shirojima Dialect the boys all spoke with each other. "This is Yukino Yuuta."

"Oh. I-I'm Kwang Chul-hee," Kwang said in a valiant attempt at a Shirojima Dialect greeting. "Yoroshiku onegashimasu."

"You mean 'o-ne-ga-i'," Mamoru corrected him. "Onegaishimasu. And you don't really pronounce the 'su' part unless you're a little kid."

"Oh."

"Don't worry," Mamoru said. *"A lot of the classes are taught in Kaigengua."* That was standard across the Empire.

By the time they reached the school, the city boy was out of breath again. The stately pillars were the first part of the building that came into view through the mist, their black finish slick with condensation, followed by the curving clay-tiled roof. Kumono Academy was built into the rock face, its inner structures carved right out of the mountain. The intricate wood and lacquer front of the building was supported by a network of pillars and beams that creaked in high winds but had held the structure in place for a hundred years.

Kwang paused at the front steps, clinging to a carved wooden railing for support, looking like he might empty his stomach into the mists below.

"Why would you build a school in a place like this?" he said in horror.

"Kumono wasn't actually built to be a school," Yuuta said. *"It used to be a monastery."*

"Oh. That explains the decor," Kwang said, eyeing the fearsome statues of Ryuhon Falleya saints standing guard at the doors.

"The place was left vacant after the fina monks built the new temple, further down the mountain in the western village," Yuuta said.

"And they decided it was a good place for a school?" Kwang said, incredulous.

"Well, Kumono is Takayubi's elite koro school," Mamoru explained as the boys mounted the front steps into the genkan. *"The village officials thought it would be appropriate if you had to be an elite koro to reach it."*

The smell of incense had never quite left the wooden halls of Kumono. The familiar scent enveloped the four boys as they joined the sleepy gaggle of students at the shoe shelves and knelt to undo the fastenings on their tabi. As Kwang, still shaking, fumbled with his shoes, Mamoru's gaze was drawn to the northern boy's feet. Instead of the two-toed tabi the Takayubi boys wore, Kwang was sporting bulky, shiny Yammanka-style shoes that fastened with magnets around the ankles. Mamoru had seen shoes like that on TV, but no one in Shirojima had ever owned a pair.

"I don't know how I'm supposed to make that climb every morning," Kwang said, cramming his oversized shoes into an open slot.

"If you want an easier walk, you could always transfer to

5

Takayubi Public High School," Itsuki suggested.

"Oh, no," Kwang laughed. *"My father won't have me in any school but the best in the region whenever we move to a new place."*

"You move often?" Yuuta asked.

Kwang nodded. *"My father's a traveling representative for a communications company, so we move all over the country, sometimes outside it."*

"Outside it?" Itsuki said in astonishment. *"Where have you been?"*

"Um…" Kwang took a moment to think. *"I've been to Yamma a few times, Kudazwe a few times, Sizwe once, for a few weeks—"*

"Boys," a voice said, "if your shoes are put away, you should be in your classrooms."

"Yukino Sensei!" Itsuki exclaimed as he and the other boys bowed. "We're sorry."

Yukino Dai was the best swordsman in the province—or the second best, depending on who you asked. There was debate about whether he could beat Mamoru's father, Matsuda Takeru, or his uncle, Matsuda Takashi in a duel. The Yukino clan had none of the Matsudas' secret bloodline techniques, but Yukino Dai was about as good as a man could get with a naked blade.

"We have a new student with us, Sensei," Mamoru explained. "He isn't sure where he's supposed to go."

"I see." Yukino Sensei looked past Mamoru at the new boy, who stuck out starkly in his bogolan uniform. "You must be Kwang Chul-hee?"

"Yes, sir." Kwang bowed and said very carefully, "Yoroshiku onegaishimasu."

The swordmaster visibly suppressed a smile at Kwang's pronunciation. *"Welcome to Kumono Academy,"* he said in Kaigengua. *"How was your first time up the steps?"*

"Super easy, sir," Kwang said, despite the obvious flush in his cheeks. *"I can't wait to do it again."*

Yukino Sensei's face broke into an open smile. *"I like you,*

Kwang," he said. *"You can follow me to the office to pick up your schedule.* Matsuda-san." He turned to Mamoru. "Run to the storeroom and find a uniform for Kwang-san. Your size should do."

"Yes, sir." Mamoru bowed and hurried to do as he was told.

He moved quickly through the narrow halls to the supply closet, his legs absorbing the shifting of the floor as the school swayed on its posts.

"Morning, Mamoru-kun!" other boys greeted him.

"Good morning, Matsuda-senpai!"

He made sure he gave each of them a bow and a smile as he went.

There was no lock on the storeroom door. Kumono was a small enough high school—Takayubi was a small enough *town*—that no one worried much about theft. Where would a thief even keep a stolen item? Where would he try to sell it? Everyone here knew everyone.

Mamoru had to clamber over a box of broken practice swords and a stack of dummies to reach the shelf of spare uniforms. Keeping his footing became a challenge as the school creaked and the dummies shifted beneath him, but what kind of Matsuda would he be if a little breeze threw him off balance? With the next gust of wind, the stack of dummies tipped toward the shelves. Mamoru leaned forward, snatched a size-four uniform from its shelf, and sprang from the top of the stack to the floor before anything fell.

After double checking the uniform size, he hurried to the office to meet Yukino Sensei and Kwang.

"Thank you, Matsuda-san," Yukino Sensei said as Mamoru handed the new boy his uniform. "Now, Kwang-san is going to be entering our second-year class, which means his schedule is identical to yours." Mamoru nodded. Being the more exclusive of two high schools in a small town, Kumono Academy had only one class per grade level. "I'm putting him in your charge. You'll look after him for today."

"Yes, Sensei."

7

"Start by showing him where the changing rooms are. And be quick. You boys only have a few *siiranu* before classes start."

Kwang took longer than Mamoru would have thought to change into his new uniform, and Mamoru found himself pacing impatiently on the creaking floor before the changing room door. When Kwang finally emerged, he was still fiddling with the waist tie as if he had all the time in the world.

"This is so funny," he said, shaking out the uniform's broad blue sleeves. *"I feel like I'm in one of those old samurai movies."*

"Well, for us, this is just a normal school uniform," Mamoru said, frowning.

"This place is weird." Kwang ran his hands over his sleeves, looking at the ornately-carved temple halls around him. *"It's like I stepped through a portal back in time."*

Mamoru felt annoyance bristle up inside him. He wasn't sure why. He opened his mouth to say something but before he could come up with the right words, the old temple bell sounded. The single ancient note reverberated through the hall, as it had done for a hundred years, calling the boys of Takayubi to class.

MISAKI

"Healthy, just like his brothers?" Hyori asked, leaning in to put a hand on the infant's head.

"Yes," Misaki said, "if a little smaller."

"I can't believe this one is your fourth!"

"Yes," Misaki sighed, trying to make her tone light, despite the heaviness in her limbs, "hopefully the last."

"No!" Hyori exclaimed, scandalized. "How can you say that?"

"Yeah, you're doing so well, why stop now?" Setsuko joked, shifting her own baby to her other hip to nudge her sister-in-law.

"Seriously, Misaki-san!" Hyori said with an ache in her voice. "You're so lucky!"

"Mmm." Misaki nodded, forcing a smile. "I suppose I am."

And Misaki *was* lucky. By Shirojima standards, she was the luckiest woman in the world. Fresh out of theonite academy, she had been fortunate enough to marry into Shirojima's greatest warrior family. And following that, she had been blessed with son, after son, after son. There had been a rough space of years, after Mamoru, when she hadn't been able to give birth, but five years ago, she had borne Hiroshi, then soon after him, Nagasa, and now Izumo. Four healthy boys, every Shirojima woman's dream.

"May I?" Hyori asked, an eager sparkle in her eyes.

"Of course." Careful to support the infant's unsteady head, Misaki handed Izumo to her friend.

"You're looking much better," Setsuko commented as Hyori gushed and cooed over an oblivious Izumo.

"I *feel* much better," Misaki said, rolling her shoulders, "at least now that you're here. I missed you two."

Normally, the three housewives spent the majority of their waking hours together, letting their little ones play together, passing around the babies as they did their shopping, laundry, cooking, and sewing. Since giving birth to Izumo, Misaki had been too exhausted to do much except look after the infant, and Takeru had insisted that she wasn't well enough for company. This was the first time Izumo was meeting Hyori and his aunt, Setsuko. He could be a fussy baby, but he didn't seem bothered by the new faces—if he could even make out facial features. He was still so young that his eyes hadn't found their focus yet.

"Four sons," Setsuko mused, burping her own daughter, Ayumi, on her shoulder. "I don't know how I'm ever supposed to catch up to that. Although, look at these chunky little arms! Ayumi could almost pass for a boy. Perhaps I'll start dressing her in boy clothes and just pretend I've given my husband a healthy son." Baby Ayumi, only two months Izumo's senior, was nearly twice his size. "What do you think?"

"I think she's perfect the way she is." Misaki was being honest, but of course, the other two women laughed.

9

When she was younger, Misaki had always pictured herself having daughters. She had enjoyed the vague fantasy of raising powerful, forward-thinking young women with the courage to amount to more than their mother, but it was just that: a fantasy. Misaki had long since let go of the idea that she could raise her children the way she wanted—or that they were even *her* children at all. Her sons were Matsudas first and foremost. Their sole purpose was to grow to be powerful warriors, like their father before them, and his father before him. They belonged to the Matsuda house, as she did.

"I'm being serious," Misaki insisted as Hyori passed baby Izumo back to her. "I would be happy to have a daughter." With a daughter, at least, she might be allowed to pass some of herself on to her own child.

"Easy for you to say when you're on your fourth son!" Hyori said indignantly.

Setsuko hummed in agreement. "You're going to have to tell us how you pulled it off."

"I want to know how she pulled it off and kept her figure!" Hyori said.

"Oh, shut up you!" Setsuko swatted Hyori on the back of the head. "The prettiest little slip of a woman in the village doesn't get to say things like that!"

"Setsuko-san," Hyori said, blushing furiously. "I'm not the prettiest—"

"Shut your pretty mouth, Hyori-chan," Misaki said fondly. "You don't need to play dumb with us. We like you better when you're smart."

Hyori was rarely smart, but Misaki thought she might as well keep encouraging her. Popular wisdom said that a woman as pretty as Hyori didn't need to be smart. 'Pretty' wasn't even the right word to describe Hyori, in Misaki's opinion. The woman was achingly, devastatingly beautiful, with an artless smile and eyes as soft as melting snow. Many Shirojima women were 'pretty,' but Hyori was the kind of legendary beauty men went to war for.

"Couple of pure-bred princesses, both of you!" Setsuko said, looking from Hyori to Misaki in exasperation. "With your smooth skin, and your teensy little waists. Don't you sit there and complain about your weight to me when I could fit the two of you inside me."

Ironically, it was Setsuko who Misaki considered to be the most beautiful woman on the mountain. When the fisherman's daughter had married into the Matsuda family, she had brought with her all the crude shameless joy Misaki missed so much from her life before Takayubi. Her sort of beauty had little to do with physical attributes. It wasn't the short hair cropped about her ears; it was the way she shook it out and sighed in pleasure when she was enjoying the weather. It wasn't her big eyes with their dark lashes; it was the way they crinkled up with mirth at the smallest things. It wasn't her bulky frame; it was the way she threw it around with careless confidence in a world where everyone, ladies and swordsmen alike, stepped so lightly.

Before they were sisters-in-law, Misaki had known Setsuko—as everyone had known her—as the fresh fish lady. Her voice could be heard on any trip to the markets at the base of the mountain. "Fresh fish! Get your fresh fish!"

It wasn't a glamorous job, but Setsuko was the kind of person who could be at her most charming elbows deep in fish guts, with loose strands of hair sticking to the sweat on her temples. Misaki had to imagine that many people had fallen in love with the stocky fisherwoman with the carefree grin, but it was Matsuda Takashi, the first son of the highest house in the region, who fell the hardest.

Misaki had first suspected the morning her brother-in-law stopped her on her way out the door and said, "You look tired, Misaki. I can go to the market for you."

For a moment, Misaki had only managed to blink up at him. "You want to go to the market?" she said blankly. Shopping for meals wasn't something a man was supposed to do—certainly not a nobleman like Takashi.

"I—uhh—I have business to attend to at the base of the

mountain anyway." Takashi didn't meet her eyes.

"I'm feeling fine, Nii-sama," Misaki assured him. "If you have important business, you shouldn't trouble yourself—"

"It's no trouble," Takashi said and Misaki realized that he was speaking in a low voice, as if worried that his father and brother would hear from inside the house. "Just give me a list of what you need."

"Alright." Confused as she was, Misaki wasn't going to argue.

"And Misaki?"

"Yes, Nii-sama?"

"If you could maybe… not mention this to my father?"

Misaki's suspicions were confirmed when Takashi returned late that afternoon and deposited eight bulging baskets of fish in her kitchen. No man but a Matsuda could have carried such a load all the way up the mountain. As strong as Takashi was, the effort had lent his face a bright flush.

"Fish," he said with a drunken smile that ill became the son of a warrior family. "You said you wanted fresh fish, right? I'm sorry. I might have missed the other things on your list."

"Um…" Misaki looked in horror at the heaping baskets on her kitchen floor. "I'm sorry, Nii-sama, what do you want me to do with all this?" The Matsuda compound didn't have freezer space to store this many fish. "Are you expecting company?"

"What? No. Why? Is this too much?"

Misaki looked up at her brother-in-law, incredulous and more than a little annoyed. *If you like the girl, just tell her straight,* she wanted to snap. *Don't blow the family fortune on fish!* But it wasn't her place to question him, and it wasn't that simple. A nobleman couldn't just propose to a fisherman's daughter and whisk her away up the mountain. Not in Takayubi. Peasants with no bloodlines to protect might marry whoever they liked, but men and women of noble houses didn't have that luxury.

"Is it too much?" Takashi asked again, still dazed and so much giddier than usual, like a love-struck teenager—like Misaki had been once. The thought pierced her chest with a sudden and unexpected pain.

Be careful, big brother, she wanted to say then*, be careful how hard you love what you know you can't have,* but that also was not her place.

So instead, she pursed her lips, looked down at the fish and said, "I'll think of something."

"Good," Takashi said, though he didn't really seem to see or hear her. "Good," and he wandered out of the kitchen, still smiling. On his way out, he passed Takeru, who regarded his older brother with the same sour expression he took on whenever he saw someone happy.

"Is my brother ill?" he asked when Takashi had gone.

No, Misaki thought sadly*, just doomed to misery.*

But Takashi had been lucky—or rather, just the right combination of lucky, reckless, and clever. He had struggled, and schemed, and spun excuses, and somehow managed to hold off marriage until his tyrannical father had passed away and there were no Matsuda elders left to tell him what to do. Then, instead of marrying a pure-blooded noblewoman of his family's choosing, Takashi married the woman he loved—the peasant with the loud laugh who sold him his fresh fish.

Takashi would never know, but in marrying Setsuko, he might have saved Misaki's life. The fisherwoman had moved into the Matsuda compound shortly after Misaki's second miscarriage, a loud burst of color when everything seemed gray.

"You haven't smiled the whole time I've been here," Setsuko had observed as Misaki helped her unpack the few belongings she had brought with her. "Why so glum, little sister?"

Misaki was two years older than her new sister-in-law, but Setsuko had married the older of the two Matsuda brothers, and in this world, the man's status was the only thing that mattered.

"I'm sorry," Misaki murmured. It had become her default response to anything over the past few years.

Setsuko planted her hands on her hips. "That's not good enough."

"Excuse me?"

"Look, you and I are going to be here in this house together until we're both wrinkly old hags with all our teeth falling out. I don't know about you, but I don't want to spend the next forty years with a woman who doesn't know how to smile."

"I know how to smile." There had been a time Misaki had been accused of smiling too much, but over the years, Takayubi had worn away at her, turning her into this quivering, brittle thing, afraid the sound of her own voice might shake her to pieces if she spoke too loud.

"*I've* never seen you smile," Setsuko said skeptically. "What's wrong with you? Are the corners of your mouth busted or something?"

No. It was the inside of Misaki that was broken. "I miscarried," she said bluntly, "twice."

"Oh." Setsuko pulled up short, her joking demeanor evaporating in an instant. "Oh, sweetheart… I'm so sorry. I didn't know."

Misaki thought she might crumble under the concern in Setsuko's eyes. The years had hardened her against her father-in-law's cruelty and her husband's indifference, but she had no armor against that honest gaze.

"You really wanted those children?" Setsuko asked, and the softness of her voice stripped Misaki bare.

"I don't know," she replied, stunned—and slightly horrified—at her own honesty. She waited, shoulders tense, for Setsuko to berate her for her selfishness, to blame her for losing the children, to tell her she was lucky to have such a tolerant husband, like everyone else did.

Setsuko only said, "Oh. Then why are you so sad?"

"I…" When, Misaki wondered, had her voice gotten so small? When had she become afraid to put a single thought into words? "I'm here to give my husband sons. I don't want to be a disappointment."

"You're not a disappointment."

"What?"

"I said, you're not a disappointment. You couldn't be if you tried." It had been a long time since someone had spoken of Misaki with that sort of simple confidence—taking for granted that she was right and good. She stared at Setsuko for a moment and realized that she had forgotten how to respond to this type of kindness. It was something she thought she had left behind nine years ago.

"Look at you," Setsuko continued earnestly. "What could a man possibly complain about? You're sweet, you're beautiful, I get the feeling you're pretty smart too, you've already borne a perfect son, and my husband tells me your cooking is to die for."

"That's nice of him to say. I do my best."

"You like cooking?"

Misaki nodded.

"Well, that's good because I'm a lousy cook."

"I'm sure that's not true," Misaki said politely.

"Oh, it is. Ask anyone who's ever eaten one of my meals. Now, why don't you make yourself useful and teach me to cook something for my fancy husband and his refined Matsuda palate."

"Matsuda palates aren't that refined," Misaki said. "Your husband likes the same food as everyone else."

"Not when I make it, he won't. Why do you think I was always the one hauling the fish to market instead of staying home to help in the kitchen? My family tried my cooking exactly once and then decided they'd rather live."

Misaki felt her face split into a smile, and for the first time in an age, she giggled.

"There's that smile!" Setsuko exclaimed, triumphant. "And look at that!" She poked a finger into Misaki's cheek.

"What?" Misaki put her hand to her face, thinking maybe there was a piece of rice stuck to it.

"You've got dimples!"

Misaki had never had any sisters, but from that day, she decided that she was glad to call Setsuko her sister. Their husbands carried with them all the tension that accompanied growing up as brothers, a first and second son competing for their father's approval, but the sisters-in-law never let any of that bad nyama in between them.

After Misaki had lived in the Matsuda compound almost a decade, it was Setsuko who made its cold halls feel like a home. When Misaki was in pain, it was Setsuko who went to the western village to buy her remedies. When she got lost in the undertow of her thoughts, it was Setsuko who pulled her back with a joke. A few months after Hiroshi was born, it was Setsuko who said, "That pretty little thing who lives in the Yukino compound. Who's she?"

"You mean Hyori?" Misaki said. "She's Yukino Dai's wife."

"Yukino who?"

"Yukino Dai," Misaki said, "the house patriarch, the Lightning Swordsman."

"I thought the Yukino patriarch was Yukino Ryosuke."

"It is—it *was*. He passed away a little while before you moved here, while you were getting ready for your wedding. Didn't you know?"

"No!" Setsuko exclaimed. "Nami, I haven't been in on the market gossip! That's where I used to get all my news. Gods in the Deep, I don't know how you noblewomen live cooped up like this!"

"You're a noblewoman too now," Misaki reminded her.

Setsuko made a dismissive, "Bah!" waving her hand.

"Yukino Ryosuke's funeral was just before you got married. Someone had to assume control of the estate, and the Yukinos' oldest son didn't want to move his family all the way back from Jungsan. Dai-san is the second son, so he moved in with his wife."

"Does he keep his wife cloistered or some kind of weird noble thing like that?" Setsuko asked. "How come we never see her?"

"I think she spends most of her time caring for Dai-san's mother. She's old and very ill, so I imagine it takes up most of her time."

"That must get lonely," Setsuko said. "We should go visit tomorrow."

That was how the sisters-in-law had met Hyori. Now, five years later, the three women were inseparable.

Hyori and Setsuko were still teasing one another about their waistlines when there was a tug at Misaki's arm. She looked down to find her third son, two-year-old Nagasa, clutching the flowered sleeve of her kimono.

"See?" he asked in his tiny voice. "See baby?" It was his favorite question since Izumo had arrived.

"Of course," Misaki said, kneeling on the tatami to place Izumo on her lap before Nagasa. "Remember to be gentle, Naga-kun. He's still very small."

"Hold baby?" Nagasa asked hopefully, holding out his arms.

"Oh, isn't he the cutest thing!" Hyori squealed.

"I'm going to hold him for now," Misaki told Nagasa gently. "You concentrate on growing a few koyinu taller and we'll talk."

"Isn't your older brother around?" Hyori asked, stooping so that she was at eye-level with the two-year-old. "Why don't you go play with him?"

"Hiro-nii-san gone," Nagasa pouted.

"Oh? Where did he go?" Hyori asked, looking at Misaki.

"Hiro-kun is at the elementary school dojo," Misaki said, jouncing Izumo on her knees.

"That's right," Hyori said. "He likes to watch the older boys train, doesn't he?"

"He's actually training *with* them now," Misaki said, "started as soon as he was big enough to lift the practice sword."

"Isn't he only five?" Hyori said in astonishment. "I thought that was against policy."

"The instructors made an exception," Misaki said. No five-year-old had ever been admitted to the elementary school's beginner sword class, but Misaki's second son, Hiroshi, was not like other five-year-olds.

"He's a serious little boy, isn't he?" Setsuko said. "Like a miniature version of his father. It's a little scary."

"How come you can't be more like that, hmm, Ryo-kun?" Hyori prodded her own son, Ryota. She said it in a joking voice, but there was a distinct undercurrent of seriousness.

"Well, he's still very young," Misaki said. "Ryota-kun, how old are you?"

"Four," Ryota said proudly.

"There, you see," Misaki said. "You may be a little swordsman like Hiroshi by next year. Who knows?"

"I *am* a sword-man!" Ryota announced, brandishing his toy katana. "I'm the best sword-man in the world!"

"Is that so?" Misaki couldn't help but tease.

"I challenge you to a duel!" Ryota shouted, seemingly to no one in particular, probably quoting a cartoon he had seen. "I challenge you to a duel!"

On a whim, Misaki pooled her jiya, pulled the surrounding water molecules to her hand and froze them into a makeshift sword— well, more of a blunt icicle than a sword—the perfect size for combat with a four-year-old.

"I accept!" she announced.

"Misaki-san, what are you doing?" Hyori asked.

"Fight me, Yukino Ryota!" Misaki intoned in her best cartoon villain voice, shifting Izumo over to her left hip where he was out of danger.

"Ryo-kun, don't," Hyori warned. "Misaki-san is a lady." But the boy, overcome with joy at having a playmate, was already whaling away at Misaki with his wooden sword.

Misaki's arm moved on an almost forgotten impulse. In two moves, she had disarmed little Ryota. With another flick of her play-sword, she had swept the boy off his feet. He landed on his back with a hard 'oof!' and Misaki pointed the icicle down at his chest.

"I am victorious!" she said dramatically. "Admit defeat or I shall tickle you!"

"Oh no!" Ryota shrieked, and scrambled away, giggling. "No, no!"

And Misaki couldn't help it. She hiked up her kimono and ran after him. The quick little boy probably hadn't expected a refined housewife like Misaki to catch up to him in three strides. He screamed when she scooped him up around the middle with one arm, and laughed, and laughed as she took him to the floor with tickles.

"Misaki-san, what are you doing?" Hyori cried, seemingly unsure whether to be scandalized or amused.

"Don't worry, Hyori-chan," Setsuko said. "This is something Misaki does every once in a while, when she's in a happy mood." What Setsuko didn't understand was that this unfamiliar creature— this fearless, ridiculous woman who ran fast and played with swords—was an echo from a time when Misaki's whole life had been happy.

Having recovered from the tickle attack, a giggling Ryota picked up his sword and came at Misaki again. This time, she gave some ground, letting the boy pick up on her rhythm and get a few good swings in before she disarmed him again.

"I'm afraid Ryo-kun is a ways away from being like Hiro-kun," Hyori laughed, "if he loses to a woman."

Misaki could have mentioned that losing a fight against her was nothing for a young boy—or even a man—to be ashamed of, but that was a part of herself she didn't talk about anymore. Takeru had forbidden it.

"Me too!" Nagasa squealed, getting his own play sword and bouncing up and down. "Kaa-chan, me too!"

"Boys, careful of the baby!" Hyori warned as Ryota and Nagasa charged Misaki at the same time.

But Misaki was more than capable of fending off two children with her right arm while keeping her infant cradled comfortably in her left. It was only when the noise became too much for Izumo that he started crying and Misaki had to call off the duel.

"Sorry, boys," she said, turning her icicle sword to vapor with a wave of her hand. "That's all for today. I yield. Good fight, Yukino-dono." She ruffled Ryota's hair. "Matsuda-dono." She chucked Nagasa under the chin. "We'll have to duel again sometime."

Smiling, she retreated to the couch to comfort Izumo.

"Oh no!" Nagasa dropped his play sword and followed his mother to the couch with a look of genuine worry. "Baby crying!"

"He's not upset with you, Naga-kun," Misaki assured the two-year-old. "He's just hungry."

Tugging the front of her kimono open, Misaki maneuvered the bawling infant inside and gave him her breast. The squalling stopped almost immediately.

"You can't be too scared of a little carnage," Setsuko teased, prodding Izumo's foot. "After all, you've got to grow up to be a great warrior, just like your grumpy father."

"Hey now, Setsuko," Misaki said with a smile. "Don't make fun of my grumpy husband. He works hard to keep that frown plastered on his face all day."

"Mattaku!" Hyori exclaimed with an annoyed 'tsk' of her tongue. "Do you know how happy Dai would be if I could give him four good sons. I tell you, he would smile all day if he had a son like your Mamoru."

"If it's any consolation, I think Mamoru would be just as happy to have Dai-san as his father," Misaki said.

"Oh yeah?" Hyori perked up.

"You didn't know? Dai-san is his favorite instructor he's ever had, for sword and jiya."

That sent Hyori into a fit of giggles. "Misaki-san, don't tease!"

"I'm not teasing," Misaki said honestly.

"His father is Matsuda Takeru," Hyori said, "master of the Whispering Blade, the greatest swordsman on the mountain."

"And a terrible teacher," Misaki said. "The extent of his instruction is to cross his arms, and glower, and say, 'Bad. Do it again.'" She pulled her face into a scowl, and plunged to the lower limit of her vocal register to affect her husband's clipped monotone. "Still bad. Do it again. Listen. Get it right or I'll gut you, you disgrace. What do you mean you don't understand? What's to understand? Just do it *right*."

"Stop! Stop!" Setsuko begged, clutching her stomach with laughter. "Your Takeru impression is too good! I'm going to die!"

"How do you even get your voice that low?" Hyori laughed.

"What? You mean like this?" Misaki thundered. "Silly woman, you couldn't possibly understand such matters. My manliness does not allow for human inflection."

The trio plunged into another fit of giggles, and because their mothers were laughing, Ryota and Nagasa ended up laughing too.

Misaki had spent years trying to belong with these people. They weren't like her friends from her school days. They weren't scrappy visionaries like Elleen, or geniuses like Koli, or unstoppable forces of energy like Robin. They would never change the world, nor understand why someone would want to, but they loved her. She could laugh with them, and that was enough.

There were days Misaki could convince herself that it was enough.

2

THE MIST

The training arena was a broad shelf of rock that the monks used to use for exercise and meditation. According to legend, the flattened half-moon had been hewn out of the mountainside by the Whispering Blades of Matsudas long dead—Mamoru's ancestors.

"Perfect weather for today's practice!" Yukino Sensei bellowed over the wind whipping across the arena. "Now we'll have a true test of accuracy!"

Mamoru heard teeth chattering and turned to see Kwang with his arms pulled all the way into his uniform.

"Is it always so cold up here?" The new boy shivered.

Mamoru almost laughed. *"Wait until the winter."*

Human-sized bundles of straw stood at intervals across the arena, frozen to the rock by Yukino Sensei's ice. Tied to each bundle was a coarse cloth sign with a number painted on it. Mamoru's jiya was already itching to surge into action as Yukino Sensei raised his voice above the wind to explain the day's exercise.

"For most of this week, we've been working on forming aerodynamic ice projectiles. Now, you boys still have a great deal of work to do on that front," Yukino Sensei said, stopping in front of Mamoru to give him a pointed look, "especially those of you who hope to one day master a certain bloodline technique."

Mamoru gave his teacher a small, determined nod, and Yukino Sensei turned to address the entire class. "Despite your sub-par forming work, I'm going to cut you all some slack so that we can train the next technique. Today, I've made your projectiles for you." He gestured to a stack of perfectly-formed ice spears, each one three strides long, with a fine point at one end and a broad base at the other to allow for a strong launch.

"What bloodline technique is he talking about?" Kwang asked Mamoru as Yukino Sensei paced further down the line of boys. "What does your family do that's so special?"

"You're joking, right?" Itsuki interjected with an incredulous look at Kwang. *"Mamoru is a* Matsuda."

No understanding registered on Kwang's face. *"Yes?"*

"The Matsudas are the masters of the Whispering Blade," Itsuki said. *"You must have heard of the Whispering Blade in the capital."*

"Well—sure—but it's just a myth," Kwang laughed, but when the serious look on Itsuki's face didn't change, his smile faded and he turned to Mamoru with wide eyes. *"Isn't it?"*

Mamoru shrugged. *"Some myths are true."*

"But it's not possible," Kwang protested. *"No jijaka can make ice strong enough to cut through steel!"*

"Some can."

"Are you one of them?" Kwang asked in awe.

Mamoru set his jaw. *"I will be."*

Kwang considered Mamoru, his eyes squinted in thought. *"I don't believe you,"* he said after a moment. *"Even Kusanagi jijakalu can't be that powerful."*

Instead of retorting, Mamoru just nodded toward Yukino Sensei and said, *"Watch."*

The master jijaka had lifted one of the spears from the pile with a gentle gesture of his hand. His two fingers were enough to keep the projectile hovering perfectly still in the air before him as he spoke.

"The strongest tajaka can throw a spear sixteen bounds," Yukino

Sensei bellowed, pointing with his free hand across the arena to the straw dummy painted with the Kaigengua numeral 16. "The best fonyaka can use wind to launch a solid projectile twenty-five bounds." He pointed beyond the first dummy to one farther away labeled with a number 25. "As a jijaka, you can do much more."

Placing a hand against the flattened end of the projectile, Yukino Sensei planted his feet and launched the ice forward. Mamoru had seen Lightning Dai's jiya in action enough times that it no longer set his heart leaping into his throat. But beside him, he heard Kwang gasp.

The spear blasted through the 16-bound dummy, through the 25-bound dummy, all the way to the end of the arena where it stuck into a third dummy marked with a barely discernible number 40.

"Holy Falleke!" Kwang breathed, gawking at the destroyed 16-bound bundle.

"Tajakalu may be able to use their physical strength to throw a projectile," Yukino Sensei said, turning back to his class, "fonyakalu may be able to use their nyama to push against one. Our nyama *is* the projectile. When a weapon is made of ice, we can control it down to the molecule. As jijakalu, we are the only race of theonite who can fight with a solid weapon that is truly an extension of the self."

Yukino Sensei gave each student a stack of projectiles and had them line up across the arena to practice firing at the army of straw targets.

Using his jiya to lift a spear, Mamoru laid his palm against the flat end and let his power rise. The ocean may not have been visible from Kumono Academy, but when Mamoru pooled his jiya in his core, it seemed to reach all the way down the mountain, to the waves that crashed at its base, and deeper than that, into the crushing depths where Mount Takayubi's roots met the seafloor.

Ryuhon tradition claimed that the great families of Kusanagi were descended from the ocean gods who had dwelt in the Sea of Kaigen at the dawn of time. Most people of the peninsula regarded this part of their tradition as more metaphor than fact. Logically, there was no way human beings could be the direct descendants of titanic fish and sea dragons.

But like many Matsudas before him, Mamoru experienced surges of madness, when the feeling of his jiya consumed him. In those moments, he knew that the power rolling through his body was born from the ancient forces that had raised Kaigen from the sea. It was more than faith. It was fact.

The power of gods rose, thunderous, like a wave inside Mamoru, and he rode the swell, moving his body with it. As the wave hit its apex, he sent its full force bursting down his arm, through his open palm, into the ice. The projectile exploded through the air, shooting farther than anyone else's, but it didn't fly straight. It glanced off the stone shelf, breaking its fletching blades, and skidded to a stop off to the side of the 25-bound target. Mamoru frowned and shook out his hands. He was just getting warmed up. With his full power, he would launch the spear so hard that it would have no choice but to go straight through the target.

Letting a new wave of nyama build in his body, Mamoru launched again. This spear managed to clip the 25-bound target, but it wasn't a clean hit, and the ice broke apart instead of penetrating.

"Stop pushing so hard, Matsuda-san," Yukino Sensei said patiently. "You have more than enough power to send a projectile clear across this arena. Relax your shoulders and focus on accuracy over force."

"Yes, Sensei," Mamoru breathed and raised another projectile.

"Slow down." Yukino Sensei reached out and placed his fingertips on the ice, stilling it before Mamoru could raise it level with the target. "Your jiya is too excited; I can feel it roaring every which way inside you. Take a moment to calm it. Focus your energy, then try again."

Mamoru nodded and Yukino Sensei moved down the line to observe the other boys, giving them each a few well-placed pieces of advice. Mamoru's mother had once said that Yukino Dai dealt his words as carefully as he dealt his cuts. It was what made him

25

such a good teacher.

"Don't over-rotate," Yukino Sensei scolded his younger cousin, Yuuta, giving the boy a hard rap on the head with his knuckles. "If you swing through without calculating your point of release, you'll crash your projectile short of its target every time."

"Yes, Sensei." Yuuta rubbed his head and tried again, this time managing to send his spear neatly into the 16-bound target.

Satisfied, Yukino Sensei turned his attention from Yuuta to Kwang, just as the northern newcomer sent his third spear spinning off course to crash to pieces on the rock shelf.

"Hmm." Yukino Sensei frowned at the new student, and Kwang cringed, clearly expecting to be mocked or smacked on the head.

But all Yukino Sensei said was, *"I bet you're very good at the spear-throw."*

"Yes," Kwang said in surprise. *"How did you—"*

"Stop trying to throw with your shoulder. Project from the hip, straight out through your palm, like you're punching a man in the solar plexus."

"Sensei," Itsuki complained from further down the line, "the wind keeps pushing mine off course!"

"These projectiles are made to cut *through* the wind, Mizumaki-san. Again. I want to see."

He paused to watch Itsuki attempt a launch, sending the spear wide.

"Your launch is weak." Yukino Sensei put his hands on Itsuki's shoulders and maneuvered him back into his starting position. "Angle your stance this way. Bend your knees. A little deeper. There."

Having given his jiya time to settle, Mamoru returned his attention to his own task. As usual, Yukino Sensei was right. Mamoru's aim got much better after he relaxed, but even with his projectiles flying straight, he still couldn't seem to get one past the 25-bound target.

"What are you scowling about?" Kwang asked him at one point. "You're shooting way better than everyone else."

Not as well as Yukino Sensei, Mamoru thought but he couldn't say that aloud, so he just clenched his jaw and raised another spear from his stack. Mamoru was almost full grown now, and 'better than everyone else' wasn't good enough. A Matsuda had to be as good as a hundred other jijakalu put together. He had to be the best anyone had ever seen.

In his frustration, Mamoru threw his whole body into the movement, *slamming* the next spear toward its target. The projectile hit the 25-bound target and went through it.

"Falleke!" Kwang exclaimed as Mamoru's projectile slid to a stop several strides beyond the target. *"What was that?"*

Not bothering to respond, Mamoru lifted another projectile from the stack. Using his jiya to keep it hovering at chest height, he backed up a few paces and ran at it. He didn't even put the whole force of his jiya into the launch, but the projectile still managed to penetrate the 25-bound target and burst out the other side.

"What did you just do?" Kwang asked in astonishment.

"Why are we planting?" Mamoru said, looking from the penetrated target to his own feet.

"What?"

"Why are we planting our feet and launching when we could add the power of momentum?"

"Um… come again?"

"The strongest waves start far out at sea."

"Mamoru-kun," Yuuta warned, recognizing the look on his friend's face. "You know what Sensei says about your ideas—"

"I know," Mamoru cut him off, raising another projectile. "Just give me a dinma." He had to try it. He had to.

Locking his jiya into the ice, he threw the projectile high into the air and released. As the projectile started to fall, Mamoru backed up as far as the shelf allowed. He would have to hit the spear on its way down. It would require perfect timing, but timing came naturally to Mamoru.

He gave the spear one last moment to descend and then sprinted at it. On his last step, he launched himself into the air and spun.

His forward momentum combined with the power of the spin and the gravity pulling him earthward. As his body whipped around, he drove his palm into the base of the projectile and launched. The force of a tsunami exploded through his palm.

All anyone saw was a flash of silver before the projectile slammed into the 40-bound target in a spray of straw. Mamoru hit the stone in a crouch and let out his breath. He had done it!

The mountainside rang with the shocked cries of his classmates, then with cheers, as they took in the destroyed 40-bound target. However, when Mamoru's eyes found Yukino Sensei, the swordmaster was not smiling.

"Matsuda!" He roared over the wind, and the class fell silent. "What in the Duna do you think you are doing?"

"Sorry, Sensei." Mamoru tried to look apologetic, but he couldn't quite wipe the smile off his face.

"Get your ego under control. You will do the drill as I instruct, or you will leave my class. Do you understand?"

"Yes, sir."

When the rest of the class finished their excited murmurings and returned to the drill, Mamoru felt Yukino Sensei's fingers dig into his ear, pulling his head back. Stifling an 'ouch,' he let his teacher drag him from the line.

"Sensei!" he started when they were out of earshot of the rest of the class. "I—"

"Mamoru-kun," Yukino Sensei cut him off in a low voice. "There is a reason we begin this drill with both feet on the ground."

"I'm sorry. I—"

"Don't interrupt," the swordmaster said mildly. "I want you to consider for a moment, that if I had the rest of these boys flying and spinning during this exercise, I would have a lot of dead boys. Do you understand?"

"Yes, Sensei," Mamoru said with a biting pang of guilt. He hadn't thought of that; he had been too focused on himself.

"Matsudas are more than flashy fighters," Yukino Sensei said.

"They are leaders, and a leader must think of those around him."

"Yes, Sensei."

"Good." Yukino Sensei released Mamoru's aching ear and raised his hand. Mamoru flinched, expecting to feel the crack of his teacher's knuckles, but the swordmaster just put his hand atop his head.

"Now," he said, "if you are going to launch from a spin, make sure the knee that you lead with stays tucked close to your body through the entire rotation. You lose momentum when you let your leg stick out. Once you have a tightly controlled rotation, try stomping backward with your right leg at the moment of the launch. Learn to put all of that together and you'll be firing spears further than mine in no time."

In his surprise, Mamoru could only say, "Oh."

"Practice at home, yes?"

"Yes, Sensei."

When the wind on the shelf reached dangerous speeds and the students started running low on projectiles, Yukino Sensei moved his class indoors for sword practice. The three hours of sparring wore most of the boys to exhaustion. To Mamoru, they felt more like a warm-up, but he kept Yukino Sensei's words in mind; he kept the other boys in mind. He had been guilty of leaving horrible bruises on classmates who were too slow to block his wooden blade—which was all of them—but he was more careful today, focusing mainly on feinting, blocking, and evading.

Mamoru found a new level of focus trying to outmaneuver his classmates without actually hitting them. His heart sank when the bell tolled, signaling the end of training. Knees shook and sweat dripped onto the tatami as the boys packed up their gear and headed to history class. To Kwang's credit, he had not passed out, as new students often did in Yukino Sensei's sword class, though he didn't seem to be able to walk without the support of the wall.

"Come on, city boy," Yuuta teased, taking Kwang's arm as they left the dojo. "You can lean on me."

"Mamoru," Yukino Sensei stopped him before he could follow

his classmates out of the room. "Excellent work today. I'm glad to see that your control is developing along with your ridiculous speed."

Mamoru nodded. From the swordsman once known as Lightning Dai, that was high praise.

"I haven't gotten the chance to speak with your father or uncle in some time," Yukino Sensei said, returning the extra bokken to the closet. "Have either of them been working on the Whispering Blade with you?"

"I…" Mamoru felt his smile fade. "My father's been trying to."

"Good," Yukino Sensei said earnestly. The pride in his eyes made Mamoru want to shrink in shame.

There was very little that did not come easily to Mamoru, but his father had been trying to teach him the Whispering Blade for almost a year now, and he hadn't come anywhere near mastering it. For centuries, the Matsuda family had passed down the secret to forming weapons of impervious ice. The technique was so difficult that no non-Matsuda had ever figured it out—and Mamoru was starting to wonder how *anyone* had ever figured it out.

It wasn't enough to be an excellent sword fighter. It wasn't enough to be good at summoning and shaping ice. The Whispering Blade came from something deeper that Mamoru just didn't understand. His father understood it, but Matsuda Takeru did not have Yukino Sensei's magical ability to put his skill into words. No matter how he explained, Mamoru just couldn't understand.

"I'm not doing well," he blurted out before thinking better of it. "My father is frustrated with me."

Mamoru regretted the words as soon as they were out of his mouth. It was beyond inappropriate for a student to discuss his problems at home with his teacher, and it was forbidden for a Matsuda to discuss the details of the Whispering Blade with anyone outside the family.

"I wish I could help you," the swordmaster said after a moment, "but I'm a Yukino, and I'm not your father. Even if it were my place to speak to you about this, I wouldn't be much help. I don't know what the Whispering Blade entails."

"I know, Sensei," Mamoru said, looking at his feet. "I'm sorry. I shouldn't have—"

"But I do know a great jijaka when I see one," Yukino Sensei said. "I know that you have the same force of nyama in you as your father and other great fighters of your line."

Mamoru nodded. But Matsuda power wasn't necessarily enough. A Matsuda's ultimate purpose was to turn himself into a weapon strong enough to defend his Empire from anything. This was what Mamoru and every man of his line had been born for. Despite this, there were many Matsudas who tried their whole lives and never produced a Whispering Blade.

Since he was old enough to picture the future, Mamoru had cultivated this image of the perfect man, the perfect warrior, Whispering Blade in hand. He was nearing fighting age, but that man still seemed so far away...

"What if it's not enough. What if..." A Matsuda was supposed to be above fear, yet here Mamoru was, too scared to finish the sentence. *What if I'm not enough?*

"Mamoru-kun," Yukino Sensei's voice softened, "Your father was sixteen when he mastered the Whispering Blade, your uncle one year older, and they were among the youngest masters in history. You have time. I promise, you will be fine."

"You can't promise that." In his anxiety, Mamoru didn't seem to be able to control the stupid things coming out of his mouth. "There have been other Matsudas with powerful jiya who never mastered it. How can you be so sure?"

"Because I know you, Mamoru-kun," Yukino Sensei said, "beyond your lineage and your raw power. In the space of time it takes a normal boy to grasp a technique, you've already improved it and expanded it to all its potential applications and then some. It's rather annoying, as your teacher."

"Sorry about th—"

"But I have no doubt that it is precisely that kind of ingenuity that gave rise to the Whispering Blade in the first place. A student like you, who can absorb what he is told but also think beyond it, is capable of anything."

Mamoru's mouth opened but he was so stunned—so touched—that he couldn't find any words to thank his teacher. How did you thank someone for praise you hadn't earned?

"Now, get to class," Yukino Sensei said, nodding toward the door.

"Yes, Sensei." Ducking his head, Mamoru gathered his things and hurried to follow his classmates.

After the heart-pumping rush of sword practice, history class was always agony. When the wind was high, the school creaked like an old ship, and Hibiki Sensei's voice had a way of getting lost in the dull moaning of the wooden beams.

"There were a number of factors that led to the Great War, or what the Yammankalu call the Keleba. Ke-le-ba." Hibiki Sensei wrote the Yammaninke letters out on the board and Mamoru sank his teeth into the knuckles of his left fist, hoping the pain might keep him awake. *"First, there was the tension between the colonial powers, Yamma and Sizwe, which were in constant competition with each other for the resources of Baxaria. Next, there was the tension created by the Baxarian colonies rejecting Yammanka and Sizwean rule. Last, of course, there was the tension between our own great empire and the extremist rebels in the west who would one day betray their emperor to establish the Ranganese Union."*

"Are you not going to take notes?" Mamoru whispered to Kwang, noticing that the new boy had not even picked up his brushpen.

"Oh, I don't have to. I'm used to learning the Yammanka way, with my ears. Besides," he murmured even more quietly, *"I've heard all this crap before anyway."*

"What?" Mamoru leaned in, unsure he had heard right. Had Kwang just called Hibiki Sensei's history lesson *crap?*

"Matsuda-san," Hibiki Sensei said sharply, "no talking in class."

"Sorry, Sensei," Mamoru said as the teacher returned to his lecture.

"Now, there are several background dates you will need to know in regard to the Keleba. The first one is 5153." He wrote the date on the board. *"This is the year of the first Abirian rebellion, when a group of violent extremists calling themselves the Longhouse Confederacy developed enough of a following to mount armed resistance against the Yammanka Empire. Abiria, despite being plagued by inter-tribal violence and not having a stable government of its own, wanted independence from Yamma. Of course, these disorganized rebels were quickly subdued by Yamma's superior forces."*

Behind him, Mamoru thought he heard Kwang make a critical, "Hmm," sound, but when he turned to look over his shoulder, the northern boy was listening quietly.

"With their inferior genes, the Abirians' defeat was inevitable. The Yammankalu are pure-blooded tajakalu, born and bred to wield the power they possess, whereas the Abirians who opposed them were of mixed blood, the product of intermarriage between the Abirian Natives, Yammankalu, Kaigenese immigrants, and most damaging of all, white slaves. This kind of impurity dilutes the divine energies that give theonites their power. Mixed theonites such as the Abirians could never hope to stand unaided against a pure-blooded tajaka army.

"Now, I want to give you several dates relating to the Yammanka-Sizwean competition over their colonial territories."

Mamoru tried to take notes as Hibiki Sensei droned on in Kaigengua and found himself doodling instead. He started out drawing the straight blade of a sword, but a gust of wind pushed against the school, his brushpen slid, and the sword became water. Mamoru followed the new curve and added lines beneath it, turning it into a rough approximation of the Tsusano wave, his mother's family crest. More waves fell in beside the Tsusano crest, some turned to fish, and Mamoru had filled half the page with stormy sea before he remembered that he was supposed to be paying attention to the lecture.

"This brings us to the dates leading up to the Keleba itself,"

Hibiki Sensei said, and Mamoru tried to refocus on the lecture.

"5286, the year that the Carythian Union formed and resisted Yammanka rule." Hibiki Sensei wrote the year up on the board.

"5287," he wrote the next date as Mamoru scrambled to catch up with his notes. *"In this year, the Sizwean colony of Malusia staged a major uprising that shook Sizwe's control of the entire region. At the same time, there was a rash of peasant uprisings in the western part of the Kaigenese Empire. These were quickly put down by our own Imperial army, but they foreshadowed bigger rebellions to come…*

"5288. Under the influence of corrupt politicians, a collection of cities, led by Ranga, rose against the Kaigenese Empire. This rebellion was put down the same year and its leaders publicly executed for their treason against the Empire.

"5289, the year that Yamma defeated Sizwe for control of Malusia and pressed to take Sizwe's other colonies, escalating the long-standing tensions between the two Kelenduguka superpowers.

"5290. Kaigen's western provinces rose up in rebellion once again. Using propaganda and false promises, the Thulanist rebels managed to trick the uneducated peasants of Ranga into following them in greater numbers than ever before. At the same time, the Longhouse Confederacy of Abiria staged a reprisal of its bid for independence in 5153, under the same flag.

"At the tail end of that year, on the twenty-eighth of Kribakalo, Ranganese terrorists attacked a graduation ceremony at Daybreak Academy in Carytha, killing principal Oyede Biida, along with several Yammanka and Kaigenese students. It was following this malicious and cowardly attack that Yamma agreed to support our great empire in its fight against the Ranganese rebels.

"5291. Early in this year, the Yammankalu allied with us, bringing foreign troops onto Kaigenese soil for the first time. In response to their involvement, Sizwe aligned itself both with our own rebel enemies and with the Abirian rebels fighting against Yamma for their independence. This led to open war between Yamma and Sizwe. Abtya aligned with Yamma.

"5292. This year marked the only time in Duna's history that all the major theonite powers—Kaigen, Yamma, Abtya, and Sizwe— were at war. It was in this year that the Ranganese fonyakalu launched their attack on Shirojima and were soundly defeated.

"In the end, victory in war always comes down to bloodlines," Hibiki Sensei said, turning to face his class with a dramatic flourish. *"We here on the Sword of Kaigen are blessed to have some of the best and purest jijaka bloodlines in the world. Matsuda,"* he said, pointing at Mamoru, *"Yukino,"* he indicated Yuuta, and then went on to point to the other great houses represented in the classroom, *"Ameno, Ginkawa, Ikeno, Katakouri, all of you belong to a chain of great fighters stretching back to mythic times.*

"Since the dawn of Kaigen, this peninsula has held its enemies back without fail. This is why we are called the Sword of Kaigen. And again, during the Keleba, the Matsudas, the Yukinos, and the other powerful jijakalu of the Kusanagi Peninsula beat back their enemies in resounding victory."

This time Mamoru was sure he heard a disdainful huff behind him, but he kept his attention on the lecture as Hibiki Sensei continued, *"For this is the Sword of Kaigen; to charge it is to die. When the Ranganese armada reached the Kusanagi Peninsula, the warriors of the Matsuda, Yukino, Ameno, Ikeno, and Ginkawa houses, along with all their vassal fighters formed a line along the beach. At the first news of Ranganese ships, our capital sent a request to Yamma for aid. But by the time the Yammanka forces reached our peninsula, the jijaka soldiers here—your own grandfathers and great-grandfathers—had already laid waste to the Ranganese invaders.*

"Yammanka pilots tell of flying the length of the peninsula to find the beaches awash in red, like the edge of the blade that has tasted victory. Prepared for battle, the men of Yamma flew lower, only to discover that the battle was done. The bodies in the sea wore Ranganese uniforms. The red staining the sand was the impure blood of fonyakalu. For the warriors of Kusanagi had

fought with such fury that there were hardly any Kaigenese casualties."

Mamoru heard Kwang let out an unmistakable huff of laughter. Hibiki Sensei heard it too.

"Is our history funny to you, Kwang-san?"

"No, Sensei. I'm sorry."

Hibiki Sensei gave Kwang a last cold look before turning back to the class to continue, this time in Dialect. "This is your past. This is your heritage. You are here at this school because you are the descendants of the greatest fighters Duna has ever seen. The best blood in the world flows through your veins. If you learn well, listen well, and work hard, the Sword of Kaigen will survive, bright and sharp, to be passed down to your sons, and their sons after them."

MISAKI

In her first year at theonite academy, Misaki had earned top grades in all her courses. In her second year, she achieved one of the fastest times on the agility course, second only to Robin Thundyil's. In her third year, she had bested some of Carytha's most feared machete fighters in single combat. As a teenager, she had worn those accomplishments with pride… never realizing that at thirty-four, her proudest accomplishment would be getting five rambunctious children to nap at the same time.

"Success?" she whispered when she arrived back home, arms full of dozing five-year-old.

"Success!" Hyori confirmed as Misaki used her toes to slide the shoes off her feet. "They're all asleep, just like you planned."

Hiroshi had nodded off on Misaki's shoulder as she carried him back from the elementary school. Fresh off of two hours of sword practice with children twice his size, even he ran out of steam. His hair was damp with sweat and his little hands were blistered from gripping the oversized practice sword, but he hadn't uttered a word of complaint, just quietly collapsed against his mother and let her carry him the rest of the way home.

He was a strange creature, her second son. She had known when he was nothing more than a small heartbeat inside her that he was his father's child. Cold. It was said that all jijakalu were born with something of the sea in them, but most seas had their warm currents and their cold, volcanic springs in the depths, free water between ice flows. Even the iciest jijakalu had some warm places in their soul—at least that was what Misaki had thought before she married into the Matsuda family. Hiroshi was born with the deadly calm of a sea frozen solid. Like his father, he was cold to the touch no matter his mood or level of exertion. Even his sweat was cool, like morning dew.

He murmured something about footwork as Misaki lay him on the futon where Ryota and Nagasa were already fast asleep.

"Shh," Misaki breathed into his hair. "We're almost five for five."

"What?" Hiroshi's eyes blinked open.

"Nothing." Misaki put a hand on his forehead, easing him down beside his brother. "Nothing, my little warrior. Just rest."

"Mmm," Hiroshi nodded and slipped off to sleep.

"And we did it!" Misaki whispered, sliding the door shut behind her. "All five of them are down."

"How long do you think it'll last?" Hyori asked.

"Probably not that long," Misaki sighed, sinking down on the cushions beside the other two women. "The boys are all properly exhausted, but the babies will wake up hungry before long."

Misaki wanted desperately to close her eyes and drop off to sleep herself, but she knew she should make use of her hands while they weren't full of squirming infant, so she hauled herself up and got out her sewing box. The family crest had begun to tear from the back of Takeru's haori and needed to be re-stitched. Carefully, she picked out the right thread to match the dark blue and white diamonds of the Matsuda crest and threaded her needle.

At the height of the Matsuda family's power, during Kaigen's wars of succession all the way through the Keleba, the ancient compound had been full of servants who did all the cooking, cleaning, and sewing for the lady of the house. Takeru's father had complained bitterly about the damn vassal houses not sending servants anymore but Misaki could hardly fault poorer koronu for deserting a house that could no longer support them.

Warrior houses like the Matsudas once made their living training sons of lesser houses in jiya and swordsmanship. Students came in droves in times of unrest, when battles were common, but peacetime was a different story. In the decades since the Keleba, even the promise of the chance to train with the greatest swordsmen in Kaigen hadn't been enough to keep most of the common koronu in Takayubi.

Still, the Matsuda crest was a mark of pride, and Misaki made sure it was stitched into every coat, kimono, and haori they owned.

"I should probably get some work done too," Hyori said, pulling her own sewing project out of the bag she had brought from home. As tired as Misaki had grown of stitching the same four diamonds into a dozen articles of clothing, she didn't envy Hyori her sewing tasks; the Yukino insignia was a snowflake.

"It's so quiet," Setsuko mused. "I can't remember the last time the compound was this peaceful. You might be a genius, little sister."

"Well, I try." Misaki smiled.

"And to think, my poor mother raised nine of us in a house the size of this room!" Setsuko said. "No wonder she's gotten loopy after all these years."

"Oh, how is your mother, Setsuko?" Misaki asked, turning to her sister-in-law. "You went to visit her a few weeks back, didn't you?" Misaki had been so busy juggling the new baby and the two older boys that she hadn't gotten a moment of quiet to ask how the trip had gone.

"My mother is fine," Setsuko said, "still in bizarrely good health, but she is getting old. Like I said, her mind is going a bit. She's convinced the Ranganese are going to come across the ocean to attack us."

"Why does she think that?" Hyori was laughing, but Misaki stilled, her grip tightening on her needle.

"She says she can feel it," Setsuko said, "an 'old fisherwoman's intuition' or something like that. She says fonyaka wind tastes different from the normal sea air."

"That's a strange thing to say," Hyori said.

"Well, Setsuko's mother has lived on the ocean for ninety years," Misaki pointed out. "She was here the last time the Ranganese came. Maybe she knows something we don't."

"You think my kooky mother is on to something?" Setsuko said in amusement.

"If the Ranganese were to attack, this area would be the first to feel it," Misaki said, "and the first hit."

The Kusanagi Peninsula extended far out into the Kaigenese Sea, barring the way to the archipelago's safe ports and beaches. Any invader from the sea had to first get past the mountainous spit of land and its inhabitants.

"But we don't have anything to fear from Ranga," Hyori said dismissively. "Our brothers and husbands are powerful enough to turn away any invaders. And anyway, if there was a serious threat from the Ranganese, the government would have told us."

"Maybe," Misaki said, doubtful.

"What do you mean 'maybe'?"

"I mean…" Misaki paused. "I just mean that the news isn't necessarily true."

"What?" Hyori looked positively stricken and Misaki wished she hadn't said anything.

"Misaki-chan says some weird, ominous things sometimes," Setsuko said with a reproachful look at her sister-in-law. "Don't worry your pretty head about it."

But Hyori was still staring at Misaki, uncomprehending. "You… are you saying our government would lie to us?"

The answer was 'yes,' of course, but Misaki couldn't say that

39

straight. That just wasn't the sort of thing you said in Kaigen.

"Misaki?" Hyori prompted, and there was so much fear and hurt in those pretty eyes that Misaki had to offer some response. She bit her lip, choosing her words carefully.

"I went to school with a lot of Yammanka jaseliwu," she said finally, "self-proclaimed keepers of Yamma's history. The funny thing about these jaseliwu was that, depending on their family, their native region of Yamma, and the koronu they served, they told vastly different histories. Sometimes two of them would sit right next to each other and tell conflicting accounts of the same event. I talked to one of these jaseliwu. I asked him how he could say that his history was true when the next jaseli over told me a different story and claimed that that was the truth. In my mind, one of them had to be lying. I told him that."

"And what did he say?" Setsuko asked.

"He said, 'there are a million ways to tell the same story. Our job as jaseliwu is to find the one the listener needs to hear. Not necessarily the one that makes them the happiest or the one that gives them the most information, but the one they need to hear to do what they need to do.' He told me that's how jaseliwu care for koronu and other kafokalu."

"Alright," Hyori said, clearly confused. "What does that have to do with our government?"

"Well, I think that's the way the Kaigenese government takes care of us," Misaki said, "the same way a jaseli in Yamma takes care of his koro." Of course, in Yamma, jaseliwu were free to decide the way they sang their songs and told their histories. They weren't issued government-approved scripts to recite, but that wasn't a discussion Hyori would appreciate. "Our Emperor tells us the things we need to hear."

From the way Hyori was blinking at her, Misaki could tell she didn't understand.

"So, do you think our government is right about how safe we are?" Setsuko asked. "Or do you think my dear old mother is onto something?"

"Well, it's been a long time since I've been out of the country," Misaki admitted, "but I know that the fonyakalu can do more than most Kaigenese believe."

"Really?" Hyori didn't look convinced. "Like what?"

"Well, back when the Ranganese first split from the Empire, warfare was different," Misaki said. "The Kaigenese Empire's military had always been based on jijakalu like us, with fonyakalu as an afterthought."

"That's only natural," Hyori said. "Fonyakalu are just untrained peasants. Jijakalu are purer, more powerful."

"Well, not really," Misaki said. "Not always."

"What are you talking about?" Hyori asked with a note of annoyance. "If fonyakalu are truly as good as we are, why would our Empire ever keep a military of all jijakalu?"

"Because the Empire's main centers of power—Jungsan, Shirojima, Haijing—have always been peopled mainly by jijakalu," Misaki said, her sewing forgotten in her lap. "The success of the Ranganese Revolution proved that a big force of fonyakalu, even a disorganized one, could defeat a jijaka army."

"But they didn't defeat us," Hyori said indignantly. "The revolution wasn't a success."

"Well," Setsuko said, "they did split the Empire in half."

"But they didn't truly best our armies," Hyori insisted. "As soon as they reached the ocean, we drove them back inland."

"Right." Misaki forgot that that was what you learned if you went to high school in Kaigen, but she didn't need to argue that with Hyori right now. "You're right, but that's part of my point. During the Keleba, the Ranganese military was not well-organized or well-trained. Fonyakalu had never worked together in those numbers, so they hadn't figured out specialized military formations to rival ours or Yamma's, but the Ranganese Union has been a sovereign power for seventy-eight years now. They've had decades to figure out how to function as a fighting force. Those groups of fonyakalu can do things no one would have dreamed of fifty years ago."

"How do you know all this?" Hyori asked.

"Hush now, Hyori-chan," Setsuko said in a conspiratorial whisper. "Takeru-sama doesn't like anyone mentioning this, but Misaki-chan actually lived outside Kaigen for a long time."

"No!" Hyori's pretty eyes widened in shock.

"Oh, yes," Setsuko said. "When she was a teenager, she attended this fancy international theonite school in Carytha."

"Carytha!" Hyori's eyes got even bigger. "So far away!"

"Yes," Setsuko said, reveling in the younger woman's shock, "and at that weird international school, Misaki made all kinds of weird international friends, including this roommate of hers, who was…" Setsuko paused for dramatic effect before whispering, "a Ranganese fonyaka!"

"No!" Hyori exclaimed again, dropping her sewing to put both hands over her mouth. "Misaki-san, wasn't that scary?"

"Not really," Misaki said, not looking up from her own work. "She was just a thirteen-year-old girl, and I think she was more scared of me than I was of her—at least until we got to know each other better."

"But you couldn't really be friends, could you?" Hyori said anxiously. "I mean, she was Ranganese!"

Misaki shrugged. "We argued a lot during our first two years. Her table manners weren't my favorite…" but she stopped before trying to elaborate any further. Trying to explain her school days to Hyori would probably do more harm than good. Misaki generally considered it a bad idea to talk about Daybreak to anyone but Setsuko—and even Setsuko couldn't really understand. There was only so much a person could understand, having lived her whole life on the same tiny island cluster.

"And your fonyaka roommate… she's the one who told you these things about the Ranganese military?" Hyori said.

"Some of them, yes," Misaki said. Of course, she had also had other Ranganese friends, acquaintances, and professors, but Hyori didn't need to know that.

"Well, then she probably made it up," Hyori said with the kind of innocent confidence that could only come from a life lived in the mists of nationalism. "Everyone knows Ranganese people can't be trusted."

Misaki didn't respond.

"And anyway," Hyori continued matter-of-factly, "it doesn't matter how strong the Ranganese Union has gotten because Kaigen is stronger now too. You can look at any news report to see that our military is bigger than ever and our economy is booming."

Misaki didn't comment, focusing instead on her sewing. Personally, she suspected that Kaigen was not actually experiencing the economic paradise that the TV reporters claimed. If they were, the wealth certainly wasn't extending to Shirojima. Setsuko's fishing village had fallen on hard times, and the last time Misaki's parents had visited, they had told her that the two biggest factories near Ishihama had closed, leaving a thousand people without jobs. Years ago, the Empire had promised a modern magtrack between Shirojima's major islands, but the project had never been finished.

"It's laughable to think that Ranga poses any threat to us here," Hyori said. "Any warrior will tell you that Kaigen has the strongest fighters."

"Any warrior will tell you that even the strong can't afford complacency," Misaki murmured.

"What did you say?"

"Nothing," Misaki shook her head. "It's not important."

As Setsuko offered Hyori laughing reassurances, Misaki stared at the blue cloth in her lap and wondered why she hadn't thought about this sooner. The Keleba had cost Kaigen its most productive agricultural provinces, most of its underpaid workforce, and many of its major trade routes—resources that now belonged to the Ranganese Union.

The fonyakalu at Daybreak had been able to do things Misaki never would have dreamed of, and that had been a long time ago. What could Ranga's armies do with fifteen more years of practice? Kaigen may have avoided total collapse the last time it went to war

43

with Ranga, but would the Empire fare as well against a new attack? When Misaki stepped back to consider all the pieces, it stood to reason that Ranga was far stronger than it had been at the time of the Keleba, and Kaigen was far weaker.

But here, high in the obscuring mists of Takayubi, where nothing seemed to have changed for a thousand years, it was easy to believe the fantasy of a stable world.

MAMORU

As the class made their way to the schoolyard for lunch, Mamoru picked up his pace to catch up with Kwang.

"What was that about?" he asked, falling into step beside the city boy.

"What was what about?"

"Back there in history class. Why were you laughing?"

"I was trying not to," Kwang said, *"and I wouldn't call the garbage that jaseli was regurgitating history."*

"What do you mean?" Itsuki demanded as he and Yuuta caught up.

"You realize that at least half the stuff he tells you isn't even true." Kwang looked around at the three Takayubi boys. *"It's propaganda."*

"Propaganda?" Mamoru had only heard the word used a few times before. People said that propaganda was what the Ranganese Union used to trick its uneducated citizens into fighting its battles. It was a distinctly Ranganese tactic. Kaigen didn't use propaganda. Everyone knew that.

"Falleke!" Kwang swore. *"You guys in this village really believe all this stuff, don't you? You believe everything the government tells you?"*

"Why wouldn't we?" Itsuki asked earnestly.

"You must see what's happening here." Kwang's voice was

almost imploring as he looked from one face to the next. *"The emperor is using you."*

"We're happy to serve our emperor," Yuuta chimed in passionately. *"How can he be using us?"*

"He can feed you lies about Ranga, and about your own ancestors. He can make you think you're invincible when you're really not."

"We are the Sword of Kaigen," Yuuta said fiercely, *"the defenders of the Empire."*

Kwang scoffed. *"That's a fancy way of saying 'cannon fodder.'"*

Mamoru's voice turned to ice. *"What did you just say?"*

From the way Kwang went tense, it was obvious that he felt the simmering fury of Mamoru's nyama. Mamoru watched the northern boy's eyes flick in indecision and then experienced a grudging flutter of admiration when the city boy held his ground and looked him in the eye.

"I said you're cannon fodder." Kwang's voice was even. *"The Emperor will give you guys any made-up story if it means you'll stay put and die for him. You may think you're great warriors with some noble purpose, but as far as the capital is concerned, you're just game pieces."*

Mamoru stood, staring down at Kwang, his eyes narrowed. The ocean seethed in his fists. *"Take that back."*

"I'm not taking anything back," Kwang said stubbornly. *"I'm going to lunch."* He started to walk away, but Mamoru stepped in front of him, barring his way out of the courtyard.

"I said take it back."

"You think you scare me, Matsuda?" Kwang's fingers curled and Mamoru felt the other boy's jiya ripple, ready for action. *"I don't care how good a fighter you are. If you take another step closer, I'll—"*

Mamoru stepped forward. *"You'll what?"*

Kwang moved fast. His ice-knuckled uppercut would have worked on just about any theonite, but Mamoru was not just any theonite. He side-stepped the punch and had the city boy on the ground in an instant. There was a satisfying thud as Kwang's back hit the courtyard stones, knocking the breath from his body.

Still stunned, the northern boy tried to draw the surrounding water vapor to his hands for another attack, but Mamoru's jiya smashed through his, knocking the molecules from his control. He hauled Kwang up by the front of his uniform. Mist gathered to form a blade of ice along the back of his free hand, protruding from the knuckles to point at Kwang's throat. It was no steel-cleaving Sasayaiba, but it would pierce a human body.

"Whoa!" Mamoru could barely hear Itsuki and Yuuta's alarmed voices through the rising swell of his rage. "Easy, Mamoru-kun! Take the edge off that blade before we get in trouble!"

"You're a good fighter," Kwang said, somehow still smug with a blade at his throat, *"and your small-town pride is cute, but it's all based on a lie."*

Mamoru's teeth ground together and his ice sharpened.

"Mamoru-kun, you don't want to kill him!"

"You're right." Mamoru let out his breath, his blade turning to water. What he wanted to do was punch Kwang in his smug face.

So, he did.

Right as the headmaster walked into the schoolyard.

3

THE ROOF

Mamoru's eyes were fixed on his knees, but he could feel the headmaster's gaze boring into him. Kwang was kneeling on the tatami of the office beside him, a cloth pressed to his face to stem the blood pouring from his nose. The blow hadn't broken anything—Mamoru had better control than that—but the northern boy would be bleeding for a while.

"Kwang Chul-hee is new here," the headmaster said, setting his brushpen aside to fold his hands on the desk before him. "It's possible that he was not taught any better at his previous school, but Mamoru, you know that this is not how the warriors of Takayubi settle their differences."

Mamoru's fists clenched on his knees, the knuckles of his right hand still stinging as his insides curled up in shame.

"I'm very sorry, sir," he said at his knees.

"*I'm* sorry that you were not able to set a better example for our new transfer student," the headmaster said and the hard disapproval in his voice was more than Mamoru could bear. "You're talented, Mamoru, but talent is meaningless without self-discipline. You will never be a fully realized Matsuda if you continuously let your pride run away with your principles."

Choked with shame, Mamoru could only nod.

"And Kwang Chul-hee." The headmaster turned to the bleeding

boy. "I want to make it clear that this sort of behavior is not tolerated in this school or this village. The sons of common peasants may come to blows in schoolyard brawls, but not warriors. We settle our differences in single combat. The next time you and Mamoru have a quarrel, you will take it to the fighting circle, or you will keep it to yourselves. Do you understand?"

"Yes, sir," Kwang mumbled as best he could with blood still running from his nose.

"As punishment, you will both stay after school and clean the entire roof—without the use of your powers."

Mamoru's heart sank. The chore wasn't insurmountably difficult—he just didn't want to do it with Kwang.

"You may use ice to anchor your feet," the headmaster continued, "but you will do the cleaning itself with your bare hands. Kwang, I will contact your father to tell him you will be staying late this evening. Mamoru..." He looked for a long moment at his nephew and sighed. "I'll let your mother know when I get home."

The shame in Mamoru's chest turned to physical pain. He had to clench his teeth to keep from blurting out 'Please don't tell her!'

He knew a real warrior wasn't supposed to concern himself with the opinions of women, but Mamoru couldn't help it. He dreaded his mother's disappointment more than any man's hard glare. She was a small woman with a sweet smile and a quiet voice, yet there was a knowing intelligence in her eyes that Mamoru had always found the smallest bit unsettling. There were times it felt as though she could see straight through him, to his beating heart and the flaws it sent pulsing through his veins.

"Now, go," the headmaster said, shaking back his sleeves and picking up his brushpen to continue his work. "Get yourselves cleaned up and don't be late for your next class."

Both boys said a quiet, "Yes, sir," and bowed themselves out of the room.

"What does he mean he'll tell your mom when he gets home?" Kwang asked as soon as they were out of earshot of the

headmaster's office. *"You live with the headmaster? Wait."* Kwang's eyes went wide. *"Is he your father?"*

Mamoru could only manage a miserable noise, putting a hand to his face.

"Is he your father?" Kwang repeated.

Worse. *"He's my uncle."*

"Wow!" Kwang laughed, surprisingly cheerful for a boy who had just been punched in the nose. *"Is everyone in this town related?"*

Mamoru didn't answer. He just said stiffly, *"Let's go to the washroom and clean off your face. You're getting your blood everywhere."*

"Technically, you got my blood everywhere," Kwang said but followed Mamoru down the creaking hall toward the washroom. *"Was the headmaster serious about challenging people to single combat? You guys really still do that?"*

"How else would we settle our differences?"

"I don't know. Talking?"

Mamoru was tempted to point out that Kwang had actually thrown the first punch, but that would have sounded childish, so instead, he countered, *"Maybe that's a luxury you have in the cities. Here, we keep ourselves and our convictions strong."*

While Kwang cleaned up, Mamoru paced the hall outside the washroom. There was no reason for him to stay really. Kwang knew the way back from the washroom, and Mamoru would still have time for lunch if he hurried. But somehow, he couldn't get himself to walk away. He couldn't unseat the feeling that somehow things weren't finished here.

As he listened to the slosh of water inside the washroom— Kwang cleaning the blood from his face—his own blood seemed to churn inside him. His fists clenched and he felt his knuckles pulsing an echo of his fist against Kwang's face. The rage echoed too, sending restless ripples through his nyama that he couldn't seem to calm.

When Mamoru's temper got the best of him, his father liked to blame it on Kaa-chan. Her clan were a wrathful, passionate lot, born of sea spray and crashing waves. Neither the most powerful nor the most skilled of Kaigen's warrior houses, the Tsusanos had made their name on the battlefield with their superhuman spirit and fury. It was said that the raw power of a true Tsusano was as changeable and devastating as a coastal storm.

But Mamoru was not a Tsusano. He was a Matsuda. And Matsudas were not made of storms. They were ice—cold in their calculations and unyielding in their integrity. He was not supposed to let his emotions whip his soul into storms.

You are ice, he reminded himself, rubbing his thumb back and forth, back and forth over his knuckles as he tried to think of the unyielding Matsuda way to deal with Kwang. The mature warrior would obviously apologize for losing his temper. Like Uncle Takashi had said, that was no way for a warrior to behave.

Then again, Uncle Takashi didn't know what Kwang had been saying before Mamoru laid him out on the courtyard floor. Kwang was a traitor to the Empire—or if not that, something dangerously close. If he was just fabricating lies to stir up conflict, Mamoru shouldn't bother apologizing; he should take the city boy straight to the arena and beat some respect into him. But if Kwang wasn't lying… If he wasn't lying… Mamoru leaned back against a wall, feeling sick.

His thoughts ran in dizzying circles. He was still trying to decide what to do when the door opened and Kwang emerged, dabbing blood from his upper lip.

"Oh," Kwang said mildly. *"You're still here?"*

Mamoru inhaled and opened his mouth, hoping the right words would come to him. They didn't. So he dropped to his knees and put his hands on the floor before him.

"Um… what are you doing?" Kwang said apprehensively.

Mamoru bowed until his forehead touched his fingers. "Kwang-san," he started, "I—"

"I decline," Kwang said quickly.

"What?" Mamoru lifted his head.

"If you're challenging me to a duel, I decline—or I forfeit, or surrender, or whatever it is you people do. I saw you in sword class. I'm not going to fight you. You can't make me."

"What? That's not what I'm doing," Mamoru said, putting his head to the floor again. *"I wanted to say that I'm sorry. I should not have said those things to you. A warrior shouldn't lose his temper like that. It was wrong of me."*

"Was it?" Kwang said.

"What?"

"You're patriotic and loyal. You're exactly what everyone's told you to be."

There was a note of condescension in Kwang's voice that made Mamoru's fingers tense, aching to curl into fists, but he was trying to demonstrate control, not to lose his temper all over again. When he couldn't think of anything to say, he pressed his forehead harder into his knuckles, worried that if he looked up at Kwang he would punch him again.

"Get up," Kwang sighed after a moment. When Mamoru didn't move a muscle, he added an impatient, *"Please. I want to show you something."*

Reaching into the fold of his uniform, Kwang pulled out the smallest info-com device Mamoru had ever seen. The rectangular screen was barely bigger than his palm.

"You brought that to school?" Mamoru said. He wasn't sure if having an info-com device was even allowed at Kumono, but he got the feeling it wasn't.

"I bring it with me everywhere," Kwang said, tapping a command into the sleek glass device. *"That's what us city kids do. Let me just see…"* He tapped around the screen, searching for something. *"Here."* He brought up the crispest holographic image Mamoru had ever seen, a tall obsidian statue in the middle of a sunny courtyard.

"What is that?" Mamoru asked.

"Near the Yammanka capital, there's this huge park filled with memorials in honor of the soldiers that died in pretty much every

battle Yamma ever fought. While my dad was doing work in Kolunjara, I had spare time to explore, and I found this memorial."

The gleaming black glass formed the shape of a fighter jet, and beside it, a Yammanka pilot—a woman—with her helmet resting on her hip, her long braids pulled back and her chin lifted toward the sun.

Mamoru had heard that the Yammanka army and air force employed females, but there was something strange about seeing a curvy young woman in full military gear. She didn't look bad, Mamoru reflected, as he considered the obsidian pilot; she looked strong. But it was still strange.

"This statue—this whole part of the park, actually—is dedicated to Yammankalu who lost their lives fighting in Kaigen."

"But no Yammankalu died in Kaigen," Mamoru said in confusion. *"Hibiki Sensei was just telling us about that. The Empire drove the Ranganese back before the Yammanka reinforcements even arrived."*

"Well…" Kwang tapped a command into the info-com device, and the image zoomed in on white Yammaninke lettering at the base of the statue.

"Bundanu… bundanuttaananu sayara ka…" Mamoru started to sound out the inscription but his Yammaninke wasn't very good.

"Bundanuttaananu sayara ka dima Kaigenka kelejonyunu ye Kusanagi Gungille la to hakili da," Kwang finished and translated for him. *"In memory of the warriors who gave their lives defending our Kaigenese allies on the Kusanagi Peninsula."*

The base of the memorial dripped with Falleya talismans, the kind family members hand-crafted and hung on the graves of their loved ones. It was clear from the photo that real people had visited the site to mourn and remember… but how could that be? How could that be? Hibiki Sensei had said that no Yammankalu died in Shirojima. Not one.

"I was surprised too," Kwang said. He seemed to be watching Mamoru's face carefully. *"I asked the park jaseliwu about it, and*

they said that over four hundred Yammanka soldiers died here."

"What?"

"Most of them were air support. Yammanka jets weren't the best back then. Apparently, the fonyakalu ripped them right out of the sky, and crashed them into the Kaigenese troops on the ground."

The school swayed, throwing Mamoru off balance, and he had to put a hand on the wall to stay on his feet. Dimly, he was aware that he couldn't just let Kwang stand there and say these things. He had to fight. A Matsuda always stood and fought, but Mamoru had never taken a hit—from a foot, fist, or practice sword—that left him this shaken. He felt sick deep in his stomach.

"I don't believe you," he said, even as the obsidian pilot stared back at him from Kwang's screen. *"That's not real. Th-that can't be—"*

"It's not the only memorial." Kwang tapped his way to another image. *"This one honors over two thousand Yammanka fighters who died helping the Kaigenese Empire defend Jungsan and push the Ranganese back to our current border."*

The thin mountain air had never bothered Mamoru. Why did he suddenly feel like there was no oxygen in his body? "No." He was shaking his head. "No, no. That can't be. That can't be right. Hibiki Sensei says—everyone knows—the Ranganese never reached Jungsan. That-that's ridiculous."

"I didn't want to believe it either, but the evidence is really solid. Our Empire wouldn't have survived the Ranganese Revolution without Yammanka aid. The Yammankalu have no reason to lie about this."

"But—*they* must *be lying,"* Mamoru insisted. *"They must be. If this were all true, if all these Yammankalu did fight here, why wouldn't we know about it? Why wouldn't Hibiki Sensei tell us?"*

"Has he ever been outside Kaigen?" Kwang asked.

"I don't think so." It was very possible that Hibiki Sensei had never been outside the Shirojima province. *"But my grandfather fought in that battle. A lot of people's older relatives were there. Why wouldn't they talk about it?"*

As he said the words, Mamoru realized that no one he had spoken to about the Keleba had ever really elaborated. His grandfather, Susumu, when he had been alive, had only ever offered the vaguest of references to the war.

"It's possible the government ordered them not to," Kwang suggested. *"It happens. If the Emperor is good at one thing, it's censorship."*

"That doesn't make sense," Mamoru said, pushing through his inexplicable dizziness to get his thoughts in order. *"This is Kaigen. We're a warrior culture. The Emperor and his officials would never disrespect thousands of fallen warriors by covering up their deaths. Kaigenese or not, those are soldiers who fought and died here. How could you think that Kaigen would show them such disrespect?"*

"Because Kaigen isn't a warrior culture," Kwang said impatiently. *"I know you think it is. I know you guys here in this village have these nice, wholesome, old-fashioned values, but have you ever been outside this province?"*

"I… no," Mamoru had to admit.

"Then you wouldn't know," Kwang said. *"You couldn't, but the rest of the Empire hasn't held old warrior values for a hundred years. The Emperor doesn't care who lives and dies—he definitely doesn't care about fighting nobly. He cares that his Empire stays intact under him."*

"But…" Mamoru floundered. *"But that can't—that doesn't explain why the government would lie to us about the Keleba."*

"Sure, it does," Kwang said. *"You guys are the Sword of Kaigen. You're the buffer between Ranga and the rest of the Empire's eastern islands. The Emperor needs you to think you're invincible. And he needs the rest of the province to believe that the Kusanagi Peninsula can protect them from anything."*

"Why?"

"So you islanders won't leave, so you'll stay here and keep fishing the coasts, and farming the land to fuel our dying economy, so you'll die protecting his lands, instead of moving into the

overpopulated cities and getting disillusioned about the state of the Empire like everyone else."

"No, no, no." Mamoru was shaking his head again. "I don't believe you." He backed away from Kwang, but the northern boy's words had already seeped into his mind like poison. He had already seen the Yammanka statues. "I don't believe you."

"Matsuda-san." Kwang reached out to him. *"It's okay—"*

"Don't touch me!" Mamoru pushed Kwang back. "Just stay away!" To his horror, Mamoru realized that his impeccably steady hands had started trembling.

"Matsuda-san—"

"I said stay away!" Mamoru shoved Kwang so hard that he slammed into the washroom door. In a few staggering steps, he was running down the hall—he didn't know where. Just away. Away from Kwang.

You are a Matsuda, he tried to tell himself. *You are solid ice,* but his inner sea had turned to roiling brine.

The floor shifted, pitching him into a wall. He stumbled to get his feet under him but the whole world seemed to be spinning. It couldn't be true—but it couldn't be a lie—but it couldn't be true, and Mamoru couldn't seem to find his balance. Kwang's words had knocked the world off its axis.

Aimless, Mamoru found himself staggering out onto one of Kumono's outdoor walkways. Wind stung his skin, scrambling his vision into a mess of bloodstained sand and careening fighter jets. He caught himself on the waist-high railing and found the mountain spinning beneath him, its mists, usually so familiar, suddenly gray and frightening. And for the first time in his three years at the swaying school, Mamoru threw up.

········

Mamoru's stomach settled after he had emptied most of its contents down the mountainside. He didn't understand what had happened to him and he decided it was best not to give it any more thought. No good could come of revisiting his own shameful weakness and Kwang's lies. It had been a mistake. All of it—the fight, the apology, that whole conversation with Kwang. No one had seen Mamoru retching his dignity over the railing. He could put it behind him.

Gathering liquid water from the mist, he washed the acid out of his teeth, shook off the dizziness, and pretended it had never happened. None of it had happened. He made himself ice. Uncompromising. Immovable. And none of it could touch him.

He didn't speak to Kwang during the second half of the day as they sat beside each other through the remainder of their classes. He didn't even look at him. Kwang—perhaps out of concern for his own safety—didn't press the issue, and Mamoru successfully pretended he didn't exist until classes finished. It wasn't until the two met after school to serve out their cleaning time that they exchanged any words.

"What is that for?" Kwang asked as Mamoru emerged from the closet with a coil of rope slung over his shoulder.

"It's for you," Mamoru said coldly, *"unless you want to walk around on the roof for a waati with no safety harness."*

"Oh."

Without meeting the other boy's eyes, Mamoru tied one end of the rope around Kwang's waist.

"So, I'm—ugh!" Kwang grunted as Mamoru yanked the knot tight. *"Ow,"* he said with a reproachful look at Mamoru. *"So, I'm supposed to trust you not to let me fall to my death?"*

Mamoru glared. *"Don't be an idiot. If you fall, so do I."*

After securing the other end of the rope around his own waist, Mamoru hauled a ladder out of the closet and motioned Kwang to follow him to the nearest outdoor walkway. Mamoru didn't need a ladder to get onto the roof, but he was guessing the soft city boy wouldn't share his agility. The wind had calmed since their midday training. *Good*, Mamoru thought. *Cleaning should go fast.*

Kwang was not looking so reassured.

"We're going to climb up there?" he asked as Mamoru

positioned the ladder against the edge of the roof.

"Yes."

"And... you're sure this isn't all some elaborate plan to have me killed for treason?" The unsteadiness in Kwang's voice suggested that he was only partially joking, so Mamoru looked him straight in the eye.

"If I kill you, you'll be facing me with a sword in your hand." He nodded at the ladder. *"Climb."*

Of all the chores to be done at Kumono Academy, cleaning the roof was the most dangerous. For the most part, Takayubi's abundant rain kept the clay tiles clean, but with the run-off from further up the mountain soil, branches, and dead leaves gathered in the curved parts of the roof. When the rooftop became visibly cluttered, sure-footed students were sent up to clear it.

Using sheets of water to wash the tiles, cleaning duty was the work of a few siiranu, but Uncle Takashi had explicitly forbidden the two from using their jiya. Instead, Mamoru and Kwang would have to scoop up the layers of twigs and grime with their bare hands and throw it off the edge of the roof. The chore would have been hard enough work with a competent cleaning partner, but Kwang was afraid of heights.

By the time he reached the top of the ladder and got onto the roof, he was shaking.

"I c-can't—" he stuttered on his hands and knees. *"I can't do this."*

Mamoru felt a surge of vindictive satisfaction at seeing the casually arrogant city boy so terrified, but he crushed the feeling before it could swell beyond his control. *You are ice. He doesn't affect you.*

"Get up," he said.

"I can't. I'm going to fall."

"I said I wouldn't let you fall," Mamoru said. *"I'm not a liar. Now stand up."*

"I can't!" Kwang called back in frustration. *"My leg muscles are all shot from your insane sword class!"*

Mamoru could sympathize. He couldn't count the number of times he had worked his legs until they wouldn't hold him up anymore—it was how he had gotten his wrought steel muscles—but it was hard to feel sorry for someone while they were whinging and whining about a simple chore.

"Just endure it," he said. *"As soon as we're done, we can go home."*

"H-how do I stand up without falling?" Kwang asked.

A fair question. While the roof wasn't dauntingly steep, the smooth clay tiles were slippery. Even a mountain-born theonite like Mamoru couldn't walk across the surface safely, and with the exception of the decorative stone dragons snaking their way across the roof's broad beams, there were no handholds.

"You have to pool water under your feet," Mamoru said, gathering mist and condensation into liquid beneath the soles of his own tabi. *"Then freeze it so you don't slide. Like this."* He waved a hand over his own feet, freezing the water into hard ice that anchored him to the steep roof tiles. *"You can do that, can't you?"*

Kwang nodded shakily and started to gather water to the soles of his shoes.

"Good," Mamoru said and turned away from Kwang, determined not to give the northern boy any more thought.

Mamoru moved across the roof with careful ease, melting his ice whenever he needed to move and refreezing it when he found a new foothold. Had he been doing the job alone, he would have finished within a waati. But he kept reaching the end of the rope and looking back to find Kwang far behind him, struggling to keep his balance on the steep surface as he collected tiny handfuls of dead leaves. A few times, Kwang let out a short cry and almost flailed off the edge roof in panic when Mamoru changed position.

"What?" Mamoru snapped the third time it happened.

"Could you just—could you just tell me when you're going to move?" Kwang said, clearly fighting to keep his voice steady. *"Just—so I can be sure I'm secure?"*

"Fine," Mamoru said, his impatience starting to wear through

58

his icy exterior, *"but hurry up. If we don't finish in the next gbaati, we'll lose the light."*

The sun was already low in the sky and trying to navigate the roof in the dark would be doubly dangerous. But despite all Mamoru's harsh words, Kwang didn't seem capable of working any faster. They still hadn't finished by the time the sun turned red and began to sink into the sea of mist.

"This is impossible!" Kwang complained for what felt like the hundredth time. *"Couldn't we just use our powers and be done with it?"*

"No," Mamoru said shortly.

"Why not? The headmaster doesn't have to know."

"He'll know," Mamoru said.

"How?"

"He's a Matsuda," Mamoru said. *"He will know."*

"Just a tiny, undetectable, bit of jiya?" Kwang pressed, *"Just to speed things along?"*

"That would be dishonest," Mamoru said.

Kwang made that little scoffing sound that Mamoru had come to hate over the past waatinu. He meant to ignore it, but he found himself turning on the other boy, bristling.

"Listen, I don't know how it works in all the fancy foreign places you've traveled, but here in Takayubi, we value honesty. We don't just make up ridiculous, self-serving lies whenever we feel like it."

Kwang looked up at Mamoru with an unreadable expression, the lines of his face colored by the setting sun. Without the blood red hue, he almost could have looked sad. *"I have been honest with you, Matsuda-san."*

You are ice, Mamoru reminded himself and returned Kwang's stare without emotion. *"Just keep working."*

"Look, you have to understand—"

"I'm not discussing this with you," Mamoru snapped. *"I don't want to listen to disgusting lies, and neither does anyone else in this village. So, if you know what's good for you, you'll stop spouting them."* Mamoru glared at Kwang, waiting for him—

59

daring him—to respond.

Maybe the northern boy had run out of energy for argument or maybe he was too scared of falling to anger the anchor at the other end of his rope. Whatever the reason, he didn't say anything in his defense. Mamoru couldn't say why, but that annoyed him more than anything.

What's the matter? he wanted to demand. *Nothing more to say now that the teachers aren't here to protect you?* But he forced himself to let the anger go. With a wave of his hand, he melted his ice anchor to allow him to edge further down the roof.

"Wait," Kwang protested, *"I'm not ready—"*

"I don't care," Mamoru said and turned to reach for the uppermost beam of the temple roof. *"Move faster."*

Kwang, of course, chose that exact moment to lose his footing. It must have happened quite suddenly because his weight jerked against the rope so hard that Mamoru was ripped right off his feet. Mamoru might have been able to recover, but the fall smacked his head into the roof tiles. Stars exploded before his eyes, costing him precious moments. When he regained his bearings, it was just in time to feel his body tumble over the edge of the roof.

His hands scrabbled for purchase, slid over the clay tiles, over the stone dragon's head adorning the corner of the roof—then caught on the dragon's snarling lower mandible.

Kwang's weight yanked the rope tight, slamming into Mamoru's stomach like a practice sword to the gut. He grimaced as stone teeth dug into his fingers, but his grip held. On the other end of the rope, Kwang was flailing in panic.

"Oh Falleke!" he gasped, his terrified voice echoing through the darkness below. *"Na-Nyaare! We're going to die!"*

"Stop moving!" Mamoru commanded.

If Kwang could just make himself dead weight, Mamoru could pull them both to safety. But the two of them were dangling by fingertips and every time Kwang squirmed, it got harder to hold on.

"Help!" Kwang screamed. *"Somebody help!"*

"No one's here," Mamoru said. The last of the staff would all have gone home at least a gbaati ago. *"Just calm down. I'm going to pull us back up."*

Mamoru had the strength in him to get them back onto the roof, but it was going to be a delicate operation. And if he tried to do it with Kwang thrashing around like an oversized fish at the end of a hook, they were both doomed. Though Mamoru's grip on the dragonhead didn't falter, his grip on his temper did as Kwang continued to gibber in panic.

"I'm too young to die! I'm too young to die!"

"Would you shut up!" Mamoru snarled. *"We're not going to die."* But as the words left his mouth, a horrible thought hit him: they were dangling from the easternmost corner of the roof, far from the steps and Kumono Lake. There was no water waiting to catch them—only jagged rocks.

"Kwang!" Mamoru exclaimed, unable to suppress a note of panic. *"For the love of Nami, stop moving!"*

If Mamoru had not been so busy shouting, he might have felt the telltale crack of breaking stone beneath his hands.

"Just don't let go!" Kwang begged.

"I'm not going to let go, but if you don't stop moving, I will cut this rope and let you fall."

Kwang uttered a terrified sound, but the threat had the desired effect. He stilled, allowing Mamoru to shift his fingers, finding a better grip between the dragon's teeth. Ignoring the whimpers of fear below him, Mamoru drew in a deep breath and started to pull up, his arms straining under the extra weight.

He gathered water and froze it around the fingers of his right hand, just to make sure that it held when he reached out for the roof with his left. Satisfied that his grip would hold, Mamoru removed his left hand and reached... but it was not his iron grip that gave.

The dragon's jaw broke off in his hand.

"No!" Mamoru made a frantic grab for the edge of the roof, but it was too far, his fingertips slid off—

And both boys plummeted into the mist.

4

THE WARRIOR

I'm not dying here!

The thought surged through Mamoru as he and his classmate plunged through open air down the mountainside. *I am not dying here!* Not because of a dinma of uncharacteristic clumsiness. Not because a lying outsider had made him lose his temper.

With Matsuda speed, Mamoru seized control of the mist around him, turned it to liquid, and slung a tendril of water upward to latch onto the nearest temple railing. As soon as the water made contact with the wood and stone, Mamoru started to freeze it, but he and Kwang were falling too fast. The tendril wasn't fully frozen when their weight jerked against it. The ice shattered and they kept falling, plummeting out of reach of the temple.

Dimly, Mamoru realized that Kwang was screaming, but the sound was lost in the roar of the wind as he scrambled for a solution. Twisting his body over in the air, Mamoru found the rope and yanked on it, bringing Kwang in close—a decision he immediately regretted when the screams got closer too, nearly breaking his eardrums. But at least this way he could protect them both at once.

Ignoring Kwang's shrieks of, *"Oh, Gods! Oh, GODS! AHHHHH! AHHHHH!"* Mamoru extended his jiya to sweep the surrounding mist into his control. Holding onto Kwang by the back of his uniform, he threw all the water he could beneath them. If they were going to hit solid rock, the best he could do was minimize the impact.

The darkness and vapor racing past on all sides made it impossible to see where they were falling, so Mamoru closed his eyes. He felt the break in the mist below, condensation-slick rock racing up to meet them terrifyingly fast, but he was faster. Pushing his jiya into action, he just managed to turn his mass of mist and droplets to snow before he and Kwang hit the side of the mountain.

The snow cushion tempered the collision, but the mountain still slammed hard into Mamoru's body, knocking the breath from his lungs. Tucking into a ball, he rolled with the fall, but they must have hit a steep slope because instead of rolling neatly onto his feet, he just kept tumbling. Rocks battered his spine, shoulders, and shins, his limbs tangled with Kwang's, and the two boys tumbled the last few bounds together before finally crashing into a solid outcropping that brought them to a stop.

Mamoru uncurled onto his back, shaking with shock, his whole skeleton ringing with the echoes of rock against bone. Closing his eyes, he assessed the damage to his own body. Broken blood vessels pulsed beneath his skin, promising dark bruises. His back and knees were scraped and blood seeped from cuts on his forearms, but he was going to be alright. He was alive.

"*Kwang-san?*" He opened his eyes. "*Are you okay?*"

The response was a muffled groan. The other boy was alive. That was enough for Mamoru to lie flat on his back for another few moments, getting his breathing under control. He didn't need his voice and limbs trembling when he rose. Once he had calmed his breathing and heart rate, he rolled over onto his hands and knees and took stock of their surroundings. They were perched on what seemed to be the only level place on an otherwise a steep incline. When Mamoru peered over the side of the ledge, he found sheer rock face stretching down into the darkness.

"*Is there any way down?*" Kwang asked gingerly.

Mamoru wasn't sure how to answer without causing more panic. "*It's not going to be easy.*" He wasn't even sure what part of the mountain they were on. Turning on the narrow ledge, he scanned the mountainside for something he recognized, but it was hard to see through the darkening fog, and nothing looked familiar. He could have used his jiya to clear the mist, but he doubted it would do much good. There wasn't enough light left.

"*Are we going to die here?*" Kwang asked.

"*No,*" Mamoru said, trying to sound more confident than he felt. "*Worst-case scenario: we'll have to wait for the morning light to find a way down, but we should try now, while there's still twilight.*"

"*Sorry,*" Kwang said. "*I don't think that's going to be possible.*"

"*Kwang-san.*" Mamoru turned around in exasperation. "*I know you're scared of heights, but—oh… oh no.*"

The northern boy was crumpled against a nearby rock. His left forearm was bent the wrong way, broken.

"*Sorry.*" Mamoru went to Kwang, who appeared to be considerably more bruised than he was. "*I should have done a better job breaking the fall.*"

"*I think you did okay,*" Kwang said, though his teeth were gritted against what must have been terrible pain, and he seemed afraid to move. "*We're alive. I've never seen someone materialize that much snow at once. I didn't know the fierce Kusanagi warriors could make such fluffy snow pillows.*"

"*Are you hurt anywhere else?*" Mamoru asked. "*Is there any bleeding?*"

"*I-I don't think so,*" Kwang stammered.

Sensing the distinct drip and flow of blood, Mamoru pulled back the leg of Kwang's hakama to reveal a deep gouge, where a jutting rock had taken a piece out of his calf. Blood was seeping freely from the injury, dripping down his shin to stain his silly Yammanka shoes.

"*Oh!*" Kwang squeaked like a girl. "*What? How did you—*

Nyaare, that looks terrible!"

"It could be worse," Mamoru said, *"but we should stop the bleeding."*

Kwang reached down to clean the wound, his hands shaky and his jiya even shakier. Mamoru pushed his hand away.

"I'll do it. Hold still." With a wave of his hand, he pulled a sheet of water from the air and ran it over Kwang's leg, washing the blood away. Kwang jumped and sucked in a breath through his teeth but managed not to squirm too much. *"This is going to feel weird,"* Mamoru warned, putting a hand to the wound before more blood got a chance to seep out. Using his jiya to hold the welling blood in place atop the wound, Mamoru began to draw the moisture from between the iron and carbon molecules, forcing the liquid to thicken and congeal.

"What are you doing?" Kwang demanded, undoubtedly feeling the crawling, needle-like itch that always accompanied accelerated healing.

"I'm creating a temporary scab," Mamoru replied. *"Please hold still."*

Kwang gaped, his pain seemingly forgotten in his astonishment. *"You can do that? You can control blood?"*

Mamoru's jaw clenched and he tried to focus more deeply on his work. *"A bit."*

"That's a rare ability!"

"Not in my mother's family," Mamoru answered without looking at Kwang. *"She's a Tsusano."*

It was Kaa-chan who had taught Mamoru how to create a makeshift scab. *For emergencies only,* she had told him sternly. *Blood manipulation is not a toy, nor is it something an upstanding Matsuda should display in public.*

Mamoru had always wondered about the extent of Kaa-chan's abilities, but it would have been inappropriate to ask. Aunt Setsuko had once whispered that his mother could use the Blood Needle—a Tsusano bloodline technique wherein the jijaka put a finger to their enemy's body and froze a drop of the victim's blood into a needle thin and sharp enough to pierce major blood vessels and lethal pressure points. Mamoru's jovial aunt could easily have been joking just to scare him; she liked to do that, and local lore had no shortage of horror stories about Tsusano blood manipulation.

There were chilling tales of Tsusano jijakalu so adept at controlling blood that they could manipulate the fluid in the bodies of other humans, using them as puppets. Unlike the Whispering Blade, Tsusano Blood Puppeteers were nothing more than a legend. No living Tsusano could attest to their existence, but it made for a good story to scare children.

"That's amazing!" Kwang marveled as Mamoru withdrew his hands from the gash to reveal a thin red scab.

"Don't touch it," Mamoru said sharply before Kwang got a chance to prod at his work. *"It's no substitute for natural healing. It won't hold under stress. And if you could… please don't mention this to anyone else."* The ability was frowned upon within the Matsuda family.

"Why not?" Kwang asked tactlessly.

"It's not…" Mamoru looked down. *"It's not an ability that a Matsuda should have."*

According to Tou-sama, blood manipulation was the reason Mamoru couldn't master the Whispering Blade. When a true Matsuda drew water from his surroundings, it was pure. The master Matsuda formed his weapon by compressing several billion water molecules to a thin blade through sheer force of nyama, creating ice as hard as metal and an edge the width of a single molecule. Mamoru always managed to catch other things up in his water—some iron particles, some dirt, some salt, some air bubbles—that weakened his ice and caused it to shatter under pressure.

"Just don't tell the other boys at school."

Kwang looked confused but agreed. *"Okay, I won't."*

Sitting back on his knees, Mamoru looked Kwang over. The broken arm needed to be set properly before his theonite body started to heal, the makeshift scab might not hold, and Kwang could have internal bruising that needed a healer's attention. Mamoru sighed.

"This can't wait until morning," he decided. *"The moon then."*

"What?"

"We'll wait until the moon is high. It's nearly full. It should cast enough light for us to climb down… or… for me to carry you down the mountain."

"We can't just call an ambulance?" Kwang asked.

The question actually made Mamoru laugh aloud. *"Takayubi doesn't have an ambulance. We don't even have a paved road."*

"Okay, but there must be a hospital, right?" Kwang said anxiously. *"Where's the nearest hospital?"*

"The medicine monks live in the western village."

"Not medicine monks!" Kwang growled, his pain manifesting in irritation. *"I mean a real hospital, with real medical equipment, and vehicles and stuff."*

"Too far," Mamoru said, *"near the Ameno stronghold on Tatsuyama."*

"Where the Hell is that?"

"At the base of the next mountain."

Kwang let out a loud groan. *"You know how many different schools I've gone to? Like twelve. And you know what? This is the worst first day of school I've ever had. Ever."*

"You're going to be okay," Mamoru said. *"I'm going to get us down."*

In his head, he tried to plot out their position on the mountain. They had fallen from the eastern side of the temple, meaning they had to be somewhere east of the lake. It wasn't a part of the mountain Mamoru had ever been before; there were no footpaths, and the steep rocks made climbing too risky for even a foolhardy adventurer. The slope they were perched on now was so steep that they probably would have gone right on rolling down the mountainside to their deaths if not for this bizarrely jutting rock formation… which, now that Mamoru was paying attention, did not feel much like rock at all. It was too perfect in its flatness. Too hard and glossy.

"What is this thing anyway?" Kwang gave voice to Mamoru's thoughts.

Kwang, who had fallen with his whole body against the smooth surface, pushed himself up with his good arm and ran a hand over the strange formation. Standing, Mamoru stepped back as far as the ledge would allow and surveyed the shape. It was darker than the rest of the mountainside, like a deep shadow behind Kwang. A flattened piece protruded from the body of the shadow, like a fin… or a wing?

"It's a plane!" Kwang exclaimed, just as the same realization dawned on Mamoru—and a smile lit his face.

"Oh!" Mamoru clapped his hands together as the pieces slid together on his mental map. *"I know where we are!"*

"What?"

"This is the black plane wreck," he explained. *"It's been here forever. You can see it from the lower steps when you look across the lake, which means we must be close to the water."* Relief coursed through Mamoru. The climb would be manageable after all.

"Oh," Kwang looked from Mamoru to the plane halfway buried in the mountainside. *"So, this has been here for a long time?"*

"Yeah." Mamoru remembered the first clear morning Yuuta had pointed it out—a smudge of dark metal lodged in the slope on the far side of the lake. *"It was here before Kumono became a school."* His father and uncle had mentioned seeing the plane when they climbed the steps as boys.

"Wait, so… how did it get here?" Kwang asked, squinting in confusion.

"It crashed during a military exercise, back when the Empire had troops in training here." That was what Hibiki Sensei had told Yuuta when he asked. *"The government was testing out some unmanned stealth aircraft. There was some kind of malfunction with this one, its engines failed, so they steered it into an uninhabited part of the mountain to crash."*

69

"Really...?" Kwang reached out to touch the plane with the fingers of his good hand, his brow furrowed. *"So that would have been when?"*

"During the Keleba." The Great War had been the last time the government maintained any military presence in Shirojima.

Kwang was running his hand in slow circles over the body of the plane, as though searching it for something. "Matsuda-san..." His voice had grown quiet and strained. *"I don't know how to tell you this... This isn't a Kaigenese plane."*

"What?" Mamoru let out an incredulous laugh, even as dread pulled at something weak inside him. *"Of course, it is! Where else could it have come from?"*

Kwang shook his head, looking apologetic, almost afraid. *"It's Yammanka."*

"Why would you say that?" Damn Kwang, Mamoru couldn't keep the anger out of his voice. *"Why would you say that!?"*

Now Kwang was definitely afraid, but that didn't stop him from explaining, *"Kaigenese planes are made of metal. This isn't metal."*

"Don't be ridiculous." Mamoru crossed to the plane in two angry strides. *"Of course, it's made of..."* But when his fingers touched the body of the plane, the words stopped in his throat. No metal was that smooth. *"What... what is this?"*

"Zilazen glass," Kwang said.

"What?"

"Zilazen glass," Kwang repeated. *"The hardest type of Yammanka obsidian. It's the strongest material in the world."*

"You're not a craftsman," Mamoru snapped in desperation. *"How could you possibly know that?"*

"Just look." Kwang put a hand against the plane and painstakingly stood to point to where its nose had rammed into the mountain. *"This jet crashed here and didn't break. It went straight into the side of the mountain and there isn't one crack in it."* And now that Mamoru looked, Kwang was right. The plane's exterior couldn't have been smoother if it were manufactured yesterday.

Even the purest Kotetsu steel didn't have that kind of durability. *"Only Zilazen glass could do that."*

Mamoru's fingers curled against the shell of the plane.

"No," he breathed. *"You're lying."* This wasn't a Yammanka plane. It wasn't Zilazen glass. *"You're lying."* He would prove it.

Mamoru dug his hands into the side of the plane until he felt his fingernails threatening to break, then dragged them down, trying to scratch the allegedly impervious glass. But even as Mamoru's nails bent and broke, he couldn't leave the tiniest mark on the plane. The surface was so perfect that in the weakening twilight, Mamoru could see his own face reflected in the blackness. Troubled. Frantic. The face of a lost child, not a warrior.

"I'm not lying," Kwang said quietly. *"You could take all the swords in Kaigen to that glass, and you wouldn't be able to scratch it."*

"Shut up!" Mamoru snarled, hating the fear in his voice.

He would *make* Kwang shut up, like he had back in the schoolyard. He would break through this black glass and prove him a liar, and this would all be over. Mamoru drew an arm back and punched the side of the plane with all his strength. A spear of pain slammed through his arm, but he didn't let that stop him. He struck again and again, in a rain of blows that would have dented any metal. Mamoru's hands could break rock and steel, but the only things that broke now were the skin and blood vessels on his knuckles.

"Matsuda-san, stop! Stop!" Kwang begged, though he didn't seem willing to put himself in range of those fists a second time. *"You'll break your hand! I'm telling you, that's the hardest glass in the—"*

"No," Mamoru growled through gritted teeth. "No, it's *not!*"

Drawing his fist back, he froze blood and mist into the hardest ice he could form across his knuckles and punched again. The ice broke, sending a shockwave of pain through his hand. The plane's shining black exterior was not even scratched. But Mamoru was shattered.

A waati earlier, Kwang's assertions had been just words and a few holographic images. Those could be faked and made up. Now a piece of his story was right in front of Mamoru. It was Zilazen glass, harder than his own ice. Unbreakable. Irrefutable.

"Matsuda-san." Kwang's voice would have sounded gentle if the words weren't twisting into Mamoru like knives. *"Just look at it for a dinma. Have you ever seen a Kaigenese jet this shape?"*

Mamoru wished he couldn't hear the words—tried not to hear them—but the plane was right in front of him. And Kwang was right; it looked nothing like any jet he had ever seen thunder overhead, nor any plane in the Kaigenese military parades on TV. It took him a moment to realize where he had seen this type of jet before: in the form of an obsidian memorial statue, with a proud woman pilot beside it. A pilot…

In a desperate lurch, Mamoru was scrambling up onto the tilted wing of the plane.

"What are you doing?" Kwang demanded, trying and failing to hold the stronger boy back with his one good arm. *"Be careful, Matsuda-san! You don't know how stable that is!"*

Hibiki Sensei had said that the black plane was part of Kaigenese forays into unmanned jets during the Keleba. Mamoru could confirm that it was the truth. If he climbed onto the top of the plane and there was no pilot's seat, he could ignore everything Kwang had said. He could lay this all to rest. He could—

The hope died as he reached the top of the plane and found a raised cockpit before him. While the body of the plane was as black as cooled coals, the cockpit was made of transparent glass so clear it could have been polished the day before. Mamoru should have stopped there. He should not have crawled forward to peer through the glass.

But he looked—and his whole body stiffened. The blood fled his cheeks, leaving him as pale as the face before him—if one could call it a face. All that remained of the pilot was a skull, lying askew atop a jumble of white bones. The shreds of fabric clinging to the warrior's ribcage were too deteriorated to identify as any kind of military uniform. The skin, whether it had been pale or dark, had decayed from the bones a long time ago.

Mamoru's first impulse should have been to start back from the human remains, but he was frozen, trapped in the emptiness of those sockets where once there had been a pilot's sharp eyes.

"Matsuda-san? What is it?" Kwang made as though to climb up to look into the cockpit too, but Mamoru shook his head. The look on his face must have said everything because Kwang stopped.

"Is it bad?" he asked quietly.

"Just... don't look," Mamoru said, though he himself couldn't take his eyes off the skeleton. *"Don't look."*

Pilots were young people with keen eyesight and quick reflexes, skilled enough to maneuver a machine many times the speed of a human, brave enough to battle far above sea or solid ground. And this young fighter had been left to rot here with no grave, no memorial, no one to remember them. Until wind and rain had washed away their face, their skin, their uniform, any indicator of who they were and what they fought for.

Mamoru looked into the sockets and wondered if the pilot had had black eyes like his. Would his face look the same stripped of all its skin? Would the mountain wash him away as easily?

He put his hand to the cockpit glass and let his fingers trail down until they ran over a series of fine grooves in the glass. Turning his attention to the shapes beneath his fingertips, Mamoru saw that the cockpit was lined with Falleya symbols of strength and protection. Among the symbols, in Yammaninke letters, was an inscription.

"N... nyama du-gu la," Mamoru read out slowly. *"N'nyama ga-na la."* He turned to Kwang, unable to keep his voice from shaking. *"What does it mean?"*

"N'nyama dugu la. N'nyama gana la?" Kwang repeated the words with the musical ease of a native speaker. *"My nyama for my country. My nyama for my king."*

The strength went out of Mamoru's limbs. Involuntarily, he found himself crumpling in something like a bow, something like pain. His forehead thudded against the cockpit. It had been decades since this plane hit the mountainside, yet Mamoru could feel it crashing through everything he knew, scattering the broken pieces to the elements.

It didn't seem to matter whether the skeleton belonged to a man or a woman, a Kaigenese pilot or a Yammanka one. A warrior had died here, and Hibiki Sensei had lied about it. The whole village had lied about it.

Mamoru's nyama seethed with something different from anger, different from hurt. It was utter disorientation. The force of his world falling apart churned the mist. Condensation writhed and slithered over the rocks.

"Matsuda?" Kwang said as the blood rose from his skin, pulled into the whirl of Mamoru's jiya. He looked on nervously—until Mamoru's turmoil tugged at the blood inside his open wounds. *"Ow! Hey!"*

The shout of pain was enough to yank Mamoru out of his confusion.

His head jerked up. A sharp gasp brought the mountainside back into focus. With a few measured breaths, he managed to bring his jiya under control. He was far from stable ice, but he managed to release the water particles around him, including those in Kwang's blood.

"Ow…" Kwang repeated, looking on in a mixture of wonder and horror as his own blood settled back onto his skin in a sticky mess. The wound in his calf was bleeding again, worse than before.

"Sorry," Mamoru breathed, shaking his head. *"I'm sorry. Here, I'll fix it."*

Jerkily, he climbed down from the plane and folded to his knees to tend to Kwang's leg. He tried to find solace in his own jiya, repairing the broken scab. But his control had fled him, his power scattering out of his grasp.

"Ow!" Kwang pulled his leg back as Mamoru's third attempt to repair the scab only made the bleeding worse.

"Sorry," Mamoru repeated in a weak voice that didn't seem to belong to him. *"I'm sorry."*

"It's okay," Kwang said, though he had put a hand over the wound, silently refusing Mamoru's help. *"I'll just cut off part of my sleeve and tie it."*

Mamoru nodded and tried to laugh it off. *"I guess I'm not as good with blood as I thought."*

"That's fine with me." Kwang gave Mamoru a strained smile. *"I don't want to wake up one day to find you using me as a puppet."*

"That's not—" Mamoru shook his head, barely able to focus on Kwang's words. *"Blood Puppetry isn't real. It's just a myth."*

"Well… I thought all the rumors about the Shirojima warriors were just myths, but you island people are more powerful than I thought." Kwang pressed his lips together and stared at Mamoru with a strange expression—something guilty and pitying that made Mamoru want to retch. *"Maybe there is some truth to what your history teacher told you. Maybe—"*

"Don't," Mamoru whispered.

"What?"

"Just don't…" His voice was strained. *"Don't speak to me."* He was one slip-up away from losing his tenuous grip on his jiya all over again. Stiffly, he turned away from Kwang and the cursed glass plane. *"I'm going to meditate."*

It was the only thing he could think of to do.

The sheer exhaustion helped. Often Mamoru could meditate better when he was drained, near sleep, when the whole world melted away except for the water all around him. Mamoru focused until Kwang disappeared. The plane and its pilot disappeared. The rock disappeared. The only thing left in the world was pure water, clear as daylight and clean as polished steel. Deep in his trance, Mamoru could feel the outline of the mountain, coated in a sheen of water droplets.

He followed the mist and condensation, sinking and trickling gently downward until he could feel the heavy ripple of liquid water—the Kumono Lake. Its weight eased a slow breath from Mamoru's body, relaxing his muscles. He settled into the embrace of the lake and nestled there for a long time, swirling with the spring water. Then, when it was time, gravity drew him to the biggest of the lake's outgoing streams, and he slipped into it.

The stream carried him down the mountain, through the dewy grasses of the western village, until it splayed its fingers over the rocks around the finawu's temple, becoming many streams, all flowing down, down, until they met the salty weight of the ocean—the primordial power that had given birth to Kaigen, humanity, and life itself. Here, even things as fleeting as mountain streams became part of eternity. Here, there was a truth that ebbed and shifted but never died. Here, he was home.

Rooted in the depths, he felt the moon rise. Drawn to the irresistible lure of Nami's mirror, he rose too, lifting fishing boats at their moorings. Tide pools filled up all the way down the coast, silver as dragon scales under the full moon, little mirrors to answer her brightness.

He opened his eyes to the sight he knew he would find—Nami's mirror held high in the sky, shining with pure light that pierced the realms of past and present. Breathing out, he was Mamoru again, but more. Whole.

"The tide pools are full," he said without emotion. *"It's time."*

"What?" Kwang started upright from where he had been dozing against the side of the plane. *"Time for what?"*

Mamoru nodded toward the sky. *"That's all the moonlight we're going to get. Don't worry. We don't have far to go."*

"Far to where?" Kwang mumbled, still half asleep.

"The Kumono Lake. It's about ten bounds below us."

"Are you sure?" Kwang asked. *"Ten bounds is a long way to sense clearly."*

Still attuned to the water all around him, Mamoru couldn't help a human smile of amusement. *"Not for me."*

"Fine. But I swear to Nyaare, if there are more rocks down there, and we jump, my ghost is going to haunt your ghost to the end of the Laaxara."

"We're not going to jump." Mamoru wouldn't admit it, but he didn't think he had the nerve for any more freefalling through the

darkness, no matter how clearly he could sense the water below. *"You're going to get on my back and I'm going to climb down."*

"I don't know if I can hold on with just one arm."

"Good thing we have a rope."

Mamoru had never tried scaling a sheer cliff face, but his mother had once told him that it was easy to climb smooth walls with only ice if your jiya was strong and you coordinated it right with your physical movements. How a housewife like Kaa-chan knew how to scale walls, Mamoru had no idea, but she turned out to be right. Recalling her instructions, he formed a disc of water around each hand and then turned the water to ice, freezing his hands to the rock. To descend, all he had to do was melt the ice beneath one hand enough to shift it down, refreeze it, and then repeat the process with the opposite hand.

A weaker jijaka might risk the ice breaking from the flat surface, but Mamoru's jiya was easily strong enough to secure him to the mountain, even with a nervous Kwang tied to his back. Hand under hand, he lowered himself and his classmate down the cliff side.

The mist grew thicker as they neared the lake, coiling tendrils reaching from the water's surface to wrap around them, smothering the moonlight. Visibility grew steadily worse as they descended, and Mamoru had to rely on his jiya to feel his way down the last few bounds to the water.

"Okay, so what's your plan now?" Kwang asked as he too sensed the lake beneath them. *"I don't know if I can swim that far with one arm."*

"You won't have to." Mamoru was already at work, freezing the lake water directly beneath them, forming a broad shape.

When he lowered them to the lake, their feet touched the bottom of a boat made of sturdy, buoyant ice.

"Oh," Kwang said in surprise and looked appreciatively at the sleek vessel. *"Well done, Matsuda-san. It would take me a whole gbaati to form a boat this nice."*

"Sit," Mamoru said, lowering himself to his knees. The boat wasn't perfectly balanced; it would capsize if either of them stood

and moved around too much.

"Okay." Kwang gingerly arranged his damaged body into a sitting position opposite Mamoru. *"Do you need me to help propel or—"*

"No," Mamoru said, and with a sweep of his hand, sent them gliding swiftly over the lake's surface. *"You don't know where we're going."*

People whispered that the moonlit curls of mist on the lake were ghosts from the next world, striding their silvery way over the water's surface. Mamoru had never feared them. The people who had lived and died here in times past were Matsudas and Yukinos. They were family.

Tonight, for the first time, they seemed like strangers.

This was the first time he had had to look at the wisps of the past and wonder what they were *really*. Were they the ancestors he had always imagined, or something entirely different? Had they fought in battles the rest of the world had covered up and forgotten? Had their lifeblood stained these waters before it was washed to the sea? If so, they must resent the living for washing away the memory of their sacrifice as easily as blood from a shoreline.

The Ryuhon monks said that spirits only ever remained bound to the Realm of the Duna unwillingly, trapped there by bitterness, regret, or simple spite. Was there anger in the silvery tendrils crowding around Mamoru? Did they resent him for his ignorance? Were they offended that he did not know the extent of their sacrifice? Or was it his treasonous thoughts that had turned them sinister?

Maybe, somehow, Kwang had really tricked him. A liar had made him doubt his family, his empire, and everything he had been taught. Now his ancestors, stung with the insult, had come seething out of the Laaxara to drag him away. Shadows wavered through the fog and Mamoru found himself pressing closer to Kwang.

"What is it?" the other boy asked, oblivious to the otherworldly presences.

"Nothing." Mamoru raised a hand, dispersing the mist before

the keel, pushing aside any ghostly faces waiting in the darkness ahead. *"It's nothing."*

Mamoru managed to keep himself calm across the remainder of the lake, but he still let out a breath of relief when their vessel bumped the shore and the two stepped out onto solid ground. His shoulders tense, Mamoru realized he was too afraid to turn and look back at the lake.

"Are you sure you're okay?" Kwang asked, peering at Mamoru's face in the low light.

"Of course, I'm okay," Mamoru said, doing his best to adopt an icy tone. *"You're the one with a broken limb. Come on."* He took hold of Kwang's uninjured arm with both hands. *"Stay close. I know the path here, but it's steep and uneven. I don't want you to fall and break any more bones."*

It was a plausible excuse, but at that moment, it was Mamoru who really needed a living thing to hold onto.

5

THE FORGE

Mamoru didn't instinctively know his way around this part of the mountain the way he did the steps, but he had deliberately brought their boat ashore near the stream that ran from Kumono Lake. He knew that if they followed the water without losing their footing, it would take them to help. Frogs chanted and dewdrops brushed their ankles as they waded into the grass alongside the stream. The fireflies bobbing along the bank didn't do much to light the way, but between the dewdrops and the running water, Mamoru was able to keep them on course without the use of his eyes.

"How much further?" Kwang asked and Mamoru could hear the fatigue in his voice.

"We're almost there. Look." He pointed down the mountain, where a red-orange glow had appeared over a rocky ridge.

"What's that?"

"Forge fire," Mamoru said, allowing himself a smile of relief. *"We've reached the numu village."*

"The what?"

"The numu village. You know, where the swordsmiths live."

"That's where you're taking me?" Kwang said, eyes wide and fearful in the firelight.

"They're knowledgeable healers," Mamoru said, *"the best we're going to find at this time of night. They'll know what to do*

about your arm."

On a map of Kaigen, the people of Mount Takayubi were lumped into a single 'Takayubi Village.' In reality, there were four distinct villages on the mountain, each populated by a different type of people.

The lowest of these settlements was the fishing village at the foot of the mountain, where Mamoru's aunt Setsuko had been born. Halfway up the mountain, surrounded by pine forests, sat the western village, where resided the influx of koro families who had moved to Takayubi over the years in the hopes of training with the great Matsudas and Yukinos.

Mamoru's own village sat high on the mountain, just beneath the cloudline. The old village was the reason the rest existed, home to the Matsudas and Yukinos who had ruled this mountain for over a thousand years. The numu village was not far from the old village, nestled among the rocks, glowing through even the coldest nights.

Kwang was still eyeing the fire like it might leap over the ridge and bite him, but the numu village was like a second home to Mamoru. His father sent him here for a few months each year to apprentice with the Kotetsu swordsmiths. In most of Kaigen, it was considered atypical—unthinkable even—for a koro to train in numu arts, but the Matsudas had a special relationship with their Kotetsu neighbors.

These days, Takayubi's numu community wasn't as much a village as it was a large cluster of houses alongside the Kumono stream. As Mamoru led Kwang onto the main path down toward the firelight, they were greeted by the sound of hammers, ringing like temple bells, pounding the impurities from metal. While the rest of the mountain slept, the smiths worked through the cool of the night when the heat from the forges was more bearable.

"I didn't realize numu villages like this even existed anymore," Kwang said as the air warmed around them. *"Aren't there, like, machines that can do their work for them now?"*

"If there were machines that could improve their work, that's what they would be using," Mamoru said. *"The Kotetsu family are*

the best swordsmiths in the world."

"If their swords are the best in the world, how come they're still here?" Kwang challenged. *"Why don't they go get jobs arming the Kaigenese military?"*

"Some of them have," Mamoru said. In his grandfather's day, the Kotetsu village had been twice its current size. *"A lot of the Takayubi blacksmiths moved north to the cities to go into manufacturing, but the best ones stayed here."*

"And they make a living on this?" Kwang said incredulously. *"How many swords can you even make per month working out of a fire pit?"*

"Three," Mamoru said, *"when they're in a rush."*

"Wait, what?" Kwang said. *"Only three? And that's all they do? Who even sponsors that?"*

"We do," Mamoru said. *"They're still here because the military can't afford them; we pay them what they're worth."*

Truthfully, the Matsuda family currently *couldn't* pay the Kotetsus what they were worth. Mamoru's last two-month apprenticeship with the blacksmiths hadn't been training as much as it had been paying off the Matsuda family's last sword order in labor.

"Any one of those swords is easily worth a whole house." The Yukino family had actually sold one of their old castles to cover the cost of the last few swords they had commissioned.

By this time, Mamoru and Kwang had reached the broad, foot-beaten path that ran the length of the village. While the rest of the mountain slept in the cool moonlight, the numu settlement was alive with the yellow-orange glow of torches. There was firelight here that never went out. No matter the hour of night, there was always someone at work.

Kwang hesitated, and Mamoru had to coax him on down the main path. His reaction wasn't unusual. Most koronu harbored a healthy fear of the numu's fiery domain, but Mamoru had walked here enough that he no longer feared the heat.

He did, however, feel a wave of prickling guilt overtake him like flames over kindling. For all his months of training here, he hadn't been able to translate the arts of steel into ice. The sound of hammers sharpened and each ring smarted, reminding Mamoru of his own efforts to create a blade—all his impurities.

They weren't far down the path when Mamoru caught sight of a figure moving in the firelight—the head swordsmith's son, carrying a towering bundle of firewood.

"Atsushi!" Mamoru called out to his friend.

The ten-year-old numu paused, looked up, and a grin lit up his face.

"Mamo—Matsuda-dono!" he caught himself, remembering his manners.

When the two were children, they had gotten away with calling each other by their given names, but now that they were both young men, Atsushi had to remember to address the son of his patron house with the appropriate respect. He fumbled with his load for a moment before depositing the firewood on the ground and bowing low.

"Welcome—I'm so sorry. We weren't expecting you." He glanced up at Mamoru. "What… what are you doing here?"

"I'm so sorry to trouble you and your family," Mamoru said. "We have a situation—"

"You're hurt!" Atsushi exclaimed, noticing the blood on Mamoru's knuckles.

"I'm fine," Mamoru said hastily, "but my classmate needs medical attention. I'm sorry to ask you—"

"I'll get my father right away." Atsushi raced off to the house before Mamoru could thank him, his firewood forgotten in the dirt.

"So, who was that?" Kwang asked.

"Kotetsu Atsushi is the head swordsmith's son," Mamoru said, stooping to gather the wood Atsushi had dropped. *"I've been apprenticing alongside him since we were young."*

"You—wait, you what?"

Before Mamoru could explain, a woman stuck her head out of the house and called, "Mamoru-dono, you silly boy, put that down!"

"It's no trouble, Kotetsu-san," Mamoru said. "I can—"

"Don't be ridiculous!" The blacksmith's wife exclaimed. "My son will get it. You and your friend, come inside."

"And who was that?" Kwang asked as Mamoru disregarded the woman's instructions and hauled the bundle of wood the rest of the way to the Kotetsus' doorstep.

"Atsushi's mother," Mamoru said, setting down the firewood, *"Kotetsu Tamami."*

"Is she a swordsmith too?"

"No, no," Mamoru laughed. Women didn't touch swords, let alone forge them. *"She makes hair ornaments."*

When Mamoru and Kwang entered the house, Tamami was at the stove cooking, while her elderly mother-in-law, Chizue, dozed in a chair nearby. Little Hotaru, Naoko, and Kyoko, whose shouts and giggles usually greeted Mamoru, were nowhere to be seen, probably in bed.

As grimy as the streets and structures of the numu village appeared from the outside, the inside of the Kotetsus' modest house was always immaculate. Mamoru had just finished properly introducing Kwang to Kotetsu Tamami and thanking her once again when the swordsmith himself stepped in through the back door, wiping his soot-stained hands on a rag.

Kotetsu Katashi was a mountain of a man. His arms writhed with hard cables of muscle and his shoulders had a way of filling up a doorway. He made an intimidating picture when he swung his hammer, his eyes furious with focus. But away from the forge, he had a warm voice and gentle smile that could put the most anxious of people at ease. It was that smile that greeted Mamoru now, wide and bright beneath the black smudges.

"Kotetsu Kama, good evening," Mamoru greeted his teacher. "I'm so sorry! I didn't mean to interrupt your work."

"Ah, it's fine, little Matsuda." Kotetsu waved him off. "Atsushi-kun can mind the fires for a gbaati. Let me wash up and I'll have a look at your friend. In the meantime, you two can have a seat in the kitchen. My wife will have tea and food ready for you in a moment."

"Kotetsu Kama, please, that isn't necessary," Mamoru protested. "We don't want to impose—"

"Nonsense, Mamoru-dono. You're not imposing. This is your house, as it is ours."

"We don't need to eat your food—"

"And what will I tell Matsuda Takeru-dono? That I sent his injured son away with an empty stomach? You'll stay for dinner," Kotetsu said with a note of finality that shut Mamoru up.

"Thank you, Kotetsu Kama," he said with another bow.

Kwang bowed too, murmuring his own quiet, "Thank you."

When the swordsmith had gone, Kwang turned to Mamoru with a look of surprise.

"You call him 'Kama'?" he said in a low voice. Mamoru could understand his confusion; the honorific was usually used by a servant or apprentice to address his master. It wasn't a title the average Kaigenese koro would use to address a sooty numu. *"I thought you were from a high warrior house."*

"I am," Mamoru said. *"That's why I owe him my respect."*

"I don't—what does that mean?" Kwang whispered as he followed Mamoru into the Kotetsus' kitchen.

"My family has a special relationship with the Kotetsus. You wouldn't understand—"

"Of course, the boy does not understand," an impatient voice creaked and Mamoru jumped, realizing that it had come from Kotetsu's mother. He hadn't known that the wrinkled old woman was awake. "How could he understand? He is an outsider." The bent woman leaned forward, her clouded eyes narrowing. "I may not be able to see anymore, but I know every speck of nyama on this mountain. *And you, boy, weren't born here. You blew in from someplace far away, didn't you?"*

Kwang only seemed to be able to stare open-mouthed at the old numu.

"Something wrong with you, boy?" Kotetsu's mother snapped.

"I thought it was your arm that broke, not your tongue."

"S-sorry, numuba," Kwang stuttered.

"Numuba?" Grandma Kotetsu cackled at the Yammaninke honorific. *"He speaks like he's from far away too. Matsuda-kun."* The woman's sightless eyes didn't move but she tilted her head fondly in Mamoru's direction. *"You can't expect a city boy like him to understand our ways, no matter how you try to explain. We're just an oddity to him. A myth. A silly fantasy from far in the past."*

"I never said—"

"Please sit, Kwang-san," Tamami said kindly. "Mamoru-dono, you too. Have some tea."

She poured them each a piping hot cup of tea before hurrying to set food on the table. Mamoru pulled some water from the air and tried not to grimace as he used it to clean his hands. His knuckles were still oozing blood, despite the makeshift scabs he had formed over them. The water stung. He could feel Kwang's eyes on him as he cast the water back into the air around him, and did his best to keep his eyes down.

"Our koro is troubled," Grandma Kotetsu muttered—it almost seemed, to herself. "His jiya could boil up and drown him."

Mamoru pretended not to hear and took a drink from his teacup. The bitter caffeine should have reinvigorated him. Instead, the heat seemed to seep into his bones, softening him like ice over a flame.

"Now then," Kotetsu said, re-emerging from the back room. *"I'm sorry I forgot to introduce myself."* He turned to Kwang with a bow. *"I'm Numu Kotetsu Katashi."*

"I'm Kwang Chul-hee." Kwang hurried to stand and bow. *"Nice to meet—"*

"Sit, sit," Kotetsu chuckled, putting a hand on Kwang's shoulder to ease him back down. *"You look like a proper mess. No need to strain yourself. Let's have a look at that arm."*

"He's also bleeding from his leg," Mamoru said. "I tried to make a scab, but it's—"

"Hush, Matsuda-kun," Grandma Kotetsu said in her creaky

voice. "Let the numu do his job."

"Yes, ma'am. Sorry."

"Here." Tamami spooned some rice into a bowl and held it out to Mamoru. "Eat."

"Thank you." As Mamoru reached out to accept the bowl, the light fell on his hands. The woman's eyes flicked to his bloodied knuckles and then to his face, filled with concern.

"Mamoru-dono… What did you and your classmate get into?"

"I…" Mamoru started, but before he could finish, Grandma Kotetsu interrupted with a reproachful click of her tongue.

"Leave koro business to the koronu," she told her daughter-in-law. "If these boys went and got bloody, it's their business, not ours."

"Of course," Tamami said demurely, though the concern didn't leave her face. "I'm sorry."

"So…" Mamoru quickly cast around for a different topic of conversation. "The little ones are all doing well?" He nodded toward the back room, where he assumed the Kotetsus' three youngest children were sleeping.

"Yes," Tamami said with a smile. "You'll have to visit some time they're all awake. They get so excited whenever you come around."

On the other side of the room, Kotetsu Kama had set about tying a splint around Kwang's arm.

"Relax," the smith rumbled. *"I know a city boy like you is probably used to brightly-lit clinics with lots of fancy equipment, but there's nothing for you to fear. I know what I'm doing."*

Kwang swallowed and nodded.

"How did a boy like you end up in a little village like ours anyway?"

*"My father works for—*ahh!" Kwang winced. *"Sorry. My father works for Geomijul."*

"For what?"

"Geomijul. It's a company that specializes in info-com technology."

"So, he's a traveling electronics salesman?"

"Not exactly. His job is to set up the infrastructure places need to use info-com devices. I guess someone in this area agreed to pay Geomijul to install satellite towers here, so you guys can get better reception with your info-com devices. He's here to oversee that."

"Does your father know that barely anyone here has *an info-com device?"* Kotetsu asked.

"Well, the company is hoping they'll sell better after the infrastructure is in place for them to actually work. Their goal is to set up enough towers in the next three years that info-com communication is possible from anywhere in Kaigen. I know my dad said something about speaking to the local craftsmen about enlisting their help. He hasn't gotten a chance to do much yet, but he'll probably come here soon looking to hire some numuwu. I'm sure building big metal towers isn't exactly your specialty, so if you guys don't want to do it, I can let him know—"

"On the contrary, it sounds wonderful. I'll send my son, Atsushi."

"What? Really?"

"Oh, yes. A young numu should always learn about new technologies. For an old man like me, that sort of thing is hard, but for a growing mind, it is essential. Young Mamoru-dono is a fair metalworker himself," Kotetsu said with a smile at Mamoru. *"If his father allows it, he might be able to help you too."*

"Right." Kwang looked from Mamoru to Kotetsu Kama in confusion. *"So, Matsuda-san says he… apprentices with you?"*

"I know it seems strange," Kotetsu said, *"but it's a tradition that predates modern Kaigenese society."*

"But… why? I don't understand."

"It's a long story. Please hold still, Kwang-san."

There was a creak as Grandma Kotetsu leaned forward. *"A thousand years ago,"* she began, *"long before metal was ever spun into conductive wires and space-going satellites, the most coveted metal in Kaigen was made by a small family of blacksmiths living here in Takayubi. Their surpassing skill in forging tools and weapons earned them the name Kotetsu, which means 'steel' in Shirojima Dialect. Though the laws of kafonu and kamaya had not yet come to Kaigen, this blacksmith family formed a close relationship of patronage with the noble house of Matsuda—a deep bond of blood and steel, which ensured that the Kotetsu smiths would always be protected and the Matsudas would always have their superior swords.*

"At this time, the Matsudas were masters of making blades and spears from ice. While these early ice weapons were rough, the fighting style served them well. Using their ice to fight long range battles, and their Kotetsu-forged steel to fight at close range, they dominated this peninsula and much of western Shirojima."

Kwang was looking at Grandma Kotetsu in confusion, but he seemed too intrigued to interrupt. For Mamoru's part, it was strange to hear a story he had heard so many times in Dialect translated to Kaigengua.

"It was at the height of the Matsuda family's reign that the first Falleya missionaries came to these shores en masse. Some came from the mainland, some came from Disa, some came from as far away as the Empire of Yamma. These missionary singers brought with them new technologies and new ways of looking at the world. Many people of Shirojima embraced the new religion, eagerly integrating it into their lives, including the Matsudas' nearest neighbor, the Yukino house.

"But the Matsuda patriarch at the time openly rejected Falleya, going as far as to send his men to behead missionaries and converts in the streets. In retaliation, a Falleya army, led by Lord Yukino Izumi, laid siege to the Matsuda castle and razed it to the ground. The Matsudas who did not die in battle were burned to death in the inferno… all except one. This was the lord's youngest son, Matsuda Takeru, for whom this boy's father is named." She nodded toward Mamoru. *"As the flames rose around the room where he slept, his mother wrapped him in an embrace of water and ice. The fire consumed wood, flesh, and bone around them, but her love protected him. When the sun rose the next day, the woman*

was dead, having finally succumbed to the heat and smoke, but in her arms, the child Takeru had survived."

Mamoru was still, his stinging hands resting in his lap. He had heard the story of Matsuda Takeru a dozen times. When he was a little boy, the razing of the Matsuda castle had moved him to tears. Now he had to look at his bloodied knuckles and wonder if the story was even true. He had never felt so empty.

"Yukino Izumi's Falleya army did their best to kill every koro they found in the castle and the surrounding houses," Grandma Kotetsu continued, *"but the resident family of Kotetsu blacksmiths was spared, their precious forges left intact. For under Falleya, it is a sin to commit violence against a craftsman."*

Kwang nodded. Having lived in Yamma, he would understand that.

"It was a Kotetsu man named Kenzou who picked his way through the ashes when the smoke had cleared. It was Kenzou who found the young Takeru in the ruins and gently helped him to his feet. By this time, Yukino Izumi had proclaimed himself ruler of the region, and Kenzou knew that if the boy were discovered, he would be killed. So, he took Takeru to his home and raised the koro as one of his own sons. And this act—this solitary act of kindness—altered the destinies of the Matsuda family, the Kotetsu family, and all of Shirojima forever.

"Hiding under a false name, young Takeru was raised to adolescence in Kotetsu Kenzou's household, under the rule of Yukino Izumi's Falleya state. As Takeru grew, he proved himself a genius.

"Despite what had happened to his family, he was able to listen to the missionary finawu and learn the value of Falleya. Despite his warrior's blood, he took to the forge like a natural numu, creating swords of excellent quality and incredible beauty. Despite his skill as a smith, he knew it was his duty to avenge his family and continue the Matsuda line. So, as a young man, he set out in disguise to train with the jiya swordsmen of the Ameno and Ginkawa clans, further north.

"No one knows exactly where he went during that time or who trained him, though many koro houses tried to claim credit after the fact. But it is the story of his return, years later, that propelled him into legend…"

Kotetsu Chizue trailed off, nodding to herself.

"So…" Kwang prompted after a moment. *"What happened?"*

"Oh, you want me to continue?" Grandma Kotetsu said in amusement. *"I thought you might be done with this old lady's foolish story."*

"No, please," Kwang said emphatically. *"You have to keep going."*

"Very well, city boy," she chuckled. *"On Takeru's return, he walked through the town gates with no weapon, only a cloth traveling pack on his back. Inside the city, he announced himself for all to hear: "I am Matsuda Takeru, Lord of Takayubi. I am here to take back my family's home." Upon hearing this, the town guards seized him and brought him before Lord Yukino Izumi.*

In Yukino's hall, Takeru faced his family's killer for the first time and repeated his challenge. Yukino Izumi was unimpressed.

"You claim to be Takeru, heir to the Matsuda house," he said, *"but I know that all the Matsudas were killed years ago. This makes you both a liar and a traitor. I have no obligation to accept your challenge. You will be executed."*

"Then I offer you a compromise," said Takeru. *"I will face you unarmed."*

"Unarmed!" Yukino laughed. *"You believe you can kill me without a sword?"*

"I do," Takeru said calmly.

"If you are so confident in your skills," Yukino said, *"then why not kill me now?"*

Takeru looked around him and replied, "Your guards are sons of this mountain, as I am. I prefer not to hurt them."

Intrigued, Yukino agreed to the duel, appointed a time, and released Takeru. When his men questioned his decision, the lord said, "He will turn tail and run or he will step into the circle with me and die. Either way, we will be rid of him."

Upon hearing of Takeru's return and the challenge he had issued, Kotetsu Kenzou hurried to his adoptive son and begged him to withdraw from the fight.

"The challenge has been made," Takeru said. "As a man and a koro, I cannot withdraw."

"Yukino Izumi is one of the best swordsmen in the region," Kenzou warned, in despair. "The sword he wields is one of mine— the best I ever made. How do you expect to protect yourself with no weapon at all?"

Takeru just smiled. "You may have given Yukino-dono a great sword, but the weapon you have given me is greater than metal. You have given me knowledge of the blade itself." With that, the young Matsuda embraced his mentor and adoptive father and promised to return to him after the fight.

Yukino Izumi appeared the next day with the sword Kotetsu Kenzou had forged for him, the best weapon of its time, folded a thousand times, sharpened to cut through five men at a stroke. Yukino met Matsuda at the center of the main square, in view of all of Takayubi…"

Kwang leaned forward, his eyes wide.

"Yukino unsheathed the great sword—and the fight was over."

"What?" Kwang said.

"In a single stroke, Matsuda Takeru's jiya sliced through the Kotetsu-forged blade and Yukino's body. The usurper was dead before he hit the ground, the first victim of the Whispering Blade."

"What? But… how?" Kwang looked from Mamoru to the numu family. *"Ice can't cut through metal. It's scientifically impossible. Even at sub-zero temperatures, under a lot of pressure, ice still can't get as dense as steel. The military has tested this in labs. Ice can't cut through metal. It can't."*

"Yet it does," Grandma Kotetsu said calmly, *"and has, time and time again since Matsuda Takeru pioneered the technique."*

What neither Kwang nor any of the Kotetsus knew was that the Whispering Blade's power didn't come from its density alone. Its cutting power was a product of the wielder's precision. The swordsman had to have such deeply perfect control over his jiya that he could sharpen its edge to a single molecule, allowing it to slide through any substance, no matter its density. The technique was a feat of human skill and focus that could never be replicated in a lab.

"You may believe the story or you may not," Grandma Kotetsu said, *"but you've held still for several siiranu."*

"What?" Kwang looked down at himself and seemed to register that Kotetsu Kama had cleaned, bandaged, and splinted every one of his injuries. *"Oh."* He let out a laugh, as a toothless grin crinkled Grandma Kotetsu's face.

"You see, an old lady has her tricks."

"Now, sit and have some food," Kotetsu's wife said, motioning Kwang to the table.

"But what happened after that?" Kwang asked as he joined Mamoru at the numuwu's scrubbed wooden dinner table. *"After Matsuda Takeru cut Yukino Izumi in half? He was just standing in the middle of the village square over the dead body of the ruling lord, right? So, what happened then?"*

"They say that the best swordsman can win a fight in a single cut," said Grandma Kotetsu. *"Matsuda Takeru won that fight and all to come in that cut, for after witnessing his power, no one dared challenge him. The only person to step forward was Yukino Izumi's son, Hayase, a boy of twelve.*

The newly-orphaned Yukino said to Takeru, "I don't intend to fight you for control of Takayubi, but I will not allow you to execute this town's finawu or destroy our Falleya temples."

In curiosity, Takeru asked, "What if I were to order Falleya purged from this region?"

"I would challenge you to single combat," Yukino Hayase said without hesitation.

Takeru was moved by the boy's bravery, and he was wise enough not to repeat his father's mistakes. Despite his power, he did not wish to rule through fear.

"I am the blood of gods," he said to the assembled crowd, *"as are all of you. The moon and ocean fear no change."*

In compliance with Hayase's request, he kept Falleya temples standing and incorporated Falleya law into his rule, eventually becoming a devout Falleka himself. Under the new laws of kamaya, he named the Kotetsus numus to the Matsuda family, binding their two houses in loyalty and mutual support for all time to come."

"And the Yukino boy," Kwang said. *"He just let him live?"*

"Not only that, he let him return to the ancestral Yukino castle and rule there. He married Yukino Izumi's oldest daughter, Mitsuki, to ensure an enduring peace between their houses. Your swordmaster, Yukino Dai, is a descendant of Yukino Hayase, as Matsuda Mamoru and his family are descendants of Matsuda Takeru. Their two families have coexisted in this region for a thousand years, never without tensions, but never without respect. For it was our ancestors—Matsuda, Yukino, and Kotetsu—who ushered in the first Ryuhon Falleya state in Shirojima."

"Wow," Kwang said. *"And the Whispering Blade has just been passed down Matsuda Takeru's line all this time?"*

Grandma Kotetsu nodded her head. *"Takeru passed the Whispering Blade down to his sons, who in turn passed it down to their sons. Ever since his time, boys of the Matsuda family are always sent to apprentice with Kotetsu smiths, in the hopes that skill in steel will lead to a Whispering Blade."*

"But... wait a second," Kwang said. *"Under Falleya, isn't it kind of weird for koronu like the Matsudas to apprentice with numuwu?"*

"The Whispering Blade is the sacred force that brought Takayubi together," Kotetsu Kama said. *"For the sake of preserving the Matsuda bloodline technique, we make this one exception. Without the combination of numu and koro arts, the technique can't be carried on. Matsuda Takeru was the sort of genius who comes around once in a millennium. Those who are able to replicate his technique are often one in a generation."*

Kwang turned to Mamoru. *"Wait. So, there are some Matsudas who can use the Whispering Blade and some who can't?"*

"Most never master it," Kotetsu Kama said, sparing Mamoru from answering, *"though it is the fate of all Matsudas to spend their lives trying. There have been weak generations in the past, during which people feared that the technique might disappear from the world. We are fortunate that this generation, we will have at least one Whispering Blade."* He gave his student a smile that Mamoru couldn't return. *"We are certain of it."*

Most days, Mamoru was certain of it too. Not right now. Now, he felt like a brittle shell, capable of nothing, containing nothing.

The moon and the ocean fear no change. "So, Matsuda Takeru ended up adopting the ideals of his parents' killer?" Mamoru said quietly.

The three adult numuwu looked at him in surprise. "Well… yes," Kotetsu Kama said. "You know the story."

"He was so strong," Mamoru murmured. "He had the blood of gods in his veins, and he just… gave way to foreign ideas?"

"He had the intelligence to see that Falleya was the way forward," Kotetsu Kama said, his deep voice that was usually so calming somehow grating at Mamoru' nerves. "While it was Falleya that killed his family, it was Falleya that spared the Kotetsus he depended on, and it is the Ryuhon Falleya he pioneered that has made this region so strong ever since."

"But how did he know?" Mamoru frowned at his knuckles. "How could he be so sure?" How could anyone be so sure of a decision that determined the fate of thousands? How?

"Are you alright, Mamoru-dono?" the numu asked gently.

Mamoru was not alright. He was churning again, his jiya agitated by the heat. "How could he just abandon everything he knew—his family's legacy—for a new religion?"

"Takeru grew up learned in the tenets of both religions. He studied both with the same diligence that he studied the blade. And as a leader, he had a decision to make." Kotetsu paused. "Are you sure you're alright? Your jiya feels unwell—"

"Kotetsu Kama." Mamoru looked up sharply. "Tell me about Yammanka obsidian."

"What?" Kotetsu said, taken aback.

"The really hard types of Yammanka glass," Mamoru said. "Are there Kaigenese craftsmen who know how to make it?"

"Of course," Kotetsu said. "Nowadays, there's so much commerce and cultural exchange between Kaigen and Yamma, there are many Kaigenese who work in jonjo glass."

"But not Zilazen glass?"

"Of course not." Kotetsu laughed. "The production of that material is a bloodline technique, like our steel folding and your Whispering Blade. Its secrets do not leave the Zilazen family."

"Oh." Mamoru hadn't realized that. "So, the Kaigenese military has never produced anything made of Zilazen glass?"

"No," Kotetsu said, "although, my cousin tells me that the Empire has been importing a lot of Yammanka bullets, so maybe—"

"What about bigger things?" Mamoru asked. "Has Kaigen ever had Zilazen glass machines? Like tanks or planes?"

"Not that I know of," Kotetsu said. "The Zilazen make machines to be operated by tajakalu, not jijakalu. Importing that kind of equipment would be nonsense. And Kaigen certainly doesn't have any craftsmen capable of creating Zilazen glass. I believe a Kaigenese smith would have to marry a Zilazen senkuli to be privy to those secrets. Even then, it might be too carefully guarded. It may be that only those with Zilazen blood are allowed to learn— so, the child of a mixed marriage, maybe?"

Tamami gave a disapproving 'tsk.' "What good theonite would want to sully their bloodline like that?"

"I don't know," Kotetsu said with a shrug. "If we ever get to see a Zilazen glass katana, the impurity might be worth it."

"Do you think that would be possible?" Kwang asked, and Mamoru couldn't tell if he was genuinely excited or just eager to steer the conversation away from planes.

"I know that Zilazen glass swords have been made in the past,"

Kotetsu said.

"Really?"

"They are extremely rare," Kotetsu said. *"There are no more than a hundred in the world."*

After Kwang had asked a few dozen more questions about sword forging and Kotetsu's wife was satisfied that both boys had eaten as much as they could, the blacksmith walked Mamoru and Kwang to the edge of the numu village and sent them on their way. Mechanically, Mamoru bowed to his teacher and wished him a good night.

As he and Kwang set off up the mountain, he expected the northern boy to give him some form of 'I told you so.' He was prepared for it, but Kwang didn't gloat. He just followed wordlessly at Mamoru's elbow up the path to the western village.

When he did speak, all he said was, *"Are you going to be okay?"*

Mamoru's voice was neither hard nor stormy. It was empty. *"Yes."*

They walked on in silence for a while. Kwang no longer needed Mamoru to lead him. The first light had crept into the sky, illuminating the way before them.

"How is your arm, Kwang-san?"

"Chul-hee."

"What?"

"Call me Chul-hee," Kwang said. *"We fell down the side of a mountain together. We can be on a first name basis, can't we?"*

Mamoru didn't turn to look at the other boy. *"If you like."*

"Thanks for introducing me to your numu friends, by the way. They were nice."

"I'm glad you liked them," Mamoru said, *"although I'm sorry you had to sit through a whole history lesson."*

"It's alright," Kwang said. *"I like listening. And your history's pretty interesting."*

If it's really history at all, Mamoru thought. If Hibiki Sensei could be mistaken about Takayubi's past, so could Grandma

Kotetsu. So could anyone.

"So, um…" Kwang must have sensed the heaviness of Mamoru's nyama because he changed the subject. *"It's pretty cool what Numu Kotetsu said about Zilazen glass weapons, right? I had no idea the Zilazen made swords!"*

"Neither did I," Mamoru said. *"I guess the world's craftsmen share things with each other that don't always concern us koronu."*

"Do you think a Zilazen glass katana would be even stronger than your magical Whispering Blade?"

"I can't make a Whispering Blade," Mamoru said, *"and anyway, there would probably never be a chance to test it. Kotetsu Kama said there are fewer than a hundred Zilazen swords in the whole world."*

Not far up the path, the two boys parted ways.

"Good night, Chul-hee-kun," Mamoru said to see how the familiar address would feel on his tongue. It felt strange until Kwang turned and smiled at him—an exhausted smile full of gratitude and fondness that he hadn't earned.

"Good night, Mamoru-kun."

Mamoru had no way of knowing that he had lived his whole life within an arm's reach of a Zilazen glass sword. The black blade had been bundled away under the floorboards of the Matsudas' kitchen shortly before he was born and had stayed there, untouched, ever since. It was a slight weapon, barely bigger than a traditional wakizashi, but it had seen more combat than any katana in the Matsuda dojo.

Of course, Mamoru had no way of knowing any of that.

His mother, after all, did not talk about her past.

6

THE PAST

Tsusano Misaki straightened up, breathing hard. She wasn't shaking. Not exactly. Thrumming was more like it.

"We did it!" She turned to the hooded figure standing further down the alley. She had never felt so alive. *"We did it!"*

"You *did it.*" Elleen Elden pulled back her hood, letting her golden hair tumble free as her eerily light brown eyes scanned the mess of bleeding and unconscious theonites. *"I just set them up."*

The littigi had her knife poised before her, but she hadn't needed it. The moment the illusion had dropped, Misaki had dashed in, felling the four men before any of them noticed the shadow sweeping through their ranks. Elleen was hardly a squeamish girl, but a frown creased her features as she stared at Misaki's work.

"Sorry about that," she said. *"I shouldn't have let myself flicker."* Elleen often did that, referring to her illusions as herself. *"I just... when they drew their machetes, I lost focus. Sorry you had to step in."*

"I'm not," Misaki said, her face alight with a delirious smile.

"We could have held them here without anyone getting hurt." Elleen's frown deepened. *"If I had just kept my nerve—"*

A crash echoed down the street beyond the alley and both girls looked to the sky. No Firebird signal yet. Robin was still fighting.

"I'm going." Misaki stepped over the nearest unconscious man,

making for the street, but Elleen caught her arm.

"What?" Misaki demanded. Elleen's weak Hadean hands weren't capable of applying much pressure, but the tension in her grip suggested that it was meant to be firm.

"What if these men bleed out before help comes?"

"Oh." Misaki turned back to look at her victims, sprawled across the grimy pavement. *"I'm sure they won't..."* She trailed off as the crawl of freely flowing blood reached her senses and, grudgingly, she realized that Elleen had a point. Some of her slashes had cut deeper than she intended. Why were human bodies so soft? Weren't tajakalu supposed to be tough? Maybe these Malusian smugglers were weaker as a result of their mixed blood.

"Fine." Misaki pulled her arm from Elleen's grasp. *"I'll make sure they don't die."*

"I'm going to go join the fighting," Elleen said. *"I'm sure you'll be close behind."*

"If I don't get there first."

"Ha." Sheathing her knife, Elleen flipped her white hood up to hide her hair and ran from the alley.

Misaki didn't personally care if these fighters lived, but she thought of how upset Robin would be if he found out someone had died during one of his missions and treated each tajaka thoroughly. She accounted for even small cuts, congealing any blood she found leaking out of them. Two were bleeding from the head where Misaki's ice-reinforced punches had hit. The third she had managed to mangle pretty terribly, slicing one of his arms nearly to the bone. He would need surgery.

As she worked on the last man's more minor injuries, he stirred and groaned. Her hand went to her dagger, but it was obvious that the Malusian was far too dazed to present a threat. Besides, she had landed a good cut to his calf. He wouldn't be walking—let alone fighting—any time soon. He blinked up at her, but he wouldn't get a look at her face. Koli had designed their fighting outfits carefully; even with her hood back, exposing her hair, the dark mask that clung to Misaki's face concealed her features.

"Wha... what's—" The man started to say, but cut off with a wince when he tried to move his injured leg.

"You are very lucky."

"Why?" he asked, still seemingly only half conscious.

"Firebird doesn't want you to die."

"Fly... bird?" he murmured. Definitely only partially conscious.

"Firebird," Misaki repeated tersely. *"If you want to make it in this part of Livingston, you'll remember the name."*

Finished with the man's leg, Misaki stood and looked around for the knife she had lost during the fray. She felt unbalanced with just the one Koumbia dagger strapped to her hip, but she couldn't find the other. Maybe one of the Malusians had fallen on top of it?

"You..." the man moved again, attempting to stand up.

"Stay there," Misaki ordered sharply. *"Your idiot employer led you into Pantera territory. Go crawling out into the open and you'll get an arrow through the neck. Lie here quietly and Firebird will make sure you're taken care of. If I were you, I'd play dead."*

"Play dead?"

"Yeah. And never take a job from Yaotl Texca again."

Deciding that the missing knife was a lost cause, Misaki pulled her hood up and took off in the direction of the real fight, cutting across the street, into the next alley. She had wasted enough time on Texca's useless henchmen when Robin and Elleen might need her.

A gaggle of homeless adyns cried out in surprise as she came barreling toward them. Inconvenient. They clogged the alley and it would take too long to detour around them. Instead, she lay into a full sprint toward them, turning at the last moment to run up the concrete wall. On her fifth step up, she pushed off with both legs. Water molecules rushed to her hands and feet. She hit the opposite wall, ice forming, and stuck there.

The adyns exclaimed to one another in shock. It probably wasn't often they saw a tiny foreign girl stick to a wall like a lizard. As they gaped in amazement, Misaki climbed. She kept the water tight to her hands and the balls of her feet, melting it each time she

101

needed to lift a hand or foot, and then refreezing it back to the building.

She was still slower than she would have liked at her newfound climbing technique, but once she fell into a rhythm—right foot, right hand, left foot, left hand—it didn't take her long to reach the top of the building. Clambering onto the flat concrete roof, Misaki turned to look over the surrounding area.

This high over the North End slums, wind whipped her hood and cloak around her. A burst of smoke a few blocks away revealed Robin's location, and there was Elleen, a bright streak in her white coat, running toward the action. Misaki could easily catch up. A human heartbeat caught her attention and she turned to find a sandy-haired adyn emerging from the doorway onto the rooftop. He had a crossbow in his hand and a Pantera yellow sash around his waist.

"Shimatta," she swore under her breath in Shirojima Dialect.

"Oi!" the man said. *"What business have you here? This be Pantera territory!"*

He raised the crossbow, but like most adyns, he was slow. Misaki shot water at him and turned it to ice with a harsh snap of her jiya.

The man cried out as the ice froze the bolt to the bow and the bow to his hand. *"Intruder! Intr—"*

The next glob of water hit him in the mouth, freezing it shut.

"Sorry." Misaki approached the adyn and pushed him back against the door, ignoring the punch he swung into her face.

She had found that a blow from an adult adyn was roughly equivalent to a blow from a four-year-old child—annoying but ultimately harmless. Her own baby brothers had been throwing harder punches than this man before they could talk. Having bruised his knuckles terribly on Misaki's cheekbone, the adyn reached for the machete at his belt. Misaki caught his free hand before it reached the weapon.

"Sorry," she repeated, gripping the handle of the machete and sliding it free of its crude excuse for a sheath. *"I'm going to*

borrow this."

Stepping back from the man was a relief, as his unwashed smell was honestly more offensive than the knuckles she had taken to the face. She gave the machete an experimental twirl and grimaced. The balance was *terrible*, but the extra reach would be a welcome change from the daggers.

"We're not here to infringe on your territory," she told the adyn, hoping the seemingly simple man would understand her through her Kaigenese accent. *"We'll be gone as soon as we're done dealing with your Malusian intruders."*

Leaving the stunned Pantera standing there, Misaki ran to the edge of the roof and leapt off. She wasn't the best jumper, but she had found that she could double her normal distance by gathering ice beneath her feet and launching off it with a repelling push of jiya. Wind roared around her in a glorious moment of flight before the concrete of the next rooftop came rushing up to meet her.

New water collected under Misaki's shoes and she turned it to snow. Not a lot, just enough to take some of the impact off her knees and ankles as she landed. Hitting the rooftop, she rolled with the momentum, regained her feet, and kept running. A few more jiya-propelled leaps, using snow to cushion landings and ice to stick to walls as needed, and Misaki dropped into step beside Elleen.

"There you are, Shadow," the littigi panted as they ran. *"Perfect timing."*

Elleen's exertion was obvious, but considering how weak most of her kind were, Misaki found it astonishing that the white girl could run as fast as she did over such great distances. Long legs and determination seemed to make up for her soft muscles as the two sprinted the last block toward the smoke.

Firebird would stop petty crimes if the occasion arose, but he only actively hunted killers. These three Malusian smugglers—Yaotl Texca, Mecatl Silangwe, and Kolonka Mathaba—had raided the homes of some of their Abirian competitors over the past few weeks, killing two people in the process. The men Misaki and

Elleen had confronted earlier had been Texca's hired help, a handful of hapless Malusian immigrants who just needed jobs. The murderers themselves were ahead.

As Misaki and Elleen sprinted for the action, they passed an unconscious Malusian, sprawled on the concrete among some shattered bottles and other garbage.

"Which one was that?" Misaki asked, only sparing a glance back at the crumpled figure.

"Silangwe," Elleen said, her photographic memory never failing to identify a face.

There were three pounding heartbeats around the corner ahead, three blazing hot spots in the cool air. Texca and Mathaba, the two serious combatants, were still in the fight.

"You ready, Shadow?" Elleen breathed.

"If you are."

The two girls burst around the corner, and immediately, Kolonka Mathaba whirled to face them, her long black braid whipping over her shoulder, hands full of fire. Beyond her, Robin was locked in combat with the infamous Yaotl Texca, but Misaki and Elleen couldn't worry about him at the moment.

Their immediate concern was the threat of Mathaba's flames—blue-white instead of orange, far hotter than the average tajaka's fire and beyond Misaki's power to extinguish. It wasn't until Elleen's hand jerked back on Misaki's cloak that Misaki realized that she had been brazenly and foolishly striding forward to rush the tajaka.

"When I say go," Elleen said, and only she could keep her tone so calm in the face of flames hot enough to melt the flesh from her bones. Behind her, Misaki felt the exhausted littigi take a deep breath, gathering her concentration. *"Steady..."* Elleen tugged Misaki back a step as Mathaba stalked toward them, then she planted a palm between Misaki's shoulder blades. *"Go!"* She shoved.

Misaki exploded forward. As she did, half a dozen Misakis burst from her, rippling illusions, all wearing her same blue and black cloak, moving with her trademark agility. Elleen's holographic Misakis scattered in all directions, momentarily disorienting Mathaba, but the tajaka was no fool. She swept her arm in a wide arc, releasing a whip of blue flame that passed through the ring of illusions.

It was an efficient way to determine which black-hooded girl was real. The moment Misaki ducked under the flames, she differentiated herself from the illusions, which were, of course, unaffected by the heat.

Ultimately, the illusions had only bought her a dinma of time, but her father always said that a great fighter could capitalize on the smallest advantage. By the time Mathaba's eyes focused in on the real Misaki, she had already gotten inside the tajaka's guard. Enveloped in the dizzying heat of Mathaba's aura, Misaki slashed upward. The machete didn't cut as cleanly as a katana, which would have easily severed the woman's arm, but it did a respectable amount of damage.

Mathaba screamed, her flames guttering out as boiling-hot blood spurted from her arm. Side-stepping a swipe of one of the woman's other arm, Misaki launched an ice-knuckled punch up into her temple. The punch itself landed hard, but Mathaba's taya was so hot that it weakened Misaki's ice, softening the attack. The tall woman staggered, dazed but not unconscious.

Flames lashed out, grazing Misaki's hand, causing her to drop the machete. Falling back, Misaki drew her knife, holding the short weapon before her in her left hand. Her stinging right hand curled into a fist and pulled back to her hip, new ice hardening across the knuckles.

The blue fire had flared to life around Mathaba again, creating intense waves of heat, but Misaki was not afraid. If anything, the heat made her blood leap in excitement like a water brought to a boil. All she had to do was open another wound with her knife, causing the woman's taya to falter again, then go in with her ice. It would be easy, satisfying. Misaki was grinning, ready to fight, ready to—

Crash!

The concrete slab, so big Elleen had barely been able to heft it, broke into several pieces against the tajaka's head. Kolonka Mathaba swayed as a cloud of rock dust crumbled into her hair and cascaded off her shoulders. She took a step... then fell to the pavement, unconscious.

"Oh..." Misaki lowered her knife as Elleen brushed off her hands. *"Thank—"*

"Help Firebird," Elleen said.

When Misaki looked toward Robin, she found him pinned to the ground beneath Yaotl Texca. She had never seen Robin down in a fight before and it sent a jolt of panic through her. She could hardly fault her friend; he had been alternately chasing and fighting these three adult theonites since leaving Elleen and Misaki to hold off the henchmen. He was usually able to stack his opponents, utilizing his speed and his knowledge of North End's streets, but it was clear that he was flagging, his hands shaking as he tried to hold Texca's machete away from his neck.

Without another thought, Misaki charged. It was unwise for a young jijaka like herself to grapple an older tajaka whose nyama could overcome hers and burn her, but Misaki had learned that she could temporarily *stun* the fire out of an opponent with a concentrated blast of cold. Reaching full speed, she mustered all the icy jiya she could and launched her body into Texca's.

The impact was painful. She and the massive tajaka tumbled over one another, scraping shoulders and elbows on the concrete. As they rolled, Texca grabbed hold of her cloak, probably thinking that his size would make it easy to pin her down, but Misaki was ahead of him. She used their remaining momentum to flip the tajaka over her hip onto his back and rolled on top of him, knife raised to strike.

Barely hearing Robin's shout of protest, she drove the blade toward her victim's chest, but Texca was fast. He struck her arm on its way down, diverting the stab. The knife stuck in his upper arm, missing his heart.

Misaki already had ice across her knuckles. She punched Texca as hard as she could, once, twice, three times. The fourth punch shattered her ice and the tajaka was still conscious. She made to slam the heels of her hands into his temples, but the moment she drew both hands back, she created an opening.

Blood dribbling from his nose and mouth, Texca lurched upward, grabbing her by the throat. His massive, blisteringly hot hand, wrapped all the way around her neck. It probably wouldn't take him much effort to snap her spine, but she didn't give him the chance. Water raced from her knuckles to her fingertips and she clawed Texca, one hand tearing across his face, the other ripping the back of the hand at her throat. He screamed, releasing Misaki's neck to clutch at his face.

Misaki's jiya moved on instinct, the claws on her right hand converging into a single long spike of ice over all five fingers. She drew the spike back, knowing that this time, blinded by blood and pain, Texca wouldn't be able to stop her—

An arm wrapped around her shoulders, jerking her back. Her ice clipped Texca's neck but didn't penetrate as she was hauled off her prey. She fought, but Robin held on with infuriating determination, putting himself between her and Texca.

"Don't!" Robin gripped her shoulders—and gods damn it, he was *strong* when he was desperate. *"Please, don't!"*

"What are you doing?" Misaki demanded in frustration.

"He's down. You don't need to do that."

"He's not unconscious," Misaki protested, yanking against Robin's grasp, barely stifling the urge to turn her ice on him. *"He's dangerous!"*

"That doesn't give us license to—" Robin cut off with a short cry of pain. As her friend buckled, Misaki looked down to find her own dagger protruding from Robin's calf. Texca had ripped the weapon from his shoulder and used it to stab Robin in the leg.

The Malusian burst to his feet in a swirl of white and orange flame. Misaki was forced to leap back to avoid being scorched as the man's fist slammed into Robin's chest, knocking him

107

backward. Robin coughed as he fell into his fighting stance, clearly winded, but Texca didn't stay to fight. As his flames broke, he turned and ran. He was going to get away!

Drawing her hand back, Misaki pulled moisture into an ice spear and shoved her palm forward, firing the projectile at Texca's back.

"No!" Robin bellowed. Flames burst from his hands, blazing so hot that they melted Misaki's thin spear koyinu from its target.

Texca whipped around a corner and disappeared. Misaki sprinted after him but by the time she rounded the corner herself, he was gone. There was no sign of which road or alley he had taken. She would have climbed for a higher vantage and tried to run him down, but she knew from watching the man run that she would never catch him. Robin might be able to if he weren't stabbed through the leg like an idiot.

She rounded on him. *"What the Hell was that?"*

"We don't kill," he said, teeth gritted as he staggered to the nearest wall and leaned against it for support.

"He would have killed us," Misaki protested. *"He was about to finish you when I—"*

"Thank you for that," Robin said and then firmly repeated, *"We don't kill."*

Misaki wanted to respond, but the aftermath of a fight wasn't the place to have a protracted argument. This was the time to get everything wrapped up as fast as possible and clear out.

While Elleen handcuffed Silangwe and Mathaba, Misaki pulled out a capsule Koli Kuruma had devised for her and shattered it on the ground. As it broke open, chemical mist poured out, colored bright green so that Misaki could easily keep track of it as it spread throughout the alley, coating the scene. Where needed, she pushed the clouds along with her jiya, ensuring that the entire alley was coated.

When that was done, she took a second capsule and hurried to repeat the process over the area where Silangwe had fallen. The chemical solution served two purposes, distorting any fingerprints she, Robin, or Elleen might have left and rendering blood unfit for

DNA testing. It was one of the ways they prevented law enforcement or anyone else with lab equipment from uncovering their identities. As Misaki finished spreading the green clouds out to blanket the last little flecks of fresh blood on the pavement, a column of fire burst from the alley where she had left Robin.

She didn't mean to get distracted—it wasn't as if she hadn't seen Robin's Firebird flare before—but her hands fell to her sides and she found herself staring as if she could drink the heat with her eyes. The flames climbed high against the clouds before spreading out into the pair of wings that had given Firebird his name. By now, everyone in this part of Livingston knew what the signal meant: criminals were ready for the police to pick up.

Of course, Firebird never just left a scene and trusted the police to arrest the catch without incident. There were all sorts of things that could go wrong: a strong enough criminal could regain consciousness and injure officers, jumpy officers could harm an incapacitated prisoner, or a third party could intervene and endanger everyone.

"Hide and watch things here, okay?" Robin told Misaki when she returned to the alley. *"I'm going to go take care of the other four."*

"You should let me fix your leg," Misaki said. Her dagger was still protruding grotesquely from Robin's calf and his light brown skin had gone pale with pain.

"Not now," Robin said. *"You've already misted the scene. I don't want to pull the blade out and bleed more."*

"I can keep your blood off the ground," Misaki assured him, *"and I have back-up capsules—"*

"We'll worry about it back in the dorm."

With that, he turned and limped back in the direction of the four men Misaki had disabled, Elleen serving as his crutch and using her illusions to conceal them from curious eyes.

Misaki found herself a hidden vantage on the roof above and settled down to watch over Mathaba and Silangwe. She didn't honestly care if the police mistreated the two criminals or if the

Pantera crept out of hiding to kill them, but Robin cared. Elleen cared. And this was their city, not hers. Before long, the Livingston police showed up in their jonjo glass patrol cars to collect Mathaba and Silangwe. They were just closing the doors on the criminals when firelight caught their attention.

Robin had sent up a second signal over the site of Misaki and Elleen's first fight—not the Firebird wings that alerted the authorities to criminals ready for arrest, but the three-pronged tajaka flare: a universal request for medical attention. As the officers' eyes turned toward the signal, Misaki quickly withdrew from the roof's edge to avoid being spotted. Her caution was probably unnecessary; no one ever seemed to notice a creeping shadow under the brilliance of Robin's flames. That was the idea.

"Do you think that's Firebird's too?" a young officer asked, clearly awed.

"Maybe," his superior said in a less impressed tone. *"It doesn't matter. It's just a medical aid flare, not the wings. He doesn't have Texca."*

"But do you think we should check it out? Or send an ambulance? Someone might need help."

"Maybe they do. Not our problem."

"But—"

"These kallaanas are killing each other all the time," a third officer spat. *"If we sent an ambulance every time, the city would be bankrupt. Now, get in the freezing car, koroden. Unless you want us to leave you here in Pantera territory overnight."*

That seemed to shut the young man up. There was a scramble of feet and the thud of a closing door. Misaki straightened up to watch the police cars speed away from the scene, wheels skidding on the poorly paved road. Even in their glass-armored cars, it seemed that the theonite officers couldn't wait to return to the blacker part of town.

Her job done, Misaki headed toward the meeting place she, Robin, and Elleen had established. When she reached the alley they had agreed on, Robin was nowhere to be seen, but she quickly found the glimmering form of Elleen Elden. The gangly girl was perched atop a short fence at the edge of a playground that looked to Misaki like the single worst place for a child to play. The metal equipment was sharp and mangled where tajakalu had twisted pieces off and borne them away to be melted into weapons. The sand bristled with arrows from some gang-related shootout.

Elleen shimmered, shifting in and out of view as Misaki approached. The littigi often did that—playing with the light across her own body, turning herself into a sort of mirage.

In elementary school, Misaki had been told that Hadeans' light colored hair and eyes were signs that they were a more primitive variety of human, closely related to dogs and monkeys who shared their coloring. She was realizing that she had been told a lot of ridiculous things.

The undeniable truth was that Elleen was beautiful—in a harsh, painful sort of way. People here always accused Shirojima Kaigenese of being stiff, but this Hadean-born girl had a different kind of stiffness about her. She had come to Carytha at a young age, as a refugee, as Robin had. She didn't talk much about what she had seen in her homeland before that, only to say that it made the streets of Livingston look like a paradise. Whatever it was, it had hardened her. Even though Elleen's gold hair and pale eyes were a bit frightening—perhaps *because* they were a bit frightening—Misaki found them beautiful. She had decided that if Elleen was related to any animal, it was something dignified and dangerous, like a leopard or a falcon.

"What do you want, Shadow?" Elleen had an interesting, highly articulated, accent that apparently came from her homeland back in Hades. She could speak Lindish like a Carythian, but she had deliberately held onto her tribe's accent all these years. Pale brown eyes turned to look at Misaki. *"I suppose you're expecting me to thank you? Fair enough."* Despite her calm voice, Misaki could sense that her friend was miserable. *"Thank you for saving me."*

"I just thought... maybe you shouldn't be sitting out here in the open?" Misaki glanced around nervously. *"This is gang territory,*

isn't it? There could be archers."

"Archers don't fire at deserted playgrounds," Elleen said dismissively. *"We can see each other, but as far as any people in the surrounding buildings are concerned, no one is here."*

"Oh." Misaki forgot that Elleen could not only weave light into images from her photographic memory but also render people invisible from certain angles.

"Please don't worry about earlier," Misaki said. *"I don't think you have anything to be ashamed of. Your illusion was incredible. It held them off until I was able to reach you. And even after it lost its clarity, they were so disoriented that my part was easy."*

"Aye," Elleen scowled, twirling a ribbon of light between her fingers before letting it vanish. *"That's what I always dreamed of as a girl: holding on long enough to get saved by a* real *theonite."*

"Ell—Whitewing, is everything alright?" They were all supposed to use their crime-fighter names when they were out in disguise—just in case a fonyaka or sondatigi was listening in—but this was apparently the wrong thing to say. Elleen let out a huff, her face pulling into a sneer.

"Have you noticed," she said, *"that every bloody crime-fighter of my complexion has to have the word 'white' in their alias. Like they need to qualify—not a* real *crime-fighter, a* white *one."*

"I didn't notice that," Misaki said.

"I suppose I shouldn't be surprised. The reporter who named me Whitewing is the same piece of xuro who decided I was Firebird's sidekick."

Elleen was typically a stoic person, making sharp quips at the expense of others, but never revealing much about herself. The day's events seemed to have peeled back the scab on a deep insecurity. This was the kind of bleeding Misaki couldn't staunch.

To any other fourteen-year-old littigi, simply surviving a fight with full theonites would have been an accomplishment to be proud of, but Elleen never seemed happy with what she was able to do. Hadeans were not built to withstand physical competition with tajakalu and jijakalu. In simply surviving one fight after another,

Elleen was extraordinary.

"If you need to thank me, then I owe you the same," Misaki pointed out, hoping it would lift the littigi's spirits. *"You saved me too."*

"I wanted to be useful." Elleen glared at the ground. *"You were ready to fight her on your own."*

Misaki didn't know what to say. She came from a culture where women were considered fragile. She was still getting used to Carytha, where there was an entire race of people who were truly more fragile than any theonite. Elleen had abilities most white people could never dream of possessing, yet she was still at a disadvantage. It must have been maddeningly frustrating.

"I thought your illusions were good—"

"Don't patronize me, Princess." Strangely, the words didn't come out with the hostile bite they should have. Instead, Elleen sounded sad.

"I wasn't," Misaki insisted. *"Truly, Elleen, I—"*

"It's Whitewing, *Shadow,"* Elleen cut her off.

"Right."

"Stay and make sure Firebird doesn't get into any more trouble, would you?" She hopped from the fence and primly straightened out her white coat. *"I'm going to head back and get some practice in before dinner."*

"Where is Firebird?" Misaki asked.

Elleen lifted an arm and Misaki followed her pointing finger to a rooftop overlooking the alley where they had fought Texca's guards. He stood right at the edge of the building, the fringe of his red coat flapping in the wind.

"See you in class tomorrow," Elleen said and vanished into thin air, the only sign of life her heartbeat slowly retreating into a nearby alley.

Realizing that Elleen's illusions would no longer protect her from the resident Pantera, Misaki hurried into the cover of another alley. Water gathered to her hands and she used it to climb the concrete wall toward Robin's position.

When she pulled herself up over the edge of the rooftop, he was still there, standing at the edge of the apartment complex, his back to her. Robin had such strong senses in some ways, yet his general awareness of nyama was lacking. If Misaki made no noise, he would undoubtedly go right on standing there, never noticing the human-shaped cold spot behind him.

He stood still against the gray sky, wind blowing through his black hair and whipping his red coat out behind him. Layers of the tough red fabric overlapped across the back of the coat forming the Firebird symbol Koli had designed.

Misaki had never understood why it had to be a bird. In Ryuhon Falleya, birds were sinister figures, heralds of disorder, disease, and destruction. In the legends of her childhood, any human who took on avian characteristics was some kind of demon. But Robin had explained that he was honored to take the bird as a symbol for his alter ego. Apparently, it was a creature of empowerment to Hadeans and Native Baxarians. Depending on the bird species and the tribe, it could stand for wisdom, freedom, or rebirth. Misaki supposed that if Robin was a demon, he did a good job looking like power and freedom in that red coat.

Koli talked about building new features into the Firebird coat—holographic fibers to make it merge with the darkness, or glow, or appear to be on fire—but Misaki thought that was silly. Sure, Robin could probably benefit from a coat with a stealth mode, but he didn't need any help glowing.

Straightening up, Misaki cleared her throat.

Robin cocked his head. *"Shadow."*

"Firebird." She folded her arms. *"I came to check on your leg, but I see you're busy brooding, so I'll just go."* She turned as if to climb back down the way she had come.

"My leg is fine," Robin said. *"It's bandaged well enough to stop the bleeding for now and I'll have someone take a look at it later. I don't think I'll need you to fix it."*

"Who said anything about fixing it?" Misaki said, turning back with an indignant toss of her hair. *"I just wanted my knife back."*

114

Robin flipped one arm upward. A silvery shape arced from his hand, spinning. Misaki caught the dagger by its handle.

"Thanks." She slid the weapon back into its sheath and then said more seriously, *"You honestly don't want me to scab it at all?"*

Robin shrugged. *"It feels alright."*

"It must feel great," Misaki said, *"given that you're trusting it to perch you there on the edge of certain death."* She came up beside him to consider the distance to the ground. *"You know you're not an actual bird, right? If you fall from this height, you'll plummet and die."*

"No." Robin rolled his eyes at her, his voice dripping with that Carythian-style sarcasm Misaki was just getting used to. *"I didn't know that."*

Blood still smeared the cement far below from Misaki's fight with Texca's guards, but the men themselves were nowhere to be seen.

"I'll be fine," he added. *"I had to stay, to make sure those men were okay."*

"Who cares if they're okay?" Misaki said impatiently. *"They were terrible."*

"They were just Texca's hired security. As far as we know, they haven't done anything except accept a job from the wrong guy."

"They pulled their machetes on Elleen," Misaki said indignantly, *"a teenage girl."*

"Well, after meeting you, I doubt they'll make that mistake again. You realize that's the idea, don't you? Not to destroy the people of this city but to make them better."

"Those men haven't even lived in this city for a week. They're foreigners."

"So are you," Robin said. *"So was I, when I first came here. We can't claim to be crime-fighters if we disrespect life just as much as the criminals we fight."*

"I don't think killing a horrible, hostile person is really disrespecting life," Misaki said. *"Most koronu would say that it's a duty."* It was agreed upon across all warrior cultures—Kaigen,

Yamma, Sizwe—that killing in self defense or defense of the innocent was a noble thing.

"I'm not most koronu." Robin said, *"and I don't want to argue this with you. You don't have to defend what you did. I understand it. It's just not... I want you to promise you won't try to kill anyone else on these missions, okay?"*

Misaki frowned. *"You know what I am, right? I'm a jijaka from a very specific family famous for killing people with swords. If you didn't want your enemies dead, why even bring me onboard? Why..."* Misaki paused, wondering if she should voice the question that had been gnawing at her these past two months. *"Why did you choose me?"*

Misaki had spent more time than she cared to admit puzzling over the question. Sure, she had already been friends with Robin and Elleen when the two orphanage buddies decided they needed a third koro on their team. But Robin, at least, had no shortage of friends, many more powerful than Misaki. It had never made much sense to her that *she* had been the one Robin and Elleen had chosen to invite into their secret world.

When Robin didn't answer for a long moment, she grew anxious and found more words spilling from her mouth. *"I mean, I assume my ability to heal people was appealing, with how you like to keep all your enemies alive."*

"They're not my enemies," Robin said, *"and it had nothing to do with your abilities."*

"Then why?" Misaki pressed.

"I picked you because of this... because you'll fight me on things like this. You see the world in a way I just don't, and that..." He glanced away from her curious gaze, seemingly not wanting to meet her eyes. *"That's important to me."*

"Really?" Misaki tilted her head. *"I would have thought you'd want to work with people who see the world the* same *way you do."* Wasn't that what everyone wanted? A community of like minds?

"I think that would be a mistake," Robin said. *"Then who would tell me when I was being stupid?"*

"Elleen would," Misaki said. *"She loves telling you you're wrong, and she's got a completely different personality from yours."*

"Sure, but we still come from the same place. We're like siblings that way. There are a lot of things neither of us would think to question that maybe should be questioned. That's a kind of blindness we can't afford."

"I don't think it would be hard to find someone willing to question what you're doing," Misaki said in amusement.

"Yes, but... not someone like you. A lot of people would argue with me just to make themselves feel better, or smarter, or nobler. You don't do that. You're a good person."

Surprise struck Misaki silent. That surprise was quickly followed by an uncomfortable pang of guilt, and she let out a sigh.

"Listen... I'm sorry I took a shot at Texca's back, okay?" she said grudgingly. *"You're right. It wasn't noble."* Her father would have been ashamed. You were supposed to look a fighter in the eyes when you killed him; everyone knew that.

"Misaki, I honestly don't care if you attack people from behind, or above, or jump out of storm drains at them," Robin said, surprising her again. *"Street fighting is always messy and full of cheating."*

"So," Misaki said, confused, *"what is the problem then?"*

Robin let out an exasperated sigh. *"You couldn't have gone for his knees?"*

"The back is a bigger target," she said defensively. *"Those ice spears are hard to aim over any distance. Look, I understand that you would rather not kill anyone, but if it's a choice between killing a dangerous criminal and letting him get away—"*

"Then he gets away," Robin said firmly.

"So, you care that everyone lives, but you don't care whether you fight clean?" Misaki asked, confused.

"I guess I always had a childish concept of a clean fight." Robin crossed his arms. *"To me, a 'clean fight' is one that leaves the world cleaner than it was, not bloodier."*

Misaki didn't mean to laugh—Robin seemed so earnest—but she couldn't help it. *"That's not just childish, you idiot. It's insane."* And yet so sweet. So *Robin. "It doesn't even make any sense."*

"What do you mean?"

"What if you let someone go and they're not just a shady one-off killer like Yaotl Texca? What if it's a serial killer, or a crazy person, or someone in the middle of carrying out a vendetta? What if letting them go puts other people in danger?"

"Then I'll take responsibility for that," Robin said resolutely. *"I won't sleep until they're caught."*

"And you think that's going to work?"

"It has to."

Misaki studied her friend for a moment. *"Robin... Firebird... people die,"* she said. *"From what I hear of this place, people die here all the time. Why is this little handful of lives so important to you?"*

"Because no one is looking out for them."

"You ever think that might be because they're not worth it?"

Robin turned to her sharply, coal eyes flashing. *"Look down there."* He pointed to the few smears of blood on the pavement where Misaki had taken down Texca's guards earlier. *"Do you know how those men got out of this alley?"*

"Well, you sent up a flair. I know the police didn't call in an ambulance, but I figured someone would." Though now that she thought about it, she hadn't heard any sirens.

Robin shook his head. *"There's an adyn-run waysis near here."*

"A waysis?" Misaki knew she had heard the Carythian term before but had never been entirely sure what it meant.

"Neutral ground," Robin said, *"a safe haven recognized by all of the major gangs. You don't attack a person sheltering in a waysis; it's against street code."*

"I didn't know there were any codes of honor here," Misaki admitted.

"None that are recognized by the government. Everyone in this

part of town has been oppressed or abandoned by theonite powers the rest of the world depends on, but they don't give up. Instead, they've made a life and a culture here for themselves. It's not perfect, but it's worth protecting, even if the ruling theonites, and the politicians, and the police have all decided otherwise."

"If the people here are honestly trying, then how come this place is such a mess?" Misaki challenged. *"How come they're still so poor and uneducated?"*

"Well, consider that at about half of North End is populated by Native Baxarians. They were doing fine until the Yammanka colonizers showed up and killed a third of them, enslaved another third, and forced the last third into Falleka marriages."

"Right." The jaseliwu back in Ishihama had always told Misaki that the natives of Abiria and Carytha had been thankful to intermarry with the more powerful Yammankalu. She had quickly gathered from the Native Baxarians she had met in Carytha that this was far from the truth. It seemed that not everyone in the world considered a strong bloodline to be a good trade for their autonomy.

"The adyns are at even more of a disadvantage," Robin continued. *"They were brought here as slaves to farm all that land the Yammankalu stole from the Natives, but when they were emancipated, they weren't given any property of their own. Some of the Native Baxarians can at least compete with the Kelenduguka physically, but the adyns don't even have that. It's easy to judge when you inherit property, and an important name, and amazing powers from your parents."* Robin's voice had grown heated. *"How easy do you think it is to build a life out of nothing?"*

"You're not just talking about the adyns and the Native Carythians," Misaki said quietly. *"You're talking about yourself."* Having come to Carytha as a refugee with nothing to his name, it was no wonder he identified so strongly with these people.

"What?" Robin looked surprised. *"No. I mean—I'm way luckier than most North Enders. Sure, Elleen and I were refugees in these slums, but not many Livingston orphans have powers good enough*

to get them accepted into a theonite academy."

"It's not your powers that make you special," Misaki said, *"either of you."*

Her father always said there were things you couldn't train into a fighter—spirit, courage, the ability to be something bigger than oneself. Robin wasn't like the hundreds of koronu who claimed bravery and selflessness. He would honestly die to protect the dirtiest beggar in this slum. It was ridiculous, it was beautiful, and it sent a terrible anxiety clawing through Misaki.

It was like Robin said: street fighting was messy and full of cheating. He might claim that gangs of North End kept to a code of honor, but Misaki was fairly sure there were no codes to protect an honest boy like him. She felt sick, standing there, thinking about all the ways the monsters of these alleys could take advantage of Robin's kindness, all the things they could do to him... It wasn't a question of whether or not he was going to die. It was a question of whether he would die quickly, with all his spirit intact, or slowly, after the evils of the world had ripped and beaten every shred of optimism out of him.

Robin was a strong fighter, but she knew better than anyone that it only took one decisively-placed needle to fell a giant. There were some fights you could only win by being more ruthless than your opponent. One moment of hesitation or gentleness against a truly dangerous opponent would cost Robin his life. That light would go out. The thought created a frantic, irrepressible panic in Misaki.

"But you would *kill,"* she said, and it came out as a plea, a demand, *"if you really,* really *had to."*

"No."

"Not even a serial murderer? A rapist? What about that witch doctor we keep hearing about who feeds his enemies to wild animals?"

Robin shook his head. *"That's not for me to do. The world doesn't need another powerful theonite trying to force his idea of justice on a city of adyns. That's not what I'm going to be."*

"And what about to save your own life?" she demanded. *"If it*

comes down to your life or your enemy's—"

"I'll find a way to stop them without any death."

"But if you can't," she pressed. *"If they're too strong, if there's no other way, will you kill then?"*

"No," Robin answered without hesitation. *"Look, Livingston's first crime-fighters killed people and they all died violent deaths before their time."*

"Oh, good," Misaki said, employing her newly-discovered Carythian sarcasm to mask her distress. *"That's very reassuring."*

"My point is that trying to stab criminals before they stab you isn't necessarily a good strategy."

"That's the dumbest thing I've ever heard," Misaki snapped, *"and you've already said a lot of dumb things today."* She didn't know how it worked with Livingston street fighters, but every swordsman knew that landing the first strike was crucial.

"I'm just trying to make things better."

"You're an idiot."

Robin shrugged. *"My brother's been saying exactly that since we were little. It's never changed my mind."*

Misaki stared at Robin for a moment, biting the inside of her cheek, an odd flavor of anger swelling inside her.

Then she pushed him.

The usually graceful fighter let out an undignified squawk and Misaki experienced a moment of heart-dropping dread in which she thought he was actually going to fall—that she had actually killed him—but he just barely managed to keep his balance on the edge of the roof.

"Misaki!" He turned on her, temperature rising in fury. *"What the hell was that for?"*

"I don't know..." It was strange how comforting it was to see the anger on his face, to know that he didn't want to die. *"I needed to make sure you were sane."*

"What is wrong with you?"

"I don't want you to die."

"Misaki." He shook his head. *"I don't know what you think*

you're doing, but I can take care of myself."

"I know you can," she said. *"I'm just not sure you will."*

"I will."

"Really? So how many times could you have taken down Yaotl Texca today before he had a machete to your neck? How many times are you going to put your own life in danger to save a criminal who doesn't deserve it? How long do you think you can keep that up before you're dead?"

"If I have to kill for this work, then I should be dead. I've seen too many theonites who put their lives before others' because they thought they were in the right. I won't be one of them."

"Do you not understand? You're going to die!"

"Then I'll die right!" He was stepping toward her when his injured leg gave out—and he fell.

"Robin!" Misaki lunged forward and grabbed his hand just as he reached for her.

Knowing she was not heavy enough to anchor them both, even in her most stable stance, Misaki threw all her weight backward. They toppled to the cement roof together, Robin falling on top of her. He caught himself on his hands, preventing his body from slamming down on hers, but Misaki realized in a rush of heat that this was the closest they had ever been.

Great Nagi! She thought dizzily. *He's so warm!* Not blisteringly, brutally hot like the blue flaming Mathaba. Just... warm. He breathed out and the heat made steam across her coldness, washing her in a cloud of steam. Misaki felt her face turn bright red.

"Excuse me!" She said very loudly.

"Sorry." Robin scrambled back off her, and she sat up with a huff, thankful that he didn't have her superior senses. If he had, he would have sensed the way her heart was fluttering through her indignant exterior. Though now that she listened for it, his heart was beating rather quickly as well. *Was he...* Well, he had just had a near-death experience. That was probably why.

"Thank you," he said earnestly. *"I—"*

"Don't ever do that again!" Misaki burst out, surprised by the

sheer emotion in her voice. It appeared to stun Robin too, and he blinked at her.

"Do what?" he asked. *"Fall off a building?"*

"Scare me like that! I told you not to stand so close to the edge, you idiot! I told you!"

It was as Misaki stared at him, her cheeks flushed, bristling with anger, that her own purpose started to take shape before her.

"You're the one who pushed me," Robin said in bewilderment.

"You're the one who invited *me,"* she snapped.

"Why are you so mad at me?"

"Because I like you!" Misaki shouted the words without thinking. As Robin's eyes widened, she felt her blush intensify, undoubtedly turning her whole face a blazing shade of pink.

"You... what?"

"I—respect you," she amended, her cheeks still burning. *"I respect that you won't kill, and I'll try to be more careful with my blades in the future, but I need you to understand something."*

"Yeah?" Robin said warily.

"If I think your life is in danger, I will kill for you."

"What? I don't want you to do that."

"Well, it's not up to you."

"I don't want you killing anyone in this city."

"Then you'd better keep yourself out of mortal danger," Misaki said.

"What?"

"It's pretty simple," Misaki said, drawing herself up to stand over Robin. *"You want to keep your precious murderers and drug dealers safe, don't let them kill you. All I'm asking is that you keep yourself alive. You can do that, can't you?"*

Robin sighed, putting a hand to his face. *"Only you could turn an offer for help into a threat."*

"Just promise me you'll be more careful with your own life."

"This is weird."

"Promise me!"

"Okay. I promise I'll do my best."

The next morning, Misaki woke early and went to see Koli Kuruma in the Fieldstone Tower. First years usually didn't get their own private workshops, but first years usually couldn't build their own computers and holographic projectors.

The tajaka was hunched over his table, broad hands skittering like spiders over his work. Most numuwu didn't have much use for their theonite speed; Koli used it to keep his fingers moving as fast as his brain.

"Numu Kuruma?" she said, nudging the door open. *"Sorry to interrupt—"*

"I told you, just Koli is fine."

"Koli..." It felt strange using the familiar address with a smith of such a famous family. *"I'm sorry but I lost one of the knives you gave me."*

"Do you know how long my Koumbia friends took forging those?" Koli was a poor weaponsmith for a numu, but he had cultivated such an extensive network of other craftsmen that it didn't matter. He would draw up designs and outsource the metalwork itself to siblings, cousins, and friends, in exchange for the complex tech work none of them understood.

"I'm sorry. Is it possible to get a replacement?"

"Those knives were twins, Misaki. You can't just replace one and expect the set to be the same."

Craftsmen, Misaki thought in exasperation. *"Okay, well, if that bothers you, I'll take a different pair. I'm happy to pay whatever—"*

"My family has more money than you've ever seen in your life, Princess."

"O-okay..." Misaki said uncertainly. She had known Koli Kuruma for months now, but his behavior still confused her to no end.

"I know you important koronu always think numuwu need to be protected and patronized, but I don't work for money."

Misaki wasn't sure what to say to that. She didn't know why he was taking such an accusatory tone; the vast majority of numuwu *did* rely on koro support to live. Koli's massively rich family was one of the few numu clans in the world who had fought for and earned the right to run their own multi-million-walla corporation. No such precedent existed in Kaigen.

"I didn't say anything about—"

"Understand, Misaki, I supply you, Robin, and Elleen because I want to. Respect that, and don't offer me money again. If you need more daggers, they're yours."

"I—um... I actually wanted to talk to you about that, Numu Ku—Koli. I was thinking I might move away from the daggers. I..." She paused. *"I want a sword."*

That made Koli swivel in his chair, raising his eyebrows.

"What?" Misaki asked, self-conscious under his scrutinizing gaze.

"Nothing. I just seem to remember suggesting a sword the very first time you came to me for arms. You told me something really inane. What was it?" He narrowed his eyes. *"Swords are a man's weapon?"*

Misaki scowled. *"You know what, never mind. If you don't want to help, I can get a new weapon myself."* She turned to go and was almost out the door when Koli spoke again:

"Specifications?"

She stilled, one hand resting on the doorframe.

"Nothing out of the ordinary," she decided after a moment. *"I just need a blade with more reach than those daggers, something that holds its edge well enough to go through a few bodies if it has to."*

"Oh dear. Planning an assassination, Princess?"

Her hand tightened on the doorframe. *"I hope not."*

Misaki's next stop that day was the main gymnasium. She had avoided open advanced sword practices since coming to Daybreak. Early in the year, she had attended a few of the novice practices for fun, but she had never felt like she should join the more serious students. Talented though she might be, the sword had never been a serious pursuit to her. How could it be? She was a girl. But that morning, she joined the advanced sword students under the glass dome of the gymnasium.

Daybreak's master sword instructor, Makan Wangara, usually delegated supervision of the novice practices to his son, Kinoro, or one of his other high-ranking students, but the weathered old koro always oversaw advanced practices himself. Today, he stood on the bleachers, overlooking the students as they filtered in. Advanced practice was open to everyone, though Wangara was known to bump students to the novice group when they were obviously out of their depth.

Misaki was confident that she could keep up with this group, some of whom had only been training with the sword for the three or four years they had attended Daybreak. She did, however, feel pitifully small as they all stood to find training partners. She was short among people her own age, and these students were all two to four years older than she was.

A brown-skinned Biladuguka girl took pity on Misaki and offered to drill with her. She looked to be about fifteen, in her second or third year.

"I'm Azar Tarore." The girl greeted Misaki the Yammanka way, taking the jijaka's hand in hers and touching her lips to the knuckles.

"Right." Misaki returned the gesture, awkwardly bumping her lips into Tarore's knuckles, and let go of her hand as quickly as she could without being rude. She hadn't gotten used to the amount of touching tajakalu did, and she wasn't sure she ever would. Inexplicably, she didn't mind the heat, but she knew her cold skin made them uncomfortable and it always left her feeling self-conscious... although Robin never seemed to mind— She shook herself and returned the girl's smile.

"I'm Misaki Tsusano. It's a pleasure to meet you, Koro Tarore."

"Just Azar, please," the girl said as they went to select practice swords from the box.

The bokken here weren't wooden like the ones Misaki used back home. Instead, they were made of some kind of synthetic material that wouldn't catch fire in the hands of an overzealous tajaka. Few things in Carytha were made of wood except the trees. The country's population was over forty percent tajaka, making wood an impractical building material.

Master Wangara called out the name of a drill Misaki didn't recognize and the rest of the fighters surged into motion, synthetic bokken clacking together. Despite her experience, Misaki wasn't used to Yammanka terminology and training methods.

"Have you done this drill before?" Azar asked patiently.

"No," Misaki said, watching closely as the pair of students next to them ran through the set of moves once, twice, three times.

"Awa, I can walk you through it."

"That's okay." Misaki's eyes followed the other two students through the sequence a fourth time. *"I've got it."*

"What—?"

"I've got it. Please, come at me, Koro Azar."

The first time Azar attacked, she did so gently, as if worried she might break Misaki if she hit too hard. Misaki was used to that, but Azar picked up her speed and power as soon as she saw Misaki in motion.

"Where did you come from?" Azar asked when Master Wangara called a break between drills.

"I'm from Shirojima, Kaigen."

"Why haven't I seen you at these practices before?"

"I—um..." Misaki shrugged, not really wanting to explain.

Other girls at Daybreak tended to react with revulsion to the idea of growing up to become a housewife. A deep, restless part of Misaki was relieved to be in a place where her viciousness was an expectation, not a surprise. Another, equally deep part of her felt a need to defend her culture from these outsiders who clearly didn't understand it.

"Who taught you?" Azar asked.

"My father."

"Oh. Is he a military man?"

"No." It was an understandable assumption. In most countries, the most skilled fighters all joined the military. The Kaigenese Empire mainly conscripted from their core provinces, leaving the koro houses of Shirojima and other provinces to arm and train their own.

Azar clearly had more questions, but Master Wangara called them back to their lines. The second drill was more difficult, and Misaki felt herself coming awake. Azar was good enough to keep Misaki engaged, though her stances were on the narrow side and she carried too much tension in her shoulders. Misaki didn't say that of course. Azar was an upperclassman; it didn't feel appropriate.

As they moved into more advanced drills, Azar started to grasp Misaki's skill level.

"Great Falleke!" she exclaimed. *"I've never seen anyone shift stances so fast!"*

"I'm little." Misaki shrugged off the compliment. *"Low center of gravity."*

Unlike some koronu, Azar's knee-jerk reaction to Misaki's skill was not to get defensive and competitive. She seemed excited.

"Next time you should drill with Kinoro or one of the fourth-year students," she said when Master Wangara called an end to the drills, *"someone closer to your level."*

Misaki had caught glimpses of Kinoro Wangara training and knew that Azar was being generous in suggesting that she was anywhere near his level. That or she just didn't understand the difference between a competent fighter and a prodigy.

After another short break, Master Wangara had the students gather around one of the fighting circles marked on the gymnasium floor.

"What's happening now?" Misaki whispered to Azar.

"Didn't you know? Advanced practice always ends with matches. Everyone fights at least once."

"Oh," Misaki said in surprise. *"Fun."*

Azar made a face. *"Sometimes,"* she said. *"Sometimes, it's scary."*

Master Wangara clapped his hands together, calling the group to attention and the conversation trailed off.

"That's enough of a break, kids." The swordmaster never spoke loudly; he didn't have to. He was the sort of person everyone leaned forward to hear. *"Time for some fights."*

"Do you want me to referee a second ring, Baba?" Kinoro offered.

"No. I'm going to referee to start off," Master Wangara said, *"and as far as fighters..."* He rubbed his hands together, turning to survey the students around the circle. *"You."* He pointed to Misaki, and she straightened in surprise. *"New kid. Are you familiar with point matches?"*

Misaki grimaced inwardly. She *was* familiar with the international style of scoring sword sparring; she just didn't think very much of it.

Tajakalu really seemed to like miserable, protracted struggles that pushed both fighters to their physical limits and provided a lot of opportunity for creativity and showing off. In sword matches, this manifested in a ridiculous points system that allowed combatants with practice swords to fight far past the point they would both have died in a fight with real weapons.

The first would-be lethal strike was worth five points. Every would-be lethal strike after that was worth two while any hit that would have drawn blood but not been lethal was only worth one point. The referee simply called out points as he saw them, with no breaks. While it *did* give that valuable five-point credit to the first killing blow, it was woefully unrealistic.

Misaki suspected it was this very approach to combat that had allowed Robin to delude himself into thinking he could get into fights with half a dozen criminals each week without dying. Any Shirojima swordsman worth his steel knew that a real fighter was one who could fell his opponent in a single cut. Then again, continuous point fighting might benefit Misaki, if she planned to go through North End, Livingston slicing and nicking criminals without killing them...

"Well?" Master Wangara prompted and Misaki realized she had been staring at him dumbly for a moment.

"Y-yes, Koroba," she said in a small voice. *"I'm familiar with point matches."*

"Excellent. Since it's your first time with us, you get first pick."

"What?"

"Pick anyone here to fight."

Misaki scanned the group, weighing her options—she didn't know any of them. She steeled herself and drew her shoulders back before naming her opponent.

"Kinoro Wangara."

The gymnasium went silent.

It was brash, arrogant, and not at all the sort of thing Misaki usually did, but she needed to become something more than just Misaki if she was going to fulfill her promise. A middle-of-the-pack sword fighter was not going to be able to protect Robin.

Master Wangara was looking at her with new interest as murmurs broke out among the other students.

"I feel that this bears asking before you step into the ring: do you understand who you are challenging?"

"Yes, Koroba."

"Good enough." Wangara nodded for his son to step into the circle, but Kinoro hesitated. His gaze flicked from his father to Misaki, back to his father.

"Are you sure, Baba?" he said.

"Yes," the swordmaster said shortly. *"Take your positions."*

The younger Wangara still hesitated. *"Are* you *sure?"* he asked Misaki.

Kinoro Wangara was sixteen—two years older than Misaki—with typically-Sizwean dark skin and a mess of black braids that he pulled back with a hair-tie when he fought. He was built like a jungle cat, long limbs thin but rippling with muscle.

"Don't be rude, Kinoro," Master Wangara scolded. *"She said she wants a fight. Show the girl some respect."*

Relenting, Kinoro stepped into the ring and Misaki took up her position opposite him. The surrounding students let out cries and clapped their hands. These non-Kaigenese had an infuriating habit of whooping, and stomping, and making all sorts of distracting noise while fighters were engaged in combat. As far as they were concerned, they were being helpful. They had this bizarre notion that praise and song could lend a person power. Much of a Yammanka jaseli's job seemed to consist of following koronu around, talking them up and singing of their accomplishments.

Misaki had never understood how a song was supposed to make a person strong. Power was born into a person and lived in the wordless depths of their soul. The strength of a bloodline wasn't something you sang about; it was something the holder knew and others witnessed. Kaigenese koronu rarely had jaseliwu follow them around. Real power needed no words. It spoke for itself.

She bowed automatically, hands at her sides, bokken resting in a reverse grip against the back of her right arm. The bow wasn't part of fighting ritual here, but it felt wrong to begin a match any other way. Kinoro returned the bow smoothly, as any Kaigenese swordsman would, and Misaki remembered that the Wangaras were famous for training in different styles across the world, from Sizwe, to Ranga, to Biladugu. This boy had almost certainly trained with Kaigenese like her before. He would know her tricks, but she was unfamiliar with his.

"Assume your stances," Master Wangara said.

As Misaki raised her bokken to mid-guard in the standard ready position her father had taught her, Kinoro dropped into a strange, catlike stance she didn't recognize. Letting out a slow breath, she tried to see him as a criminal. She had to stop him from hurting Robin. She had to—

"Fight!"

Kinoro exploded forward as if shot from a canon. His bokken slid across Misaki's middle before she could even start to defend.

Master Wangara called out, *"Five points - Kinoro!"*

And the end of the fight, Misaki thought with a sick feeling in her gut that had nothing to do with the practice sword that had just thumped into it.

But these were tajaka rules and the fight went on. Misaki tried to return the favor, slashing her own bokken at Kinoro's neck, but he sprang back so fast that he was out of range by the time the weapon swung through. She was in the process of flipping the blade around for a second cut when he hit her again, this time in the leg.

"One point, Kinoro!"

The swordmaster's son had every possible physical advantage over Misaki—size, strength, speed, flexibility—and the most infuriating thing was that he didn't need any of them. His skill so far outstripped her own that he probably would have been able to trounce her with any number of physical handicaps. Each feint was perfectly placed to trip her up, each strike impeccably placed. His footwork was so inscrutably tricky that at times, he seemed to be teleporting from one side of Misaki to another.

As soon as she thought she had him with a cut, he was suddenly gone—only to reappear half a heartbeat later and score a point as her blade swung wide, exposing her center. He didn't hit her hard, but each stroke of his bokken left her feeling shaken. The students on the sidelines were stomping and shouting so loudly she could barely think, and he was *so fast—*

No, she thought as he flashed through her guard again to strike her shoulder. *It's not just speed. It's foresight.* Kinoro Wangara moved with perfect timing, forecasting her every movement and striking in the split dinma she was vulnerable. She just had to be less predictable, trip him up.

The next time she advanced, she made the same decisive slice toward his neck she had attempted several times now. He evaded as she knew he would: falling back just far enough to be out of her swing radius, but still close enough that a powerful launch off his back leg would shoot him back in for an attack. However, instead of facing him as he sprang forward, she spun, letting the momentum of her follow-through carry her into another, downward slice in the same direction as the first.

A surprised Kinoro only avoided a blow to the head by inexplicably changing directions mid-stride. There was a smack as Misaki's bokken caught one of his braids, and an appreciative roar swelled from the fringes of the circle. Apparently, even an almost-point against Kinoro was cause enough for them to celebrate. Not for Misaki. She had to do better.

She had always been a quick learner, but this Kinoro Wangara, it seemed, learned even faster. The second time she tried to feint into a spin, he responded by dropping into a spin of his own, sweeping a leg around to take Misaki's feet out from under her. Her immediate impulse was to tuck and roll out of the fall, but Kinoro had somehow hooked her ankle with his toes, making that impossible. She caught herself on her forearms with bruising force, barely avoiding breaking her nose on the jonjo glass floor.

"Two points, Kinoro!" Master Wangara called as the tajaka's bokken touched the back of Misaki's neck and rested there.

"Yield." Kinoro said.

Misaki wanted to. She was painfully out of breath and both arms throbbed from taking the impact of Kinoro's swings. But Robin would get back up. Robin would still be fighting, and Misaki had to be there to protect him. Bracing her left hand against the floor, she gritted her teeth. Then she slammed her bokken into Kinoro's, knocking it away from her neck.

The other students cheered and sang as she staggered to her feet, but it wasn't long before Kinoro had her on the floor again. This time, she landed on her back, stars careening across her field of vision as Kinoro's bokken touched her throat. She had to blink hard to bring the tajaka's dark face into focus above her. To his credit, there was nothing gloating in his expression. Misaki herself was never so gentle with inferior fighters.

"You did well," he said, his black eyes soft with a sympathy Misaki didn't need. *"You have my respect."*

I don't want your respect, she thought bitterly. *I want to be better than this!*

"Do you yield?"

Misaki clenched her jaw. She hadn't landed a hit yet. Kinoro looked to his father. *"Baba, can you call off—"*

Misaki swung her bokken with all her strength. It struck Kinoro's bare ankle with a loud crack.

"Ow!" Kinoro cried out. The sudden pain caused his grip on his own bokken to loosen and Misaki twisted it from his hand. She rolled backward into a crouch with two weapons.

"That was uncalled for!" Kinoro exclaimed, clutching his ankle.

"One point, New Kid," Master Wangara laughed.

"Baba!" Kinoro looked at his father, betrayed, and his temperature rose. It was hard to tell if he was more annoyed with Misaki or his father, but annoyed was good. Maybe it would make him sloppy. He turned back to Misaki and pointed to her. *"I'm going to hit you for real now."*

Normally, Misaki enjoyed getting a rise out of another fighter. She had gotten a lot of good laughs punching Robin and tripping Kazu onto his face, but she didn't feel like smiling now.

As Kinoro, now weaponless, coiled into a fighting stance, Misaki weighed her options. An honorable fighter would throw the tajaka his weapon back, but she had forgone honor when she took that swing at his ankle. Nobody cared about rules of engagement on the street; if she wanted to succeed where she was going, she couldn't afford courtesy.

Throwing the extra bokken at Kinoro as a distraction was out too. His reflexes were so fast that he would snatch it right out of the air. She didn't even trust herself to hurl the practice sword out of the ring without the tricky boy somehow managing to catch it.

Her only option, it seemed, was to hold onto both bokken and see what she could do. She had never properly learned to dual-wield swords, but the twin daggers she took out crime-fighting had given her a sense of balance with a weapon in each hand. Keeping the right bokken clutched in a forehanded grip for longer-range strikes, she flipped the left one into a reverse grip, to use in defense if Kinoro got too close.

The tajaka's keen eyes followed the movement, undoubtedly reading her train of thought. He didn't ask his father to break again. He was engaged now. The noise from the crowd focused into rhythmic clapping, like a heartbeat, gradually quickening as the two fighters circled.

With the sword in her left hand as a backup defense, Misaki was able to slice at her opponent more freely. Mobile as Kinoro was, she managed to trap him against the edge of the ring. Even cornered, Kinoro still managed to block her attack, taking the hit on his forearm instead of his ribs, before darting past Misaki, out of range.

"One point, New Kid!" Master Wangara declared.

The crowd of students roared in approval, but the sound only grated on Misaki. One point wasn't good enough. She needed a killing strike. She would have to swing faster to have any chance at a decisive, fight-ending hit. No hesitation.

Kinoro shook out his arm and then came at her.

There! She swung—and missed. Somehow, Kinoro had managed to duck faster than she could think. Her left hand, which should have raised the second bokken to defend her center, was caught in Kinoro's burning hot grip. She tried to bring her right hand back up to slash again, but she had swung so hard on that first slice that she had thrown herself off balance. Kinoro used that momentum to flip her over, making to slam her onto her back.

Misaki managed to twist in the air and get her feet under her, but it didn't do her any good. She had barely touched down when Kinoro's palm slammed into her chest, throwing her backward. Both bokken flew from her grip. She heard them clattering away as her own body crashed to the floor and slid a bound. The glass dome spun above her. She couldn't breathe.

"Kinoro!" A reproachful voice said—one of the older students. *"That was too hard!"*

"Sorry!" Kinoro said, and Misaki was dimly aware of his quick footsteps approaching. *"Are you—"*

"She's fine," Master Wangara said. *"Leave her."*

The footsteps stopped. *"But Baba—"*

"Take over running matches, Kinoro. Use the next circle."

With eye-watering effort, Misaki managed to draw a breath. She was only winded. Wangara was right; she would be fine. She didn't feel fine though. She felt panicked, inadequate. Fighting—even losing—had never made her feel this way before.

Until now, swordplay had always been an experience of pure joy. Her natural talent and her access to her father's instruction automatically put her above ninety percent of the other fighters she encountered. And if she lost a fight every now and again—if Kazu got a lucky hit in or if some boy knocked her down—well, what did it matter? She was a girl, and no one staked a girl's worth on her swordplay. It was all just a hobby—a delight if she did well, unimportant if she didn't. But if one of those slip-ups meant the difference between Robin living and dying... there was no joy in that thought. Only pain.

As she lay staring at the gymnasium's ceiling, slower footsteps approached and she found Master Wangara standing over her.

"You did not enjoy that," the swordmaster said lightly.

Misaki didn't respond for a moment. She was still focusing on taking in deep, full breaths.

"Sh-should I have?" she grunted finally.

"A lot of fighters thrill in the challenge of trying to land a hit on Kinoro. Others enjoy getting a rise out of him, but every moment of that was grueling for you. For someone so proficient at fighting, you certainly seem to loathe it."

"I prefer to win."

"A lot of koronu prefer to win," he said. *"Most of those aren't stupid enough to challenge my son to single combat."*

Misaki just lay still, breathing slowly.

"Get up."

Misaki tried, but without the driving force of combat behind her muscles, she couldn't manage it. Everything hurt.

With a sigh, Master Wangara opened his hand and shot *fire* at her. Misaki yelped and rolled onto her feet just in time to scramble clear of the flames.

"I haven't seen you here before," Master Wangara said. *"Who are you?"*

"Tsu—Misaki Tsusano," she said, just remembering to order her name the Yammanka way—given name and then surname. *"I'm a first year in Limestone Four."*

"Tsusano," Master Wangara said with a knowing nod. *"I see. I'm going to hazard a guess you have no brothers?"*

A good guess. It would explain why a girl had ended up training the sword with her father, but that was not Misaki's situation.

"I have three," she said with a note of pride, *"just none as good as I am."*

"And you're here," Master Wangara said, *"which means your parents can't be entirely traditional people."*

"They're pretty traditional," Misaki said. *"They're still going to marry me off when I'm done with my schooling here."* A few months ago, the thought wouldn't have pulled at this strangely painful feeling in Misaki's chest. Why was Robin's face suddenly filling her mind?

"Interesting," Master Wangara said, crossing his arms.

"Is it, Koroba?"

"I just wonder," he said, *"why would a future housewife need to be a skilled fighter?"*

Misaki frowned stubbornly. *"Maybe it's fun for me, Koroba."*

"Oh, I'm sure it is, but you didn't come here today for fun. You came here out of need."

Misaki eyed the swordmaster in surprise. *"How do you—"*

"You came here for a purpose today. I could see it on your face. It must be something very important for you to challenge my son, of all people."

"Maybe I'm just an idiot with an oversized ego."

"If you had stepped into that ring to sate your ego, your attitude would be uglier right now," Wangara said confidently. *"There are few things uglier than a wounded ego. You honestly wanted to see how you measured up, and you honestly wanted to do better."*

Misaki nodded.

"The sword for its own sake is a beautiful thing but I like a sense of purpose in a student." Master Wangara considered Misaki for a moment and she was nervous that he would ask her to elaborate on why she had come to the practice. She couldn't tell him what had given her purpose. She couldn't tell him about Firebird, but he didn't pry. Instead, he said, *"I have time this Suradon at the tenth waati."*

Misaki looked up sharply. *"What?"*

"I'll try to find you a training partner closer to your size and strength. Until then, I'm afraid you'll have to make do with Kinoro."

"What are you..." Misaki suddenly felt dizzier than she had any time Kinoro had knocked her down. *"A-are you offering to train me?"*

"Not offering, Tsusano. Insisting."

"B-but..." Better fighters than Misaki competed viciously for the privilege of training with Makan Wangara. *"But you don't train first years,"* she said blankly.

"I train students who need me." Wangara put a toe under Misaki's fallen bokken and flipped the weapon into his hand. *"Most first years don't have enough experience to benefit from my instruction any more than they would benefit from Kinoro's or that of some other, less experienced fighter. If you want to advance beyond what you've already learned from your father, then you need me."*

"Wangara Kama, I-I don't know what to say. Thank—"

"You know your Tsusano-ryuu katas?"

"Yes, Koroba," she said, though she hadn't practiced them in a long time, *"all except the Stormblade forms."*

"Good." He threw the bokken at her with blinding speed for a man his age and seemed pleased when she caught it. *"Practice those. Have them ready to demonstrate for me by Suradon—and don't try to cut corners. I know what they're supposed to look like."*

Misaki clutched the bokken and found herself smiling. *"Do I need to bring anything, Koroba?"*

"Nothing except that smile."

"What?"

"If you want to be a great swordswoman, you'll need to find purpose and joy in your fighting at the same time. Now if you'll excuse me, I'm going to go oversee a few more matches."

Misaki nodded. *"Suradon on the tenth waati,"* she said, just to make sure she hadn't imagined it. *"Tsusano-ryuu katas."*

"And a smile," Wangara said and strode off to referee the next match.

7

THE SUN

When Misaki hid her sword, she nailed the floorboards down over it. It was a promise to herself. She might never be able to destroy the part of her that was aggressive and willful, but she could bury it. That was what she had thought at the time.

"A jijaka is a fine thing to be," Master Wangara had once told her, *"undoubtedly the best theotype for a swordfighter."*

"Why?" she had asked.

"Most strong things are rigid. If you are water, you can shift to fit any mold and freeze yourself strong. You can be strong in any shape. You can be anything."

I can be strong in any shape, Misaki told herself as she packed the hammer and nails away. *I can be anything.* If she had adapted to the dangers of Livingston's dark alleys, how hard could it be to master marriage and motherhood?

"As Nagi smiles on strong men, Nami smiles on patient women," her mother had told her on her wedding day, all aglow with pride.

"It will all be worth it when you hold your child in your arms," her father had said. "It will be worth it when you watch them grow."

And Misaki had believed them. Not because it made any sense. Because she had to. Because if she didn't believe it was worth it, then what had she done?

So, when her new husband barely even looked at her in the aftermath of their wedding, she kept smiling. When her father-in-law snapped at her, she bowed, and spoke sweetly, and did as she was told. It would all be worth it. When her husband's frigid nyama made her skin crawl, she gritted her teeth and endured his touch. It would all be worth it.

She did not fear physical intimacy, but she liked to melt into the sweet sting of heat, not grate and buckle under ice colder than her own. She needed warmth to soften her jagged edges, and Takeru's nyama was as far from warmth as a distant planet. She did her best to yield to his touch. There were a few times, she couldn't help it; she recoiled, her arms moving automatically to shield herself. Wordlessly, Takeru took her wrists in his firm, freezing cold grip, placed them on either side of her as if positioning a doll, and continued.

All her life, Misaki had been told she was beautiful. Her husband must not have thought so, because he never looked her in the face, instead fixing his eyes on the pillows beside her. Though their skin was touching, they might as well have been a galaxy away from one another. Eventually, she resigned herself to the idea that she was nothing more to him than a vessel, a womb to carry his sons—but that was alright. It would all be worth it when she held her child.

As she reached out to hold Mamoru for the first time, she forced a smile. But as his tiny body curled up against her breast, he was as cold as Takeru. She held him close and waited, but the joy she was supposed to feel never came. All she felt was a frigid echo of her husband's jiya, pulsing from the little body, reminding her that the child she held in her arms was not truly hers. He was a Matsuda.

It was then that she should have realized that the divine light she had been promised was not coming. It was never coming. But Misaki had always been too stubborn—or too stupid—to acknowledge her mistakes. So, she forced down the tears, smiled her sweetest smile, and held the infant closer, even as the feel of him made her want to shudder and retch. She forced herself to love him.

As Mamoru grew, so did his jiya. By the age of three, he had the aura of a much older theonite. Morning mist would reach out to touch his skin with reverent fingers, standing water would freeze at his touch, and dew drops would slide from blades of grass to dog his footsteps. Misaki had grown up in a household of powerful, purebred jijakalu, but even she had never heard of such nyama in such a small child.

"Were you and Takeru-sama like this when you were little?" Misaki asked her brother-in-law one evening as Mamoru splashed in a puddle in the courtyard. His little hands sent the water flying high into the air. A few drops turned to ice and pinged off the roof while others burst into puffs of fog. "Was your jiya this strong when you were three?"

"Ah…" Takashi scratched the base of his neck. "To tell you the truth, I don't really recall. My first memory of using my jiya was when Grandfather Mizudori started training me for combat."

"How old were you?" Misaki asked.

Takashi shrugged. "Five? Six, maybe? You could check with our father. Then again…" *maybe don't* were the words Takashi meant to say but couldn't. Matsuda Susumu tended to get particularly ill-tempered any time someone raised the subject of his sons' overwhelming power. It was a sore subject for him.

"So, you didn't start properly training your jiya until you were school age?" Misaki said.

"That's the way it's usually done."

"Usually," Misaki repeated, "but Mamoru is an unusual child. Shouldn't someone teach him to control that power before he hurts himself?" The average three-year-old theonite didn't manifest enough power for this to be an issue, but Mamoru's abilities were rapidly approaching a point where they would become genuinely dangerous.

Takashi shrugged. "When the boy starts his training will be up to his father." A gentle reminder that Misaki was overstepping her authority.

"Of course, Nii-sama," she said, bowing her head.

"And, knowing Takeru, he won't want to train Mamoru-kun himself until the boy has at least learned his fundamentals at school," Takashi continued. "I don't—oops!" He lifted a hand to stop an arc of half-frozen water droplets before it hit himself and Misaki. "Careful there, little one!" he laughed, vaporizing the drops with a flick of his fingers. "You almost hit your sweet mother! My, my..." he mused, staring at Mamoru. "Maybe he could use a little help. You should ask Takeru if he can start training a little early."

Misaki did, but as usual, Takeru had no interest in his child's parenting and even less interest in his wife's opinions on it. As Takashi had predicted, he said, "I am a master jijaka and swordsman. I don't train little children."

"But—"

"I'll train him once he's worthy of what I have to teach. Now, bring me more tea."

Misaki nodded and did as she was told, but she decided that someone had to teach Mamoru control. If his father, uncle, and grandfather weren't going to, why shouldn't she? She was his mother, after all, and whether or not it became a lady, she had plenty of techniques worth teaching.

She started out with the simple games she had played with her brothers as a child, racing ice chunks down the floor like cars, building snow towers, tossing a ball of liquid water back and forth without spilling any on the floor. Mamoru excelled at and quickly tired of the games that occupied most jijaka children for years, and Misaki found herself walking him through more advanced techniques.

"You want to make sure you leave a little cushion of snow between your knuckles and the ice," she said, guiding Mamoru's jiya as he froze water over his small fist. "That's it. Now try again."

Mamoru hesitated, but obeyed his mother and swung his fist into the rock. "Oh!" His little eyebrows shot up in surprise. "It doesn't hurt!"

"That's the idea." Misaki smiled. "This way, even if you've got delicate little fingers like Kaa-chan's, you can punch just about anything without damaging your hand."

"I want to try again!" Mamoru exclaimed, shaking the water from his hand.

Mamoru practiced hitting the boulder again and again while his grandfather watched from across the courtyard with a sour expression. Misaki had noticed that her father-in-law's permanent scowl seemed to deepen whenever he watched her showing Mamoru a technique, but she had elected to ignore it. A reasonable man couldn't possibly be angry with a mother for teaching her child to control his power. Of course, Matsuda Susumu was not a reasonable man.

He finally spoke up the day Misaki taught Mamoru to congeal blood. The boy, then five, had skinned both knees on the path in front of the house. Worried that his crying might set off his temperamental grandfather, she had shown him the advanced technique to distract him—not realizing that that would displease her father-in-law far more than the noise.

"Misaki!" the old man snapped just as she told Mamoru to try the next scab on his own. "A word."

"Of course, Matsuda-sama." Misaki hurried to kneel before her father-in-law, just out of earshot of Mamoru. "What is it?"

"What do you think you're doing?"

"Teaching my son how to deal with an injury," Misaki said.

"That is not your place."

"But," Misaki protested before she could stop herself, "scabbing is a useful technique for a warrior to know."

Matsuda Susumu's face twisted. "Know your place, you stupid woman. What would you understand of a warrior's jiya?"

What would you *understand of a warrior's jiya?* Misaki thought savagely. "I'm sorry." She bowed her head. "I was out of line. I won't do it again."

"I should hope not," Susumu huffed. "Matsudas fight with pure, untainted water. We have no use for your filthy Tsusano blood magic, and a warrior has no use for a woman's input."

Misaki caught her rage and ruthlessly smothered it before it could rise to the surface. "Forgive me, Matsuda-sama."

Every time Misaki's sense of duty failed her and she had the urge to lash out at her father-in-law, she stopped her tongue through sheer vindictive cruelty, reminding herself that her sharpest barbs couldn't inflict worse than what this man had already suffered. He had spent his whole life a disappointment—an heir to the Matsuda name too weak to produce a Whispering Blade, despised by his parents, surpassed by his sons.

As the only boy among many daughters, Matsuda Susumu had been his generation's sole hope of carrying on the Matsuda techniques. The family had poured years into his training, but he never displayed the power or talent of his forebears. He never achieved a Whispering Blade. In desperation, his aging father taught the technique to Susumu's sons as soon as they were old enough. Both Takashi and Takeru proved superior jijakalu to their father, mastering the Whispering Blade in their teenage years.

And what happened to a man who devoted his entire life and soul to a single pursuit only to fail entirely? Misaki supposed, after so many years of disappointment, he turned into a wrinkled husk of a human who could only find solace in tormenting those younger and better than himself. The cruelest thing Misaki could do to a bitter creature like her father-in-law was keep serving, smiling, and pushing out babies like nothing bothered her. The cruelest thing she could do was serve her purpose—like he never could.

She bowed herself out of Matsuda Susumu's presence with a demure smile and returned to her son.

"Look, Kaa-chan!" Mamoru beamed. "I can do it. I'm doing it!"

"Stop." Misaki put her hands over the boy's, stopping his jiya.

His smile disappeared. "Why?"

"I shouldn't have showed you... This is not a technique you should use. Please... forget that I taught you."

145

"You mean I can't use it again?"

Misaki hesitated. "Maybe…" She lowered her voice to a whisper. "Maybe keep it on hand for emergencies." Jiya blood clotting could save a fighter's life on the battlefield, and she would be damned if she was going to tell her son right to his face that the purity of his technique was more important than his life. "For emergencies only," she said sternly.

"Yes, Kaa-chan."

From that day on, Misaki was careful to remember that Mamoru was not hers. His accomplishments didn't belong to her. They belonged to his father and grandfather. Having taught Mamoru the basics of control, Misaki stopped meddling in his development. Soon, he went off to school, where proper fighters—men of the Matsuda, Ikeno, and Yukino lines—taught him to use his powers as a man should.

Misaki was pregnant again. She felt the nyama of a child growing inside her and plastered her smile in place to do it all again. She had borne the pain once without a single tear or word of complaint; she could do it again. She didn't realize that the only thing more painful than bearing another Matsuda son would be failing to do so.

"You lost it?" Matsuda Susumu snarled. "What do you mean you lost it?"

"I…" Misaki tried to answer but a wave of dizziness overtook her. The lines of the tatami crawled and swam beneath her knees. The room was tilting. She had dragged herself from the blood-soaked birthing bed, washed herself, and dressed when the midwives said that her father-in-law demanded an audience. The finawu hadn't even finished the purification rites. She had always had exceptional stamina and pain tolerance, but that had been the end of it. Her body was shaking. The tatami swirled and became waves. Maybe if she fell forward, they would swallow her up and wash all of this away…

"You stupid, selfish woman," her father-in-law was saying somewhere in the distance. She tried to hear him but only made out fractured pieces. "Sons"… "strong sons"… "the reason"… "the only reason you are here." He sounded angrier than usual. Misaki caught herself with a hand on the solid floor before she could fall face-first into the welcoming waves.

"Pathetic! You've just cost me a grandchild and you're too arrogant to even speak. You really are a selfish woman."

"I…" Misaki struggled to make her voice work. "I'm sor—"

CRACK!

She registered the impact before she felt the sting in her cheek. Credit where credit was due; Matsuda Susumu hit *hard* for an old man.

"If you can't give this family sons, you are worthless." Through her haze, Misaki caught the note of satisfaction in Susumu's voice. She had finally proven herself the disappointment he had always said she was. She had failed in her only purpose. Finally, she was truly lower than he was. "Don't forget why you are here."

Misaki had lifted herself onto her elbows, but couldn't find the strength to push herself up onto her knees.

Above her, Susumu let out a disgusted noise. "She's your woman. You deal with her."

"Yes, Tou-sama," a second voice said.

Takeru.

Misaki was so disoriented that she hadn't even realized that her husband was in the room. He was so still, his icy nyama was so like his father's, that he simply disappeared into the background. It wasn't until the older man had hobbled out of the room that Takeru moved, taking slow steps until he came to a stop over 'his woman.'

His bare feet swam into focus before Misaki, followed by the hem of his hakama—and suddenly she felt the warmth of tears in her eyes. It was almost a relief. She had spent so many years playing the good wife, smiling, holding back her grief, but she was not a good wife anymore. Now, she had failed him. Now, surely, it would be alright for her to cry. It was the expected thing, wasn't it?

Even if she had had the strength to lift her head, she wouldn't have looked up at him. How could she? She had just lost his child.

He must be furious—

"Come, Misaki." His voice was calm. "You need to get some rest."

She didn't move.

Crouching down, Takeru cupped her cheek where his father had hit her. The gesture was utilitarian—a cold object to bring down the swelling. He did not even try to meet her eyes.

"Can you stand?"

"I'm sorry," Misaki said, her voice small as it strained against the tears trapped in her throat. "Takeru-sama, I'm so sorry."

"That's alright," he said, sliding one arm beneath her knees and putting the other around her shoulders. "I'll carry you."

Takeru, as always, handled her as if she were a particularly fragile doll. Maybe he could feel how rigid she grew under his hands and didn't want to scare her. Maybe he truly thought all women were so frail a simple touch could break them. It was impossible to tell what Takeru was thinking behind that impassive expression. Sometimes Misaki considered it a mercy. Now it made her unbearably lonely.

She was limp as he lifted her in his arms and carried her from the room. She didn't know if she started shivering in response to his nyama or for some other reason, but once the shaking started, it wouldn't stop. It was more than just cold, more than grief. It was panic, as she realized that he wasn't going to yell at her. She wasn't going to cry. And if she couldn't even cry… if she couldn't even cry, what kind of monster was she?

"Pull yourself together." Takeru didn't quite look at her, staring ahead at the floor just past her shoulder. "You're going to be fine."

But Misaki was not fine. She was weak, worthless, selfish, and every other demeaning thing Matsuda Susumu had ever called her. She was a monster who couldn't even shed a tear for her lost child. What kind of husband said that was 'fine'? What man with a beating heart could say that?

When Takeru lowered her onto the futon, Misaki found her fingers tangling in the front of his haori, gripping with all the strength left in them.

Stay, she thought desperately. He couldn't leave her alone here with her darkness, strangled, unable to cry, unable to move. *Stay, stay.*

"Let go," Takeru said without emotion.

But Misaki's hands curled tighter. If he walked away now, she would turn to stone.

"Misaki, this is unseemly," Takeru said coldly. "Let go."

"Takeru-sama…" She searched his face one more time for some hint of grief, or empathy, or rage, anything. *Gods, anything.* "I'm sorry, I failed you. I—"

"We'll try again." He said it as if she had just dropped some eggs on the way back from market. "After you have your strength back." Icy hands closed over hers and effortlessly pried her fingers loose. "Rest."

"Takeru," she whispered as he walked away. "Please—"

"Do as you're told." He closed the door, and in that moment, he might as well have been the one who slapped her. Nami, he might as well have taken his Whispering Blade and carved everything from inside her.

Something in Misaki was dead after that day. She no longer saw her husband or Mamoru as they passed through the house around her. Every night, Takeru clinically opened her kimono, pushed her down, and lay with her. He put another baby in her, and she lost that one too.

After the second miscarriage, she began to think that she really was a doll—stiff, unfeeling, incapable of producing life because she was not really alive. There were horror stories of Tsusano puppet masters, manipulating the blood in the bodies of others— dead and living—making them dance like dolls. Sometimes Misaki wondered if she had subconsciously become one of them, puppeting her own gutted body through each day.

It wasn't until Setsuko married into the family that a pulse flickered to life in the doll's chest. Setsuko was the first person who had ever talked to Misaki about the miscarriages. It had been the subject of their first argument... the first real argument Misaki had had in years. Misaki couldn't even remember what she had said to set her sister-in-law off—some innocuous thing about being stupid or useless—and Setsuko had slammed her spatula down on the stovetop.

"Stop that!"

Startled, Misaki could only stare for a moment before stammering, "S-stop what?"

"You keep saying such horrible things about yourself!"

"Well... that's because—"

"I don't care why," Setsuko snapped. "I won't have you calling yourself useless or evil anymore, you understand? I won't have it!"

"But it's true," Misaki protested. "I haven't given my husband a son in years. I've miscarried twice now. What do you call a woman like that?"

"Not useless," Setsuko said. "Not evil. A miscarriage doesn't make you a bad woman."

"Doesn't it? My husband is a powerful jijaka, from a line that has never had any trouble producing sons. If his babies are dying before they're born, it's not a problem with him. It's me."

The more Misaki had thought about it over the years, the more it seemed that it *must* be her fault. She hadn't really wanted the babies after Mamoru. Not with the passion she was supposed to. That in itself was a sin against Nagi and Nami.

A strong jijaka like Misaki could drown a child inside her if she didn't want it enough. She had no recollection of trying to end the pregnancies; both times she had *meant* to carry the babies to term. Even if she had felt no excitement at the prospect, she had fully expected to give birth, but there was so much bitterness trapped inside her. Could she have caused the miscarriages in her sleep? While she dreamed? Had her subconscious risen like a sleep-walking demon and drowned the babies?

"You didn't do it," Setsuko said firmly. "Anyone who tries to tell you that you did is an idiot."

"But... our father-in-law thought..." Misaki choked as his voice rang through her head. *You selfish, stupid woman, you did this! You killed my grandchildren!* For years, she had sat still with those words permeating her mind like poison—*you killed my grandchildren.*

"Our father-in-law is dead. What he thought doesn't matter anymore. If it did, I wouldn't be here." Setsuko's okonomiyaki, forgotten on the stove, had started to smoke. "The only thing that matters is what you think. Do *you* think it's your fault you miscarried?"

"I hope not." Misaki was surprised at how easily the truth fell out of her mouth.

"Then it's not your fault," Setsuko said resolutely.

One of the okonomiyaki in the pan caught fire.

"Oh no—" Misaki started toward the stove, but Setsuko stopped her.

"Let it burn!" Setsuko said savagely. "It was going to taste terrible anyway. Look, I know I look like a dumb country girl— and I am—but I know a thing or two about the messy business you nobles don't like to talk about. My auntie is a midwife. She'll tell you a woman can't get rid of a healthy baby unless she really tries—and more often than not it'll kill her. I reckon getting rid of a Matsuda baby would be even harder. If you were the reason behind the miscarriages, you would know it."

Having said her piece, Setsuko turned to clean up the mess she had made of the stove, leaving Misaki to stare at her in a mute stupor. It had been a long time—such a long time—since anyone had had that kind of faith in her. She wasn't sure what to do with it.

"But if it wasn't my jiya…" she said, hating that she could hear the fear in her own voice, "then I'm broken. What if I can't have any more children?"

"Then your husband still has a perfectly good heir in Mamoru, and you have nothing to be ashamed of. I thought you said you didn't really want more children anyway."

"But that's the only reason I'm here." Misaki's voice shook.

"My marriage wasn't like yours, Setsuko. I'm not here because my husband loves me. I'm here to give him sons."

"What are you? A baby dispenser?" Setsuko laughed, scrunching up her nose.

Misaki would have laughed too—except that that was exactly what she was. And over the years, the thought had crushed her into something small.

"That's why he married me."

"Well, you married him back, didn't you?" Setsuko said.

"I didn't have a choice." It was a weak lie. If Misaki wanted, she could have fled all of this and set fire to the bridges behind her. It just hadn't been that simple...

"I swear, Misaki, I know you're smart—with your big vocabulary, and your noble upbringing, and your fancy theonite academy education—but sometimes you're the dumbest woman I've ever met."

"E-excuse me?"

"Why don't you try taking responsibility for the things you *can* control instead of the things you can't?"

"I…" Misaki considered arguing for a moment, then cocked her head at Setsuko as the other woman's words sank in. "Are all Takayubi fisherwomen this smart, or just you?" she asked finally.

"Just me," Setsuko said with a self-satisfied grin. "How do you think I landed me a handsome husband so far above my station?"

"Good point."

"Listen, little sister." Setsuko took Misaki's hands. "I know we haven't known each other for long, but you don't strike me as someone so childish she can't take control of her own happiness."

"I don't know what you're—"

"You can play weak and dumb with me, but it's not going to work. There's a bright, strong woman in there." Setsuko put a hand on Misaki's chest. "I'd like to meet her."

Misaki let out a chuckle—the most genuine sound that had come out of her in a long time. "Careful what you wish for. You don't…"

She paused when she realized that she had very nearly told Setsuko about the sword hidden beneath the floorboards at their feet. That had to stay buried. No matter how close she got to Setsuko, that was part of her that she could never revisit. But even with the sword firmly boarded up beneath them, Misaki felt a piece of her old smirk turn the corner of her mouth.

"Careful what you wish for."

While the floorboards stayed nailed firmly in place, Setsuko had broken through Misaki's stupor, bringing a part of her to life again. Maybe it wasn't a perfect life, maybe she wasn't truly happy, but she had found it in her to produce three more children— Hiroshi, colder than Mamoru and even more powerful for his age, Nagasa, with his sharp eyes and infectious energy, and now Izumo.

Misaki's fourth son wasn't as deathly cold as his brothers had been. Maybe that was a bad thing; maybe he didn't harbor the kind of frigid power his father was looking for, but it certainly made him easier to hold close to her breast.

"Yosh, yosh," she murmured into the infant's soft hair in between humming. "You're alright, Izu-kun. You're alright."

It was only the third time he had woken up that night. Not bad.

"Nenneko, nenneko yo," she sang softly.
"The moon shines down on dewy fields.
In my hometown,
Beyond this mountain and the next,
An old man used to play a driftwood flute.
The sun, long since sunk beneath the sea,
Shines in the Mother's mirror through the night.

My grandparents are dewdrops on the grass and notes on the wind.
Whisper, little sound, through the field,
Murmuring of all that we cherish,
Sighing for all that we mourn.

My parents are dewdrops on the grass and notes on the wind.
Quiver, little sound, through the field,
Weeping for what is past,
Laughing for tomorrow's joy.

You and I are dewdrops on the grass and notes on the wind.
Echo, little sound, through the field,
All the things that are forever,
All the things that fade away.

Nenneko, nenneko yo.
Catch the moonlight and shine, little dewdrop,
For beyond this mountain and the next,
The old man plays on,
The old man plays on…"

As she finished her lullaby, Izumo let out a tiny breath against her shoulder. He was asleep. She brushed the tears from the baby's face and slowly, slowly lowered him into his cradle.

"There you go, little one. Sleep well."

She had just straightened up when a muffled sound made her stiffen. Someone was in the hall. Stepping out of the room, she peered down the corridor and caught movement in the shadows. Her hand flew to her hip, but of course, there was nothing there. Stupid. There hadn't been a sword there for fifteen years.

"Who's there?" she demanded.

"Sorry, Kaa-chan."

"Mamoru." She let out her breath as her oldest son stepped into the lamplight. Somehow, she hadn't recognized his nyama or his outline. In the dark, he almost cut the figure of a grown man…

"I was trying to walk softly," Mamoru said. "I thought you were all asleep."

"And I thought you must have snuck in and gotten to bed some time during the night," Misaki returned, trying to sound reproachful rather than shaken. "You know it's nearly morning?"

"Yes, Kaa-chan. I'm sorry."

"Your uncle told me he had consigned you and the new boy to roof cleaning duty. Don't tell me it took you this long to finish a simple chore."

"We ran into a problem." Mamoru looked at his feet. "We didn't actually finish."

"So, not only did you get yourself in trouble, but you also failed to carry out your punishment?" That wasn't like Mamoru. "Come here." She motioned him further into the light.

He stepped forward and her eyes passed over him, taking in his bruised face, and dirt-smudged uniform. She had been so preoccupied with the new baby, and Mamoru had been so busy with school, that it had been a while since she had really looked at him. He had grown so much while she wasn't paying attention, standing almost as tall as his father. His skinny limbs had started to fill out with the muscles of an adult fighter, but his scrapes and bruises spoke of a boy's carelessness.

"I'm confused," Misaki said. "Your uncle told me you gave the new kid a beating, not the other way around."

Mamoru fidgeted. "This wasn't—none of this is from him. We fell off the roof."

"What did you do that for?"

"It was a mistake."

"Matsudas don't make mistakes." It was what Takeru always said to the boys, but she regretted the words when she saw the shattered expression on Mamoru's face. He really took them seriously. Of course, he did. "Hey, Kaa-chan was just joking." She offered him a smile. "Change your clothes and I'll get you something to eat."

"I already ate," Mamoru said, "at Kotetsu Kama's house. Kwang-san—the new boy—was injured from the fall, so we stopped to get his arm fixed, and they insisted we stay for dinner."

"Oh." It sounded as though Mamoru had had quite the night. "Well, change out of your clothes anyway. You need to let me wash that uniform before you're seen in it again."

"Yes, ma'am." Mamoru nodded and moved down the hall to his room.

He emerged clad in his blue house kimono, washed clean, bandages wound around his knuckles.

"Uniform," he murmured, handing his school clothes to his mother.

Misaki expected him to retreat to his room to get some sleep while she worked, but he knelt and looked on in tense silence as she gathered water into the laundry tub. Tossing the uniform into the vessel, she added soap, and began spinning the water with her dominant right hand, holding her left just above the tub to keep any wayward drops from sloshing over the edge.

Once she was satisfied that she had spun all the blood and dirt from the fabric, she streamed the dirty water into a second tub and replaced it with fresh water. All the while, Mamoru watched her work, though he didn't really seem to see her. His mind was somewhere else.

"Is Tou-sama... does he know?" he asked finally.

"Your father isn't home," Misaki said, working the clean water into a spin. "He's sleeping overnight at the office, so you're off the hook for tonight."

Not that Takeru was a particularly frightening disciplinarian. Despite his power and his intimidating demeanor, he was not as harsh as many parents in Takayubi. He didn't beat Mamoru.

"I just..." Mamoru said. "I thought... you might...?"

"I might what?"

"Give me a talking to."

Misaki looked at her son in surprise. Was he *asking* her to be angry with him?

"My role in this house is to rock the babies to sleep and comfort the little ones when they skin their knees. Are you a little baby?"

"No, Kaa-chan."

"When it comes to business like this—men's business—that's for your father to handle. But," she continued before she managed to stop herself, "if you want someone to scold you, I'm annoyed enough to stand in for him at the moment."

"Oh—I-I didn't mean—"

"It seems like you've made one stupid mistake on top of another today," she said, pulling the water from Mamoru's uniform. "How do you intend to fix it?"

"I've apologized to Kwang Chul-hee," Mamoru said. "I thought I would go to school the short way, a bit early, and finish cleaning the roof on my own."

Misaki looked out at the sky and raised an eyebrow. "It's dawn, son. When are you planning to sleep?"

"Oh." Mamoru blinked. "I guess, I'm not."

"I don't think that's a brilliant idea," Misaki said. "Sleep is important for a growing young man." Of course, she wasn't one to talk considering the way she had spent her nights at fourteen—and Great Nagi, was Mamoru really the age she had been back then? When had that happened? "You should lie down and rest for at least a little while."

Mamoru shook his head distractedly. "I don't think I can."

It was only then that Misaki looked more closely at his face and realized that he wasn't just exhausted. He was in pain.

What's wrong? She wanted to ask, but that wasn't the sort of thing you asked a man and a warrior, even if you were his mother.

"It's not like you to get into a fight with another student," she probed finally.

"I know." Mamoru looked down at his knees. "I…" He fidgeted. "Can I tell you why?" The question seemed to tumble out of his mouth unbidden, before he could stop it.

"What?"

"Can I tell you why I hit him?"

"If you weren't able to control yourself, I don't care to hear any excuses," Misaki said sternly, "and neither will your father. When he hears about this—"

"Please." Mamoru's voice was strained. "It's not—I'm not trying to make excuses. I just…" There was a desperation in his eyes that Misaki couldn't remember ever seeing there before. What in the realms had happened to him?

Before she could think better of it, she said softly, "Tell me."

"Kwang-san was saying bad things—treasonous things—against the Empire. He said the history Hibiki Sensei teaches us isn't true. He said that during the Keleba, a lot of men died here on the Kusanagi Peninsula and other places in Kaigen, and the Ranganese had to be driven back by the Yammanka reinforcements. He says the Empire covered up the deaths of all those people." Mamoru was watching her face. Intently. Waiting for a reaction.

"I see," she said stiffly.

"You see?" Mamoru's voice broke. "That's all you're going to say?"

"What else would I have to say about it?"

"You... you..." Mamoru looked at her like a drowning man watching the shore recede—and Misaki realized that he was waiting for her to tell him what to think. She was his parent, after all; she was supposed to have the answers; she was supposed to steer him right. "You must have something to say," he implored.

"I..." Misaki opened her mouth, closed it, bit the inside of her cheek. Finally, she said, "Your father would be very unhappy to hear you repeating those things in his house."

Mamoru's gaze dropped in shame and she felt a sudden surge of guilt. It was up to her to steer him right...

"The things that boy tells you are certainly treasonous."

"I know, Kaa-chan. I'm sor—"

"But they are true."

Mamoru's head snapped up, bloodshot eyes wide with shock. "Kaa-chan—!"

"You are not to repeat this," she said quickly, "to anyone. I should not need to explain that that kind of talk is not becoming of a Matsuda."

"But..." Mamoru looked like he was on the verge of a panic attack. His eyes glazed like the whole world had started reeling before them. "But if it's all true, then..." Misaki watched the wheels turn in the boy's head and felt a bit of panic bubble to life in her own chest. What had she done? What had she been thinking? Mamoru was fourteen—unstable, impressionable—and he was a *Matsuda*. What had she been thinking telling him the truth?

"Why did you say that?" Mamoru demanded alongside the admonishing voice in Misaki's head. "Why—why would you tell me that?"

"Because I assumed you were man enough to handle it." Misaki masked her anxiety under a harsh tone of voice. "You're a Matsuda, aren't you? Pull yourself together."

"B-but… but…" Mamoru was so shaken he couldn't get ahold of his words, let alone his tumultuous nyama, which pulled at the water in the laundry tub, splashing some over the side. "You're saying Hibiki Sensei really wasn't telling the truth about our history. The Empire has been lying—"

"I just told you not to repeat any of that!"

Mamoru flinched as though struck. "I'm sorry." He bowed his head. "I-I won't forget again. I'm sorry."

He clutched one bandaged hand in the other and hunched in on himself. Misaki could feel the pain radiating from him. Not just physical pain; he had taken worse beatings than this in training. His nyama was churning, all that terrifying power he had inherited from his father writhing like a knotted serpent trying to free itself from its own coils, strangling and biting itself in confusion.

Her boy was in agony.

And Misaki experienced a stab of something she had not felt in a long time: protective instinct, an overwhelming desire to shelter, to comfort, to heal at any cost. She supposed this was what a good mother was supposed to feel toward her children every waking moment, but she had not felt it since Daybreak. Since she had something worth protecting.

Gently, she reached out and gripped Mamoru's arm. "Sit with me," she said.

"Wh-what?"

"If you're going to take the shortcut to school, you can spare a few siiranu to sit with your mother. Come. We'll watch the sunrise."

The front deck of the Matsuda compound had a clear view down the mountainside. When the day was bright and cloudless, Misaki could see all the way down to the twinkling ocean. On chilly mornings like this, the lower half of the mountain disappeared in a sea of fog that changed color with the growing light. Right now, it was a pale blue, verging on lavender.

Misaki sat with her knees tucked beneath her, hands folded in her lap, the picture of the demure housewife she had cultivated over the past fifteen years. Beside her, Mamoru crossed his legs in a rigid approximation of his father's posture, but his heart was beating faster than Takeru's ever did.

Despite the serenity of the mountain around them, Misaki was anxious. Mamoru's predicament placed her in a confusing position. She had it in her to ease his pain, but she couldn't do it with a housewife's soothing touch and meaningless reassurances. For this, for once, she needed to be honest. And her honesty was rusty.

"You know, I…" She started with a small truth, just to see how it would feel. "I never liked the cold."

Mamoru turned to look at her with a question in his eyes.

"I'm a cold enough person—in my nyama and my personality— that I can get quite enough of it all on my own. When it comes to the rest of the world, I like a little heat to offset all the ice in me. I know jijaka koronu are supposed to hate fire, but I envy you whenever you leave to apprentice at the forges. Warmth is so hard to come by in this village… That's why I watch the sunrise out here whenever I get the chance."

Misaki gazed wistfully over the mist. "I like how I can feel the sun simmering on the horizon even before it comes into view. I like the moment it lights up the fog and then burns through it. That brightness reminds me that there's a world beyond this mountain, beyond Kaigen. No matter how cold the nights get here, the sun is rising somewhere. Somewhere, it's making someone warm."

"You've been out there," Mamoru said after a moment. He

spoke cautiously too, hesitantly venturing out after her into this new territory. "You never talk about it, but Aunt Setsuko says you went to theonite academy outside of Kaigen, all the way on the other side of the world."

"It was a long time ago," Misaki said. "I was the age you are now."

For a long time, they were quiet. More than once, Mamoru took a breath as though steeling himself to speak, then seemed to think better of it. His body was still, his eyes focused ahead, but the tension in his hands and the thud of his heart betrayed him. He was afraid, Misaki realized, afraid to ask what she knew of the outside world.

His fear wasn't misplaced. There was a reason Takeru had forbidden any discussion of Misaki's school years. A good deal of what she knew was not only against the Matsuda creed; it could be considered treason against the Empire. She couldn't give Mamoru her knowledge from Daybreak any more than he could ask for it.

But she had to say something.

"Listen, son... when I was your age, I had to face truths that seemed to break the world. That's what happens when you come into contact with people who aren't quite like you. You learn over time that the world isn't broken. It's just... got more pieces to it than you thought. They all fit together, just maybe not the way you pictured when you were young."

"But how?" Mamoru's voice cracked. "I don't understand. How do I fit them together? If *nothing* is what I thought... Kaa-chan, please... what am I supposed to think?"

"That's something you'll have to decide for yourself," Misaki said. "That's part of becoming an adult."

Mamoru shook his head. "What is that supposed to mean?"

"A child doesn't have to take responsibility for his decisions. A child can trust in his parents to tell him what to do. A man trusts himself."

"But... aren't we all children of the Empire?" Mamoru asked, and of course, he would think that. That was what he had been told in every story and song since he learned to speak. "Don't we *have* to trust our government?"

"I suppose so," Misaki said, and before she could stop herself—"if you really want to be a child forever. Do you, son?" She looked sharply at Mamoru in the growing light. "Or do you want to be a man?"

"I want to be a man," Mamoru said determinedly. "It's just that—I don't understand, Kaa-chan. I'm a koro, a Matsuda. When I grow up, I'm supposed to be a man of action with the power to shape history. H-how am I supposed to do that if I don't even know what's going on?"

A fair question, one that had no simple answer. "See, that's the hard part," Misaki said, "coming to terms with what you don't know, finding the answers, and acting on them without regret. Some people never learn. Some people learn too late. Nami, I wish I…" Misaki pulled up short, shocked that she had let the thought even start to come out of her mouth. Because what had she meant to say? *I wish I had had the courage to go against my parents and the Empire? I wish I had made my own decisions when it mattered?* If she had, the boy looking anxiously into her eyes would not exist. Gods, what kind of mother was she?

"What do you wish, Kaa-chan?" Mamoru asked with such innocent interest that Misaki could have curdled her own blood in shame.

"Nothing, son." She touched his face. "I've borne a powerful Matsuda heir. What else could I wish for?"

"A smart one?" he suggested.

Misaki laughed. "You're smart, Mamoru—or you're starting to be. I'm sure you'll grow into a fine man."

"Will I?" He asked with genuine worry. And Misaki had no idea how to answer.

"I…" With her words failing, she borrowed some from her swordmaster. His wisdom may not have saved her, but maybe Mamoru could make more of it than she had.

"I know you might feel broken, but we're jijakalu. We're water, and water can shift to fit any mold. No matter how we're broken and reshaped, we can always freeze ourselves strong again. It's not going to happen all at once," she added. "You have to wait for the turn of the season to see what shape the ice will take, but it will form up, clear and strong. It always does."

Mamoru nodded. "But I... I'm not to repeat anything you or Kwang-san told me?"

"No," Misaki said, "but that doesn't mean you can't listen. You can learn a great deal listening to people with different experiences from your own. A jaseli once told me, listening never made any man dumber, but it's made a lot of people smarter." She waved a hand. "That wasn't a very good translation. I promise, it sounds more poetic in Yammaninke."

"Like Matsuda Takeru the First..." Mamoru murmured, staring hard into the fog below.

"What?" Misaki didn't follow his train of thought, but he seemed to have reached some kind of revelation.

"He learned from people who weren't like him. Even though he was a koro, he grew up with blacksmiths. He was willing to learn from them, and the foreign missionaries, even the son of his greatest enemy—and in the end, it made him stronger."

For a moment, Misaki could only stare at her son. She had never thought of Matsuda history that way—in any way that related to her own experience—and here her bloodied, sleep-deprived fourteen-year-old boy had just connected two pieces of the world she never would have thought to fit together.

Maybe she still had some growing up to do herself.

"Thank you, Kaa-chan." Mamoru turned to her with a wide smile. "I think I learned something."

Misaki only stared.

"What?"

She tilted her head. "You have dimples."

"I got them from you."

The sun was visible now, burning through the mist, and Misaki brushed Mamoru's bangs back from his face.

"You know, Mamoru… you'll be a man sometime soon. But just for today, let me be your mother, and tell you in all my motherly certainty that everything is alright. The world is whole. You are on the right path. Everything is going to be alright."

He nodded.

"And Mamoru…" She took his chin in her hand, turning his face toward hers. "You're a good person. I trust you to grow up well."

"Thank you, Kaa-chan."

The slopes below had turned gold with sunlight. The sun set off the dewdrops like sparklers in shimmering waves up the mountainside. Beside her, Mamoru made a concerted effort to keep his eyes open, but as the sun warmed the world, his head sank against her shoulder. His nyama, finally relaxed, started drawing him into the embrace of sleep.

"Someday, will you tell me about your foreign school?" he murmured. "About all the things you did when you were young?"

Misaki was not prepared for the ripple of warmth that touched her heart. She had never thought that anyone here in Takayubi would ask about Daybreak. Hearing the words from her own child was more than she ever would have wished for.

"Someday, Mamoru-kun. Not today. Right now, you have your own future to look toward."

"Mmm…" Mamoru breathed out, his eyes falling shut.

This is it, Misaki realized. This was the joy they had all promised, in a single, simple hope: Mamoru might grow up to be different from his father.

The sound of small feet interrupted her thoughts.

"Good morning, Naga-kun." She recognized the springy bare-footed steps of her third son before she turned to look at him. "Did you sleep well?"

"Kaa-chan…" the toddler slurred, rubbing his eyes. "Baby crying."

"I'll be right there," Misaki said softly.

Mamoru was so deeply unconscious that he didn't even stir as she laid him down on the wooden deck and went to comfort

Izumo. She hoped that Mamoru would be able to sleep for a little while before heading to school, but when she emerged from the childrens' room with Izumo in her arms and a sleepy Hiroshi following after her, she realized that this had been a foolish hope.

"Nii-san up!" Nagasa giggled. The three-year-old had clambered on top of his big brother and was alternately tugging his hair and slapping his face. "Wake up!"

"Kaa-chan," Mamoru grumbled, his eyes blinking open. "I'm being attacked by a demon."

"No!" Nagasa laughed in delight. "No demon! It's me!"

"Hmm." Mamoru sat up, pitching his giggling brother into his lap. "That's just what a demon *would* say."

"No!" Still laughing like a maniac, Nagasa squirmed out from under Mamoru's arm and made a break for the kitchen.

"Not so fast, abomination!" Rolling onto his feet, Mamoru caught up to the toddler in two quick strides and scooped him up. "I bet you haven't brushed your teeth yet—or I'm sorry—your *fangs*." He prodded his brother's cheek and Nagasa snapped playfully at his finger. "Yeah, let's brush those little demon fangs, shall we?"

As Mamoru slung Nagasa over his shoulder and carried him toward the washroom, Misaki was overtaken by a memory more distant than Daybreak—giggling through wood-paneled halls with her own brothers. Takashi said that he and Takeru had never really played as children—or rather that Takeru had never wanted to play with him.

For fifteen years Misaki had lamented being fated to raise her husband's sons. All that time, she hadn't considered that these boys might have something of her in them too.

She wondered, *what else could I wish for?*

8

THE LETTER

Frost crept up the tree branches as the month of Koronkalo froze into a sparklingly cold Sibikalo. The sun set early, the numu village burned bright in the frozen evenings, and Misaki was thankful that this new baby wasn't quite as cold as the others. Mamoru, Hiroshi, and Nagasa had all gotten progressively icier as they grew stronger, but Izumo's little body stayed warm, even as his muscles came in, and Misaki found herself genuinely enjoying holding him close through that first month of the cold season.

According to the news, some other villages and cities along Kaigen's western coast had been ravaged by storms. But Takayubi remained a picture of a small-town peace as Nagi cast his first snow on the mountain. Izumo's eyes came into focus on a world cloaked in white.

Where previous winters there had been a solitary set of footprints through the first snow, now there were two. Kwang Chul-hee showed up at the doors of the Matsuda compound each morning to meet Mamoru, and the two made their way down the mountain together, talking. When it came time for Geomijul to begin construction on its info-com towers, Mamoru begged his father to let him join Chul-hee and Kotetsu Atsushi on the construction team during his winter break. Misaki hadn't expected Takeru to agree, but he allowed it, on the condition that Mamoru keep up with his training and schoolwork. So, under mounting snow-cover, Mamoru, Chul-hee, and little Atsushi began work on the towers that would change communication in Takayubi forever.

If Misaki had been a better mother, maybe she would have discouraged her son's friendship with the opinionated northerner. But Mamoru was a young man now, she told herself in justification. He could befriend whoever he wanted.

She didn't know what he talked about with Kwang Chul-hee. True to his promise, he never brought any of those conversations home with him, but the change in her son was visible. It was the marked difference between a carefree man and a thinking one. A swordsman was supposed to be wary of his surroundings. But it was one thing to be attuned to wind and water droplets; another to analyze and understand human actions. As Izumo's new eyes started to bring the physical world into focus, Mamoru's eyes were changing too. There was a sharpness to the way he looked at everything around him—a hunger—as he scrutinized the rough edges and shifting layers of his world, trying to make the pieces fit together.

Misaki should have realized that it was only a matter of time before he did something stupid. He wasn't a jaseli, trained to retain and process the truths of the world, nor was he a peaceful craftsman. He was a fighter, with a fighter's ferocity. And there was a reason the jaseliwu, finawu, and numuwu of the world kept certain things from their koronu. Jaseliwu had the power to wrangle ideas without spilling blood. When koronu clashed, the results were always ugly.

MAMORU

"You seriously forged all of these yourself?" Chul-hee said, raising his eyebrows at Atsushi. *"Without any help?"*

"I'm in training to make the greatest swords in the world," the

blacksmith's son said indignantly. *"I don't need help to forge a few nuts and bolts—especially since your company provided the steel and molds."*

"Whose idea was it to have the local numuwu work from Geomijul molds?"

"My father's," Mamoru said. *"He said it was the only way to cut costs enough to make the towers affordable."*

"Well, they look great." Chul-hee examined one of the screws with an appreciative smile. *"I know numuwu in Yamma who would kill to be able to do this."*

The three boys had already aided in the construction of two info-com towers further down the mountain, near the village hall. This was the first time Atsushi had forged components without his father's help as well as the first time the youngsters were being allowed to work construction without supervision.

The foundation had been set—cement solution poured into deep holes—earlier that week. All the boys had to do now was assemble a three-bound-tall tower on top of it, working from the Kwangs' blueprints.

"Do you know if they got the first two towers working?" Atsushi asked as they moved the first beam into place.

"My father told me they already have all the utilities set up," Mamoru said. *"They were hoping to get it working today."*

Since Mamoru was a little boy, his father had worked an administrative job at the village hall. In the old days, Matsudas hadn't needed regular jobs; the surrounding koro houses had provided them with everything they needed in return for the privilege of sending their sons to train in their dojo. But as the population of Takayubi dwindled, the Matsuda family had had to turn to other means of making a living.

After the Keleba, Matsuda Mizudori had become a sword instructor and then the headmaster of Kumono Academy. His son, Matsuda Susumu, followed in his footsteps, and his son, Matsuda Takashi, followed in his. As Takashi's younger brother, Takeru had spent a few years serving as the head sword instructor at

Kumono, but after his father passed away, he had ceded the position to Yukino Dai to take a government job at the village hall.

Mamoru wasn't entirely sure what his father did at work—just that it involved lots of paperwork and numbers, and kept him extremely busy. And whenever the government or a business introduced something new to the village—like new roads, or trash disposal systems, or info-com towers—Tou-sama was there to facilitate the process.

"So, once it's working, the computer at the village hall will be able to send and receive messages from anywhere?" Atsushi asked.

"Not anywhere," Chul-hee clarified. *"To start with, probably just other places nearby with working towers."*

Atsushi looked excitedly down the mountain toward the village hall. *"Do you think it's working yet?"*

Chul-hee pulled his info-com device out of his pocket and glanced at it. *"Not yet."*

"How do you know?"

Chul-hee held up the device to show Atsushi the screen. *"No signal."*

"So, that thing... that info-com device will just connect automatically if there's a working tower around?"

"That's the idea."

"So, for an info-com device to work all the time, there would have to be towers all over the world?"

"Not necessarily," Chul-hee said. *"The Yammankalu have satellites that send and receive info-com signals from space."*

"What?!" Atsushi dropped the end of the beam he was carrying and Mamoru just barely managed to catch it in a pillar of ice before it crushed the blacksmith boy's toes.

"Careful!"

"Sorry, Matsuda-dono!" Atsushi bowed to him. *"Sorry, I just... you're joking, right?"* he turned to Chul-hee. *"Right, Kwang-san? You can't send communication signals that far!"*

Chul-hee smiled at the boy's disbelieving face. *"It's not a joke, numuden."*

As Chul-hee explained Yamma's satellites to Atsushi, the boys maneuvered the first beam into place.

"Is everything lined up?" Mamoru asked from where he stood, supporting the heaviest part of the beam while the other two tugged it into alignment with the base.

"Perfect," Kwang said. *"Go ahead, Mamoru."*

Nodding, Mamoru let his jiya surge into action. The snow around them rose to encase the base of the beam in ice and form pillars to hold the top of it in place. This was a system the three of them had worked out over a week of working together: Mamoru maneuvered the pieces of the tower into place and held them there with the huge ice formations that only he could make, Chul-hee and Atsushi inserted the screws, and then Atsushi welded the pieces together with his blowtorch. As they worked their way upward, Mamoru started forming steps of ice for the other two to climb to reach the tower's joints.

"So, no matter where you go in Yamma, there's always a signal?" Atsushi asked as he and Chul-hee sat atop one of Mamoru's ice platforms a bound and a half from the ground, screwing a beam in place.

"Almost," Chul-hee said, *"not underground."*

"Wait." Atsushi paused. *"Does that mean these towers will be obsolete in a few years?"*

"No. Why would you say that?"

"Well, if Yamma has already had info-com satellites in space for years, Kaigen can't be far behind, right?"

Chul-hee pressed his lips together and focused on tightening the screw before him. So far, he had avoided sharing any of his anti-government thoughts with Atsushi. Maybe because the numu was younger than Mamoru—and he seemed so bright-eyed and innocent. *"Satellites are expensive,"* he said finally.

"But Kaigen has more money than Yamma," Atsushi said. *"The economy's the best it's ever been."*

"Well..." Chul-hee started. *"The thing about that is—"*

Mamoru coughed. The ice under his control cracked violently, nearly pitching Chul-hee and Atsushi from their perch—nearly; he wasn't irresponsible. Atsushi screamed and grabbed onto Chul-hee, who grabbed onto the nearest beam.

"Sorry!" Mamoru cleared his throat and righted the ice platform beneath them. *"I just—inhaled some snow."*

While Atsushi reoriented himself, Chul-hee stared over the edge of the platform down at Mamoru. Meeting his eyes, Mamoru shook his head. Atsushi wasn't soft-minded, but he was only ten; he wasn't ready to have his world ripped apart and turned upside down.

Mamoru knew by now that he couldn't stop Chul-hee's dangerous mouth by yelling at him, or punching him, or pleading with him to be more careful. He suspected as he held Chul-hee's gaze that it was only a matter of time before little Atsushi was treated to the same horrible revelations he had experienced the day he met the northern boy. But for the moment, Chul-hee relented with a roll of his eyes and changed the subject.

The three were just discussing heading back to the village hall for lunch when Mamoru caught sight of a pair of figures coming up the mountain toward them. Even at a distance, Mamoru recognized his father's even, deliberate gait—eerily smooth over uneven ground. The other figure, trudging and stumbling along behind him could only be Chul-hee's father, Kwang Tae-min. Despite his breadth of knowledge and worldly air, the traveling Geomijul representative was not a sure-footed creature. It was easy to tell that he was a stranger to snow and mountains.

"Oh—Matsuda-dono," Atsushi said as he too caught sight of the men. "What is he doing up here?"

"I don't know." Mamoru's brow furrowed. Tou-sama wasn't known for leaving his desk during work hours. After Chul-hee and Atsushi finished securing the beam they were working on, Mamoru used his ice to lower them to the ground.

Atsushi scrambled down, as the adults approached, and bowed deeply.

"Appa, Matsuda-sama, good to see you," Chul-hee said with a more casual nod. *"What are you doing up here?"*

"Unfortunately, I need to collect my son and head home," Tou-sama said. *"Something has come up."*

"Oh—it's going to be difficult to keep working without him," Chul-hee said. *"He's been doing most of the heavy lifting."*

"It's fine," Kwang Tae-min said. *"I was going to call you boys down to the village hall anyway. I need your help with a few things."*

"Are the towers working?" Atsushi asked excitedly.

"That's where I need your help, kid," Kwang said with a smile. *"We have some frozen components—mostly wires. I was hoping you could help me find some better insulation."*

"Oh. Of course, sir."

After Chul-hee and Atsushi packed up their tools, the group made their way back down the footpath toward the village.

"I've never personally overseen construction in a place this cold," Kwang Tae-min said, carefully picking his way through the snow. *"As a jijaka, I suppose I should be embarrassed; after years of setting up Geomijul infrastructure in Yamma and Sizwe, I've completely underestimated the destructive power of ice."*

The Kwangs and Atsushi went on discussing wiring, insulation, and a lot of technical things Mamoru only half understood until they reached the break in the path. One fork led toward the snow-covered village hall and the much bigger info-com tower looming beside it. The other led back down to the village itself.

"Goodbye, Matsuda-dono," Atsushi said, bowing to Mamoru and his father.

Kwang just punched Mamoru in the arm. "See you tomorrow, Mamoru-kun."

"See you tomorrow."

Mamoru was so sure-footed that he was used to being the fastest up and down the rocky mountain paths, but Tou-sama didn't bother with the rocks at all. Ice changed shape to form level steps beneath his feet with each stride. Deep snow parted before him like it couldn't wait to clear his way.

Like most jijakalu, Mamoru needed to put in visible effort to manipulate water. Tou-sama's power was on a level where water scrambled to obey him, and Mamoru found himself struggling to keep pace.

"That boy is very familiar with you," Tou-sama said without looking back at him.

"We're classmates."

"Yukino Yuuta and Mizumaki Itsuki are your classmates too. You haven't been spending much time with them this winter."

"We still train together sometimes," Mamoru said. "I just wanted to work on the info-com towers with Chul-hee and Atsushi." He paused, glancing nervously up at his father's face. "If you want me to stop, I will, Tou-sama. I only joined the construction team because you said it was alright—"

"It's fine with me. Just as long as you stay focused on your true purpose."

His tone made Mamoru's gut clench in guilt. He still hadn't gotten any closer to mastering the Whispering Blade.

"Yes, Tou-sama," he said. "So… can I ask why we're heading home so early?" he ventured, eager to change the subject.

"I was going to leave early anyway. I have a meeting with my brother at the eleventh waati at his office, but a letter just arrived for your mother, from Ishihama."

"Oh." Mamoru still didn't understand why that was cause for them to head back to the compound. It wasn't unusual for Kaa-chan to receive letters from her family in Ishihama. The post workers at the village hall sometimes gave Tou-sama the family's mail to take home with him rather than delivering it to the door, but Mamoru had never known his father to rush them straight home.

"This letter was marked as urgent," Tou-sama explained at Mamoru's look of confusion. "It was sent through the one-day express post with Lord Tsusano's personal seal, which means it must contain news he needs delivered right away."

And Mamoru found himself picking up his stride, wondering what news from his mother's home was so urgent it couldn't wait a day.

MISAKI

"You're home early," Misaki said in surprise. "I'm sorry—I just put Izumo down for his nap, so I haven't prepared any lunch yet."

"Where are the other two?" Takeru asked. He tended to do that—talk about the boys like they were items on an inventory.

"Hiroshi is at the elementary school for extra training, and Nagasa is napping." After an uproarious three waatinu chasing Ryota around in the snow, she was hoping he would stay down for a while. "Give me a siira. I'll make you tea and put some lunch together."

"Before that," Takeru said, "there's something you need to see." He pulled a scroll out of his sleeve and held it out to her. "This is why we came back early. It's from your brother."

"Oh." Misaki took the kayiri scroll from her husband. While Ishihama had working telephone lines, Takayubi did not, so on the rare occasions that Kazu contacted her, it was always through letters. But this was the first time one of them had ever been marked as express mail. She tore through the Tsusano seal and unrolled the scroll.

Dear Misaki,
I hope this message reaches you in time that you don't have to worry. Yesterday, our hometown and the neighboring area was hit by a coastal storm. Many homes were devastated, including our own Arashiki, and over 100 people have turned up dead so far. I just want to let you know before you hear about it on the news, that our family and friends are all alive and safe.
Kaito and I sustained some minor injuries, but Kaa-san, Tou-

sama, Raiki, my wife, and all the little ones are unhurt. After all, we would hardly be Tsusanos if we couldn't weather a bit of wind and rain.

All jokes aside, it seems like these storms have been especially bad recently. See if you can talk your husband into a vacation further inland. I hear the capital is lovely this time of year.

Nyama to you,
Your brother, Tsusano Kazu, Lord of the Arashiki

"What does Lord Tsusano say?" Takeru asked.

Misaki suppressed a smile. Even though it had been years since her father passed on the title, it was still funny to hear people refer to her silly baby brother as Lord Tsusano.

Misaki handed Takeru the letter. His eyes flicked up and down, reading through it.

"What's this part at the end? Why is he recommending we go inland?"

"I don't know," Misaki said honestly. "Sometimes Kazu... has an odd sense of humor."

"He knows we live on a mountain, right? We're hardly in danger of flooding."

"I know. It's strange." The whole thing was strange.

The Arashiki was an old castle built into the rock face overlooking the sea. The power of the Tsusano clan made it the only safe landing place along a coast of wave-beaten rock. In the old days, the inhabitants of the Stormfort had used their jiya to bring trade ships from the mainland safely into port. During the Keleba, when the mainland became the enemy, the Tsusanos of the Arashiki made a new name for themselves dashing Ranganese ships to pieces on the rocks and raising the sea to swallow the survivors. Now the Stormfort served as the Empire's guard tower, a watchful eye looking ever westward toward the Ranganese Union.

While Misaki had reason to doubt her grandfather's stories that the Tsusanos had single-handedly wrecked half the Ranganese armada, it was hard to imagine any seafaring force passing their coast intact. But the ocean was a fickle ally. And for every day of diving gulls and bright sunshine, Misaki remembered a night of thunder and crashing waves that shook the cliff side. Tou-sama and the servants would go around shuttering the windows while Kaa-san took Misaki and the two boys into the safe stone rooms deep inside the house. Misaki remembered gritting her teeth against the plaintive creaking of the walls, huddled into her mother's arms, her hands over little Kazu's ears.

The storms, Kaa-san said, were a reminder of their place in the world. "Ours is borrowed power," she would say, "a gift and a blessing. The true power belongs to the gods."

But Nami and Nagi were always merciful to their Tsusano children. Despite the noise and terror, none of the storms had ever taken more than a few shingles and shutters off the mighty Arashiki. Misaki couldn't imagine a storm powerful enough to damage the stubborn barnacle of a fortress, much less destroy it. And Ishihama was in Shirojima, not far down the coast from Takayubi. If they had just suffered waves big enough to take out the Arashiki, how could the waters here remain undisturbed? How could the sky above the mountain be so clear?

"We should put on the news," Takeru said, "to see if there's any more information on the storm."

It wasn't unusual for the Matsudas to have the TV on while they ate meals. Most of the time, it was background noise—an endless procession of ignorably bland propaganda. But recently, Misaki had noticed Mamoru giving the screen his full attention, watching the billowing flags, pontificating jaseliwu, and military demonstrations with almost predatory fascination.

"*I'm here in Ishihama,*" a reporter jaseli told the camera in Kaigengua, "*where many homes were recently devastated by a terrible storm. Our imperial troops have been working tirelessly to provide aid to the displaced and retrieve survivors from the wreckage.*"

Misaki watched anxiously, hoping they would show some of the damage—and at the same time hoping they wouldn't. Ishihama was the place of her earliest, most innocent memories. She didn't know if she could bear to see it in ruins. But they didn't show any footage. The reporter went on talking in front of a white winter sky, her hair and tasseled hanbok blowing in the wind.

"Out of concern for our safety, the soldiers have not allowed my camera crew any closer to the destruction than this hill. We are truly lucky to have their help in this time of need and to have a leader who cares so deeply for all of our well-being. For some words from the capital, I give you to Jali Ban-hyang Jee, Voice of the Emperor."

"Greetings, people of Kaigen, children of the Empire." Ban-hyang's entrancing voice was as silky and strong as ever, though it carried a note of solemnity. *"Today, His Majesty's heart is heavy with the tragedy that has befallen his children in Ishihama."*

As the Emperor's jaseli spoke, the screen finally began displaying still images of the destruction in Ishihama—houses reduced to rubble, forests flattened, cars floating in flooded streets, then soldiers arriving in their crisp blue uniforms to help people out of the rubble, carry the wounded, and cradle lost children.

"That's not real," Mamoru said quietly.

"What?"

"That," Mamoru pointed just as the image disappeared from the screen. "That photo of soldiers handing food out to civilians. They used it a week ago when they reported on the storms in Heibando and Yongseom."

"I'm sure you're mistaken," Misaki said with a nervous glance at Takeru. "A lot of coastal towns look similar."

"I'm not mistaken," Mamoru insisted. "That's the third time they've used it."

By this time, the broadcast had switched to different footage—decimated houses and flooded streets. As Misaki looked more closely at the wreckage on the screen, she couldn't say that the landscape and architecture looked particularly familiar. It had been a long time since she had been to Ishihama, but she was sure that the landscape was rockier than the place they were showing.

"Why do you think they're not using real footage?" Mamoru asked.

"Mamoru," Misaki said warningly, "this isn't the time to be worrying about tiny technicalities—"

"It's not a tiny technicality. They're not showing us any video footage. All the images could be faked—"

"Mamoru," Takeru said. "Your mother's hometown was just struck by a terrible tragedy. Show some respect."

"Is that respect?" Mamoru demanded, pointing to the screen. "They won't even give us the truth about what happened to those people. Do you call that respect, Tou-sama?"

Misaki felt the bottom drop out of her stomach. She looked at Takeru and realized that she had no idea how he would react. She had never said anything like that to his face. She wasn't an idiot.

"Mamoru, I-I don't think you know what you're saying," she scrambled to repair the damage. "His Majesty, the Emperor tells us what we need to know. It's not so much a matter of literal truth—"

"I want to know what Tou-sama thinks." Mamoru looked to Takeru.

"I think… you must be running a fever," Takeru said after a measured pause. "Kotetsu Atsushi was sick with the flu last week and now he's passed it on to you. Are you feeling unwell?"

He was giving Mamoru a chance to back down—a chance any sane person would take under the weight of that icy stare. But Mamoru had apparently gone insane.

"I'm feeling fine, Tou-sama," he said without hesitation. "Respectfully, I just want to know how you feel about your government lying to you."

Takeru's expression barely changed—except for a deepening of the crease between his severe eyebrows. It was the scariest thing Misaki had ever seen.

"It's that Kwang boy, isn't it?" he said darkly. "He's the one who's put these ridiculous ideas in your head."

Mamoru took a breath and held his father's gaze. "Does it matter where the ideas came from if there's truth in them?"

"What has he been saying to you?"

"A lot of things. He says the hurricanes the government keeps reporting aren't really natural storms; they're Ranganese attacks."

The feeling in Misaki's stomach turned from anxiety to pure dread.

"Then he's either a liar or an idiot," Takeru said dismissively. "The Ranganese aren't powerful enough to cause that much destruction, especially in places like Ishihama and Yongseom, where there are strong warriors to oppose them."

But he was wrong. The Ranganese Union was—and always had been—more powerful and cunning than the ruling Kaigenese were willing to admit. It was an arrogant misconception that had already cost them two thirds of the Empire.

Buildings damaged by fonya looked different from those damaged by natural storms. Could that be why the news crews weren't allowed at the scene of the disaster? Was that why they weren't showing real footage?

"Kwang Chul-hee says the Emperor doesn't want us to know how strong the Ranganese have gotten so we won't panic, so we'll stay here and die defending his coastline."

"You sound angry," Takeru said evenly. "It is our duty to defend Kaigen, no matter what information the Emperor chooses to share with us."

"But... doesn't that just make us cannon fodder?"

"It makes us the cannon."

Mamoru faltered. "But—that's not— If the Emperor won't even tell us—"

"What the Emperor does or doesn't tell us is irrelevant," Takeru said. "None of it changes the fact that we are here to lay down our lives for the Empire. We are the Sword of Kaigen."

"You say that—everyone says that—but in the end, a sword is just a tool."

In one motion, Takeru stood and backhanded Mamoru across the face.

Mamoru looked surprised. He shouldn't have.

"You will not say such things in my house. Do you understand?"

"Yes, Tou-sama. I'm sorry."

"I thought I was raising a warrior, but your words reflect the ignorance and weakness of a child."

"Tou-sama—"

"A warrior's sword isn't made of ice or metal. It is his soul, his focus, his conviction. That is what makes a Whispering Blade and it's why you continuously fail to produce one."

"Yes, Tou-sama." Mamoru's voice was choked with guilt. "I understand—"

"If you understood, you wouldn't let such disgraceful nonsense pass your lips. The Empire depends on us to be stronger than doubt, stronger than fear. As long as we are not broken, the Sword of Kaigen will not break, and the Empire will stand. Only a weakling would let himself doubt that. Are you that weakling?"

"No, Tou-sama."

"We'll see," Takeru said icily. "Get your sword. I'll be in the dojo," and he swept from the room.

Still stunned, Mamoru lifted a hand to his face. He didn't touch his cheek where Takeru had struck him. Instead, he brought his fingers to his mouth, as though unable to believe what had just come out of it.

"I just said that." He looked at Misaki, wide-eyed with horror. "I just said those things to my father."

"You did," Misaki said, rather stunned herself.

"Am I an idiot, Kaa-chan?"

"You might be." Misaki offered her son a smile, even as fear twisted in her stomach. "Now, do as your father says. Go defend your idiocy."

"Is he going to kill me?"

"If he is, you'd better die like a man, on your feet."

Nodding, Mamoru rose, squared his shoulders, and walked out of the room.

"Glory to Kaigen!" Jali Ban-hyang bellowed at his back. *"Long live the Emperor!"*

9

THE FIGHT

The Matsuda dojo occupied over half the compound. In centuries past, it had accommodated fifty students at a time. These days, the only people who trained here were the Matsudas themselves.

Women weren't allowed on the floor, and Misaki made a concerted effort not to hover at the door too often. A lady was not supposed to take an interest in sword fighting. It wasn't supposed to make her eyes light and her blood surge. When she watched others in the heat of combat, she teetered close—much too close— to her old self, and she found it best to avoid the edge altogether.

But for once, it wasn't hunger that drove Misaki to follow her husband and son to the dojo doorway; it was pure motherly concern. There was a deadly edge to Takeru's nyama that made her want to stay close to Mamoru. Just in case. Takeru had never been excessively violent with his children, never seriously injured Mamoru in training. But just in case.

She knelt in the dojo doorway to watch as Takeru and Mamoru prepared to fight. Most practice matches were fought with wooden blades, but this wasn't a normal training exercise. The two had brought out their steel katana, placing them on the floor before them and bowing to the weapons in silence. It was a ritual that marked the beginning of a duel.

Outsiders assumed that traditional steel didn't mean much to a

182

master of the Whispering Blade. It was only after marrying into the family that Misaki herself realized how much the steel katana meant to the Matsudas. A Matsuda man's katana was his dearest companion up until and even after he achieved a Whispering Blade. It was only through rigorous daily training with that steel that he instinctively knew how to shape the blade and distribute the weight when it came time to form his Sasayaiba. A Matsuda who didn't train with an excellent metal sword stood no chance of making even a halfway-decent one out of ice.

Takeru, usually so calm and precise in his movements, tied his katana at his hip faster than normal, yanking the strings taut with uncharacteristic ferocity. His sword was Numu Kotetsu Katashi's proudest accomplishment, an elegant, minimalistic weapon, with a circular guard of unadorned steel, and a handle of pearl white lacquer. The blacksmith had named the weapon Kyougetsu, the Moon Spire—a blade so bright and clean that it could cut through the dark of night like Nami's mirror.

Mamoru's katana, which he had helped to forge himself, was almost as long as Kyougetsu, making it a positively massive sword for such a young fighter. Nami and Nagi's serpent forms entwined in two-toned silver and bronze to form the guard above a handle bound in dark teal wrapping. The young sword didn't have a name yet. That was something it would have to earn in its koro's hands—hands that faltered slightly as Mamoru slid the sheath into the belt of his hakama. Fingers fumbled with the string for a moment before managing to tie it properly.

Takashi claimed that there were days that Mamoru could fight on almost even footing with his father. But Misaki could see when Mamoru took up his starting stance that this was not one of those days. He did a good job making his apprehension look like determination. It would have fooled the untrained observer, but his upper arms were too tense. His grip wasn't quite steady. They were the kind of cues Misaki used to look for when she needed to dismantle another fighter—which meant that Takeru could see them too.

"If you think you're man enough to preach truth to me, you'd better be ready to back it up in combat," Takeru said, fixing his son with an icy glare. "Are you ready?"

Mamoru nodded. "Yes, Tou-sama."

"Good," Takeru said and shot forward. The first clash made Misaki's heart leap in something between terror and excitement. The ring of steel blades was like electricity in her veins. With a clang, Takeru knocked Mamoru's sword aside and sliced downward, bringing his sword to a stop a hairs-breadth from Mamoru's neck.

"Your defense is terrible," he spat, smacking Mamoru's cheek with the flat of his blade. "I hope you can do better than that."

Takeru came at Mamoru again and again, each clash ending ruthlessly fast.

"Sloppy!" He struck Mamoru's knuckles.

Takeru had excellent control. Like any decent teacher, he would hit Mamoru with enough force to let him know he'd made a mistake, never enough to cause permanent damage or overwhelming pain. But today, he was hitting harder than normal—harder than he needed to.

"Still sloppy! Your defense is pitiful!" Takeru blasted through Mamoru's guard and struck him in the sternum with the hilt of his sword. Too hard.

Mamoru doubled over. For a moment, Misaki thought his knees were going to give out, but he inexplicably managed to stay on his feet.

"Stand up," Takeru said coldly. "If I wanted to end this fight now, I'd have hit you with the sharp end. Stand and face me."

Mamoru tried to straighten up, staggered, gagged, and clapped a hand over his mouth. Misaki was certain for a moment that he was going to throw up, but after a few deep breaths, he swallowed and lifted his gaze to meet Takeru's. Gripping his katana like a lifeline, he resumed his fighting stance.

Takeru took the invitation without waiting for Mamoru to regain his bearings. Their blades crashed together so hard that Misaki felt the impact in her bones, her forearms twitching as she imagined the damage her own body would take under that force. The collision sent Mamoru's katana spinning out of his hands.

On a normal day of training, they would stop after someone was disarmed. But Takeru kept going. Before the katana had hit the dojo floor, he was attacking again. Mamoru caught on just in time to form an ice shield across his arm.

Takashi talked about how creative and skilled Mamoru was with quickly-formed ice shields, but Misaki hadn't understood what he meant until she watched the boy summon ice to defend against the Moon Spire. Takeru's blade glanced off the shield once, twice, and then stuck in the softer outer layer of ice.

Misaki recognized the sophisticated disarming technique. She had never mastered it even at her prime, but Mamoru pulled it off neatly. His jiya swallowed the Moon Spire and froze around it. Then, cranking his body around, he spun the sword from his father's hands.

Takeru let it happen. His jiya was easily powerful enough to override his son's, but he loosened his grip and allowed Mamoru to fling the sword away.

"Alright, boy." Takeru flexed his fingers and the temperature plummeted. "If this is the way you'd rather fight…"

The Whispering Blade flashed out of nowhere. Mamoru ducked under the cut and rolled to retrieve his katana—only to meet a wall of ice.

"I don't think so," Takeru said. "If you're man enough to stand and insult me to my face, then you're man enough to face me jiya to jiya."

What came next was painful to watch.

Mamoru had mastered every jiya attack in the Kumono curriculum and then some. He could shoot projectiles with pinpoint accuracy, sling whips of water at blinding speeds, and raise walls as thick as tree trunks. He was smart enough to use everything in his arsenal to keep Takeru and his Whispering Blade at a distance.

None of it made a difference.

Takeru cleaved through his defenses like they were rice paper, closing the distance between them within moments. In close, Mamoru had no choice but to try to match his father's ice katana with his own. In a seemingly perfect imitation of Takeru's technique, he opened his hand and let jiya pour out of his palm to form a sword of solid ice. It looked like a Whispering Blade—straight, sharp, and clear—but Takeru sliced through it in a single stroke.

"Weak," he scoffed as Mamoru scrambled to reform the blade from where it had been severed. "Muddy intentions produce an impure ice."

Mamoru took a swing with his reformed sword. All Takeru had to do was raise his own Whispering Blade in defense and Mamoru's ice broke against it. The process repeated again and again until Takeru lost patience and shattered Mamoru's entire sword, leaving him with a handful of splintered ice.

Weaponless, Mamoru started to form a shield, but Takeru punched through it, knocking him to the tatami.

"I y—" Mamoru started, only to have the breath knocked out of him as Takeru's foot slammed into his chest, pinning him to the floor. "I yield!" he managed to shout at last.

"Do you?" Takeru growled and stabbed downward.

Misaki screamed.

For a single moment of blind terror, she saw Takeru plunge his blade into Mamoru's mouth—but that wasn't quite what happened. As Takeru's fist shot forward, his Whispering Blade collapsed into harmless liquid. It refroze across his knuckles just as they connected with Mamoru's face. The boy's head snapped back, blood blossomed from his mouth, and he lay there stunned.

Takeru let out his breath.

For a moment he looked like he was going to hit Mamoru again. Then he paused. "What are you doing, Misaki?"

"What?" Misaki looked down and realized that she was on her feet. Not only that, she had taken two steps onto the dojo floor. Ice had formed on her fingernails in the beginning of claws. "Oh…"

she said blankly. "I-I'm sorry, I... Sorry." She quickly backed off the forbidden floor and folded to her knees, shaken. "I'm sorry, Takeru-sama. Continue."

Takeru stared at her for a long moment before turning his gaze back to Mamoru. The boy was still lying flat on his back, mouth and nose red with blood. His eyes had a blank, shell-shocked look about them, and Misaki wondered if he had thought the same thing she had for that split dinma: that Takeru was actually going to kill him.

"A Matsuda does not yield," Takeru said. "He fights through the enemies before him or he dies in the effort." Takeru's fist was still clenched, the ice still cold on his knuckles. "If you're too afraid to face the Empire's enemies, you have no right to call yourself part of this family. You have no right to stand before me in this dojo."

Misaki barely heard the words coming out of Takeru's mouth. All her attention was on his fist as her mind screamed, *don't hit him again. Gods in the Deep, don't you dare hit him again.* She didn't think she would be able to hold herself still if she had to watch Mamoru take another blow. She was so intent on Takeru's icy knuckles and the red of Mamoru's blood that the sound of approaching footsteps made her jump.

"Setsuko!" she exclaimed as her sister-in-law came to stand in the doorway beside her.

"Sorry." Setsuko bowed to Takeru. "I—uh…" She paused as she took in the mess of ice strewn across the dojo, and the blood on Mamoru's face. "I didn't mean to interrupt anything."

"What do you want?" Takeru snapped.

"My husband wanted me to remind you that you have a meeting with him at the eleventh waati at his office."

"Tell him I'll be late."

"You're already late." Only Setsuko would dare take that tone with Matsuda Takeru while he stood, prickling with jiya, spattered with blood and ice crystals.

He glared at her for a moment before turning to look down at Mamoru. "Clean up this mess," he said. "Practice on your own until I get back. You do not leave this dojo until you've fixed your sloppy technique."

"Great Nami, what happened here?" Setsuko whispered to Misaki.

"I'll explain later," Misaki said in a low voice.

She and Setsuko got to their feet and parted to make way for Takeru as he stepped out of the dojo.

"I'll go with you to Kumono," Setsuko said to Takeru. "My husband forgot his lunch, so I'm going to take it to him. I just have to get Ayumi bundled up for the cold—"

"Go on ahead," Takeru said disinterestedly. "Pack up whatever you need. I'll be with you when you're ready to go."

Setsuko took the hint to clear out and bowed herself out of his presence. When she had gone, Takeru turned his icy glare on Misaki.

"Is this your doing?" he asked in a low voice. "Or just that city boy?"

"I…" Misaki didn't know what to say. She may have been guilty of putting dangerous thoughts in Mamoru's head, and she didn't know how much influence Kwang Chul-hee had on him; it was hard to say who was to blame for his doubts. But the gall to challenge his father wasn't something he could have picked up from either of them. Mamoru's rage was his alone. "I'm sorry. I don't know—"

"I don't care." Takeru turned away from her. "Just fix it."

"What do you mean?"

"If you had some hand in this… this weakness that's overtaken him, you set it right. Do you understand?"

"Yes, sir," Misaki said timidly.

She stood stiffly in the hall as Takeru walked away, taking the worst of the cold with him.

In the dojo, Mamoru had gotten to his knees but didn't seem to have found it in his legs to stand. Misaki itched to go to him, to pick him up, to heal the bruises. Instead, she just asked softly, "Are you alright?"

"Yes." Mamoru stood gingerly, his mouth and nose dripping blood on his hakama. Putting his hands to his mouth, he glanced to the doorway. "I'm sorry." He said into his hands. "Sorry you had to see that."

It wasn't clear if he was referring to his attitude, his sloppy fighting, or the blood. Misaki realized, with a bit of very misplaced amusement, that Mamoru probably thought this was the most violence she had ever witnessed.

She finally came up with what she hoped was a reassuring, "I've seen worse."

Mamoru stood alone in the middle of the dojo with his hands covering his mouth until he heard the sound of Takeru and Setsuko's footsteps leaving the compound and the thud of the sliding door closing behind them.

Then he moved his hands, waking his jiya. Misaki watched in surprise as he drew the blood from his face and clothes then formed a scab over his split lip. She knew that as a child, he had shown promise in blood manipulation, but she hadn't realized that he still remembered the little she had taught him all those years ago. Not only that, he had clearly taken the time to get better at it. She had to wonder, that all these years, this boy had been growing up right in front of her—and she had missed it.

His lip mended, Mamoru walked around the dojo, melting down and evaporating all the ice left over from the fight. He didn't work with his usual speed and power, but Misaki was glad that he was at least walking and breathing normally. Once he had extracted the last bits of moisture from the tatami, to prevent any mold from forming, Mamoru picked up his katana and shifted into his starting stance. With a slow breath, he started running through his katas.

Even without a real opponent in front of him, Mamoru moved with a ferocity that brought the sequence of movements to life. Misaki could feel each breath in her own lungs, each shift and explosion in her own muscles. She found herself matching his steps in her mind, striking and parrying the blade with her eyes. Slowly, she started to pick out the weak spots, the lagging movements, the openings… The form was beautiful. Not perfect.

"Not enough."

Misaki didn't realize she had said the words aloud until Mamoru turned to look at her.

"What?"

"It's…" *nothing*, Misaki meant to say. *It's nothing.* After all, what would a woman know of fighting? "You won't fend off your father fighting like that."

"I know that, Kaa-chan." Mamoru let his sword arm fall. "It's obvious how much better he is." Misaki never would have guessed it from the boy's beautiful, fluid movements, but the irritable note in his voice betrayed the depths of his frustration. "I don't know how to close the gap. I can't fight like he does."

"Yes, you can," Misaki said. "You fight exactly like he does— just not quite as clean. That's your problem; you're trying to imitate a swordsman with many times your strength and nyama. You need to play to your advantages."

"What advantages?"

"Your range of movement, for one. You're quicker and lighter on your feet than your father."

Mamoru was shaking his head. "That's nice of you to say, Kaa-chan, but I'm not. If you knew anything about fighting, you'd have seen when we fought—I'm not fast enough to counter him."

"Yes, you are." Misaki stood. "Your reaction time is noticeably shorter than his, but you waste movement when you hold all that tension in your shoulders. That's how he keeps getting through your guard."

Mamoru stared at her and she could see the wheels spinning in his head—as he registered that what she said made sense, but couldn't figure out how she knew. "If… if it's so obvious that I'm doing that—if even you can see it—then why didn't he tell me?"

"He's been trying," Misaki sighed. "That's what he means when he keeps saying 'sloppy.'"

"Oh…" Mamoru looked down at nothing for a moment, thinking, visualizing. Then he made two cuts—in such quick succession that Misaki could barely follow the blade with her eyes.

"Better," she murmured. Not perfect. "Better…"

Mamoru tried again, and Misaki found that she had taken a half-step forward.

"Don't swing so hard," she said. "If you have the angle right, the cut will go through without you throwing your whole body behind it."

"Yukino Sensei says it isn't easy to cut through bone and sinew," Mamoru said, his eyes still focused forward. "It takes a lot of power."

"Power," Misaki said, "not muscle. If you trust yourself and your blade… you'd be surprised how easy it is to cut through a human body."

Her toes curled at the threshold. She tipped forward ever so slightly. Teetering.

"Kaa-chan…" Mamoru was starting to look worried. "What on Duna are you talking about?"

"I can't tell you…" Misaki tilted, trying to will herself back from the edge. *This is wrong. This is wrong, you stupid woman. Know your place*—"but I can show you." And she was over the edge, striding across the dojo floor, light with an idiot's elation.

Mamoru's eyes were wide. "Kaa-chan, what are you doing?"

"Something I probably shouldn't." She smiled as she reached the sword rack. "But given your behavior today, you're not one to judge now, are you?" She stood with her hands on her hips for a moment, surveying the rack of Kotetsu swords in their refined lacquer sheaths. The swords at the top of the rack belonged to Matsuda patriarchs past. Having never seen the men's weapons so close, she took a moment to admire them.

Beside Takeru's white Moon Spire sat Takashi's matched katana and wakizashi, Nagimaru and Namimaru. Named for God and Goddess, both weapons had leaping fish carved into their hilts and ocean blue wrapping knotted around their grips. Higher on the rack rested the ancestral sword Kurokouri, Black Ice, wielded by Matsuda Susumu and great Matsudas past. Above that sat Matsuda

Mizudori's sword, the Mist Cutter, Kirinagi, his father's sword, the Cloud Whip, Kumokei, and *his* father's sword, the God Fang, Senkiba.

Just standing before the blades of legend put a tingle in Misaki's fingertips. She would never dream of putting her hands on such sacred weapons, but further down rested lesser weapons—katana, wakizashi, and tanto that were worn, damaged or otherwise inferior, but still functional. From those, Misaki selected a slender wakizashi and tested its weight in her hands.

"Kaa-chan!" Mamoru exclaimed sheathing his own katana. "I-I don't think you should be touching those."

Misaki ignored him. "Heavy." She frowned. "I suppose Kotetsu weapons are always on the heavy side. No wonder your shoulders are so tense."

"Kaa-chan, those blades are all sharp," Mamoru said in mounting anxiety. "I don't want you to hurt yourself."

"You're right." Placing the wakizashi back on the sword rack, Misaki crossed to the dojo supply closet and rummaged for a pair of bokken. "Put away your katana, son."

Misaki knew she was violating sacred space. She knew she should leave the dojo now and pretend this had never happened, but her resolve only hardened as her hand found the hilt of a wooden sword. Takeru had told her to fix Mamoru. Well, she couldn't fix the fact that he was confused and angry. She couldn't fix the fact that he was fourteen. What she could fix was his technique.

After some coaxing, Mamoru put away his metal sword and took the wooden one Misaki offered.

"I don't understand this, Kaa-chan? What is going on?"

"You asked what I was up to at that foreign school all those years ago." Misaki gave the wooden sword a twirl, loosening up her joints. "Your father doesn't like it when I talk about it, but this won't require any talking. Go on," she nodded to Mamoru. "Take a swing."

He looked aghast. "You can't be serious! Kaa-chan, I'm not

going to—"

"Don't want to attack a little old lady?" Misaki smiled. "Fine. Then defend!"

10

THE REASON

Misaki wasn't half as fast as she had been back in Carytha, but Mamoru was so startled that he just barely raised his bokken in time to block. The hard thwack of wooden blades against one another woke an old joy in Misaki, and suddenly she was moving on pure unfettered instinct, driving her opponent back.

Mamoru was strong, but Misaki had made a name for herself fighting theonites physically stronger than herself. If she met him muscle-to-muscle, the impact would devastate her joints. Instead, she let her blade ricochet off his and turned the energy back on him in her own strikes—a trick she had learned over years of fighting Kinoro Wangara. Wood had a spring to it that metal didn't. The harder Mamoru hit, the more speed he gave her.

She could see on Mamoru's face that his mind had gone numb with shock. His body moved on muscle memory, automatically matching each of her steps in perfect form, neatly countering each strike. But as quick as his reflexes were, that kind of conditioned movement had its limits. For one thing, it was predictable.

Misaki feigned a thrust. The movement was ridiculously slow compared to her feints of fifteen years ago, but Mamoru fell for it, which was all that mattered. As he brought his blade across to block, Misaki flipped her bokken over and struck him in the ribs.

Mamoru uttered an undignified yelp—more out of surprise than pain; Misaki very much doubted that she could hurt him with a wooden sword.

Stepping back, she clicked her tongue. "Now son, you shouldn't have fallen for that."

Mamoru's eyes were wide, his hand on his side where she had hit him. "Kaa-chan... this... *this* is what you did overseas, when you were at school? You *fought?"* Mamoru shook his head, seemingly struggling to fit this new piece of information in with everything he knew. He brought a hand to his head, pushed it back through his bangs, and stared at his mother. "I... I guess I shouldn't be surprised."

"You shouldn't?"

"Well, Chul-hee has been telling me about the places he's been—Yamma, Sizwe, and Kudazwe. In all those countries, female koronu are allowed to fight and serve in the military."

Misaki nodded. "That's how it is in most of the world."

"Right," Mamoru said slowly, "and you went to school outside of Kaigen, which means that you went to school with those warrior women, when you were getting to be fighting age. Aunt Setsuko is always saying you did really well there. So, I guess, it makes sense that you'd be able to fight just as well as anyone else. I just can't believe I didn't know... How did I not know?"

"No one does," Misaki said.

Honestly, she wasn't entirely sure that was true. It was common for one fighter to be able to spot another just by the way they moved, and Takeru and Takashi were two of the most perceptive fighters she had ever known. Sometimes, she found it difficult to believe that the brothers could have shared a roof with her all these years and not picked up on her combat background. Then again, it was very possible that the sexism inherent to their upbringing had created a blind spot so opaque that they weren't capable of recognizing those abilities in a woman. In any case, it was not something she would ever discuss with her husband or brother-in-law.

"You understand why your father doesn't know—why he *can't* know," Misaki said seriously. "He would never approve."

Takeru would reject her love of fighting like he rejected everything from her past. She waited for a painful moment for her son to reject it too. Everything in his upbringing suggested that women shouldn't fight, couldn't fight. They were precious dolls to be protected—

"Why wouldn't Tou-sama approve?" Mamoru asked. "I mean, I know it isn't normal for women to fight, but everyone always talks about how important it is for Matsudas to keep the bloodline strong by marrying women from powerful families. If you can fight, doesn't that just prove that Tou-sama married a powerful woman?"

"So… you're not upset?" Misaki asked, surprised at how fragile her voice had become. In that strange moment, she realized that, however improper it was, the idea of Mamoru's disapproval was far more upsetting to her than Takeru's. "Knowing I can fight doesn't bother you?"

"Why would it bother me?" Mamoru said. "This is good news. I'm the son of two great fighters, instead of one. This is good. It means that I must be strong. I should be proud."

Misaki stared. It defied logic. How had a soulless block of ice like Takeru and a selfish thing like her created something so bright? Somehow, despite everything, despite this tiny village, his frigid father, his bitter mother, his brainwashing school, despite all of it, Mamoru was growing up into a good person.

"Kaa-chan?" Mamoru said uncertainly. "What is it?"

"Nothing." She shook herself. "We have work to do. You're going to need to take a proper swing at me."

Mamoru looked nervous. "I don't want to hurt you."

Misaki smiled. Eighteen years ago, if a boy had said that to her, she would have bared her teeth and said, 'Try it.' Now, she just smiled. "They're just wooden blades, son. I trust you." She took up her stance and gave Mamoru an encouraging nod. "I trust you."

After a moment, Mamoru returned her smile—and attacked. He didn't come at her full speed. If Misaki was being honest with herself, she probably couldn't handle him at his full speed. But if he was going to give her openings, she was going to make him sorry. Side-stepping a particularly hesitant stroke of Mamoru's bokken, she struck him across the knuckles.

"*Ow!*" He stepped back, shaking out his hand. "How are you so strong?"

"I'm not. I'm bouncing off your misplaced force and redirecting it against you. I'm sneaky like that."

"You're amazing!"

"Maybe for an old lady." Misaki rolled her shoulder and felt a few joints in her back pop. "You should have seen me in my prime. I would have eviscerated you."

"You were that powerful?" Mamoru said and—bless his heart—he didn't even look skeptical.

"No," Misaki said honestly, "I was never as powerful as you, nor as talented. But I was decisive and willing to fight dirty."

Of the three friends who had taken up crime-fighting on Livingston's streets, Misaki was the only one who had never had her picture on the news or trading cards. There was a good reason for that. Firebird and Whitewing were symbols meant to draw attention. They stepped onto a street intending to be seen, heard, and feared. Nobody thought to fear their creeping Shadow until it was too late.

Misaki was an ambush predator. Her preferred tactic was to take out a criminal's Achilles tendons before he noticed her crouched in the shadows. If he saw her before she could spring her trap, she still had the element of surprise, as few fighters ever expected a diminutive Kaigenese girl to have her unflinching ferocity. And if it came to a head-on clash, blade-to-blade—well, she still had plenty of surprises.

In the next bout, Misaki used one of her favorite maneuvers. She took a swing and missed. Like everyone, Mamoru moved to take advantage of her moment of imbalance. But on the follow-through, she flipped the bokken into a reverse grip. While Mamoru was still starting his swing, she shot forward to meet him. His bokken thumped into her calf; in a real fight, she would have suffered an ugly leg injury—but her blade was at his throat.

197

"I win," she breathed as Mamoru uttered a short gasp. "Why did you let me in?"

"I fell for the feint."

"Only for a dinma." She had watched his eyes closely. "You had a moment to correct, and with your speed, a moment is all you should need."

Mamoru shook his head. "It wasn't enough. You were too fast."

"No," Misaki said. "Ten years ago, I might have been too fast. Right now, you're just slow."

When Misaki attacked again Mamoru blocked the strike to his neck—perhaps only because he was already expecting the feint. His counter was terrifyingly fast, but Misaki anticipated it and ducked. Mamoru's bokken whistled through the empty air above her head. As always, he swung too hard, needlessly throwing himself off balance. In the split second before he recovered, Misaki spun into his ankles, taking both his feet out from under him with a sweep of her bokken.

Mamoru landed hard on his back, but it was Misaki who grunted in pain as they both straightened up. She hadn't put that kind of strain on her knees in years and they were shrieking in protest.

"Are you okay?" Mamoru asked.

"I'm fine," Misaki said tersely. "You, on the other hand, are an idiot. Your father and I are both slower than you. Do you know why we can both get through your defenses?"

"I…" Mamoru looked down at his arms. "I'm too tense."

Misaki nodded. "And you swing too hard on your attacks. It creates an opening, during your follow-through in which you're vulnerable."

"I'm not sure what you're—"

"I'll show you. Come at me."

Mamoru did as he was told and Misaki realized, with a ringing pain in her forearms, that he was starting to fight her in earnest. She stayed on the defensive until inevitably, he swung too hard.

"There!" she exclaimed and darted forward.

Mamoru, with his superhuman reflexes, managed a quick back-step. Misaki's bokken brushed the front of his kimono.

"Oh." Understanding lit his face as he looked down at his own chest.

"You see?" Misaki said.

"I do!" Mamoru exclaimed happily. "I see!"

Against someone with faster legs or longer reach, he would have been cut in half.

"So, how do I fix it?" he asked, looking at her with eager eyes.

"The first thing you need to do is relax your shoulders and stop gripping your sword so tight."

"Right." Mamoru let out a breath. "I'll try."

"Then you have to keep your body relaxed all the way through your cuts," Misaki continued. "You're trying to slice through your target, not smash it with a cudgel. You don't need to swing so hard."

"But if I don't swing hard, how will I ever cut through anything?"

"With *confidence*," Misaki said. "If your stroke is fast and decisive, you won't have to throw all your muscle behind it." If she had been fighting as hard as Mamoru, she would have completely worn herself out by now. "A cut is the quintessential final decision—your life or your opponent's. If you don't have confidence in your choice, you won't commit to it. And if you don't commit, you will fail."

"Then…" The tension returned to Mamoru's body, his hands clenched around the wooden sword handle. "I'm a failure."

"What? I didn't say that."

"But I am. I'm a failure!" Mamoru hit himself in the head with his bokken. "I have too much doubt in me. Tou-sama said my doubt is making me weak, and he's right. I can't—"

"Mamoru, Mamoru!" Misaki caught the bokken before he could hit himself in the head again. "I think you're making this more complicated than it needs to be."

"What?" He blinked at her, a red welt forming between his eyes.

"You feel disillusioned with Kaigen. I understand that. But just think for a moment; does that really change your reason for fighting?"

"I... I guess it doesn't?" Mamoru frowned. "It just doesn't feel right, thinking that people have fought and died and we'll never know the truth about it. I don't know if I want to fight for an Empire that disrespects its koronu like that. There are warriors who aren't remembered for what they did—"

"Well, do you fight to be remembered?" Misaki asked.

"I... I didn't mean that—"

"I'm asking honestly," Misaki said. "Do you fight for personal glory? So the name Matsuda Mamoru will go down in history? Or do you fight for the thrill? Or the privilege of serving your Emperor? You need to ask yourself these questions. The only way to find that conviction you're missing is to know beyond a doubt what you're fighting for."

"Well... where did you find your conviction, Kaa-chan?" Mamoru asked. "Back in your school days, when you were at your best, what did you fight for?"

Finally, a question that was easy to answer. "I fought to protect the people I cared about," Misaki said. "It was simple. My friends had grand ideals they represented. I just didn't want them hurt. Some people called me selfish—and they were right—but I was honest with myself, and it made me unstoppable. I never had any doubt about why I was fighting, and there was nothing I couldn't cut through."

"Kaa-chan..." Mamoru's voice had gotten quiet, like he was afraid to ask the question on his tongue. "Did you ever kill anyone?"

"No."

At Daybreak, Misaki had taken a combination of combat and medic classes, then trained herself to cut with clinical precision. She would strike a criminal's weak points, rendering them unable to fight, and then clot the blood to prevent them from bleeding out before the authorities got there. She had taken tendons, eyes, and limbs, but never a life.

"I never had to kill anyone, but…" Misaki paused to rub the skin between her thumb and forefinger where a blister was forming.

"But what?"

"I would have." Misaki lifted her head to look her son in the face. "If it came to it, I would have killed without a second thought. If it was to save Robin, I would have killed as many people as I needed to."

"Who's Robin?" Mamoru asked.

"He's…" *Warmth. Hope. The sun burning through the fog.* "A robin is a Carythian bird. It's a metaphor."

"Oh."

"I know everything seems complicated now," Misaki said, "but I suppose the only question that really matters is… If strangers came here intending to kill you, and me, and all your little brothers, what would you do?"

"I would kill them," Mamoru said resolutely. "I wouldn't have to think about it. I would kill them all."

"There." Misaki pointed to his chest. "That's all you need."

"Really?" Mamoru thought for a moment. "It's that simple?"

"It was for me. Then again… you may not want to take your old lady as an example." After all, Mamoru wasn't much like her. Now that Misaki thought about it, he was more like the people she would have killed and died for. "You may well find that you have a higher ideal that you want to fight for. You're a nobler person than I am."

Mamoru looked surprised. "You're noble, Kaa-chan."

"That is the dumbest thing you've said all day. Square up."

Now that Mamoru had absorbed the fact that his mother could indeed fight, his koro's brain had started to pick apart the *way* she fought. As he caught on to her tricks, she had to pull out more and more creative ways to counter him. It was a dance she had once danced with the most important people in her life—her teachers, her closest friends, her most dangerous enemies. But her body had changed since then. Her blade didn't cut as fast as her thoughts, and her joints screamed more insistently with each bout until finally, she couldn't bear it any longer.

Realizing that her muscles would give in the next few dinmanu, she parried Mamoru's overhand strike and went for one of her spinning attacks—just to see if she could still do it. She fumbled the stepping and came up short, but she could see on Mamoru's face that he was impressed.

"I've never seen anyone fight in that style," he said, "not even Uncle Kazu. Those aren't Tsusano techniques."

"No, they're not." Misaki put her hands on her knees and tried to conceal how painfully winded she was.

Her first teacher had been her father, who had trained her alongside her brothers for fun, not realizing he was planting the seeds of what would become a deeply rooted love for fighting in his daughter. But he was not her greatest influence. That distinction went to Master Wangara, the wild swordsman of Yamma.

"Where did those techniques come from?" Mamoru asked.

Misaki shook her head and managed to gasp between heaving breaths, "We don't talk about it."

"Are you alright?"

"Yes." She nodded, kneading her right forearm, "just at the end of my strength. Sorry, son. I think that's all I have in me. The muscles aren't there anymore."

"Have you not trained in all these years?"

"Of course not," Misaki said. "Housewives don't fight."

"I'm sorry," Mamoru said. "I didn't realize—That must have been hard for you."

"Don't be ridiculous," Misaki laughed. "This is the most fun I've had in years. You're going to have to keep practicing on your own until your father gets home. If anyone asks, I was never here."

"You really love fighting," Mamoru said. It wasn't a question. "How could you give it up?"

"I…" Misaki paused, still massaging her arm, trying to come up with an answer that would make sense to her son. "Something I learned is that the act of fighting in and of itself isn't important.

What was really important to me was protecting the people I cared about. I've never needed a sword to protect you—to raise you the way your father wanted. Caring for my family meant putting away the fighter, so I did."

Mamoru was quiet for a moment and Misaki looked up to find him staring at her with a confused expression on his face.

"What is it?" she asked.

"Why do you call yourself selfish?"

Before Misaki could think of a way to answer, a whimper echoed down the hall and Mamoru turned to the sound. "Izumo."

"That's for me to worry about. Eyes forward, now." Misaki put the tip of her bokken to his jaw, turning his face forward. "You just worry about what's ahead of you."

. . . .

Izumo's crying had woken Nagasa, but both boys had slept far longer than Misaki expected.

"Thank you," she murmured, ruffling Nagasa's hair before reaching into the cradle to pick up Izumo. *Thank you for giving me that time with Mamoru*, was what she meant, but the two little boys were far too young to understand that kind of sentiment.

"You're welcome, Kaa-chan," Nagasa responded politely as Izumo kept crying.

After feeding Izumo, Misaki tied the infant to her back, helped Nagasa into his coat, and swung by the elementary school to pick Hiroshi up from training. Having Nagasa along slowed her progress through the snow, but today, she was thankful for the little boy struggling along beside her. It gave her a periodic excuse to rest her own worn-out legs.

"Uh-oh!" Nagasa exclaimed as he fell down in the deep snow for a third time. "Too slippery!" Misaki took his arm and lifted him to his feet. "Snow on me," he observed and shook the snow from his sleeves, his jiya sending it wide in twinkling clouds.

The toddler had long since developed the ability to move water particles but he lacked the control to move them where he wanted them to go. He still needed his mother to clear the path before him and to hold his hand where it was too icy. Mamoru and Hiroshi had both been more powerful and skilled than Nagasa at three, but what Matsuda Takeru's third son lacked in jiya, he made up for in chatter.

"I fell down, Kaa-chan," he explained as Misaki picked him up and brushed the snow from the front of his coat. "Three times." He held up three fingers. "I fell down three times. If it's again, then it will be four times. Now we're walking more. I can see our house."

Misaki had learned that he didn't really need her to respond; he kept going all on his own. She had no idea where Nagasa had inherited his overgrown vocabulary and love of talking, but it could be convenient to have a child capable of entertaining himself with his own running monologue.

"Hey, there are birds up there. Those birds can fly, way up there. Maybe Izumo can see the birds. There's Ryota's house!" he said, happily pointing at the Yukino compound. "See? Izu-kun, see Ryota's house? Can we go see Ryota?"

"We already saw Ryota-kun today," Misaki pointed out. "You played with him for a long time, while Hyori was visiting."

"I like playing with Ryota," Nagasa said. "Ryota has toy cars at his house."

"I know, but right now we have to pick Hiroshi up from training."

"Okay," Nagasa said and then promptly launched into another ramble about where all the birds might be going.

When they reached the elementary school, Ameno Samusa was waiting at the door to see his youngest student off.

"How did he do?" Misaki asked.

"He's getting stronger," Ameno said. "It'll be quite a while before he's ready to be taking on serious opponents, but it's very unusual for someone his age to have such good control. I've been teaching here for two decades now and I don't think I've ever seen his equal."

"What about Mamoru?" Misaki asked, just out of curiosity.

"Mamoru was exceptional," Ameno said. "This one may be better." He shrugged. "Only time will tell."

"Thank you, Ameno Sensei," Misaki said, bowing. "Hiro-kun, get your shoes on. Time to go."

"What does 'only time will tell' mean?" Hiroshi asked as they made their way back to the Matsuda compound.

"I think Ameno Sensei means, we'll have to wait until you're big enough to fight your brother."

"He thinks I could beat him?" Hiroshi seemed vaguely fascinated by the idea.

"In ten years, maybe," Misaki said with a laugh.

"Mamoru-nii-san is strong," Hiroshi said. "He is bigger than I am."

"He is," Misaki said.

"But I could grow. I could beat him."

"Maybe."

"Like Tou-sama beat Uncle Takashi?"

"Hiro-kun!" Misaki stopped so quickly that Nagasa ran into her legs. "Who told you about that?"

"The teachers talk about it sometimes," Hiroshi said.

"Oh—well—just, try not to mention it in front of your uncle, alright?"

"Yes, Kaa-chan."

The results of the Matsuda brothers' last duel were common knowledge throughout the village, though most were polite enough not to discuss it. The fight had been years ago when Takeru had wanted to leave Kumono Academy to work in the mayor's office and Takashi had wanted him to stay. Their father, by that time very old and uninterested in their professional careers, had crossly demanded that they settle the matter in single combat instead of bothering him with it.

Only a few people had witnessed the fight itself—Yukino Dai, who served as the referee—and a few other men, but people talked. One Whispering Blade was not necessarily equal to another.

Takashi was a creative, devastatingly powerful swordsman with an explosive fighting style and a thousand tricks up his sleeve. But when it came down to jiya against jiya, his ice was not a match Takeru's focus.

"But you know, Takashi-nii-sama has had his share of victories against your father in the past," Misaki pointed out. That was the fate of all male Matsuda siblings, wasn't it? To beat each other into greatness like hammers on steel? "They've always been close in combat ability, but you should keep in mind that they are close in age. It will be ten years before you're big enough to challenge your older brother and even then, he will be much more experienced than you."

When Misaki looked down at Hiroshi, she was unnerved to find that her ever-serious second son had something like a smile on his face.

"I'm going to grow as fast as I can," he said.

11

THE PATRIARCH

It was dark by the time Takeru came back from Kumono Academy. He appeared distracted. The anger wasn't gone—if anything his frown had deepened—but it was dispersed. It was only when he walked past the dojo and saw Mamoru practicing that he seemed to remember his threat from earlier.

"Are you ready, son?" he asked.

"Yes, Tou-sama," Mamoru said with a small smile. As exhausted as he was, his shoulders had relaxed.

Misaki hovered at the dojo doorway to watch the fight, Izumo perched on her hip.

In a flash, Kyougetsu was out of its sheath.

His muscles loosened, Mamoru responded just as fast, drawing his own katana in the perfect defensive position. The two swords rang against one another, Mamoru absorbed the impact and returned with his own clean cut, grazing the front of his father's kimono—a split dinma before Takeru's blade came to a stop at his neck.

Takeru took two measured steps back, glanced down at the cut across the front of his kimono and uttered a neutral, "Hmm," before lifting his eyes back to Mamoru.

"Again," he said.

This time it was Mamoru who attacked first. Misaki felt her own rigid shoulders relaxing as she saw that he had processed everything from her brief lesson. Freed from the tension that had tied him up earlier, he had become a new creature—liquid lightning. In his movement, she saw the promise of a fighter as fast as Yukino Dai, as powerful as Takashi, and perhaps one day as precise as his father.

The volley was long and ferocious, each man gaining and losing ground as fast as Misaki's eyes could follow.

At last, a particularly savage stroke of Kyougetsu sent Mamoru stumbling. Instead of pressing in for the finish, Takeru drew back. Mamoru regained his footing in a single step and snapped back into his fighting stance.

For a moment of stillness, father and son stared at one another.

Mamoru was coiled deep in his stance, ready to spring back into motion at the smallest twitch of his father's blade. Takeru appeared to be thinking. Hunger had brightened Mamoru's eyes, and the smile of a fighter's high had turned the corner of his mouth. He wasn't dreading his father's next move; he was looking forward to it.

But instead of attacking again, Takeru gave a curt nod and said "Good."

"Good?"

"Yes. You're dismissed."

"Really?" Mamoru looked almost disappointed. "You didn't—"

Takeru slammed the Moon Spire back into its sheath with a clang that made Mamoru flinch. "I said you're dismissed."

That night, Takeru wasn't in the bedroom or his study. Misaki found him standing on the front deck.

"Wind."

Misaki glanced around them. The breeze was light and the bare branches were calm. "Is there?"

"At sea," Takeru clarified.

Misaki had keen eyes and ears, but her senses were nowhere near as sharp as her husband's. Takeru could feel a dewdrop slide off a blade of grass halfway across the village—and cut it in half before it hit the ground. If he felt something more than natural air currents disturbing the ocean, it wasn't something he would discuss with his wife. That sort of thing, he would say, was not a woman's business.

So instead of pressing, she leaned into the railing and studied him. She may never have loved Takeru, but he fascinated her, in the way that powerful theonites always fascinated her. It was why, when her parents told her she was going to marry a Matsuda, she thought she might grow to love him. Love might grow out of awe. But after all these years, Misaki still studied her husband the way one studies an animal from afar. Searching. Searching for understanding or common ground. Never quite finding a connection.

In an objective sense, Takeru was perfect. From the precise lines of his face to the powerful ligaments of his arms, his whole body could have been sculpted by a numu angel of the ancient world.

The perfect weapon.

Like all men in Takayubi, he wore his hair long and tied back from his face. While Takashi was just starting to show wrinkles from a human combination of smiling and sleepless nights, Takeru's face bore few extraneous lines. It wasn't that he looked young—*ageless* was probably a better descriptor. Misaki figured that when she grew old and shriveled, Takeru would look just as he did now, a god of ice.

The thought would have made a normal woman insecure, but Misaki doubted age would do anything to affect her standing with her husband. He had never seemed particularly interested in her appearance. Early on, it had offended her. There were certain qualities she had known her Matsuda husband would never appreciate—her swordsmanship, her skill in chemistry, her affinity for foreign languages—but a man was supposed to care that his wife was beautiful. For all her strange and mannish habits, she was still a woman, and it still wounded her pride to think that her husband did not find her desirable—that was until it occurred to her that, if Takeru desired her, he would be moved to touch her more often. And she was content to have him keep those frigid hands to himself.

As her eyes trailed down to the hands in question, Misaki realized that they were clamped rather tightly on the wooden railing. The knuckles were bruised, and she was suddenly reminded of Mamoru's bloody-knuckled fists clenched too hard on his knees. For a long time, she had believed that Matsuda Takeru was more ice than man, but he had been different today. She had never seen him hit Mamoru that hard. Was it possible that there were cracks in the ice?

"Did you have a good day, Takeru-sama?" she asked softly.

The wood uttered a creak of protest under his grip. "Not really."

"What did Takashi-nii-sama want to speak to you about?"

Her husband often told her to keep her nose out of 'men's business,' so she wasn't really expecting an answer. For a moment, he looked as though he was going to rebuke her for the question, but then he said stiffly, "He wants me to quit my job at the mayor's office."

"What?" Misaki couldn't keep the surprise or the anger out of her voice. "Why?"

"He wants me to teach combat at the school."

"But Kumono already has a sword instructor," Misaki said. "They have Dai-san."

"Nii-sama is going to make Dai a part-time instructor. He says that Dai is too soft with the students. He's concerned that the standard is going down."

"What?"

That was patently untrue. Misaki could tell just from the few times she had watched Yukino Dai teach that he was as brilliant an instructor as he was a swordsman. He may not have been able to win a jiya-to-jiya fight with one of the Matsuda brothers, but as far as passing on knowledge, he was worth several Takerus.

She knew exactly why Takashi wanted his younger brother back at Kumono and it was purely selfish. Takashi wasn't cut out for administrative work. He had stepped into the role of headmaster because his father and grandfather had held the position before him, not because he had any desire to run the school. When Takeru had worked at Kumono with him, Takashi had relied heavily on his younger brother's sense of organization and professionalism. Misaki could see why he wanted Takeru back—but that still didn't make it a good decision.

"And what is Dai-san supposed to do?" she demanded. "He has a wife and a small child at home. How is he going to support them on a part-time salary?"

"That is not my brother's concern," Takeru said coldly, "nor is it yours."

"Of course it is! Hyori is my friend."

"It's not your place to criticize the head of this household."

Misaki bit down on her pride, as she had for so many years. "You're right. It's not," she conceded, "but am I not allowed to worry about my friend's happiness… and my husband's?"

"Happiness?" Takeru's tone was not so much bitter as baffled. "What does any of this have to do with happiness?"

"You love your job at the village hall. You love crunching numbers." Love was perhaps a strong word. All evidence suggested that Takeru was incapable of love—but the only times Misaki could ever remember him being remotely animated were when he talked about his work at the mayor's office. It was usually mind-numbingly boring stuff like budget management, but it seemed to give him satisfaction.

"Surely you can convince him otherwise."

"I asked him to reconsider," Takeru said. "He's made up his mind."

"You can still say 'no.'"

Takeru gave Misaki a look—that look like he was contemplating having her committed. "My brother is the head of this house. It's not my place to question him, and it's certainly not yours."

"But you…" *You just lectured Mamoru about not being strong enough to fight through his doubt. You'll beat your son into the ground, but you can't be bothered to fight for yourself?*

"What is it, woman?" Takeru snapped, and Misaki knew she had no choice but to back down.

"I'm sorry. I shouldn't have contradicted you."

If he wanted to make himself miserable, so be it. It wasn't her place to argue.

....

If Takeru was still angry the next day, he didn't show his displeasure any more than Misaki showed hers. At breakfast, she served him his tea with her usual smile and he accepted it with his usual straight-faced indifference.

"Good morning, Misaki!" Takashi greeted her as though nothing was wrong.

"Good morning, Nii-sama," she said and poured the hot tea in his cup instead of his lap.

"No tea, Misaki." He pushed the cup away. "This is a day for celebration."

"Oh—um… Why?"

"What? He didn't tell you? You didn't tell her, Takeru-kun?" he looked at his brother. "Takeru is coming back to teach at Kumono Academy!"

"Oh—yes, he did mention that, Nii-sama." Misaki screwed her face back into smiling position. "It's wonderful news. We're so thankful."

"You see, this is a happy day!" Takashi beamed. "Today, we drink!"

Judging by the color of Takashi's cheeks and the volume of his voice, he had already gotten started.

"Of course," Misaki said. "I'll go get some sake."

When she retreated to the kitchen, Setsuko was there, ladling the miso soup Misaki had prepared into bowls.

What is going on? Misaki wanted to snap the moment she saw her. *What the hell is wrong with your husband?*

A moment later, she realized how unfair that was and wanted to slap herself. Setsuko might have a better relationship with her husband than most women, but she couldn't control what he did at work. His decisions weren't hers.

"Good morning, Setsuko," she said.

"Morning, Misaki." One look from Setsuko told Misaki that she already knew about Takashi's decision—and understood how disastrous it was going to be. "Listen, I—"

"Kaa-chan, I'm hungry!" Nagasa whined, tugging on Misaki's apron.

"Sit." Misaki nodded to the kitchen table, where she, Setsuko, and the little ones ate whenever the men were using the main table. "I'll get you some rice as soon as I—"

"Kaa-chan," Mamoru stuck his head into the kitchen. "Izumo is crying. Oh." He looked back over his shoulder. "And so is Ayumi."

"Just a dinma," Setsuko said, as she helped Misaki load up a tray with rice, soup, and sake for the men. "I'll go get them."

"Miii-sa-kiii!" Takashi sing-songed from the other room. "Where is the saaa-ke?"

"Coming, Nii-sama!" Misaki picked up the tray and started toward the dining room, only to have Setsuko stop her with a hand on her shoulder.

"Ah-ah. Before that..." She took a third cup and put it to Misaki's lips.

"What? No. Setsuko—I can't—"

"You need it."

"Okay." Misaki relented and allowed Setsuko to tip the sake into her mouth.

"Atta girl." Setsuko grinned as Misaki squeezed her eyes shut and swallowed the fire.

"Thank you," Misaki breathed as the liquid burned down her throat deep into her chest. "I needed that—"

"I know." Setsuko smacked her on the back and hurried off to get the babies.

"Is that Mamoru back there?" Takashi asked, leaning over to look into the kitchen as Misaki set his soup and rice before him. "Hey, Mamoru! Come out here!"

"Why?" Takeru asked stiffly.

"He's a young man now. He should sit with the men."

"He's only fourteen," Takeru said.

"You're just upset because he's better than you. Misaki, go tell Mamoru to come out here—and bring him some sake."

"No need," Takeru said. "He can have mine."

Misaki was never sure if Takeru refused to drink because he was worried about dulling his senses or just his ability to frown. Today, it might have just been his small way of slighting his brother.

"No, no. Don't be a stick in the mud," Takashi said. "Drink it."

"Nii-sama, it's not even noon yet."

Takashi slammed his palm on the table so hard that Misaki jumped. "I said drink."

Takeru held his older brother's gaze and for a moment, Misaki thought he was going to object. She wanted him to. He lowered his gaze and knocked back the cup in one gulp.

"There you go, little brother!" Takashi clapped Takeru on the shoulder.

Clenching her jaw, Misaki turned to leave. Before she reached the kitchen, Mamoru appeared in the doorway, holding Izumo. "You asked for me, Uncle?"

"Give the baby to your mother, boy," Takashi said. "Come sit with us."

"Thank you," Misaki said as she shifted the tray to one arm to accept a fussing Izumo with the other. "Don't try to swallow too much at once," she whispered to Mamoru.

"What?"

"It's going to feel like a punch to the nose, but try to keep a straight face. If you don't, your uncle will mock you for the rest of the week."

"Come, Mamoru," Takashi said, motioning him to the table. "Have a drink with us. There…" he beamed as Mamoru knelt

214

down at his left hand. "Look at you. Look how tall you've gotten. You're growing up into a fine man, aren't you?"

Mamoru didn't seem sure how to respond. "Um—I hope so, Uncle."

"Fine young man," Takashi mused as Misaki retreated to comfort Izumo. "You must make your father so proud."

"I-I hope to someday," Mamoru said, audibly uncomfortable. "I don't think I've earned—"

"Oh, you'll earn your father's pride"—There was a clink as Takashi poured himself more sake—"or spend the rest of your life trying, like he did, like our old man did, like his old man before him. You'll grow, and you'll train, and grow, and train with all your soul until one day you'll be sitting behind the Kumono desk wondering why the hell you took all that time to become such a powerful fighter. So you could do battle with schedules and registration forms? So you could pass all that tedious nonsense on to your own son?"

"Nii-sama." Takeru's voice was so rigid it sounded like it might snap. "Please don't speak that way about our family's legacy."

"Quiet, Takeru-kun. I wasn't talking to you. I'll tell you something, Mamoru-kun—" a pause for a deep swig—"I'm glad I have a little girl."

There was a confused silence.

"You're looking at me like I'm crazy," Takashi laughed, "but I'm serious. Girls are made for peacetime. A girl can thrive in peacetime. It comforts me to think my little Ayumi won't have to put up with all this nonsense. Training until you bleed, only to be left in a sheath to rust…"

"I-I'm not sure I understand, Uncle."

"I hope you never do. You're too bright to rust." Takashi let out a sigh that was almost a moan. "I was bright too, once, you know."

"Uncle—"

"That's enough talk," Takashi said abruptly. "Have a drink, nephew."

There was a pause, a painstaking gulp, and Takashi burst out laughing. "Oh, Mamoru-kun! You should see your face!"

. . . .

"I'll talk to him," Setsuko promised Misaki and Hyori later, "for both of you. Just not right now. I think I'll wait until his head is on straight."

The three women had just settled down to a rare moment of peace. Mamoru was studying in the next room with Kwang Chul-hee. Hiroshi, Nagasa, and Ryota were scrambling across the floor alongside the older boys, deeply absorbed in the ice car racing game Mamoru had taught them, Izumo was asleep, and Ayumi was quietly feeding at Setsuko's breast.

"Oh, you don't have to speak to your husband on our account, Setsuko-san," Hyori said earnestly. "That sort of thing is men's business."

"Hyori-chan is right," Misaki said wearily, selecting a needle from her sewing box. She wasn't at all in the mood to talk about the situation with Takashi and Takeru; all she really wanted to do was catch up on her sewing, so she was eager to shut down the subject as quickly as possible. "Kumono is Takashi-sama's school. If he wants to change the staff, that's his decision."

"Sure," Setsuko said, "but it's a stupid decision, and *someone* ought to tell him."

"Setsuko-san!" Hyori gasped. "How can you say such disrespectful things of your husband?"

Setsuko shrugged. "He knows I love him."

"I'm sure Dai-san has already raised his objections," Misaki pointed out. Dai was enough of a man that he could speak up for himself. "If he or my husband have a problem with Takashi-sama's decision, it's their job to take it up with him. They're grown men, aren't they?"

"Wait. Why would *your* husband have a problem with the change?" Hyori asked, confused.

"Takeru's not a big complainer," Setsuko said, "but he *really* didn't like teaching at Kumono."

"Really?" Hyori looked shocked. "My husband talks about it like it's the best job in the world. Surely, a great swordsman like Takeru would love it too."

"Well, there's a difference between being great at fighting and being great at teaching it," Misaki said. "Takeru-sama would much rather be behind a desk doing paperwork than teaching students. That's why Takashi-sama really wants him around, to help him with the administrative work he hates so much."

"I don't know…" Hyori looked doubtful. "Should you really make those assumptions about the head of your family?"

"No, Misaki's right," Setsuko said and heaved a sigh. "Poor Takashi-sama has really never enjoyed being the Kumono headmaster. Sometimes I think what he should really do—what he really *wants* to do—is just pass the job off to Takeru or Dai. They would be good at it."

Misaki couldn't stop the incredulous laugh from escaping her. "Dai-san, maybe, but Takeru…" *Takeru couldn't lead his way out of a paper bag,* she very nearly said aloud. *You need a spine to lead.*

"Takeru has those nobleman book-smarts," Setsuko said, "which is more than I can say of my poor man."

"Setsuko-san!" Hyori's beautiful doe-like eyes had widened in horror. "You really shouldn't speak that way about your husband!"

Misaki looked down at her sewing, glad that she hadn't chosen to voice any of her thoughts on Takeru. She didn't want poor Hyori to have a heart attack.

"I didn't mean it in a mean way," Setsuko said quickly. "My husband is a great man with his own strengths, but he isn't a perfectionist like Takeru. He doesn't get any satisfaction from clerical work. It just makes him bored, and cranky, and less fun in bed."

"Setsuko-san!" Hyori clapped both hands over her mouth and blushed so furiously Misaki was afraid she might faint from all the blood rushing to her head.

"What?" Setsuko said and Misaki wondered if her sister-in-law had taken a few swigs of the sake as well. Even Setsuko usually had more delicacy. "He's so much more energetic when he's been in the dojo training than when he's spent the whole day in the office. I'm sure Dai-san is the same way—"

"I don't think we need to talk about Dai-san," Misaki said hastily casting around for a change of subject. "Um—Hyori-chan, you wouldn't happen to have any dark blue thread to spare?"

"Oh—s-sure," Hyori stuttered. "I don't use nearly as much blue as you." The Yukino family colors were white, silver, and sage green.

Rummaging in the drawer of her sewing box for a moment, Misaki came up with a spool of pale gray thread and held it up. "Trade you."

"Oh—Misaki-san, there's no need—"

"Trade you," Misaki insisted and tossed the spool into Hyori's lap.

"Oh… Thank you." Hyori picked up the spool and clutched it to her chest like it was a treasure. "You're always so kind, Misaki-san." The blush hadn't quite faded from her cheeks, and Misaki wondered how a married woman with a child could be so ridiculously innocent.

"Give me a dinma." Hyori rose to search through the bag she had brought with her. "I'm going to find some blue for you."

Normally, Misaki didn't mind sewing, but today she found herself frustrated. "Mattaku mou!" she swore. "This is a mess. I might just have to pass this one on to Tamami-san." Kotetsu's wife was a far better seamstress than any of the koro women.

"What happened to it?" Hyori asked.

"Fight," Misaki said.

"Oh. But—Dai hasn't trained with your husband in months…" It was common knowledge that Dai was one of the few swordsmen ever to get through Takeru's guard with a steel katana. "So, who did that to his kimono?""

"Mamoru."

Hyori gasped. "He's really gotten that skilled?"

For the first time that day, Misaki found herself smiling. "Not *that* skilled." She held up Mamoru's kimono from the same day, which was so sliced up it was barely holding together.

"Oh dear!" Hyori exclaimed with a laugh. "That is going to take a lot of thread, isn't it? Is this a good shade?" She held up a spool.

"That looks perfect," Misaki said and reached out to take it.

"Oh, Misaki-san!" Hyori exclaimed suddenly, pulling up short. "What happened to your hands?"

"What?" Misaki's heart dropped. "Oh—! Nothing." She pulled her hand back quickly. She knew she should have spent more time healing the blisters! "I think I had an allergic reaction to this new soap I tried using. It gave me a rash."

"I didn't see any new soap," Setsuko said. She and Misaki bathed, did their laundry, and washed their dishes in all the same spaces.

"Well that's because I threw it away," Misaki said. "It wasn't any good."

"You know, it almost looks like you're blistered," Hyori said in concern. "It's weird... sometimes my husband's hands get like that."

"Really?" Misaki's heart started to thud faster. Takeru was already unhappy with her; the last thing she needed right now was for someone to find out that she had been in his dojo putting her hands on his weapons. And if gullible, naïve Hyori was the one who caught her at it, she didn't think her pride could take it.

Hyori had moved closer, reaching out to take one of Misaki's hands. "Why would you have blisters like Dai's?"

Misaki's mind was scrambling to generate a lie when—"Takeru-sama!" she exclaimed in relief. She usually wasn't so happy to feel her husband's unpleasant coldness fill a room. "You're home early!"

"Shimatta—!" Setsuko swore under her breath and pulled her kimono up to cover her breasts.

"I didn't realize we would have company," Takeru said without bothering to greet any of the women. "Why is Kwang's boy in our house?"

"He has a deal with Mamoru," Misaki said.

"What?"

"Mamoru helps him with his combat training, and in exchange, he helps Mamoru with his Kaigengua homework."

Poor Chul-hee usually didn't last more than a waati in the dojo before he was too exhausted to lift his bokken, and the two would retire to the family room to run through Kaigengua vocabulary until the sky grew dark. It was how the boys had spent most of their mid-winter break.

"Hmm." Takeru huffed, then turned his cold gaze on Hyori. "And you... shouldn't you get home and prepare dinner for your husband?"

"Oh—y-yes, Matsuda-dono." Hyori scrambled to gather her things before bowing herself out of the room.

"That was rude," Setsuko muttered.

"Misaki," Takeru said, "see your friend off and then come to my study."

His impenetrable monotone made it hard for Misaki to tell if she was in trouble or not. Either way, she thought it would be best to do as he said without asking questions.

Ryota cried when Hyori told him it was time to go.

"Yosh, yosh," Misaki soothed the toddler, patting his head. "Naga-kun will still be here tomorrow."

"Thank you for having me, as always, Misaki-san." Hyori bowed. "Oh, and don't worry about Mamoru's kimono," she said with an uncharacteristically mischievous smile.

"What?"

Hyori patted her bag. "I'll have it back by next week."

"Hyori-chan, I can't let you do all that work!" Misaki reached for Hyori's bag, but the younger woman clutched it to her chest.

"No, please!" she said earnestly. "Please let me do this for you, Misaki-san. Dai keeps all his clothes in such good condition, it's not like I have a lot of my own mending to do."

"Fine," Misaki sighed. "I'll owe you. You'll have to let me help you with your laundry later."

While Hyori came from a good family, her own jiya was weak. The kind of heavy water-moving work that came easily to Misaki tired her out quickly.

Hyori gave her a loving look that Misaki neither understood nor deserved. "You're always so kind to me, Misaki-san."

"Have a good night, Hyori-chan." After she bowed, Misaki couldn't help it—she reached out and gave her sweet friend a short pat on the cheek. "I'll see you tomorrow."

"Good night, pretty girl!" Setsuko said, waving Hyori off.

With the smile fading from her face, Misaki crossed through the family room and made her way to Takeru's study.

"Takeru-sama," she said softly when she reached the door. "You wanted to see me?"

Takeru didn't acknowledge her presence except to wave her inside. He was still absorbed in the kayiri on the desk before him, so Misaki bowed herself into the room and approached quietly. She knelt before Takeru—the way she used to kneel before his father—until he was ready to speak to her.

Finally, he set his brushpen down and looked up.

"There was another letter addressed to you." Reaching into the folds of his kimono, he produced a scroll and handed it to her. The rolled kayiri was battered and smudged as if it had come a long way.

"It's from Kolunjara!" Misaki exclaimed when her eyes fell on the sender's address.

There was no name. Her fingers passed over the seal and paused when they found it unbroken. Her gaze lifted to meet Takeru's in a moment of surprise. He hadn't opened it.

Misaki had the feeling—no, she was certain—that Takeru had spent the first few years of their marriage intercepting her letters from overseas. Only the blandest of congratulations on her wedding had ever reached her, nothing of substance. Nothing that really mattered.

There were letters that should have come that conspicuously never made it into her hands. She already knew what most of them would say. Elleen would stiffly express less sadness than she really felt before saying that she respected Misaki's judgment. Master Wangara would tell her to look out for herself. Koli would go on a tirade that started out making sense before devolving into ramblings on the nature of human ambition and free will. And Robin... well, she tried not to imagine what he might have written. It hurt too much.

She could have objected—and if she'd really wanted to, found a way to get to the letters before Takeru did—but in a way, it was a kindness. It made it easier to forget the life she had left behind... or at the very least, push it to the back of her mind.

Perhaps she should have been grateful that, after a decade, her husband finally trusted her enough to give her a foreign letter without looking at it first. But when she searched her bitter little heart for a drop of gratitude, she came up empty.

"Why would you be getting mail from Kolunjara?" Takeru asked.

Misaki couldn't read any suspicion into his voice, but his presence spoke clearly enough: he trusted her enough to let her have her mail, but he was going to stand over her while she read it.

"I don't know," she said honestly.

"You have no acquaintances there who might have sent this?"

Last Misaki had heard, Koli Kuruma was still living in the Yammanka capital, but the handwriting on the scroll was far too neat to be his. She shook her head.

"Honestly, I have no idea who this is from."

Curious, she broke the seal and unrolled the letter. The writing was in Yammaninke—no. Not exactly. The letters were Yammaninke, but the words themselves were in Lindish, a language Misaki had not seen or heard since her school days.

The only nagiji on the kayiri were a set of familiar characters—a signature at the bottom of the text. Misaki felt herself draw in a gasp.

"What is it?" Takeru asked. "Who is it from?"

"My... my old roommate," Misaki said. She neglected to mention that her roommate was Ranganese.

Dear Misaki,

It's been a while. I know you told me it would be better for your marriage if we did not have any more contact, and I'm sorry to breach that. I myself am risking more than I would like to say to get this message to you, but I could not live with myself if I didn't send it. I am loyal to my country, but you are my friend, and I don't want any harm to come to you or those you love.

If you are no longer living on the Kusanagi Peninsula, this letter will probably not reach you and thank the Gods that you are out of danger.

However, if you are reading this, I can only assume you are still at your address in Takayubi. If that is the case, you are not safe. I don't know what information the Kaigenese government has given you about the state of Ranga or the possibility of war, but whether they have told you or not, you are in serious danger. Take your family and leave Takayubi as soon as you can.

And if you do survive the coming weeks, if you could send a letter back to this address, so I know you're alright.

Nyama to you. A million times, nyama to you.

Nami, don't let this be our last contact.

Your devoted friend,
Guang Ya-li

Misaki felt as if she had turned to stone.

"What is it?" Takeru asked, reading the shock on her face. "What does it say?"

"Please, Takeru-sama, sit down," she said quietly.

"What?"

"You need to hear this."

Kneeling opposite her husband, Misaki translated the letter

aloud. Takeru listened without expression.

"And who is this Guang Ya-li?" he asked.

"I told you, she's a friend from school," Misaki replied in the vain hope that Takeru wouldn't press her further.

"And where was she born?"

Guang was a common family name across Namindugu. There were as many Guangs in northern Kaigen as there were anywhere in Ranga, but, "Ya-li is Ranganese."

"Then this letter should be destroyed and forgotten," Takeru said calmly. "Nothing she says is to be trusted."

"She was a close friend—" Misaki protested.

"You're speaking nonsense, Misaki. Even if this Guang Ya-li really was your friend, how would a woman know the plans of the Ranganese military? It's impossible."

"It's more than possible," Misaki said, trying to keep the indignation out of her voice. "The year Ya-li and I graduated, her sister was promoted to general in the Ranganese army."

Takeru let out a disdainful noise that made Misaki's teeth clench. "Her sister? What kind of joke of a military are they running over there?"

Misaki ignored her husband's comment. "Ya-li would know, and no matter what you think, she wouldn't lie to me. Not about this. I understand if you don't want to take the word of a Ranganese woman, but it isn't just her. Kazu—Lord Tsusano—also warned us, in his own way."

"All your brother said was that we should take a vacation to Jungsan."

"It was a strange thing to say. He meant to tell us something."

"It was a coincidence."

"Respectfully, Takeru-sama, I know my brother. And I know this woman. I think the Ranganese really might be planning something."

"And what if they are? If the Ranganese are coming, they are coming to their deaths." He spoke with the same stupid confidence that seemed to possess everyone in Takayubi. "This is the Sword of Kaigen. To make a run on it is to die."

"Those are pretty words," Misaki said, "but you haven't seen what's out there."

"It doesn't matter," Takeru said, rising to his feet to tower over his wife. "The Empire depends on us to hold back any threat from the west, and we have done so without fail for centuries."

"I know." Misaki stayed on her knees, hoping that if she kept her temper in check and spoke softly, she could make him see reason. "You and the other men here are great fighters, but you aren't an army. This peninsula isn't the theonite powerhouse it was the last time the Ranganese attacked."

"Maybe not," Takeru conceded, "but it will be far worse off if we leave. Did you ever think that perhaps this old friend of yours is trying to talk you into treason?"

"What?"

"She knows who it is you married, yes?"

"Yes."

"Then it's a good plan, isn't it?" Takeru said. "Get you to leave the peninsula, along with your family—perhaps the whole extended Matsuda family—when the Empire needs us here the most. Ranganese people are devious."

What would you know about Ranganese people? Misaki wanted to snap. *You've never met one*, but she held in her anger. A woman didn't speak to her husband that way.

"I don't think those were her intentions—" Misaki began evenly, only to have Takeru cut her off again.

"I don't want to hear any more of what you think!" His voice rose in a rare moment of anger. "Clearly, you don't understand the first thing about what is coming out of your mouth. It doesn't matter whether this Ranganese woman is lying or telling the truth. To flee when our country needs us would be treason, and you will not say another word about it. We are the Sword of Kaigen. If we've let it rust, then we deserve to die on it, along with our enemies."

"Including your sons?" Misaki demanded. "Your little

children?"

"Yes," Takeru said without irony or hesitation. "Who do you think you married?"

Misaki's fists clenched. Now was the time to apologize to her husband and ask for his forgiveness. Now was the time to look down in deference and shame. Instead, she stood and looked up, directly into Takeru's eyes. In a breath, the rage of fifteen years filled her chest, lifting her chin and pulling her shoulders back.

"I'm taking the boys."

"Excuse me?"

"I'm taking my sons and going away—to Ishihama to visit my parents," she decided as the words were coming out of her mouth.

"Don't be ridiculous. Your parents no longer have a house to visit. If anything, they should be coming to stay with us—"

"You can come with us if you like," Misaki said, "but I'm taking them."

"Misaki." Takeru took a step forward, staring down his wife with a glare that had made hardened men tremble. "That is not your decision to make."

Unintimidated, Misaki held his gaze. It had been too long since she had had the courage to fight for something. If she couldn't fight for her own children, then who was she? What had she become?

"You can try to stop me," she said and headed for the door.

"Misaki—" Takeru grabbed her arm. She made herself water and slid through his fingers before his iron grip had a chance to tighten.

Ducking under his arm, she darted for the door, but he was faster. Misaki knew the moment his bruising grip closed around her wrist that she wouldn't be able to twist free, but she wasn't out of defenses.

Moving on reflex, she focused all her jiya into her free hand and drove her first two fingers into Takeru's arm.

Outside the myth of the Blood Puppeteers, it was impossible for a jijaka to control a significant amount of the blood inside another person's body. Nowhere was a theonite's nyama more powerful than in their own veins. But what Tsusanos had learned centuries ago was that a minuscule amount of blood, manipulated with pinpoint accuracy, could be the deadliest weapon of all.

Misaki's power narrowed to a needlepoint. Takeru's strong body and even stronger jiya made him difficult to penetrate, but Misaki managed it. For a split dinma, his blood became her needle, striking a pressure point deep inside his arm. Takeru's arm jerked, stiffening for a moment, before going absolutely limp.

His hand slid from her wrist, and Misaki almost wished she could stand there and relish the look of utter shock on his face.

"Was that—?"

"Blood Needle," she said with a breathless smile. More specifically, it was a combination of the traditional Tsusano Blood Needle and the medical acupuncture she had learned from Ya-li. "Your arm will work again in five siiranu—four if you relax." She crossed to the door.

"Misaki," Takeru's voice was pure ice. "You—"

"Oh, and I wouldn't use my jiya during that time if I were you," she added. "Not unless you want to risk permanent damage to the muscles in that precious sword arm."

"You will regret—"

Before he could finish, Misaki slammed the door and sealed it shut with a thick layer of ice. The part about not using his jiya had been a spur-of-the-moment lie—the kind she had always been good at. Whether Takeru called her bluff and freed himself with his jiya, kicked down the door, or waited the four siiranu for the effects of her Blood Needle to wear off, Misaki had only moments.

Hiking up her kimono, she sprinted down the hall. Pausing at the boys' bedroom, she took Izumo from his cradle. The sudden movement mixed with his mother's frenzied jiya woke him and he started crying, but Misaki had no time to worry about that.

"Yosh, yosh, Izu-kun. It's alright, it's alright," she chanted as much to herself as to her baby as she ran to the family room. "Kaa-chan is going to make this all alright."

"Kaa-chan!" Mamoru exclaimed when Misaki burst into the

family room, visibly shaken, her jiya radiating panic. "Are you—"

"Help your brothers get their coats on," Misaki said. "We're leaving."

"We're what?" Mamoru said blankly. "Kaa-chan—"

"Chul-hee-kun," Misaki addressed the northern boy, who was still kneeling at the study table opposite Mamoru. "You're going to want to run home, get your father, and get off this mountain."

"Matsuda-dono, what is this? Did you hear something—"

"There will be time for you to ask questions later," she said— and Gods, she hoped it was the truth— "Right now just do as I say!"

Setsuko appeared at the door. "What's going on?"

"You too, Setsuko. Get Ayumi and let's go."

"What?"

"There's no time to explain," Misaki said, finagling Izumo into his coat and handing him off to a confused Mamoru. "We just have to get out of here, off of this mountain."

"What? And go where?"

"I don't know—your parents' house," Misaki said as the thought occurred to her. "We'll stop there first." The fishing family would give them shelter if they needed it, and Misaki was sure Setsuko wouldn't be willing to flee Kusanagi without them.

"Why?" Setsuko demanded. "Are we in danger?"

"Sort of—yes." The answer was yes. Misaki just didn't mention that the most immediate danger was from her own husband.

"Well, I can't leave without Takashi," Setsuko protested. "He isn't home yet."

"He's fast," Misaki said. "He'll be able to follow us if he needs to. With the little ones, we're slow. We need to leave here now!"

Misaki had never seen Setsuko look so scared.

"A-alright," she said, "but what about your husband? Where is Takeru?"

"He'll be along in a siira."

If Misaki had truly wanted to buy herself the time to escape with the children, she should have done more to incapacitate her husband. During his moment of surprise, she should have tried to take out his knees or render him unconscious with a blow to the temple. But she wasn't at the point where she was willing to commit outright violence against her husband... was she?

Was she?

Now that she considered the situation, Takeru was certain to follow them. He was certain to be furious. It was unlikely that Misaki would be able to talk him over to her side after she had so openly defied him. Inevitably, he would catch up to them. He would try to force them back. Then, would she hurt him? Would she fight him in earnest? Out of that train of thought rose a darker question: would it even make a difference?

Misaki had fought her fair share of terrifying theonites, but Takeru was more powerful than any of them. Should she go back and properly disable him now? This might be her only chance— now, while he didn't have the use of his right arm and might hesitate to use his jiya.

"Kaa-chan," Mamoru's voice shook her from her thoughts. "Hiro-kun and Naga-kun are in their coats. Chul-hee says he won't leave until someone explains something to him. What should I do now?"

"Mamoru..." Misaki said, turning slowly to stare at her son.

In all her anxiety about Takeru coming after them, she hadn't considered that in any of those scenarios, Mamoru would be there too... Mamoru, who was powerful enough in his own right to tip the scales in either direction. Factoring in everyone's level of skill, power, and experience, it was very likely that the confrontation would come down to whichever parent Mamoru sided with.

But that couldn't happen.

Not to Mamoru who was earnest, and loyal, and cared about both his parents. No child should have to make that choice. But the reality was that if Misaki and Takeru engaged in combat right in front of him, he would have to choose. If she fled with the boys now, knowing Takeru would follow, she would be condemning Mamoru to the sin of raising his sword to one of his parents.

She couldn't do that to him.

Her decision was made.

"Mamoru."

"Yes, Kaa-chan?"

"Those ice sleds you make for Nagasa and Ryota—can you make one big enough to hold your aunt and all four little ones?"

"Um… sure. I think so."

"Good. You're going to make that sled, get everyone into it, and take it down the mountain as fast as you can without crashing."

"What—now?"

"Yes, now. Go!"

"Wh-what about you, Kaa-chan?"

"I won't be far behind you." Squaring her shoulders, Misaki turned back toward the hall. "There's just one more thing I need to take care of."

Before Mamoru could protest, she was off down the hall, her resolve hardened to ice.

She had to go for Takeru's head, she decided. He wasn't like the enemies she'd dealt with in the past, who could be disabled by a single severed tendon or well-placed blow to the knee. His nyama ran so deep that he could move water with only his mind. A Takeru with all his limbs shattered was still dangerous. A Takeru who could *twitch* was still dangerous.

Her heart rate picked up as her mind raced to map out every possible reaction he might have, any attack he might launch, and how she might counter it.

She turned the last corner—and found her path blocked.

"Nii-sama!"

She had been so wrapped up in her own anxiety that she hadn't even sensed the swirl of Takashi's nyama entering the compound.

"Misaki, what on Duna is going on here?" Takashi demanded. "Why is my brother's study door frozen shut? Why is everyone in a panic?"

Misaki's ice broke into disarray. Her heart threatened to beat out of her chest. Takashi was here. Takashi was here. That changed everything. If her chances against one master Matsuda were slim, her chances against two were infinitesimal.

"What is going on?" Takashi repeated more insistently.

Misaki's jiya seethed inside her, knowing it had to leap into action, unsure which way to go.

"I…" Misaki's head spun. The words wouldn't come.

"Your jiya is behaving strangely, little sister," Takashi said, his brow creasing in concern. "Are you alright?" He reached out to her.

If she struck at him now, before he had a chance to anticipate it—but, no. If she raised a hand to Takashi, Setsuko would never forgive her, let alone follow her to safety. And she couldn't go without Setsuko…

"Answer me, Misaki."

Misaki opened her mouth, but before she could lie, there was a crash.

Takeru's study door exploded, flinging pieces of broken wood and ice in all directions.

"What was that?" a voice said, and Mamoru raced into the hallway, Setsuko and Chul-hee close behind him. "Kaa-chan, are you…"

But all voices fell silent as Takeru appeared in the study doorway. The force of his anger was so heavy that no one could speak or even breathe beneath it. He took a step into the hallway, and everyone stepped back—everyone except Misaki, who had lost the ability to move.

Takeru's right arm still hung motionless at his side, but he didn't need it to hold Misaki down. His gaze pinned where she stood, like a blade through the gut. His voice could have frozen the sun when he spoke.

"Misaki…"

And with those three syllables, she was certain for the first time that her husband could feel an emotion. He could hate.

She waited, rigid, for Takeru's glare to turn to physical ice and end her life. Unable to look him in the face, she closed her eyes.

She knew the sound of a sword piercing a human body. She knew the deathly cold of the Whispering Blade. She knew what it was like to bear that ice inside her. She was ready...

But the next sound to hit her ears was not the sickly crunch of ice through bone. It was the tolling of a bell. The next thing she felt was not hard ice through her abdomen, but the tender touch of breeze on her cheek. Faint. So faint, but distinctly alive. And in a moment Misaki's jiya, Takeru's, Takashi's, and Mamoru's were all swept away by something foreign—something lighter and faster, but every bit as powerful.

Misaki's eyes snapped open to a new and terrifying clarity. The world reoriented. Dread expanded like a dilating pupil as the threat shifted from the two Matsuda men to something so much bigger, so much worse...

Takeru's gaze released her as his attention turned to the unexpected sound. "Is that the temple bell?"

"That's what it sounds like," Setsuko said, her head cocked to the side.

"Why are the finawu ringing it now?" Mamoru asked. "Is there a storm?"

"There must be," Takashi said. "The news has been warning us about storms hitting the coast."

"That's not a coastal storm, Headmaster." Kwang Chul-hee spoke the realization Misaki was too frozen to voice. "That's fonya."

"Kwang-kun," Takashi began in exasperation, but whatever reassuring thing he had meant to say was swallowed by a sound unlike anything any of them had heard before, a roar—not quite animal, nor human, nor divine, but some shuddering thing in between.

The sound shook the mountain, rattling the floorboards beneath their feet. The fina's bell, meant to toll steadily through the ages, quickened, faltered, and drowned in a howl so savage and hollow it might have been the yawning mouth of the Laaxara itself.

Misaki knew for certain when the wind raked her skin that Ya-li's letter had come too late.

"They're here."

12

THE RANGANESE

Misaki's world tilted. It was a strange lurch—shifting from the thought that she might die to the realization that they were *all* going to die. Siiranu ago, she had turned her Blood Needle on her husband, she had been ready to raise her jiya to her brother-in-law, and Takeru had looked at her with murder in his gaze. But the moment the wind hit the house, the world tipped like the deck of a ship, pitching them all in the same direction.

In the midst of groaning wood and foreign nyama, Mamoru was the first one to find his feet. Turning, he raced down the hall toward the front deck. Misaki followed, Takeru and Takashi close behind her—fighters who had been dinamu from turning their blades on each other, all running the same way. Because suddenly, none of their quarrels mattered. None of it would ever matter if they were dead.

When Mamoru threw the door open, biting wind burst in on them.

"Oh!" he exclaimed, seemingly remembering that he had an infant in one arm when Izumo started to cry. "Sorry, Izu-kun!" Hastily, he wrapped the baby in his sleeves, shielding him from the wind.

The sky was the wrong color—not the blue twilight or misty gray native to Takayubi. This was foreign darkness, dingy like rust, veined with day-old blood.

"Give the little one to your mother, Mamoru-kun," Takashi said as he and the rest of the family came out onto the deck.

"Yes, Uncle," Mamoru said and carefully handed his wailing brother to Misaki.

She patted Izumo on the back in a weak attempt to comfort him, but her eyes were on the horizon. Out at sea, a universe away, Misaki could make out a sliver of sunlit sky, but the window was fast disappearing behind a wall of clouds. As the storm front loomed closer, the wind picked up, causing the beams of Kumono Academy to bend and whine so loudly the sound echoed across the mountain. The usually placid Kumono Lake writhed with waves, and further down the mountain, the pines around the western village whipped spinelessly as if they were blades of grass.

Nagasa toddled out onto the deck, only to be knocked off his feet by the wind.

"Careful!" Mamoru exclaimed, picking up his crying brother and nudging him back into the house.

Hiroshi was smart enough not to walk directly into the wind as Nagasa had but stayed at the threshold, gripping the doorframe for balance, his unnervingly intent stare fixed on the gathering clouds.

"Setsuko, Misaki, get the children inside," Takashi said. "Shut all the doors and windows."

Shut all the doors and windows. Misaki could have let out a hysterical laugh. *What good is that going to do?*

"Look!" Chul-hee exclaimed, pointing down the mountain.

"What in Nami's name is that?" Setsuko cried.

The darkest of the clouds were massing just offshore, near the fishing village at the base of the mountain. Misaki realized what she was seeing before she was ready to believe it...

Chul-hee seemed to be having a similar thought. "No..." he said under his breath. "There's no way..."

At Daybreak, it had been common knowledge that wind funnels could not be taken into battle. No solitary fonyaka was powerful enough to generate one, and no team was coordinated enough to control one they had started. Many skilled fonyakalu—including some of Misaki's fellow students—had been injured or killed attempting to weaponize wind funnels. And those had been small funnels, no bigger than a dozen bounds across.

Judging by the way the cloud cluster dwarfed the fishing village below, this was something far bigger.

"They're not..." Chul-hee's voice had taken on a note of horror. "They're *not.*"

Yet, before their disbelieving eyes, the clouds swirled together and formed a funnel above the shore. Even though Misaki knew it was human fonya, even though she did not believe in sky gods, it looked for all the world like the dark finger of a god, extending earthward.

"No," Setsuko said as she realized what was happening. "Wait! They can't!"

The attack was strategically placed, Misaki realized. The fonyakalu had formed their storm system out at sea where it wouldn't draw immediate attention, but the tornado was only going to touch down now that they had reached dry land. That way, they avoided bringing seawater ashore and giving their enemies more to fight with—as if the poor coastal fishermen would have stood a chance either way.

"No!" Setsuko screamed as the roaring column descended on her family's village. "Wait! Wait!"

Ignoring her cries, the sky god rumbled and put its fingertip to the shore.

They were too high up to see the houses break into splinters or hear the screams of the fishermen inside them. But Misaki felt it. The death of a single theonite could cause a disturbance in the atmosphere. The deaths of so many—all in the same moment—hit her like a physical blow. Normally, she couldn't sense nyama at such a distance, but the snow acted like spinal fluid, shooting the agony up the rocky backbone of Takayubi. She felt it shudder, like a sob, in her veins before dropping into silence. Dozens of pulses. Gone. In a single beat of her own heart.

Misaki had not known her sister-in-law could make such a sound.

"Setsuko—" Takashi started, his own voice strained. As he reached for his wife, she lurched forward, into the wind, as if to run down the mountain. "Setsuko, wait!" He caught her before she could lunge off the edge of the deck and held her tight.

She shook in his arms. Her jiya, usually as light as shallow waves bubbling over sand, could have churned blood. Takashi held her tight. His eyes were squeezed shut like he could feel every drop of her pain, like he could take it all into his own chest if he only willed it hard enough.

"Don't look." He placed a hand on his wife's head, wrapping his nyama around her like a blanket as the last of the houses below were consumed by the wind.

He made his power a solid wall, shielding Setsuko from the tremors of destruction, but she didn't stop shaking. Burying her face in Takashi's chest, she screamed. A shrill, raw sound made of more than just grief. Made of rage. Takashi bent his head and spoke soft words into her hair before turning to the others.

"Misaki, take her inside. It isn't safe out here. Takeru-kun…" He looked to his brother. "We have some Ranganese to kill. You too, Mamoru-kun. Let's go."

Misaki's blood seemed to still in her veins.

No.

Not Mamoru. Not Mamoru.

She opened her mouth to raise an objection—he's too young, or he should stay here and protect his brothers—but she abruptly found her arms full of a sobbing Setsuko. Shifting Izumo to one hip, she found her sister-in-law's shaking hand, held it tight, and guided her inside. They were barely through the door when the men swept past them.

It was customary for a Shirojima warrior to pray to his sword and his gods before battle. But there was no time for ritual. Takashi barely paused to bow at the dojo threshold before racing to the weapons rack and grabbing two swords in each hand—Nagimaru and Kyougetsu in his right hand, Namimaru and Mamoru's sword in his left. Turning, he tossed his brother and nephew their katana.

Nobody seemed to notice that Takeru caught his Moon Spire with his left hand. He held the pearly sheath still at his side while Takashi and Mamoru hurried to tie their swords in place. The fingers of his right hand were twitching. They would be in working condition soon, but he evidently didn't trust them to tie a knot yet.

Mamoru's hands moved fast, almost manically so, driven by an energy Misaki recognized. She used to feel it too—a cocktail of adrenaline, determination, and fighter's madness that could drown out fear and better judgment—whenever she gambled her life against an enemy who outclassed her. Maybe she would have felt that same rush now if she were the only one in danger. But that was her son. That was her son, who was bright, and growing, and a better koro than she had ever been. His life was too precious to gamble.

"Mamoru…" she started, but everyone's attention was on Takashi, as the Matsuda patriarch tied his wakizashi in place alongside his katana and turned to give his commands.

While the mayor was the official head of the village, the Matsuda patriarch was the closest thing Takayubi had to a military commander. Not just Mamoru and Takeru—every fighter on the mountain would answer to Takashi before anyone else. It was the way their people had done things since long before Jungsan had ever sent bureaucrats to oversee them.

"That tornado can't come up the mountain," Takashi was saying. It was a reasonable assumption; naturally occurring tornadoes were characteristic of western Ranganese desert country and flat Abirian plains, not rocky Kaigenese coast. "As soon as it reaches the base of the mountain, the uneven terrain will break it apart. Whoever is making it will have to touch down on solid ground, and we'll be there to meet them."

"I don't know about that, Headmaster," Chul-hee said.

"Kwang-kun, this isn't the time for your weird—"

"He's right, Nii-sama," Misaki interjected. "That thing outside is not a natural wind funnel." She couldn't fathom the amount of precision and teamwork it must take to not only generate a tornado that size but then control it. This was no gaggle of mercenaries or ill-trained peasants' sons on their doorstep; it was a highly organized military unit. "An army of fonyakalu strong enough to manipulate that much wind is strong enough to bring it up a mountain." There was no doubt in her mind. "That tornado will be at the village gates in siiranu."

"Even better," Takashi said and Misaki was mildly horrified to find him smiling.

"What?"

"Saves us the trouble of taking the fight to them." Takashi turned to face Takeru and Mamoru, looking more alive than Misaki had ever seen him. "These Ranganese dare to attack my wife's people, our fishermen, on our coast. They dare to mock the gods of our ocean. Let's show them the real power of gods. And you, city kid." He pointed to Chul-hee.

"People are still calling me that?"

"You have that thing Takeru and Mamoru keep talking about—that little telephone rectangle?"

"Yes, Headmaster," Chul-hee said, pulling the info-com device out of his pocket.

"Can you use it to call the government?"

"Um—not from here. So far, the towers we set up are only working further up the mountain."

"Then you'd better get up there now," Misaki said. "Assuming the wind doesn't take out the towers, that rectangle may be the fastest way for us to let the Emperor know that this is happening."

She didn't trust the Kaigenese government by any stretch of the imagination, but right now, they were Takayubi's only chance at reinforcements.

"Head up the mountain," Takashi said, "and take this." He took a spare wakizashi from the rack and tossed the sheathed weapon to Chul-hee, who just managed to catch it. "In case you run into trouble."

"I get a girl sword?"

Takashi snorted. "I've seen you fight, Kwang-kun. Our full-sized katana are too much for you."

"Ah." Chul-hee glanced from Mamoru's sword to Takeru's even bigger Moon Spire. "Touché. But if we need someone to get to the towers as fast as possible, should I really be the one? I mean—isn't Mamoru faster?"

"Mamoru is much faster," Takashi agreed. "He is also a Matsuda. He was made to face the enemy, not run the other way."

"Face the enemy?" Chul-hee said incredulously. "I don't know if you noticed, Headmaster, but the enemy is a tornado. What are you going to do?"

"Kill it," Takashi said. "Now, go!"

"Right." Chul-hee's tone was casual, but he was clutching the wakizashi's sheath so tightly that his knuckles had turned white. "It was good to… I-I'm glad to have met all of you." His eyes met Mamoru's for a moment before he ducked his head in a deep bow. "Thank you for everything. And don't worry." He straightened up. "I'll get you those reinforcements. Just hold on." Turning, he ran from the house, calling back to the Matsudas. "Hold on!"

When Chul-hee was gone, Takashi turned to hold Setsuko one last time.

Tenderly, he touched her face. "No more tears, my love. Your parents and brothers and sisters are about to rest so peacefully. I'm going to send them off with the butchered corpses of all their enemies."

Setsuko nodded with a savagery Misaki had never seen in her eyes. "Do it," she whispered.

"I'm going to throw so many Ranganese souls at their feet that they'll be able to walk over them like a bridge into the Laaxara. Don't fret, sweetheart," he added to Ayumi, crying in Setsuko's arms. "Your father is going to protect you."

And they were moving. They were leaving. Misaki felt the world slipping through her fingers.

"Wait!"

"We don't have time, Misaki," Takashi said.

She ignored him and grabbed Mamoru's arm. *Stay!* She wanted to beg. *Stay where I can protect you!* But that was a ridiculous thought. Mamoru was a strong fighter. If he couldn't protect himself, she was hardly going to be any help.

"Pay attention to your distance," she said instead. "Fonyakalu are most dangerous at mid-range—two to three bounds. That's where their attacks land the hardest. Stay well back or in close, with your sword. Don't linger in their mid-range striking zone."

Despite his uncle's impatience, Mamoru was listening intently. "Yes, Kaa-chan."

"And look at the color of their uniforms," Misaki added. "Rank and file Ranganese troops wear yellow. Their elite fighters wear black. If you see yellow, you stand a chance. If you see black, I want you to run."

"Kaa-chan, you know I can't do that."

"But…" *I want you to* wasn't a good reason.

"Kaa-chan." Mamoru held her shoulders in a firm grip—and when had his hands gotten so big and strong? "I'm a Matsuda. Wasn't I born to do this?"

The answer was yes. This was the reason she had left everything she loved to marry into this family, the reason she had endured her father-in-law's abuse, and her husband's indifference all these years, so that the Matsuda family would have a powerful heir, so Kusanagi would have its blade edge.

This was as much purpose as any of their lives had ever had, and now was the moment Mamoru was supposed to live up to that purpose—to give all of it meaning. She couldn't take that from him.

So, all she said was, "Yes." Her heart overflowing with pain, she squeezed her son's arms. "Yes, my son. I'm proud of you."

"I'm not sure I'm worthy of your pride," Mamoru said with a smile, "but I will be. Just wait."

Mamoru broke away from her, but Misaki found her legs carrying her after her son and husband, her hands reaching out, not ready to let go, not ready… There had to be something else, some way she could save them. She was the only one who had ever encountered fonyakalu. She had spent years watching them, training with them. She knew the theory behind wind funnels, even if she had never seen one successfully mastered. There had to be something in her memory…

Think, Misaki. Think!

"Don't try to attack the wind itself," she said, catching Mamoru's sleeve. "It's stronger than any individual theonite."

"Misaki," Takashi said. "We really don't have time for this. Say your goodbyes–"

"No!" Misaki growled, past caring about propriety. "Listen!" She had never heard of anyone stopping a tornado once it got going. If anyone was going to do it, it would be these men, but only if they had a working understanding of what they were facing.

"These wind funnels are created by two-part teams. One group keeps cool air circulating around the outside while the other forces warm air into the center to feed the updraft."

Takashi was looking at her in confusion. "How would you know—"

"You're not going to stop the tornado by taking out the fonyakalu on the outside," Misaki continued. "All they're doing is streamlining wind that's already moving. The updraft is what powers the cyclone. The strongest fonyakalu will be there, inside the funnel, forcing that hot air upward. If you want to stop the tornado, they're the ones you have to take out. You'll have to find them, inside the wind."

"Alright…" Mamoru said, but she could see on his face that he wasn't following.

"Wind is faster than blood or water—more sporadic—but you can still pick out the bodies in it, like little fish in a stream—"

"That's enough," Takashi said, pulling Mamoru away, out of her grasp. "We have to move."

Desperate, Misaki shouted out the last thing she could think of. "Takeru-sama!"

Her husband didn't turn. She had no right to expect him to listen, no right to speak to him at all—but he was her last chance to save her son.

"It has vital points, like the human body… Like your arm."

Mamoru looked back at her in utter confusion. "What—"

"Come," Takeru grabbed the front of Mamoru's kimono in his left hand and hauled him out the door. "Your mother is talking nonsense."

MAMORU

Mamoru moved without thinking. His body knew what to do. Every man and boy knew what to do once the alarm bell sounded, the same thing their forefathers had done during the Keleba: the men of the old village would converge at the gates, then head down the mountain to join forces with the fighters from the western village. As the Matsudas sprinted toward the village gates, Yukino Sensei fell into step beside them, along with his older cousins and the fighters of the Mizumaki house. As one, they raced down the mountain to meet their enemies.

This scene had played a thousand times in Mamoru's daydreams in class, on the dark ceiling before he fell asleep, and in his dreams after… since he was old enough to dream at all. He had spent his whole life preparing for this moment, fearing it, hoping for it. But even as his legs carried him down the mountain, he couldn't quite believe that it was real.

The copper-colored sky tinted the whole village, making the familiar houses seem alien and far away. The deafening sound, like a thousand fighter jets, felt like it could tear the boundary between this world and the next. Even Mamoru's own flesh didn't seem quite real. The wind made his body by turns slower and lighter than it should have been. It roared across his skin, making it numb and tingly, more like the skin of a spirit, as if his body belonged to that grown warrior from his dreams—far away, far in the future, on that day that might never come…

"I need numbers, Takeru-kun!" Uncle Takashi shouted over the wind as they ran. "How many men of fighting age do we have between this village and the western one?"

"Two hundred and four," Tou-sama said without missing a beat.

"Ha!" Uncle Takashi let out a laugh. "More than enough!"

But the sight that greeted them at the edge of the village caused them to pull up short, tabi skidding to a stop in the snow. The smile disappeared from Uncle Takashi's face.

He swore under his breath and turned to Tou-sama. "Your wife was right. The damn thing is coming up the mountain!"

Not only that; the tornado was advancing faster than Mamoru had ever seen any theonite move over land. It had already swallowed the forests on the lower slopes. In moments, it would be at the edge of the western village.

"We have to get down there, Matsuda-dono!" one of the Mizumaki men cried. "Now!"

But not all the men were assembled yet, and it was already too late.

"No!" Mamoru made to run toward the western village before it was gone, only to be jerked back.

Yukino Sensei had a handful of the back of his kimono.

"Wait for orders," the swordmaster said.

"But we have to help them!" Mamoru's upsurge of adrenaline mixed with a keening strain of pain as the wind reached the lowest houses. "Itsuki-kun is down there! Yuuta-kun! Your family—"

"We can't do anything to help them now." Yukino Sensei pulled him back, and for a moment, Mamoru felt an unbearable pang of the swordmaster's pain. But it was only a moment. Yukino Sensei had enough control to keep his emotions under the surface. "The only thing we can do now is avenge them."

Yukino Sensei was right, of course. Even sprinting, unimpeded, down the mountain, they would never reach their sister village in time. All the men of the old village could do was watch as the majority of Takayubi's population was ripped from the side of the mountain. Mamoru tried to power down his jiya, to feel as little as possible, but the adrenaline in his veins wouldn't allow it. He couldn't shut out the death any more than he could look away from the destruction.

The koronu fought. Even at a distance, Mamoru felt their jiya gnash like teeth against the wind. Spikes of ice jutted into view between the buildings before falling to pieces, along with everything else. But of course, it wasn't just those who fought who died. Mothers and children were torn from their homes and dashed against the rocks. The temple where Mamoru had prayed every holiday and learned the names of his gods burst apart, clay roof tiles scattering into nothing.

Even though the wind felt like nyama, Mamoru couldn't believe that it was human. What human with a soul of nyama could kill koronu and non-combatants in the same breath? This was the work of demons.

As the agony receded, Mamoru realized that Yukino Sensei had never let go of him.

It wasn't just Yuuta and Yukino Sensei's other cousins who had disappeared in that wind. Almost all of Yukino Sensei's students came to Kumono from the western village. Mamoru was the only one left. Around them, other men cried out in rage. Some shed tears. Some fell to their knees. Yukino Sensei didn't buckle or cry. He didn't scream the way Setsuko had. He stood perfectly still, his shoulders back, his eyes fixed ahead, but somehow, he had never seemed so fragile. It was as though he had turned himself to ice. If he moved, it would crack.

"Sensei…" Mamoru started, his own voice shaking, but he didn't know what he could say. He blinked and felt tears slide down his cheeks. He had grown up with the boys from the western village, and he felt their loss like a hole in his chest. But Yukino Sensei was their teacher. He had devoted years of his life to nurturing them, pushing them, and watching them grow. They were his pride. To have all of that vanish in a moment… Mamoru could only imagine how it must feel.

"Takeru-kun…" Uncle Takashi's voice had sobered, "numbers. Who do we have left? How many from each family?"

"Ikeno: twelve, Katakouri: nine, counting the thirteen-year-old and the cripple, Ginkawa: nine, counting the twelve-year-old, Ameno: six, Mizumaki: five, Yukino: four, and Matsuda…" Tou-sama looked from his son to his brother, "just the three of us."

"So, how many in total?"

"Forty-eight, Nii-sama."

"Good." Uncle Takashi turned to face the assembled men. Despite the destruction they had just witnessed, not one had turned back. "Ameno, Ikeno, Ginkawa, to the northern pass! Form a line—two deep, Ameno and Ginkawa up front, Ikeno behind! Katakouri, keep watch on the cliff. Shoot down any fonyaka who tries to scale the rocks."

Uncle Takashi's voice—as loud as it was—couldn't carry to all the men over the wind, but in moments, fighters were repeating his orders across the group.

"Wait…" Mamoru said as the Ameno, Ginkawa, and Ikeno swordsmen, and the Katakouri archers raced to follow orders. "Who's going to guard the southern pass?"

The southern pass was the wider of the two avenues up the mountain, and Uncle Takashi had just sent more than two thirds of their fighting force in the other direction.

"We are," Uncle Takashi said. "Yukino, Mizumaki, with me!" he called and the eleven remaining fighters followed him down the slope toward the southern pass.

Mamoru had walked this path almost every day of his life. It was the path that he took every time he visited the Kotetsus in the blacksmith village, every time he met up with Yuuta and Itsuki before they headed up to Kumono Academy. Yet it looked unfamiliar now, stained with the rust-colored light of the storm. Snow and dust thrashed like fitful ghosts, like the Laaxara rising to snatch at the fighters as they raced to face their enemies.

"Hyousuke!" Uncle Takashi called to the nearest Mizumaki as

they passed the numu village. "Go tell the blacksmiths to stay inside their houses with the doors closed!"

The man nodded and split from the rest of the group.

Uncle Takashi called the men to a stop at the narrowest point in the pass. With a sweep of his arm, he cut a straight line through the snow extending from the jagged rocks to their right, to the base of the slope leading up to Kumono Academy on their left.

"We hold them here!" he bellowed. "No fonyaka crosses this line!"

The line he had drawn looked to be at least thirty bounds long. Mamoru imagined that a general who hoped to defend such an area would have sent in fifty-some soldiers.

There were twelve of them.

The men automatically arranged themselves by skill, with the younger Mizumakis placing themselves on the more defensible edges, and the powerful Yukinos covering the open ground near the middle of the pass, where the Ranganese were most likely to break through. Realizing that he had lined up in between his uncle and Yukino Sensei, Mamoru stepped back, thinking he should cede his position to a more experienced fighter.

"Stay where you are, Mamoru-kun." Yukino Sensei's voice was firm but gentle. "You're a Matsuda, aren't you?"

Swallowing, Mamoru nodded. He felt a hand clap onto his shoulder and turned to find his uncle smiling at him.

"It looks like you won't have to see rust, after all, nephew." Uncle Takashi squeezed his shoulder and Mamoru felt a disorienting jolt of pure elation. His uncle wasn't just smiling to raise the spirits of the other men. He was excited.

The mountain shook beneath their feet as Uncle Takashi took up his position between his brother and nephew. The tornado had consumed all of the western village and the surrounding forest without slowing down and was now no more than a hundred bounds from where they stood—twelve men against a towering column of wind.

"We hold this line!" Uncle Takashi boomed.

"We hold this line!" the other fighters echoed, matching his ferocity.

"We are the Sword of Kaigen!"

"We are the Sword of Kaigen!"

"We hold this line!"

The wind rose as if in response to their voices, trying to deafen them and rip the skin from their bones. But the men of Takayubi stood strong, rooting their feet in the snow.

"Fire at will!" Uncle Takashi roared into the wind.

Mamoru raised his jiya and tried to form a spear, but it was difficult with the wind trying to tear the snow from his grasp. And even if he could form a proper projectile, what was he supposed to fire at? They faced a solid wall of wind. It was impossible to discern anything through the whirl of snow.

Yukino Sensei was the first to take a shot. Raising a bound-long spear from the snow, he launched three spears—one after another—with all his strength and precision.

As far as Mamoru could tell, all the projectiles did was disappear into the vortex, but when he looked back toward his teacher, Yukino was smiling.

"I hit something."

"You did?"

"Yes." Yukino Sensei flexed his calloused fingers and raised another ice spear from the snow. "Just not hard enough to do damage. It's difficult to sense the target and attack at the same time. I could use a bit of Matsuda power."

"What?"

Yukino Sensei made a sweeping movement with his hands, positioning the spear so that it hovered in front of Mamoru.

"Running start, Mamoru. Then spin."

It took Mamoru a moment to catch on. Then he smiled in understanding. "Yes, Sensei!" He backed up, counting his steps. Then he ran at the ice spike.

Launching off the snowy ground, he spun in the air, and slammed the heel of his hand into the projectile, channeling all his jiya through his arm. At the last moment, he felt Yukino Sensei's jiya join his own in an unbelievable burst of power. His teacher's more controlled jiya entwined with his, guiding the spear through the wind to its target. Mamoru started as he felt it make contact with something solid.

Yukino Sensei's senses were so sharp that he could detect the bodies through the swirling snow, just like Kaa-chan had said—like fish in a stream.

"Again!" Yukino Sensei shouted before Mamoru could stand and marvel any longer.

"Yes, Sensei!"

Mamoru had practiced his spinning launch in the months since Yukino Sensei had told him how to perfect it. His aim still had room for improvement, but he could fire projectiles at full power for a waati without tiring.

All along the line, other jijakalu had replicated their technique, forming pairs to fire projectiles into the whirlwind. Only Tou-sama and Uncle Takashi were powerful enough to line up and launch their attacks without assistance. In a siira, a steady barrage of well-aimed ice was raining into the oncoming tornado.

Mamoru could tell that they were hitting bodies. Even if he was relying entirely on Yukino Sensei's superior aim, his jiya still picked up the vague sensation of ice thudding into flesh—over and over again. They were felling fonyakalu, but somehow, the wind wasn't slowing.

At a hand signal from Uncle Takashi, Tou-sama, Yukino Sensei, the most senior Mizumakis, and Mamoru all gathered to him. Even right up close, it was hard to hear anyone's voice over the roar of the wind.

"We're hitting fonyakalu," Uncle Takashi said. "Why isn't it stopping?"

"They must have replacements," Yukino Sensei said. "As soon as one soldier drops, another takes his place."

"What do we do?" Mizumaki Hyousuke asked.

"We need to get rid of the ones who can't be replaced," Tou-sama said. "We need to destroy the source of the funnel's power."

"How?" asked Hyousuke's older brother, Toki.

Tou-sama's murmur was so quiet that Mamoru almost didn't hear it over the wind. "Needles."

"You mean spears, Matsuda-dono?" Toki said. "That's what we've been trying! The wind is too strong! We're hardly getting through the wind surrounding the funnel."

"Mizumaki-san is right," Yukino Sensei said. "How are we supposed to pierce the center?"

"None of you can." Tou-sama was massaging his right arm, his eyes fixed on the oncoming tornado. "I'll do it."

"What?"

"Keep firing your spears," Tou-sama said. "Take out as many fonyakalu as you can." Turning his back on the tornado, he took a knee, laid his open palms on the ground, and closed his eyes. In an instant, his jiya dropped from fighting aggression to perfect calm.

"What is he doing?" Mizumaki Hyousuke demanded. "Matsuda-dono!" He reached out to touch Takeru's shoulder.

"No, wait!" Mamoru grabbed Hyousuke's sleeve, stopping him. "He's meditating."

"Meditating?" the Mizumaki said incredulously. "Prayer isn't going to do us any good now! We need him to fight!"

"Just wait," Mamoru insisted.

It took Mamoru waatinu to reach his deepest state of meditation, but in it he could sense every water drop and snowflake that moved on the mountain. If his father's legendary focus was enough to reach that state within these precious few moments, they might stand a chance.

Uncle Takashi seemed to agree. "Return to your position. Root there until the wind dies."

"Until it dies?" Hyousuke said, incredulous.

"You trust your lords, don't you, Mizumaki-san?" Yukino Sensei challenged.

Hyousuke hesitated but nodded and stepped back to return to his place alongside Toki and the other Mizumakis.

Mamoru and Yukino Sensei tried to fire more projectiles into the tornado, but the wind had grown so strong that neither jijaka could take a step without risking being swept off their feet.

Yukino Sensei shouted something that Mamoru couldn't hear through the deafening roar, but from the movement of his lips, it looked like, "Root!"

Mamoru did as he was told, raising the snow around him up to his knees and hardening it to ice, freezing himself to the side of the mountain. He could no longer hear anything. His own hair lashed his face hard enough to leave cuts.

As strong as his stance and his ice were, Mamoru realized that if he stood against the wind any longer, he would simply snap off at the shins. It took all his strength to curl his body forward and sink to his knees. Huddling into the snow, Mamoru made a protective cocoon of ice around himself. Tou-sama still had not moved—still as the mountain itself before the wind.

The funnel was almost on top of them now. Mamoru wondered what it would feel like to die by tornado. Would he be ripped from the snow like a tree from its roots and then smashed into the mountainside? Or would it be slower than that? What if he was more stubborn? If he refused to let go of the mountainside, would the wind strip the flesh from his bones? He was certain he was about to find out—

Then Tou-sama moved.

Physically, it was the tiniest of movements, a sharp twitch of his fingers. But it was as if a thread had snapped. Something changed. The wind still spun, but suddenly it had weakened, lost its otherworldly fury.

When Mamoru dared to lift his head, he found the wind funnel falling apart, dispersing into scattered shreds of cloud. Debris rained across the mountainside.

Most of the men didn't seem to understand what had happened, but Uncle Takashi turned to his brother with a smile. "Well done, Takeru-kun!"

In the snow below, Mamoru could just see two black-clad bodies lying crumpled and motionless. A moment later, a third body thudded to the ground before them, making Mamoru jump.

As Mamoru backed away from the fallen fonyaka, Uncle Takashi strode toward it. Putting a foot under the limp form he turned it over to reveal the wound that had brought the man down. The puncture itself was barely visible, but Mamoru could feel the blood seeping from the fonyaka's chest to soak into the black cloth buttons of his uniform. The man's face had been smashed beyond recognition in the fall, but his hair was still neat, pulled back into the long braid characteristic of Ranganese warriors.

Mamoru found that he couldn't take his eyes off the broken body—the flesh, and blood, and hair. No matter how long he looked, it was a man. Just a man. That wind that had darkened the sky and roared like a god... the heart of it had been human.

"Is this how you killed all of them?" Uncle Takashi asked, considering the hole in the fonyaka's chest.

"There were just the three at the center of the funnel." Tou-sama rose smoothly to his feet and straightened his hakama. "Sorry, Nii-sama. It took me a while to pinpoint their bodies all at once."

It was difficult for Mamoru to process what his father had just done. In order to lance those fonyakalu through the chest, not only did he have to track the movements of a million flecks of snow moving at unbelievable speeds—he had to take control of them. It was super-human. This was why it was said that the Matsuda veins ran with the blood of gods.

"I still don't know how you do that," Uncle Takashi said with an admiring shake of his head.

"I listen to the mountain."

"And what did the mountain tell you, little brother? Other than where to strike?"

"We are outnumbered," Tou-sama said, "twenty to one."

Mamoru stared at his father in amazement. He hadn't just killed the fonyakalu creating the updraft; while deep in that state of meditation, he had had the presence of mind to count the number of foreign bodies on the mountainside.

"Twenty to one?" Takashi scoffed. "The Ranganese are idiots if they think they can challenge us with those numbers."

"I'm not worried about numbers," Yukino Sensei said. "It all comes down to the quality of the fighters they've sent."

"Resume your positions!" Takashi called to the Yukinos and Mizumakis staggering to their feet in the surrounding snow. "This fight isn't over. We have enemies incoming!"

"I don't see that many," Mamoru said, squinting into the whiteness.

In response, Tou-sama raised a hand, lifting the fog and snow before them.

Before the ruins of the western village, stood a wall of yellow—hundreds of rank and file soldiers standing in formation. Banners unfurled, revealing the black dragon of Ranga rearing against a blood red sun. These men must have followed the tornado up the mountain, stepping over the bodies and leveled houses.

With a prickle running up his spine, Mamoru realized that the moment they could see the yellow-clad soldiers was the same moment the Ranganese could see them.

The eye contact created a beat of perfect stillness.

Then a sound rose from the Ranganese. A war cry—raw and human—that shook Mamoru more than the roar of the tornado. For the first time, his rust-colored dream hardened into reality.

The Ranganese surged up the mountain.

13

THE DRAGON

The charging Ranganese had many bounds of snow to cover, but they were moving fast.

With the roar of the tornado gone, Uncle Takashi could make his voice heard again. "Hold the line!"

Of the twelve men who had formed the line, two were nowhere to be seen—blown away in the high winds. Of those who had managed to stay anchored in the snow, only some were getting up.

"We hold the line!" Uncle Takashi bellowed again and those who could still stand repeated his call across the pass.

"We hold the line!"

Uncle Takashi seemed only vaguely annoyed by the thinning of his forces. "You three," he addressed Tou-sama, Yukino Sensei, and Mamoru. "Spread out further. Cover for those we've lost."

Four, Mamoru thought, his eyes scanning the line. We've lost four fighters. There were only eight of them now—the three Matsudas, Yukino Sensei, two of his cousins, and the two most powerful of the Mizumakis. How could eight men defend this pass against an entire army?

As if in response to Mamoru's thought, Uncle Takashi lifted both arms. With them rose a swell of nyama so powerful it shook Mamoru's body. Throwing his hands forward, Uncle Takashi sent his nyama down the mountain in a single massive wave. Pushed by his power, the snow rose to form an army of spikes, jutting upward from the ground toward the oncoming army of men.

If Tou-sama was a paragon of Matsuda precision, Uncle Takashi was the embodiment of Matsuda power. His was the only nyama Mamoru had ever known to echo the crash and pull of the ocean itself.

Uncle Takashi's spikes met the fonyakalu's front lines in an explosion of ice and flesh. It was like watching a white crest form atop a breaking wave—only this wave crested red. Blood burst from the front line as fonyakalu were impaled or cut into pieces on the spikes, but some of them evaded. At first, Mamoru didn't understand how, with Uncle Takashi's spikes covering nearly every koyin of flat ground. Somehow, they were shooting up over the forest of ice.

"They can fly?" He blurted out in a mixture of wonder and horror.

"No," Yukino Sensei said, his intelligent eyes trained on the fonyakalu's movements. "They're keeping themselves aloft by throwing their fonya against the ground."

As the soldiers drew closer, Mamoru could see that he was right. The Ranganese were not truly weightless. As each started to fall toward the spikes, he threw a palm strike or a thrusting kick at the ground, releasing a concentrated burst of wind that propelled him back into the air.

"They're like leaves..." Mamoru said. A flurry of yellow leaves, buffeted by breeze, never quite touching the ground.

"Well, they've come in the wrong season. Autumn dies in the teeth of winter." Uncle Takashi nodded to his brother. "Let's put some more red in all that yellow."

As a fonyaka toward the front of the group started to descend between two of Uncle Takashi's spikes, a third suddenly burst from the ground, impaling him through the stomach. In the next moment, three more fonyakalu tried to touch down, only to be lanced on spikes so clear and perfectly straight they could only be the product of Tou-sama's jiya.

This was how the brothers usually worked together, Uncle Takashi leading with his decisive personality and overwhelming power, Tou-sama following, filling in the gaps with his signature precision.

The brothers fell into rhythm with one another, Uncle Takashi erecting walls of spikes that caught the clumsier fonyakalu on their way down, Tou-sama sending spears up in the openings when more careful fonyakalu tried to exploit them.

Yukino Sensei took a different approach, forming and firing spears that took the enemy soldiers out of the air. Some of the other jijakalu tried to do the same, but the problem with firing at fonyaka targets was that they *moved*, using air currents to sharply change direction in midair. Yukino Sensei might be landing hits, but the Mizumakis who lacked his impeccable control weren't having as much luck. And no matter how many yellow clad soldiers they killed, the army kept advancing. For every soldier that fell to their ice, there was another right behind him. The closest of the fonyakalu were now mere bounds away—close enough to return fire.

The first blast of wind knocked one of the Mizumaki fighters off his feet. Mamoru was scanning the advancing fonyakalu, trying to figure out where the attack had come from when he suddenly found himself on his back in the snow.

It was disorienting to be hit by something he could neither see nor hear coming. If oncoming fonya made an impression in the atmosphere, it was too difficult for Mamoru to distinguish between that and the confusing swirl of air all around him. He wasn't trained to perceive it.

"Back on your feet!" Uncle Takashi's voice roared. "Don't let up!"

Rolling onto his hands and knees, Mamoru started to rise, an ice spear at the ready—only to be knocked down again by another blast of wind, this one stronger than the first—and he remembered Kaa-chan's warning: *Fonyakalu are most dangerous at mid-range—two to three bounds. That's where their attacks land the hardest.*

The closest fonyakalu were still several bounds from Mamoru and the other swordsmen. Once they got closer, their invisible wind attacks would do more than just knock men down. They would be fatal.

In a stroke of genius, someone—Tou-sama judging by the quiet effectiveness of the maneuver—lifted the snow beneath their feet, creating a veil of water particles. The jiya-made fog wasn't so thick as to obscure the view of the oncoming soldiers. Just the opposite: it brought blessed clarity.

The next time a fonyaka fired an attack, it billowed through the water molecules, creating a visible break in the veil. Seeing the wind coming, the targeted Mizumaki Hyousuke evaded and returned fire, spearing the fonyaka through the chest.

Mamoru dodged a blast of air and rallied his jiya for a counterattack, but no sooner had he formed the spear than he found himself dodging another dangerous burst of wind. Even with the snow veil lending insight into the movements of the air, it was too much. The fonyakalu were piling into their optimal striking distance too fast.

"Don't let up!" Uncle Takashi commanded again.

But with so many fonyakalu coming at them, flying over and dodging between spikes, climbing over ice formations, it was impossible to attack and defend at the same time.

Recognizing this, Uncle Takashi changed his orders. "Shield!" he called down the line. "Shield and hold your positions!"

Mamoru raised the snow before him to form a thick wall just in time. Two separate bursts of wind slammed into the other side. The ice cracked and Mamoru rushed to mend it. Bracing his hands against the shield, he gathered a layer of softer snow on the outside, hoping to cushion the impact of the next attack, but defending against wind turned out to be different from defending against blades or blunt objects. The next attack blasted the snow away, nearly shattering the ice beneath. Only the stubborn force of Mamoru's jiya kept the shield from breaking into a thousand pieces.

Ice shields cracked and shattered all down the line, but Yukino Sensei spent his days teaching and training on the Kumono ledge, one of the windiest place on the mountain. He knew how to shape a shield that stood strong before the gale.

Mamoru felt his teacher's jiya rise before him, reshaping his insufficient shield into a thick wedge designed to divert even the strongest wind.

"Good thinking, Dai," Uncle Takashi said, lifting his hand.

Combining their jiya, the two master jijakalu erected wedged shields all the way down the line, protecting their fellows.

"Stay behind the barrier!" Takashi bellowed. "Brace!"

"Brace!" the men's voices echoed his down the line. "Brace!"

It wasn't until a hand closed on the back of his kimono and Yukino Sensei repeated the order, "Brace!" that Mamoru realized he had just been standing there.

Yukino Sensei pushed him into the barrier and Mamoru put his hands against it. It was only by virtue of mechanical reflex that he managed to lock his jiya into the wall before him, lending his own strength to the ice. The explosions of wind had gotten more powerful, but with eight strong jijakalu supporting Yukino Sensei's well-designed barrier, their defense held.

It wasn't until Mamoru tried to speak that he realized that he was shaking. "N-now what?" he asked.

"We hold here and wait for the enemy," Uncle Takashi said.

"So, we're just going to let them come?" Mamoru asked blankly. "We're just going to let them past the barrier?"

"In close," Uncle Takashi said with a nod. His hand had moved to the blue-wrapped handle of his wakizashi, Namimaru. "Where we want them."

The fonyakalu were almost on top of them now. Mamoru could hear the foreign whoosh of their fonya and the crunch of their feet across the frozen ground. Taking a slow breath, he gripped the handle of his own sword. The feel of the weapon in his fingers usually lent him strength, made him calm...

The first yellow-clad soldier came flying over the barrier—
and Mamoru froze.

Moving had never been difficult for Mamoru. He was always the first to react, the first to jump into action. But suddenly, at the moment it mattered most, it was as if he wasn't Mamoru at all. Just a shell of himself, watching a muscular Ranganese soldier descend before him and charge.

Pure reflex jerked his sword out of its sheath in a slashing motion, causing the fonyaka to jump back. If he had been focused and ready, Mamoru would have easily been able to deliver a lethal cut, but he *wasn't* ready. The tip of his sword only grazed the front of the fonyaka's uniform.

As his enemy stumbled, Mamoru's conditioned hands flipped his sword over into position for an overhanded cut, but his mind couldn't finish the attack. He couldn't swing.

The moment of hesitation was all the fonyaka needed to throw a kick into Mamoru's stomach, slamming pain through his skeleton. His back hit Yukino Sensei's barrier, and his head cracked backward into the ice, spilling stars across his vision. Blinking, he tried to get into a defensive stance, but it was too late. The fonyaka was already lining up an attack, which at this distance, would certainly kill him. His head spinning, his jiya in disarray, he wouldn't be able to defend or counterattack in time.

The fonyaka raised a hand.

Then his body jerked. The curved blade of Nagimaru stuck through his chest. In another flash, the sword's shorter companion, Namimaru, cut the man's head from his shoulders.

The katana was yanked free and the two pieces of fonyaka thudded to the ground to reveal Uncle Takashi, splattered with blood, a sword in each hand, looking furious.

"What are you doing, boy?"

"S-sorry, Uncle! I—"

"If you're not going to fight properly then get out of the way!" Hooking the handle of blood-slick Nagimaru behind Mamoru's head, Uncle Takashi pulled him away from the barrier and threw him back, just as a fresh group of fonyakalu came vaulting over the wall.

Unlike the typical, right-handed Matsuda, Uncle Takashi was completely ambidextrous. With his katana, Nagimaru, in his right hand and his wakizashi, Namimaru, in his left, he cleaved through all five fonyakalu in a single spin.

As he stumbled to avoid the sudden spray of blood, Mamoru found a firm hand on his arm.

"Be my second line," Yukino Sensei said, his voice as firm and calm as ever.

"Wh-what?"

"Stand there," Yukino Sensei said, pushing him further back from the barrier. "Watch my back. Clean up if any fonyakalu get past me or my cousins."

"Y-yes, Sensei," Mamoru managed, but Yukino was already turning to face the fonyakalu, his katana drawn.

Yukino Sensei's sword was Takenagi, the Bamboo Cutter, an elegant weapon with a handle wrapped in sage green and a guard of silver bamboo leaves. It was the oldest of the Kotetsu-forged weapons still in use, passed down the Yukino line through several generations, but Mamoru couldn't imagine it suiting any wielder better than Yukino Dai. Shorter than Tou-sama's Kyougetsu and slighter than Uncle Takashi's Nagimaru, Takenagi was built for speed—like its master.

In his prime, Yukino Sensei had been one of the fastest swordsmen ever recorded. Now, at twice Mamoru's age, his speed was still unmatched among the fighters of Takayubi. His art was not in complex technique or flashy tricks; it was in perfect execution of the basics, at three times the speed of the average swordsman.

It was strange how natural Yukino Sensei looked as Takenagi sliced through the first unlucky fonyaka, painting the snow with his blood. Mamoru had sparred and drilled with this man for so many years now that he knew his movements like the steps of a dance. It was mesmerizing to watch those comfortingly familiar steps and strokes, separate heads from bodies, spill organs, and sling arcs of blood across the whiteness.

In his light gray kimono and hakama, Yukino Sensei blended in with the snow. Many fonyakalu who came in his direction probably fell to his blade without ever registering his presence. He moved efficiently on his quick feet, positioning himself so that no more than two fonyaka ever reached him at once, turning a many-on-one fight into many one-on-one fights. And one-on-one, there were few living fighters who could contend with Yukino Dai. Mamoru noted with awe that it never took the swordmaster more than a single cut to fell a soldier. No swing was wasted.

The white of the mountainside gave way to seeping red.

Despite their numbers, the fonyakalu were fighting at a deadly disadvantage. Unable to penetrate Yukino Sensei's wind-repellant barrier, they had to jump over it, landing in a dangerous position—jijakalu before them, an unbreakable wall of ice at their backs. Between the barrier and the swordsmen, the Ranganese didn't have the two-bounds of distance necessary to throw their wind attacks at full power, and they weren't prepared for a close-range fight with men of Takayubi.

Every Ranganese soldier carried what appeared to be a standard issue sword and a shorter dagger, but their steel was inferior. Their weapons broke so easily against the jijakalu's Kotetsu steel that they might as well have been fighting with sticks.

Some of them might have been able to propel themselves further up the mountain and attack the jijakalu from behind, but there was a reason Uncle Takashi had chosen this place to make a stand. The slope behind them was steep and slick with ice. Lacking jiya to give them a foothold, the few fonyakalu who tried to make the jump ended up sliding back into the danger zone, if Matsuda or Yukino ice didn't jut from the ground to spear them first. Dozens upon dozens of the yellow-clad soldiers leaped into the death trap, and the bodies began to pile up on the reddened snow.

While Yukino Sensei methodically disposed of his enemies one well-placed cut at a time, Uncle Takashi was savagely butchering fonyakalu almost faster than they could come at him. He spun, snarling and smiling at the same time, one blade flashing after the other, as if trying to see how much blood they could spill at once.

When Nagimaru stuck in one fonyaka's ribcage, Uncle Takashi simply let go of the weapon. The poor fonyaka who had darted in to take advantage of the break in momentum abruptly found himself skewered on the end of a Whispering Blade. Laughing, Uncle Takashi spun, cleaving another soldier in two with his ice blade and throwing Namimaru into the chest of another oncoming fonyaka. He came out of his spin with a Whispering Blade in each hand.

Uncle Takashi was the only man in history ever to dual wield Whispering Blades. Apparently, his master, Matsuda Mizudori, had disapproved, complaining that Takashi's double Sasayaibas weren't flawless manifestations of the technique—not as perfectly sharp as they would be if he focused his jiya on just one. But they seemed to serve their purpose well enough, slicing through fonyaka muscle and bone like it was nothing.

The Matsuda patriarch roared, and the energy in his voice was nothing like hatred. In fact, from the smile on his face, Mamoru almost would have thought that his uncle *loved* these Ranganese invaders—more than he loved his wife, his baby girl, or anything in the realm of Duna.

"Come on!" he bellowed, coming out of another bloody spin with that manic light in his eyes. "Is that all you've got, Ranga? Come on!"

But no more fonyakalu came vaulting over the wall to meet him.

Quite suddenly, everything had gone quiet.

The only sound was the heavy breathing of the Takayubi swordsmen and the horrible gurgling breaths of the few Ranganese still dying at their feet.

Mamoru's eyes swept across the blood-stained snow, trying to estimate the number of Ranganese corpses. There were so many—dozens upon dozens—but the soldiers who had charged up the mountain toward them had numbered in the hundreds. So why had they stopped coming?

"What are they doing?" Mizumaki Hyousuke asked warily.

"They're shaken," Yukino Sensei said. "They probably expected to roll over us with ease. If they're smart, they'll fall back to regroup and reconsider their strategy." He turned to Uncle Takashi. "We might do same, Matsuda-dono?"

"Yes." Uncle Takashi nodded, though his eyes were wild and faintly glazed, seeming to look through Yukino Sensei instead of at him. His mind was still lost somewhere in the thrill of the battle. He was drenched in blood. "Yes, we might." Blinking his way down from his fighter's high, he swept some of the blood from his clothes and turned to his men. "We still have our eight, yes?"

"Yes, Matsuda-dono," Yukino Sensei said.

Mizumaki Toki was wounded, but everyone was still on their feet.

"Mamoru-kun," Uncle Takashi said with a glance at Mamoru's clean blade. "You didn't kill any fonyakalu." His tone was more surprised than anything else.

"You didn't leave me any," Mamoru said weakly.

Uncle Takashi laughed—a loud, half-mad sound he usually only let out when he was drunk. "We didn't," he laughed. "I suppose that was rude of us, na, Takeru-kun?"

Tou-sama glanced up at his brother but didn't dignify the joke with a response. He appeared to have slaughtered a ridiculous number of fonyakalu in his quiet, efficient way. Judging by the number of corpses at his feet, he had killed as many as his brother—yet he had somehow managed to do it without getting nearly so much blood on his person.

The fighting had altered Uncle Takashi and Yukino Sensei, making Uncle Takashi's eyes turn wild and Yukino Sensei's jiya hyper alert, but Tou-sama was virtually unchanged. Except for the smattering of red and the slightly accelerated rise and fall of his chest, he looked no different from his usual immaculate self. It was as if cutting through a small army didn't affect him at all.

Sublimating his Whispering Blade, he crossed to where his

Moon Spire protruded from a fallen fonyaka's chest and pulled it free. He swept his sword clean of blood, restoring the weapon's celestial shine before returning it to its sheath.

The trouble with steel swords—even ones as good as these—was that they could only go through so many bodies before they started to lose their edge. A Whispering Blade bore no such drawbacks. It was customary for a Matsuda to switch to his Sasayaiba after felling ten men. Mamoru guessed that Nagimaru, Namimaru, and Kyougetsu had all been pushed far beyond the eight-body standard by now. There were so many bodies…

Mamoru had been here on the battlefield many times in his dreams, but those childish dreams had not accounted for all the blood. He was accustomed to the feel of blood in all its consistencies, but he was unprepared for a world soaked in it. It felt heavy, sickening. This was Takayubi, a clear place, a clean place of crystal springs and pure white snow. It felt wrong with the heavy iron of so much red sinking into it, and for the first time in his life, Mamoru thought he understood why Grandfather Susumu had always called blood and its manipulation 'dirty.'

"Resume your positions," Uncle Takashi commanded.

Mamoru had to step over a severed arm and a puddle of organs he couldn't identify when his uncle motioned him back to his place in the line.

The finawu said that jijakalu and fonyakalu had seethed together in the same primordial sea before Nagi's spear touched the waters and stirred them into human form. Was this what they had all looked like at the dawn of the world? Before Nagi's power made them human? A frothing mess of flesh in the seafoam? Absently, Mamoru found his thumb tracing the god-serpents that formed the guard of his sword. *Nami. Nagi. Is this all we are? Just flesh and blood? So much blood...*

"Mamoru-kun," the voice brought him sharply out of his red-stained trance. Yukino Sensei was looking at him in concern, but somehow the only thing Mamoru could see were the flecks of blood on his teacher's face. "Our numbers are too few for me to keep protecting you. You are a strong enough fighter to face these soldiers. You are. But you need to be ready—"

Yukino Sensei was interrupted by a crash that made them both jump. Ice shards flew in all directions, and Mamoru watched his teacher's eyes widen. Someone had broken through the barrier.

"But—" one of the other Yukinos started, "How—?"

Before he could finish, there was a second crash. This blast of wind was so powerful that it not only blew apart a whole bound of the barrier but knocked Mamoru back a few steps. Chunks of ice rained down around them. With the middle part of the barrier down, Mamoru and the others could once again see down the mountain.

Yukino Sensei had been right about the fonyakalu falling back to regroup. The yellow-clad soldiers, their numbers diminished considerably, had fallen back several bounds down the mountain— only now they were not alone. There were new soldiers with them. Soldiers in black.

A prickle of apprehension ran down Mamoru's spine as he remembered his mother's words. *Rank and file Ranganese troops wear yellow. Their elite fighters wear black. If you see yellow, you stand a chance. If you see black, I want you to run.*

His hand tightened on his sword.

"The ones in black are supposed to be strong, right?" Uncle Takashi said with a hungry look in his eyes.

"They broke through Yukino-dono's barrier," one of the Yukino cousins said as the newly reformed lines of Ranganese burst into a charge, "at such a great distance... They're monsters."

"Their strategy has changed," Yukino Sensei mused as the black-clad fonyakalu broke out ahead of their yellow-clad inferiors. "They're sending their best fighters ahead to clear the way for the rest. This is about to become a fair fight."

A fair fight? The black shapes moved so fast it was impossible to count them, but there were far more than eight of them.

Tou-sama and Yukino Sensei lifted a new veil of snow particles just in time. The fonyaka at the head of the group turned a flip in the air, spinning as Mamoru sometimes did to generate power, and threw an attack. If Mamoru had not seen the wind disturb the mist, he never would have been able to avoid it. As it was, he barely managed to spring clear before the wind slammed into the side of the mountain. Even the fonya coming off the fringe of the attack sent Mamoru tumbling in a spray of snow. Rolling back onto his feet, he couldn't help but wonder if the fonyaka knew—even at that distance—to aim for the weakest link.

Both Uncle Takashi and Yukino Sensei's cousin, Shiro, took shots at the lead fonyaka. The man in black deflected them both before a smaller ice bolt from Yukino Sensei struck him in the throat, and he dropped.

As the black-clad soldiers closed in, Yukino Sensei became a blur of movement, firing spears so fast Mamoru's eyes could barely follow them. The lightning swordsman sacrificed the normal impressive size of his spears, substituting smaller projectiles that he rained on the attackers like arrows. Even with his speed and reflexes, Mamoru couldn't imagine charging into such an onslaught. Yet the men in black kept coming, dodging, deflecting, even taking bolts to the limbs and shoulders and pressing on anyway.

"What do you think, Takeru-kun?" Uncle Takashi glanced at his brother. "Shall we see if these monsters are strong enough to face a god?"

Tou-sama offered a nod. "I'm ready, Nii-sama."

At that moment, Mamoru realized that he was about to witness one of the Matsuda family's most advanced techniques in action.

Unlike the workings of the Whispering Blade, the theory behind this technique was no secret. It was a structure of interlocking ice pieces, joined at the seams by mortar of liquid water. When done correctly, it created a weapon with the fluidity of water and the strength of ice. There were many master jijakalu who could achieve it with a modest amount of water. An Ice Snake, it was called.

But when two fully realized Matsudas combined their power, the resulting creature was greater than any snake.

The full power of the Matsuda line surged into motion as Uncle Takashi took hold of what remained of Yukino Sensei's barrier and turned it to water. Tou-sama followed, lacing his brother's stream with ice, forming scales as hard as steel and spines as sharp as swords. Uncle Takashi's fury intertwined with Tou-sama's cold precision to form a new creature, long enough to cover half the pass. It was the teeth of winter. It was poetry. It was God in water.

The Matsuda Dragon reared up to tower over its enemies, ice shard eyes flashing with power beyond simple jiya. It gnashed its teeth, and the sound of its several thousand scales shifting against one another produced a hungry hiss.

The fonyakalu pulled up short.

These men could create tornadoes, but even they faltered when faced with a god.

"Ji xu!" one of the black-clad fonyakalu said roughly, seemingly ordering the others forward. They hesitated. *"Ji xu!"*

One of them took a step—and the dragon struck.

In an instant, the fonyaka was gone, leaving only a bloody smear on the snow. Black shapes scattered into motion and the Matsuda Dragon plunged after them. Uncle Takashi led the water, slinging the dragon's coils with his trademark speed and unpredictability. Tou-sama followed, spinning the blades, keeping the ice of its scales hard and sharp.

A pair of fonyakalu dodged the crash of the dragon's teeth, only to find themselves sliced apart by the rush of scales along its body. The dragon's head, while a formidable weapon on its own, mainly served to distract from its equally dangerous coils. It was in those coils that Uncle Takashi's power spun fastest, lending deadly speed to Tou-sama's razor-blade spines. Mamoru resisted the urge to flinch as a fonyaka made the mistake of trying to spring off the creature's body with his feet. His legs weren't so much cut up as they were pulverized, turned to a fine spray of blood and bone fragments.

Multiple fonyakalu threw wind attacks at the dragon. They were strong, and a few managed to blow pieces of its body apart, but this had little effect on the creature as a whole. The dragon's true body was made of the unspoken understanding between Uncle Takashi and Tou-sama. As long as the brothers stood back-to-back, wrapped in one another's jiya, their creation could not be destroyed by any amount of blunt force. Most of the attacks on the dragon backfired as dispersed scales acted like shrapnel, striking unfortunate fonyakalu in range of the blasts.

Several fonyakalu tried to get past the dragon itself to attack the Matsuda brothers directly, but with the dragon's central coils encircling its creators, this was impossible for even the fastest elite fighters. It wasn't enough to dodge the sporadically lashing body of the dragon. The whole thing was coated in ice scales that Tou-sama could shoot out to pierce the flesh of anyone within a several-stride range. The fonyakalu's powerful long-range attacks had little effect, and any fonyaka who got close to the dragon put himself at the mercy of its projectile scales.

Mamoru realized that he had started backing away from the Matsuda Dragon as the god feasted on its prey. Not because he feared it. Why should he fear the power of his own blood? But what help could he offer alongside such power?

Further down the line, Yukino Sensei had kept up his rain of spears, supported by his cousins, just managing to hold the remaining lines of elite fonyakalu at bay. Mamoru had just taken up position alongside the Yukinos, readying his own spear, when he saw something that made him pause in confusion: a black shape, so fast he might have mistaken it for the shadow of a diving hawk, was zig-zagging between the spears of ice. It took Mamoru a moment to realize that the shape was another fonyaka, and he wasn't just weaving in between Yukino Sensei's projectiles, he was springing off of them on the balls of his feet, simultaneously nudging them off course and using them as steps on his way up the mountain.

"So fast!" one of the Yukino cousins exclaimed in shock.

"Keep firing," Yukino Sensei ordered his cousins, lowering his jiya and reaching for his sword.

The fonyaka may have been fast, but he was charging straight toward certain death—in range of Takenagi. In a flash of black, he was on the swordmaster. Takenagi whipped out of its sheath and Yukino Sensei made his cut—quick and clean as lightning.

The fonyaka *dodged.*

Mamoru felt like his brain had short-circuited. It was barely possible for a quick-footed fighter to evade Yukino Sensei by staying out of his cutting range. It wasn't possible for someone to dodge his blade in that close. It wasn't possible.

Yet the fonyaka had done it, deftly tilting his body to avoid the bamboo-splitting lightning strike of Yukino Sensei's blade. Takenagi sheared off the tip of the man's braid as his foot shot upward, slamming into Yukino Sensei's chest. The swordmaster flew backward, springing off one hand to land on his feet.

Coming out of his kick, the fonyaka caught his braid as it whipped around. Seemingly unconcerned with the second Yukino swordsman advancing on him, he took a dinma to frown at the cut-off ends of his hair. Without so much as a sidelong glance at his new attacker, he evaded the first swipe of Yukino Kiyomu's blade and pulled out what Mamoru realized was a spare hair tie.

As Mamoru watched in utter disbelief, the fonyaka started tying off the end of his braid. Out of curiosity, Mamoru raised a spear and fired at him. The Ranganese soldier casually stepped out of the way without taking his hands or his eyes from his work. A moment later, Yukino Kiyomu attacked again. In one movement, the fonyaka ducked under his swing and spun a hooking kick into his jaw, knocking him sideways into the snow.

Straightening back up, the fonyaka finished tying off his braid, tossed it over his shoulder, and turned to face Yukino Sensei.

"*Ni qie le wo de tou fa.*" He scowled and strode purposefully toward the swordmaster.

Mamoru and Yukino Kiyomu both started forward to stop him. With a disinterested flick of his wrist, the fonyaka released a wave of air pressure so strong that it knocked them both back. As he fell in the snow, Mamoru watched the inhumanly fast fonyaka break into a run. Reaching to the back of his belt, he drew a pair of twin daggers.

Yukino Sensei calmly shifted into his stance. White met black in a thunderclap of steel. Even as Mamoru struggled to keep track of the clang and flash of blades, something was horribly apparent: Yukino Sensei was *losing*. Mamoru had never really thought about the fact that the lightning swordsman was past his prime, the peak of his physical ability behind him. Like most of the Ranganese soldiers, this fonyaka looked to be in his early twenties, at the height of his speed. It made a difference.

Yukino Sensei hit the ground, a dagger buried in his left shoulder. He had deflected the stab so that it missed his heart, but he was now on his back, bleeding, Takenagi pinned under his enemy's boot. The fonyaka drew his other dagger back to deliver the finishing blow.

"No!" Mamoru scrambled forward, raising a hand to form an attack—

The Matsuda Dragon reared out of nowhere. Jaws of water and ice crashed together on the black-clad soldier, eating him whole. Yukino Sensei let out his breath as the dragon slithered back to coil around its masters, resting its head between Tou-sama and Uncle Takashi.

"That was a bit dramatic, Matsuda-dono."

"You're welcome," Uncle Takashi smiled.

"Nii-sama," Tou-sama said, his voice suddenly urgent. "Something is wrong."

"What?" Uncle Takashi turned to his younger brother. "What do you—"

The dragon's head exploded, sending a shower of splintered ice and water droplets in all directions.

Unbelievably, the fonyaka emerged, shaking, drenched in water and blood but still breathing. Not only had this Ranganese soldier bested Yukino Sensei in single combat. He had destroyed the Matsuda Dragon—from the *inside*.

The Matsuda brothers should have been able to reform their dragon with a thought, but the fonyaka had burst from its head directly between them, disrupting the intrapersonal flow of jiya that kept the creature intact. The dragon's teeth had opened cuts all over his body, leaving his uniform shirt hanging in dripping black strips. His own teeth chattered from cold for a moment before he shook himself and threw an attack. Uncle Takashi dodged the burst of wind and he and his brother simultaneously returned fire.

The fonyaka spun, and though it may have been impossible for a single theonite to make a tornado, this one could create a miniature whirlwind powerful enough to repel both Tou-sama's and Uncle Takashi's attacks at once. He was so fast! But there was no time to stand and watch.

With the dragon gone and both Uncle Takashi and Tou-sama occupied with a single opponent, the rest of the Ranganese elite pressed forward, emboldened. Yukino Sensei stood, tearing the dagger from his shoulder, and rained spears on them, but they kept coming.

Five fighters advanced on Mamoru's position. Mamoru readied his sword, but Yukino Sensei moved in front of him, releasing a hail of small close-range projectiles. The first soldier took ice to the eye and went down, but the other four either deflected or dodged. In the scatter of movement, one managed a counterattack that hit Yukino Sensei in his right arm, knocking Takenagi from his hand.

But that didn't stop the swordmaster. He might not have had a Whispering Blade to fall back on, but he was far from defenseless in an empty-handed fight. He slammed an elbow into the first fonyaka's temple, knocking him unconscious, then swung the man's limp form into his nearest fellow, buying him a moment to snatch his sword from the snow. He turned, Takenagi in hand, and engaged two of the others—but the fifth dodged past him, heading straight for Mamoru.

This fonyaka wielded a sansetsukon—a three-segmented Ranganese staff—a weapon Mamoru had heard of but never seen in use. The bizarre apparatus consisted of three short staffs, each about the length of a man's forearm, connected end-to-end by a pair of chain joints.

Mamoru attacked first, hoping that his speed would be enough to end the fight in one move, but the fonyaka moved fast too, deftly parrying with one segment of the staff before swinging the entire weapon around like a whip. Unfolded to its full length, the sansetsukon covered too much distance for Mamoru to clear its range with a quick back-step. He dropped to a crouch, nearly flattening himself to the snow to avoid having his head taken off. The jointed staff whooshed over him, sending up a spray of snow.

As soon as it had passed, Mamoru burst to his feet, lunging forward to take advantage of the moment of follow-through. Against a swordsman, it would have worked, but the sansetsukon wasn't a rigid blade with a single trajectory to follow. As Mamoru aimed a stab beneath the fonyaka's ribs, the sansetsukon curled around its wielder's body, the end segment whipping around to slam into the top of his katana, knocking it off course yet again.

Before Mamoru could regain his balance for another attack, the sansetsukon was unfurling toward him again in a hard snap, like a striking snake. He blocked, but he wasn't used to countering a weapon with joints. When he intercepted the middle segment, the end segment swung around into the fonyaka's free hand—and Mamoru realized he had played right into his enemy's trap. The sansetsukon tightened around its prey, trapping his sword.

With a hard twist of his body, the fonyaka jerked the segments of his weapon in opposite directions, trying to snap Mamoru's sword in two, but it took more than that to break a Kotetsu blade; the movement jolted Mamoru's arm, nearly wrenching it from its socket, but his steel remained intact. When the fonyaka realized he wasn't going to be able to break the sword, he seemed to settle for breaking its wielder.

With an eerily high-pitched snarl, the fonyaka snapped his head forward, into Mamoru's. Stars sprayed like blood across Mamoru's vision, knocking the world off kilter. Through his dizziness,

Mamoru registered the stomping kick to his knee a split-dinma before it made contact. Unable to evade or counter, he turned his knee inward and let it buckle under the force. It put him in a horribly vulnerable position, down on one knee with his sword trapped, but at least the blow hadn't shattered his kneecap.

Hoping for the best, he gripped his sword with both hands and slammed it against its prison, and for probably the thousandth time in history, a Matsuda had a Kotetsu to thank for his life. Even though the strike was clumsy and poorly-aligned, Mamoru's superior steel severed the chain links of the fonyaka's sansetsukon.

With his katana free, Mamoru spun in an attempt to cut the fonyaka's legs out from under him, but the black-clad soldier was too quick to counter. Wielding the broken sansetsukon like a nunchaku, he slammed the weapon into Mamoru's face.

When Mamoru's back hit the ground, his blood was splattered across the snow beside him, along with at least one of his teeth. He couldn't feel his mouth. Before he could rise, the fonyaka was on him again, pinning his sword arm down under a knee. Metal clinked and slithered against Mamoru's neck.

Dizzied, Mamoru didn't register what was happening until the chain yanked tight and he couldn't breathe. The sansetsukon was around his neck and the fonyaka was leaning his weight into it, strangling him. Panic flooded Mamoru, jerking his body uselessly against the ground.

His free hand scrabbled against the fonyaka, but the movements were frantic and haphazard. He knew that his only chance was to draw on the snow beneath him for a counterattack, but blood was pounding in his ears, disorienting him. The ice he formed spasmed and cracked before he could use it to strike.

The fonyaka leaned in harder and chuckled. Even through his dizziness, the sound made Mamoru blink, and a confusing thought flashed through his mind: *Kaa-chan?*

But his mother wasn't here. Why did that laugh bring her to mind?

Mamoru blinked again, and in a strange moment of clarity, his eyes found the fonyaka's. He had been so preoccupied by the color of the uniform and the strange weapon that he hadn't actually looked into his opponent's face. Now that he did, he found a soft jawline and delicate features. *Beautiful*, he thought before blackness swarmed from the edges of his vision to swallow him.

A silver blade flashed into view.

Takenagi cleaved through the black shape above Mamoru, slicing straight through the soldier's spine. Wind blew Mamoru's hair back. Abruptly freed from strangulation, he coughed, wheezed, and heaved ice-clear awareness back into his lungs. Yukino Sensei kicked the body off of his student and calmly watched it fall.

Then something on his face changed. His expression turned to shock and then to horror, as he realized what Mamoru had just moments earlier:

The fonyaka was a woman.

Her sweet face was pretty even as the color drained from her cheeks and her eyes glazed over. She looked to be about thirty, no older than Yukino Sensei's own wife, Hyori—and though her dark chuckle had reminded Mamoru of Kaa-chan's, she really did look like Hyori…

The hands on Takenagi shook.

"No…" Yukino Sensei said in a low voice. "I didn't…"

Sensei, Mamoru tried to say, but he choked and had to turn onto his elbows, coughing flecks of blood into the snow.

"I didn't…" Yukino Sensei whispered and Mamoru hadn't known his teacher could look so lost. The swordmaster didn't see another black-clad soldier advance in his periphery, didn't sense the blast of wind.

Even if Mamoru had been able to get his lungs working, the warning would have come too late.

Air pressure slammed into Yukino Sensei with a horrifying crunch of bone. The force sent him flying several bounds to crash in a spray of snow further up the slope.

"No!" Mamoru scrambled to his feet.

He almost made the same mistake as his teacher, but he registered the fonyaka lining up an attack, just in time to dive out of the way. The concentrated wind hit the slope where he had been a moment earlier, blasting it clear of snow and cracking the rock beneath.

"*Ni hao kuai,*" the Ranganese soldier said, barring his way.

A childish, panicked part of Mamoru couldn't move past the crunching sound Yukino Sensei's body had made when the attack hit him.

Run! Kaa-chan's voice begged as he wheezed air into his lungs and his heart hammered. *If you see black, I want you to run.*

But this man stood between him and Yukino Sensei.

Mamoru let out a slow breath, cleared his mind of emotion, and sized up his opponent. This one was decidedly male, heavier set than the other elites Mamoru had seen. He didn't carry any weapons, suggesting that he specialized in bare-handed attacks. With that bulky build, he couldn't be a highly mobile fighter like the woman with the sansetsukon or the man with the double daggers. Mamoru guessed that his primary method of attack was the thrusting palm strike that created that concussive burst of air pressure.

As Mamoru watched, the fonyaka sank into his stance and drew a hand back to his rib cage, gathering all his fonya to his core for an explosive release. One of the first things Mamoru had ever learned from Yukino Sensei was that attacks with that much wind-up couldn't be fired off in quick succession. The fonyaka had to plant deep in his stance to pool that much power, which left him immobile. In between those rock-shattering palm strikes, there was a window of opportunity... Mamoru just had to get close enough to take advantage of it.

Fonyakalu are most dangerous at mid-range—two to three bounds. Don't linger in their mid-range striking zone.

Mamoru estimated the bounds between himself and the fonyaka with his eyes. He was standing just over three bounds away, just out of the optimal striking zone. The fonyaka was waiting for him to get closer.

Sorry, Kaa-chan.

Mamoru stepped into the striking zone.

The fonyaka attacked immediately, but the charge had been no more than bait, and Mamoru sprang left. Even the fringe of the attack was enough to knock him off his feet. Instead of wasting precious time trying to maintain his footing, Mamoru moved with the wind, letting it throw him into a forward roll. As he came out of his roll, the balls of his feet dug into the snow. Pushing off with legs and jiya, he burst forward with a single thought: *close the distance. Close the distance as fast as possible.*

The Ranganese man was already planted in his stance, winding up for a second palm heel strike. As his hand drew back, Mamoru flipped his katana into a single-handed grip and extended his free hand, raising the snow at the man's feet. He didn't have enough control to form a spear while sprinting—but he could form simple ice.

A bound from the fonyaka, Mamoru darted right, narrowly avoiding the second attack. The wind threw him off balance again, but he didn't let the physical disturbance break his focus. As his feet stumbled beneath him, he maintained his control over the snow and turned it to ice around his enemy's boots.

The ice hardened just as Mamoru came up beside the fonyaka. The man tried to turn and face him, but of course, with his boots frozen in place, he couldn't. He started to swing an arm around to hit Mamoru—with a closed fist, an elbow, or some kind of wind attack, no one would ever know.

Mamoru made an upward cut. Steel hit flesh, crashed through bone, and the fonyaka's arm flew from his body. Kaa-chan was right; it really was easy with a clean stroke. Mamoru followed his sword through its arc and spun his body into a second cut, slicing the immobilized fonyaka open under the ribs.

The man made a terrible choking sound, the air around him jerking as though itself in pain as he tried and failed to draw breath. Mamoru turned away from the sight, as he shed the blood from his katana and slid it back into its sheath.

He had just defeated his first serious enemy in single combat. His nameless sword had tasted its first kill. It should have been a proud moment, but Mamoru didn't feel any pride—just the sickly hammering of his own heart—as he turned and raced up the slope toward Yukino Sensei.

He knew before he reached the body that it was too late. The swordmaster's nyama was powerful and distinctive, yet there was no hint of it when Mamoru fell to his knees beside his teacher. Yukino Sensei lay on his side, Takenagi still resting loosely in his hands. The wind had hit him so hard that his skull had caved in. One of his eyes had come partway out of its socket.

Had Mamoru been a dignified warrior, worthy of his name, he might have taken a moment to pray. He might have considered that this man was the last of the true Yukino swordsmen, that his passing ended a line that stretched all the way back to Takayubi's founding ancestors. He might have found some words of respect to ease his teacher's way into the Laaxara.

Instead, he just shook, like a child, and said, "I'm sorry, Sensei," his voice ragged and small. "I'm so sorry." He reached out and touched his master's hands—the hands that had taught him how to hold a sword. "Don't go."

He didn't consider how lucky he was that no fonyakalu attacked his unguarded back. He didn't notice when the whirl of wind and clang of blades died down around him. He didn't even move when a hand rested gently on his head.

Uncle Takashi.

He should say something. He should face his uncle and commander, but he couldn't muster any movement.

"Mamoru," a voice said, and Mamoru blinked in surprise when he realized that it didn't belong to his uncle but to his father. He didn't think Tou-sama had ever touched his head like that... affectionately. "It's time to stand up."

"Yes, sir," Mamoru said mechanically, but couldn't quite get his body to obey. His hands were frozen atop Yukino Sensei's, unable to let go.

He expected his father to grow impatient and scold him, maybe yank him to his feet. Instead, Tou-sama's voice was soft. "He died fighting, Mamoru. It's what he was born to do."

Mamoru bowed his head in a nod but found that he couldn't lift it again.

"The fonyaka who did this…"

"I killed him," Mamoru said numbly.

"Then you've done right by your teacher," Tou-sama said with a calm certainty that Mamoru wished he could share. "He can move on in peace, but our work is not finished. The Ranganese started bringing boats ashore as soon as the tornado cleared the fishing village. These waves of soldiers are not going to stop. The next will be on us in a siira."

"He died protecting me." Mamoru didn't know why he needed his father to know. "If he hadn't stopped to save me, he would still…"

"Then he's left what remains of this fight to you," Tou-sama said. "Will you disappoint him?"

Mamoru closed his eyes. Of course, Tou-sama was right. He dragged his hands from Yukino Sensei's, fists clenching in the snow. What was he doing crying on his knees? Certainly, Yukino Sensei had taught him better than that. Certainly, he had expected better when he gave his life for his student…

"Stand up," Tou-sama said once more.

This time, for Yukino Sensei, Mamoru obeyed.

14

THE SWORD

Misaki wasn't surprised at the calm sense of purpose that had overtaken her. What *did* surprise her was that Setsuko seemed to have fallen into it with her. The stout fisherwoman moved around the house with energetic determination, barricading all the windows and doors against the growing wind. Since watching her husband head down the mountain, she hadn't shed another tear. The tremors had left her breath and hands, replaced by wide-eyed, ferocious focus.

"Alright." She pushed a table against the last door and turned to Misaki. "What do we do now?"

"We need to take the children and hide in the cellar," Misaki said.

"The wind seems to be slowing down," Setsuko said, looking around at the surrounding walls, which had stopped creaking. The storm still howled, but it no longer felt like it was moments from ripping the Matsuda compound off its foundations.

"You're right..." Misaki opened her hands to the fitful air, feeling for the terrifying roar she had sensed earlier. It wasn't there. "The tornado is gone!" she exclaimed. They had done it! A tentative hope swelled in her chest. If the men had overcome the tornado, they stood a chance.

"Well, if we don't have to worry about the tornado, wouldn't it make more sense to take shelter here, near the central courtyard?"

Setsuko said.

"Oh, Setsuko." The fisherwoman was so clever and wise about so many things that Misaki sometimes forgot that she didn't know the first thing about battle.

"What?"

"This compound might be defensible enough in a jiya-on-jiya fight, with a full retinue of guards, but these walls won't do us much good against fonyakalu."

Setsuko still looked confused.

"Ranganese koronu can jump like nothing you've ever seen," Misaki explained. "These walls won't slow down a determined fonyaka—or honestly a jijaka who can climb worth a damn."

"Kaa-chan said a bad word!" Nagasa exclaimed.

"But you know what?" Misaki moved one of the tables, slid the door open, and stepped onto the deck overlooking the courtyard. "You raise a good point."

Shifting Izumo to her left hip, she extended her dominant right hand and activated her jiya. Taking control of the snow covering the courtyard, she formed arm-length spikes of ice, pointing skyward. "We'll see how they like landing on this."

As she worked, Misaki was surprised to feel Setsuko's jiya surge into motion beside her. Setsuko raised the snow, forming a spike of her own.

"Setsuko, you don't have to—"

"I want them to die," Setsuko growled and pushed her jiya into a second spike.

She wasn't very good. Fishing jijakalu mainly used their power to corral fish into nets and gut them once they were caught. There was rarely any call for them to make human-killing spikes, and Setsuko's came out rather lumpy. A fonyaka would have to fall very hard on one of them to work up a decent bruise. But Misaki didn't say anything to that effect. She knew what it was like to feel useless among powerful fighters who needed help. It was why she had started serious combat training in the first place.

With that thought, she noticed a pulse of tensely cold jiya at her elbow. Hiroshi was standing beside her. His hands were on Nagasa's shoulders as if to comfort the confused younger boy, but his eyes were fixed on the discolored sky. Of the little children, he was the only one old enough to have some understanding of what was happening.

"Hiro-kun, be a dear and give your auntie a hand," Misaki said.

"Yes, Kaa-chan." Hiroshi moved to obey immediately, seemingly relieved to have something to do.

Misaki returned to her work, driving more spikes skyward, the formations growing taller and stronger as her jiya built momentum. If she was honest, it was unlikely that these spikes would do any good, even if any fonyakalu were reckless enough to leap directly into the center of the compound. But it was something to do with the nerve-splitting stress of the past waati. It was a good way to loosen her limbs, see what her jiya could still do... if she needed to use it for real.

"Is this good, Kaa-chan?" asked a small, monotone voice.

Misaki turned and felt her mouth fall open in surprise. She hadn't expected any more out of Hiroshi than she did out of Setsuko. Yet, at five years old, he was living up to his name. The spikes he had formed were nearly as tall and sharp as her own. If it came to it, they would draw blood. They might even kill.

"Yes," she said blankly. "That's very good, Hiro-kun. Thank you."

She brushed Hiroshi's bangs back from his face and looked down at the boy.

"Is there anything else I can do, Kaa-chan?" There was a rare note of emotion in Hiroshi's voice. Frustration.

At his age, it was very possible that Hiroshi grasped only the one thing about his existence: that he was born to fight. His uncle, his father, and his older brother had all gone down the mountain to fulfill that purpose. But Hiroshi was too small. It had to be a horrible place to be—old enough to understand what was happening but too young to do anything about it.

"Not today," Misaki said, putting a hand to his ice-cold cheek.

"But Kaa-chan—"

"Not today," Misaki repeated, but she couldn't bear the strained look on her son's face, so she added, "but someday."

She decided then, with ferocious certainty, that someday would come. It had to. She could still feel Mamoru's shoulders sliding from her fingers, the moment she let him go. Because he was a warrior. And a part of her understood that there was nothing crueler than denying a warrior the fight he was born for. That, in its own way, was worse than death.

These boys had the same blood in their veins, the same power, the same need. But they were still years from being able to realize it. If she couldn't deny Mamoru his fight, how could she let these boys die without ever having a chance at theirs? What kind of mother would she be?

"You're good boys," she said. "All three of you. You're going to grow up strong." She gave Nagasa's head a reassuring pat. "You're going to find something worth fighting for and you're going to get your chance to fight for it. Someday. Kaa-chan is going to make sure of it." Then she straightened up. "Setsuko, I'm going to need you to take Izu-kun."

Setsuko looked uncertain as she took her sister-in-law's baby. Little Ayumi was still tied safely onto her back. She opened her mouth as if to ask why when a sound made her stop.

A crash. It came from somewhere close. Far too close.

"What is that?" Setsuko asked.

"That's the sound of fonya hitting houses," Misaki said as screams pierced the din. "They're in the village."

"D-does that mean... the men—"

"Don't think about that now," Misaki said, smothering her own emotions before they could swell out of control. She herded her boys back inside, slammed the door shut, and froze it in place. "Take the children, and hide in the cellar! Now!"

"Wait—where are you going?" Setsuko demanded as Misaki turned and ran back into the house.

"Don't worry about me!" Misaki called over her shoulder. "Just hide!" This time, Misaki didn't hesitate at the threshold of the dojo. She bowed herself in, sprinted to the sword rack and snatched up the first weapon she could find. Too heavy. She knew without unsheathing it that it would only slow her down in combat. She would be better off empty-handed; at least she would be mobile.

Casting it aside, she took the next sword down and pulled it from its sheath. Also far too heavy. She bit her lip as more screams pierced the air. At her best, she might have been able to fight with one of these weapons, but she was far, far from her best. Disuse had made her instincts dull and her muscles soft. She couldn't afford a handicap.

Turning, Misaki ran from the dojo toward the kitchen.

"Misaki!" Setsuko intercepted her on her way—alone this time. She must have bundled the children into the cellar already. "What are you doing?"

"Don't mind me." Misaki didn't break stride, forcing Setsuko to run after her. "Just go hide with the little ones." Reaching the kitchen, Misaki dropped to her knees on the floorboards and was faintly annoyed to find Setsuko still at her side. "I said go!"

"Are the cellar doors really going to protect us?" Setsuko asked, flinching as fonya crashed into something not far from the compound.

"No." Misaki froze ice across her knuckles. "I am."

"What—?"

Misaki hauled her fist back and, with a concentrated burst of jiya, punched through the floorboards. It was so easy, she could have laughed. She had fixed the boards in place with such a sense of finality all those years ago. Yet, armed with her claws and a sense of urgency, it took her only dinmanu to tear through the wood.

Forgotten, she had tried to tell herself. *It was forgotten, along with everything from her life before.* But the little blade had never left her mind or her heart. Her hands found the weapon as easily as if she had put it there yesterday.

"What is that?" Setsuko asked as Misaki straightened up on her knees and brushed a cloud of dust from the sheath.

"This..." In spite of everything, Misaki found a smile on her lips. "This is Shadow's Daughter."

Encircled with delicate vines and blossoms, the sheath had the appearance of burnished wood, though in reality, it was made of something far stronger.

"Like you," Koli had told her in delight. *"Pretty flowers on the outside."*

"And inside?" Misaki asked, raising an eyebrow at the numu.

"Inside..." he beamed, *"just like you."*

Tentatively, Misaki gripped the handle and pulled the blade halfway out of its sheath. Her eyes widened. She felt the breath catch in her chest.

"Is this..." Her voice was barely a whisper. *"Koli, this* isn't *what I think it is!"*

"I told you, I have all the connections."

Misaki fought hard to keep her face impassive. *"So... I'm pretty on the outside, but hard and dark on the inside."* She shot Koli a look, even as her treacherous fingers tightened possessively on the weapon. *"I feel like I should be insulted."*

"As a lady of Shirojima, you certainly should be. As a fighter, you have no room to talk."

"Does she have a name?" Misaki asked softly, afraid that if she spoke louder, Koli would hear the tremor of excitement in her voice.

"While we were working on her, we nicknamed her Misaki-denyaa. Once you put her to use on the streets, that name might put your secret identity in jeopardy. I thought we might throw in your code name instead, call her Sirawu-denyaa. Maybe Siradenyaa for short?"

"Shadow's Daughter?" Misaki raised an eyebrow. *"A little dramatic, don't you think?"*

Koli crossed his arms petulantly. *"I'll take a thank you."*

"Koli... I can't accept this."

"Too bad. She's made for you."

"But... this is such an amazing weapon—"

"One of a kind," Koli said proudly.

"Shouldn't you give it to a koro who will get more use out of it? I mean—I'm not even supposed *to fight..."* She trailed off as Koli rolled his eyes. *"What?"*

"That's like saying a knife isn't supposed to cut."

Misaki considered the numu for a moment. *"Sometimes I wonder if you're a human, Koli."* She was aware that this was part of the reason the two of them got along so well.

"What do you mean?" He didn't sound offended. He had already resumed tinkering with the machinery strewn across his desk.

"Do you see people beyond their physical function? Or are we all just... things *to you? Just tools, and weapons, and baby-making machines?"*

"I'm a numu." He shrugged, heating his fingers to weld two components together. *"The gods wired me to see the world in terms of raw material."*

"Well, my *gods wired* me *to look pretty, marry well, and make babies,"* Misaki said.

Koli snorted. *"If you say so. Though that claim makes your precious Nami and Nagi look like some lousy craftsmen."*

"Excuse me?"

"A competent god would never make a housewife with your skill and hunger. You might look like a decorative flower, but you're more sword than anything else."

"You're doing it again," Misaki said, pointing an accusing finger. *"You're calling me a weapon."*

"An effective one," Koli said. *"It was supposed to be a compliment."*

"I'm just... not sure I can take it." The compliment or the sword.

"Then don't," Koli said impatiently. *"All I can say is that it will be a terrible waste. When you get into your next fight—and let's be honest, Misaki, you* are *going to get into another fight—you'll do better with that blade than any other. Like I said, the girl was made for you. She won't be as good in anyone else's hands."*

"But—"

"That sword was a gift, not an invitation to tedious conversation," he said shortly. *"You want to debate religion and philosophy, go find yourself a jaseli. Everything I have to say is right there in your hands. Do what you will with it."*

"Misaki, wh-what is this?" Setsuko was stuttering, caught between her fear and confusion, as she stared at Siradenyaa. "What are

you—"

"Don't worry." Misaki tied the obsidian sword at her hip and realized how much she had ached for its weight there. A baby just wasn't the same. "I know what I'm doing."

"You mean... you know how to fight? How?"

Misaki watched the pieces come together for Setsuko, as they had for Mamoru. But this time she couldn't wait in anxious silence for approval. What Setsuko or anyone thought of her unladylike behavior didn't matter anymore. What mattered was that Misaki and her dishonest black blade were all that stood between her family and certain death.

There was a crash from the front of the house and both women jumped. Someone was trying to break down the doors.

"You need to hide now!" Misaki hissed urgently. "Make as little noise as possible. Fonyakalu have excellent hearing. It'll be easier for me to draw them away from you if they don't know you're there."

"Draw them away from us?" Setsuko had a pained look on her face. "Misaki, I can't—I don't want to leave you alone out here."

"You have to."

Another crash shook the house. Setsuko's eyes had gotten impossibly wide. She was terrified. The predator in Misaki could see her itching to bolt for safety. But frustratingly, she didn't.

"Misaki, I can't leave you alone," she whispered. "I know I won't be any use in holding them off, but—"

"That's not it," Misaki said, looking at her knees.

There were obvious reasons Misaki had kept her history of fighting hidden beneath the kitchen floorboards: violence was a wildly improper hobby for a well-born lady and her husband had strictly forbidden any talk of her time overseas. But if propriety and obedience had made her nail the boards down, something stronger had kept them in place, a deeper sense of shame.

The fact was that even if she had been a man, with pure blood and great power, she wouldn't be the sort of fighter a respectable Matsuda would want to consort with. Takayubi swordsmen were noble warriors who met their opponents face to face on the open field and had the raw power and discipline to back up their reputation. Misaki was just the opposite: a weak, deceitful ambush predator who rarely gave her victims the dignity of a clean fight. Because in a clean fight, she would lose.

What she did was an insult to truly noble koronu. The people who had known her for what she really was had been able to forgive it... though she wasn't sure it was something that should be forgiven.

"Setsuko, I would like it if you... didn't watch what I'm about to do."

"I'm not scared," Setsuko lied, even as the next crash at the doors made her flinch. "I-I've gutted so many fish; I can't imagine fonyaka blood looks too different."

"That's not it. I don't want you to see... *me*." Not as she really was. Not what she would become as soon as Siradenyaa tasted blood. The people she had fought alongside in the past had reined her in, preventing her from indulging her killing streak, but if she *had* to kill...

"I don't understand."

"You..." Misaki's words caught in her throat and she had to swallow. "You think I'm a good person." She touched Setsuko's hands. "That saved my life."

"What?"

"I never admitted it because I'm proud and stupid—" and they were running out of time. Misaki blinked rapidly. No time for tears. "You saved me. I'm going to return the favor, but I need you to trust me and *hide*."

Setsuko hesitated for a moment. Then she nodded, squeezed

Misaki's arm, and leaned forward. Their foreheads touched, pressing together in a moment of silent support. Then the two parted ways, Setsuko rushing back toward the cellar and Misaki turning to face the threat. She might not be worthy of belonging to this family, but she was going to protect it with every bit of venom, and bloodlust, and underhanded trickery in her.

Fonya crashed against the doors, cracking them, as Misaki stepped into the front hall. There was nothing she hated more than meeting her opponents face to face. Every instinct in her screamed to hide and set an ambush, but she needed to draw the soldiers away from Setsuko and the children, and to do that, she needed their attention.

The double doors blew open. As splintered wood clattered to the floor, Misaki found herself face to face with four men in yellow uniforms—well, not quite face to face. Her body was angled slightly to hide the sword at her hip, giving her the appearance of a diminutive housewife. In its own way, that was better cover than any shadow.

MAMORU

The mountain had gone from rust to red. With the last of the fonya-made clouds gone, the sky was clear again, but it wasn't the bright light of day that shone through. Instead, sunset touched every koyin of snow not already soaked with blood, bathing the corpse-strewn mountainside in red.

Among the mess of yellow and black-clad dead, Mamoru found two crumpled forms in sky blue—the Mizumakis—and two in light gray—Yukino Sensei's cousins. Uncle Takashi stood two bounds away, looking significantly more exhausted than before, but still smiling. He and Tou-sama were the only fighters left standing.

"You... you killed all of them," Mamoru murmured in awe. "All those elite soldiers."

"Our Yukino and Mizumaki comrades did their part before they succumbed," Tou-sama said. "Their families can be proud."

"And the fast one?" Mamoru asked. "The dragon killer?"

Uncle Takashi let out a chuckle. "The 'dragon killer,' huh?" There was a touch of annoyance behind his smile, but Mamoru thought a fighter who had bested Yukino Sensei in single combat and held off both Matsuda brothers more than deserved the title. "Your father took care of him," Uncle Takashi said with an appreciative smile at Tou-sama.

"Almost." Tou-sama flexed the fingers of his right hand with a distant, faintly irritated look on his face. "He didn't die."

"Really?" Uncle Takashi said. "It looked like a direct hit."

"My aim was a bit off," Tou-sama said. "The spear connected but missed his heart."

"Well, it still sent him flying a good distance," Uncle Takashi said dismissively. "So long as he was sufficiently stunned, the fall will have killed him."

Far down the mountain, Mamoru could make out movement— yellow-clad figures climbing through the ruins of the western village, coming for them.

"Take these siiranu to gather your strength," Uncle Takashi told his brother and nephew. "The fighting will only get harder from here."

At that moment, a scrabble of movement on the nearby rocks drew Mamoru's attention. Instinctively, he and his uncle reached for their weapons, jiya rising, but Tou-sama held up a hand.

"It's one of ours."

And sure enough, the figure that appeared over the rocks was dressed in a kimono and hakama. His hands clutched a bamboo longbow.

"Katakouri Senpai!" Mamoru said in surprise.

Katakouri Hakuzora was the youngest of the archers who had gone to cover the northern pass, a slight, quiet boy one year ahead of Mamoru at Kumono Academy.

"Why have you abandoned your line?" Uncle Takashi demanded.

"Th-there *are* no more lines, Matsuda-dono," the boy said. His hands shook on his bow.

"What?"

"I'm the only one who..." his voice broke and tears ran down his face through well-worn tracks. "Forgive me, Matsuda-dono. I'm the only one left."

"What?"

"They broke through within siiranu. My father sent me to tell you... The line is gone."

"What do you mean, Senpai?" Panic flooded Mamoru. "You mean they're in the village?"

"We tried to stop them—"

"Takeru," Uncle Takashi said immediately. "Go back to the house."

Tou-sama froze, an uncharacteristic flicker of hesitation crossing his face. "Nii-sama—"

"Now!" Uncle Takashi commanded. "You need to protect Setsuko and the others."

"There are still the advancing Ranganese to deal with," Tou-sama said. "I should stay and help you hold them here. Mamoru should go back."

"We can't gamble the fate of our family on a fourteen-year-old boy, no matter how skilled. You're the strongest fighter, so you will go. Ensure that our family survives."

The logic was sound. Mamoru had never known Tou-sama to reject sound logic... or to question orders. Yet he made no move to obey. His eyes flicked to Mamoru, then back to his brother.

"Nii-sama... please."

"What?" Uncle Takashi snapped, looking ready to hit his brother.

"I'm... not that strong."

"You are," Uncle Takashi's tone somehow came off harsh rather than encouraging. "You have your orders."

Tou-sama's jiya rose, as if in rebellion. For a disconcerting moment, Mamoru was certain that his father was about to attack his uncle—then Tou-sama's jiya dropped back to its flawless calm. An invisible tension left his body.

"Yes, Nii-sama," he said without emotion, his gaze down. He didn't even look at Mamoru as he told him, "Hold the line."

"Yes, sir," Mamoru said.

Without another glance back at his brother or son, Tou-sama turned and tore up the mountain. There was no time to watch him go. The next wave of Ranganese was almost on top of them.

These soldiers mostly wore yellow but a figure in black led the charge, brandishing a pair of swords.

"I-I'm sorry, Uncle," Mamoru said as he took up his fighting stance. "I don't know how to help you with any advanced attacks or—"

"You won't have to," Uncle Takashi said, eyeing the oncoming soldiers. "Just take care of the four furthest to the left. Leave the rest to me."

"Yes, Uncle."

Katakouri Hakuzora had taken up a position as well. Though the boy's quiver was empty, he formed an arrow from ice and nocked it to the string.

"Don't bother, Katakouri-kun," Uncle Takashi said.

"Matsuda-dono?"

"This fight is beyond you. Head up the mountain and do what you can to protect the women and children."

Unlike Tou-sama, the young Katakouri didn't need telling twice. "Yes, Matsuda-dono." He bowed and turned to run up the mountain.

And the fonyakalu were on them.

This time, Mamoru didn't freeze. Something in him had hardened when the life left Yukino Sensei—as if a piece of the swordmaster's powerfully calm nyama had passed into him. His blade had already tasted blood. Now that he knew the feeling, the movements came more easily. The first fonyaka caught his katana in the stomach, falling into two pieces across it. The second wisely drew back, out of Mamoru's cutting range, and pulled his arm back for an attack. Too slow. Mamoru shot a spear of ice into his throat.

The next two fonyaka fired blasts of air pressure at him

291

simultaneously. He jumped clear of one attack, only to have the other catch him full in the chest, knocking the breath from his body. As he stumbled, one of his enemies took advantage and darted in to grab his sword arm, immobilizing it in an iron grip.

Smart move, Mamoru thought ruefully. He was faster than he was strong; he couldn't fight his way out of the grip of an adult soldier.

The fonyaka drew his own sword back for the killing blow. And even if Mamoru had had the physical strength to contend with a full-grown theonite, he didn't have the time to spare wresting his sword arm free. But what he lacked in strength, he could still make up for in speed.

Before the man could complete his swing, Mamoru snapped an ice-knuckled punch into his face. The jab had been more of a distraction anything else. It didn't break the fonyaka's nose or even cause his grip to loosen significantly. What it did was buy Mamoru a moment to draw the surrounding water molecules into formation.

The water gathered to his left hand formed a weapon to mirror the metal one in his right. And Mamoru sliced upward. It was no Whispering Blade. Mamoru knew that. His ice wasn't sharp enough to cut through steel, but he felt a savage thrill of pride when he confirmed that it *was* sharp enough to cut through human muscle. The fonyaka screamed, dropping his own sword as blood spurted from his shoulder. Annoyingly, he didn't relinquish his grip on Mamoru's right arm.

Lifting a foot, Mamoru slammed a kick into the bleeding man's stomach, knocking him back. The fonyaka's grip was so stubborn that he ended up ripping Mamoru's katana from his hand as he fell. It didn't matter. Mamoru's right hand instinctively moved to join his left on the handle of his newly formed ice sword, and he shot forward, slicing the man's throat open.

As the next soldier was coming at him, sword drawn, Mamoru's eyes flicked to his steel katana, lying less than a bound away in the snow. He might have time to retrieve it... but he felt so strong here in the high of battle. *Maybe...* He brought his ice sword around to meet the fonyaka's metal one, and the crash sent a shockwave through his arms.

Both blades broke.

Not quite. Mamoru gritted his teeth in frustration. *Not quite good enough.* The stumbling fonyaka was so surprised to find his steel snapped off that he couldn't rally any sort of defense before Mamoru's ice reformed and drove through his chest.

Having carried out his orders, Mamoru turned to help his uncle, but there wasn't much left to help with. At least a dozen yellow-clad soldiers lay dead at Uncle Takashi's feet. The only fonyaka still standing was the black-clad elite, and he didn't look like he would be standing much longer. His left hand was clenched hard around the handle of a broad-bladed Ranganese sword but his right arm was sliced open to the bone, pouring blood. Uncle Takashi would be able to cut him down in a single stroke.

However, it seemed to take the Matsuda patriarch a considerable amount of effort to step forward and swing his katana. When he did, the stroke was weak. The wounded fonyaka managed to block with the sword in his left hand. Nagimaru screamed against the Ranganese blade and bit into the fonyaka's shoulder. Then, with a primal roar, Uncle Takashi flipped Namimaru around in his left hand and plunged the smaller blade into the soldier's stomach.

The air writhed as the fonyaka lurched forward, snarling, striking at Uncle Takashi with astonishing power for a dying theonite. Steel clipped Uncle Takashi's arm before he stepped back, ripping his own swords free and ending the fonyaka's life in a burst of blood.

The wound in Uncle Takashi's shoulder was shallow, but as he staggered back, Mamoru realized why his movements had been slow. Amid the haze of fresh blood, Mamoru hadn't sensed it, but he could see now: a deep wound ran the length of Uncle Takashi's torso, from his left shoulder to his right hip—and it was gushing blood.

"You know..." Uncle Takashi smiled through clenched teeth, even as his dark blue kimono turned a darker shade of red. "I've never fought another dual wielder. Bastard got me good, didn't he?"

"Uncle!" Mamoru hurriedly shed the blood from his own sword, sheathed the weapon, and ran forward. He reached his uncle just as the bleeding man listed and fell into him.

"I'm fine," Uncle Takashi protested as his nephew caught him, but he was leaning far too heavily on Mamoru's shoulder for that to be true.

Uncle Takashi was still muttering blatant nonsense about a shallow papercut, but Mamoru knew he had to do something. Apologizing profusely, he yanked open the front of his uncle's kimono and scrambled to apply pressure to the wound. He grimaced as his hands slid in the blood and the sleeves of his kimono quickly became soaked with it. There was no way he would be able to stem the flow with his hands alone. And Mamoru realized he was going to have to disobey his mother again.

He took a shaky breath.

"Don't be a girl, Mamoru," Uncle Takashi scoffed, his words slurring as if he had consumed too much sake. "It's just a bit of blood."

It would have been inappropriate to do anything but agree, so Mamoru just nodded. "Of course, Uncle. Please—please hold still."

With a sweep of his hand, he pulled the excess blood from his Uncle Takashi's chest. *So much of it. Far too much.* But he couldn't think about that now. Putting both hands over the deepest part of the wound, he poured all his focus into his palms.

"What are you doing, boy?"

Mamoru didn't have the attention to spare on an answer. He had never congealed this much blood at once. It consumed every bit of his concentration. Uncle Takashi was quiet for a moment, still as he felt Mamoru's jiya struggling to solidify the blood leaving his chest.

"Where did you learn to do that?" he finally asked in confusion.

Mamoru wouldn't have answered if he could. He had promised Kaa-chan he would never—

"Misaki," Uncle Takashi murmured, arriving at the only logical conclusion himself. Matsudas and Yukinos never so much as dabbled in blood manipulation. Kaa-chan was the only person who could have taught him. "Strange little woman, my sister-in-law. I think... I would have liked to know her better."

Mamoru squeezed his eyes shut, tuning out his uncle's murmurs along with the rest of the world as he fought to control the blood beneath his hands. This was nothing like scabbing his own damaged knuckles or the cuts on Chul-hee's legs. Mamoru had never encountered blood that so adamantly fought against his jiya, so eager to leave the body. The fonyaka's sword must have hit a major blood vessel near Uncle Takashi's heart. In trying to stem the flow of blood, Mamoru was fighting against the pumping core of all his uncle's power—and that was inevitably a losing battle.

"I'm sorry." Mamoru opened his eyes, knowing that the weak scab he had managed to form would never hold. "I can't do it. I'm not strong enough. I'm sorry."

Nagimaru fell to the snow beside them and Mamoru was surprised to find Uncle Takashi's hand atop his head. "You can do it," he murmured very quietly. "You worry too much, Takeru-kun."

"I'm not..." Mamoru trailed off as something yellow moved in his periphery, far down the mountain. "Oh no."

"There are more headed our way, aren't there?" Uncle Takashi sounded calm.

"Yes, Uncle."

"Hmm," the man breathed out. "You see how many?"

"I... It looks like twenty? Maybe more."

Yukino Sensei and Tou-sama were the jijakalu with truly superior senses. Without them, Mamoru and his wounded uncle were blind to most of the mountain around them.

"Alright. More than twenty," Mamoru said as the group drew closer.

"I should hope so." Uncle Takashi stooped to pick up Nagimaru and a bit of blood spurted from a weak place in the scab across his chest. "This time I'll try to leave a few more for you, kid. No promises though."

Mamoru unsheathed his sword, but before he could take up position beside his uncle, a shrill sound echoed down the mountain. Screams. Mamoru and his uncle both looked up sharply. Those weren't battle cries, Mamoru realized with sinking dread. Those were screams of terror—of women and children. The sound was too close to have come from the main village, but...

"The blacksmiths!" Mamoru gasped.

How? Had some Ranganese gotten past them in the chaos, while Mamoru sat frozen by Yukino Sensei's body? Or had they cut across to the numu village from the northern pass after breaking through the lines there? It didn't matter. The blacksmiths were in danger.

"Go." Uncle Takashi nodded in the direction of the numu village, where plumes of smoke rose against a darkening sky.

"But..." Mamoru looked from the smoke to the charging Ranganese. The wave of soldiers would be here in a siira. Without Tou-sama to back him up, Uncle Takashi couldn't make his ice dragon, and he was bleeding so much...

"Go and protect the smiths." Uncle Takashi said. "I'll thin these fools out for you."

Thin them out?

"Uncle..."

"Hey!" Uncle Takashi grabbed Mamoru's face in a bone-crushing grip that sent a jolt of pain through his mouth—a sharp reminder that one of his teeth had just been knocked out. "You don't worry about me. That isn't your place. Those numuwu, on the other hand, are under your protection. They need you!" He shoved Mamoru from him. "Go!"

"Yes, sir." Mamoru's legs obediently stumbled into motion and he ran. A selfish part of him was glad that there was no time for him to bow or wish nyama to his uncle. If he had lingered another moment, he would have had to acknowledge the horrible truth unspoken in the air:

He was leaving his uncle to die.

15

THE KILLERS

The Ranganese hesitated in the doorway of the Matsuda compound, regarding Misaki with expressions that ranged from apprehensive to amused. Had she been a man or even a more imposing woman, they surely would have attacked by now, but they hung back, seemingly confused to find a tiny housewife standing before them. The hallway was too narrow to accommodate all four of them shoulder to shoulder. Someone had to make the first move. Her victim stepped forward, unknowingly sealing his fate.

He looked to be nearing middle age—in his late thirties or early forties—yet he still wore the colors of a low-ranking soldier. He must not have been particularly skilled or powerful to have gone so long without a promotion. One look into his face and Misaki could see through him, to the internal mechanisms that moved him. This man was insecure, looking for an easy way to feel powerful, like picking on a defenseless housewife.

Robin would have seen the humanity in that kind of cruelty, even if it was turned on him. He would have seen a way to make this man better. Misaki saw only eye sockets, a throat, a sensitive groin, a hundred points of attack to choose from.

Instead of drawing her shoulders back as the fonyaka approached, she cowered. Like dropping bait in the water before a clueless fish. He smiled— the smile of a weak man seeing a very rare chance to feel powerful.

"Don't hurt me," she whimpered in Shirojima Dialect. She knew how to say the words in Ranganese, but why let on that she knew their language? Why let them see any of her before it was too late? "Please, don't hurt me."

Drawn to her lure, the man closed the distance between them with hunger in his eyes. Misaki waited until he was almost on top of her, then opted for the simplest point of attack. Why waste her best material on this idiot? She snapped a kick into his groin. With a high grunt, the fonyaka doubled over.

The kick was by no means incapacitating, but it bought her the moment she needed to gather ice to her fingertips. And before the man could straighten up, she had him by the throat. Misaki's hands were so delicate that her grip was not particularly dangerous in and of itself. That was why she had invested so much time and training in her claws. It was these men or her children. Robin would forgive her. Five nails of ice pierced deep into the man's neck.

His eyes widened in shock. He opened his mouth as if to scream and blood bubbled from between his lips, dribbling down his chin. Curling her fingers in as far in as they would go, Misaki ripped her hand free. His windpipe shredded in her fingers.

Like that, she was a killer.

The remaining men let out cries of alarm as their comrade fell, but Misaki didn't give them time to take stock of the situation. Before the body had thudded to the floor, she was moving, sprinting on bare feet toward the next nearest soldier. She picked up speed and focused on her target's face, reading his expression. He fell for it. He thought she was stupid enough to charge him.

Looking confident, he drew his arm back and threw a palm strike. Just before the burst of fonya left his hand, Misaki veered right, running up the wall. In the end, Misaki never did find out if her legs had the strength to carry her to the end of her old maneuver. The peripheral wind off the blast pushed her body, flipping her over onto her feet directly behind the fonyaka. Realizing his mistake, the soldier started to turn, but it was too late. Siradenyaa was out of her sheath. A single stroke severed his spinal column.

In the same spin, Misaki turned and cut through the next soldier. Only a few steps behind his comrade, he probably didn't even see what had happened before Shadow's Daughter separated his torso from his legs.

One more to go.

Misaki made her cut, but this last soldier was a *young* man— fast—and he stepped back, out of range. Wary eyes flicked over her, taking in her stature, her weapon, her stance, sizing her up. She couldn't allow that, so she pressed in, black blade flashing in a second attack meant to drive him up against the wall and into a corner.

Infuriatingly, he evaded again, backing through the genkan and partway out the door, drawing his own inferior sword. Smart boy. The aggressive part of Misaki itched to follow him, but she knew that if she let him take the fight outside, onto open ground, she was a dead woman. So instead, she darted right, through the nearest side hallway, disappearing as was her way.

The windowless hallway was so dark it might have been one of Livingston's alleys, and it was going to stay that way. Misaki formed a block of solid ice over the light switch. As she went, she slid all the doors open, coating the doorframes in ice. Then she flattened herself against the wall, melting into the shadows, and waited.

The soldier moved down the hallway on cautious feet. If he was smart, he was listening closely, his hands open, trying to detect her breath stirring the air. But Misaki could hold her breath for a long time. This was where the dark put a fonyaka at a serious disadvantage: despite their acute hearing, fonyakalu had no sense of a person's heat signature or blood flow, making them blind to a stealthy enough opponent. Misaki, on the other hand, could feel every inch of her prey as he approached—a pulsing network of arteries, capillaries, marrow, and spinal fluid.

As the fonyaka neared her position, Misaki flicked her fingers, using the ice she had formed on one of the doors to slam it shut.

Instinctively, the man whirled toward the sound, turning his back to her.

Misaki peeled from the shadow and stabbed.

There was a crunch, accompanied by a choking grunt of surprise, as Siradenyaa hit her mark. The fonyaka didn't have to linger long in his pain. Darkness lent Misaki's attacks unparalleled precision. Without the distraction of clothes, skin, and other visible features, she could hit the exact internal part of a person she was aiming for. Unhindered by the bones that would have stopped a lesser sword, Siradenyaa had driven directly through the young man's heart.

Misaki slid the blade free of the soldier's chest and felt his blood pour onto the floor as he fell. She stood still for a moment, absorbing sensation. She had always wondered what it would feel like to stab someone through the heart, but this... this was disappointing.

She had assumed, for some reason, that killing a person would be hard. But it wasn't. When you were used to slicing tendons, of course cutting a man in half was easy. When you had trained to stab between major arteries, of course piercing a whole organ was easy. With a blade like Siradenyaa, killing was obviously going to be easier than not killing. She should have understood that, but she couldn't explain the emptiness that suddenly overwhelmed her.

The line between wounding and taking a life had been such a concrete and non-negotiable thing to Robin and Elleen. Yet Misaki had just crossed that line without experiencing so much as a tug of resistance. She had *wanted* there to be resistance. Deep in her heart, she had hoped there was something of Robin in her.

The young man's blood spread from his body to seep between her bare toes, still eerily warm from a life that was no more. He had been someone's son. Why couldn't she feel anything? As a mother, a woman, a *human*, how could she feel nothing?

Unbidden, her free hand lifted to touch her waist.

How could she?

A shuffle of movement from the hallway drew Misaki's attention. As her hand left her stomach to grip Shadow's Daughter, she welcomed the emptiness. It didn't leave any room for fear as she went to face her next victims. Three yellow-clad fonyakalu faced her in the front hall.

And for the moment, Misaki let herself be thankful for the thing she was. After all, a lady wouldn't have been able to slice a man's legs out from under him and then plunge a blade into his mouth when he opened it to scream. A mother wouldn't have been able to cut a young woman's head from her shoulders. A human being wouldn't have been able to turn from their dismembered corpses without a single pang of guilt.

Thank the Gods she was a monster.

The third soldier managed to catch Misaki in the arm with a burst of fonya, knocking Shadow's Daughter from her hand. Back in Livingston, she had always had her daggers to fall back on if she was disarmed. *"But your greatest concealed weapons aren't really this or this,"* Koli had told her, holding up each of the knives in turn. *"They're your ingenuity… and your brutality."*

Snatching one of the long pins from her hair, she darted toward the last fonyaka. He threw a palm strike, but it was telegraphed. She evaded and drove her hairpin into the side of his neck, burying the hair ornament all the way up to the flowery bauble at the end. He choked, blood spattering from his mouth, and clawed at his throat. Not wanting him to suffer longer than necessary, Misaki jabbed a fingertip of concentrated jiya into one of his eyes. The Blood Needle pierced deep into his brain, killing him instantly.

She let out a breath as the man's body crumpled to the floor. He twitched and then lay still, blood running from his neck and eye onto the flowers of Misaki's hairpin. Like all of Kotetsu Tamami's work, the ornament was a masterpiece, a sensitive composition of pearls and pink lacquer blossoms. Blood ran in between the petals, accentuating the beauty of all their details for a moment before consuming them in red.

Misaki's hair, now free of its tightly pinned bun, stuck to her neck, and she realized just how sweaty she had gotten. In Livingston, disabling seven enemies would have been a warm-up for her. Now, she was breathing as if she had just sprinted the length of a city.

Trying to ignore the burning in her muscles and the growing stitch in her side, she picked her way through the corpses to retrieve Siradenyaa. She kept a wary eye on the broken-down doors as she swept the blood from the blade but no more soldiers appeared. She had just set the top of Siradenyaa against her left knuckle to return the weapon to its sheath when the air stirred through her loose hair, making her stop. Fonya. *Strong* fonya. She returned both hands to her sword handle as a pair of uniformed figures appeared in the doorway.

"Oh, *xuro.*" Misaki's heart dropped.

These soldiers wore black.

MAMORU

Mamoru ran faster than he ever had in his life. He didn't have time to pick the easiest path up the snow-covered rocks, so he did what his father did, making ice steps for himself as he ran. In his haste to reach the blacksmith village, he nearly tripped and fell over a body that lay crumpled in his path.

It was Katakouri Hakuzora, dead in the snow.

On his way back to the old village, the archer must have heard the screams or seen the smoke and detoured to help the blacksmiths. His bow lay splintered beside him, his sightless eyes squinted slightly as if he had been lining up a shot when he died.

There was no time to collapse and mourn. Mamoru had done enough of that over Yukino Sensei's body. In all likelihood, that was when the fonyakalu had broken through to the numu village—while Mamoru had knelt crying like a child. Dropping briefly to one knee, Mamoru took Katakouri's hand and wrapped it around the grip of his bow where it belonged.

"Nyama to your soul, Senpai," he murmured, and he was back on his feet, sprinting.

As he neared the numu village, Mamoru felt for the second time that day, that his skin might peel—not from wind this time, but heat. He was used to the distant warmth the forges, the way it built as he neared the little village, but the fire-dried waves of air rushing over him were far hotter than they should have been.

He leaped over the final ridge to the village and crashed into a wall of heat so intense it felt like it might knock him back down the slope. He had known from the oversized columns of smoke that something would be on fire, but nothing could have prepared him for the inferno that spread out before him now. For a moment, he could only stand transfixed and terrified as the smoke took his breath and the heat sucked the moisture from his skin.

"Fire is like an animal," Kotetsu Kama always told him. "If you feed it, soothe it, and treat it with care, it need not bite you."

The first few times the smith master had had him stoke a fire, Mamoru had accidentally put it out when his jiya jumped in response to the heat.

"Easy, koro," Kotetsu had snapped, smacking his hand back with a pair of tongs. "This isn't a fight. Do you understand?"

"Yes, Kama." Mamoru rubbed his smarting knuckles, pulled the moisture from the kindling he had just doused, and picked up the striking stones to start again. But each time the flame swelled, Mamoru's jiya surged up against it out of reflex—like water rushing back to fill the space left by a stone when it was dropped in a pool.

"What are you afraid of?" Kotetsu asked after Mamoru's fourth failed attempt.

"I'm not—" Mamoru started to protest. It was unseemly for a koro to admit fear, but he stopped short at the knowing look on his mentor's face. "It's just... isn't fire what Hell is made of?"

"Not just fire. There are boiling seas in Hell also," Kotetsu pointed out.

"Oh." Mamoru hadn't thought of that. "I didn't..."

"You misunderstand the order of the world. Hell is fire without the calming influence of Nagi and Nami. Fire without the power of gods to balance it. And what is our jiya?"

"The power of gods," Mamoru said.

"I know you koronu like to frame relationships between opposites in terms of conflict," Kotetsu said, drawing a piece of glowing hot metal from the coals. "Fire against water, light against darkness, day against night, but one who hopes to create must understand that opposites exist to balance and complement one another. This is why the tide-bringing moon follows the drying sun, why day follows night, why men marry women. I believe this is why the two greatest empires are Yamma, built on the power of fire, and our own Kaigen, built on the power of water. The two exist in this realm, not to destroy one another, but to create a balance between jiya and taya."

He paused to douse the red-hot metal with water. "In this balance, there is creation." Steam hissed from the metal, dispersing to reveal the twisted serpents that would one day form the guard of Mamoru's sword. "As a warrior endeavoring to draw on the numu arts, it is vital that you understand this."

"What about fonya?" Mamoru asked, staring at the serpents, made of two different metals but wound so tightly together. "The finawu say that the fonyakalu were born from this ocean, just like our ancestors. They were born from gods too."

Kotetsu made a thoughtful noise. "I believe that fonyakalu... whatever divinity they hold has been corrupted into a type of power that was never meant to be. Not in the realm of the Duna."

"I don't understand."

"Based on what I know of wind—what it does to fire, and oceans, and empires—I would say that fonya is the power of chaos. Anyone who wields the power of wind, whether he realizes it or not, is a sort of demon."

Mamoru had not understood his mentor's logic at the time. Fonyakalu controlled air, an essential part of water and fire. Kotetsu himself had taught Mamoru to use the bellows to ensure a fire was properly oxygenated. Every living human, including jijakalu and tajakalu, breathed air to survive. He had never understood how something so vital to all life in the realm of the Duna could be a force of Hell.

He understood now.

The fonyakalu couldn't have reached this place more than a few siiranu ago, but the blacksmith village was already consumed. Even with the forges smashed to pieces, the fire never could have spread so fast or grown so furious without wind behind it. Mamoru had come to know fire as an animal that could be tamed with jiya, but this fire was uncontrolled—an animal fed to bursting, whipped to a rage, and set loose on its keepers.

This was the power that had ravaged the order of the world, destabilized Yamma's Namindugu colonies, ripped the Kaigenese Empire in two... This was the power of chaos.

With a sickening feeling in his stomach, Mamoru remembered that Uncle Takashi had ordered the numuwu to stay in their houses. He wondered how many of them had been able to outrun the flames, and of those, how many had escaped the Ranganese soldiers.

He tried to run straight for the Kotetsus' house, but the moment he approached the nearest structure, the flames leaped at him like hungry demons, simultaneously lashing at his skin and evaporating his only means of defense. Pressing forward, he raised his jiya and threw snow into the fire in an attempt to clear a path through the flames. It was no use. Most of what he threw evaporated in an ineffectual hiss. The Matsuda Dragon itself would have had its jaws full fighting this creature. Overwhelmed by the heat, Mamoru had no choice but to double back and go around the worst of the fire.

The best he could do now was find any survivors and get them out. As he ran into a part of the village where the fire was less intense, a sound drew his attention. Crying. The sob broke off abruptly in a crunch of bone. He rounded a burning house to find a Ranganese soldier standing over a prone woman. Her face was so bloody that it took Mamoru a moment to recognize her as Kotetsu Saori, one of Kotetsu Kama's cousins. She was the one who did the lacquer work on the sheaths. She had spent over a year designing his mother's sewing box, agonizing over each iridescent flower petal.

The fonyaka's boot was on her neck. Seemingly unaware of Mamoru's presence, he lifted his foot to stomp again.

Mamoru had never formed and fired a spear so fast in his life. The water jumped into formation before his thoughts had even solidified into an attack, propelled forward by pure rage. The fonyaka barely had a chance to lift his head before he was impaled through the chest. As the icy projectile jutted out of the soldier's back, Mamoru was already racing forward.

"Kotetsu-san!" He fell to his knees beside the woman and touched her shoulder. "Kotetsu-san, can you hear me?" But the blood in her veins had slowed. Her nyama didn't stir. She was gone.

Her young daughter lay a bound away, her spine twisted at a horrible angle, broken. Further down the foot-beaten path through the center of the village were other bodies—big and small, men and women. Kotetsu Saori's oldest daughter, Kasumi, lay dead beside a tiny bundle of a body. Her newborn son. A *baby*. No older than little Izumo.

A few siiranu ago, Mamoru hadn't thought there could be anything worse than staring down at his teacher's still fingers and shattered skull. But Yukino Sensei was a warrior. He had lived to fight. It was one thing to kill a koro, who faced you with pride and purpose. But death in battle held no meaning for a numu. What had been done here was unthinkable. Unforgivable.

Beside Mamoru, the fonyaka jerked against the ground, coughing blood. Not quite dead. Rage flooded Mamoru and he brought his sword slamming down on the man's exposed throat. The awkward angle and sloppy technique caused the blade to stick in the fonyaka's spinal column. Mamoru jerked it free with a snarl and stood.

For a moment, he felt an overwhelming urge to lift his own foot and stomp on the fonyaka, feel his body break beneath his heel. Crush him. Break him until he was as shattered as the women and little children he had killed.

But there were more numuwu in this village, and if even one was still breathing, Mamoru had to protect them. Fists clenched, he stepped over the fonyaka's corpse and moved on to look for survivors. He scanned every piece of wreckage as he went, but found no movement except the hellish thrashing of the flames. It seemed that whatever Ranganese had been here had moved on after ensuring that their victims were dead. Kotetsu Saori's killer must have been a straggler.

Halfway through the village, Mamoru encountered a thick wall of ice. It was mostly melted, but it had succeeded in holding the flames back from the easternmost houses in the village. Mamoru let an open hand trail over the water-slick ice and felt relief wash over his singed nerves. He knew this ice, recognized its stable underlying structures. Rounding the end of the wall, he finally found human movement in the rubble. His face broke into a smile of relief when he recognized the soot-stained face of his mentor.

"Kotetsu Kama!" His voice cracked. "You're alive!"

The ice wall had prevented the fires from reaching the Kotetsus' wooden house, but the fonyakalu had decimated the structure, reducing it to a pile of rubble.

"Matsuda-dono." The blacksmith looked up as Mamoru ran to him. "You have to help me!"

"What is it?" Mamoru asked.

"My son." Kotetsu's usually steady hands shook and Mamoru realized that they were smeared with blood from clawing through the rubble. "Atsushi is trapped under the house."

"And the rest of the family?" Mamoru asked.

Kotetsu Kama swallowed. "Th-they..." Mamoru had never heard Kotetsu struggle to control his voice. "The little ones were able to crawl out and run after..." He swallowed. "A-after the soldiers were gone. I think they made it to safety."

"What about your wife?" Mamoru asked. "Your mother?"

Kotetsu shook his head. "It was so fast. There were only a few of them, but they brought the fire out of the forges. Then when people came running out of the houses, they killed them. Kaa-san knew. She told us not to stay inside from the beginning..." He put a hand

307

to his eyes. Mamoru had never seen his mentor this way, as a husband and son, as someone who could feel lost.

"Kotetsu Kama." Mamoru had no idea how he kept his own voice from trembling. "You have to get out of here. There are still Ranganese coming up the mountain. Uncle Takashi said he would hold them, but I don't know how long—"

"I won't leave without my son."

Mamoru found himself wanting to nod in agreement. Something in him didn't want Kotetsu to go. The numu had always been a source of comfort and guidance, but he was a blacksmith. It wasn't within his power to stop the threat coming up the mountain, nor was it his responsibility; it was Mamoru's.

"I will protect your son," Mamoru promised. "But I need you out of danger. I'm just one fighter. I don't know if I can protect you both at once."

"Surely you're not on your own," Kotetsu said.

"The Yukinos and Mizumakis are all gone. My father was sent back to the main village to protect the women and children, and my uncle..." Mamoru couldn't understand how he suddenly knew. "My uncle is dead," he said softly.

"What?" The stricken look on Kotetsu's face reminded Mamoru that the blacksmith had once helped train a young Takashi at the forges. They had been friends since childhood. "He can't be..."

Despite Kotetsu's denial, Mamoru knew. He still wasn't sure how. Maybe the certainty came through his subconscious awareness of the nyama around him. Maybe it was the simple logic of how much blood Uncle Takashi had lost, how many enemies he had been facing, and how long it had been.

"The Ranganese will be here any dinma," he told Kotetsu with fresh urgency. "You need to be gone before they get here. I'll take care of Atsushi. Go!"

"But—"

"Do what I say!" Mamoru bellowed, surprised at the strength in his own voice.

In the forge, he was Kotetsu's student, but the forges were gone now. This village had turned into a battlefield, and on the battlefield, the koro's command ruled.

Kotetsu only hesitated for a moment, considering Mamoru as though seeing him for the first time. "You're a fine koro, Matsuda Mamoru." He bowed his head in acceptance. "I leave my son to you."

Mamoru nodded, silently accepting responsibility.

"Nyama to you, Matsuda-dono." Kotetsu said, and fled up the mountain.

Immediately, Mamoru got down on his hands and knees and peered into the darkness beneath the rubble.

"Atsushi-kun?" he called to his friend. His voice shook at first, but he pushed the tremor down with a smile. "Atsushi-kun?" his voice was stronger now, more encouraging. "Can you hear me?"

He couldn't quite make out words, but there was a muffled response from under the broken wood and stone. Wind whipped the flames on the other side of Kotetsu's ice wall. The fonyakalu had almost reached them.

"Hold on, okay? I'm going to get you out of there. I just need to take care of some fonyakalu first. Hold on."

Gripping his sword, Mamoru ran to the edge of the village, far from the flames, where he could meet his enemies with the full frozen power of his jiya. If there had been some small hope that his uncle would survive to help him, it disappeared when he reached the ridge overlooking the southern pass.

He had always heard that a theonite's nyama could do strange things at the moment of death. He had felt the air spasm when he killed fonyakalu, but the gruesome sight below was unlike anything he had ever heard of.

It was as if every drop of Uncle Takashi's godlike nyama had manifested in ice at the end—in some sort of final defiance. The resulting formation was not a recognizable shape like a katana or a dragon. It was something primal and raw.

An explosive personality in life, Matsuda Takashi had *become* an explosion in death, frozen branches and blades bursting from his body in all directions—crystal ice veined with blood. Unwary fonyakalu who had been too slow to jump clear were speared through limbs, chests, and abdomens by the force of his dying jiya. Some had been hoisted off their feet high into the air, creating a tree of corpses that glittered red against the sunset.

Those who had survived the carnage were charging up the slope toward Mamoru.

With a slow breath, Mamoru raised his sword. Atsushi and Kotetsu Kama were behind him, counting on him to protect them. Beyond them, his mother and father were counting on him. Beyond this mountain, the fishermen of the Shirojima islands, and the farmers of Yuwei and Hakudao were counting on him. His Empire was counting on him.

He took in his enemies—one, two, three, four, five fonyakalu—as they flew up the slope. Any one of these soldiers who got past this point would kill Kotetsu Kama on the path. They would kill Atsushi too, if they found him, and then move on to the main village to kill more. And after that, after everyone in Takayubi was dead, these soldiers would press inland, bringing the same fate to hundreds more.

Unless the Sword of Kaigen served its purpose.

So I will.

With that thought, Mamoru's limbs seemed to grow light, buoyed by new energy. Yukino Sensei had given his life so he could fight on, and Uncle Takashi had given his last moments to make the job easier. Their strength was in his limbs, pumping from his heart into his veins. There were no longer any confusing ambiguities or difficult choices. There was only what Mamoru had been bred and trained for since he was old enough to hold a practice sword—to charge down the mountain at his enemies and kill.

Kill.

Kill.

16

THE SOUL

For the second time that day, Misaki shrank away from the Ranganese at her doorstep, but this time her fear was not pretend. Even at her physical prime, she wouldn't have dreamed of challenging a member of Ranga's special forces in combat. Now she faced two.

The taller of the pair was a towering man with a spray of shrapnel scars across half his face, a sign that he had survived battles in the past. The smaller was a woman with the sort of legs Misaki would have killed for when she was at Daybreak—long and well-built. At first glance, neither fonyaka had any weapons, but Misaki noticed that the woman had a pair of strange straight knives tucked into her belt, one at each hip. No, not knives, Misaki realized. Fans.

Misaki had once made fun of Ya-li for fighting with a folding fan, but she had shut up after she saw the way a deftly-wielded fan could amplify fonya, doubling its range and power. To a jijaka, a fan was an aristocrat's accessory to go with fine inkstones and scented stationery. To a skilled fonyaka, it was the difference between a strong attack and a devastating one.

The black-clad Ranganese stepped forward and Misaki stepped back. Just from the fonya radiating from them and the powerful grace of their movements, she knew that facing them in combat was not an option. The only thing she could do was try to draw them

311

away from the cellar where her family sheltered.

Turning, Misaki ducked into the nearest side hallway. The female fonyaka darted after her, gaining on her with alarming speed. Damn those legs. The male fonyaka smashed right through a wall to cut off her retreat. Misaki stumbled to a stop, her heart pounding, trapped between two fighters far stronger than herself. The man took a menacing step toward her while the woman drew the fans from her belt.

Thinking fast, Misaki drew all the water she could from the surrounding air. She raised the liquid on either side of her, as if ready to form twin ice shields, as if she had anywhere near the power of jiya to withstand what they would throw at her. The female fonyaka let out a derisive huff of laughter. One of the fans flipped open and struck.

Instead of bracing her defenses, Misaki let go of them. As the water dropped, so did she, flattening herself against the floor. There had been a time she could drop into a full split cold; now just a low crouch strained her muscles and sent a burning pop of pain through her hip, but it effectively put her below the trajectory of the air pressure.

The male fonyaka probably would have been able to dodge his comrade's attack in an open fight, but Misaki's water had obscured his view of the fan-wielder until it was too late. The wave of amplified fonya slammed into his body at full force, knocking him through the nearest wall and, judging by the crashing sounds, probably the two behind it as well.

"*Aiya*-!" The female fonyaka uttered a gasp of alarm.

Misaki's impulse was to use her enemy's moment of surprise and distress to close the distance between them, but a twang of pain in her hip told her that wasn't going to be possible. Instead, she slung a whip of ice-laced water at the woman's ankles.

Too slow. The fonyaka was light on her feet and leaped over the arc of the attack. The wind enhanced jump sent her spinning through the air toward Misaki. One of those long legs swung toward the ceiling and then dropped, heel first, like a hammer.

Misaki's days of springing around with that kind of elastic agility were passed; she had to clumsily throw herself to the side to avoid the attack. The axe kick landed with terrifying force, splintering wood and shaking the whole house. If the woman's foot hadn't broken clean through the floorboards, Misaki probably would not have survived the next two dinmanu. The moment the woman took to extract her leg from the planks gave Misaki time to scramble into a ready stance. Even so, she just barely managed to dodge the following slash. Fan blades clipped her sleeve, tearing the blue fabric.

As the fonyaka swung through her missed attack, Misaki turned her body into an upward cut, aiming for the brachial artery under the woman's extended arm. But rather than trying to reset, the woman spun *with* the momentum of her missed attack. Her body turned before the blade reached it, removing Misaki's target.

Misaki's cut brushed the back of the elite's uniform without hitting flesh, but that was the beauty of a little sword like Siradenyaa: she could change directions on a neye. The moment Misaki's cut missed, she flipped her sword over for an overhanded slice to her opponent's neck.

As the woman completed her spin, a closed fan clanged into the side of Siradenyaa, knocking it off course. Misaki pulled Shadow's Daughter back to her hip as the fonyaka did the same with her closed fan. In a strangely mirror-like moment, both women launched off a back foot, going for the stab.

Stupid girl, Misaki thought, almost disappointed with her young opponent. The fonyaka might have speed and strength on her side, but it wouldn't matter; Siradenyaa's stabbing range was so much longer than that of a fan, there was no way the Ranganese woman's attack could land first. Siradenyaa drove toward her victim's chest, aimed past the black buttoned uniform, past the breast to the beating heart beneath.

But in her haste to end the fight, Misaki had forgotten about the other fan. It appeared in the way just before her blade could strike its mark. Siradenyaa, of course, passed through the thin metal, but the stab had been diverted, missing the woman's heart to tear harmlessly through her sleeve.

Misaki made to slice free, but before she could adjust her stance to do so, the fan snapped closed, trapping the Zilazen glass blade in its folds. Gripping the closed fan, the woman twisted the sword from Misaki's hands, sending both weapons spinning away.

The moment she realized she was being disarmed, Misaki relinquished her hold on the sword and changed her stance to aim Blood-Needle-ready fingers at the woman's neck. Even with the opening, she still wasn't fast enough. The fonyaka bent out of the way of the attack, effortlessly drawing Misaki into a joint lock.

Against a stiffer fighter, Misaki would have tried to relax her muscles and slide free, but this woman was so flexible, she might as well have tried to escape the coils of a python. In a heartbeat, Misaki found herself slammed against the wood floor, her arm twisted painfully behind her, a knee crushing down between her shoulder blades. Fifteen years ago, she would have bladed ice across the bottom of her foot and snapped a scorpion kick into the woman's face, but she knew without trying that she no longer had the flexibility in her spine to make a move like that work.

The woman twisted her weight against Misaki's arm, wrenching a roar of pain from Misaki's throat.

Think, Misaki! Think, before your arm is broken!

This fonyaka was sharp. She would notice any overt movement, in either Misaki's body or the surrounding water. Thankfully, the Tsusano Blood Needle was not the only needle in Misaki's arsenal. With two fingers, she drew together a sliver of water molecules a stride from herself and the fonyaka: a tiny version of the mighty ice spears the men of Takayubi were so fond of.

Most fighters would choose a forbidding spear over a needle, but the nice thing about needles was that they could slide through cloth, flesh, or air unnoticed, and they took only a tiny movement to direct. The Ranganese woman didn't notice anything as Misaki's water thread froze to a hard point. She cranked Misaki's arm further. As the pain spiked, Misaki snapped her two fingers inward, yanking the ice needle toward them.

The shriek was as gratifying as it was terrible; it let Misaki know that her attack had found its mark in the fonyaka's eye. As that snakelike grip released, Misaki rolled free and staggered to her feet.

Impressively, the fonyaka found her way to her feet as well, a hand over her bleeding eye. Her scream of pain rising to one of rage, she lunged for Misaki. The remaining fan flashed forward and had the woman's depth perception not been compromised, Misaki would have been sliced to pieces in the ensuing fit of slashing and screaming. As it was, she had to deflect a few of the attacks with her forearms, shredding her sleeves and splattering her blood across the floor.

The woman drove her out of the hall, into the kitchen, and Misaki knew she had to end this while the advantage was still hers. Her eyes darted to where she and Setsuko kept the knives, but her brain canceled the thought before she risked her neck trying to go for the cupboard. She hadn't been able to kill this woman with a Zilazen glass sword; what good was a little kitchen knife going to do? Even injured, this woman moved so much faster than she did; she would have to immobilize her to kill her. Misaki was at the end of her stamina, her overtaxed legs ready to buckle beneath her, while the fonyaka's fury seemed to be making her stronger by the dinma.

Stumbling back from her crazed enemy, Misaki fell against the counter, careful to place herself directly in front of the sink. The woman swung her fan, releasing a burst of fonya, and Misaki dove sideways, letting the air pressure slam into the sink. Water exploded through the room, pouring from the broken faucet onto the floor and spraying high into the air.

The fonyaka let out a cry of surprise as the spray caught her in her good eye. Misaki took advantage of the woman's moment of blindness and moved in. Not trusting her shaking muscles with a sweep kick or any of the more advanced takedowns in her repertoire, she launched her whole body forward in a tackle. The taller fighter was so well muscled that it felt like ramming her shoulder into solid rock, but Misaki's momentum managed to take her off her feet.

Both women crashed to the floor as water spread out beneath them and rained from above. Instead of trying to pin the stronger woman down with her weight, Misaki landed with her palms on either side of her victim and forced her exhausted jiya into motion. As the fonyaka's good eye snapped open, her grip tightened on her fan and her fonya swirled back into motion with a vengeance—but it was too late. The fight was over.

The same clinging ice Misaki once used to scale walls was also excellent for immobilizing an opponent. Where most jijakalu required a considerable amount of water to freeze someone's body in place, Misaki needed only a thin sheet. In the moment after they hit the wet floor, she had frozen the fonyaka's hair, skin, and uniform to the floorboards with ice strong enough to stick a human to the side of a skyscraper.

Misaki watched the woman's working eye widen as she registered the biting cold and realized that she couldn't move. Her face twisted into a snarl. Fonya whipped Misaki's hair and kimono, but without its wielder's limbs to give it direction, the wind was no more than impotent bluster.

Reaching to the woman's right hand, Misaki pried the fan from her fingers. It might be a messy instrument of execution, but her muscles and jiya were so exhausted that she didn't think she had it in her to form an ice spear or even stand up and search for Siradenyaa. Flipping the fan open, she tried to find a comfortable grip on the base with her left hand; her right arm had been twisted so hard, she didn't trust it to hold a weapon.

"You slimy Kaigenese sea slug," the woman spat, resorting to racist insults, as so many fighters did in defeat. Not good ones either. *"You cheated."*

Indignant, Misaki scowled down at the fonyaka. "*You* try fighting fair after pushing out four babies," she panted in Shirojima Dialect she knew the woman couldn't understand.

As soon as the words were out of her mouth, a thought made her pause and stare down at the fonyaka. She was certainly younger than Misaki, but not too young to have children of her own... She had stopped struggling. Instead, she lay under Misaki, still except for the rise and fall of her chest. Her jaw was set in determination. It was the look of a woman steeling herself for death, the look of a woman who knew—who had always known—what she was getting into.

If she had children... well, then she shouldn't have traveled over the ocean to kill someone else's. She had no one to blame but herself.

Misaki raised the fan to strike.

"You're holding it wrong."

The unexpected words only made Misaki pause for a dinma. It was a mistake.

In that moment of hesitation, the woman *moved*. An animalistic shriek rent the air as her right arm ripped free of the ice, leaving her sleeve and most of her skin behind. In a lurch of horror, Misaki realized that the woman hadn't been steeling herself for death but for the worst pain imaginable.

Roaring in agony, the fonyaka caught Misaki's face in an iron grip, fingers slick with blood. Misaki tried to jerk her head back, but the younger woman was too strong. Powerful fingers dug in, levering her jaw open, and the fonyaka *pulled*—not on Misaki's body, but the air inside it.

Breath rushed from Misaki's lungs, dizzying her, and a sharp pain drove through her chest like knives. Panic took hold as she realized what was happening to her: *Lazou Linghun*, the Ranganese called it—the Soul Pull—a bloodline technique as rare as the Whispering Blade and as feared as Blood Puppetry. It took a tremendous amount of power to vacuum the air from another theonite's body, but with enough training, there were members of certain bloodlines who could do it. And in her pain-spiked rage, power did not seem to be an issue for this woman.

Misaki tried to fight the pull, tried to expand her lungs in a deep breath, but the moment she did, the rib-splitting pain nearly made her faint. In dinmanu, her lungs would be sucked empty, reduced to crumpled tissue. Unable to claw the stronger theonite's hand from her face, she slashed the bladed fan across the woman's throat. Blood spurted from the fonyaka's neck and her body convulsed against its ice prison.

Horrifyingly, her death throes only caused her grip to *tighten*, her nails drawing blood from Misaki's cheeks, and the pull intensified. It was as if the fonyaka's soul itself had dug claws into Misaki on its way out of the living world, determined to drag her with it.

Pain splintered through Misaki's chest and sides as her lungs started to collapse. Blind with panic, she struck again, driving the fan so deep into the woman's neck that it hit her spine and stuck there. The fonyaka's hand stiffened around Misaki's face, twitched... then finally, finally slid away.

Too late, Misaki thought as the world blurred. *Too late*. Her aching jaw opened wide, but no air came. Only suffocating darkness.

MAMORU

Mamoru made such quick work of the five fonyakalu that it didn't seem real. Was this what it was like to be Uncle Takashi, he wondered as he whirled, cutting through two yellow-clad soldiers in the same slash. If it was—if this was how *good* it felt—then he supposed he was happy his uncle had died fighting.

The bodies hit the snow and lay still. Mamoru stood among them, shoulders back, breathing hard in a mixture of exertion and exhilaration. After confirming that there were no more fonyakalu advancing up the slope, he ran to the Kotetsus' house and started digging through the rubble. Reaching out with his jiya, it didn't take him long to find Atsushi.

"Mamo—Matsuda-dono!" the boy's voice broke in relief.

Atsushi had always been quick with his jiya for a numu and it had saved his life. He had braced the debris off of his body with a pair of thick ice pillars. He didn't have the strength to push it off him entirely, but Mamoru did.

"Atsushi-kun. On three, we're going to lift together. Ichi... ni... *san!"* Their combined jiya shoved the debris upward and Atsushi scrambled out from underneath.

Mamoru grabbed his hand and pulled him to safety. Before he let the load back down, Mamoru stuck his arm underneath the house one last time, extending his fingers, feeling for the pulse of living blood. If Atsushi had survived the collapse, maybe someone else had too. *Maybe...* but no pulses pulled at Mamoru's fingertips. Only a slow, iron-laden ooze he was coming to recognize as blood leaving a corpse. Closing his eyes, he withdrew his arm and released his jiya, letting what remained of the house crash down.

Atsushi was clinging to his sleeve, shaking.

"Mamoru!" the little blacksmith gasped, forgetting formality in a mixture of anger and hysteria. "My mother is still under there! My grandmother—"

"Listen to me Atsushi-kun." Mamoru held the boy firmly by the shoulders. "Your mother is—" The words caught in his throat. He couldn't say it. He couldn't imagine hearing those words, so he chose different ones. "All your mother would want is for you to live." And that was worse—because he didn't have to imagine. He had seen the look on Kaa-chan's face when he pulled himself from her hands, watched her fingers grasp at the air where he had been. "That's all she would want. Your grandmother too. You know that."

Atsushi was shaking his head in denial, his eyes shining with tears. And, perhaps because he suddenly felt tears threatening in his own eyes, Mamoru slid an arm around Atsushi and pressed the little blacksmith to his shoulder.

"For your mother, Atsushi-kun. Head up the mountain. Catch up with your father if you can. If you can't, find a safe place to take shelter. You know this mountain better than the fonyakalu. If you hide..."

Mamoru trailed off as something caught his attention: a flash of black on the rocks above—too fast to be a passing bird. His heart dropped.

"Run, Atsushi-kun!"

"What—"

"Run!" Mamoru threw the boy from him.

He had barely flung his own body backward when the fonya hit. The wave of air pressure struck the snow where he and Atsushi had been with a sound more like thunder than wind.

Mamoru tucked into a ball and rolled as he hit the ground. When he uncurled onto his feet, tabi skidding through the snow, Atsushi was still tumbling from the force of the attack. The wind had thrown the two of them several bounds apart.

The elite fonyaka landed in a crouch between them, torn black cloth fluttering about him like feathers before settling about his form. Mamoru hadn't gotten a close look at the man's face before, but his eyes passing slowly over the man's body, confirmed his worst fear. There was the sloppily retied braid cut by Yukino Sensei's first swing. There were the thin cuts where the Matsuda Dragon's teeth had sliced through his clothes into his skin. There was the bleeding puncture wound in his left shoulder where Tou-sama had aimed to kill him... and failed.

The dragon killer uncurled into a standing position with lazy grace.

On the other side of the fonyaka, far beyond Mamoru's reach or the range of his jiya, Atsushi struggled to his knees. The ten-year-old numu was shaken and disoriented. Easy prey. Helpless, Mamoru watched the dragon killer's eyes flick from him to Atsushi in playful indecision, as if he hadn't quite chosen a victim yet. If his injuries had weakened him, it didn't show in his posture, and if he was still at full strength, Mamoru knew that there was nothing he could do to protect his friend.

"Run, Atsushi!" he shouted as Atsushi tried to stand. "Run!"

Atsushi was fast for a numu. Of course, that wouldn't save him from this demon who seemed to move at the speed of sound.

If I run, Mamoru thought frantically, *if Atsushi and I break in opposite directions, maybe I can get the fonyaka to follow me.*

Running would cost him his life, he knew. You couldn't expose your back to a superior fighter and expect to live, but that wasn't the point. Mamoru was fast. He might be able to buy Atsushi enough time to get to safety.

Then he remembered his first encounter with the dragon killer, remembered how the black-clad demon had brushed right past him and the Yukino cousins, heading straight for Yukino Sensei. This fonyaka was like Uncle Takashi; he had a hunger for a good fight that eclipsed everything else. Where lesser predators were drawn to the weak and wounded, this one was drawn to strength.

The realization snapped into place right as Atsushi found his feet and ran. Like a tiger triggered to motion by scattering deer, the fonyaka darted after him.

"No!" Panic lent speed to Mamoru's jiya as he raised the snow and fired a pair of spears at the fonyaka. The dragon killer must not have been sufficiently impressed because he blew Mamoru's attacks away without so much as a glance in his direction, and took another step after Atsushi.

"NO!"

The power of a dozen jijakalu seemed to fill Mamoru's limbs. The ice wall was bigger than anything he had ever formed in one shot. It exploded from the snow like a geyser and rose to tower over the dragon killer, stopping him in his tracks.

Mamoru was well aware that the fonyaka could break through the wall or vault over the top if he really wanted to. It was a simple show of power, something to draw the man's attention from Atsushi.

It worked.

The fonyaka turned to Mamoru as if seeing him for the first time. He wore a strange expression, as if he hadn't decided if he was impressed or just exasperated.

"If you even think about following him, I'll fill your back with spears." Mamoru knew the fonyaka didn't speak Shirojima Dialect, but he was certain that the threat carried in his tone.

The dragon killer raised an eyebrow as if to say, '*Are you serious? You're sure you don't want to run?'*

I wasn't made to run, Mamoru thought. "Face me, fonyaka."

Realistically, Mamoru wasn't a match for this man, who had fought Yukino Sensei, Tou-sama, and Uncle Takashi to a standstill. But that was exactly why he had to win. There was no one further up the mountain who would be able to stop this creature. Dozens— possibly hundreds—of innocent people would die if he was allowed to continue on his way.

Maybe I can't kill him, Mamoru thought, drawing his sword. *Maybe I can't kill him, but I can do* something. *I can wound him badly enough that my parents will have no trouble finishing him off.*

"*Hao.*" The fonyaka rolled his neck with a resigned sigh that seemed to say *Let's get this over with quickly.*

Mamoru bent his knees, ready to spring out of the way of one of the long-range attacks these fonyakalu seemed to favor. Then he remembered how hungrily this particular fonyaka had devoured the distance between himself and Yukino Sensei—not once but twice. His weapons, before he had lost one in Yukino Sensei's shoulder and the other in the maw of the Matsuda Dragon, had been a pair of daggers, which worked best in a direct physical clash. For whatever reason, this man preferred fighting in close. But that didn't mean he *couldn't* fire off longer-range attacks. Mamoru had to be ready for an attack at any distance.

The fonyaka came at him, shooting over the open snow so fast his feet didn't even seem to touch the ground. More arrow than man.

Mamoru's first instinct was to coil back into his stance and look for the perfect place to strike, like Tou-sama. End the fight in one cut, like Yukino Sensei. But Tou-sama and Yukino Sensei had already failed to kill this man, and Mamoru was not their equal. There was no precision or intelligence in Mamoru that this man hadn't already seen from Tou-sama, no speed or perfection of technique he hadn't seen from Yukino Sensei, no raw ferocity he hadn't seen from Uncle Takashi.

Eyes forward, Kaa-chan's voice reminded him, quelling his panic. *Focus on what's ahead of you.*

Mamoru breathed out and Yukino Sensei's voice joined hers. *A student like you, who can absorb what he is told but also think beyond it, is capable of anything.*

Mamoru's only chance—if he stood any chance at all—was to be that student and hit this man with something he wouldn't expect.

So, instead of setting a stance to wait for fonyaka, Mamoru ran to meet him.

Unlike the other elite soldiers Mamoru had faced, the dragon killer didn't need to plant his feet to throw an attack. He fired off a palm strike mid-sprint. The lightning-quick blast didn't land with enough force to throw Mamoru off his feet or shatter bone, but the moment it hit, Mamoru realized its intended purpose—too late. The wind had already struck his right arm, sending his katana spinning from his hand, high into the air.

Losing his sword should have thrown him off, but he had built up too much momentum to let anything slow him down. He was a Matsuda. His sword wasn't made of ice or metal. It was his soul. Mist and snow rushed to his hands as the last of the distance between himself and his enemy collapsed.

The fonyaka's next palm strike hit the best impromptu ice shield Mamoru had ever formed. The shield's hardened outer layer shattered, while the snow cushion beneath absorbed the impact, blunting the force of the palm strike before it reached the innermost ice sheet that protected Mamoru's arms. The techniques canceled each other out, causing both fighters to stumble back only a few steps instead of sending them both flying.

Regaining his footing, Mamoru threw what remained of his shield at the fonyaka. In the dinma the black-clad man took to swat the inner layer of the shield aside, Mamoru raised his hands and locked his jiya into the still airborne pieces of the outer layer. The ice had broken along planned seams, creating sharp-edged shards.

Let's see you dodge this, Mamoru thought, and yanked his hands inward, bringing those hundreds of sharp pieces racing toward the fonyaka. Even the most agile fighter couldn't dodge his way through a hail of projectiles this thick.

At the glint of approaching ice, the fonyaka let out a short sound of surprise. Then he spun. *Damn!* Mamoru had forgotten he could do that! The rotation created a protective whirlwind around the fonyaka. The cyclone wrapped around him like a cocoon, catching Mamoru's hundreds of tiny projectiles and flinging them away. Some of the ice shards flew wide. Most of them, however, shot straight toward Mamoru, propelled by a deadly combination of his own jiya and his enemy's fonya.

He had to push sharply outward with his jiya to avoid getting hit by his own projectiles. His reflexes saved him from fatal injury, though some of the ice struck him in the shoulders and thighs. His opponent didn't leave him time for the pain to set in.

The fonyaka's pivoting feet were as subtle as they were quick. Mamoru wouldn't have picked up the movement with his eyes alone, but he was so attuned to the water around him at that moment that he felt the shift in the snow beneath the soldier's boots. Even knowing the spinning kick was coming and having seen it in action, Mamoru barely managed to drop into a crouch in time to avoid it. He let out a breath of relief as the kick whooshed over his head, missing him completely. What he hadn't counted on was the second kick.

He registered the black boot snapping toward his head too late to evade. All he could do was bring an arm up to protect his head. The roundhouse crashed into his forearm, which then crashed into his face, throwing him sideways. His head rang as if it had taken a full force kick and his *arm*—he was fairly sure something in his arm had broken. But oddly, it didn't hurt. Flooded with fighter's madness, he was far past feeling any pain. He spun out of the blow smiling, his fists up, ice sharpening across his knuckles.

The fighter's high must have lent him speed because he managed to deflect the snakelike hand technique the fonyaka aimed at his neck. He feinted a punch at the fonyaka's face with one hand, using the other to target the man's injured shoulder. If Tou-sama had already done half the damage for him, maybe— The dragon killer saw through it. He barely bothered to dodge the feint, letting the weak blow clip his cheek, and parried the stronger punch Mamoru aimed at his shoulder.

Sensing the fonyaka shifting back, Mamoru seized a handful of the man's black uniform. He couldn't let the dragon killer out of close range. He had seen the kind of attack this man could throw from his optimal striking distance and had no intention of letting him set up another one. Mamoru yanked the man forward.

The dragon killer didn't seem to mind, drawing his arm back to throw a punch—a bizarrely telegraphed move for such an apt fighter. Mamoru brought his right hand up to block, but somehow—inexplicably—the fonyaka's punch passed *through* it.

The blow caught Mamoru in the stomach, bringing the world to an abrupt halt.

A dull throb pulsed through his abdomen as a smile twisted the corner of the dragon killer's mouth.

"Got you," he said in broken Kaigengua.

For a moment, Mamoru was so surprised to hear words—words he *understood*—coming out of the demon's mouth that all he could do was blink.

Then he felt the blood soaking into his hakama, and it dawned on him that the attack he had just taken hadn't been a punch at all. Shock melted into dread as he looked down.

The thumb and first two fingers of his sword hand were gone, sliced off at the second knuckles. There was a blade lodged beneath his ribs—long, bright, and strangely familiar. Mamoru couldn't understand where the weapon had come from until his eyes fell on teal wrapping and serpent's coils. It was *his* sword. The dragon killer had caught it on its way down.

Mamoru's mind stuttered, confusion, denial, and begrudging awe grinding against one another like wedges of ice on a breaking river. His own sword... Did that mean the fonyaka had planned this whole exchange of blows? From the moment he knocked the weapon from Mamoru's hand? Was he really that good? If so, Mamoru had never stood a chance. Then again, maybe the wound wasn't as deep as it looked. Maybe he could still fight. He could still—

The dragon killer ripped the blade free and Mamoru watched his own insides spill from his body. Reality overcame him like river waters breaking through the last of winter's ice. *I'm dead,* he realized with chilling clarity.

I'm dead.

17

THE END

"Misaki?" a voice said above her. Why was her chest full of knives?
Gods, it hurt so much! "Misaki!"

Her eyes blinked open and she was surprised to see that there
were not, in fact, several blades buried in her torso. She was in one
piece, the only bleeding from the jagged cuts on her forearms.
Setsuko was staring down at her with tears in her eyes.

"Misaki! Oh, thank Nami you're alright!" Before Misaki could
react, the other woman had wrapped her in a crushing hug that sent
new spikes of pain through her ribs. And Misaki remembered: the
flash of fan blades, a skinless arm, *Lazou Linghun* sucking the
breath from her lungs.

What are you doing? Misaki tried to say. *Get back! Go back and
hide!* But when she opened her mouth, only a wheezing groan came
out.

"Yosh, yosh," Setsuko soothed, rubbing her back. "You're going
to be okay."

"H-how..." Misaki whispered and felt her eyes watering with
pain. How could making a single sound hurt so much? "How... lo-
ong...?"

"How long were you out?" Setsuko said. "Just a few dinmanu, I
think. I just heard all this terrible screaming, and I know you said to
stay in the cellar, but I had to... I'm sorry. I'm sorry," she babbled,

"But I had to make sure you were alright. You passed out just as I came into the room. And-and there's so much blood in here! I didn't know whose it was and I-I thought you might be dead, Misaki! What happened?"

Mutely, Misaki shook her head. Setsuko wasn't supposed to know. She wasn't supposed to know any of this.

"So, this girl here..." Setsuko said, nodding to the partially beheaded, partially skinned mess that had been the fan-wielding fonyaka. "Did you kill her?"

Squeezing her eyes shut against the pain, Misaki nodded.

"And all those men in the halls? Was that you too?" Setsuko spoke slowly, as though she was almost afraid to know the answer. But there was no point trying to lie, so she nodded again.

"Great Nami, Misaki!"

Misaki kept her eyes shut, not wanting to see Setsuko's expression of horror. She waited in agony for her sister-in-law to recoil, push her away. Instead, Setsuko clutched her tighter.

"I'm so glad you're here!" Setsuko's voice broke into a sob. "What would we have done? What would we have done without you?"

That was when Misaki felt it: a vague sense that there was still a living fonyaka nearby. She gripped Setsuko's shoulders and gritted her teeth, trying to form words.

"Get... back..." she managed finally. Setsuko wasn't safe here.

"I'm sorry," Setsuko said as Misaki's feeling solidified into a certainty. Somewhere in the next room, a fonyaka was winding up for an attack. "I know you said to stay hidden, but when I heard the screams, I just couldn't—"

"Back!" Misaki shoved Setsuko with all the strength left in her body—just as the neighboring wall exploded.

The wind sent Misaki tumbling across the wood. She put her hands over her head, hoping that her push had been enough to put Setsuko out of range of the debris biting into her forearms and clattering across the floor around her.

Get up! Her mind screamed even as the numbness of shock and impact pulsed through her limbs. *Get up and fight!*

Her body wouldn't do it. Everything hurt so much.

All she wanted was to lie down and let this new attacker kill her. Let it end. But her life wasn't the only one in the balance. Because Setsuko was there—perhaps *only* because Setsuko was there—she planted her hands on the floor and tried to stand. She never did make it to her feet.

Instead, a hand seized her loose hair and yanked her upward, wrenching a cry from her damaged lungs. It was the scarred fonyaka. The blood dripping from his head made Misaki glad she hadn't taken the full impact of the fan-wielder's attack, as he had. The impact had likely left him unconscious for a few siiranu, but it didn't seem to have weakened him. With what seemed like an effortless swing of his arm, he hurled Misaki across the kitchen.

She hit the table where Mamoru and Chul-hee had been studying and tumbled across it, shattering teacups and scattering scrolls. When she collapsed onto the tatami on the far side of the table, her whole body seemed to pulse with forming bruises. Her scalp stung and there was now a screaming pain in her neck to rival that in her lungs. Fighting the stars crowding her vision, she gripped the side of the table and tried to stand, but her body was shaking so badly she couldn't do it. Blinking through the stars, she could just make out the scarred fonyaka striding toward her.

"Stop it!" a voice shouted and Misaki turned to see Setsuko brandishing a kitchen knife. "Leave her alone!"

"No!" Misaki's eyes widened, panic driving her to her feet. "Setsuko, don't!"

Too late. Setsuko had already run at the soldier, raising the knife to stab. The fonyaka's casual backhand sent her smashing through the kitchen's back door.

"No!" Misaki screamed. "No! No!" She rushed forward—to go to Setsuko? To attack the man? With her mind scrambled from the impact, she wasn't even sure, but the fonyaka moved faster.

He caught her around the throat and slammed her back down on the floor. At this point, Misaki didn't even know if killing this man would make a difference. She would live, yes, but when the next soldiers entered the house, she would be far too weak to fight them off. She was tempted to give up, let him kill her—but he had hit Setsuko, so he was going to die.

She didn't resist as he straddled her and put both hands around her neck to strangle her. Instead, she focused her jiya into two fingers. As he pressed his considerable weight down on her windpipe, he put himself close enough to give her a clear shot through his left eye.

Blood Needle ready, she drew her hand back and—

A blade struck the man in the neck.

Misaki started. Her immediate thought was that Setsuko had woken up and come to her aid. But when her eyes flicked from Siradenyaa's glass tip to her hilt, it wasn't Setsuko she found clutching the handle.

It was Hiroshi.

The five-year-old was barely big enough to hold the lightweight sword in both hands, but his stance was solid and his gaze fixed.

Above Misaki, the fonyaka's face twisted in a grimace. He was wounded but not dead. Blood squirted grotesquely from the cut in his neck as he straightened up and turned to face his attacker. Hiroshi didn't flinch as the drops spattered his face and chest.

"Hiro—" Misaki started, but the fonyaka put a foot on her chest, slamming her back down so hard her head spun.

Still holding Misaki to the floor with his boot, the soldier looked down at Hiroshi, incredulous. Offended almost. Misaki's heart lurched in panic, but there was no fear on Hiroshi's face, no hesitation. He didn't even pause to adjust his grip on the weapon before he slashed again, opening a clean cut from the man's hip to his collarbone.

The fonyaka made a strange noise and reached out as if to grab at Hiroshi. Shoving the boot from her chest, Misaki scrambled to her feet to defend her son. But the man only stumbled and crashed to the floor. His fonya rose for a moment, rushing through the room in a howl of denial, then went still.

Hiroshi had killed him.

Blood dribbled down his blank face as he turned to face Misaki. "You're safe now, Kaa-chan."

With something like a sob, Misaki snatched the sword from his hands and flung it away. She grabbed her son by the shoulders—roughly, her breathing too quick, near hysteria.

Why would you do that? she wanted to scream, to shake him. *Why would you do that?*

But Hiroshi was only five. He had only done what he had been taught by his teachers, his distant father, and his monster of a mother. They had created a little boy who was ready to give his life to kill his enemies. A true Matsuda. Misaki's head dropped onto Hiroshi's tiny shoulder. The monster crumbled and she was just a woman, just a mother who had failed her son.

"Hiroshi..." her voice broke. "Come here."

Gathering the boy into her arms, she held him tight, and loved him, loved him as hard as she could, and hoped it would be enough to wash everything else away.

Hiroshi, as always, was cold.

MAMORU

The dragon killer stepped back and cast aside the nameless sword, now red with its owner's blood.

Mamoru swayed.

Blood drizzled from the stumps of his fingers onto the frozen ground. It was a strange sensation, feeling the liquid that carried his nyama leaving him to seep out onto the mountain. His vision slid. But it couldn't be over. It just couldn't. If he could just force himself to move, push through it, it would all be alright. He took a step... and another... fell to one knee. His mangled hand hit the snow—

And the world snapped into focus.

The pain was sharp, but small, unimportant somehow. Suddenly, it wasn't as though he was missing fingers. His fingers were the snow. They were the rivers, reaching all the way down the mountain to sink into the ocean and grasp the power of gods. He wasn't bleeding out. He was the mountain. For the first time in his life, he was perfectly, overwhelmingly whole.

He smiled.

A decade later, a fifteen-year-old Hiroshi would become known as the youngest swordsman ever to master the Whispering Blade. What the world would never know, was that he was the *second* youngest.

By the time the Ranganese soldier registered the blood-red flash of ice, it had already passed through his body. The sword was pure Matsuda—half Takayubi snow, half Mamoru's own blood—and it cut through the dragon killer like he was no more than air.

Alone on the mountainside, a Whispering Blade caught the last rays of a dying sun. It gleamed once, pointed skyward, as its first and only victim hit the snow. Then, its work done, the sword fell to mist. The sun sank to the sea.

Mamoru didn't feel the jiya ebb from his body, didn't feel himself fall. All he knew was that his cheek lay numb against the icy ground as the last of the red left the sky.

I did it, he thought, and the blood spreading from his body seemed unimportant. *Tou-sama, Kaa-chan, I did it!* He couldn't wait to tell them!

If part of him was lucid enough to understand that he was never going to see his parents again, he ignored it. The power that had just filled him was too big not to be remembered. He had touched divinity, held it in his hands. He didn't hear the thunder of approaching planes or the loudspeakers announcing the arrival of reinforcements.

As he and the dragon killer had fought, their feet had churned the surrounding snow into waves, like the brine at the beginning of the world. Red from Mamoru's fingers snaked through those waves to mix with the blood slowly seeping from the other man's body.

Blood became snow, became blood, became ocean... and Mamoru found his eyes frozen open, staring into the dragon killer's face.

It wasn't a frightening face or even a particularly foreign one—pale skin, black eyes, and sharp features, much like Mamoru's own. In a different uniform, the man could have been an upperclassman or a young teacher at Kumono Academy. People always said the Ranganese were demons of a different breed from the Kaigenese, but their blood seemed to be the same color, now that they lay still, letting it run together. They had all come out of the same ocean, hadn't they? At the beginning of the world?

The dragon killer didn't look like he had felt any pain. If anything, he looked faintly surprised, his eyes wide and his lips parted. Just a human. Here with Mamoru at the end of the living world. As his body grew warm and numb, Mamoru wondered if this fonyaka had someone to remember him across the ocean—a father, a mother, someone who would be proud to hear that he had died on the Sword of Kaigen.

18

THE SHELTER

Misaki started at the sound of a crash, clutching Hiroshi tighter to her. But the young fonyaka who appeared in the doorway was already dead, his spine snapped by a single pale hand around his neck. A wave of icy jiya overtook her as Takeru threw the boy's limp body aside and stepped into the room.

"You're a mess," he said by way of greeting. "Both of you. Where are Setsuko and the other children?"

"S-Setsuko is unconscious," Misaki said, pointing to the next room. Her jiya had quickly confirmed that her sister-in-law's heart was still beating, but she wasn't sure what damage she might have sustained. She hadn't quite gotten herself to move, not wanting to let go of her son. "Izumo, Nagasa, and Ayumi are hidden in the cellar."

"Well, what are you just sitting there for?"

"Mamoru," Misaki started desperately. "Where is—"

Then a roar tore through the sky outside. Another tornado? No. *Planes.*

"Citizens of Takayubi," an amplified voice split the night in Kaigengua. *"In the interest of national security, his Imperial Majesty has ordered an airstrike on the area. You have ten siiranu to reach the nearest bomb shelter."*

Chul-hee had done it! Reinforcements were here.

"His Imperial Majesty has ordered an airstrike on the area," the voice repeated. *"You have ten siiranu to reach the nearest bomb shelter."*

"Well, we have our orders," Takeru said as if the mayor had just instructed him to file a bit of paperwork. "Let's go."

"What about the others?" Misaki asked. "Your brother?" *What about Mamoru?*

"They'll hear the announcement too," Takeru said in the same uninterested tone. "They're fast. They'll meet us at the shelter. Get the rest of the children."

Nodding, Misaki got to her feet and ran to the cellar. When she threw the doors open, the three smallest children were huddled among the food stores. Ayumi fussed on the floor, still half-wrapped in the cloth Setsuko had unslung from her shoulder. Nagasa was curled up at the back of the shelter with Izumo in his lap, his hands over the infant's ears.

"Come, Naga-kun," she said, kneeling to comfort little Ayumi. "Bring the baby to me."

Takayubi only had the one bomb shelter, further up the mountain by the mayor's office, and they only had ten siiranu to reach it.

"Naga-kun, I'm so sorry." She stroked a hand across Nagasa's bangs before picking up the babies, one in each arm. "I'm going to need you to run. You can run on your own, right?"

"Yes, Kaa-chan," Nagasa said, his eyes wide with confusion as the planes tore lower outside. Misaki wasn't sure if he really understood or the response was just automatic, but she only had two arms.

"Hiro-kun," she said as she emerged from the cellar with Nagasa and the babies, "hold your brother's hand and don't let go. Make sure he keeps up."

"Yes, Kaa-chan." Hiroshi slid his blood-smeared hand into Nagasa's and held tight, pulling him after Misaki as she made for the front doors. Misaki led them through the back hallways of the house, avoiding the kitchen and the main hall where most of the butchered bodies lay. Nagasa didn't need to see that.

When they stepped out into the genkan, Takeru was waiting for them, Setsuko's limp form slung across one shoulder as if the hefty woman weighed nothing at all.

"Is she—"

"She'll be fine," Takeru said. "Let's go."

The dusk outside was chaos. Women screamed and scrambled to find others. Children didn't know where to run. Misaki scanned anxiously for Ranganese soldiers, but the only ones she found were already dead, lying motionless in the snow while the scene around them swirled with the chaos they had created.

"Did you kill all the Ranganese in the village?" she asked.

"Every one whose feet touched the snow," Takeru replied.

Of course. A Matsuda's power flowed through the snow of the mountain. No soldier standing outside in that snow would have escaped Takeru's ice. But that meant that there were almost certainly soldiers he had missed, those who had entered homes to dispose of women and children.

Planes roared closer to the mountainside in the dark, the swooping, scraping sound so big it seemed to exist in multiple dimensions. Nagasa stared, wide-eyed, up at the jets as Hiroshi pulled him along.

"Birds?" he asked in excited curiosity, seemingly oblivious to the pandemonium of adults around him.

"Planes," Hiroshi corrected. "The Emperor sent his pilots."

"Why?"

Hiroshi's answer was simple but accurate: "To kill."

"You two!" Takeru called to two Mizumaki women—a mother and daughter—nearby. "My wife is injured. Help her carry her children to the shelter."

"What?" Misaki started to resist as the women moved to obey. "What are you talking about? I'm not—"

"Don't listen to anything she says," he told the Mizumakis without looking at her. "She has a concussion."

"What...?" Misaki realized that he was probably right, but it was hard to say if he could tell or if he was just using it as an excuse to ignore her words.

As the women took Izumo and Ayumi from her, a figure approached—notable because he was moving in the wrong direction, down the mountain instead of up toward the bomb shelter.

Takeru recognized him before she did.

"Kwang Chul-hee," he said.

The northern boy still had the wakizashi Takashi had given him tied at his hip, but he didn't appear to have met with any Ranganese. Other than being out of breath, he seemed unhurt.

"Matsuda-dono," he panted. "Are all of you alright?"

"We're fine," Takeru said. "Well done contacting reinforcements, by the way. You have our thanks."

"My father took a census from the mayor's office and he's been checking people in as they reach the shelter," Chul-hee said. "I came to look for the families we're still missing." He looked down at his info-com device, the display illuminating his face in the growing dark, and tapped at the screen. "Now that all of you are on your way up, I can check off your family... except..." He looked up at their small party again. A pained expression crossed his face. "Where's Ma—"

"Who else are we missing?" Takeru demanded, starting up the slope toward the bomb shelter. "Other than warriors?"

"Um... half of the Mizumaki family is unaccounted for," Chul-hee said. "We're missing all but one of the Katakouris, and no one has seen a single member of the Yukino family."

"What?" Misaki stopped in her tracks. "Are you sure?"

"Sorry," Chul-hee said. "No one has seen Yukino Hyori or her son."

"No!" Misaki put a hand to her hip, only to have her fingers brush the lip on an empty sheath. She had left Siradenyaa in the house. Weaponless, she turned imploringly to her husband, still armed with Kyougetsu. "We have to go back! We have to find her!"

"My brother ordered me to get you, Setsuko, and the children to safety. Come now. We have to move."

"She's our friend. How can you—"

"These are my orders," he said, "and I have given you yours."

Misaki clenched her jaw. "Yes, sir." Then she swayed, putting a hand to her head. "Sorry, I... I feel dizzy. Kwang-san, could I have your arm?"

"Of course," Chul-hee said and rushed to support her.

Takeru must have noticed her eyes flicking to the wakizashi at Chul-hee's hip. He stepped forward to stop her. Knowing she was not physically fast enough to outmaneuver him, Misaki spun. Instead of going straight for the weapon, she turned her body into Chul-hee's in a move that put the young man between herself and her husband.

"W-wait—what?" The northern boy stuttered in surprise.

As Takeru's hand closed on Chul-hee's shoulder instead of hers, Misaki seized the handle of the wakizashi.

Then she shoved off Chul-hee's body, simultaneously throwing him backward into Takeru and propelling herself forward. The wakizashi slid from its sheath and she was sprinting, weapon in hand, toward the Yukino compound.

She didn't look back to see if Takeru was following her.

He could either leave Setsuko with Chul-hee, hoping the boy would be able to get her safely to the shelter, or he could try to pursue Misaki while carrying their sister-in-law. Either way, the Yukino compound was close enough that he wouldn't catch up to her before she got there.

The double doors at the front of the house hung open, knocked from their hinges by the same blunt force fonya that had breached the Matsuda compound. Not far from the entrance, Misaki found a tiny body in a light gray kimono. Ryota. The four-year-old lay face-down on the genkan step. Blood had seeped from his back to stain the Yukino snowflake insignia, but Misaki could feel that the blood in his veins had stilled.

She looked away quickly, knowing there was nothing she could do for the sweet little boy.

"Sorry, Ryota-kun," she murmured and tried not to think about his bright-eyed smile or his infectious giggle as she pressed on. She had to find Hyori.

The first thing Misaki saw of the Ranganese soldier was his back. He was on top of Hyori, straddling her. Her kimono was torn open, exposing her pale legs.

Misaki was on him before he could turn. Takashi's spare wakizashi might not have been as light or sharp as Siradenyaa, but Misaki's slice was clean, cleaving through muscle, windpipe, and spinal cord in one strike.

At this point, Misaki was becoming familiar with the wind off a dying fonyaka—a haunting but harmless breeze from the weaker soldiers and an outright howl from the black-clad elites. None of that prepared her for the power that burst from this man the moment she cut through his neck.

The wind flung its host's blood in all directions, shattered a few nearby vases, and threw Misaki to the floor, reawakening the stabbing pain in her chest. She struggled to her hands and knees amid porcelain shards as the last of the man's fonya roared through the rest of the house, making the walls creak.

With a horrified sound between a shriek and a sob, a blood-splattered Hyori kicked, trying to drag herself out from underneath the headless body.

"Sorry!" Misaki exclaimed and scrambled forward to haul the corpse off her friend. "I'm sorry, Hyori-chan. That was... messier than I anticipated."

Hyori was bloody, her face streaked with tears, but Misaki flooded with relief to feel that her friend's nyama was still strong. Most of the blood on her had come from her attacker. Sobbing, Hyori tried to rearrange her kimono to cover herself, but her hands were shaking so badly that she couldn't do it.

"Hyori, I'm so sorry," Misaki said, touching the other woman's shoulder. "I'm sorry I didn't get here sooner."

Considering the power of the soldier's dying fonya, it was unlikely Misaki would have been able to kill him without the element of surprise, but she should have tried. Or someone should have tried. Somehow. This should never have happened.

Pulling water from the air, Misaki swept it down her friend's body, clearing away the blood, and everything else the Ranganese soldier had left on her. Then she tried to close up Hyori's kimono for her, but the garment was so ripped, it didn't cover her breasts—bruised where fingers had clawed at them.

Misaki clenched her teeth. Until now, she had not felt true hatred for the Ranganese, but suddenly, she wished she hadn't killed the man so quickly. Wistfully, she thought of all the things she could have done to him before he died, how many times she could have stabbed him, how many pieces she could have cut off... but no amount of violence would heal Hyori.

Despite her rage, Misaki forced her voice to be soft as she rubbed her friend's arms. "It's alright, Hyori-chan. He's dead now. He's gone. It's going to be alright."

"No, it's not. It's not." Fresh tears spilled from Hyori's eyes and rolled down her cheeks. "He killed my son! My son! My baby boy!"

Part of what had always made Hyori so beautiful was her simplicity. Those soft eyes were as clear as spring melt, concealing nothing. In love, in joy, in mirth, she was pure. Her pain was the same. Undiluted. And it was unbearable to look at.

Misaki ruthlessly forced back her own tears. They weren't out of danger.

"You're still alive," Misaki insisted. "You're going to survive this."

"I don't want to." Hyori's voice was broken. "I don't want to, I don't want to."

"I'm so sorry, Hyori-chan." Misaki tucked a strand of the woman's hair behind her ear. "I know this isn't going to be easy, but I need you to stand up."

There would be time to come undone after everyone was safe. Pulling off her own coat, Misaki wrapped it around her friend, tying it closed to cover what the ruined kimono couldn't.

"Yosh, Hyori-chan." Misaki pulled Hyori's arm, doing her best to be gentle in her urgency. "There's a good girl. Stand up."

"I can't." Hyori was shaking her head. "It hurts."

"You have to. Bombs are going to start raining on this mountain any siira now."

"I don't care. Just leave me."

"I can't do that," Misaki said. "What will I say to Dai-san when he gets back?"

"He won't want me," Hyori sobbed into her hands. "I'm disgraced. I'm ruined."

Ignoring her friend's protests, Misaki draped Hyori's arm across her shoulders and stood, pulling the other woman up with her. Hyori let out a pitiful cry of pain, her legs buckling beneath her.

"Please! Misaki, just leave me! Let me be with my son!"

"No," Misaki said through gritted teeth. "No. You're not going to die here. Neither of us are."

By the time Misaki got Hyori to the broken doors of the Yukino compound, the woman had fainted. Takeru was waiting there, still holding an unconscious Setsuko.

"We don't have time for this," he said. Shifting Setsuko onto one shoulder, he reached out to pick up Hyori.

"No." Misaki bent over and hoisted Hyori's limp form on her own shoulders. "I've got her. Just run."

"Misaki—"

An ear-splitting explosion shook the ground, and Misaki's stomach dropped. The airstrike had started. She ran. Hyori was considerably taller than Misaki, but Robin Thundyil, Elleen Elden and several other people would be dead if Misaki couldn't make good time carrying a person bigger than herself to safety. Takeru was running too. And even if there had been time for them to argue, they would hardly have been able to hear each other.

Bombs rocked the lower slopes like thunder, shaking the ground beneath Misaki's feet. In the distance, men cried out. She could only hope that the screams belonged to Ranganese and not villagers unable to reach the shelter. Amid the deafening noise and darkness, there was no way to tell.

Ahead of her, Takeru skidded to a stop in the snow. Misaki nearly stumbled into him before she saw why he had stopped. A skinny figure stood in the dark before him—Atsushi, the swordsmith's son.

"M-Matsuda-dono!" The boy yelped. He had an ashen look on his face, as if he had just witnessed sights that struck the soul from his body.

"Atsushi," Takeru said. "Where is your family?"

The little smith's lip trembled. "M-my father..." He pointed toward the southern pass. "One of the bombs hit him. H-his leg is gone. H-h-he told me to run. I-I couldn't help him. He's still on the path and I'm not strong enough to carry him. Please—Matsuda-dono. You have to go back. You have to save him."

Takeru stared at the numu boy for a moment. Then he scooped him up around the waist and kept running.

"Wait! Matsuda-dono, no!" Tears streamed down Atsushi's face as he struggled, kicking ineffectually at Takeru. "Please! Please!"

"This is unseemly, boy," Takeru said coldly. "Don't make me knock you unconscious."

With a last sob of despair, Atsushi stopped fighting and clung to Takeru, burying his face in his lord's kimono—as if there was a drop of comfort to be found there.

Atsushi's cries hurt Misaki's heart, but she couldn't fault her husband for this particular decision. Her detour to save Hyori had already put their lives in danger. Heading back down to the southern pass in the middle of a dusk airstrike would mean almost certain death. Even to save Takayubi's greatest swordsmith, it wasn't worth it.

The shelter was in sight, only a few bounds ahead, when the sound of a low-swooping jet split the air. Deafened by the sound, Misaki stumbled from the force of the wind. Then a bomb hit— mere bounds from her. Had she been unburdened, she might have kept her footing, but with the wind and Hyori's dead weight throwing her off balance, she fell.

Pilots had good eyesight, but the sun was gone. And in the dark, fonyakalu were indistinguishable from jijakalu.

Misaki rolled over onto her hands and knees. Unable to find the strength to stand, she crawled toward Hyori. The other woman groaned, mournful eyes blinking open as Misaki gripped her arm. Through the ringing in her ears, Misaki could hear her whimpering.

"Why? Why are they firing on us?"

Because we don't matter, Misaki thought numbly. *The only thing the Empire cares about is stopping the Ranganese here. It doesn't matter how many of us get caught in the crossfire.*

Before Misaki could pull Hyori up, she felt Takeru's jiya rising around them. The snow beneath her turned to a plane of ice as smooth as the surface of a frozen lake. Most jijakalu couldn't create ice formations strong enough to lift multiple people, but Takeru was not most jijakalu. He lifted his hand and the smooth ice tilted, sending everyone on it sliding toward the shelter entrance.

A shower of bullets shattered the ice where Hyori had just been, but the formation itself held. A moment later, Misaki, Hyori, Atsushi, and an unconscious Setsuko tumbled to the bunker's jonjo glass floor. The hands of the other villagers immediately grabbed them, pulling them the rest of the way in.

"Kaa-chan!" a relieved voice said and Misaki found Nagasa clinging to her arm.

"Atsushi," Chul-hee said, helping the battered young smith to his feet. "Are you okay, numuden? Where's your family?"

Atsushi shook his head. His sob became one of many filling the small bunker. As Misaki got to her feet, Takeru slid into the shelter on his own ice, a hail of bullets following him almost to the threshold. He managed a smoother landing than the rest of them, even as gunfire sent up a spray of cutting ice shards all around him.

"Back!" he ordered the rest of the villagers, outstretched hands stopping the ice shards before they could shoot into the bunker.

"What about your son, Matsuda-dono?" Chul-hee looked from Takeru to Misaki. "Where's Mamoru?"

"He's not here?" Misaki scanned the huddle of people in the dark confines of the shelter and didn't see him. By her quick count, there were no more than thirty-five, most of them women and children. Surely there had to be more survivors than that! But when she turned back toward the town, no one was following them up the mountain.

"Matsuda Mamoru is still missing," Chul-hee's father, Kwang Tae-min, said. "Along with his uncle, Yukino Dai, and almost all the men."

"What?" Hyori said weakly.

Takeru grabbed hold of the heavy shelter door, ready to slide it shut.

"Wait, wait!" Hyori clutched at Takeru's sleeve. "Matsuda-dono, my husband is still out there!"

Takeru ignored her and started to close the door.

"Wait," Misaki insisted in a stronger voice. "Hyori's right. What about all the fighters?" *What about Mamoru? Where is Mamoru?*

Takeru didn't look at her. "No one else is coming," he said in a flat voice.

Misaki felt the whole world gray. The maddened energy that had kept her moving stilled. "What?"

"When I left the line, my brother and son were the only fighters left alive. There were still over a hundred Ranganese advancing on their position. No one else is coming."

All the strength went out of Misaki's limbs.

"No... no..." Hyori's voice started as a low methodical moan that rose in pitch until it was a shriek. "No, that can't be right! *That can't be right!*"

"You should be proud, Yukino-san." Takeru looked down at the wrecked woman. "He died with his sword in his hand."

Hyori screamed.

....

That night in the bunker was as close to Hell as any night in the Realm of the Duna. The darkness stank of blood and vomit. Hyori screamed for her son and husband. Ameno Samusa's wife insisted that her daughter had been awake when she brought her to the bunker, even as those around her tried to tell her that the girl's skull was shattered. One of the Ikeno elders died right there in the crowded darkness while her daughters-in-law tried to patch her injuries with the meager medical supplies in the shelter. Through the noise, Misaki was dimly aware of Izumo wailing in her lap, but she couldn't seem to lift her arms to hold him.

It was only now that she was coming down from her fighter's high, that she understood what had kept her body moving through this whole ordeal, through injuries that should have put her out of commission. It was more than adrenaline. There had been a hope, however ridiculous, that they would all make it through this alive. That hope had started to die in the Yukino compound when she saw little Ryota's body. The clunk of the closing door had fallen like a sword, killing it entirely. The shelter was sealed and Mamoru was not there. Mamoru was not coming.

After being held back so long, exhaustion rushed over her with a vengeance, weakening her to the point of paralysis. Grudgingly, she realized that Takeru had been right about the concussion. Her head pulsed. Shapes that should have been clear blurred in the dim light.

Even her jijaka senses, which never failed her, started slipping away. The human heartbeats that were usually so distinct in the dark, warped and mashed together with the pain in her own pulsing head and chest. Tears, saliva, blood, sweat, and stomach acid became indistinguishable as they moved through people's bodies and oozed out of them.

"Kaa-chan?" Nagasa's terrified voice at her shoulder was the only thing keeping her tethered to reality—a thin thread preventing her from falling into the formless chaos. "Kaa-chan, what's happening?" The toddler tugged on her sleeve, trying to pull his mother back to him. "What's happening?"

She couldn't make her voice work to answer him. She couldn't even lift a hand to offer him comfort. Not when skin disappeared and Misaki couldn't even tell what liquid was moving inside all the bodies and what was spilling out.

"Kaa-chan, Baby crying!" Nagasa's little voice broke. "Baby crying!"

When he couldn't get his mother to respond, Nagasa cried too.

Eventually, the sobs, and screams, and moans of pain all coalesced into a sticky sea of sound, varying only when the boom of bombs too close to the shelter caused it to swell. The sea consumed Misaki. Fire and acid seemed to leach into her lungs, reawakening the stabbing in her chest. The pain immobilized her like a spear through the torso, pinning her back against the bunker wall.

She needed someone to speak to her, a calm voice to ground her in reality before everything merged into this soup of blood and sound, but Setsuko was still unconscious, Hyori had crumpled to the floor, seemingly too deep in her own agony to register anything around her, and Takeru... well, Takeru, of course, didn't even turn to look at his wife. He stood with his back to the other villagers, facing the bunker door, an immovable stone figure in the dark.

Misaki had the strange feeling then that he was the key. If she could reach out and grab onto him, he might stabilize her. His rigid form was the only thing that seemed to be motionless in the writhing, weeping crawl of human flesh. But he was as distant as he was still, and Misaki knew from years of experience that reaching out and calling to him wouldn't make a difference.

He was untouchable.

She was alone, drowning in screams.

19

THE LANTERN

The fire in Robin's hand guttered as a roll of thunder graced them with another shower of rain. He made a dissatisfied noise in his throat.

"We might have to switch to that thing soon," he said, nodding to the unlit kayiri lantern swinging from Misaki's fingers. *"If it rains harder, I won't make a good light."*

"You've been a fine light, Robin. We're already there." Misaki pointed to the small light ahead—the street lamp that marked Ishihama's only bus stop.

"Your father predicted this," Robin said, staring up at the evening sky, now nearly black with clouds. *"Right down to the volume of the thunder and the size of the raindrops."*

"He does that."

"How?"

"If I knew that, I'd have applied for a job in weather forecasting instead of emergency medical treatment."

"I should have asked him to teach me," Robin mused as they reached the bus stop, marked only by a wooden sign affixed to the lamppost.

"I don't know how that would have gone."

"Because I'm a tajaka?"

"No. I think it's a matter of experience. He was born in the

Arashiki, you know. The more storms you experience, the more you pick up on the signs."

The rain fell harder and Robin's flame finally went out, leaving only the light of the bus stop's solitary street lamp.

"Sorry about this," Misaki laughed. She extended an open hand above Robin's head—no easy feat as the tajaka was several koyinu taller than she was—diverting the raindrops around him. *"We really should have tried to come up with an umbrella for you."*

"Hindsight." He shrugged, seemingly not at all bothered as the ocean wind blew rain through Misaki's guard to spray his neck and face.

They were quiet for a moment. Misaki stood close in order to shield him from the rain, close enough to feel the heat radiating from his body through his black coat. She sighed, melting into the warmth, trying to let herself savor it, just in case this was the last time... but, no. She wouldn't think about that. Robin couldn't know she was thinking that. If she was going to do this right, he had to go on ahead.

"So?" he said, and she blinked up at him, coming out of her darkening thoughts. *"Did I do alright? Or were they just pretending to like me?"*

"Pretending? Robin, no. They loved you—Kazu especially."

"He smacked me around a lot for someone who likes me," Robin said, rubbing a bruise on his chin where Kazu's fist had clipped him in a hand-to-hand bout.

"You accepted the invitation to training," she pointed out. *"Anyway, he's a sixteen-year-old Tsusano. That's how he shows affection. I'd be more worried if he hadn't bruised you a bit."*

"Alright then," Robin laughed. *"I'll take your word for it and be flattered."*

"Thank you for not burning him," she said, *"and for giving him a few wins. That was gracious of you."*

"Giving *him?"* Robin repeated. *"He fought well."*

Misaki just raised an eyebrow at her friend in a knowing expression.

Robin sighed. *"He was trying so hard,"* he said and Misaki rolled her eyes.

"Gods, you're soft, Thundyil."

Tsusanos were masterful with the sword, but hand-to-hand combat was Robin's domain. Kazu had been far out of his depth challenging their foreign guest to an empty-handed match. While Robin was not one to back down from a challenge, he was also not the sort of person who reveled in humiliating a younger fighter who was doing his best. Where Misaki was used to simply thrashing Kazu and walking out with an imperious toss of her hair, Robin had let the boy have his pride.

"Besides," Robin added after a moment, *"I thought the idea here was to get your parents to like me. I thought throwing their heir all over the dojo was maybe not a good way to do that?"*

"Oh, Robin," Misaki laughed a sigh. *"You really don't understand Shirojima culture. Being the strongest is a* good *thing. That's why all these powerhouse Shirojima families are always intermarrying. I would say letting Kazu get a few hits in was a mistake except that my father knows a thrown fight when he sees one. He was sufficiently impressed."* She hoped.

"Power," Robin said. *"That's really the thing people use to decide who they marry?"*

Misaki nodded. *"This whole betrothal business..."* She had avoided bringing it up this whole time; she didn't know why she brought it up now. *"My parents scoured the region for the most powerful house that would take me."*

"And did you land a good house?" Robin asked casually, but Misaki could sense the tension in his voice.

"Who do you think you're talking to? Of course, I did," Misaki said, equally tense, though she tried to pass it off as indignation. *"Matsuda, House of the Whispering Blade."*

"Langana, Misaki, not bad!" Robin was still trying a little too hard to sound casual. He shook his head. *"It just all seems so... old-fashioned."*

The observation made Misaki laugh in earnest. *"You're just now noticing that we're old-fashioned? Did you not notice how we light our house?"* She jiggled the kayiri lantern in her left hand—her right was still guarding Robin from the rain—*"Or the fact that my father kept calling you Son of Kri?"* a title that had been used centuries ago to address tajakalu of unknown parentage. *"We keep to the old warrior traditions the rest of the world has forgotten and we're proud of it."*

The rain thickened from a patter to a deluge and Robin caught her hand, letting the water pour down on him. Creatures of fire usually wilted and shivered in the rain, but Robin Thundyil never seemed to fit in with the rest of his kind. His Disanka skin, so much darker than Misaki's but lighter than a Yammanka's had a luminous quality to it, like the aura of a littigi but warmer. He *glowed* in the downpour. Raindrops evaporated as they fell on him, hissing softly. The mist they created caught the fiery light of his skin, cloaking him in flame-like vapors.

"I don't want to leave without you," he said.

Misaki looked at him through the rain and saw an unfamiliar emotion in those coal black eyes. Robin Thundyil, Firebird, the crime-fighter who made hardened criminals quake at his shadow, was afraid.

"I'll be right behind you." She squeezed his arm. *"Just like we planned."*

"One week," Robin said firmly. *"You'll be back in Carytha in one week?"*

"Yes." If everything really does go to plan. *"I will."*

If this *didn't* go to plan... well... Misaki couldn't think about that now. If she let her mind wander in that direction, she would never be able to let go of Robin's sleeve.

"Right." Robin was nodding, seemingly more to himself than Misaki. *"You're smarter about this stuff than I am. I trust you."*

Stupid boy, a voice in her head scoffed, but it was drowned out by a part of her that hoped to all the gods that Robin was not being stupid, that his trust was not misplaced. Still caught in her thoughts, she didn't notice Robin leaning in until his lips met hers.

She stiffened with a small noise of surprise. The water that had managed to seep into Robin's clothes, heated by taya, hissed to steam when it touched Misaki's cold skin. Instead of recoiling from the threat of frostbite like a sane tajaka, Robin sank into it, drinking the cold like a parched man at a half-frozen river. Misaki melted.

Kissing was one of those bizarre Carythian practices that had first repulsed Misaki and later seduced her. Apparently, the romantic custom had been introduced to Carytha by the white slaves imported from Hades during the height of Yammanka colonialism. Most tajakalu did not kiss, but Misaki remembered thinking the first time Robin's lips met hers that she had never been happier that this particular tajaka had grown up in a barbaric white slum.

Wound up in his heat, she had to wonder what appeal this held for the white adyns with no jiya or taya. Where was the magic in something that didn't seethe between extremes? Where was the excitement in a kiss that didn't spark, and steam, and *burn* like this? Robin held her there, wound in tendrils of steam, before breaking the kiss.

"Sorry," he said as Misaki raised a hand to tingling lips, doing her best to look affronted rather than melted. *"I just had to—just in case—I'm sorry. I'm just nervous."*

"Why?" Misaki laughed to cover the fact that she was just as anxious, if not more so. *"You did your part. You were wonderful."*

"What if it wasn't enough?" Robin asked. *"What if they say no?"*

"They won't."

"But if they do?"

Misaki shrugged. *"Then the answer is no."*

"It just seems weird to me that you would let someone else have the final say on who you spend the rest of your life with."

"Not just anyone else," Misaki said. *"They're my parents. They know me better than anyone, and I trust their judgment. That's how I knew they would like you."* She smiled.

"If you say so... I guess I'll have to defer to your expertise," Robin laughed. *"I don't have much experience with... family stuff."*

Robin had lost both his parents and all his siblings except his twin brother, Rakesh, in the border skirmishes between Ranga and Disa when he was only five. A loss like that was enough to shatter a child beyond repair, but somehow Robin had put those pieces back together into a broad smile and a heart open to everyone. *A voice for the silenced, a shelter for the defenseless, a pair of fists for the powerless.*

It happened against Misaki's better judgment: she tipped onto her toes as if falling upward and caught Robin's mouth in another kiss. The lantern slipped from her fingers and splashed to the ground, forgotten, as her hands tangled in Robin's hair. Coarser than Kaigenese hair, straighter than Yammanka curls—an anomaly, like everything about him. Her fighter who preserved life. Her theonite who kissed like an adyn. Her tajaka who drank the cold like it could sustain him.

They broke apart just as the bus came rattling up the path, headlights glowing in the rain. Cheeks flushed, they scrambled to stand an appropriate distance apart as the headlights brushed over their dispersing steam and the bus squeaked to a halt. The driver stepped out, squinting to see the teenagers through the driving rain.

"Two?" he asked in Shirojima Dialect, rounded with a full Ishihama accent.

"No." Misaki shook her head, indicating Robin. "Just the one. He doesn't speak Kaigengua or Dialect, so please make sure he doesn't miss his stop. Shirojima Grand Station."

"Of course, Ojou-sama," the driver spoke respectfully, noting the Tsusano crest on Misaki's yukata. "He'll be taken care of. Any big bags?" he asked, gesturing toward the luggage compartment under the passenger seating.

"No," Misaki said as Robin picked up his single waterproof bag and slung it over his shoulder. While the Thundyil twins had recently come into a ridiculous amount of money, Robin's habits had not yet adjusted for it. He still packed like a boy who had grown up in an orphanage.

"Well," Robin straightened out his thoroughly sodden coat. *"Goodbye,* Ojou-sama." He bowed at the waist and put his first two

knuckles to his lips in a charmingly strange combination of a Yammanka parting and the Kaigenese one he had just learned.

"Ah, wait!" Misaki snatched the lantern from the puddle where she had dropped it. *"Wait, Robin!"* She dried the lantern with a quick pull of her jiya and held it out. *"Before you go..."*

"Oh." Robin smiled. *"Of course."* Putting his hand into the lantern, he struck a flame at his fingertip. Steam hissed and he ignited the little wick inside.

The lantern illuminated Robin as he boarded the bus and gave her one last smile. The doors closed and the vehicle rolled away, gravel crunching beneath its tires.

It was a long way back to the Arashiki, but Misaki's lantern stayed alight the whole way, even as the rain persisted. The kisses lingered, tingling on Misaki's lips, along with her promise: *I'll be right behind you.* As she came out of the trees near the cliff's edge and picked her way down the rain-slick staircase carved out of the rock face, more lantern flames winked in return, illuminating the windows of the mighty Stormfort. Most of the region used electricity to light their houses these days, but the storms that battered the Arashiki made electricity unreliable. They still used portable kayiri lanterns for light.

The stairs down to the Arashiki had a sturdy railing running alongside them, to keep the Tsusanos and their visitors from plummeting to the ocean below. Misaki no longer worried about falling as she had when she was a child. She no longer formed the thin layer of clinging ice beneath her tabi to keep each step anchored to the stone in the wind. Things like rocks and heights had ceased to frighten her. Somewhere in the past four years, her fears had grown bigger and less physical.

"Ah, Misaki." Tou-sama gave her a broad smile as she came in. "Did your friend make it to the bus alright?"

"Yes." Misaki's hair and yukata were soaked, but a quick wave of her hands turned the water to vapor.

"For his sake, I hope you got there before the rain."

"No, but he'll live. It does rain, on occasion, in Carytha. He just isn't used to the amount we get here."

Robin had spent a week at the Arashiki. Several people had commented that it seemed silly for someone to cross the world only to stay such a short time, but there was only so long Robin could stay away from his city without things starting to fall apart. In the few days he had stayed in the Tsusanos' home, he had managed to make friends with everyone, despite the language barrier. That was what Robin did. He had done his part to make this work. Now Misaki just had to do hers.

She took a breath, sick with nervousness.

"Is something wrong, Misaki?"

"Now that he's gone, I... I need to talk to you, Tou-sama."

She had planned to wait until the next day. It was late now and her father would want to sleep soon, but she couldn't wait. She wouldn't be able to rest if she had to lie down with the question still squirming through her mind.

"The storm is just beginning," he said. "We should talk further inside."

Misaki followed her father into one of the Arashiki's interior sitting rooms, so deep that it was essentially a finished cave, carved into the cliff side. Even here, the sheets of rain were still loud against the Arashiki's walls, mixing with the sound of waves on the rocks below. Misaki knelt opposite her father, setting the lantern between them.

"Now, Misaki," Tou-sama said gently, "what is it, child?"

"Tou-sama... I don't want to disrespect you..."

"You haven't, Misaki." His tone was light, humorous. "Are you planning to?"

"It's just... I know you went to a lot of trouble to secure my betrothal to Matsuda Takeru. I don't want you to think I don't appreciate that. I do. But... I-I just..." Nagi's Sky, why was she stammering so much? She took a breath to collect her words. "I know Robin told you—I had him tell you—that he was here as part of a research project."

"That's not why you brought him here." Tou-sama had probably seen through the lie the moment she told it; he could read people as he read weather patterns, like no one else.

"I'm sorry for lying, Tou-sama." She bowed her head. "I needed you to meet him, so you would understand what I... what I'm about to ask you."

"Well, flower, you've got me curious now. Spit it out."

"I um... I don't want to marry Matsuda Takeru." She said it all in one breath, her eyes closed. "I want to follow Robin back to Carytha."

She opened her eyes and found Tou-sama's expression unreadable in the wavering lantern light.

"He's agreed to marry me," she added hastily, feeling light-headed, as if there wasn't enough breath in her chest for all the words she needed to make her father understand, "since I know Kaa-san really wants me to marry young, and you're concerned about my future being secure. You saw what a good fighter he is, he's just inherited more than enough money to support a family, and I would still be marrying according to my station—technically, *above* my station, since the Thundyils are honorary manga koronu in their homeland. Of course, you're my father. I wouldn't without your permission..."

She looked to Tou-sama, anxious, aching. Her fists were clenched so tightly that her nails were driving crescent moons into her palms.

"Oh, Misaki... he is a good boy." Tou-sama's voice sounded sincere, so why did he seem so deeply sad?

"So," she said when she could bear the silence no longer. "Your answer?"

"No."

Misaki fought back the surge of anger—of *grief*—that rose in her chest. She had expected the answer. She had known there was only a slim chance. She couldn't be angry at her father. She could only be angry at herself for hoping, for letting *Robin* hope. When the Thundyil twins had found out about their inheritance, Misaki had seen a chance. Robin was a good fighter, the son of a good family, heir to a good fortune. Suddenly, he had met all the qualifications for marriage to the daughter of a great house. There had been a chance...

"Misaki," Tou-sama said and even through the irrational anger, she couldn't bear to hear him sound so sad. "I'm sor—"

"Please," Misaki said in a small, strained voice that seemed too fragile to belong to her. "Don't apologize, Tou-sama. I understand."

She really did. Robin was Disanka. His people had inherited their powers by mixing with their Yammanka conquerors, meaning his blood was impure. Misaki had of course seen enough to know that bloodline purity didn't have nearly as much bearing on a person's ability as people here thought, but she hardly expected her own experience to change deep-seated Kaigenese notions of propriety.

If Misaki were to marry Robin, their children would be even more mixed, and thereby worse off by traditional standards. Fire and water might balance each other, but they didn't mix well when it came to offspring. She knew that. Why had she done this? How could she have even entertained the thought that her parents would allow her to marry a foreigner? Why had she thought this would work? Why had she thought meeting Robin would change her father's mind?

"So..." She tried to breathe normally. "You're going to force me to marry the Matsuda?"

"No, Misaki. I have no illusion that I can force you to do anything you don't want to do. You're a Tsusano—tamable as a storm—but I order you to marry Matsuda Takeru."

His meaning was clear. She *could* abandon her betrothal. She *could* go to Carytha with Robin, but she would do so in defiance of her father. The realization twisted like physical pain in her chest. Why? Gods, why would he do this to her?

"Misaki..." Tou-sama's voice was not stern or cruel. In his quiet way, he sounded like he was in as much pain as she was. "I don't do this to hurt you."

"But why?" Misaki couldn't stop the tears from running down her cheeks. "Is this just because Robin's not a jijaka? Because his powers aren't genetically compatible with mine? Why should that matter? I'm a girl; I wasn't going to continue the Tsusano line anyway—"

"That doesn't matter to me," Tou-sama said resolutely. "He could be another jijaka or he could be an adyn with no power and no family name; my answer would be the same."

"I don't understand. If it's not about blood, then what is it? What's wrong with him?"

"Nothing, sweet girl. Nothing. I didn't need to meet him in person to know that. I may not have been a perfect father to you, but Nagi knows I didn't raise an idiot. You would never attach yourself to anything less than brilliance—and he *is* that. Brilliant, and driven, and kind..." He sighed, "but you must not follow him down the path he walks. You certainly cannot be allowed to marry him."

"Why?"

"That boy—the man he is going to become—would lead you into danger and, inevitably, to tragedy. I haven't pressed you about the violent business you've gotten yourself into at Daybreak Academy, but he is the source of it, isn't he?"

"I..." Misaki couldn't deny the observation, but neither could she voice the deeper problem. *I'm attracted to danger.* "Yes, Tou-sama," she said quietly.

"I understand," Tou-sama said, "that this is part of the allure. Don't think I can't recognize that. When I was your age, training to wield the Riptide, I wished for another war."

"You what?" Misaki said in surprise. Tou-sama had always been something of a pacifist, as forgiving as he was strong. Wishing for a war didn't sound like him at all.

"I was raised on the glorious stories of the Keleba and the days before it, when our people sank ships and battled invaders. As I trained, I thirsted for a chance to flex my skill in battle like the heroes from our legends. I dreamed of the Ranganese or some as-yet-unknown enemy sailing against our Stormfort, just so I could slake that thirst. Then one day, the thirst disappeared. Do you know what day that was?"

Misaki shook her head.

"It was the day you were born, Misaki. Since I started building something better and more beautiful than a fighter's glory, the idea of war has made me sick. The idea that my little girl might suffer or that my boys would be forced to go to war... That's not something a loving parent wants to contemplate, even the most hardened warrior. Now that I'm an old man, far past my fighting prime, I consider it a great blessing that I have never had to unsheathe my sword in a real battle. I would not see you or your brothers in danger for all the glory in the world."

"I understand, Tou-sama," Misaki said, the tears still wet on her cheeks. At the very least, she understood the logic of it. "But what does that have to do with—"

"A life of dangerous adventures might seem worth it now, when you are young and seemingly invincible, but one day, you will have children, and you will not want that life for them."

"Robin wouldn't endanger his children," she protested. "The work he does is all about *saving* children. He would never put his own at risk."

"Not on purpose, I'm sure. But men like that one... evil follows them everywhere. He is a good boy," Tou-sama said again, "but he is a gamble, and I can't gamble my daughter's life. You'll understand when you have children of your own."

Misaki ducked her head to conceal the pain on her face. She had lost the argument. Had she expected anything else? Her father was wiser and more methodical than anyone she knew. He thought through everything. How could she have expected to overcome that with nothing but a full heart and her tears?

"Matsuda Takeru has all the capabilities of a warrior, but he also has the good sense to give you and your future children a stable, peaceful life," Tou-sama said. "He is not the sort of person who will seek out trouble and bring it down on you. He will keep you safe."

Tou-sama seemed to sense the agony in his daughter and to understand, resigned, that there was nothing he could say to ease the pain.

"I will let you be," he said and left the room, as the storm rose to a howl.

The light in the lantern flickered out.

....

A month later, Misaki was married to Takeru, second son of the Matsuda house, master of the Whispering Blade. Takayubi was eerily quiet. She ached for the Arashiki's crashing waves or Livingston's constant traffic, anything to stave off the silence pressing around her. Perhaps it was thanks to that silence that a footstep on the front deck immediately drew her attention. She went and opened the door, expecting to find another neighbor with another belated wedding gift. She was unprepared to find the glow and smoky scent she had been trying so hard to forget.

"Robin!" Her heart jumped with too many emotions—shock, horror, and something that should not have been there at all. Hope? That wasn't right. That didn't make any sense.

"Misaki!" His face split into a smile of relief. *"So, that does say 'Matsuda.'"* He glanced from a note in his hand to the stone sign above the compound doors.

"What are you doing here?"

"I had to see you."

"So, you came to my husband's house? All the way from Carytha? Are you insane?" Even with Robin's newfound fortune, it was an expensive trip, one he appeared to have made alone.

"I had to make sure you were okay... and help you get away if you weren't."

"Help me get away?" Misaki meant it to sound indignant, but it came out too high—breathless, helpless. *"Robin, I married Matsuda Takeru. This is my home now. I can't leave."*

"Of course, you can," Robin said, his eyes alight with that ferocious determination that had first drawn Misaki to him. *"You're no one's prisoner. You're Sirawu, the Shadow. You can go anywhere."*

He reached out to take her arm but she snatched it back.

"Don't touch me. You can't—I mean... Robin, I'm married."

"I know. I tried to get in contact with you as soon as I heard. Misaki... why?" His voice broke and she looked away, unable to meet his eyes. *"How did this happen?"*

"It... it doesn't matter," she said toward her feet. *"It happened. It's done now."*

"No." Robin was shaking his head. *"I don't accept that. You can't just give up."*

"Who said anything about 'giving up'? I made a decision."

"Why didn't you tell me?" For the first time, the hurt leached into Robin's voice. *"You just disappeared. Why?"*

Hope and denial tangled in Misaki, grappling as she tried to find words. But there were none. There was no way she could explain...

"You need to leave," she said stiffly.

"No. Misaki, I won't. I can't."

"I'm fine here, Robin," she lied. *"You need to go now. I promise, everything is okay."*

"That's what you said last time." He sounded so betrayed. *"I shouldn't have left you then, and I won't do it again."*

Of course, a simple 'you need to leave' wouldn't be good enough for Robin. If she wanted him to walk away, she had to wound him, make herself the enemy. That way he could steel himself against her and overcome. Robin could always overcome an enemy; he had just never been good with guilt. She had always been more eloquent and ruthless than her friend. For years, she had used that to support him, filling in the gaps his temperament left in his work. Now she would use it to hurt him.

"I said I would talk to my parents. I never made any promises to decide on you, or to tell you when the decision was made."

"That's ridiculous. You—"

"I humored you, Thundyil," she said, *"out of respect for the experiences we shared in Carytha, but you should have known this couldn't happen. Did you really think I would marry a Disanka orphan? A boy who grew up on the street?"*

Robin twitched. *"Don't,"* he said very quietly. *"Don't do that."*

"Do what?" Misaki snapped. *"Tell the truth?"*

"Try to protect me."

"Protect you?" Misaki scoffed, trying to conceal the way his gentle words shook her. *"I'm trying to get you to leave—"*

"You're trying to hurt me," he said, *"so I can leave you here without any guilt."*

Her jaw clenched.

"I know your tactics, Misaki. They won't work on me." His voice had gotten so tender, so unbearably understanding—

"And I know yours," she said sharply. *"Don't use that voice on me. I'm not a crazy person with a machete to someone's neck."* But she might as well have been. The tension and frantic, impotent fury between them could have rivaled any hostage situation. "You're *the one who traveled all this way to barge in where you weren't invited. If anyone needs talking down, it's you.*"

"You didn't respond to any of my messages."

Misaki hesitated for a moment in confusion. She had never *gotten* any messages. Why? Had her husband or father-in-law been intercepting them? Would they really—? No. It didn't matter. She wouldn't have responded anyway.

"Did you ever consider," she said, *"that I just didn't feel like talking to you?"*

She had thought she could avoid upsetting anyone. If she did as her father said and then just never had any contact with Robin again, her old friend would forget about her, move on, and she would never have to confront him. Damn Robin for ruining that. Damn him!

"I just need to understand," he said. *"I need you to be honest with me. Is this what you want?"*

Misaki drew herself up, employing the posture she had learned to tower over taller theonites. *"It is,"* she said, voice icy. She didn't feel tall.

"I don't believe you." His gentle tone sent a spike of rage through Misaki.

361

Her fists clenched. *"How dare you?"*

"What?"

"How dare you claim to respect my choices and then deny them because you don't agree with them? How dare you claim to respect my autonomy and then deny it because it means you don't get to keep me."

"I—That's not what I—"

"Which is it, Thundyil? Do you respect my decisions or not?"

"I do," Robin insisted, his own voice rising. *"You know that, Misaki! That's why I'm worried about you. This..."* he gestured vaguely around him—from Misaki's restrictive kimono, to the rest of the quiet little village, and the frigid mountain surrounding it— *"This doesn't seem like something you would have chosen of your own free will."*

"Well, it is," Misaki said stubbornly—and damn it, why were there tears pressing at the back of her throat? Why had Robin come here? Why was he doing this to her? *"Maybe you don't know me as well as you think."*

"But—"

"You presume to understand me because we went to school together for a few years?" She hardened herself against the tears. *"Who do you think you are?"*

"Your friend," Robin said earnestly—and Nami damn it, Misaki had never seen so much pain in his piercing black eyes— *"We didn't just go to school together; we fought together, learned together, saved each other's lives—"*

"I'm a daughter of the Tsusano house." Misaki's voice rose and she struggled to keep it under control. *"You assume your uncivilized little alleyway brawls were ever more than a hobby to me? You really expected me to stay there, in that dirty, adyn-ridden city?"*

That struck a nerve, sending the first flicker of genuine anger through Robin's expression. *"Don't say that."*

"I'm sorry," she said placidly, pressing her advantage, even as something in her screamed. *"I thought you wanted honesty, but clearly, you don't understand—"*

362

"Then explain it to me," Robin said, his voice simultaneously pleading and forceful. *"Honestly. Because it looks an awful lot like a forced marriage."*

But Misaki *couldn't* explain honestly. To do so, she would have to admit that she still loved him. And she couldn't do that. Not to him. Not to herself. Not to anyone.

"Xuro, Misaki, I knew you loved your family. I didn't think you were a coward."

"Oh, is that what I am? I made a decision you don't like, so I'm a coward?"

"This isn't about me!" Robin burst out. *"You don't have to marry me if you don't want to. You don't have to come back to Carytha or ever see me again if you don't want to, but please... you can't stay here. As your friend, I can't let you."*

Misaki didn't recoil as Robin took her arm and tugged. She *did*, however, flinch at the wave of nyama that swept onto the front deck a moment later. *Takeru.*

"Misaki," her husband said, appearing at her shoulder in a wall of solid cold. "What is going on here? Who is this person?"

"Oh—!" Misaki yanked her arm free, looking from Takeru to Robin in panic. "This is... um..."

Robin's hands curled into fists. He was glaring at Takeru with a blazing fury he usually reserved for murderers, and Misaki realized that he must have noticed her flinch and inferred the worst. Gods, why had she flinched? Why?

Takeru's jiya had crushed the temperature down to a shivering degree. He and Robin didn't speak the same language, but the glares they exchanged needed no translation. Both said plainly that someone was about to die.

"Wait..." Misaki started weakly, but she had no idea what to say. What was she supposed to do in this situation?

Robin was doing a good job not trembling under the force of the cold, but Misaki could see on his face that it had him disconcerted. Theonites as powerful as Robin were not used to having their nyama completely overwhelmed by another.

"So, you're Misaki's husband, huh?" Robin switched to Yammaninke, though it was unlikely to do much good; Yammaninke instruction in rural Kaigen was not good enough to produce fluent speakers. *"What are you, like, twice her age?"*

Takeru took a step forward and sparks crackled at Robin's fingertips.

He wouldn't win.

Robin was a handy street fighter, far better than a self-taught orphan had any business being. His natural grace and his above-average taya made him unstoppable to the untrained, low-powered criminals of Livingston, but this wasn't Carytha. This was the seat of a power that had guarded an Empire for years. Robin's mix of critical thinking and inexhaustible willpower were good for fumbling through a fight with a stronger theonite, but Takeru was a caliber of fighter Robin had never encountered before. A direct clash with the Matsuda, here among so much ice and snow, would be a death sentence.

"Robin, don't," Misaki warned in Lindish. *"You're no match for him."*

"Is that why you're staying here?" Robin demanded, looking disgusted. *"Because you're afraid of him?"*

The look on his face spelled disaster. He was ready to beat someone bloody, but Takeru wouldn't go down like a Livingston brawler or machete fighter. He would *kill* Robin if it came to it.

"Tell this man he isn't welcome here," Takeru said. "He should leave before he finds his head separated from his body."

The words chilled Misaki. She tried not to look frightened as she translated them to Lindish for Robin.

"You're afraid of him," Robin said. *"I can't leave you here."*

Misaki's mind reeled. There was now a very real threat to Robin's safety. She wouldn't convince him to back down by telling him that Takeru was too strong; she had to employ a different tactic. *Stay calm, Misaki. Stay calm.* Lifting her chin, she adopted the most scathing tone she could manage.

"Really, Robin? You honestly think I'm stupid enough to marry

someone who might hurt me? Since you apparently need this spelled out for you, my husband is trying to protect me from a raving lunatic who showed up out of nowhere to harass me."

Robin's darkly glowing eyes, like live coals, flicked between her and Takeru. She knew that look. When he was searching for the right thing to do. Not the easy thing, but the right one. For the moment, he seemed stumped, but Robin always did the right thing, no matter how hard it was. That was why Misaki had always followed him, why she loved him.

"You are not welcome here, outsider," Takeru said again and this time Robin could not miss the meaning. "This is your last chance to leave unharmed."

"I..." Robin seemed uncertain. *"Misaki, I'm not leaving without you."*

Takeru took another step forward, the air grew colder. Robin shifted into a fighting stance—

"No!" Before she could stop herself, Misaki had grabbed the wrist of Takeru's sword hand, disrupting his jiya before the fabled Whispering Blade could form in his fingers. Her new husband—still such a stranger—looked down at her in mild surprise.

"H-he's just a boy," she scrambled to explain. "He's not right in the head. It wouldn't be right for you to kill him, Takeru-sama. Please... I don't want you to have that on your conscience."

Matsuda Takeru stared down at her, his expression unreadable. "Can *you* compel the madman to leave you alone then?"

"Yes, sir."

Misaki leveled a frigid glare at Robin, her best friend, the only person she had ever wanted.

"My husband is understandably concerned for my safety, but he has generously agreed not to kill you if you leave immediately and never show your face here again." Robin still hesitated, so she made her voice ice. *"If you really don't respect my decision, then go ahead. Fight him. Die."*

Robin's flames flickered his uncertainty. His wide eyes reflected confusion and betrayal, but Misaki had seen him fight his way through worse than that. Against all the odds, he always fought. He always did the right thing.

The flames between his fingers guttered and went out as he lowered his gaze. *"If this is really what you want."*

"It is," Misaki said through her teeth.

"Then I'm sorry I disturbed you." Head down, Robin turned and walked away.

Beside Misaki, Takeru's jiya eased back, the frigid bite receding from the water molecules around him. But Misaki found everything in her suddenly straining, frantic.

Robin was walking away? Robin was *walking away*.

Misaki opened her mouth to call after him—*Come back! Come back! Please, Robin! Take me with you!* But no sound came out. The breath had frozen in her chest.

Takeru's hand closed on her arm. "Come, Misaki. You should be inside, where it is safe."

She was numb, unable to resist as the cold creature she had married pulled her into the Matsuda compound and shut the doors.

Why did he walk away? an agonized voice screamed through Misaki. *He's Robin. Robin saves everyone. Robin never leaves a friend behind. Why did he walk away?*

But the smothered, honest part of her knew the truth: he *was* just a boy. For all his abilities, and accomplishments, and superhuman spirit, Robin Thundyil was only nineteen. He had been out of his element, in a culture he didn't understand, caught between people older and, he mistakenly thought, smarter than himself. By all accounts, he had done the right thing—the only thing he *could* do when she looked him in the eye and told him to leave.

Robin had always deferred to her when it came to matters of protocol, politics, and people. Why had she expected him to magically grasp things she barely understood herself? Why had she expected him to read her and react like a man? The answer lurked, unwelcome: *because you're too afraid to do it yourself. You are a coward, Misaki.*

If she wasn't woman enough to fight her own battles, then what right did she have to Robin's help? How could she expect him to save her when she wasn't willing to lift a finger to save herself? What had she thought Robin was going to do anyway? Fight the Whispering Blades and the rest of the mountain and then whisk her away? That wasn't within his ability. He had never had any power to change this situation... only she had. And she had been too weak to make it happen.

A coward like her had no right to someone like Robin, no right to the future she had let herself imagine with him. Still, she crumpled in on herself and wept for it. Loud sobs would have disrupted the silence, drawing the attention of the men of the Matsuda house, so she smothered the sounds in her long sleeves.

Takeru found her there a waati later, curled up in the middle of the bedroom, shaking.

"Misaki...?" his usually frigid voice had taken on a note of worry. "Are you well?"

"Yes." Hiding her face, Misaki forced her tears into water vapor and willed herself to stop trembling. "Yes, Takeru-sama."

It was not until the next day that Misaki found the bag Robin had left her, tucked into a corner of the front deck. It contained only one thing: the sword that had been her companion through all their adventures—one last plea to remember everything they had had together.

She had knelt, holding Shadow's Daughter for a long time, fingers playing over the Zilazen glass handle. Tou-sama said that there were better and more beautiful things than the rush of battle. *You'll understand when you have children.* It would be worth it when she had children.

Tou-sama had promised.

20

THE LAST TIME

Misaki came to the logical conclusion that she was in Hell. In her addled brain, it was the only thing that made sense; no Dunian night could stretch as long as that night in Takayubi's bomb shelter. Somewhere in the chaos, a bullet had hit her and sent her soul spinning into the fires of eternity. A twisted soul like hers couldn't possibly pass into the peace of the Laaxara. It made sense.

But in the morning, the loudspeakers declared the area secure, and the bunker doors opened to the daylight of the mortal realm.

The brightness was blinding at first. Misaki blinked around her, confused to find herself in the real world, hurting and alive. In her daze, she looked down and realized Izumo wasn't in her lap.

Panic jolted her to her feet, sending splinters of pain through her chest. Her hands groped around her, fumbling over Siradenyaa's empty sheath, but there was no baby.

"Izu-kun?" She turned, frantic. "Naga-kun?"

Her adjusting eyes found Ayumi in the arms of one of the Mizumaki women, but where were her sons? She had just taken a breath to scream when she found them. Her shoulders relaxed and she let out a soft, "Oh."

Izumo was cradled in a pair of soot-stained arms, sound asleep against Atsushi's chest. At some point in the night, perhaps in search of human contact, or to quiet the crying Misaki was too far gone to hear, the blacksmith's son must have taken the infant. Nagasa had wormed his way under one of Atsushi's arms and fallen asleep with his head resting against Izumo's, while Hiroshi leaned against the huddle with his back to the other children.

They made a strange picture, the Kotetsu boy in his smith's tunic, and the Matsuda boys in their fine kimono, all tangled together, splattered with blood and dirt. Tears had dried in the ash on Atsushi's cheeks, indicating that he had cried himself to sleep. Yet the ten-year-old had held the Matsuda boys through the night, while their parents were too frozen to do so.

Hiroshi was the first to blink awake in the brittle morning light. Or maybe he had never been asleep. The circles under his eyes suggested that he had spent the night as Misaki had, staring ahead into the darkness.

"Are you alright, Hiro-kun?"

Hiroshi's eyes were veined with blood as he looked up at his mother. Stiffly, he nodded. If some part of her second son had ever truly been a child, it was gone now.

Misaki's eyes moved to the numu boy, holding her two youngest. She didn't want to wake him.

"Atsushi." Reaching out, she gently touched the boy's shoulder. "Atsushi-kun."

He stirred. His lips moved. "Kaa-chan?" he said softly, and Misaki had to swallow an unbidden swell of guilt.

"No, Atsushi-kun," she said as he blinked bleary eyes. "It's me."

Grief fought with embarrassment on his face. "Oh... I... M-Matsuda-dono. I'm so sorry."

Misaki wanted to be able to give him a smile. Her face wouldn't do it. "It's alright, Atsushi-kun. Thank you for looking after my sons."

She bent to take Izumo, but stopped with a grimace as the pain in her chest flared.

"Are you alright, Matsuda-dono?" Atsushi asked.

"Yes," Misaki said, though just getting the one word out hurt.

"I can carry the baby if you need me to."

"I'll take him," another woman said—the younger of the two Mizumakis who had helped carry the Matsuda babies the previous night. Fuyuko. That was her name. Her father and brother hadn't come back from the frontlines.

"If you don't mind, Matsuda-dono?" the girl said, holding out her arms for Izumo.

"Y-you..." *You don't have to do that*, Misaki started to say, but her abused lungs stopped her again.

"It's no trouble," Fuyuko said and carefully gathered Izumo into her arms.

Misaki let the other woman carry Izumo as the villagers started to venture out of the bunker. She even took the arm Atsushi offered her for support as what remained of Takayubi stumbled out of the shelter into the light.

Destruction spread out before them, smoking. The mayor's office near the bomb shelter's entrance had been obliterated, as had the info-com tower beside it.

"Try to watch your step, boys," Fuyuko warned Atsushi, Hiroshi, and Nagasa, lifting the hem of her own kimono to step over a beam from one of the fallen info-com towers.

"*At least we got one good use out of these towers, huh?*" Chul-hee said to his father in Kaigengua. He sounded numb.

"*I don't know if I would call this* good," Tae-min said.

Bombs had left gaping holes in some houses; most had been completely destroyed, reduced to splinters. Bodies littered the mountainside, many of them in pieces, Kaigenese and Ranganese all jumbled together in bits of blood and bone. As they walked, Misaki pulled Nagasa to her hip and put a hand over his eyes, as if she could truly shield him from any of this.

The airstrike, while devastating, may not have been excessive. Judging by the number of yellow and black uniformed bodies strewn throughout the rubble, it seemed that the Ranganese had kept advancing up the mountain into the night, giving the pilots something to fire on. The result was that the village had been decimated.

What remained of Takayubi's population spread out slowly, sluggish with grief and shock. Some clawed through the ruins of their houses for the bodies of their loved ones. Some simply stood where they had lived and raised their families, faces blank with disbelief.

The village had been a necessary sacrifice. Misaki understood that, from a tactical standpoint. That was why she couldn't explain the rage and horror rising like bile in the back of her throat.

She had seen devastation before. She had been in Livingston at the height of Kalleyso's reign of terror, but somehow, back then, it hadn't seemed so bad. With no small amount of shame, she realized that, to her, those horrors belonged in violent adyn countries, far across the ocean. Not here. Not where she had rocked her babies to sleep and taught them their first words. Not where she had met Hyori. Not where she had laughed at Setsuko's jokes and cooking.

For so many years, Misaki had thought she would never belong in Takayubi, but somehow, while she hadn't been paying attention, this place had become home. Someone had dropped bombs on *her home*.

Hyori, whose wobbly legs had barely supported her down from the shelter, collapsed before the blackened ruins of the Yukino compound. The carved stone Yukino insignia that had been mounted above the doors now lay cracked in the snow. Hyori's fingers traced the stone grooves, shaking.

Misaki felt a tug at her fingers and looked down to find that Nagasa had pulled her hand from his eyes. He was looking toward what remained of the Yukino compound, where he had spent so many days playing.

"Ryota-kun?" he asked in a small voice.

Hiroshi had stopped beside them, following his younger brother's gaze to the Yukino compound. "I think Ryota-kun is gone," he said slowly.

"Where?" Nagasa looked from his big brother to his mother, eyes pleading. "Gone where?"

"Um..." Mizumaki Fuyuko said nervously, "maybe we should get your boys away from here, Matsuda-dono?" She looked to Misaki. "Maybe into your own house?"

"No." Misaki put up a hand to stop Fuyuko before she could guide Hiroshi and Nagasa in the direction of the Matsuda compound. "Not until it's cleaned up."

What Misaki had left inside the house was easily worse than anything the children were going to see outside it.

"How...?" The young woman looked around. "How is it going to get cleaned up? There are so few of us, and..." *So much destruction.*

"The Imperial army should be here to help soon," Misaki said. She wasn't expecting much in the way of aid from the Kaigenese military, but it would be strange for them to make no appearance at all. At the very least, they would provide the manpower to move some of the bodies.

But the first aid to arrive didn't come from the government. It came from the surrounding villages. Fishermen, farmers, and smiths, who had seen the tornado advancing from the coast in their direction, who had seen where it had stopped. They appeared as the sun cleared away the last of the mists. When the Takayubi residents went to meet them, they saw, with a swell of hope, that some of the volunteers were carrying survivors from further down the mountain.

Atsushi was the first one to find the face he was looking for.

"Tou-san!" he cried out.

Kotetsu Katashi was being supported up the path by two fishermen. He was barely conscious, missing his left leg below the knee, but he still managed a wide smile as his son came running to meet him. Atsushi's younger brother and sister were alive as well, being carried by a pair of fisherwomen. A single, bruised fina and a pair of frightened children were the only survivors anyone had found in the leveled western village.

There was no sign of Mamoru.

"We've left a few men further down the mountain to keep searching for survivors," the oldest of the fishermen explained.

"Very good," Takeru said. "Thank you for your help."

"It's all of us who need to thank you, Matsuda-dono." The man got on his knees, and the rest of the volunteers followed suit, bowing low in the snow before Takeru. "You and your people stopped this army before it could reach the rest of us. We can never thank you enough."

As villagers tearfully reunited with their family members, a surprisingly lucid Kotetsu Katashi explained that the numuwu with good enough legs had scattered when the Ranganese attacked. Of course, many had been caught and killed, but those first Ranganese to break through had been few enough that a good number of smiths escaped.

"Our house was destroyed almost immediately," he said, "before we could think of fleeing. Fortunately, my two little ones were small enough to crawl out from under the debris and run before any fonyakalu found us."

With the possible exception of the Matusdas and Yukinos, the old blacksmith families knew the mountainside better than anyone. Atsushi's younger siblings, along with several other numuwu had taken shelter in caves that were all but impossible for an outsider to find.

After applying a tourniquet to his own exploded leg, Katashi had managed to drag himself to the safety of the nearest cave with his powerful arms. Takayubi's rock formations had acted as natural bomb shelters, protecting the numuwu not only from the Ranganese, but also the subsequent airstrike. They had stayed hidden underground until they heard the Kaigenese voices of the fishermen calling out for survivors.

Astonishingly, three men had survived the carnage at the northern pass: thirty-two-year-old Ginkawa Aoki, forty-three-year-old Ikeno Tsuyosa, and his seventeen-year-old cousin, Ikeno Shun. During the initial clash with the fonyakalu, Ginkawa had taken a blow to the head that had rendered him unconscious and had lain ignored for the rest of the attack. He had regained consciousness at the beginning of the airstrike and then risked the bombs to crawl among the corpses in search of survivors. In the dark, he had managed to drag the two wounded Ikenos to safety.

Somberly, he told the desperate group of wives and mothers that there had been no other beating hearts in that darkness. Ikeno Tsuyosa had lost an arm, and the seventeen-year-old was even worse off, having suffered multiple stab wounds to the torso and severe head trauma that had left him delirious.

"We brought them here, hoping you might have medics to tend to the wounded," the elder fisherman told Takeru, "maybe a building to set up operations..." He looked around at the smoldering remains of the main village. "I'm so sorry, Matsuda-dono. We didn't realize this place had been so badly bombed."

"We will set up a base of operations in my home," Takeru said, indicating the remaining half of the Matsuda compound. "We may have to clear out some Ranganese corpses and brace parts of the roof with ice, but I believe it is the building with the most structural integrity at this moment."

Turning from the fishermen, Takeru raised his jiya where a portion of the compound's outer wall had been destroyed. He knocked out some of the loose bricks and then flattened a sheet of packed snow over the fallen pieces of wood and rock, creating a path into the part of the compound that was still standing.

"You and you." He pointed to two of the tallest fishermen. "Come help me clear out the bodies and debris."

"Yes, Matsuda-dono!" the men said and scrambled to obey.

"We'll freeze the fonyaka bodies in the courtyard until we have occasion to dispose of them," Takeru said, not looking back as the men followed him into the compound. "Make sure you clean up as much blood as you can after you move each corpse. The place must be properly sanitized before we move in the weak and wounded."

The fishermen left outside quickly set about helping the people of Takayubi form makeshift benches and shelters of ice against the compound's outer wall. For a different community of theonites, shelter would have been a more immediate concern in the midst of a mountain winter, but Kusanagi jijakalu were different. Their subconscious jiya allowed their blood to keep circulating even when their body temperature dropped below freezing. It was how Misaki had spent the entire night barefoot without suffering frostbitten toes. Even a baby as young as Izumo, now asleep in Fuyuko's arms, was in little danger from the cold.

Of course, even well-bred jijakalu could not survive forever outdoors in the winter. Within a few days, they would start to run out of energy and freeze. Without food, it would be sooner. Blankets were recovered from ruined houses and draped over ice wedges to form comfortable seats for the elderly and injured to rest on while they waited for the Matsuda compound to be cleaned out. Fisherwomen formed cradles for Izumo, Ayumi, and the other babies, padding them with blankets and spare clothing.

By the time the fishermen had set up in the Matsuda compound, more volunteers had arrived. These were warriors and blacksmiths from Takayubi's two nearest neighboring mountains. The Tetsukai blacksmith family had brought medics with them, including two city-trained doctors. The professionals immediately took control of first aid, directing others what to do. The representatives from the Ameno stronghold on the neighboring mountain of Tatsuyama had brought baskets of food and a dozen warriors to assist in the search for survivors.

Misaki and the children were guided into the compound. Takashi's study, which the man had barely ever used anyway, had been converted into a small hospital. Setsuko was already lying on some blankets, still unconscious, as two medics bent over her.

"None of us are seriously injured," Misaki assured the Tetsukai medic as he guided her into the room and asked that she sit.

"Sorry, Matsuda-dono. Your husband insisted that we examine you."

The most concerning of Misaki's injuries was the persistently painful stabbing in her chest from the fan-wielder's *Lazou Linghun*. If her lungs were truly damaged, it would take more than a few bandages to fix it, but she humored the numu anyway, allowing him to disinfect and bandage the cuts on her arms.

As soon as the medic had moved on to check Nagasa for injuries, Misaki knelt forward and tugged Hiroshi toward her.

"Keep an eye on your little brothers and cousin," she whispered in his ear. "Kaa-chan should be back soon."

"Where are you going?" Hiroshi asked.

"I'm going to go find your brother." Misaki rested a hand on his head for a moment before slinking out of the room and down the hall. She made a stop at a surviving closet to hide Siradenyaa's sheath and get herself a pair of tabi.

"Hello, Matsuda-dono," Kotetsu Katashi said when he noticed her stepping lightly toward the compound's back door. The swordsmith had Atsushi and one of the fishermen cleaning his wounded leg and taking steps to prevent infection, while his younger children sat nearby. "And where are you headed?" he asked, managing quite the amicable tone for a man who had just lost a leg and a third of his family.

"I—um..."

Katashi's smile faded and he lowered his gaze. "You won't find him on the front line where the others died."

"What?"

"Atsushi was the last one to see him, I think." Katashi looked toward his son, who nodded.

"At the blacksmith village, ma'am, near our... wh-what used to be our house."

"Thank you," Misaki said with as much affection as she could muster, and slipped out of the compound.

She was under no delusion that she would blend in on the slopes with the volunteers. It wasn't that she was the only woman—there were other wives and mothers eager to find their warriors—but she *was* the only noblewoman.

"Please, Matsuda-dono," one of the fishermen said, noting the insignia on her kimono. "You should go back and rest. We'll carry the dead and wounded back to you. This is no place for a lady."

"I've seen..." *I've seen worse,* Misaki meant to say, but the words stopped painfully in her throat.

The slope leading down to the frontline was terrible. Here lay the blacksmiths who had run for the caves but never made it. Further down lay the bodies of warriors. It was hard to tell if they had been pushed back from the northern pass or if they had come up the slope deliberately when they heard the screams of civilians further up the mountain. There was Ameno Samusa, the elementary school sword instructor who had taught Hiroshi and Mamoru before him. There was the numu woman who had crafted Misaki's wedding jewelry, hand in hand with her husband, who came around every three months to clean and repair the Matsuda compound's roof.

Volunteers paused hopefully at each body, checking for signs of life, but so far it seemed that they hadn't had any luck. Anyone who had fallen to injury out here on the open slopes had almost certainly been hit by the Imperial army's bullets or debris from their bombs.

Misaki had seen dismembered bodies before, messes of blood and internal organs, people hacked into pieces by machetes. But she hadn't felt it then. After all, Livingston, Carytha had been an exotic land of morbid curiosities and exhilarating danger. That had been the real difference between herself and Robin Thundyil: for him, the tragedy of Livingston's slums had been real. To Misaki, the privileged daughter of an untouchable noble house a world away, it had only been a game, a passing thrill to sate her thirst for adventure. It hadn't quite been real.

This was real.

"Please, Matsuda-dono," one of the fishermen was saying, his voice very far away. "A lady shouldn't have to see this."

"No," Misaki said quietly. "No one should have to see this."

How had she been so cavalier with lives that meant something to Robin? How had she shrugged off atrocities and then called it strength? Here on the slopes of her mountain, where every corpse was a personal loss, she did not feel strong at all.

"Why don't you go back to your family, Matsuda-dono?" the fisherman asked.

"I'm missing a part of it," she replied. "I need to find my son."

"Then—at least let me accompany you, ma'am. Parts of this slope may still be dangerous."

Misaki didn't need an escort to find her way, but she thanked the fisherman anyway and let him follow along. He might not have the authority to order her back to the main village, but it simply wasn't good manners to let a lady wander into the aftermath of a battle alone.

"What's your name, fisherman?" she asked as they picked their way down the steep path. It may have been a strange time for small talk, but Misaki found that she couldn't bear the silence. It left her too much room to contemplate where she was going, what she would inevitably find.

"Chiba Mizuiro, Matsuda-dono." His voice carried the eager anxiety of a man who did not often get to talk to members of high houses.

"Chiba." Misaki smiled in a weak attempt to put the man at ease. "My sister-in-law is a Chiba, you know."

"Matsuda Setsuko-sama," he said. "Yes, I—I heard about that marriage." Of course, he had. It had been quite the scandal. "My branch of the family is—*was*— close with hers."

"The fishing village at the base of this mountain," Misaki said, "where the tornado touched down first; what kind of shape is it in?"

"It's... not in *any* shape, Matsuda-dono. It's gone. If it weren't for the little pieces of wood and the odd scrap of netting, you would never know there was a village there at all."

"I'm so sorry to hear that." Misaki tried to focus on that, on the tragedy of the lost fishing village and her sympathy for Setsuko. It was by no means a pleasant thought—in fact, it was quite painful, but that was the point; it was almost painful enough to take her mind off where her feet were carrying her. Almost.

"So, I assume there are no survivors?" she asked.

"Not that we could find," Chiba said, "though a few of us stayed behind to look, mostly people hoping to find their lost relatives."

Misaki nodded. Poor Setsuko. Poor Setsuko.

"I saw the tornado," he said. "My wife and daughters were crying by the time it touched down. We thought we were all going to die."

"I'm sorry," she said quietly. "That must have been terrible for you."

"Please don't apologize, Matsuda-dono," Chiba said fiercely. "If it weren't for you and your family, none of us would be here now. I only regret we can't do more to help."

Misaki cast a glance at her escort, meeting his earnest gaze.

Matsuda Susumu had always complained that the peasants and lesser houses of the peninsula were not loyal the way they had been when he was young. He talked about the days when all the people of Kusanagi had respected and revered the Matsuda house. During the Keleba, the great families of Shirojima had earned their vassals' loyalty through their indisputable shows of strength against Kaigen's enemies. The Matsuda house might have raised powerful fighters every generation since the Keleba, but no one in Misaki's generation had witnessed the proof of that power... until now.

It seemed that a fragment of that ancient wonder had stirred from sleep when the people of Kusanagi's coast saw a tornado fall before the power of Takayubi. Loyalty was born of the awe shining in this fisherman's eyes. And now, koronu poured up the mountain, eager to serve however they could.

"Your son and your brother-in-law—all of you who fought here—are heroes," Chiba said fervently. "We owe you our lives."

She couldn't say whether it made her happy or sad that Matsuda Susumu had not lived to see this loyalty revived. She wished she could feel something... *anything* other than the inevitability of each step down, down toward the end of her world.

By this time, the charred remains of the blacksmith village were in sight, growing closer with each step.

"You know, I've never had much occasion to visit the other fishing villages in this region," Misaki said too quickly, her voice high with strain. "Tell me more about your village."

"Oh." The man looked surprised. "But Matsuda-dono, don't you think we should look for your—"

"Tell me," Misaki demanded sharply, "about your house, your boat, your family. Talk to me about something." *Just take me away from here.*

They were skirting the smoking remains of the numu village,

where the familiar smell of burned wood and coal had mixed with the insidious stench of charred flesh.

"Your most successful fishing excursion," she said desperately. "Tell me about that."

"Alright, Matsuda-dono," Chiba said uncertainly. "Um—most of my family's income doesn't come from fish. My wife is an excellent pearl diver, a skill she's started to pass on to my daughters. We sell the pearls to numuwu for them to use in their jewelry and baubles for ladies like you."

Misaki tried to focus on Chiba Mizuiro's words even as her eyes had started to scan the ashy, bloodstained snow. She tried to be there with the pearl diver and her daughters on that boat.

"I worry about my wife sometimes, the way she dives so far down into the dark on days when the waters are violent. My mother died diving for pearls, you see. So do many women every year. I worried more than ever when my oldest daughter started going out with my wife. And when we decided my youngest was ready to try, well, I thought I might die from nerves. But the water was so placid and clear that first day all three of them dove together.

"It was like Nami was so happy to see them that she cleared the coast of waves, and sharks, and sharp rocks just for them. I barely caught any fish that day, but the Goddess filled my girls' hands with pearls."

"That sounds wonderful," Misaki said, trying with all her might to feel a sliver of the fishing family's joy. Of course, she couldn't. She had never had to dive for her riches. If she wanted pearl necklaces or hair ornaments, someone brought them to her. She had never given much thought to the pearls themselves or the people who risked their lives to gather them from the ocean floor.

"I think that was the day I understood that this peninsula really was blessed by the blood of gods. City people come through sometimes and say it's dying, but divinity lives here."

"Divinity?" Misaki's voice seemed to come from somewhere far away. Her eyes had fallen on a thin shape in the snow—Mamoru's sword. The blade was drenched in blood.

"I watched a *tornado* stop here," Chiba said earnestly, "before it could reach my village. I think this is a place of miracles. Just like my mother used to tell me... for every diver the ocean takes, there is a perfect day, when she showers a family with bright pearls and love."

Misaki's feet crunched to a stop in the snow and the fisherman's gaze followed hers.

The black-clad soldier before them was in two pieces, cut in half by what must have been a brutally decisive stroke of the katana. And there, facing him in the snow, barely a stride away, was Mamoru.

The indiscriminate spray of bullets had left holes in the back of his kimono, singed circles piercing the diamonds of the Matsuda crest.

"Merciful Nami!" the fisherman exclaimed in undisguised disgust. "Those pilots just shot right through him! What if he was still alive?"

"He wasn't," Misaki said softly. Thank the Gods for that. There wasn't space in her heart for any more rage.

"How can you tell?" Chiba asked.

"There's barely any bleeding from the bullet wounds," Misaki said numbly.

"What?"

"There was no blood flow when the bullets hit his body. His heart stopped beating long before that."

The fisherman was eyeing her, visibly unsettled. "How can you tell—"

"Before I married into the Matsuda family, I was Tsusano Misaki. I know blood." She noticed the man shift a fraction of a step back. Superstitious. "Could you please give me a moment with my son?"

"Yes—of course, Matsuda-dono. Just..." Chiba Mizuiro got down on his knees and bowed before the body until his forehead was buried in the snow. A quiet prayer passed his lips. Then he shuffled to face Misaki and bowed again, just as deeply. "Nyama to you, Matsuda-dono, and to your son."

"Gods willing," Misaki murmured, and he withdrew, leaving her alone with the body that was no longer Mamoru.

In her mind, Misaki had compared the bomb shelter to Hell. But this—this clarity of stillness—was worse. The bizarre thing about Misaki was that she could be at home in Hell. Chaos had its own calming effect on her. In the bunker, the screams, the pulsing blood, and the gunfire had drowned each other out, smothering her in a daze. Here, there was no fluid crawl of blood or dribble of tears to consume Misaki's attention; this blood had frozen into something solid and irrefutable. There was no movement to spur her to action, nothing to mend or destroy. There was only the frozen truth of her son's death.

Slowly, Misaki sank to her knees beside the corpse.

Her eyes traced the details, preserved in the cold. The bullet wounds may not have bled, but there was plenty of frozen blood to survey, a map of Mamoru's struggles leading up to his death. Minor cuts littered his face and forearms, bruising and raw skin around his neck suggested that someone had tried to strangle him, and his lip was split from a blunt blow to the mouth, but none of that had killed him. It was clear that his death had resulted from the deep blade wound in his side.

Misaki wished she hadn't seen wounds like that before, on the victims of machete attacks in Livingston. She wished she hadn't witnessed firsthand how excruciatingly long it took those people to die.

The fonyaka opposite Mamoru had been cut cleanly in half by a sword stroke that ran from his right hip to just beneath his left arm—the sort of cut that ended a man's life instantly. Even the greatest fighter in the world couldn't get up for a counterattack after that. Mamoru's blow had been the final one... which could only mean that her boy had fought through the injury that ended his life. Even with that hideous wound in his side, draining his blood and disabling vital organs, he had fought.

His right hand was mangled, missing two fingers, so she reached out and touched his left, smoothing a gentle touch over his battered knuckles. The first time Misaki had held Mamoru, as a tiny baby, she had hated the feel of his jiya simply because it reminded her of his father's. It had made her want to retch and recoil. Now she reached for it, her fingers grasping and senses straining for the smallest trace—but of course, there was nothing. The life force that had made him Mamoru had departed, on its way to a different realm of existence.

A breathless sob escaped Misaki. Her ice-laced fingers dug into the back of her son's kimono and she wished, she *wished,* from the depth of her aching chest, that her claws could pull a life back to the Duna as easily as they could tear one out of it.

The next breath that came out of her was more of a scream than a sob, and the pain it sent through her lungs was so pitifully small next to the sheer absence beneath her hands. She would let a fonyaka pull her life from her mouth, she would give her soul a thousand times over, if she could just bring Mamoru's back.

It wasn't until she felt liquid blood on her fingers that she jerked back and realized what she was doing. As she longed to feel Mamoru's pulse and nyama, her own subconscious had risen to pull at the lifeless body. It hadn't restored a true pulse, of course. All it had done was unfreeze arteries and disrupt rigor mortis, causing Mamoru's bullet wounds and other injuries to bleed anew.

Horrified, Misaki scrambled a pace back from the body.

"Sorry!" She gasped, wiping the blood from her hands in the snow. "I'm so sorry!" She bowed down, crushing her forehead into the frozen ground until it hurt, until ice and then rock ground into her brow. "I'm so sorry."

She stayed there for a long time, pressed to the ground in apology as if there were enough apologies in the Duna to make up for how she had failed him. Closing her eyes, she prayed to Nagi for strength and Nami for calm. Neither obliged. Her bloodstained hands shook, even as she braced them against the ground for some semblance of stability. The sobs wouldn't stop, but she had not come here to confuse Mamoru's spirit and pull it in two. She had come here to help him, to be a good mother, if the Gods would give her this last chance.

One didn't need to be a fina to understand that regret was like poison to the spirits of the dead. A spirit who regretted what he hadn't accomplished in life would be unable to pass into the peace of the Laaxara. Those spirits became trapped in the burning realm on the fringe of the Duna, unable to truly die, their suffering intensifying as their regrets festered. It was a horrible existence. And it was the souls of those who died young, in the midst of hope, unfinished business, and unfulfilled potential who were in the most danger.

Through the shaking, Misaki found the voice to speak to her son.

"Kotetsu Katashi and Atsushi both lived, you know," she said softly. "The Kotetsu line survives, with all its knowledge, because of you." That was the first thing he needed know: that he hadn't died for nothing. To Misaki, at this moment, the lives of the Kotetsus seemed irrelevant, but Mamoru was a better person than she was. It would matter to him.

"I know you doubted. I know you worried that you wouldn't know what to do. But look at you... you fought so well." And with the grief, Misaki realized that there was also pride welling up in her throat. It intertwined with the pain, amplifying it. "You're only a boy, but you fought to the last like a man. You did well here. But I'm sure you know that..." A painful, nearly hysterical smile jerked at the corners of Misaki's mouth. "No warrior could have fought through injuries like yours without being sure of himself."

Misaki bit down on her trembling lip as her throat closed up. There were no holy men here to offer the perfect, enlightened words to send Mamoru's spirit on its way. As his mother, as the only living person here, Misaki had to find the words. This was the last thing she could do for him. So, even though it shook her body and hurt beyond imagining, she forced herself to keep speaking.

"You did right by your family and your country, even though, I think... none of us did right by you. There is nothing in this world for you to regret. Nothing at all."

But it wasn't *Mamoru's* regret Misaki truly feared. Her son had been honest with himself and others. He had lived well and died with purpose. Right now, Misaki herself was the greatest threat to her son's spirit. The regrets of a spirit's loved ones could also tie it down. The bitterness that consumed her could doom him to an eternity of fire—unless she found some way to be better.

With a last bracing breath, she lifted her head to look into Mamoru's face and was surprised to find a kind of peace there. Somehow, the horrific damage to his body had done nothing to contort his features, as pale and clean as his father's, but gentler— like the bright edges of a moon barely softened by mist. His jaw wasn't clenched, nor was his brow crunched in pain. Instead, he had the innocently wondering look of someone halfway woken from a dream. His eyes, glazed and frosted from the cold, no longer functioned, but somewhere in the space between space, his spirit still saw her. He still listened. She looked into those eyes, using them to ground her, as she started to speak.

"Mamoru-kun..."

The sound of her own voice wavering in uncertainty brought her back to the first time she had truly talked to her son: that dawn on the front deck mere months ago when they watched the sunrise. She hadn't quite known what to say then either, to help him on his way.

Start small, she told herself, as she had then, *conversational.* The right words would follow if she just loosened her time-stiffened lips.

"Do you remember that morning, Mamoru? After you had that fight with Kwang Chul-hee and asked for my help? You asked me if... if one day I would tell you about my school days, about my life before Takayubi.

"It made me so happy to hear you ask that, and I was looking forward to telling you those stories. They were going to be fun stories, adventure stories. I'm sure you would have liked them, but now I think... maybe those stories about Tsusano Misaki—Sirawu, the Shadow—didn't have as much value as I put on them. Maybe they weren't worth retelling or holding onto the way I did.

"See, Mamoru, there were certainly people in those stories who knew what they were fighting for, heroes who were noble and strong-willed, and worth remembering... like you. But I wasn't one of them. Sirawu was just that. A shadow. It was someone else's story and I was just passing through it. This... *you* are my story... and I was so selfish, so tied to that shadow that I *missed* it. And my son, I— I'm so sorry it took me this long to understand. I'm sorry—" the words caught in her throat, choking her, until pain shot through her chest, forcing her to let them out. "I never loved you the way I should have."

Tears rolled down Misaki's cheeks. For the first time since coming to Takayubi—perhaps the first time in her life—she knew she was human. Acutely, unbearably human. Now that it was too late.

"Your mother is a selfish woman, Mamoru." She clutched a sleeve in her hand and wiped the tears from her eyes, only to have new ones well up in their place. "I won't deny that. I've lived my life unable to let go of all the 'what if's, the 'if only's. For my husband, I couldn't let go of them. For the love of my life, I couldn't let go of them, and we've all suffered for it. It was the poison of my regret that killed my unborn children, those who would have come after you and before Hiroshi. My regret has poisoned this family for years, but I swear, Mamoru, I won't let it touch you.

"The thing is... you're more important than all of them. So, what I couldn't do for my parents, or Robin, or Takeru, or my unborn babies, I'll do it for you. My son, I'll do it for you. You've done more in this world than anyone could have asked. This once, let me be the mother I should have been from the beginning. Let me take care of the rest, alright?"

She crept forward to touch his hand again, but this time, she did not sob or pull. Her jiya was under control. She cried quietly, her tears falling without disturbance. She let him be still.

"I know I have no right to ask anything of you, but please... if your poor, stupid mother can ask one last thing of you... let me hold you one more time. Just one more time, you're going to let Kaa-chan hold you and treasure you the way I should have the day you were born. Then I'm going to let you go on with all my blessings. Is that alright?"

Finawu said it was not good for a woman to touch the dead, but Takayubi's finawu had all been lost in the tornado with their temple. There was no one to judge Misaki as she gathered her boy into her arms and settled down to hold him for the last time.

Please Nami, please Nagi, she prayed through the tears. *He's such a good boy. Don't let his stupid mother ruin this for him. Please... give me the strength to let him go.*

A mother was supposed to go to the temple after the death of a child. She was supposed to speak to the spirits of the Dead until she had said all she needed to say to the child, until all her unresolved feelings were spent, all conflicts resolved, all grudges laid to rest, until the finawu were satisfied that the deceased could move on in peace. But the temple was gone, along with all the masks and wise monks in it.

The best Misaki could do was hold her baby, and love him, and love him, and hope it was enough that she could let him go.

"You have no debt to pay the Duna." She murmured, resting her cheek against his cold head. "It is enough that, even for a moment, I had a son like you. It is enough that Hiroshi, Nagasa, and Izumo will have a brother like you to look up to as they become young men themselves. It is enough," she told herself, even though she would never hear him laugh with his little brothers again, never watch him bring beauty to another kata, never see that boyish smile, with those dimples, deepen into the smile of a man. For a moment, her hands had been full of pearls. She rocked and repeated, "It is enough.

"It is enough.

"It is enough.

"It is enough," until Chiba Mizuiro returned with a group of volunteers to help her carry the body up the mountain.

Before they left, Misaki paused before the corpse of the Ranganese soldier who had killed her son. Kneeling down, she passed a hand over his eyes, closing them, letting herself forgive him. It was easy to forgive a young man following orders.

Too easy.

And it didn't lift any of the weight from Misaki's chest—because this Ranganese stranger wasn't the one who really needed forgiving.

21

THE STORMLORD

Setsuko woke later that day, complaining of a splitting headache with her usual good humor. When Misaki softly told her what had happened to her husband, she got very quiet. It was plain that she had been expecting the news. If Takashi had survived the battle, he would have been the one at his wife's side when she woke.

"How did he go?" She asked finally. "Was it possible to tell?"

"Fighting," Misaki said. That much had been easy to deduce. In fact, it was a bit of an understatement. *Decimating* or *slaughtering* might have been a more apt description of the scene Takashi had left on the southern pass. "After sending Takeru up to the village to protect us, he was one of the last of our men standing." He and Mamoru.

"His body?" Setsuko asked, strangely calm.

"Well... there isn't really a body," Misaki explained. The volunteers had formed slabs of ice inside the Matsuda compound walls, where they placed the collected bodies. But there hadn't been much of Matsuda Takashi to collect. His bones had been placed in a woven basket.

"The volunteers retrieved his swords, but it seems like his death jiya was so strong, it turned all the blood in his body to spikes of ice. It was *spectacular*," Misaki added on a whim. Maybe it wasn't a very ladylike way to describe something so violent, but she thought Setsuko would want to know.

"Spectacular, huh?" the satisfied look on Setsuko's face told Misaki she had thought right.

"And terrifying."

"Well," Setsuko managed a laugh. "Coming from you, I take that as high praise!"

The corner of Misaki's mouth twitched, but she couldn't quite return Setsuko's smile. Part of her had hoped that the blow to Setsuko's head had knocked out the memory of what she had witnessed during the attack on the Matsuda compound, the carnage Misaki had created, but if Setsuko was uncomfortable sharing her makeshift rubble bench with a monster, she didn't show it as she leaned forward.

"Tell me more," she said.

More? She wanted to know *more* about her husband's gruesome death?

"I've never seen death jiya like it," Misaki said and did her best to describe the bloody formation of spikes. "I've never known a fighter who was absolutely indomitable right to the last. From the look of the battlefield, he managed to take several fonyakalu with him at the moment of death, and that's to say nothing of the hundred or so he killed before that."

Setsuko smiled a strange smile that teetered on a blade edge between savagery and adoration. "That's my husband," she said, her eyes full of tears.

And that's my Setsuko, Misaki thought as she clutched her sister-in-law's hands, *vibrant, unbroken, even in the face of the unthinkable*.

"You hear that, Ayumi-chan?" Setsuko beamed through her tears as her baby woke and started fussing in her arms. "Your father's a hero and a god!"

Misaki wished she had Setsuko's strength. She had thought for so many years that what she had was strength—faking a smile through pain and anger—but this honest ability to smile from the heart was something beyond anything she had ever had. It was why she had followed Robin like a moth to a flame. It was why Setsuko was and always would be the most beautiful woman in the world.

"Come, little one." Setsuko stood, nuzzling Ayumi to giggles. "Let's go pay our respects."

"I told you, there's no body," Misaki said.

"Yes." The smile faded from Setsuko's face as she looked at Misaki. "But I have to say goodbye to my brave nephew, don't I?"

Misaki looked up at her sister-in-law in surprise. She had only just woken up. "H-how did you...?"

Setsuko put a hand to Misaki's face, ran a gentle thumb beneath one of her eyes. "You're not much of a crybaby, little sister," she said softly. "I've never seen your eyes so red."

Something in Misaki's expression must have broken through Setsuko's calm because for a moment, she looked sadder than Misaki had ever seen her. The hand on Misaki's cheek tugged her in. She took the invitation and leaned her head into Setsuko's chest.

No words. Just silent support.

Misaki closed her eyes, reminded of the way her mother used to hold her during a storm, assuring her children that the wind and thunder could never hurt them. It was a comfort Misaki knew she would never feel again, one she could never offer her own children.

"I think I should apologize to you," Setsuko said finally, "since my husband isn't here to do it himself."

"What do you mean?"

"Takeru came back to protect us on his orders... He could have sent Mamoru, and..." *and Mamoru would still be alive.* It was something Misaki had been trying not to think about. "I'm sorry."

"It's not your fault," Misaki said. It wasn't even Takashi's, really. He must have realized that staying to hold the line meant certain death, that whoever he sent back up the mountain would have to head up the Matsuda house in his absence. Takashi himself could have exchanged places with Takeru, but Mamoru was too young. A fourteen-year-old could not lead the family, let alone the whole village, in a time of crisis.

She ignored the little voice in her head that demanded to know why Mamoru couldn't have gone up the mountain *with* his father. Why hadn't Takeru insisted on it? How could he have left his own son to die without argument? How?

"It was necessary," Misaki insisted as if it would do anything to lessen the ache. "You don't need to apologize to me."

"Mmm." Setsuko rubbed Misaki's back. "But someone should."

A steady stream of corpses on stretchers came up the mountain all day. It was horrible to hear the cries of grief and denial from family members that greeted each new body, but Misaki found that it was more horrible still to watch a body appear over the ridge to silence. Some of these people had died along with everyone who might remember them. They lay alone on their ice slabs, with no one to mourn them.

As Setsuko went to speak to the fishermen who had collected her husband's bones, Misaki stood before Mamoru's body, one hand on Nagasa's head, one on Hiroshi's shoulder, and tried to explain to her sons. Nagasa didn't understand. How could he at his age? He kept shaking Mamoru, asking why he wouldn't wake up.

While Nagasa kept clutching at Mamoru's sleeve, Hiroshi's hand trailed down slowly and rested on the lacquer sheath of his brother's sword.

"Mamoru-nii-san was firstborn..." he said slowly.

"Yes," Misaki replied.

"And... Uncle Takashi was firstborn."

"He was," Misaki said, looking at Hiroshi. She watched his eyes narrow as his five-year-old mind carefully worked its way up the hierarchy he had been born into.

"So, I am..."

Hiroshi did not yet know the words 'heir' or 'inheritor,' but it was clear from the questioning way he looked up at Misaki that he had some notion of the concept.

In the space of a single day, he had gone from being the second son of a second son to the Matsuda heir. Even if he couldn't fully understand the shift, he could feel it. His little shoulders had stiffened as if a physical weight had dropped onto them. His fists clenched and Misaki realized that her secondborn, who had been as steady as solid ice from the day he was born, was shaking. When she looked into his eyes, she saw something she had never seen there. Not even as he faced down a Ranganese soldier four times his size. Fear.

"I'm not big enough yet," he said. "I'm not strong enough."

"No." Misaki tried to smile at Hiroshi as she stroked his hair and put a hand on his shoulder. "You're not big enough, but you're plenty strong. If nothing else, Hiro-kun, you are strong."

Hiroshi didn't seem to hear her. "He can't go yet." He stared through her, looking almost fevered. "He can't."

"He's already gone, Hiro-kun. There's nothing we can do about it."

"But he *can't*." Hiroshi's face twisted in anger, his eyes still unfocused. "I didn't catch up to him yet."

As Nagasa sobbed and Hiroshi shook quietly under her hands, it occurred to Misaki what a big piece of their world Mamoru had been. Not just a firstborn son, but a decade older than his younger brothers, he must have loomed so large to them. He had been a landmark and a bulwark between them and the far-off adult world. For Nagasa, he had been a friend and protector. For Hiroshi, maybe he hadn't been a friend, but something more important; he had been something to chase after.

"I didn't catch up to him yet."

"Listen, Hiro-kun, that's alright. You don't have to stop chasing him. He won't be here with us anymore, but I'm sure his spirit would be happy to know you kept following his example. You can still grow up strong, like him, in time."

"But—I'm not firstborn," Hiroshi protested, his voice strained with anxiety. "I'm not big enough."

Misaki understood at that moment that Hiroshi was struggling to voice a terror beyond his vocabulary. The firstborn Matsudas—Takashi and Mamoru—had been 'big' to Hiroshi in more than their age and physical size. He was talking about the size of their skill, their strength, their responsibility. They had both been massively powerful figures in Hiroshi's world, responsible for dealing with the nondescript adult dangers the rest of the family could not. Now, both of them had died facing those dangers, leaving Hiroshi standing where they once had. Still so small.

"I'm not ready."

"I know, Hiro-kun. None of us are. But we're going to do our best together, alright?"

Drawn tighter than a Katakouri bowstring, Hiroshi nodded.

"Right now, we have to give Mamoru our prayers and help him on his way. The only thing we can do now is let him go without worrying too much about us. If you have anything you would like to say to your brother, any last things you feel he should know, you should offer them now."

Hiroshi stood, considering his brother's body for a long moment. Then he stepped back and knelt down with his forehead to the ground.

Misaki could only guess what passed between Hiroshi and his brother's spirit. It was impossible to tell if he berated Mamoru for leaving him, if he asked for strength, if he asked forgiveness for taking his place, if he made promises to grow strong and protect the family, but whatever he prayed, he must have felt it deeply, because his jiya rose with palpable force, turning the snow around him to ice. The whole time, Nagasa didn't stop crying.

"What are we going to do about the funerals?" Setsuko asked as she and Misaki sat on the half-destroyed front deck of the compound with their children.

"I don't know." Misaki was rubbing slow circles over Nagasa's back. For a long time, the boy had sobbed uncontrollably, but she had let him hold Izumo, which seemed to have calmed him down for the moment. "I don't actually know how Takayubi deals with mass death like this."

"You nobles probably have a lot of extra fancy ceremonies, right?"

"We do." The day after Matsuda Susumu passed away, it had seemed as if every monk in Takayubi showed up to dress the body, sing Donkili, fuss over the ornamentation of the coffin, and prepare the cremation site. Misaki herself had spent waatinu making sure her hair, obi, and bone white kimono were all arranged just so, to avoid offending the spirit of her embittered father-in-law. After each of her miscarriages, the finawu had led her through so much prayer, and fasting, and purifying that she had thought it might never end.

"We should have covered the house shrine to protect it from evil spirits," Misaki said, recalling the one ritual that was always observed after a tragedy.

"Oh." Setsuko's shoulders slumped. The Matsuda shrine was in the part of the house that had collapsed completely.

"We could salt the area?" Setsuko suggested.

"Right." Misaki sometimes forgot that the lower classes considered salt a catch-all antidote to the supernaturally sinister. On a peasant's budget, that was far more doable than sending for an exorcist monk every time a ghost came calling.

"Is my low breeding showing?" Setsuko asked at the look on Misaki's face.

"No, it's not a bad idea," Misaki said wearily, "but the salt is in the kitchen."

The kitchen, while it had not been hit by any bombs, had been utterly destroyed in Misaki's fight with the two elite fonyakalu. The broken faucet had continued spewing water well into the night, flooding the floor and the surrounding rooms. When Takeru and the volunteers cleaned the house, someone had frozen the spigot shut and erected an ice wall to prevent the water from spreading throughout to the rest of the compound, but the kitchen itself was unsalvageable.

"We also have no cemetery," Misaki said. "The fishermen who were helping search for bodies said it was destroyed." The tornado had advanced well past the western village before the men of Takayubi managed to stop it, leveling the cemetery, shrines, and trees further up the slope.

"So, we don't have any place for the ashes of the dead?" Setsuko asked.

Misaki shook her head. There had been graves ready for Takashi and Takeru beside their father's since the brothers reached their thirties, but the wind had scattered headstones, ashes, and bones of ten generations of Matsudas across the mountain.

"I heard the Amenos have sent for monks to help with all the ceremonies," Setsuko said.

"That's good," Misaki tried to sound reassuring. "They'll know what to do." But how much good could any fina really do in this situation? So many dead children. So many dead without warning. Was there any ceremony that could purge the miasma of so much pain?

"Where is Takeru-sama?" Setsuko asked.

"I don't know." Misaki shrugged. "Still giving the volunteers directions, maybe. I don't know." Frankly, she didn't care. He had left Mamoru to die. And for what? So he could arrive in the village just in time to try to stop Misaki from going to save Hyori?

"Has he prayed for Mamoru?"

"I don't know." Misaki shrugged again. "It doesn't matter."

"Of course, it matters..." Setsuko trailed off, staring at Misaki in confusion. "You're upset with him," she said after a moment.

"And you're not?" Misaki said. "He left your husband to die."

"He also saved me."

"Your husband saved you," Misaki snapped. "Takeru was just following orders."

"Well, you can't exactly blame him for leaving the frontline then, can you?" Setsuko said. "If he was just following orders?"

Misaki didn't answer. She did, however, tug Setsuko's arm when she noticed Yukino Dai's body passing on one of the stretchers. The swordmaster's face was covered with a cloth, which would have made him indistinguishable from the other Yukino men who had died holding the line, but Misaki recognized his katana resting in the stretcher at his side. Of all the beautiful swords in Takayubi, Takenagi was the one Misaki had envied. Lighter than other Kotetsu swords and so breathtakingly fast in Dai's hands. She knew with a sad certainty that no swordsman would be worthy of the weapon again.

"We should go," Setsuko said softly.

Misaki nodded. Leaving their children under the watchful eyes of the Kotetsus and some fisherwomen, the sisters-in-law went to be with Hyori.

They found her where she had collapsed that morning, half draped over the fallen stone Yukino insignia. Her head was resting in the crook of her arm as if she were sleeping, but Misaki knew before crouching down to Hyori's eye level that she wasn't asleep. There was a brittle tension in her shoulders that could only come from waking pain.

"Hyori-chan?" Misaki rested a hand on her friend's back.

She was so stiff and still that for a horrible moment, she reminded Misaki of the corpses in the snow, rigid with a combination of ice and rigor mortis. She didn't move as the men lowered Dai onto the ice slab next to the bundled remains of his son.

"Hyori-chan?" Misaki said again.

Dazed eyes blinked and she said miserably, "What?"

"They've found your husband's body."

Hyori turned away from Misaki with a strained sound of denial, like the bleating of a lamb in the wolf's jaws. "No." She buried her face in her arms. "No."

"You should at least give him your prayers, Hyori-chan," Setsuko said softly, "so he can move on in peace. He loved you so much."

Hyori only curled more tightly against the stone, her knees twitching up to her chest. "I can't."

"What do you mean, Hyori-chan?"

"I'm not worthy," Hyori said in a voice smothered with pain and muffled in her sleeves. "I shouldn't touch him. I shouldn't even look at him."

"Hyori-chan, what are you talking about?"

"I failed him."

"What?" Setsuko looked confused. "Are you talking about Ryota-kun? Hyori-chan, that wasn't your fault—"

Hyori flinched away from the hand Setsuko tried to lay on her shoulder and huddled into herself, shaking her head. Misaki hadn't told Setsuko about what that last Ranganese soldier had done to their friend—and she never would. That wasn't the sort of a thing that a Kaigenese lady would ever put into words. The shame was too deep.

Misaki waited until Setsuko had stepped away to pay her respects to Dai before kneeling in the snow to put an arm around Hyori's shoulders. She tried to make her voice low and soft, as her mother always had, trying to capture that magical power to comfort.

"Hyori," she murmured, putting her forehead to her friend's hair. "It wasn't your fault."

Hyori didn't pull away. She curled up tighter with a tiny, miserable noise, but Misaki refused to let her friend shrink away into the darkness. Not because of one man's disgraceful behavior.

"He was stronger than you. There was nothing you could have done, for your son or yourself. Your husband, of all people, would understand that. Any warrior who knows victory and defeat would understand."

Hyori sniffed and though Misaki couldn't see the tears, she could feel salty water seeping from Hyori's eyes into her sleeve.

"Dai-san treasured you. He would never have stopped loving you for something that wasn't your fault."

"Y-you think..." Hyori stammered, and through the grief, there was the faintest flicker of something that made Misaki melt with relief. *Hope*. "You think he could... forgive me?"

"No, Hyori-chan," Misaki lifted a hand to stroke her friend's head. "He doesn't have to. There is nothing to forgive."

"But I'm not—I'm not pure anymore."

"Someone took that from you," Misaki said fiercely, "dishonorably. Just like someone took his life from him."

"You think he was killed dishonorably?"

"Don't be ridiculous, Hyori-chan. Who could kill Lightning Dai in a fair fight?" Misaki didn't mention that Dai's head appeared to have been shattered by an attack from behind. That was the sort of detail a delicate thing like Hyori wouldn't appreciate—and apparently, it wasn't necessary, because the most fragile of smiles had crossed Hyori's face. It was the most beautiful thing Misaki had ever seen and she squeezed her friend, desperate to hold onto it.

"I suppose you're right..." Hyori said hesitantly.

"The people who did this—who fought without honor and destroyed without conscience—they are the ones who will burn in Hell's fire for this. Not your husband. Not you."

"A-are you sure?"

"Positive," Misaki said. "If there is anyone here now who need's Dai-san's forgiveness, it's me."

"What are you talking about?"

"I should have gotten there sooner. I knew you could be in danger; I should have gone to check on you as soon as I knew my children were safe. Nami forgive me, I knew the Ranganese attack might be coming. I... I had so many chances to do something, but I failed you. I failed everyone. So, let *me* ask Dai-san for forgiveness, and you..." Misaki drew back to hold Hyori's shoulders in a bracing grip, trying to will strength into her. "You just send him all your love. Alright?"

Hyori was shaky, tears still trembling in her eyes, but she nodded. "Alright."

After Hyori finished praying, Misaki and Setsuko sat with her. Neither had any words to ease her agony. But in the end, the words they chose didn't seem to matter. Hyori just knelt and stared numbly at the body, seemingly unable to see or hear what was around her. They stayed anyway and held her hands as if their presence could make her any less alone.

Misaki was still murmuring soft reassurances when the flutter of familiar colors caught her eye.

"Oh." She stood, wondering if she had imagined the symbol, but it was real. The white-crested wave of the Tsusano family, rising among the Ameno banners.

Setsuko nodded to Misaki as if to say, *I'll look after her.*

Misaki squeezed her arm in a silent 'Thank you.' "Hyori-chan, excuse me a moment." She brushed a hand over Hyori's back before hurrying as quickly as was ladylike to meet the Tsusano party.

Her eyes fell immediately on her father's blue and silver haori, but when the Tsusano leader turned to face her, it was not her father.

"Kazu-kun!" Her voice broke.

She had never been so happy to see her dumb baby brother, and she found herself lurching toward him. Maybe the emptiness of letting Mamoru go was too fresh in her heart, maybe Kazu's face was just a reminder of a time before any of this. Before she found the self-control to stop herself, she had thrown her arms around him.

The Lord of the Stormfort grunted in surprise, opened his mouth as if to say something but ended up coughing as Misaki crushed him tighter in her arms. He smelled like salt and sea wind, like a home that no longer existed. She had to let Mamoru go, but at least Kazu was here. She could hold him like this, like she had when they were little children and he had run into her room afraid of the thunder.

"Nee-san!" Kazu could not have sounded more shocked if she'd punched him in the face.

When they were young, she had always been the one scolding him for breaches of decorum. If he had ever clung to her this way in public, she would have smacked him away and hissed that that was no way for a young lord to behave.

"Nee-san... are you alright?" he asked as Misaki drew back. "Are you...?" *Insane?* The implication was there. "What happened?"

Misaki shook her head, unable to voice it. Kazu's men were staring, their expressions ranging from shock to worry. Through her haze of emotion, she realized that she recognized some of them. They were members of the Tsusanos' vassal families, who had served her father and trained in his dojo as children.

"Umiiro-san, Hakuyu-san." She detached herself from Kazu to bow properly. "It's good to see you again."

"Matsuda-dono." They bowed deeply.

"H-how are things in Ishihama?" Misaki asked, turning from the vassal men back to her brother. "How is our family?"

"Our parents are comfortably set up with our cousins and

everyone else has a place to stay in the short term at least."

"Good," Misaki nodded. "Good, I'm so glad."

Unlike Takayubi, which was surrounded by poor fishing and farming villages, Ishihama had neighboring towns capable of accommodating a small influx of refugees.

"But Ishihama was only attacked a short while ago. How—"

"I know what you're going to say, Nee-san," Kazu said with a guilty smile. "I probably shouldn't have left home so soon after the—after the disaster, but I've left Kaito and Raiki to look after the family."

"Right." Misaki had forgotten that even her youngest brothers were well into their twenties now, perfectly capable of looking after the family in Kazu's absence. "Still..." The timing didn't add up. "How did you get here so fast?" Ishihama wasn't that close to Takayubi and the roads weren't good. "How did you—"

"We started traveling two days ago," Kazu said, "by sea."

"By sea!" Misaki exclaimed in surprise.

A group of powerful jijakalu could propel themselves across a body of water on hydrodynamic ice formations faster than any car or train. But despite its speed, free ocean travel was a dangerous method of transportation, usually reserved for emergencies. Even the most powerful jijakalu were foolish to put themselves at the mercy of the ocean. Kazu and his men must have crossed hundreds of clicks of open sea, far from the coast, to get here so fast. It certainly explained why they all looked so exhausted.

"You must have left Ishihama before the Ranganese even got here," Misaki said in confusion.

"We'll talk about that later," Kazu said. "I'm sorry it has to be under these circumstances, but it's good to see your face, Nee-san."

Misaki nodded and took a moment to look her brother up and down. At thirty-two, this Kazu was far removed from the giggly, hyperactive boy who had cried at the sound of thunder. To Misaki's surprise, he looked... well... *lordly*, with his benevolent gaze and his shoulders filling out the haori that had once belonged to their father. The Tsusanos' massive ancestral sword, Anryuu—the Riptide—was tied to his back, marking him not only as the head of his house but Ishihama's foremost warrior.

His skin was littered with cuts and bruises that looked like they had come from falling rubble. A few of the deeper wounds on his face were obviously going to scar, despite the well-knit scabs he had formed over them. Amused surprise flickered through Misaki as she realized that Kazu wasn't going to look bad with scars. He was going to look hardened, *intimidating*. Eyes trailing down, she tilted her head at a deeper wound across his right collarbone that looked suspiciously like the work of a blade.

"Ah..." Kazu quickly pulled the neck of his kimono up to cover the injury. "You know, I forget how *cold* it is up here."

Misaki gave him a knowing look. None of her younger brothers had ever shared her proclivity for deception, but Kazu had always been the worst liar of the bunch.

"And you look like you had some... fun?" Kazu's eyes passed over Misaki's bruises and the cuts the fan-wielder had left on her forearms. A normal brother would have worried for his sister, but Kazu undoubtedly remembered all the times Misaki had trounced him in the Tsusano dojo and knew to worry for her enemies more than anyone else.

"Misaki-nee-san..." He lowered his voice so the others wouldn't hear. "You *didn't* go to the frontlines?"

"Oh, Kazu-kun, I'm flattered that you assume I would have survived that, but I didn't have to." She gestured to the wrecked village behind her. "The frontlines came to me."

"We should have gotten here sooner." He sounded pained. "Have the military representatives arrived yet?" He glanced around him and Misaki saw an echo of the jumpy boy who had been so scared of the thunder.

"No. I mean, planes showed up to bomb every last fonyaka off the mountainside, but no one has spoken to us yet. I haven't seen any imperial troops on the ground."

"Good."

"What?"

"Not here," Kazu said quickly.

"So... did you know?" she asked. "The storm you wrote me about... was it really a storm or—"

"I said not here," he repeated more firmly. "Misaki-nee-san, I'm sorry. I know this is a difficult time for you, but I need to speak privately with your brother-in-law. Can you take me to him?"

Misaki shook her head. "Matsuda Takashi didn't survive the battle. My husband is the head of the house now."

"Oh..." Kazu said as a few of his men uttered sounds of surprise and denial. "I'm so sorry. Can you take me to your husband, then?"

"Yes." Misaki nodded. "Yes, of course. I'm so sorry. You and your men must be tired and hungry. I would invite you inside for tea, but there isn't much left of my kitchen... or the whole house, really." She nodded toward the Matsuda compound.

"What about your family?" Kazu asked anxiously. "Other than your brother-in-law—nyama to his soul—is everyone alright?"

Misaki looked down, pressing her lips together.

"Nee-san?"

"Come with me," she said softly.

Kazu and his men followed her through the breach in the compound wall to where the volunteers had laid the dead. Mamoru's body had been covered, but the boy's katana rested beside him, and Kazu knew his nephew's sword.

"Oh, Nee-san..." His voice shook.

For a moment, he looked as he had when he was a boy, on the verge of tears. A lord of the house did not cry in front of his men, of course, but Misaki found herself feeling ridiculously grateful for her brother's moment of weakness. It was good to know that one of the men in her life cared that Mamoru was gone.

One by one, Kazu and his men paid their respects to Mamoru, bowing before the body and offering their prayers. Unable to watch, Misaki turned from the scene and went to find her husband, as Kazu had asked.

She hadn't spoken to Takeru since the previous day when he had tried to stop her from going back for Hyori. He must have heard by now that Mamoru's body had been found. His firstborn son was dead. But the knowledge didn't seem to affect him as he swept about the village, organizing supplies and ordering volunteers around.

"I'm busy," were the first words out of his mouth when he saw her.

"I know, Takeru-sama." She lowered her gaze, made her voice soft. It was the only way to hold off the anger simmering in her throat. "I'm sorry, but my brother, Lord Tsusano, is here to see you. He says it is urgent."

"Ameno-san," Takeru addressed the lead representative from the Ameno family. "Please, take over operations here."

"Yes, Matsuda-dono." The man bowed.

"I hope to be back shortly," Takeru said and followed Misaki to where Kazu was waiting. He walked right past his son's body without so much as glancing at it.

"Tsusano-dono," he said with a cordial bow. "It has been a long time. I am glad to see you here."

"Likewise, Matsuda-dono," Kazu said, dipping into his own bow, notably lower than Takeru's. Misaki knew that her brother had always been intimidated by Takeru, but he did an admirable job hiding it as he straightened back up. "I am deeply sorry for your loss."

Takeru offered a gruff nod.

"But it is good to see that my sister's husband, at least, survived the attack," Kazu added. "I'm relieved to know she will be taken care of."

Another nod.

"Is there someplace more private we could talk, Matsuda-dono?" Kazu asked.

"Regrettably, my house is occupied by the wounded at the moment."

"Somewhere else, then? Out of earshot of everyone?"

Takeru nodded. "Follow me, Tsusano-dono. Misaki, you may leave us," he added over his shoulder.

"No—I would prefer that she come along, if that's alright with you, Matsuda-dono," Kazu said haltingly. "She is my sister, so I'd like her to hear what I have to say as well. I would think, as her husband, you wouldn't mind—"

"Fine," Takeru said with a dark look at Misaki, "but you will keep your mouth shut."

"Yes, sir," she said quietly.

Kazu's eyes flicked from his sister to Takeru in obvious discomfort, but he didn't say anything. It wasn't his place to say anything. Not only was Takeru the new Matsuda patriarch, but he was also more than ten years Kazu's senior. A young lord didn't comment on an older lord's treatment of his woman—even if the woman in question was a sister who had once rocked a certain young lord to sleep and taught him his first sword forms.

"Do you have anyone else you would like to include, Matsuda-dono?" Kazu asked.

"What?"

"I'm sure you have other men you trust?" Kazu said. "Men you would like included in this meeting?"

Kazu was so ready to accept Takeru's authority, it probably didn't occur to him that the secondborn Matsuda hadn't even been the head of the house for a full day.

"My brother's closest confidants were myself and Yukino Dai," Takeru said. "The latter is dead."

"Lightning Dai?" Kazu said in shock. "He's gone too?"

"We lost most of our best." Takeru slowed his steps before what remained of the Mizumaki house, where Kwang Chul-hee and his father were helping the Ameno men organize and distribute the meager supplies the volunteers had brought up the mountain. He seemed to consider for a moment, his eyes passing over each of the high-ranking Ameno men, the two surviving Mizumaki elders, and the crippled Katakouri man, who had been unable to join the fight.

The visiting Amenos, while they were doing a wonderful job helping, were not typically very involved in Takayubi affairs. The Mizumakis and Katakouris were close and trusted allies, but these remaining men were not their leaders. Katakouri Hisato, with the twisted leg, was a fifth son who had spent his entire adult life working as a cashier in the western village's convenience store. The Mizumaki elders had been fine men in their prime, but these days one could only remember half of what he heard, and the other could not hear at all. Takeru's eyes narrowed in thought.

Then he made up his mind. "Kwang Tae-min."

"Yes?" The northerner looked up.

"Your son can take over the work you are doing, yes?"

Tae-min glanced at Chul-hee. "Sure."

"You will come with me."

"Oh—" Tae-min looked surprised. "Of course. Just give me a moment."

"He's... a northerner," Kazu whispered with an apprehensive look at Takeru. Kwang Tae-min may have forgone his hanbok and bogolan vest in favor of a Shirojima style kimono, but his accent was unmistakable. "He's not one of us."

"He is a citizen of the Empire, as we are," Takeru said, "and he is well-traveled, giving him insights we might not have." Misaki had plenty of the same insights, although Takeru didn't seem particularly interested in listening when they came from her mouth. "He is also one of the few men of sound mind who survived."

"He didn't fight, I take it?" Kazu said.

"His strengths lie in other areas," Takeru said. "The two of us have spent a few months now working together on one of the mayor's projects."

All Misaki knew of her husband's relationship with Kwang Tae-min was that the two had worked together closely on the plan for the info-com towers. She knew that Takeru had been the one to suggest the project in the first place, and he had evidently grown close to the northerner as they worked together to make it a reality.

Takeru was always pressing for more modern development—a paved road one year, better power lines the next—and on the rare occasions his projects were approved, he was always the one who ended up managing them. The mayor was—or rather had been—

more of a figurehead, a dull but harmless government official, content to let his staff do his job better than he could. The Empire didn't typically send its best and brightest to oversee tiny mountain villages.

"And the mayor?" Kazu asked.

"Dead," Takeru said, displaying no emotion for the man who had employed him for many years. "He was at home in the western village when they came."

Having finished giving instructions to his son, Kwang Tae-min hurried over.

"Tsusano-dono, this is Kwang Tae-min, a representative from Geomijul Communications," Takeru said. "Kwang-san, this is Tsusano Kazu of Ishihama, Lord of the Arashiki and my wife's brother."

After the two men bowed and exchanged greetings, Takeru led them out of the village, up toward the mountain's summit. The snow grew deeper as they ascended, but it parted before them at the touch of Takeru's jiya.

Two of Kazu's men followed them up until Kazu turned to them. "Stay here," he ordered. "Ensure that nobody follows us."

"Yes, sir."

As the men took up position in the snow, Misaki had the feeling that her suspicions were about to be confirmed. This attack and whatever had taken place in Ishihama were connected, and the government was going to considerable trouble to hide it.

Takeru led them to a snowy clearing overlooking Kumono Academy. The temple-turned-school was the only structure that seemingly hadn't been touched by bombs or fonya. It stood as proud and serene as ever against the rock. Perhaps it was too high up the mountain, too removed from most of the action, for anyone to have bothered with it. The climb had certainly taxed Misaki's aching lungs.

"Now then, Lord Tsusano." Takeru turned to Kazu. "What was it you wanted to discuss?"

"I..." Kazu started hesitantly. "First, I wanted to apologize, for not warning you properly."

"Explain."

"As I'm sure you've guessed, Takayubi wasn't the only town the Ranganese attacked in these past few weeks. They came to Ishihama as well. That was what destroyed the Arashiki and the surrounding town, not a storm as the news reported."

Takeru nodded as if he had suspected this the whole time, as if he hadn't slapped his son around the dojo for suggesting it.

"Based on where all the other so-called storms hit the coast, we—my father and I—figured the Ranganese were targeting Kaigen's old warrior houses. We thought Takayubi might be next. Of course, we hoped not, but..." Kazu shook his head. "The least I can do is warn you about what is going to happen next."

"What do you mean?" Takeru asked. "Should we be expecting more attacks?"

"No, no, Matsuda-dono," Kazu said hastily. "Nothing like that. I wanted to warn you about the Kaigenese military, before they get here."

At the look of confusion on Takeru's face, Kazu continued, "There is a reason I couldn't explain our situation in the letter I wrote my sister. As soon as the Kaigenese troops arrived in Ishihama, they made it clear that we were not to discuss the attack amongst ourselves or tell anyone else what had happened."

Takeru's brow had furrowed in thought. "Why?"

"I don't know." Kazu shook his head. "They wouldn't tell us, but it was clear that they were trying to keep news of these attacks contained. The Emperor's soldiers even moved us all into the neighboring town while the Yammanka troops helped them clean up the damage."

"The Yammankalu are involved?" Misaki asked.

It wasn't unusual for Kaigen's more powerful ally to give them military support, especially where Ranga was concerned, but it added a new level of complexity to the situation. Yamma was its own player, with its own motives.

"Yes. The Yammanka soldiers were there almost as soon as our own military."

"How did they act?" Misaki asked. "Did they say anything to you, or—"

"You were told not to speak," Takeru said shortly.

"Um—" Again, Kazu's eyes flicked uncomfortably between Misaki and her husband. He might not have had the courage or authority to speak up for his sister, but he did answer her question. "The Yammankalu barely interacted with us. Most of them communicated only with the Kaigenese military and then went to help with the clean-up, or... whatever it is they're doing in the area affected by the attack. We haven't been allowed back in to find the bodies of family members or retrieve belongings. I don't know if anything's changed, but that was where things stood when I left."

"And you think we can expect something similar here in Takayubi?" Takeru asked.

"Maybe. I just wanted to warn you before the Kaigenese troops arrived. I'm so sorry my men and I didn't make better time," he added earnestly. "I'm sorry we weren't able to offer more meaningful support."

"Don't apologize," Takeru said. "As you saw, our warriors were more than sufficient to hold the hostiles back until the Emperor's forces arrived." He said it with his usual disinterest, as if the deaths of his brother, his son, and so many civilians meant nothing.

"We didn't face anything like this in Ishihama," Kazu said.

"The Ranganese didn't send as many soldiers?"

"I don't know. I think most of the Ranganese involved in the attack never actually reached us."

The Tsusanos' town, perched high atop that sheer cliff, was far more defensible than Takayubi—or indeed any place in the world, as far as Misaki knew. No army in history had ever breached it, and she was relieved to hear that even this terrifying new Ranganese force was no exception.

"Did they attack with a tornado?" Takeru asked.

"Initially, yes. When we saw it forming over the water, my father realized almost immediately that it was the Ranganese."

"Oh? Had your father encountered fonyakalu before?" Takeru asked, probably thinking of how he and Takashi had been uncomprehending in the face of the tornado for several siiranu until Misaki and Chul-hee had convinced them that it was the work of the Ranganese. She wondered with annoyance if he had the decency to be embarrassed.

"No, Matsuda-dono."

He's just not an idiot. Misaki thought angrily.

"I think," Kazu said more tactfully, "my father had just seen so many hundreds of storms in his life that he could sense right away when one was not behaving normally. Knowing that the houses nearest the edge were lost, we evacuated as many homes as we could and gathered the warriors to face any Ranganese who made it ashore."

"And?"

"The tornado broke apart when it hit the cliff," Kazu said and it didn't surprise Misaki that the Ishihama Cliff had done what even the jagged rocks and steep slope of Mount Takayubi could not. "Obviously, our Arashiki was destroyed, along with the houses that sat near the edge. The wind off the tornado threw some of the Ranganese over the lip of the cliff—about two dozen, I think. We killed them." That explained the blade wound across Kazu's clavicle. "The rest of the Ranganese, I assume, tried to scale the cliff, but they didn't make it before the Yammankalu showed up to shoot them down."

Takeru nodded. "So, you did not suffer heavy casualties?"

"Only two of our warriors died in combat, but the flying debris caused devastation for clicks around. Unfortunately, there wasn't time to evacuate the entire area, and the tornado shattered the weaker parts of the cliff's edge, raining rocks on us, some as big as houses. Many people were killed by those rocks—we think close to a hundred."

"You think?"

"That's how many were missing after we reached safety and took count, but like I said, we haven't been back to our houses and the soldiers won't tell us anything." He shook his head. "I just wonder what they stand to gain from covering all of this up."

A sense of security, Misaki thought. If news of the attacks spread, people might panic and become more difficult to control. Then again, that didn't explain what secretive business the Yammankalu were up to.

"It doesn't matter," Takeru said. "Thank you for the warning, but it is not our business to question the will of the Emperor. If these are his orders, our only job is to obey."

"Matsuda," Tae-min said, looking uneasy, *"I get the feeling you may not like what the Emperor asks of you."*

"What are you talking about?" Kazu asked, shifting to Kaigengua as he turned to Tae-min.

"I know that the media would suggest that the heart of the Empire is strong and overflowing with resources, but I'm a native of Jungsan, and I just think..." Tae-min paused, looking apprehensively between the two Shirojima men. He was taking a gamble; he didn't know Kazu, and how well could one really know Takeru? *"The reality of the Imperial army is very different from the image it projects."* He turned to Kazu. *"If the military has already made an appearance in Ishihama, you already have some idea."*

"Well..." Kazu was frowning. *"I didn't interact with the soldiers very much."* The hesitation in his voice revealed that there was some truth to what Kwang Tae-min said.

"I don't say this to belittle the Empire or to upset you, Tsusano," the northerner said carefully, *"but Matsuda..."* He looked to Takeru. *"Your village is in a difficult position at the moment. So far, we've accounted for forty-two living, many of whom are injured. You have only what remains of the Matsuda compound and the very little that remains of the Mizumaki house to accommodate all those people. My son is still inventorying the food we've recovered, but it isn't going to be enough to feed many—"*

"I'm aware of that, Kwang," Takeru said tersely. *"What does this have to do with the military?"*

"I just want to warn you... I don't want you to make the mistake

of assuming you can rely on the Empire to support your community through this time. I've been around enough to know that you will be disappointed."

"You shouldn't say such things of the Empire," Kazu said, his frown deepening.

"So, your town has received the aid it needs, Tsusano?" Tae-min asked.

"I didn't stay long after the attack," Kazu said. *"I'm sure they have by now."* He didn't sound sure. *"Besides, Ishihama didn't need aid the way Takayubi does. My people still have roofs to sleep under, a way to get back on our feet. If this village doesn't get help..."*

It will cease to exist, Misaki thought grimly.

"Whatever the Emperor orders, our only job is to obey," Takeru reiterated firmly. His words made it sound simple, as if lives didn't hang in the balance. "It is a privilege to serve the Kaigenese Empire in whatever way we can."

"Of course," Kazu agreed, "but I will admit that all of this is strange. Not just the business with the Imperial troops and the Yammankalu; the attacks themselves don't seem logical."

"What do you mean?" Takeru asked.

"A smart fighter strikes at his enemy's weak points."

"Yes?"

"So, what is Ranga doing launching these concentrated attacks on the towns of Kaigen's most powerful fighters? If their goal was to penetrate into the interior and they had the element of surprise, why target the homes of the people most likely to repel them?"

Kazu made a surprisingly good point. It was like deliberately aiming a sword stroke at armor or a Blood Needle at bone. At worst, doomed; at best, wasteful. There were so many places a Ranganese force of this size and skill could have come ashore and killed everyone with ease, or even snuck through completely unnoticed in the night.

"Maybe penetration wasn't their goal," Misaki suggested, even as Takeru shot her a disapproving look. "These attacks could be part of a more complicated plan. Maybe their intention was to weaken the great houses."

"At the cost of so many soldiers?" Kazu said incredulously.

There again, he had a point. There were ways to do away with your enemies without losing hundreds of good fighters. Granted, none of the ways that came to mind were particularly honorable— most of Misaki's immediate thoughts involved assassins and poison—but slaughtering children was not honorable. Burning blacksmiths in their homes was not honorable. Raping your enemy's women was not honorable. If the Ranganese were willing to commit those atrocities, why not stoop to poison or a single well-placed bomb? Why sacrifice so many fighters?

The rank and file soldiers in yellow may have been an expendable resource to the Ranganese Union, but those soldiers in black were one in ten thousand. When Misaki had been at Daybreak, Ranganese special forces had been limited to Ranga's strongest bloodlines—Sheng and Tian. Soldiers of their caliber were incalculably valuable assets. Why send dozens of them to die in a head-on battle?

Before the men had a chance to discuss further, one of Kazu's fighters ran up the slope to them and stopped, panting, winded from the climb.

"I'm s—" He cut off, struggling to catch his breath, his lungs unaccustomed to Takayubi's thin air. "S-sorry to interrupt, Matsuda-dono, Tsusano-dono." He bowed.

"What is it, Hakuyu-san?" Kazu asked.

"The Imperial troops have arrived. They're asking for the head of the village." Hakuyu looked to Takeru as he straightened up. "I told them that was you, Matsuda-dono."

"I'll be right there."

22

THE SOLDIERS

The Imperial troops had not come alone. As in Ishihama, they had Yammanka soldiers with them. It had been a long time since Misaki had seen Yammankalu—or any non-Kaigenese people for that matter. For some residents of Takayubi, the sight of a foreigner was a complete novelty. Women and children gathered to gawk and murmur, though they hovered a careful distance from the Yammanka lines as if worried the fire-wielding soldiers might spontaneously combust.

"I didn't know they'd be so tall," one woman marveled.

"They're beautiful," another woman sighed. "Such dark skin! Like in the movies!"

"And their hair looks so... fluffy," Mizumaki Fuyuko added, scrunching up her nose. "Do you think I could get one of them to let me touch it?"

"Don't be stupid, Fuyu-chan," another teenage girl said. "It would burn your fingers off."

Fuyuko cocked her head. "I thought they had to be on fire to do that."

"No. I'm pretty sure the fire is inside them, under their skin, like we've got blood inside us."

"And—wait a dinma—are those *women?*" Mizumaki Fuyuko gaped as if that was somehow more outlandish than the idea of people with fire for blood.

"They can't be," her mother said dismissively. "They have spears."

"They've also got breasts, Mizumaki-san," Setsuko said in amusement. "I'm pretty sure they're women."

"Nonsense. Women can't—"

"Look!" Setsuko said, seemingly delighted at the opportunity to scandalize her already traumatized neighbors. "That one has really *big* breasts!" She pointed to a nearby Yammanka.

The soldier in question looked toward the chattering Kaigenese women and rolled her eyes with a long-suffering sigh. Being stationed in Kaigen had to be a tiring experience for a female soldier. Misaki was ready to feel sorry for her until she saw the patterns on the woman's uniform—pilot patterns. This woman and the tajakalu standing around her were responsible for bombing Takayubi to pieces.

In the darkness and confusion of the previous night's airstrike, it had been impossible to tell which country the planes belonged to, but it didn't surprise Misaki that the Yammankalu had responded faster than the Imperial army. Yamma had military bases scattered across the Kaigenese Empire, and they were famously quick to respond to crises. Still, it was unsettling that the Emperor would allow foreign planes to rain bombs on his own land.

"They all look rather upset," one woman commented, looking down the line of Yammanka soldiers.

"They're tajakalu," Misaki said. "It's the middle of winter and they're up here on a freezing mountain."

The dark-skinned tajakalu shivered in their bogolan uniforms, looking determined but deeply miserable in the shin-deep snow. At least they hadn't shown up in forty-year-old uniforms, which was more than Misaki could say of the Kaigenese troops. They wore the same blue and tan hanboks they had since the Keleba.

The first person to address Takeru was a stocky Kaigenese officer with a bit of a belly, who introduced himself as Colonel Song. He was accompanied by a Kaigenese jaseli wearing the robes of a military translator, which annoyed Misaki slightly. How uneducated did these men think they were?

"I'm told you're the head of the village?" Colonel Song said in Kaigengua.

"Yes, sir," Takeru answered slowly, the Imperial standard more awkward on his tongue than his native Shirojima Dialect, *"as of some time yesterday evening."*

"Really?" Colonel Song raised his eyebrows. *"Yesterday?"* Misaki didn't care for the note of condescension in his voice. *"Can you explain to me how that came to be?"*

"The mayor is presumed dead, as we have not yet found many survivors from the western village where he lived. I was his accountant, administrative assistant, and the person responsible for running his office whenever he had to report to provincial headquarters. So, for the time being, I will assume his responsibilities until he is found or replaced. My brother, the head of the resident ruling warrior house, was confirmed dead a few waatinu before you arrived, so I take his place as the leading—"

"I see," Colonel Song said, evidently growing bored with Takeru's slow, over-pronounced Kaigengua. *"So, these people will all answer to you?"*

"Those who live here in Takayubi, sir, yes."

"You can keep them under control?"

Misaki didn't like how Song referred to them as if they were a troublesome herd of livestock. She liked it less when Takeru responded with an unhesitating, *"Yes, sir."*

"Very good. The first thing I am going to need is for your people to bring all the bodies to the remains of the settlement southwest of this village."

"You mean the blacksmith village?"

"Oh, is that what it was?" Colonel Song said, with an amused quirk of his mouth that made Misaki want to punch the teeth out of it. *"Then, yes, the uh... blacksmith village. Our Yammanka allies have begun to set up their equipment there."*

"Their... equipment?" Takeru repeated slowly.

"Their equipment," the translator said in Shirojima Dialect and Takeru favored him with a cold look.

"The Yammankalu are conducting an important forensic investigation for our Emperor," Song said. *"You and everyone in this village are to give them your full cooperation."*

"Of course, General," Takeru said, though this was the first order that seemed to give him pause.

The Yammankalu might have been Kaigen's allies since the Keleba, but they were still foreigners, and villages as ancient and isolated as Takayubi didn't take well to foreigners interfering in their affairs. This was a village where the mere presence of *Kaigenese* outsiders like the Kwangs could cause a stir.

"I understand you've been having your people transport bodies to this building?"

"Only the bodies of our own," Takeru said, *"those with friends and family who need to lay them to rest. We've been waiting for finawu to arrive from the neighboring mountain to administer the proper rites."*

"I understand," Colonel Song said, *"but we will need all the bodies brought to the Yammankalu at your blacksmith village— Kaigenese and Ranganese."*

There was a pause. *"You... what?"* Takeru said blankly.

The translator, who was either extremely determined to condescend or just extremely bad at his job, piped up, "The colonel said, 'all the bodies, Kaigenese and Ranganese.'"

Takeru was still staring at Song. *"I don't understand."*

"You will direct your people to bring the bodies of every person killed during the attack to the Yammankalu. That includes the bodies they mistakenly brought here." He jerked his head toward Mamoru's covered corpse. *"In cases where only pieces of a body remain, they will need whatever can be recovered."*

Misaki didn't blame Takeru for standing in shock.

"Have I said something confusing to you, Matsuda?"

"You want me to take the dead from their grieving families?" Takeru's voice was as emotionless as ever, but more than that, it

417

was empty.

"This is the will of the Emperor."

"I apologize, sir. I just..." Takeru had started to stumble over the Kaigengua he rarely used. *"I don't understand."*

"The colonel says 'This is the will of the—'"

"Are you stupid?" Misaki snapped at the translator. *"He clearly knows the phrase 'will of the Emperor.' We have a TV."* Getting a chance to use her fluent Kaigengua after so many years of speaking Dialect should have been a pleasant experience, but she found herself baring her teeth around the syllables. *"Learn to read the situation, you moron."*

All three men stopped, staring at her.

Oh Misaki, you idiot.

"Chou, you may go," Song said after a moment. As the embarrassed translator bowed and took his leave, the colonel turned to Takeru. *"You said you could control this village. Would you mind controlling your wife?"*

"Yes, sir. I apologize." Takeru said, placing himself between Misaki and the colonel. *"She is suffering from shock and a mild concussion."*

"I'm sure all of you have suffered greatly, but take comfort knowing it is all in service of the Empire."

"Of course."

"Now that we understand each other, I'll have my soldiers start collecting the bodies." Misaki felt her world splinter as the colonel turned toward Mamoru and put a hand on him. *"We'll start with this one."*

"That's Mamoru," Takeru said as Colonel Song motioned some of his men forward. *"That's my son."* There was no protest in his tone, but there was something. Misaki had to believe there was something. There was no way he could allow this...

"Very good then. We'll start with your son."

"Yes, sir." Takeru bent and took the sheathed sword from beside Mamoru, just as the soldiers lifted the body. *"Glory to Kaigen. Long live the Emperor."*

Rage pulsed through Misaki, driving her forward. *"No,"* she growled through gritted teeth, *"You can't—"*

Kazu moved shockingly fast, catching her around the waist before Takeru or the soldiers seemed to have noticed her advancing.

"Nee-san, don't!" he hissed hauling her back.

"Let go!" Misaki lunged to break free, but Kazu's grip held, jolting her back again. *Nami,* when had her little brother gotten so *strong*? "They can't do this! They can't—"

Takeru's jiya slammed down over hers, a freezing shockwave through her blood and bone marrow. Her husband hadn't touched her—he had barely even *moved*—but the impact left her stunned. It was common knowledge that a strong theonite could force his power over that of a weaker one, neutralizing it, but Misaki had never come up against jiya so devastatingly stronger than her own.

"Matsuda-dono!" Kazu's voice said very far away, sounding startled and a little horrified.

Dimly, Misaki felt her husband's nyama, so much colder than her brother's, push in between her and Kazu, enveloping her like the waters of a frigid lake closing over her head. The sensation left her so dazed that she didn't register what was happening until Takeru's cold hands were guiding her onto her knees on singed tatami. She was inside the compound, in the room where Kotetsu Katashi was resting.

The blacksmith's children and her own huddled together on the nearby futon.

"He can't come back," Atsushi was struggling to explain to a crying Nagasa and his own younger siblings.

"Why not?" his little sister, Naoko, demanded.

"People don't come back from the Laaxara. I mean—they do sometimes, but..." Atsushi shuddered, pulling Naoko closer. "Not in a good way. They don't come back as... *them.* They're something different, something bad."

"My brother is not bad," Nagasa said.

"No, he's not," Atsushi agreed, "or—he *wasn't*. That's why we're not going to see him again."

"It's good that you were at least able to keep his sword, Matsuda-dono," Katashi was saying to Takeru.

"It would have been wasteful not to," Takeru said. "It's an excellent weapon."

"It is a *hero's* weapon, Matsuda-dono," the swordsmith said. "It should be kept in your family for future generations to wield and admire. Its name should be repeated proudly alongside the likes of Kurokouri and Kumokei."

"My son's sword doesn't have a name."

"Of course it does, Matsuda-dono," Kotetsu said in his singularly gentle, rumbling voice. "It gave its maker and wielder to earn it. That is Mamoriken," he nodded to the sword, "the Protector."

For a moment, something almost like an emotion flickered across Takeru's features. Almost. Misaki wondered why trying to find emotion on that man's face felt like trying to grab the thread of a spider web, like trying to remember a dream...

"Thank you, Kotetsu Kama." Takeru bowed.

Before he left the room, he paused where Misaki knelt and crouched down to her level to whisper, "Your behavior has been disgraceful. You will rest here in silence until you are able to conduct yourself in a respectable manner. Do you understand?"

"Of course, sir," Misaki slurred, mocking Takeru's low voice and Shirojima accent. *"Glory to Kaigen. Long live the Emperor."*

If he was going to kill her, he might as well do it now. After all, it seemed that the loss of his closest family members meant precisely nothing to him. But he didn't raise a hand to her. He simply pressed one down on her shoulder, as if to confirm that she would stay.

"You are not well," he said. "Rest."

Then he left, as he had the day of Misaki's first miscarriage, as he always did. She watched him go, wishing he had hit her.

23

THE RIPTIDE

The Yammankalu did not let any civilians near their tents for the next two days. Misaki tried to speak to one of the Yammanka soldiers, hoping he would be more helpful than Colonel Song and his imbecile translator. To his credit, the tajaka was significantly friendlier and more respectful than the colonel, but she still couldn't get much out of him.

"I'm sorry, Koroyaa," he repeated each time she tried to ask what they were doing with the bodies. *"I can't tell you any specifics at this time."*

Yammankalu tended to stand closer to one another than Kaigenese during conversation. This allowed Misaki to stand just close enough to the man to sense his heartbeat—the heat wasn't unwelcome either.

"We are here to help you," he said earnestly. *"I swear it on the Falleke. If our work here is successful, it will prevent any further attacks on this village and others."*

His pulse remained steady, meaning he was either honest or a very good liar.

The impulsive spy in her considered sneaking into the encampment. Tajakalu were irritatingly difficult to sneak past in the night, due to the fact that their first response to any strange sound was to flame up and illuminate the space. Misaki was very good at moving quietly, of course, and she could easily bring her body to the same temperature as the snow, erasing any heat signature a tajaka might detect, but there were almost certainly Imperial jijakalu in the camp as well, who might sense her jiya.

After running through several scenarios in her head, Misaki looked down at Izumo sleeping in her arms and wondered what in the realms she had been thinking. It was the selfish, thrill-seeking girl, Sirawu, who risked lives to sate her curiosity. Hadn't she explained to Mamoru how despicable and naïve that girl had been? Hadn't she learned better? This wasn't the Livingston adventure story where her actions had no consequences. Here, her children could die.

"I'm sorry," she murmured toward the encampment and bundled little Izumo closer to rest her cheek on his soft head. "Kaa-chan wouldn't do that to you. Not again."

She retreated back up the mountain without another look back at the Yammanka tents, but her curiosity didn't abate. That night, she saw Mamoru's body when she closed her eyes and sleep wouldn't come. Dawn found her on a ridge overlooking the remains of the blacksmith village. The mist obscured nearly all of the encampment far below, but the wavering light of flames in the quiet blue of the mountainside suggested that the tajakalu had been at work through the night. Snow crunched softly beneath tabi and Misaki felt her brother come to stand on the ridge beside her.

"Good morning, Tsusano-dono," she said, not taking her eyes from the firelight gradually growing sharper as the mists thinned. Takeru had insisted that she use Kazu's 'proper title,' though it still felt funny on her lips. An amused breath at her shoulder told her that Kazu felt the same way.

"Morning, Matsuda-dono," he returned. "Your ladyship couldn't sleep?"

"Your lordship can't mind his own business?" Misaki was still annoyed with him for holding her back from Colonel Song. She knew she shouldn't be—he had been the prudent one in that situation—but she was.

Kazu laughed. "I don't know why I thought you'd be nicer to me when I became the head of the house."

"Neither do I," Misaki said lightly. "What a silly thing to think."

"Are you always going to be this mean to me?"

"Until I die."

"Misaki-nee-san... are you alright?"

"What am I supposed to say to that, Kazu-kun? I've just lost my son."

"Sorry. Of course, you're not—I wasn't talking about that. I meant..." Kazu paused for a moment, clearly unsure if he should elaborate. He swallowed. "Is everything alright... with your husband?"

"Excuse me?" Misaki raised her eyebrows, honestly surprised at her brother's forwardness.

"Is he... has he been good to you?"

"Don't be stupid, Kazu."

"What?"

"A smart koro needs to consider his position before he goes and asks a question like that."

Kazu stared at her, uncomprehending. "My position?"

"Say I *did* complain about my husband? Say I told you he was evil incarnate, possessed by a demon, and you were compelled to defend me in combat. How do you think that would go?"

"I..."

"Could you win?" Misaki asked. "If the answer is 'no,' you might consider keeping your mouth shut."

"I'm a pretty good fighter," Kazu protested, sounding endearingly as he had when he was ten.

"You're a *very* good fighter," she said, "and a lousy tactician."

"What is that supposed to mean?"

"A good tactician knows when he's outmatched."

Kazu gave her a sour look. "I see why Tou-sama still misses you so much. You two sound exactly alike. Could it hurt to have a *little* confidence in me?"

"Alright." Misaki folded her arms, willing to bite if it meant a chance at shifting the topic of conversation. "Inspire me, Tsusano-dono. What's your master tactical plan? Hypothetically, if you had to face a Whispering Blade, what would you do? You haven't even brought a proper sword of your own." It hadn't escaped her notice that Kazu carried only the giant Anryuu, forgoing the regular-sized backup katana a Tsusano leader usually carried.

"I have my Riptide," Kazu said defensively, reaching back to pat the forearm-length handle of Anryuu.

"Ah yes," Misaki said, affecting a mockingly dramatic tone, "Mighty Anryuu, the Undertaker, Sinker of Ships."

The ancestral sword was a weapon of ridiculous size, so big it could only be carried across a Tsusano patriarch's back, fixed in place with a broad leather strap so it didn't bump and drag along the ground. According to legend, it had been forged by Ishino smiths for the war hero, Tsusano Raiden, a contemporary of Matsuda Takeru the First. Raiden was said to have stood over two stories tall, allowing him to wade into the sea and cleave whole ships in half with his Stormblade. Misaki had always found this particular legend amusing, considering the modest stature of modern Tsusanos, but it did provide an explanation as to why anyone would forge such a ludicrously large sword.

Misaki envied her younger brother for many things, but learning to wield the Riptide had never been one of them. Her shoulders and forearms burned just thinking about trying to maneuver such a massive weapon.

Like laymen couldn't understand why master Matsudas trained with steel swords, many couldn't understand why the Tsusanos trained with the Riptide. If a man could slice and spin with Anryuu in hand, he was unstoppable with a regular sword. It was a simple matter of conditioning for maximum speed and strength, much like training with weights on one's wrists and ankles. Anryuu was a glorified training tool. Though the Ishihama smiths kept its blade sharp, wielding it in an actual fight was folly.

"Don't tell me you expect to be dueling anyone with that monstrosity?"

Kazu shrugged. "It worked well enough on the Ranganese."

"What?" Misaki's eyes widened. "Kazu, it's not good for a Lord to make up stories."

"I'm not making it up," he said in genuine annoyance.

"But that's impossible," Misaki said. "I fought the Ranganese too. Even the rank and file soldiers weren't exactly slow. I know you're strong, but no one could wield such a heavy weapon fast enough to fight those fonyakalu."

"Tou-sama could," Kazu said. "You know that, Nee-san. You've seen him do the Stormblade katas."

"Yeah..." Of course, she had. She remembered kneeling a safe distance away as her father sliced and spun through the ancient sword forms composed by Tsusano ancestors specifically for the use of the Riptide. As a child, she had viewed her father as a god and hadn't questioned the fact that he could swing a sword as heavy as a grown man as if it weighed nothing at all.

"But... he's Tou-sama," Misaki said, "and he was younger then."

"Right," Kazu said. "I forgot you haven't seen him in a while. Did you know that now, in his sixties, he still moves just as fast as he used to? He can still use Anryuu—I mean, not just lift it, but wield it faster than a twenty-something wields a normal sword."

"What? *How?"* Misaki asked, stunned.

"That's what I always wondered," Kazu said. "I've been asking him about it for years, but he'd never give me a straight answer, just vague platitudes about willpower... He said that, in order to wield Anryuu, 'a man must be bigger than himself,' which never really made sense to me. He said I might understand when I grew up. Then, when the Ranganese attacked, suddenly it made sense. I fought them, Nee-san. I fought them with Anryuu."

"Seriously?" Misaki exclaimed. "Your arms must be wrought steel!" She had been impressed by her brother's strength when he held her back from Song and his soldiers. But to wield the Riptide in battle...

"It's not in the arms," Kazu said, flexing his fingers. "I've been wanting to talk to you about it, actually."

"To me?" Misaki said in surprise.

"Well... everything was so chaotic after the attack. I didn't get a chance to discuss it with Tou-sama. I figured, you're the only other person who might understand."

Misaki's only intention in bringing up Anryuu had been to divert Kazu's attention from Takeru. Now that it had worked, he had her genuinely interested. Still, there was propriety to be upheld, so she forced herself to click her tongue reproachfully.

"Kazu-kun, you know I don't do that anymore. I'm a mother and a housewife."

"Of course." Kazu gave her an exasperated smirk. "So, you won't mind if I do this." He poked Misaki in the arm, right on one of her deep cuts.

"Ow!" She snatched the arm back and held it protectively to her chest, glaring at her brother. "Point taken. What is this *amazing revelation* you need to brag about?"

"I know better than to brag to you, Nee-san. There isn't a technique in my arsenal you hadn't already figured out when you were seven. If you fought to defend the people you love, I'm sure you've experienced it too."

Misaki only stared at him blankly. "Experienced what? Super strength? Ascension to godhood? Can't say that I have."

"Really?" Kazu looked surprised. "But Setsuko-nee-san told me you fought off a whole horde of Ranganese—including elite soldiers—without having practiced with the sword in years. How did you do it?"

"Sloppily." Misaki held up her fan-sliced arms. "As you can see. How did *you* do it?"

"It started with a mistake," Kazu said, "just me being too impulsive, like always. When the first Ranganese came up over the cliff, I let my adrenaline run away with me and went ahead of the rest of the men. I didn't realize there would be so many, and I got myself surrounded. Right away, a fonyaka—one of those monsters in black—hit my sword arm, sending my normal-sized katana flying and breaking my wrist. It should have been over then. I should have died..."

"But?" Misaki prompted.

"But my family, my wife and children, hadn't gotten to safety yet. The men were still scattered, disorganized. I realized that if I let myself fall there that Ishihama would fall with me. I felt my jiya rise like it never had before. Not broader, but deeper, stronger inside me. I unsheathed Anryuu and suddenly, I just wasn't hurt anymore. The sword's weight didn't matter anymore. I was faster than I ever had been, faster than any of the Ranganese. I did things that a man just can't do—cut through five fonyakalu in one stroke, punched one so hard my fist came out of his back. One of my men got his leg pinned under a boulder the size of a small house, and I lifted it off him like it weighed nothing. It was like... the kind of thing that happens in legends."

Misaki would have accused him of telling tall tales, but Kazu was a terrible liar, and he didn't speak like he was bragging. Instead, he sounded awed, as if he himself could still barely believe the things he was recounting.

"How?" she said.

"*Blood*, Nee-san." He turned to her with an excited look in his eyes. "We can manipulate blood. It's so simple! When I used Anryuu against those fonyakalu, it wasn't the work of my muscles. It was the blood in my veins—*all of it*, moving in direct response to my will."

"What?"

"I think there's a reason Anryuu is our ancestral sword," Kazu said, "and it's not because one of our ancestors was a giant demigod. I think that a fully realized Tsusano—and *only* a fully realized Tsusano—can wield it. We're the only great house whose jiya can move our own blood. And apparently, at a high enough level, the force of that blood manipulation can overcome normal physical limitations."

"Gods, Kazu," Misaki breathed. "That's incredible!"

So, that was how Tou-sama had always gotten his body to do the impossible, and continued to do so into his old age. He wasn't just physically strong. He turned his blood into a direct extension of his will. With the flow of blood moving his body for him, his aging bones and muscles didn't have to bear the strain.

"You're so skilled, Nee-san," Kazu said, staring at Misaki. "I'm surprised you didn't figure this out years ago."

"I'm not," Misaki said.

What Kazu was describing was clearly a matter of willpower as much as skill, and willpower had never been her strong suit. Now it seemed that her little brother had gone and grown up while she still had the shallow jiya of a child. Sure, she could wield it more deftly than any child, but jiya was supposed to deepen as a person matured. Somewhere in her soul, Misaki was still a little girl.

"But you've always been so good with blood," Kazu said in confusion.

"Little tricks of blood," Misaki said, "claws and needles that require a lot of precision and barely any power. And it's always other people's blood," she added, "not my own." Misaki rarely turned her jiya inward. She didn't much like thinking about what lay deep inside her. From what she could tell, it was twisted, evil, and best left untouched.

"Anyway," Kazu said, "a week ago, I wouldn't have dreamed of challenging a Whispering Blade. Now... I can't explain it, but I'm something more now. I'm more than Tsusano Kazu."

"And you're sure that thing you did on the battlefield wasn't just a fluke?" Misaki asked. "The result of an intense fighter's high?"

"It wasn't."

"How can you be so sure?"

"My right arm is still broken. Have you noticed?"

"No," Misaki said. "Not even when..." Not even when he physically restrained her back at the compound. "You've been compensating for the injury by manipulating your own blood?"

Kazu nodded. "Like Tou-sama compensates for his aging body. This power... I might not understand it completely, but I know that it comes from my will to protect the people I love. I could do it for you, Nee-san. I know it's not my place, but I *will* protect you if you need it."

She laughed to hide her sudden swell of emotion. "You're so dramatic."

"I know," he said apologetically, "but I'm being serious."

"You shouldn't get involved in another lord's marriage."

"I know," Kazu said resolutely, "but you say the word and I will."

He held her gaze with an intensity somewhere between the expectant trust of a child and the resolve of a man. Her little brother still trusted her to know what was best—like Robin had, like Mamoru had...

Misaki looked at her feet. "My word isn't worth much, Kazu-kun. I'm just a stupid woman."

"Misaki." Something in Kazu's tone darkened. "He hasn't hurt you?"

"No." *Not physically.* Physical violence was something Misaki could cope with. It was something she understood.

She should have scolded her brother again, told him that what a lord did with his woman was his own business, but motherhood must have made her soft. She couldn't find it in her to be short with Kazu when he looked at her with such open concern.

"You've grown up into a good man, Kazu-kun," she said, "but part of being a great leader is understanding where your real responsibilities lie. Your concern is touching, but you have your own family and your own village to take care of now. Let your big sister take care of herself, ne?"

Kazu looked like he wanted to say more, but closed his mouth with a stiff nod. He really had grown up.

"And what about you?" Misaki asked. "I haven't gotten a chance to ask after your wife and children. How are they?"

She watched with warmth and a bit of envy as her brother's face lit up. The question set him babbling happily about his daughter's high grades in school, his toddler's first words, and the new baby that had arrived back in the summer.

"Kaida is so headstrong now that she's getting older. Thank the Gods for Aicha and her infinite patience. I don't know how I would ever wrangle all three of the little ones like she does. That woman is a saint."

"Do you love her?" The question dropped from Misaki after building behind her lips for several dinmanu. Maybe it was an odd thing to ask, but she needed to know.

Kazu paused, nonplused. "What?"

"Your wife, Aicha. Do you love her?"

Kazu blinked. "I..." From the way his brow furrowed in thought, Misaki got the feeling it wasn't a question anyone had ever asked him. "I do," he said after a long moment.

"Did you just figure that out?" Misaki's tone was joking, but her curiosity was genuine. "You've been married to the girl seven years now."

"Well, it wasn't right away," Kazu said. "Obviously. We were practically strangers when we married. In the beginning, she was a source of worry for me, more than anything else. That first year, she was so homesick. She missed her family and their fields back in Hakudao. I grew up in the Arashiki, so I suppose I didn't realize how unpleasant it would be to someone afraid of heights, and storms, and the ocean."

"You were scared of the storms too, when you were little," Misaki couldn't help pointing out.

"But you always knew what to say to calm me down. Actually, remembering that—remembering the way you used to talk to me— was a big help, when I needed to comfort my wife."

"Seriously?" Misaki said in surprise. She recalled being vaguely impatient with Kazu when he would cry.

"You were always patient... So, I was patient with her, and after a year or so, she turned out to be fine."

"I'm impressed," Misaki said. "Patience has never been your strong suit."

Kazu shrugged. "Well, I knew our parents had chosen us specifically for each other. And Tou-sama and Kaa-san are so wise and good; I trusted in their judgment, and in the end, they were right about her."

"Yeah?" Misaki cocked her head. Kazu had been married a long time now, but it was still strange trying to think of her little brother as a husband and father. Not that he would be bad in either capacity. It was just strange.

"Once Aicha stopped being scared we were all going to fall off the cliff side, she actually turned out to be a really calm person— smart too. She balances me when I'm..."

"Overexcited?" Misaki suggested.

"They really did make me a good match."

"Hmm," Misaki said thoughtfully.

"They thought they had made you a good match too," Kazu said after a moment.

"Is that what they thought?" Misaki knew the bitterness had leached into her voice. She didn't care.

"I remember when they were planning the marriage, while you were still away at Daybreak," Kazu said. "Tou-sama went out of his way to find you the most powerful husband he could. The first thing he told the matchmakers was not to bother with any house weaker or lower-bred than our own. When they'd ask why, he'd say 'Misaki is stronger and more skilled than most men. She won't respect a weak man.'"

"I... didn't know that."

Misaki had never brought herself to talk to her parents about how they had arranged her marriage into the Matsuda family. There had been too much hurt there. She wanted to be able to love them, thank them, make them proud. That got harder when she thought about the fact that they had been shopping her around to men she didn't know while she was still a girl in school, in love with someone else.

"I wasn't involved in the process, of course," Kazu said. "I was too young at the time, but I'll admit now that I snuck around and listened in on a lot of it."

"Of course, you did." Misaki smiled.

"I remember, early on, there was talk of you marrying Matsuda Takashi."

"*What*?" Misaki said in utter surprise.

It made sense, she supposed. A father with his daughter's best interests at heart would try to marry her to a firstborn son. That way, her husband would inherit, securing her future.

"But Matsuda Susumu turned them down, huh?" Misaki said. Her father-in-law had complained so incessantly about her unclean Tsusano blood. Surely, he wouldn't have wanted her to mix with his precious firstborn son.

"No," Kazu said, looking at her in surprise. "Matsuda Susumu was very receptive. He offered Tou-sama a choice between his first and second son."

"Really?" It had never occurred to Misaki that Susumu could have been in favor of her marrying into his family; he had always seemed to hate her so much. Then again, the man had seemed to hate everyone, including his own sons, so she supposed it wasn't that strange. He probably would have been just as cold and disdainful toward any daughter-in-law.

"So... it was our father who chose Takeru?"

Kazu nodded. "Of course, initially, he and Kaa-san agreed that it would be best for you to marry the firstborn Matsuda. Then we traveled here to meet the whole Matsuda family, Matsuda Susumu introduced our parents to both his sons and after that Tou-sama changed his mind. He said... well..."

"What did he say?" Misaki asked, suddenly burning with curiosity.

"I—uh... I probably shouldn't repeat it," Kazu said apologetically, "out of respect for Matsuda Takashi's spirit."

"His spirit can take it," Misaki said dismissively. "Tell me."

Kazu sighed. "Kaa-san liked Takashi better. She and Tou-sama argued about it the whole way back. 'Takashi is so handsome,' Kaa-san kept gushing, 'and such a powerful jijaka!' Tou-sama seemed to think Takeru was actually the better fighter of the two. I don't know how he figured—"

"Tou-sama was always perceptive about that kind of thing," Misaki said, with a nod. "He was right. And that was it? He just boiled it down to a question of who was stronger?"

"I don't think it was quite that simple. He also seemed to think Takeru was more level-headed and responsible. He said, 'We can't marry our smart girl to a big dumb flake.'"

Misaki felt a laugh burst from her and didn't even care that it shot needles of pain through her lungs.

"But, Nee-san, you can't ever tell anyone I told you this," Kazu said, looking slightly panicked. "Promise—"

"Don't worry, Tsusano-dono," she laughed. "I won't tattle."

The smile faded from her face, but the pain lingered in her chest as she stared down at the daylight creeping through the mists. Her father had chosen Takeru for her... She didn't know whether to feel touched or deeply, furiously hurt. Tou-sama had loved her, joked with her, taught her to use a sword. He was supposed to know her. He was supposed to be wise.

In the remains of the blacksmith village below, morning light revealed movement.

"And this is the same thing they did in Ishihama?" she asked as Kazu followed her gaze down to the encampment.

"I think so. Again, we never really got a look."

"What do you think they're doing?" Yammankalu moved between bogolan tents like ants, their activity indiscernible from this distance. "What do they need those bodies for?"

"I don't know," he said. "It's probably best not to question it."

"It must be very important," Misaki said a bit petulantly, "for them to expend all their energy on that rather than helping us rebuild or gather supplies."

The Kaigenese and Yammanka troops had been in Takayubi for two days and so far, they had done nothing to deliver on the propaganda image of helpful soldiers handing out food and blankets. They hadn't provided medical attention, food, or help repairing the damage their own bombs had caused. The only thing they seemed interested in was collecting all the bodies for the Yammankalu. A few soldiers had gathered up broken beams and slats from the houses, helping to clear the area, but nothing more.

"I've sent some of my men out to the surrounding villages to gather more supplies," Kazu said, "and the Amenos sent one of their men to the mountain strongholds further inland to request aid from the Ginkawas. We heard from the fishermen that the main Ginkawa branch keeps large food stores for crises like these, so that should help keep your people fed for a while."

"If they're willing to help," Misaki said.

"Of course, they'll help," Kazu said. "We're all the blood of gods."

Misaki didn't share her brother's confidence, but he turned out to be right. The next day, new banners crested the ridge bearing the silver river dragon of the Ginkawa family.

Centuries ago, the great houses of Shirojima—Matsuda, Tsusano, Ginkawa, Yukino—had fought bitterly for supremacy. It was strange that now they were all one people, struggling for survival against the Ranganese and an Empire that seemed determined to disregard the way of life they represented.

In the immediate aftermath of the attack, Misaki had not been very conscious of her brother-in-law's absence, but it became more palpable as the days passed. Takashi may not have been perfectly equipped to manage the village in the aftermath of disaster, but he at least would have taken command of the situation. All Takeru ever offered the arriving volunteers was a coldly formal greeting and minimal instructions.

Takeru was in the middle of greeting a new group of volunteers when Mizumaki Fuyuko came running into their circle.

"Mizumaki-san," Takeru said in surprise as the young woman fell to her knees in the snow before him. "What are you doing? We are in the middle of—"

"Matsuda-dono!" she gasped shrilly, so out of breath that for a moment, she could barely speak. "I'm sorry to interrupt. You need to come right away."

"Come where?"

"The blacksmith village," Fuyuko gasped. "The soldiers, th-they're... You have to see what they're doing!"

Takeru and the other men followed Fuyuko. Hastily tying Izumo to her back, Misaki followed as well. They came to the blacksmith village to find that the Yammankalu had cleared away their tents and dug a massive pit. The hole, while barely a bound deep, spanned the entirety of what had once been the blacksmith village. Into it, the soldiers had thrown the hundreds of bodies they had collected over the past few days—Ranganese and Kaigenese, warriors and civilians, all piled together.

Among the yellows and blacks, Matsuda blue was easy to pick out. Mamoru lay among a tangle of fonyaka corpses, his head resting against the shoulder of one of the butchered numuwu. A small child's body lay across him, so badly burned that it was not identifiable as belonging to any kafo or family.

If the sight had not choked her with horror, Misaki would have had to admire the efficiency. Only the Yammanka military could move so much earth and so many human bodies in a few waatinu, and it was clearly something they had wanted to get finished as quickly as possible. The wave of villagers Mizumaki Fuyuko had brought down the mountain immediately began shouting in horror, demanding to know what the soldiers were doing.

The few remaining Yammankalu hurriedly packed up their equipment and left as the villagers descended. Evidently, they were finished in Takayubi now that their secret investigation had concluded and they had done the heavy lifting that Colonel Song's Imperial troops were too weak and disorganized to do themselves.

"Colonel Song," Takeru said, striding up to the smug man where he stood above the dirt in his pristine hanbok. *"What is happening here?"*

"If you would step back, Matsuda," the colonel said, not seeming particularly interested in Takeru's presence, *"and tell your fellow villagers to return to their work. They do not need to see this."*

"I can't," Takeru said.

Colonel Song raised an eyebrow. *"I beg your pardon?"*

"The bodies of their family members are down there," Takeru said. *"I can't demand that they step back."*

The colonel gave Takeru a sour look, as if the Matsuda patriarch were a fly he had just found in his tea. *"Fine,"* he said and gave a signal to his soldiers. They moved forward and grabbed the crying women, forcibly hauling them back from the pit.

Nearby, one of the Ginkawa Aoki intervened, trying to pry a soldier off a screaming woman. The soldier struck him. Not a proper punch, but a backhanded slap—like one might strike a misbehaving child. The sound cut through the rising chaos, making everyone stop and stare for a moment in indignant disbelief. The Ginkawa man looked more shocked than anything else.

It was one of the women who spoke up first.

"How dare you?" she snarled at the soldier. "Do you know who he is? He fought to protect this empire! How *dare* you?"

Jiya rose among the villagers and their helpers. Hands on both sides went to swords.

"Disarm anyone who resists," the colonel said coolly.

The vicious, irrational part of Misaki wanted Colonel Song to go ahead and try it. Let him see how his brainwashed excuses for soldiers fared against *real* fighters. These hundred-some Imperial soldiers would be lucky to survive an honest fight with the dozen Ameno and Ginkawa swordsmen before them. Gods help them if they faced Takeru or Kazu.

"Stand down!" Takeru commanded, his voice booming across the pit. "Ginkawa, Ameno, people of Takayubi, stand down!"

There was a moment of tense stillness.

Then, slowly, the grieving women and the volunteers stepped back, hands withdrew from sword handles and the swell of their collective jiya eased back like a retreating tide. Colonel Song raised his eyebrows, looking mildly impressed at how quickly they obeyed.

"You have not explained yourself, Colonel." Takeru's voice had taken on a dangerous edge. *"What do you think you are doing here?"*

"These bodies are going to be burned," the colonel said as if it were perfectly normal to throw the corpses of fallen warriors into a pit like trash.

"All the bodies?"

"This is standard procedure, to prevent disease."

It was only then that Misaki noticed the layer of boards and beams laid out beneath the bodies, at the bottom of the pit. The soldiers who had come around to take wood from the ruined houses hadn't been helping clear Takayubi of debris; they had been gathering kindling.

"But the Kaigenese should be returned to their families for proper funeral rites," Takeru said.

"This is the will of the Emperor. We need to keep your village clean."

"I understand that," Takeru said, *"but surely you can at least let the grieving families have their relatives' remains. I can assure you, they will be properly cremated straight away."*

"Sorry, Matsuda," the man said gruffly. *"It's standard procedure."*

"Our son's body is in there!" Misaki burst out, unable to hold her tongue any longer. Takeru had never even prayed over Mamoru. What kind of person burned a boy's body without allowing his father to pray? *"Yukino Dai is in there. You can't—"*

"Quiet, Misaki," Takeru hissed. *"General, I apologize for my wife's behavior."*

"Don't worry about it," the colonel said with entirely fake sympathy. *"She's been through a lot."*

"But if these bodies are all going to be burned here, how are my people supposed to lay their dead to rest properly?" Takeru voiced the question screaming through Misaki's mind. *"We need to give them graves."*

"There aren't going to be marked graves," Colonel Song said, *"and these are not your people, Matsuda. You and all these villagers belong to the Emperor."*

Misaki looked toward her husband, watched his hand clench. She didn't know why she expected him to speak up against this insufferable man. He had taken worse from his father and brother without protest. He had taken the order to leave his son to die without protest.

"I meant no disrespect, General." Takeru bowed his head. *"I'm sure the Emperor has his reasons."*

The man's mouth twisted in a condescending smile. *"You're a smart man, Matsuda. I think we're going to work well together."*

Takeru nodded. Across the pit, the few remaining tajakalu were lighting torches for the Kaigenese soldiers.

"In the absence of the government-approved mayor, you agree to take responsibility for this village in the coming months?"

"Of course, sir."

"Then you will see to it that these people understand one thing: no one is to speak of the Ranganese attack. If any outsider asks, the dead here were victims of another coastal storm."

"They died in battle," Takeru said.

"No." Song nodded to his men and they threw their torches in, setting the pyre ablaze. *"They died in a storm."*

Flames crept onto yellow fabric. As the crack and peel of burning flesh started to rise from the pile, Misaki finally understood. The bodies weren't being destroyed to prevent disease. The Empire was burning all evidence of the attack.

"The Emperor knows of your sacrifice here, and he is thankful for your service. Surely, for such loyal subjects, that is enough."

"Of course..." Takeru said, emotionless, *"it is enough."*

"The Yammankalu leave this evening, and I move my men out tomorrow."

"Tomorrow?" Takeru looked at Song in surprise. *"Are none of your troops staying to help us rebuild?"*

"Sadly, the Emperor's forces have a great deal to take care of at the moment. My superiors from the capital will be back in two months to see that everything is proceeding according to the Emperor's will."

"Can we expect aid then?" Takeru asked. His voice, of course, didn't register any desperation, but their situation was truly desperate. It was the middle of winter and most of their people had no houses to stay in. Volunteers from the neighboring areas might

be happy to help them for now, but Takayubi couldn't rely on their generosity for the rest of the winter.

"Aid may be a possibility then." Colonel Song crossed his arms. *"We will see if everything is proceeding according to the Emperor's will."* His meaning was clear: *keep quiet and you may get the aid you need to survive. Be a good dog, and you may live.*

Takeru was still for a moment, staring down at the flames as they climbed the pile of corpses toward Mamoru's body.

"Excuse me," he said after a moment. *"I have some things I need to take care of."*

Turning on his heel, he swept away, leaving Misaki at the edge of the pit with Colonel Song, surrounded by the wailing sobs of Takayubi's women.

"It really is a shame about your son," the colonel said, *"but I'm sure a good Kaigenese boy like him was more than happy to die for his Emperor. Surely, you're proud that your family was able to serve the Empire."*

Misaki took a breath, ready to tell the colonel exactly what she thought of the Empire, but at that moment, Izumo shifted softly against her back, and she realized that she couldn't. This man represented the Empire itself. If she insulted him, if he deemed her a traitor, he would be justified in putting her entire family to death. She would be single-handedly responsible for the end of the Matsuda and Tsusano lines, and all this suffering would have been for nothing.

Colonel Song turned a placidly expectant expression toward her as if daring her to say what was on her tongue. She clenched her teeth on the words. Pain flared in her chest from when the fan-wielder had tried to pull her soul from her body.

This is where Ranga started, she realized. *With a breath held too long, with a people who couldn't bear to answer to men like this any longer.*

But Ranga had been bought with hundreds of thousands of lives, and Misaki couldn't sacrifice any more. She closed her mouth and lowered her gaze to the rising fire.

"You've had a difficult few days, Matsuda," the colonel said. *"Maybe you shouldn't watch this."*

"Mmm," Misaki said without taking her eyes off the pyre. *"Maybe I shouldn't."*

She kept her eyes open and watched Mamoru burn. It was the only defiance she could afford.

24

THE EMPIRE

More committed attempts than Takeru's were made to talk the colonel out of the mass burning. Kwang Tae-min, Kazu, and the high-ranking Ameno representatives all begged him to stop as soon as they realized what was happening, but by that time, the flames had already turned most of the bodies to blackened husks. In a few waatinu, they would be nothing but ash.

Takeru was conspicuously missing when the colonel called the villagers and volunteers together and gave them the Emperor's orders. There were protests. Even the most loyal and brainwashed Kaigenese citizens weren't willing to sacrifice the dignity of their fallen loved ones without argument.

But all Colonel Song had to do was repeat, *"This is the will of the Emperor. Surely, you don't want to displease the Emperor,"* until the protests dissolved into quiet tears.

With Takeru still gone, Kazu and the high-ranking volunteers from the Ameno and Ginkawa houses did their best to calm people and keep order. In Takeru's absence, people even started turning to the women of his house for guidance.

That evening found Misaki and Setsuko surrounded by women who either wouldn't bring their grievances to the men out of propriety or had been unsatisfied with their responses. The women clustered close in the temporary sleeping quarters that had been the

Matsuda dojo.

The men—survivors and volunteers who didn't have a nearby village to go home to at night—just barely managed to squeeze into the compound's intact bedrooms and studies at night. The dojo was a sacred male space, but it was the only indoor chamber big enough to house all the women and children who had no roof to sleep under. Takeru had removed the shrine and the weapons rack.

Now every night, the dojo built to accommodate fifty sword students became a sleeping area for twenty-some women and all their children—and this evening, a place for them to hold their own assembly.

"How could they do this?" Mizumaki Fuyuko asked for what felt like the tenth time. "They burned our dead and now they won't even let us remember them?"

"We can still remember them, Mizumaki-san," Misaki tried for a comforting tone, but it was difficult to maintain a reassuring air when her words were so obviously empty. "We'll always remember... We're just not supposed to talk about the way they died."

"That's *not* remembering them," Fuyuko's mother, Fuyuhi, said angrily. "Not as they were. My husband and son, your son—" she turned to Misaki, "—and your husband—" to Setsuko, "—and yours—" to Hyori, "—all of our men were warriors. If we don't remember the way they died, then we're not remembering them for who they were."

The women were quiet. No one could deny Mizumaki Fuyuhi's words.

"And don't try to tell me we can remember without speaking of what happened here," the older woman said, smashing down Misaki's pitifully weak response before it could even take shape on her lips. "A warrior's legacy is essential to his soul. To deny what happened here—to ourselves or to anyone else—is the greatest disservice we could do our dead."

"And that's to say nothing of the defenseless who were killed," added Mayumi, one of the few surviving Katakouris, "our fellow women, the numuwu, and finawu, and small children." The archer's widow was crying but the tears only seemed to make her voice stronger. "Are we supposed to deny what they suffered?"

For so many years, Misaki had looked down on these people for soaking up the Empire's propaganda. For so many years, their small-minded ignorance had frustrated her. It was a strange experience—strange and sad—to watch a whole village full of people realize what she had a long time ago: that the Emperor was more of a selfish tyrant than a protective father.

In the face of the horrible revelation, the women of Takayubi were stronger than she would have anticipated. For all their softness and demureness, these noblewomen were well-educated, versed in Kaigenese poetry, history, and philosophy. They may have grown up in a culture of denial, but when the bloody truth stared them full in the face, they were more than capable of comprehending it. They were more than capable of anger. Misaki wished she knew how to calm that anger. If she had, she would have saved herself years of pain.

"It's like the Empire doesn't even care!" Mizumaki Fuyuhi's voice rose as her eyes filled with tears. "How could they do this? How could you *let them* do this?" she demanded, turning her fury on Misaki. "Your house is supposed to protect us! Your husband vanishes as our dead are taken from us, and now you're telling us to just forget—"

"Hey," Setsuko cut the other woman off sharply. "You don't need to speak to her that way."

"She's telling us to deny what happened to our families. She's a coward—"

"Watch your mouth!" Setsuko shouted out and Mizumaki Fuyuhi wasn't the only one who started. No one had ever heard Matsuda Setsuko, the cheery, simple fisherwoman take that tone with anyone. "I know you're angry, but we're all ladies here and you'd do well to watch your tone," she said, proving that she could be just as imperious and commanding as any high-born koro. "Misaki is the wife of the head of this village. You'll talk to her with respect."

There was a stunned silence.

Then Fuyuhi inclined her head toward Setsuko. "Apologies, Matsuda-dono."

"I don't need your apology, Mizumaki," Setsuko said. "I'm just a widowed fisherman's daughter. Apologize to her." She pointed to Misaki.

Mizumaki Fuyuhi bowed. "My apologies, Matsuda-dono."

"The whole damn world seems to want us to die," Setsuko said, ignoring the few women who cringed at her coarse language. "We can't afford to start tearing each other down like a pack of rabid dogs. Now, if you knew what you were talking about, Misaki-sama would be the last person you'd be yelling at. She's fought harder to defend this village than any of us."

"It's true," Hyori said softly. It was the first she had spoken. "During the attack, Misaki-san came back for me, even though the bombs were already falling. When I was too weak to stand up, she carried me to the shelter. If she hadn't come back for me, I would have died with my son."

"Sorry... I didn't realize that," Fuyuhi said.

"She even tried to warn us," Hyori said, "months ago before there was any news of storms, she tried to tell us the Ranganese might be coming—me and Setsuko-san. We didn't listen." Hyori was looking into her lap, eyes soft and sad. "Whatever she has to say, you should listen to her now."

"So, you knew our Empire was feeding us lies?" Mayumi demanded. "You knew we were going to be attacked?"

"No," Misaki said. "I only suspected."

"Then why didn't you say anything?" Mizumaki Fuyuhi asked.

Misaki took a breath and then replied, "For the same reason you're not going to."

"What?"

"The Empire might not be as strong as we thought it was, but it *is* dangerous. The Emperor may not retain the most competent military, but he *does* employ competent assassins. If we are outspoken about our disapproval, I worry that people will start to disappear."

"But... the Emperor wouldn't do that to us!" Katakouri Mayumi protested. "Our men protected his borders!"

"And then he had their bodies burned without rites," Setsuko said. "I don't think he cares about their service. I don't think he cares about us at all."

"Well, that's not right!" Mayumi said while others exclaimed their agreement. "We need to do something. We need to stop them."

Misaki shook her head. "Defying the Empire won't change anything; it'll just get us killed."

"So, what can we do?" Mizumaki Fuyuko asked, and Misaki recognized the tremor in the girls' voice... the unbearable shiver of rage giving way to helplessness. "What can we do for our dead? How can we do right by them?"

"We can live," Misaki said. "We can keep Takayubi alive for them."

It felt like such a pitiful offering.

"But..."

"Listen, Fuyuko-san," Misaki said gently. "A few months ago, my son, Mamoru, came to me for guidance. The circumstances aren't important, I suppose, but he had found out certain things about how the Empire had lied to us. He asked me how he could fight for an Empire he couldn't trust."

"And what did you say to him, Matsuda-dono?"

"I confess, I didn't have a good answer to give him at first. But he was a smart boy—smarter than his mother, I think. The last time I spoke to him, he had decided that if enemies came to Takayubi, he would fight them no matter what. Whether the Emperor commanded it or not, whether he was remembered for it or not, he would fight to protect the people of this mountain and all the farmers and fishermen behind it. And that was what he did. He..."

Misaki paused, swallowing hard. She did not want to cry in front of these women, not when she was trying to give them strength. But they needed to know.

The daughters, wives, and mothers weren't the only ones hanging on Misaki's words. Hiroshi knelt nearby, listening with a desperate sort of intensity. No one had spoken to him about Mamoru's death except to tell him that his older brother was not coming back. He was only five, after all. But he had already seen things—*done* things—no five-year-old should. Maybe he needed to hear. If he was going to take Mamoru's place and chase his image, that image needed to have meaning. If he was going to move forward in the knowledge that he was a killer, that killing needed to have meaning. Every pair of eyes locked on Misaki was pained and straining. For all of them, all of this had to mean something.

"Mamoru died fighting, with multiple injuries, including missing teeth and a gut wound so deep it should have disabled him instantly. He stayed on his feet and fought."

The tears she wouldn't let herself cry were rolling down other women's faces.

"Takayubi alone was important enough for him to fight through that much pain. I have to imagine that many of Mamoru's fellow warriors—your husbands, fathers, brothers, and sons—felt the same way. Empire or none, I think many of them would have died to protect this mountain."

She could see from the women's faces that she had connected with them. They understood.

"They gave their lives protecting Takayubi," Misaki continued, her voice stronger than she expected. "Now it's time for us to protect it. That's what we can do for them."

"So... do nothing?" Mayumi said.

"Surviving isn't nothing, Katakouri-san," Setsuko said. "We're going to survive."

"How? Without government aid, we'll never make it through the winter."

Setsuko laughed. "Of course, we will, silly girl."

"How can you be so sure?" Fuyuhi asked.

"Because I've done it before..." Setsuko took a moment to count on her fingers, "twenty-four times. Remember, before I married my Takashi-sama—*nyama* to his soul—I lived in the fishing village at the base of this mountain. There wasn't a lot of food to go around some winters and you'd better believe my family's shack had as many holes in it as we've got bullet-holes here, but we always managed somehow."

"But... we're not fisherwomen," Fuyuko said.

"You're right," Setsuko said cheerfully. "You're better bred than fisherwomen. You come from warrior stock, every one of you. The same blood that made your fathers, brothers, and sons such powerful fighters flows through your veins, doesn't it?"

"Yes." The women nodded hesitantly.

"Right." Setsuko beamed. "So, if a bunch of low-bred fishermen can live through a Takayubi winter, it should be no problem for you ladies. I know you nobles aren't used to lean times, and getting stepped on, and sleeping twelve-to-a-room, but you're a tough bunch. You'll all be fine."

As Misaki watched hope slowly return to the room, she thought again that it was a bit of a shame that Takashi hadn't traded places with Takeru. Setsuko would have made—*was* making—a wonderful head woman of the village. There weren't many fisherwomen who could stand before a room full of noblewomen and command their loyalty.

"Thank the Gods for Setsuko," Misaki sighed as she sat on the front deck with her brother that night. She was putting off going to bed, and conveniently, Kazu also seemed too restless to sleep, giving her someone to talk to.

"It wasn't just Setsuko-san," Kazu said. "I also heard a lot of people talking about how you inspired them and put them at ease."

"Me?" Misaki said in surprise.

"You're good with people, Nee-san."

"I'm what?" Misaki laughed.

"You're good at talking to people—lifting them up, breaking them down. You've always been good at that."

Now that she thought about it, she realized that Kazu was right. Back in Ishihama and all through Daybreak, she had approached interactions with others confident that she would find the right words to say. Somewhere in Takeru's frigid disregard and Matsuda Susumu's abuse, she had lost that.

"I wish I had your skill," Kazu sighed. "I wish I could have done more to reassure these people."

"Well, it's not your job," Misaki pointed out. Honestly, it was Takeru's, but he was still nowhere to be found.

"I'm just... still so shaken myself," Kazu admitted. "I didn't know the Empire would do this. You went to school overseas, Nee-san. Did you have any idea?"

"Not really," Misaki said. "I mean, I knew our government wasn't transparent—What government is?—but I never imagined anything like this... Maybe if I'd been paying more attention."

"It doesn't make sense to me. I thought the Emperor valued us, wanted us strong. What is going on?"

"I don't know," Misaki sighed. "There are obviously political forces at work here that we just can't see."

"Sure, but... Is there any political agenda that would justify this?" Kazu asked.

Misaki just shook her head. She had no answer.

"I feel sick." Kazu grimaced. "Like my own father stabbed me in the back."

"Kazu," Misaki said. "If this is what's happening in Ishihama, you have to go home."

Kazu didn't respond. He stared ahead, his jaw set, and Misaki could tell from the look on his face that he had been thinking the same thing all day but just hadn't wanted to say it.

"You said your wife is afraid of storms," Misaki said. "I'm sure she wishes you were with her."

"But things are so much worse here, Nee-san," Kazu protested. "Your people need help—"

"I know. I'm not going to argue that," she said, "but this isn't your responsibility."

"And if this *is* what's happening in Ishihama, what can I do?" Kazu clasped his hands in front of him and twisted them together, knuckles white. "I mean—it's the *Imperial army*, Nee-san. What can I do?"

"You can be there for your people," Misaki said. "You can lead. The families of Ishihama won't blame you for what the Empire does. They'll be thankful that you're there, doing whatever you can."

Kazu pressed his lips together, frowning. "You're right, Nee-san," he sighed finally. "You always are. If only you'd been my big brother—"

"You don't give yourself enough credit," Misaki cut him off, "and neither does Tou-sama, if he's still on about that. The work you've done here—the leadership you've shown—has been admirable."

"Don't tease, Nee-san. I was trying to pay you a compliment."

"I was being serious," Misaki said. "I wouldn't want anyone else at the head of my old house."

Kazu shook his head, eyeing his sister as though sure this was some kind of trap. "What—"

"You have something a lot of powerful theonites lack, including your own big sister." She looked into his eyes. "You're a good man, Tsusano-dono." She used his title, for the first time without irony. "You really have become what Tou-sama was, something bigger than yourself. I may not understand it, but I'm very proud of you… whether you believe me or not."

Takeru was still not there the next morning when Misaki said goodbye to her brother.

"I'm leaving behind some of my men to look after you and your people," Kazu said.

"Don't they have families to get back to?" Misaki asked.

"Hakuyu-san isn't married, and the two Umiiros volunteered."

"Fine." Misaki smiled. "It's really not necessary—"

"But it is," Kazu said seriously. "I need to make sure you're taken care of."

The first thing Kazu's men ended up doing was sweeping the mountain in search of Takeru, who still had not returned at noon.

It was Misaki who eventually found him, in the snowy clearing above Kumono Academy. No one else had thought to look that far up the mountain. He perched near a ledge in his favored meditating position, down on one knee, head down, both palms pressed to the ground.

"Takeru-sama?" she said when she had gathered enough air into her aching lungs.

His jiya was so still, his body so cold, that he seemed like part of the snow. Misaki's blood-sensitive jiya barely picked the inhumanly-faint heartbeat and blood flow. If not for the blue Matsuda haori, she might have missed him entirely.

"Takeru-sama," she said more loudly.

A twitch of his shoulders—an unsettling flicker of motion in the picture of perfect stillness. Then, slowly, he straightened up. As his palms came away from the snow, his eyes opened and his nyama returned to normal, a proper human heartbeat and blood flow registering in Misaki's senses.

"You know you're not to bother me when I'm meditating," he said.

"Is that what you've been doing this whole time?" Misaki fought to keep the anger out of her voice. "Meditating?"

"Yes," Takeru said without even the suggestion of an apology in his voice.

"You've been up here for more than a day."

Standing, he strode past Misaki and down the mountain without another word. Misaki's fists clenched.

"We needed you, you know?" she shouted at the Matsuda insignia on his back. "Your people needed you!"

He just kept walking.

25

THE GODS

In the next few days, droves of finawu arrived, shuffling up the mountain in their long red robes. They apologized profusely for taking so long, but they had had to travel a long way. The Ryuhon religion practiced by the great houses of Shirojima was an ancient form of Falleya distinct from the Nagino Falleya practiced in most of Kaigen. Takayubi's temple had been one of the last true strongholds of the religion.

The pyre where Mamoru, Dai, and hundreds of others had burned to ash had been covered with soil and packed down in a neat circle. Colonel Song had forbidden anything that might mark the site as a grave, but the finawu gathered around it in reference and spent days singing their prayers as the villagers and volunteers took it in turn to join them.

Misaki visited the grave herself on the second day with her sons, a white cloth tied into her hair. Traditional mourning outfits were entirely white, but few of Takayubi's residents had even one change of clothes, let alone a full set of proper mourning attire. Instead, they improvised, wrapping strips of white cloth around their waists or tying them into their hair.

Ironically, their visit fell on the New Year, usually a time for bright decorations, colorful sweets, and hopes for the future. But the New Year was also an important time to drive away bad spirits, so

Misaki considered it as good a day as any to bring her family to pray.

The Matsudas went through the rituals, songs, and recited prayers for Mamoru, though Misaki politely declined the masked spirits' offer to act as intermediary in conversation with her son.

"I spoke to his spirit at length, Fina-sama," she explained with a low bow to the senior monk, "as did his little brothers, shortly after his death. There is nothing more we can offer him."

"And the boy's father?" the bald man asked in a voice wobbly with age. "He has also prayed already?"

"I... I don't know, Fina-sama." It didn't make Misaki sound like a very good wife, but it wasn't smart to lie to a Ryuhon high monk. "He has been keeping to himself since the storm."

"Mmm. Meditating, I heard?"

"Yes, Fina-sama."

"He will join you here then?"

"Ano..." Misaki licked her lips. "I don't think he was planning on it, Fina-sama." She hadn't spoken to Takeru since she had found him meditating near Takayubi's summit.

"Hmm." The wrinkles on the man's face arranged themselves into what Misaki took to be a frown. "This is not good, young Matsuda. A man and his wife should be together after the loss of the child. The boy, when he lived, was of both of you. You hope to keep his spirit from being torn in two pieces, yet you do not come here together."

"I'm sorry, Fina-sama. I will try to talk to my husband, and bring him here tomorrow."

"No, child," the fina said with a slow wave of his withered hand. "This thing, if it is forced, will do your son's spirit no good. Your husband must come here for himself, because he wishes it."

Misaki nodded, secretly relieved that she would not have to attempt that conversation with Takeru. "If I could, I would like to speak to a mask for my brother-in-law, Matsuda Takashi."

She needed to see if she could forgive him for his last orders.

When her prayers were done, Misaki gathered her children and prepared to head back up the mountain with the Kotetsus, who had shown up to pray at the same time. Kwang Chul-hee was with them, mainly to serve as Kotetsu Katashi's crutch, while Atsushi corralled the younger children. Kotetsu was in the process of designing himself a chair that he could easily move around with his jiya, but while he lacked the supplies to finish it, he still relied on Atsushi and others to help him move around. With the master swordsmith relatively immobile, the numu family had only just gotten the chance to pray over the resting place of those they had lost.

Throughout the rituals, Chul-hee had waited on the fringes of the circle. His purpose was only to make sure that he was there to help Kotetsu back up the mountain when he needed it, but the inquisitive boy had quickly become fascinated by the proceedings. He seemed grateful when Kotetsu opted to rest for a while on a bench of ice before tackling the steep path up to the main village—now the only habitable place on the mountain.

"I don't understand," the northern boy murmured, staring at the chanting monks in their blood-red robes. "Why the special finawu?"

"Monks who practice the Imperial standard Nagino Falleya would not be able to administer the proper rites," Misaki said.

"There's a difference?"

Misaki, Kotetsu, and even Atsushi laughed at the question.

"What?"

"Ryuhon Falleya is *very* different from the religion you know, boy," Kotetsu said.

"How so, Numuba?" Chul-hee asked.

"Numuba." Kotetsu chuckled again at the title. "You'll notice we don't use those fancy Yammanka addresses the rest of the world is so fond of?"

"Yeah." Chul-hee looked self-conscious. "I thought it was a dialect thing."

"It is indeed 'a dialect thing,'" Kotetsu said, "because we Shirojima Dialect speakers do not put much stock in the Yammanka version of the world's origin and its order."

"But... Yamma is the place of First Planting," Chul-hee said in confusion.

"If you believe that," Kotetsu said.

"How can you *not* believe that, Numu Kotetsu? You still worship Nagi and Nami, like the rest of us, don't you?"

"And what are Nagi and Nami to you, Nagino Falleka?" Kotetsu asked.

"They're children of the mangrove seeds planted by the Falleke—Kiye, God of Soul and Fire and Nyaare, Goddess of Flesh and Substance," Chul-hee recited what was obviously a deeply ingrained story from many repetitions in school. His voice even took on the vaguely musical lilt of the Falleya myths imported from Yamma.

"The mangrove was the sixthborn seed of human ancestors, after Kri and Sura of the first baobab seed, Bemba and Sibi of the second baobab seed, Nege and Joya of the first acacia seed, Nyanga and Chaka of the second acacia seed and Sayandana, the Death Bringer, of the sycamore seed."

"Sixthborn, hmm?" Kotetsu said, looking faintly amused.

"Yes. Their pods didn't split open until after Kiye and Nyaare sent fire to purge the land of the Death Bringer's evil. Bemba shielded them from the fire with his body until Kri tamed the flames and became the first tajaka. Then, when Sura's song summoned the rains that flooded the world, they broke out of their seeds and took the form of giant fish so they could bear their seed siblings above the water. After saving the other human ancestors from drowning, they lay down and swam east with the receding water, carving Yamma's Great Twin Rivers into the land."

Recounting the story seemed to give Chul-hee comfort as he stared into the chanting mass of strange finawu. "They continued swimming beyond the edge of Kelendugu, pulling with them the water that became the world's oceans. They didn't stop until they came here and raised Kaigen from the waters. Then they created the first Kaigenese people from seafoam—Why are you laughing?"

"Nagi and Nami are gods of the ocean," Kotetsu said.

"Yeah," Chul-hee said.

"And we are to believe that they are the mere children of deities of earth and fire?"

"Well... I..."

"This conceit that all the races of humans came from seeds is ridiculous to us," Kotetsu said. "It is an irrefutable truth that all life came from the ocean. Thus, it stands to reason that the original gods are those of the ocean. Nagi and Nami were not children of any Yammanka gods. Nami and Nagi *are* God and Goddess supreme, parents to us all."

"Wait—you deny the existence of Kiye and Nyaare?" Chul-hee looked utterly scandalized. "*That's* what Ryuhon Falleka is?"

"Oh, no," Kotetsu said earnestly. "None of these monks would go so far as to say that the Kiye and Nyaare you all worship do not exist. We accept that the version of events in Yamma *did* unfold more or less the way it is told in the Donkili; the Yammankalu simply misinterpreted it."

"They what?"

"Nagi and Nami weren't *children* of Kiye and Nyaare. They were the originators themselves, just reborn in a different form."

"So, it's basically... you think the mother and father of everything were the gods of the ocean, not gods of earth and fire?" Chul-hee said slowly. "I guess that's not the craziest thing I've ever heard."

"Singing sky heralds, tamers of wild brushfire; these things all sound nice in songs—and perhaps they did exist at some point, but these were not the first beings on Planet Duna. Before anything else—plants, humans, and other creatures—there was the endless water. The ocean is the ultimate source of power and life. It has been obvious to us here in Shirojima since long before the fossil record started to prove us right."

The appeal to scientific evidence seemed to give Chul-hee pause. "But... the fossil record also suggests that modern humans originated in Yamma and then migrated across the rest of the world like the songs say."

"I suppose that would be relevant," Kotetsu shrugged, "if our power had its origins in human life."

"I... wh-what?"

"Another essential part of Ryuhon Falleya is the knowledge that we are the blood of gods. Nagi and Nami didn't just whip humans up out of seafoam. They made life from water long before that, beginning with the simple, wriggling creatures of prehistory. Some of these early creatures were made of pieces of the originators themselves—children of gods, who then went on to have innumerable generations of their own children, who all bore some sliver of the originators' power.

"That gods' blood still flows through the greatest of the ocean creatures—the giant sharks, squid, and long forgotten monsters who live in the deep. Perhaps the descendants of Nagi and Nami first took human form in Yamma, among other lesser humans. It is not important. Many humans may have different kinds of power now, but it is only the direct descendants of Nagi and Nami who wield the truest power of the ocean.

"This is why we in Shirojima are such devoted practitioners of Ryuhon Falleya and why we guard our bloodlines so carefully. We guard the blood of gods."

Chul-hee looked skeptical but faintly awed. If nothing else, the sheer audacity of the swordsmith's words had him impressed. "So, Ryuhon Fallekalu really believe that the Matsudas and these other jijaka families are directly descended from the gods of the ocean?" He looked from Kotetsu to Misaki.

"More or less," Misaki said with a smile. "Some bloodlines are purer than others. The Matsuda bloodline is famously the purest throughout history, followed closely by the Yukino and Ginkawa lines. Then there are the families regarded as having a lesser but significant amount of gods' blood, including Kotetsu, Ishino, Ameno, Katakouri, and Tsusano." She lay a hand on her own chest. "There are some branches of the Mizumaki family, like the one here in Takayubi, who are thought to have gods' blood in them while others are just regular jijakalu."

"You're talking about this like it's a measurable thing, Matsuda-dono," Chul-hee said incredulously.

"Well," Misaki returned, jouncing Izumo on her knees, "your Nagino Falleya mythology presumes to count the ancestors of all humanity on ten fingers."

"Sixteen, Matsuda-dono," he said indignantly. "There are *sixteen* human ancestors."

"Oh, right. I apologize. It's been a while since I brushed up on my heresies."

Chul-hee looked as if she'd slapped him. "Well, now I know where Mamoru got his—" He stopped short with a look of consternation. "Sorry."

"Oh no, go on." Misaki smirked, feeling strangely delighted by this small diversion Chul-hee was providing. "Where Mamoru got his what?"

"With respect for his spirit, Matsuda-dono... his *attitude*," Chul-hee said. "Anyway, the sixteen ancestors are a *metaphor*. Everyone knows there probably weren't just eight married pairs of people, all at the same time. The myth just explains the origins of the different types of theonite. I mean—tajakalu don't go around claiming to be more descended or less descended from Bemba and Kri."

"No," Misaki said, "just their millennia-long parade of queens, kings, and generals."

"Yes, but that makes sense," Chul-hee protested. "That's well-kept orature that only goes back a few thousand years. They don't think they're the descendants of... prehistoric god-fish."

"It's not something one *thinks* so much as something one *knows*," Kotetsu said calmly, "as surely as the return of the snow and the tides. It is a feeling."

"Convenient," Chul-hee smiled, comfortable enough with Kotetsu by now to know that the swordsmith wouldn't mind his irreverent quips. "It's something you know because you feel it. It can't be proved."

"If you doubt, you must never have witnessed a Matsuda draw on the powers of the deep."

Chul-hee was quiet for a moment. His eyes flicked upward, toward Kumono lake and the now-deserted school above. "I think I have."

"Oh?"

"I watched Mamoru meditate once."

"And?"

"He... he seemed to see things he couldn't possibly know. It was dark, but he mapped out the whole mountain in his head, just from the mist on the rocks, the dew on the grass, and the flow of streams. It was amazing."

Kotetsu shrugged. "If you think that could be done without a sliver of gods' power then, by all means, keep to your Nagino Falleya."

Chul-hee was quiet, his gaze seemingly lost in the mists around the lake.

"These finawu are here because they are the only ones who know how to send the souls of our dead on to the place they belong, into the arms of their true mother in the deep."

"Your version of the Laaxara?" Chul-hee said, still staring at the lake.

Kotetsu nodded. "The Ocean of Souls." He reached out a broad hand and clapped it down on Chul-hee's shoulder, causing him to start out of his daze. "Now, be a good boy and help lug this old bag of gods' blood up the mountain."

26

THE SPIRIT

The Ryuhon finawu were gracious and careful, taking the time to listen to each grieving villager and lead them through the appropriate prayers and rituals. Some even agreed to stay, taking up residence in the old temple that had been Kumono Academy. But their noble efforts hadn't put all the spirits to rest.

Misaki saw Mamoru when she slept. Sometimes she was the Ranganese soldier who had killed him—thrilling like a maniac in the high of combat—only sobering when she found her son bleeding before her and the pain cleaved her in two.

Sometimes he stood in one of the compound's hallways or in the dojo, seemingly close enough to touch, but somehow out of reach. Another time, she relived the fight in the darkened hallway. She stabbed the soldier through the chest, only to find Siradenyaa buried to the hilt in the center of the Matsuda crest. She slid the blade free and it wasn't the Ranganese boy but Mamoru who fell to the floor at her feet, eyes wide in betrayal. She wanted to hold him, patch his bleeding heart, comfort him, but she couldn't. She could only stand there as the blood seeped in between her toes. She could only watch him go.

One night, the dream did allow her to move. She tried to staunch the blood from his wound, only to pull it from his body, killing him. She woke to screaming that time, but it wasn't hers. When her eyes snapped open, she found Nagasa thrashing on the blankets beside her, his back arched, small heels beating against the dojo floor with bruising force. Hiroshi was already gripping his shoulders, trying to shake him awake.

"It's a nightmare, Naga-kun. Wake up!"

"Nii-san! Nii-san!" Nagasa whined, but when his eyes opened, he looked surprised to see Hiroshi above him. "Nii-san?"

"I'm here, Naga-kun," Hiroshi said.

"No. Where is...?" Nagasa's wide eyes flicked around, searching the dark, as Misaki put a soothing hand on his head. "Where is Nii-san? Where is Mamoru?"

"He's not here, Naga-kun." Misaki stroked his hair and found his bangs damp with sweat. "He's gone."

"No, *no!*" Nagasa's small voice rose in anger. "He was *here!*"

"No, little one. No." She gathered her third son to her chest, still petting his hair. "It was just a dream."

She would have worried about waking the others, but Nagasa wasn't the only one crying. There were so many nightmares in the dojo that one crying child barely made a ripple. Misaki did her best to soothe Nagasa, but her soft words masked a deep dread and sorrow. The fact that not one but two of them were seeing Mamoru so vividly was a sure sign that there was a ghost in the compound. Some part of Mamoru was still here, bound to the Duna, suffering and dangerous.

Setsuko was coping the best of any of the Matsudas. Every day, when the work had wound down, she carried little Ayumi to the mass grave.

"See that?" she would say, bouncing her daughter on her hip. "Your father lies here. Your father was a hero, Ayumi. Never forget that. Your father was a hero, so we're going to be strong for him, ne? We're going to make his spirit proud."

The stout woman was the only person who seemed to have drawn strength from the tragedy. She seemed to have decided that she was going to get back at the Ranganese by living with a vengeance. A lesser woman might have lamented no longer having a man to look after her or resented Misaki for taking her place as the head lady of the Matsuda house. But far from sulking or eyeing Misaki with envy, Setsuko positively leaped with energy, asking "What can I do to help? What do you need me to do?" With Ayumi on her back, she carried as much as any of the men.

The only people who worked as enthusiastically as Setsuko were, surprisingly, the Kwangs. Misaki had expected the father and son to leave the village as soon as they could arrange it. The info-com towers may have saved the village, but they were destroyed now, and she couldn't imagine anyone wanting to linger at the site of such trauma.

But the city boy and his father threw themselves into rebuilding the village as if it were their own. Kwang Tae-min assisted the numuwu in disassembling the broken info-com towers so the metal could be repurposed to build new houses while Chul-hee volunteered himself for the building efforts. The northern boy had barely spent two seasons on Mount Takayubi, but the time had transformed him. His soft limbs had filled out with muscle from months of sword training with Yukino Dai and Mamoru. He may never have achieved the combat prowess to be of any use against the Ranganese, but his newly forged strength made him invaluable in rebuilding in the wake of the attack.

He ended up spending most of his time helping Hyori build a new home with the help of Atsushi. She was one of the few women left behind with no resident or visiting male relatives to help her rebuild. Her sister and parents had lived in the western village. They had been killed in the first moments of the attack, their houses ripped right off the side of the mountain before anyone had a chance to defend themselves. Neither her husband nor her younger brother had returned from the battle, and her little son had been killed right in front of her eyes. She had no one left to care for her in her grief.

Misaki and Setsuko did their best to visit her often. And in the meantime, Chul-hee and Atsushi did an admirable job trying to keep her in good spirits. The boys pointed out to her that the foundations of the Yukino compound were still usable, but they respected her wishes not to live in the place where her son had died and started erecting a shack for her near the Matsuda compound, where Misaki and Setsuko could more easily look after her.

One day, she appeared while Setsuko and Misaki were picking through the ruined part of the Matsuda compound with splinter-pricked fingers, trying to determine which pieces of wood could be repurposed and which were beyond use.

"Hyori," Misaki said in surprise. "Is something wrong?"

"Misaki..." Hyori's hand was over her stomach.

Sensing that Hyori wanted her closer, Misaki clambered down from the wreckage and went to her.

"What is it?"

"I..." Hyori's hand crunched in the front of her kimono, shaking. "Misaki... I'm pregnant."

"What?"

"I didn't know who to tell. I..."

"Are you sure?" Misaki asked. It had only been four weeks, but jijaka women could almost always tell.

"Wait. You're pregnant?" Setsuko exclaimed, bustling over to them.

"Y-yes," Hyori murmured, shrinking in on herself.

"That's wonderful news!" Setsuko beamed. "It means Dai still has a child! You'll still have part of him. What a happy day!"

But there was no happiness on Hyori's face when her eyes met Misaki's, only horror.

Setsuko ran off to tell the neighbors, and Misaki had to ask, even though the look on Hyori's face made her fear the worst. "*Is* it Dai's?"

"I don't know," Hyori said in a hopeless whisper. "The timing... There is no way to know."

"Oh, Hyori-chan." She reached out for her friend's hands, but Hyori pulled away. Horrified, Misaki watched the little hope Hyori had accumulated over the past weeks evaporate.

"I should have died," she said.

"Don't say that!" Misaki exclaimed. "You said there was no way to tell. It might be Dai's baby—"

"And then what?" Hyori demanded. "Then what? Even if it is his, how am I supposed to care for a child? I'm disgraced, I have nothing, no husband—"

"We'll take care of you," Misaki promised, "me and Setsuko."

"How?"

Hyori had a point. Aside from a few standing walls and one very detached man, the Matsuda house didn't have many more resources than she did.

"I'll make it happen," Misaki said stubbornly. "I'll make sure you and this child are taken care of. I swear it."

Hyori was shaking her head. "I should have died."

"*Stop* saying that!" Misaki begged. "Hyori, please!"

But the thought seemed to have taken root deep inside Hyori, and nothing Misaki or anyone else said could shake it out.

"It would have been better if I had died," she kept saying in the same empty voice. "I think when that soldier came into our house, he was supposed to kill us both. I was supposed to die."

"Don't say such things, Yukino-san!" the neighbors and volunteers kept saying. "You must live. You are carrying your husband's child."

That particular attempt at comfort usually prompted a fit of moaning and hair clutching so unnerving that everyone stepped back from Hyori and decided to give her space. They didn't realize they were twisting the knives deeper.

Four weeks after the attack, there were enough ramshackle shelters that people started moving out of the Matsuda compound. Misaki should have felt relieved to know that the residents of the village at least had the beginnings of new homes. And she had always liked her space; it should have been nice to see the wounded numuwu, crying women, and shouting children filtering out of her home.

"Feels a little lonely, doesn't it?" Setsuko said after she and Misaki had helped the Kotetsus pack up and bid them farewell.

"Yes," Misaki murmured. That was the word. Lonely.

"For a while there, it reminded me of home—of my parents' shack," Setsuko said. "Twelve of us all squeezed into the same two rooms to sleep. That was the worst thing when I moved here... all the quiet, empty space. Guess I couldn't understand why you would need so much space for just a few family members."

"Right." Misaki remembered those first days after Setsuko had moved in. Setsuko had stuck to her like glue, insisting that she talk and smile. It hadn't occurred to her that Setsuko might have been reaching out for something too. "On the bright side, a good piece of the house is gone now."

A good piece of the family was gone too.

When the halls had been filled with the temporarily homeless people of Takayubi, nursing injuries, giving each other comfort, and sleeping on folded blankets, there was no room for the memories. The emptiness left the house open to too many memories, where Ryota always liked to chase around with Nagasa, where Takashi had liked to lounge after his evening drink, where Mamoru had gotten ready for school, studied with Chul-hee, played with his brothers...

The nightmares got worse.

Misaki was dismayed when one day, she came back to the compound to find the bedroom she had shared with Takeru before the attack empty. On the floor of the dojo, among many shocked and grieving people, it was not out of place for one to mutter in her sleep or wake up shouting. She didn't want Takeru to hear that. She didn't want to sleep beside him at all.

She was still standing in the bedroom doorway, gripping the doorframe when she felt the touch of Takeru's nyama on the back of her neck.

"Misaki," he said and his tone of voice suggested that he had already repeated himself several times.

"Sorry—" she turned from the bedroom doorway to face her husband. "What is it?"

"I found something in the wreckage."

"Oh?"

Takeru took a step forward and Misaki fought the urge to step back. When Mamoru was born, she had hated the way his nyama reminded her of his father. Now she hated the way Takeru's nyama reminded her of Mamoru. She didn't want to look at him. She didn't want him anywhere near her.

"What is this?" he asked, holding up Siradenyaa.

"That..." Misaki said, looking at the weapon, "is mine."

Lying had barely crossed her mind. There had been a time when she had feared her husband's disapproval, times she even thought he might hurt her, but after seeing him bow to a man who had stolen and burned his son's body, she couldn't seem to take him as seriously. What did she have to fear from a coward with no soul and no spine?

"A friend of mine had it made for me at Daybreak Academy," she explained, brazenly disregarding her husband's rule about talking about her past. "I hid it under the kitchen floorboards after we got married. It's funny; I thought I would never need it. I thought surely Matsuda Takeru, the greatest swordsman in Shirojima, would be powerful enough to protect his own family without his wife taking up arms. I guess I was wrong."

Takeru opted to ignore the blatant insult. Wordlessly, he extended a hand and dropped Siradenyaa. Misaki's hand shot out possessively and caught the weapon before it could fall to the floor, automatically assuming her favored reverse grip, perfect for attacking an opponent standing close in an enclosed space like a hallway.

"Hiroshi said he recognized that blade. He said he used it to kill a man in black."

"He did," Misaki said. Why bother lying—why bother watching her words at all—if her husband clearly didn't care. "Nice thing about that blade is that she isn't just light; she's got a razor-sharp edge that makes cuts easy for an undersized woman or, as it turns out, a small boy."

"You should never have allowed something like that to happen," Takeru said stiffly. "He is too young."

Misaki was so indignant that she could only stare at him.

"You should have ensured that the children stayed hidden," he said. "Your job as a woman is not to fight—"

"And what about your job?" Misaki found herself demanding. "What about your responsibility to keep this family safe?"

"My orders were to protect you, Setsuko, and the children—"

"*I* protected Setsuko and the children." Misaki felt her face twist into a snarl of rage. "Five people were here in the house with me when the Ranganese broke down the doors, and all of them are with us now." Her snarl turned predatory and she felt the need for blood in her teeth. *"One* of our sons was with you. Just one. And where is he now?"

"Misaki—"

"Where is he now, Matsuda Takeru?" she demanded savagely. "Where is he now?"

Predator's eyes searched his expression, mad with hunger. She hadn't just insulted him now; she had bitten into the rawest nerve she could find. There had to be anger there. There had to be something.

He just stared at her flatly, completely emotionless. "I don't need you speaking to me that way," he said. "Pull yourself together."

Misaki's fists clenched, a new army of insults crowding to the tip of her tongue, but she stopped at the sound of bare feet padding across the floor.

Hiroshi rounded the corner into the hallway. "Kaa-chan?"

The boy stopped, staring up at his parents. Expressionless, he looked from Takeru, to Misaki, to the black sword clutched in his mother's hand. If seeing the weapon he had used to cut into another human had any effect on him, it didn't show on his face. He did, however, seem to realize that he had intruded on a sensitive conversation between his parents because he dropped to his knees.

"Sorry, Tou-sama, Kaa-chan." He bowed with the poise of a grown swordsman. "The baby is awake."

"Tell Setsuko to deal with it," Takeru said disinterestedly.

"No," Misaki said before Hiroshi could move to obey. "It's

alright. I'll take care of it."

"We're not done here." Takeru took a step toward Misaki, as if to back her into the bedroom, trapping her.

Misaki brought Siradenyaa up between them in a reverse grip, handle first. Takeru's chest hit the blunt butt of the Zilazen glass sword and he stopped. Misaki met his eyes in challenge. At the moment, her position wasn't aggressive—barely even defensive—but that could change with the smallest flip of the blade. Another fraction of a step forward would force Misaki to either give ground or turn her wrist and cut him. It was his gamble.

He didn't move.

That's what I thought, a vicious part of Misaki growled.

"I think we are done."

Lowering Siradenyaa, she strode past her immobile husband, past a very confused Hiroshi, and out of the hall.

Izumo was squirming in his cradle—well it wasn't really a cradle but a bureau drawer padded with spare clothing. Misaki had given his old cradle to a woman with a much younger infant whose home had been destroyed.

"Hey there, little one." She patted Izumo's stomach but she couldn't pick him up with Siradenyaa in her hand. "I'll be right with you."

Reaching behind the drawer cradle, she pulled Siradenyaa's flowered sheath from its latest hiding place. A quick swipe of her jiya cleaned the dried fonyaka blood from the blade. Having sheathed Siradenyaa, she hid the weapon again and knelt to pick up Izumo.

"Yosh, yosh," she soothed, rocking him.

The baby's arms moved as he cried, swiping aimlessly at his own face. As Misaki watched, a few tears jumped from his cheeks, drawn to his tiny fingers by the pull of his jiya. The salty droplets tumbled through open air, twinkling, for a moment, before falling to the tatami.

Mamoru and Hiroshi had also been moving tiny amounts of water by the time they started to teethe; Nagasa around the time he started to walk. Unlike the three before him, Izumo did not seem to grow colder as he grew stronger. He didn't scald like a little tajaka, but his modest human warmth was like that of the few adyn children Misaki had held.

It wasn't just Izumo's body temperature that was pleasant. Misaki had come to love the feel of his nyama—not hard but fluid, never grating against her coldness, but swirling about it until slowly, they melted together and both became liquid. He brought back a long gone feeling of being adaptable, fluid, and free.

Misaki let the feel of her fourth son at her breast calm her, ease the anger.

She had planned to spend the rest of the day helping Takeru and Setsuko continue the grueling work of cleaning up the wrecked part of the Matsuda compound, but when she contemplated the prospect of seeing Takeru again, she found that she couldn't face it. Instead, she bundled Izumo into a cloth sling against her chest and slipped out of the compound to visit Hyori.

Visits to Hyori's little hut were hardly joyful experiences, but her friend needed companionship. And at this moment, Misaki felt like she would be ready to walk into Hell itself so long as Takeru would not be there.

Hyori greeted her with her usual politeness, inviting Misaki into the cold, cramped space, and apologizing that she didn't have any food to offer—as if any of them had food.

"Sorry about the cold," she said. "The boys are still helping me with the insulation."

"I live with Matsudas," Misaki said, "I'm used to the cold."

"I'm worried," Hyori admitted once they were kneeling together on the tatami.

"Why?"

"This baby... it doesn't feel like Ryota did inside me."

"Well, none of my boys quite felt the same as one another," Misaki said. "Hiroshi was so much colder than the others—"

"It doesn't feel like a jijaka."

Misaki paused. "It's barely been long enough for you to tell that you're pregnant at all, Hyori-chan. I'm sure it's too early to tell something like that."

"Maybe..." Hyori's hand rested on her waist, her thumb rubbing nervously back and forth across her obi.

With all the heart-twisting chaos of Misaki's own life, she still found it sobering to consider what Hyori was facing. If the baby was her husband's, life would be difficult. Without any family to support her, she would have to work to support the child—a daunting prospect for a noble girl raised to be a housewife. And it wasn't as if there were an abundance of employment options in Takayubi.

If the child was not Dai's, everything would be so much worse. Misaki had spent a good portion of her sleepless nights, trying to figure out what could be done to help Hyori in that worst-case scenario. What could she do to make life easier for her friend? All her consideration had yielded little. Everyone would know what had happened. Hyori would live the rest of her life bearing shame that wasn't hers to bear. And the child... Misaki shuddered to think how these people would treat the child, but she couldn't show her apprehension. Hyori hardly needed Misaki to add to her stress.

"I'm sure everything will be fine." Misaki did her best to project reassurance she didn't feel. What she *did* feel was anger. A pressing, seething abundance of anger. It swelled in her chest, causing a flare of pain that made her grimace.

"Are you alright, Misaki?" Hyori asked, shuffling over on her knees to put a hand on Misaki's back.

"I'm fine," Misaki said, clutching her chest.

"Your lungs are still bothering you," Hyori said. "I know there isn't a lot of money right now, but maybe several us could pool our funds and try to get you to a city hospital for an x-ray. At the very least, we should try to get an expert here to examine—"

"Nami's wrath, Hyori, are you honestly worrying about *me*?"

"Of course," Hyori said.

"You're so good Hyori..." She couldn't find comfort in Hyori's touch. Instead, she saw the Ranganese soldier on top of her friend, holding her down, and she felt *hatred*. "You're so good. No man should be allowed to diminish that. No man."

"Misaki, you're not making any sense—"

"Listen, Hyori-chan." Misaki gripped Hyori's arm. "Maybe it *is* your husband's child. Maybe it's not. That doesn't matter."

"How can you say that?"

"Because the child doesn't *belong* to its father!" Misaki burst out, surprised by the rage in her voice. "Who says that children belong to their fathers? We carry them, we nourish them inside us, we bring them into the world, we do all the work in raising them. Then these men—these men think they can just take them and kill them?"

"Misaki..."

"What claim does that Ranganese bastard have to a child from your womb? What right do any of them have? As much as Ryota was Dai's, he was yours. As much as Mamoru was Takeru's, he was mine. He was *mine*!"

A slamming pain made Misaki look down and realize she had punched the tatami, breaking the bamboo reeds and cracking the wood floor beneath. In his sling, Izumo started crying.

"Sorry." Misaki put a hand to her eyes. "I'm so sorry, Hyori-chan. I'm not helping. I... I should go." She bowed. "I'll replace the tatami and boards. Give Chul-hee and Atsushi my apologies."

"Misaki..." Hyori was looking at her friend in a mixture of concern and fear, but no intervening emotion seemed to be able to drive the deep sorrow from her eyes. Misaki couldn't bear to look at it any longer.

"I'm so sorry." She bowed one last time and fled the hut.

After leaving Hyori, Misaki wandered. Under the pretense of checking on the neighbors, she made her way throughout the entire village. She visited Katakouri Mayumi and her crippled father, Hisato, who had just finished putting the roof on their makeshift house, the Mizumaki women who had almost finished theirs, and the Ginkawa volunteers who were just starting work on a shack to house the several children orphaned in the attack.

The Ameno men gathered near the beginnings of the orphanage

greeted her and bowed, but she decided not to bother them when she noted that they appeared to be at their wits' end trying to ration supplies for distribution. From the way they struggled with the numbers, it sounded like they could have benefited from Takeru's help, but he had been barely involved in the larger rebuilding efforts since returning from his little trip up the mountain. He would correct numbers, but he didn't take an active role in any of the planning, leaving coordination to Kotetsu Katashi, who was still recovering from the loss of his leg, and Kwang Tae-min, who still struggled to communicate with the Kusanagi natives.

Not wanting to think about Takeru anymore, Misaki forcibly inserted herself into the conversation between Kotetsu and Kwang about plans to construct more lasting dwellings in the coming months, despite understanding next to nothing about carpentry or village planning. By the time the sun had set and lights started going out, Misaki was out of people to visit and there was only one place left to go... back to the house, to the bedroom. To Takeru.

The compound was dark when she crept in. Izumo, who had long since fallen asleep in his sling, went into his drawer without much fuss. In the dark, Misaki found four other sleeping pulses—Hiroshi, Nagasa, little Ayumi, and Setsuko. The woman had taken to sleeping in the same room as the children since the house had emptied. She no longer had a husband to sleep beside, and Misaki supposed it must comfort her to sleep among her family, as she had when she herself was a child.

Setsuko stirred as Misaki straightened up from the drawer.

"Hey, pretty girl," she mumbled—a funny thing to say in the dark—"You're back late." She sounded exhausted, but in the satisfied, happy sort of way that came from a day of hard work.

"I know," Misaki whispered, wishing more than anything that she could join Setsuko on the floor and share in her content. "I'm sorry. Please, go back to sleep."

For a moment, she entertained the idea that it might be alright for her to curl up here with her sister-in-law and children, and sleep soundly, surrounded by love. But that was out of the question. A woman who slept outside the main bedroom was one who had been rejected. And Takeru had not rejected Misaki. Not yet.

Stepping back from Izumo's drawer, she left the room of soft breaths and sweet heartbeats. Even in the dead of winter, the room where Takeru slept was always a few degrees colder than the others. Most powerful theonites, including Takeru's own brother, had powerful pulses that Misaki could sense from bounds away. Takeru's heartbeat was as faint as it was steady. His breath barely moved the air. If not for the skin-crawling cold he exuded, Misaki would not have been able to tell that her husband was there, asleep on their futon. She was thankful that the Gods had graced her with the stealth of a snake. She slid under the blankets beside Takeru without disturbing him.

She dreamed of the day she sparred with Mamoru in the dojo. Only the weapons in their hands weren't bokken. Mamoru held his beautiful serpent sword. Misaki held Shadow's Daughter.

"Careful," Misaki said, dimly aware that sparring with such weapons was not safe. "I don't want to damage your sword."

"I'm sure it will be alright," Mamoru said in a reassuring voice that somehow made Misaki's dread grow. "Mamoriken is strong."

"Mamoriken...?" Misaki repeated slowly. "That's not... your sword doesn't have a name." *Not yet*, a faraway part of her screamed. *Nami please, not yet. Let this moment stay. Let me stay here with him.*

"Of course, it does. It's the Protector."

"No..."

"Isn't that what you told me to do?" Mamoru said. "Protect the people who are important to me, no matter the cost?"

"I didn't say that." *I never said no matter the cost. I never—*

"But you named me, didn't you?" Mamoru said. "When I was born?"

"No!"

"You knew this is what I was when I was still in your womb. Before I was born, I was already—"

"No!" In her distress, Misaki lashed out, forgetting that

Siradenyaa was still clutched in her hand. Glass hit flesh. She and Mamoru both looked down to find a gaping sword wound in his side. She had killed him.

"Kaa-chan..." Mamoru wasn't angry when he looked into her face. Worse. He looked bemused. "Why?" he asked in a voice full of hurt. "Why?"

Misaki's eyes snapped open and she sat up—only to find Mamoru standing at the foot of the futon. Oh, Nami—

"You shouldn't have left me," he said accusingly, and now he was angry. "Why would you leave me alone out there?"

Misaki wanted to speak, but she seemed to be frozen from the inside, rigid, like all the times she had held herself beneath her husband, trying not to recoil. Could it be that, after so long lying still against this futon, she had forgotten how to move altogether? Even for her son?

"Why are you doing this?" Mamoru demanded, his nyama rising, freezing cold like his father's. "Why are you keeping me here? Why are you doing this to me?"

I didn't mean to, Misaki tried to say as Mamoru's frigid jiya crawled up the walls, forming spikes of ice. *I'm sorry! My son, I'm so sorry!* But no sound would come out of her open mouth.

Flesh peeled from his neck and face, crackling as it burned away. He had been dead and still when his physical body burned, but not this Mamoru. This Mamoru *screamed*.

"WHY DID YOU LEAVE ME?"

Ice shot toward Misaki, sizzling with Hellfire—

She jerked awake. This time it was real—real sweat clinging to her skin, real tears on her face, and a terribly real ice spike pressed against her stomach, not quite hard enough to break the skin. Breaking the spike with her jiya, she sat up and looked around her in horror. She had heard of sleep-forming before, the phenomenon in which a jijaka dreamed so vividly that their jiya activated, but it had never happened to her before. Her sleeping jiya had raised ice all along the walls of the room, forming long spikes that pointed inward toward the futon.

A ragged breath beside her drew her attention to her husband. Takeru was up on his knees, eyes wide in the moonlight, and he was—oh Nami!—he was bleeding! One spike seemed to have pierced his right arm while another had clipped his side. He was holding a hand to the side of his neck. When he lowered the hand, it was covered in blood.

Misaki knew with heart-dropping certainty that she had done this. In sleep, her jiya had risen against Takeru, as it had once risen against his unborn offspring inside her. And he was bleeding from the neck. The poison in her had grown out of control.

Takeru looked at the red on his hand, then at Misaki. His eyes were no longer emotionless. They were wild as he growled, "Get out."

"Takeru-sama, I—"

"*Get out!*" he roared.

And Misaki was on her feet, scrambling backward out of the room. She didn't stop running until she had reached the front deck, as far from the bedroom as she could go without leaving the compound. Part of her wanted to keep running, through the rocks and snow in her bare feet, down into the ocean, where she could drown in the arms of the Gods. But she was shaking violently and her legs gave out beneath her.

Alone on the deck in the biting winter air, she curled into a ball. One hand fisted hard in her own hair, the other curling into her middle, sinking into the flesh of her stomach.

How had this all gone so wrong? Fifteen years ago, she had turned her back on Carytha, to go to her future in Takayubi. It was supposed to be the right decision—for her family, herself, her country—so why had it all turned into this?

She had thought she was water that could adjust to fill any container, be as strong in the shape of a mother as a warrior, but in the end, maybe Koli had been right about her. She was a knife, a sharp edge, that killed or cut anything it touched. The babies she hadn't killed in her womb had been born into a world of blades that cut them down before they had a chance to grow. Now the evil in

474

her had risen out of her sleep and turned its wrath on her husband.

Part of her expected Takeru to come after her and punish her, maybe—finally—kill her. A growing part of her prayed to feel the Moon Spire or the Whispering Blade against the back of her neck. She had raised her jiya against him twice now. He was well within his rights to take his revenge, so why not? It would be so easy for him. One stroke. It was all she deserved.

Instead, the touch on the back of her neck was gentle.

"Misaki?" Setsuko's voice—a tender, familiar sound, offering reassurance that Misaki did not deserve and never had. "Sister, what happened?"

Misaki shrank from the touch. She had never deserved it.

"You shouldn't come near me, Setsuko," she said, her voice strangely clear through the tears—as if it was coming from someone else's mouth. "Something is wrong with me."

"What do you mean?"

"Do you still see him, Setsuko?"

"What?"

"Your husband. Does he haunt you?"

Setsuko shook her head. "I know who I married, and I know how lucky I am to have married him. A marriage like ours is something I never would have thought to hope for all those years ago at the fish market when I made eyes at the pretty nobleman from up the mountain. I'm a simple country girl who never expected to marry well or marry for love, so when I did both, I guess I understood that every moment of it was a gift. Takashi, this life, this place, is all something I never expected to have. He died fighting. That was who he was. I'll miss him, but I suppose... it's enough that I ever had him at all."

"A handful of pearls," Misaki murmured.

"What's that?"

"Nothing... You're a remarkable woman."

"Nah." Setsuko shrugged. "I'm just too dumb to overcomplicate things."

Misaki tried to chuckle like she used to at Setsuko's jokes. The smile wouldn't come.

"I know who I married," Setsuko said again, more seriously. "There was an itch in him. Age, boredom, rust, he'd use different words for it. It's hard to believe my man could fear anything, but I think he feared growing old in this house without ever fulfilling his potential. The way he went... I think that was a kinder end for him than that slow rust. He wanted to mean something."

"And sticking around to be a husband to you and a father to Ayumi?" Misaki couldn't help but ask. "That wasn't enough meaning for him?"

"You know what he was like," Setsuko said with a fond smile. "So dramatic. It wasn't enough for him to love us. He had to show it in the biggest, most ridiculous way possible."

"But it wasn't just you he left," Misaki said. "He left this whole family—this whole village—with no leader when he sent Takeru back. Isn't that a bit selfish?"

"No," Setsuko said stubbornly. "It wasn't. Not *just* selfishness, anyway. It was trust."

"What?"

"You never heard him talk about Takeru behind closed doors. He believed in his little brother, more than he ever believed in himself."

Then he was even more delusional than I thought. Takeru still had not emerged from the house to retrieve her. What kind of leader couldn't even control his own wife?

"My husband knew exactly what he was doing when he died," Setsuko said resolutely. Then she paused, pressing her lips together. "I think... Mamoru-kun had some of that same magic in him. I know he was too young, but you said yourself that he died with purpose. Shouldn't his spirit be alright?"

"It's me. It's my fault he can't move on."

"Why do you say that?"

"Because I'm *angry*, Setsuko," Misaki breathed. "I know it's not right, but I'm just... I'm angry all the time. It's eating me alive."

"Then you have to do something about it," Setsuko said in a resolute way that made it sound simple.

"I know," Misaki said miserably. "I just... I don't know what—or how."

"Well... do you know what's making you so upset?" Setsuko asked. "Are you angry with the Ranganese?"

"No, no." Bizarrely, Misaki hadn't given the Ranganese much thought since the attack.

"Are you angry with Takashi?" she asked more gently. "For sending Takeru back to us instead of Mamoru? It's alright if you say yes."

"No," Misaki said honestly. It didn't make sense, but she wasn't angry at Takashi.

"Then who?"

"I don't know," Misaki said, clutching her head. "I don't know." But that wasn't true.

"Well, once you figure it out, maybe you should confront the person—or spirit—or whoever it is. Cleanse your anger."

"Maybe..."

"I bet that after that, you'll be able to rest, and so will Mamoru."

Misaki nodded. Setsuko's advice may have been simple, but it was sound. If Misaki didn't do something with this anger, it was going to kill her. Mamoru would never be at peace and their family would be poisoned forever. Any warrior knew that death by slow poisoning was worse than death by the blade.

After Setsuko had gone back to bed, Misaki took a brushpen and a sheaf of kayiri from Takashi's old study. Lighting a lantern, she knelt on the floor and started writing.

27

THE DUEL

Snow fell softly on the buried pyre. The earth Song's soldiers had packed down over the pit had been visibly different from the rockier ground around it, but once Nagi finished laying his shroud of new snow over the ground, it would be indistinguishable from any other part of the mountain.

Takeru approached the circle in measured swordsman's steps, his left thumb resting on the guard of Kyougetsu, ready to flick the weapon out at the slightest hint of danger. Then his eyes fell on his opponent.

"You?"

Misaki stood slowly, her own left thumb resting on Siradenyaa's glass guard. As she had expected, Takeru hadn't kept her waiting long. The snow had barely started to gather in her hair and the folds of her clothing. She had borrowed a ceremonial women's hakama from one of the fina nuns. While the loose garment was not intended for combat, it allowed for more movement than the restrictive obi and kimono she usually wore.

"Misaki..." Takeru didn't quite seem to have put the pieces together. "What are you doing here?"

"I have an appointment," she said calmly as his eyes flicked to the sword at her hip. "I challenged another warrior to a duel." She placed her right hand on Siradenyaa's handle. "Evidently, he

478

accepts."

Takeru's reaction was disappointing but predictable.

"This is ridiculous, Misaki. You will return to the house immediately."

"No." She was done sitting with her disappointment. Here, on the snow-covered grave of her son, someone was going to pay for it. "We're going to duel."

"We will do no such thing," Takeru said firmly. "A man doesn't fight his wife."

"You forfeit, then?" she demanded. "That would be a first in Matsuda history, wouldn't it? I also believe it entitles me to your head if I want it."

"I can't forfeit if it's not a real duel," Takeru snapped. "You have to be a warrior to issue a challenge and you are not."

"Am I not? Would you like to tell that to the Ranganese who got past your lines?" She thumped a heel against the ground beneath which her victims were buried. "I believe I killed eight before you arrived to 'protect' me, and one more when you refused to protect Hyori. Or did you think they had all dropped dead of their own accord?"

"It is not your place to take up arms," Takeru's voice rose, as did his jiya, crushing down on her. "You are a woman. Your only job is to look after the children."

"And why is that again?" Misaki asked, her voice full of venom. "Oh yes. Because my husband, the greatest swordsman in Shirojima, is supposed to protect us all."

"Misaki." His voice had grown dangerous. "You will not speak to me that way. You are my wife—"

"I never wanted to be your wife!" Misaki burst out and found her voice breaking into a scream. "I never wanted any of this!" Gods, it had been so long since she had screamed. The sound was so visceral, even Takeru took a step back. "I didn't want any of this, but I birthed that boy, and nursed him, and loved him—all because my parents wanted me to marry a Matsuda! The only reason I am here is that you are a strong theonite who was supposed to keep me

479

and my children safe! That's what I gave up my life for. Safety."

"I will not hear any more—"

"I left everything behind to marry you! I have been an obedient wife, I have borne you children, I have done everything that was asked of me, so why did this happen? Why is my son gone?" Misaki finished, breathless, feeling like she could fall into a thousand pieces, like she could eat the world. She was ready to fight.

"I had my orders," was all Takeru said.

"Like you had your orders when Colonel Song burned the bodies of our dead and then turned his back on us?" Misaki snarled.

"A Matsuda obeys his superiors. When I left the frontline..." Takeru's voice seemed to falter. "Nii-sama was clear—"

"I don't care about Takashi," Misaki spat. "He isn't here anymore. Neither is Colonel Song, or your father. You're all out of people to hide behind. I married *you*, I had a son with *you*, and *you* left him on the frontlines to die when you had a chance to save him. Takashi is not going to answer for his death. You are." She whipped Siradenyaa from her sheath and leveled the blade at her husband's chest. "Draw, Matsuda Takeru!"

"I will not hear any more of this, woman!" Takeru bellowed, as if sheer volume could silence her now. "This is your last chance to obey—"

"You lost your right to my obedience when you stopped being a man!" Misaki cut him off. "If you want me to go back to the house, you'll have to fight me. I've stood by too long while you disgraced yourself, but this—this is the last time you will be weak in front of me. One of us is going to rest here with our son. Draw!"

Takeru held her gaze. There was no indication that the storm seething in her had prompted so much as a ripple in him. For a moment, the only movement between them was the slow undulation of falling snow.

"You shouldn't yell so much." His voice was suddenly quieter. "It's not ladylike."

Indignation twisted in Misaki's throat, and she shifted into her stance, preparing to attack. Her anger was itching to burst into action, and she had given him ample warning—

"Besides," he said in that same subdued voice, "you made your case better in the letter."

"What?" Misaki's fingers squirmed in their grip on Siradenyaa's handle. Her body was heartbeats from surging out of her control— like the lurch that had sent her into Kazu's arms, the fury that had driven her toward Colonel Song's throat—and it took all the willpower she had to hold it back. Takeru still hadn't drawn Kyougetsu or summoned his Whispering Blade. If she was going to follow through with the formalities of the duel she had called for, she couldn't attack him until he had a weapon in hand.

"It is customary," Takeru said, "for the challenge to be reviewed before a duel commences."

Misaki glared up at him, eyes narrowing. "Does this mean you *accept* my challenge?" she asked. "If so, I don't need anything reviewed. I know what I said." After fifteen years of holding still, she didn't feel like she could take another moment. She wanted to *fight*.

Ignoring her, Takeru reached into the fold of his kimono and produced the anonymous letter of challenge Misaki had left on the door of the compound. Nami's sake, wasn't that just like him? He couldn't even fight without making sure the paperwork was all in order. Emotionless, he read aloud:

"Matsuda Takeru,

I am one of many who lost my family, my home, all that was precious to me, to your cowardice and poor judgment. In abandoning the frontlines during the battle, you condemned other warriors to die, including your own brother and son."

"I told you, you don't need to read it," she said, but Takeru kept going:

"Since our village has been ravaged, you have not spoken to the government on our behalf. When the bodies of our dead were disrespected, you did not speak up. When the authorities refused us aid, you did not dispute their decision. When we needed you most,

you disappeared up the mountain, leaving others to assume your responsibilities.

At every turn, you have proven yourself incapable of standing up to authority when those beneath you depend on you to do so. It is my belief that a coward like this is unfit to lead our village in its time of need."

There had been so much righteous anger in Misaki as she wrote. Takeru's deep, calm voice stripped the words of their emotion, sharpening them to their simple cruelty.

"For these reasons, I challenge you to single combat, at the ninth waati, on the ground where the numu village once stood. If you would prove yourself a man, do so in single combat."

Takeru finished, still staring at the letter.

"Incapable of standing up to authority," he repeated, strangely pensive, rather than angry. "Is this in reference to Colonel Song... or to my brother?"

"Both," Misaki said, her sword still drawn. "I stand by what I said and what I wrote. Do you deny any of it?"

Takeru did not answer. When he reached to his hip, Misaki twitched, ready to defend herself, but instead of drawing Kyougetsu, he slowly untied the white string holding it in place and slid the pearly sheath from his belt. Then, just as slowly, he knelt and placed the Moon Spire off to the side.

So that's how it's going to be, Misaki thought, shifting her grip on Siradenyaa. *He's starting right off with the Whispering Blade.*

Legend said Sasayaiba could cut through anything. It remained to be seen whether it could cut Zilazen glass. Misaki was ready. She had thought through every maneuver she had ever seen Takeru employ. She had planned counters for all of them. She was ready—

But she hadn't planned for what he did next.

Having set his sword aside, Takeru rested his palms on the snow-covered ground... and bowed.

"What are you doing?" she demanded.

"I admit to all of the accusations the challenger has leveled against me. So..." He scooped his hair to the side, exposing the back

482

of his neck. "I forfeit," he bowed lower, offering his bare neck to the blade, "and offer my life in atonement."

Misaki felt like the world had come to a halt. She might have thought she was dreaming, but she never could have dreamed this. Even at her most delirious, she would never invent a Takeru who ceded a fight, who knelt before a woman, who asked to die.

"What the hell do you think you're doing?"

"I'm accepting the terms of your letter," Takeru said. "I'm forfeiting and surrendering my life."

"I d-didn't... I didn't mean all those things in that letter," she stammered, backpedaling in her confusion. "I only wrote what I thought would bring you here."

"All you had to do to bring me here was issue the challenge," Takeru said. "You must have known that."

The pang of guilt was disorienting. Misaki swayed, utterly lost. How had this stand-off she had planned so carefully slid out of her control in a matter of moments?

She had thought Takeru might try to force her back to the house, prompting her to resist, or walk away in disdain, prompting her to chase him. She had known that the chances of him accepting her challenge like that of an equal were slim, but if he did, she had been certain he would defend his manhood and put her in her place. All paths ended in a fight. That was how she had planned it, how it *had* to be, so what in all the realms was happening here? Why was he on his knees?

"Why?" The question came out strained.

"What?"

"Before I kill you," she said, "I have to know why... If you understand all my accusations, if you agree, then why did this happen? Why didn't you stand up to Colonel Song? Or to your brother? You bastard, how could you let all of this happen?"

"I..." Takeru's voice was so quiet it barely broke the silence of the falling snow. "I have no answer."

Misaki's mouth opened in disbelief. *Isn't this what you wanted?* asked a voice in her head. *Didn't you want to bring him low? Didn't*

483

you want to kill him? It wasn't until she stood over her husband, staring at his exposed neck that she realized that the answer was no. She didn't want his life. But what did she want then? Why was she here?

"I felt them die." Takeru spoke the words toward his knees, his face hidden.

"You what?" Misaki's voice that had been a screaming storm only moments earlier was no more than a whisper.

"Sometimes... I am not a man," he said slowly, "I am the mountain," and for a dinma, Misaki wondered if he had gone insane—if they had both gone insane—but he kept speaking. "It is a state I have been able to effect since I was a child. I retreat deep into the snow and rivers, and sink myself into the ocean below, and everything on this mountain becomes me, and I become the mountain. It looks like meditation, but it is more. It is becoming a different sort of being..."

"A different sort of being?" Misaki repeated.

"A *bigger* being," he said, "so big that I, Matsuda Takeru, cease to matter. The first time it happened to me, I was very young. On that day, the snow fell thick, as it does now. My father was beating me for something. He knocked me down in the snow in the courtyard. And with my palms to the ground, I realized that I could disperse myself into the snow, spreading all across the mountain, even to the sea below and deeper, deeper... until the pain diffused through my new being, like a drop of blood into a pool. Maybe the pain and shame were too much for a small boy to hold, but the mountain... the mountain could bear it all, so I became the mountain."

Misaki could only stare down at her husband in awe. She had never experienced anything like what Takeru was describing, nor could she fathom why he was telling her about it now.

"As the mountain, I am hyper-aware of some things. I can feel every molecule of water, from the rivers, to the snow, to the subtlest movements of the mist all around. In the midst of so much sensory input, any feeling in my human self—physical or emotional—

becomes insignificant, and therefore bearable."

"You're telling me that when your feelings are inconvenient to you, you just... get rid of them?"

"I let the size of the mountain dull them to the point of insignificance."

It was bizarre to be vindicated in her suspicion that Takeru was not quite human. All those times Misaki had looked into his face and felt as though she could find no emotion there... she had been right. But why was he telling her all this now?

"Other Matsudas have been known to achieve this state too, through intense meditation, but I can slide into it like a glove, on a whim."

It shook Misaki for a moment that she had even contemplated fighting a man whose power was as big as the mountain itself. The poison had consumed her, turning her completely foolhardy—like a small, rabid creature thinking it could take on an animal forty times its size.

"Matsudas past deemed this ability a gift from the Gods," Takeru said, "but I have used it to hide. Since I was a child, using it to escape my father's wrath, I have used it to hide. When it is too much to be a man, I am the mountain. I have done this my whole life—when there was a truth I didn't want to acknowledge, a decision I didn't want to face, a pain I didn't want to endure. It is easier to enter a state in which I am spared human emotions like regret, or shame, or love."

"Do you *ever* feel love?" Misaki demanded. She didn't know if the question came from spite or genuine curiosity. It said too much that they felt like the same thing.

Takeru did not answer her question. It was a moment before he spoke again, leading in with a deep—rather human—breath.

"When Takashi-nii-sama ordered me back to the village, I became the mountain. It was the only thing I could do—the only way I could obey."

Misaki was silent. The simple admission that he had struggled to leave Mamoru should have come as a relief. Instead, it just lay a new pain atop the old. Her husband had been human the whole time.

"But I made a mistake," Takeru continued. "I retreated into the mountain to spare myself the reality of leaving my brother and son without considering the fact that they were born of this mountain too. Their jiya was bound to the same snow, and ice, and moving water as mine. I didn't realize that, in that state, I would *feel* them die."

Misaki felt her hands shake on Siradenyaa.

"I was on my way back to the village when my brother died— and—" His eyebrow twitched, as if his face was trying to find an expression for the pain, but had forgotten how. "It was sharp, Misaki, just a pinprick on the mountain, but it hit like a Blood Needle. Such a tiny thing... and I was paralyzed."

For so many years, Takeru's silence had infuriated her. Now, he was speaking freely and she would have given anything to have him stop.

"I wish I could explain it—My brother was my shelter in all things. His death left me shaken, flayed, like nerve and muscle exposed to the air."

The words were too raw, too near. When you spent years in the company of Takashi, who wasn't much for fancy words, and Takeru, who wasn't much for words at all, it was easy to forget that the Matsudas had a tradition of poetry as old as their tradition of the sword. Takeru might only stumble his way through Imperial Kaigengua, but his Shirojima Dialect was vivid and concise, like the simple clarity of Hyori's eyes. Unbearable.

"I felt after that—as I imagine a skinned man must feel—but I was the mountain, and I couldn't move, not backward toward Mamoru nor forward toward you and the little children. I could not act on my brother's orders or my own impulses. And then..."

"Then Mamoru died," Misaki whispered.

Her grip on Siradenyaa had gone slack. As tears clouded her eyes, she remembered staring through a similar fog in the dark of the bunker. The haze of her concussion or perhaps the tides of her own stubborn denial had drowned the memory, submerging it deep in the

486

back of her mind, but it came bobbing back now: Takeru, resting his head against the bunker door as his shoulders shook. In the dark, the low sound had mixed with the weeping all around them, and gone unnoticed. She hadn't reached for him or spoken his name, even when she knew she should. Why hadn't she reached for him?

"It's..." *It's alright*, she meant to say, *I forgive you*, but she couldn't. Even now, part of her was still too prideful. Too cruel.

Taking a deep breath, she tried again. "I know that a Matsuda's job is to defend the Empire, even at the expense of his sons." Snowflakes caught in her tears as they ran down her cheeks, making them slow with cold. "I know who I married."

"Who *did* you marry, Tsusano Misaki?" Snow had gathered in Takeru's hair in the stillness. "Who did you marry?"

"I was supposed to marry a man with the strength and sense to keep my children safe."

"Then I have failed you completely."

"You didn't..." Misaki stumbled over her words, lost between her overgrown anger at Takeru and this new and foreign urge to defend him. "You didn't know that was going to happen. You didn't know you would be immobilized."

"That's no excuse. It doesn't change the fact that I couldn't carry out my brother's orders when they mattered, nor challenge them when it was needed, so cut me down. Even though you are a woman, you issued a formal challenge, so your hands and conscience should be clean in the eyes of the Gods. You can rid the family of my spiritual impurity."

That part surprised Misaki. "Your spiritual impurity?"

"I harbor anger toward my brother and regret for not protecting my son. That weakness has kept them both from passing to the next world. Perhaps the Gods will allow me to take their place in Hell, knowing my bitterness has passed out of the living realm."

"You... you think Mamoru's ghost stays because of you?" Misaki didn't understand. *She* was the one who had suffered for nights with terrible visions. *She* was the one who couldn't let go.

"I never prayed for him."

"Why not?"

"How do you face a son—an honest, brave warrior—who was killed while you stood and did nothing? I have been unable to send his spirit off, so he has haunted us all this time, stealing your sleep and Nagasa's. Last night, he caused my jiya to rise out of my sleep and it nearly killed us both."

"That wasn't..." *That wasn't you,* Misaki had started to say, but she trailed off. Now that she thought back to the previous night, she remembered waking up drenched in sweat and tears. That water on her skin would have been the first to turn to ice if her jiya had been active. The ice spikes protruding from the walls had been straight and clear, much more like Takeru's clean blades than her own imperfect creations.

"You *stabbed* yourself!" she exclaimed in horrified realization. There were accounts of theonites subconsciously wounding themselves with their own untamed nyama, but it was only supposed to happen to children, whose powers were not developed enough to be lethal. In an adult, it was treated as madness.

"It was lucky that you screamed," he said. "The sound woke me before my jiya had a chance to hurt you."

Misaki realized then that when he had shouted at her to get out, it hadn't been anger in his eyes but panic. He had been worried for her safety.

"With that in mind, you should be careful in this endeavor." Takeru lowered his head again, voice peaceful. "I doubt my death jiya will manifest as dramatically as my brother's, but it may still be extremely dangerous. Make sure you get clear as soon as you've severed my spinal column."

How could he speak so calmly about his own death? Why was his heartbeat so steady?

"You're doing it now, aren't you?" Misaki accused. "Retreating into the mountain, so you won't have to face this like a man."

"I am not."

"Then how are you so calm all of a sudden? You had emotions a moment ago, when you were talking about Mamoru. How can you ask your wife to kill you as if it means nothing at all?"

"Because... This does not upset me."

"I don't believe you." How could someone as powerful as Takeru just give up on his own life without resistance?

"I'm telling you the truth. I haven't tried to enter that state since..."

"Since Colonel Song burned the bodies," Misaki spoke the realization aloud as it hit her. "You couldn't face it so you ran away, to retreat into the mountain."

"I tried," Takeru said. "The anger didn't go away."

"Oh, Takeru-sama..." Misaki breathed, voice high in a mixture of exasperation and grief. "The anger isn't going to *go away.*"

For a moment, she couldn't name the emotion welling up inside her. When she did identify it, an insane part of her wanted to laugh—because it was *pity.* For this ridiculous man on his knees in the snow, for this blind, self-centered woman who had been married to him for fifteen years and never seen him for what he was. Fifteen years and she had never once looked at Takeru as someone who might need her help. Or if she had, she had shut it down—*it's not my place, not my responsibility, not my family.*

"Well?" Takeru asked, his voice as placid as ever. "Are you going to do it?"

"No." She lifted her head and felt something flare to life in her chest, a fresh determination.

You've always been good with people, Kazu had said. If she could pull others out of their despair, she could do the same for Takeru. As she had just learned, he was just as human as anyone else.

"The anger is not going to go away," she repeated in a stronger voice, "but you are going to face it and tame it, like a man."

"What?" Takeru looked up at her, confused.

"You're guilty of the same thing I am—trying to please and obey your elders." Misaki shook her head. "Maybe that was a mistake. Maybe not. It doesn't matter anymore. None of them are here to give us the answers anymore. We're all out of parents, and grandparents and brothers... It's just us..." She paused, unsure where she was going. Maybe setting aside her own regret wasn't enough. Maybe this was the last thing she needed do for Mamoru.

Find the words, Misaki.

She took a painful breath. "When you left Mamoru to hold the line, you were just a second son, following orders, but you're more than that now. You're the head of the Matsuda house."

"But I was never supposed to be. It was peacetime. None of this was supposed to happen."

"I know." Emotion choked Misaki and she was overcome by a sudden urge to do something she had never remotely wanted to do before. She wanted to rush to Takeru. She wanted to *hold* him... and to have him hold her. In the same moment, she realized that that was not an option. They weren't children. They needed more than a protective pair of arms. They needed to *be* more.

"Whether or not my failures are forgiven, I am not equipped to protect our village," Takeru said, his frustration palpable, painful. "A force of fighters, I might be able to lead, but I don't know how to care for a group of widows and orphans with no homes, no resources, and no support from the Empire."

"But you have to. You realize that, don't you?" Misaki said. "If you don't assume the role of village leader, the government will send someone else. We'll be at their mercy and that will be your doing."

That gave Takeru pause.

"Look. Maybe you're not at fault for everything that's happened up until now. Maybe I can't hold you responsible for the decisions of your father and brother, but you *are* responsible for what happens next." As was she. She understood that now, and she wouldn't fail. Not again.

"Fighting the Ranganese is one thing—it is what I was born to do—but defying the Empire..." Takeru shook his head, "that is beyond my ability. It's impossible."

"It is *impossible* for ice to cut through steel. It is *impossible* for a jijaka to stop a tornado. You're a Matsuda. The impossible is a day at the dojo for you."

"But—in the letter you wrote—"

"Forget what I wrote!" Stepping forward, Misaki tore the letter from Takeru's hand and ripped it apart. "I rescind my challenge."

"You can't just—"

"Here is my new challenge." She pointed her blade at him as the torn pieces of kayiri fluttered to her feet. "You agree to be a man and make this up to me. You are going to do whatever you have to in order to protect this family and this village, with or without the support of the government.

"Misaki—" Takeru started to rise, but she put Siradenyaa to his neck and he froze.

"No," she said coldly. "You don't stand up until you are ready to accept my new challenge. Do you accept, Matsuda Takeru?"

"I have already told you that I don't know *how* to protect Takayubi, woman." Even in his self-doubt, Takeru somehow still managed to sound condescending. "I can't—"

"You can," Misaki cut him off angrily.

"What makes you so certain?"

"Because this time, when we head up that path, we do it together. This time, you will have me. Do you accept my terms and my help?"

"I accept," he said, but his face was blank. There was no fear, but no conviction either. It was not enough.

"Then prove it," Misaki said.

His brow creased in confusion. "What?"

"I can't take your word that you will accept my help when you have done nothing but disregard my advice and my feelings since I married you," she said coldly, "and I can't take your word that you will stand to defend Takayubi when you won't even stand to defend yourself."

"What do you want from me?"

In answer, Misaki put the flat of Siradenyaa to his cheek. "Do you know what this is?" she asked.

His eyes flicked to the black blade pressed to his pale skin. "Yammanka obsidian?"

"It's Zilazen glass. Experience, science, and ancient Yammanka religion say no other weapon can put a scratch on it. When you get up, you're going to prove yourself equal to the challenge. Prove that you're ready to do the impossible. If you can't manage that..." *Nami, I hope I know what I'm doing.* "Then this village has no use for you, and neither do I."

She slashed downward.

Takeru moved so fast it might have been pure reflex. Misaki barely saw the Whispering Blade before the icy weapon rang against Siradenyaa, knocking it away from its target. The impact of ice against glass was so intense that Misaki had no idea how she kept her grip on her sword.

Takeru was on his feet.

As the snow rose around him, Misaki's jiya rose as well, not around her, but *inside* her.

She was still in the dark halls of the Matsuda compound, fighting for her family. In her mind, she had never left. She couldn't, she now realized, until she faced this last and most dangerous opponent.

The enemy that loomed before her now was not Matsuda Takeru himself, but the bitterness of silence that had built up between them over fifteen years. She would fight it, kill it. And when she was done, she would have a husband. Her children would have a father. Takayubi would have a leader. Mamoru could rest.

Their blades crashed together, and Misaki experienced a moment of satisfaction when she realized that Takeru had not held back but struck with full, bone-breaking force. This was followed by a moment of utter surprise when she realized that her bones were *not* broken. She and little Siradenyaa had withstood a stroke of Takeru's Whispering Blade. Not only that but, as the Zilazen glass guard locked with Sasayaiba's ice one, Misaki stepped forward and with an inhuman burst of power, shoved Takeru back.

He recovered smoothly, his feet quickly finding their stance again in the gathering snow, but he looked stunned. The feat of strength, from such a diminutive theonite, should not have been possible.

"What *are* you?" Takeru whispered.

Something bigger than myself, she realized. "I'm Matsuda Misaki," she said with pride and honesty she never attached to those words before. "I'm your wife."

And she attacked him.

The speed of her youth seemed to surge into her limbs—but more than that. She was something more than Tsusano Misaki or Sirawu, the Shadow. She was fighting for something greater than one life, or five, or ten. Takeru's will to live, Mamoru's soul, her family's future, the survival of Takayubi itself, all hung on her blade edge. That was something the Shadow, in all her blind love and ruthlessness, would never have understood.

Like Kazu, Tou-sama, and the Giant, Tsusano Raiden, had borne the weight of Anryuu in battles past, she bore Takeru's attacks and forced him back. Takeru responded with his flawless form, leaving no openings, but he was on the defensive as Misaki drove forward.

In all her years of training at Daybreak, Misaki had never had the skill to match a master swordsman in combat. But unencumbered by the tight kimono or the childish cowardice that had bound her for years, she had become a new creature, more fluid and boundless than a girl but more solid than a shadow—a *woman* of lightning sinew and roaring blood.

For once in her life, her body kept pace with her mind. The moment she visualized a swing, the blade was there. The moment she registered an opening, she was inside it. If she willed her stance to hold, it held. She was breathing hard, but it occurred to her that for the first time since the Soul Pull, the heaving breaths were not hurting her lungs.

Three times, the Whispering Blade cracked, but Takeru was quick to reform it. *Good.* If he could withstand Siradenyaa, if he could fight through this, then there was hope for Takayubi yet. Snow whirled faster around them as Misaki crashed into the Whispering Blade a fourth time—shattering it.

The moment was jarring. With her blood serving as an extension of her will, Misaki didn't feel the impact in her muscles and joints. Instead, she felt it in her soul—and it felt unnatural. The Whispering

Blade was not supposed to break. She may have extended her willpower throughout her own body, but that still was not good enough. She needed it to reach beyond herself. She needed it to reach *him*.

Show me better, she willed Takeru as she pressed forward. *Show me the impossible.*

He gave a calculated amount of ground, but instead of using the retreat to reform his Sasayaiba, he changed tactics, making a broad sweeping motion with his open hands. Snow rose to the flow of his jiya and a serpent reared from the ground before Misaki—not quite a Matsuda Dragon; that technique required the power of two full-grown Matsudas, but the creature was far bigger than any ice snake Misaki had ever seen an individual jijaka form.

The serpent slung razor-scaled coils protectively about Takeru and then raised itself up to face Misaki, ice shard eyes gleaming. It was taller than a house, its fanged jaws open wide enough to bite her in half. It was a good attempt at intimidation but Matsuda Takeru needed to be more than outwardly intimidating; he needed to be invincible to the core.

Misaki hoped the icy creature was as mighty as it looked, but there was only one way find out. As the creature struck, she stood her ground. Ice met glass.

In two lightning strikes of Shadow's Daughter, Misaki shattered the serpent's head. Flipping Siradenyaa into a single-handed reverse grip, she extended her open hand to the creature's headless neck and seized control of the water inside it. Even at her strongest, she could not fight Matsuda Takeru for control of the snake's spines and scales. Ice was his undisputed domain, but Takashi had been the one with the decisively fluid energy to power the inside of the Matsuda Dragon, and Takashi was gone.

With a roar, Misaki heaved her arm back. Her jiya ripped the liquid interior from the serpent as if pulling the spinal cord from a living snake. The formation collapsed like a skeleton with no spine.

Do better. Misaki exploded through the rain of scales. *Give me more.*

TAKERU

Matsuda Takeru buckled.

He had never lost control of the dragon's armor. Even when Takashi's water moved at blinding speeds or changed direction sharply, he had been able to move with it. Following had never been difficult for him.

He had assumed that Misaki, like most fighters, would attack the dragon's invincible exterior, but she had gone for the unstable interior—for Takashi's *absence*. The emptiness shook the heart of him while the impact sent his armor scattering in all directions.

Flayed and boneless, he faced the creature he had awakened, this woman of gods' blood and fury.

Her face was flushed, strands of hair flying free of her bun, as she swept her glass sword through what remained of the dragon. Then she came at him, black eyes gleaming as bright and sharp as the obsidian. So many years, he had avoided touching this porcelain doll he had been given for fear of breaking her. He hadn't wanted to see this beautiful, strange woman crumble the way his mother had. Somehow, he had broken her anyway, but she hadn't broken quietly like porcelain. She had broken like black glass and ice—jagged and more dangerous than ever.

Takeru summoned enough willpower to pull some of the dragon's scales toward his hands to form his Whispering Blade. The reflexive cold and pressure of his jiya produced a sword hard enough that it wouldn't break against Misaki's glass weapon, but it would never cut through the Zilazen glass. He knew that with damning certainty before their blades even met again.

A true Whispering Blade required pure focus and resolve. The blades he was forming now might cut through flesh and bone. They might even cut through metal, but they were not perfect Whispering Blades. They were off by a few molecules.

The black sword slammed into Takeru's guard and he stumbled

back. He had never had any trouble focusing his jiya before. His blade had been perfect since he was a teenager. It had been perfect when he fought the Ranganese, perfect when he faced Mamoru in the dojo that day and called him weak. The irony was that Mamoru had been right—about the Empire, about the Kwangs, about the Ranganese—and Takeru had called him weak.

In the uncertainty of youth, Mamoru had been closer to true clarity than his father ever had been. Takeru had demanded that Mamoru stand and fight for his truth. Now that his wife was asking him to stand, all he could do was shatter, and shatter, and shatter.

Misaki didn't slow, didn't give a koyin of ground. Something had taken place inside the woman's body—some deep Tsusano blood magic that Takeru didn't understand—lending her inhuman strength. But strength alone couldn't move a fighter with such grace. As the tiny woman matched his steps, Takeru was forced to realize that he had spent fifteen years sleeping obliviously next to a combatant very nearly his equal in skill.

How had he never noticed? Or had he noticed and turned a blind eye to it, as he turned a blind eye to everything that unsettled him? So much of his life had been lost in the haze of snow, mist, and meditation that he didn't even know.

Sasayaiba cracked against a brutal blow of Misaki's sword. Instead of taking a moment to recover from the impact, she sped up with fresh fury, spinning into a stab. Takeru blocked and his ice broke apart, barely deflecting the obsidian sword before it could drive into his chest.

She wouldn't really kill him... would she?

He had never truly grown to know the woman who lived inside the doll, and it was hard to fight an enemy one didn't know. He attempted an offensive cut with a new Sasayaiba, only to have it break against his wife's more decisive counterstrike.

Matsuda Takeru the First had found his Whispering Blade in perfect clarity. He had studied every corner of his world, from the koro's castle to the numu's forge, from the old religion to the new, and understood it all intimately. Unlike his ancestor, Takeru had only ever found the focus to form a Whispering Blade by retreating into the obscuring white of the mountain, where he was blind to his country, his wife, even his own emotions. What sort of a man closed his eyes to the world and called it clarity?

All Takeru could see of this woman was that she was angry—and each time something cracked or shattered, she seemed to grow angrier, her movements more erratic, more ferocious, harder to read. There was pain in her fighting, coursing alongside the strength, pitching and rising like storm waves with each stroke of her sword. She was in agony, and it was his fault. He had never meant to do this to her, but with each defensive step back, he only seemed to make it worse—and he couldn't bear it. In her growl, he heard his father's bitterness, his mother's tears. Mamoru boiled from her eyes.

He had to make it stop.

He searched for an opening to grab hold of her, but she was too fast and showed no signs of tiring. If he pressed in with his imperfect Sasayaiba, her obsidian blade would take his arm off. Shifting tactics, Takeru used his physical body as a focal point for her attacks while raising the snow around her in a trap.

At the touch of his nyama, the frenzied snow rushed to answer its master. Despite the physical strength Misaki had manifested, her sense of the water around her was still dull compared to a born Matsuda's. In the spinning confusion of snow, she didn't notice the water molecules massing behind her.

Letting his blade shatter against hers, Takeru opened both hands and pulled the water toward them in a broad wave. Misaki screamed in surprise as the wave engulfed her from the shoulders down. She reacted with the speed of a trained fighter, dropping her sword to use both hands in an attempt to throw the water from her body. But Takeru was already freezing the liquid and her jiya was nothing against his. The wave froze solid, immobilizing her.

"Yield," Takeru said, covering his fatigue under a commanding tone.

Her glare pierced him—not like a blade, but like *claws* that dug in and held tight, making it impossible to pull free.

"That was underhanded, Matsuda Takeru," she hissed as they locked eyes, equally immobilized. "I would be impressed if it weren't such an obvious sign of weakness. I didn't take you for a cheater."

"You never specified terms of combat," Takeru said. It was a pitiful excuse. Few terms of combat allowed techniques that restrained the opponent. Then again, jijaka terms of combat had never been intended for duels between spouses. "I don't want to hurt you."

"*Hurt* me?" Misaki's breath, cold as it was, made steam in Takeru's sub-zero aura. She looked, if possible, more agonized than she had in the flurry of combat. "This..." Her eyes flicked down to the ice encasing her body. "*This* is how you try to ease my pain?"

"I..." Takeru had the feeling he was missing something. "I can't bring Mamoru back," he said.

"But you can be better." She glared at him again, *and merciful Nami, wouldn't those claws loosen their grip?* "You can be better than the man who couldn't save him."

"I will," Takeru promised. "I'm not going to hurt you again."

"If you don't want to hurt me, you will face me like a real fighter," Misaki's teeth ground together in a snarl, "with respect."

Takeru was used to other theonites' nyama falling still once they were encased in his ice. Unable to move their limbs, most had trouble using their powers to affect the world around them. But Misaki's power was not around her; it was *inside,* lending her little body godlike strength as it strained against its prison. Her pain screeched against him like claws on stone and he struggled not to cringe.

"This fight is over, woman," he insisted as though speaking the words aloud could make them true. "You have no weapon. Yield."

"I won't. I can't. You haven't accepted my challenge yet."

"I have—"

"You haven't fought me like a Matsuda."

Her body heaved against the ice—and *cracked* it.

The break sent a jolt through Takeru's soul. He was a little boy, curled up on his side, shaking with the aftershocks of his father's fists, unable to understand where his mother had gone, why she had left, why his father hated him so much. Tou-sama had stomped on him twice, leaving a heel-sized bruise on his cheek and a lance of pain in his ribs.

Knowing he would not be able to stand, he rolled onto his side and crawled. He was distantly aware that his brother must have stepped in to protect him, which meant that Takashi was probably hurt worse than he was. It wasn't a comforting thought. Guilt wound itself in with the confusion and broken blood vessels, creating a new, worse kind of pain.

He knew that if he lay still and listened, he would hear Takashi crying, feel his brother's pain answering his own like an echo. So instead of listening, Takeru crawled faster, fingernails scratching across the tatami in desperation. Hand over hand, he dragged himself forward until he reached the deck overlooking the snow-covered courtyard. Hauling himself to the edge, he rolled over it, into the white embrace below.

He landed hard on his side, probably adding to the bruises, but everything was alright now. The moment he hit the ground, the snow rushed to cradle him like his mother's arms, and he was safe. Spreading his fingers out in the whiteness, Takeru let everything flow to the mountain. The pain dispersed into a thousand snowflakes, then ten thousand, thinning like mist to the morning.

For his whole life, Takeru had been certain that he was right to cast his pain off on the mountain, that it was the only way—because how could one possibly hold so much suffering in something as small as a human form?

Yet here was this this woman who held everything inside a little body of flesh and blood without breaking. It was as though all that pain had compressed in her small figure like the molecules of a Whispering Blade or thousand-fold steel beaten to a blade in the forge. She had taken every drop of hardship like a stroke of the hammer, turning it to strength, and she was stronger than Takeru. She was breaking him.

"Stop," he commanded, but she continued to struggle.

The splitting ice screamed with Takashi's voice, with Mamoru's, everything he had tried so hard to push away. He held his open hand ineffectually before him.

"Stop!" He bellowed, his voice no longer commanding. Begging. "Stop! Stop!"

One of Misaki's hands burst free. The ice had left scratches on her arms, red over the white scars from her fight with the fonyakalu. Crashing out of her restraints, she raced forward. She had no weapon, but she came at him anyway.

In that moment of awe, Takeru realized how much he owed this woman, who had borne his children, who had fought, and fought, and fought for a family she had never asked for. She had given him her life and demanded nothing in return. Mamoru hadn't inherited his strength from his father. It had come from her.

Perhaps she was stronger than he was. Perhaps it was impossible for him to overcome this woman who seemed to carry the force of an army inside her. But she was right. A Matsuda didn't balk before the impossible.

Takeru extended his jiya to form a blade, but Misaki was ahead of him. She tore the sheath from her hip and slammed it into Takeru's face. The sheath must have been made of the same Zilazen glass as her blade because it hit harder than any ice or metal Takeru had ever encountered.

As he reeled, she threw a kick into his stomach. It had been decades since someone had struck him hard enough to knock him down, but in Misaki's monstrously powerful state, her foot slammed the breath from his body and sent him tumbling through the snow.

When he uncurled onto his hands and knees, Misaki stood before him, breathing hard, her hair flying freely in the wind. She had retrieved her sword, though the sheath was still clutched in her left hand like a second blade. Through the knives of pain in his ribs, Takeru recognized a stance similar to Takashi's and wondered where she had learned to dual wield... Where had she found so much strength? No one had hit him this hard since his father.

The snow pulled at Takeru, offering tenderly to take the pain away. His fingers spread out in its beckoning cold, ready to oblige—but Misaki was still looking at him with expectation in her eyes. That gaze clutched him like claws—or a pair of arms—holding him.

So, instead of giving himself to the snow, Takeru dug his hands into it hard. His fist tightened and the snow rushed up to him. In an agonizing surge, it seemed to give back everything he had sent out into it over forty years: his brother's bruises, his mother's screams of impotent anger, his nineteen-year-old bride, holding her face in her hands as she fought to stifle her sobs, his father holding a bamboo rod and cracking it down on him.

The stick hit his ear and became the crash of bombs on Takayubi's slopes. It hit his back and became Kotetsu Atsushi's fists as he begged Takeru to go back for his father—*"Please! Matsuda-dono! Please!"* It hit his arm and became Misaki's Blood Needle. It hit his knuckles and he felt them crash into Mamoru's teeth, bloodying the boy's mouth.

Hold the line, he had said as his son looked at him in fear.

And Mamoru had. He had protected Takayubi with everything he had.

Now it was Takeru's turn.

Clutching the truth of his life in his hands, he stood.

Misaki was rushing toward him now, the final, most important part of his life bearing down on him. And he saw them both for what they were: a woman who needed her husband, and a man who needed his wife.

That clarity sharpened to an edge.

The Whispering Blade met Misaki's obsidian sheath and sheared through it. Her eyes went wide, and she smiled—Gods in the Deep, she *smiled*—a raw, open smile, and it was the most beautiful thing in all the Duna.

Her sword hit the broad side of Takeru's Whispering Blade, knocking it off course, but this time, the ice didn't shatter. It didn't even crack.

Discarding the sliced-off half of her sheath, Misaki attacked Takeru with new energy. For the first time, they met each other—not a frozen mountain and a doll, but living flesh, a man and a woman. Misaki's smile grew. She had what she needed from him.

But in his new clarity, Takeru realized that there was one more thing he needed from her—as a man. She spun in to cut at his neck and he lowered his arm.

MISAKI

Misaki threw her entire body into the attack, knowing the Whispering Blade would be there to meet her, ready to smash through it or break in the effort.

The impact didn't come.

Panic jolted through her fighter's high. Even in her state of heightened reflexes, she barely managed to jerk to a stop before her blade sheared Takeru's head from his shoulders. The black glass bit into his neck, and the world spun to a halt, the snow itself seeming to pause in shock.

Misaki stood there, breathless, heart hammering, as two drops of blood beaded on Takeru's neck. Two drops. She hadn't killed him. But it had been a close thing.

Why? She thought furiously. *Why didn't he block?*

He should have had time to counter, so why hadn't he? Had he been trying to *trick her* into killing him? Had he been *testing* her?

But when she looked into her husband's face, his expression wasn't smug or knowing. It was openly surprised. Then, as she watched, that surprise melted into something softer than triumph.

Relief.

They looked at each other, chests heaving with exertion, Siradenyaa still resting at his neck. Then the Whispering Blade turned to snow, fluttering down to rest at their feet. Takeru's fingers touched her sword hand.

"I accept," he said and for once, his voice was full—overflowing with gratitude, and strength, and the determined bite of winter.

And Misaki somehow understood why he had given her that last opening. If she truly wanted to kill him, then he was alone. He was willing to stand and fight, but he would rather die than do it alone. It wasn't just the challenge of responsibility he was accepting as his hand touched hers; he was accepting *her*.

Cool fingers ran over Misaki's sword hand, over her sleeve to brush the hair back from her face. In the falling snow, Takeru stared at the woman he had married and saw her for the first time.

"I accept."

28

THE STRANGER

Takayubi legend said that a Matsuda had never walked away from a duel without first spilling his opponent's blood on the ground. Takeru and Misaki broke that tradition that day.

She caught the drops of blood before they could fall and placed a gentle hand over the cut on his neck. He didn't push the hand away, even as her jiya tugged at his open wound, knitting the liquid into a scab.

"You're stronger than I thought," Takeru said.

Misaki made a dismissive noise in her throat. "It was a fluke. I've been in far better shape."

"I wasn't talking about your swordplay. I always knew about that."

Misaki blinked in surprise, snow fluttering from her eyelashes. "You did?" Then she sighed. "I suppose I underestimated your powers of perception."

"No. Your father mentioned it when he first described you to us."

"You never said anything." Misaki paused. "Why didn't you say anything?"

"I don't know..." That thoughtful crease appeared between Takeru's eyebrows. "I'm sorry, I never asked."

"I never offered." Instead, she had boarded her real self up behind a stiff façade, hoping that somehow she could turn herself into something else. "I'm sorry." Misaki rubbed her open palm over Takeru's neck one last time before letting it trail down to rest against his chest. The cut had scabbed over, stopping the bleeding.

"Thank you," Takeru said, "for offering now."

He lifted his hand to touch the cut on his neck—not the one Misaki had just scabbed over but the one Mamoru's ghost had left during that last nightmare.

"I think I should stay a while," he said, "and say goodbye to my brother and son."

Misaki nodded. "Of course." But she found that the thought of leaving Takeru alone on the mountainside upset her. He had spent too long alone in the snow, hadn't he? Meditating the humanity out of himself, sinking deeper into a refuge that was now stained with his family's blood.

"Would it be alright if I stayed with you, Takeru-sama?" she asked softly.

Takeru was quiet for a moment. Then he nodded. "Please."

. . . .

The sky was darkening by the time the two stood to make their way back home. Misaki had frozen the two pieces of Siradenyaa's sheath together to hold the blade. It was cold enough that the ice would stay strong, but eventually, she would need a new sheath.

"I asked Setsuko to watch the boys while we were gone," Misaki said. "I told her I might be a while, but I hope she hasn't gotten worried."

"I think she has," Takeru said. "She seems to have sent someone to find us."

"What?"

"Someone is coming down the mountain toward us." Takeru cocked his head as though listening. "Two people."

"We should go to meet them," Misaki said, brushing the snow from her knees, "let them know we haven't vanished." It was bizarre how she still didn't feel any physical pain, even after fighting and then sitting with her legs folded beneath her for so long.

They had barely started up the southern pass when Misaki's eyes landed on a figure carefully shuffling down the mountain toward them. Kwang Chul-hee had gotten better at keeping his footing on Takayubi's slopes, but he still made his way around more slowly than the native villagers.

"Oh!" the boy said when he caught sight of Misaki and Takeru through the falling snow. "It's you."

"Kwang," Takeru said, effortlessly covering the distance to the stumbling boy with his smooth stride. "What are you doing here?"

"Setsuko-sama said you had both been gone a long time and she was getting worried. She asked if I would go looking for you."

"We are well and on our way back, as you can see," Takeru said, though Misaki noticed Chul-hee's eyes brush uneasily over the fresh cuts on Takeru's neck.

"Alright. I—" Chul-hee stopped short. His eyes had fallen on the sword at Misaki's hip. "What is that?"

"That is my wife's business," Takeru said a little sharply. "As a lady of a noble house, she can bear a sword if she—"

"No, I've seen women with swords before," Chul-hee clarified, "just not swords like *that*. Matsuda Misaki-dono-sama..." he fumbled his Shirojima honorifics in his excitement. "Is that what I think it is?"

Misaki glanced down at Siradenyaa. "You have a good eye."

"You mean... that's..."

"Zilazen glass?" Misaki said. "Yes."

"You're joking!" Chul-hee exclaimed, slipping into his native Kaigengua in his disbelief. *"Kotetsu said there were no Zilazen katana!"*

"Do you want to see for yourself?" she suggested in Kaigengua.

Chul-hee looked breathless. *"Could I?"*

With a smile, Misaki untied Siradenyaa and handed the sheathed weapon to Chul-hee. He bowed, accepting it with both hands.

"Careful," she warned as he gripped the handle and slid it

partway out of the sheath. *"It's sharper than most swords, but it doesn't rust, so you can touch the flat without worrying about leaving finger oils."*

"Oh," Chul-hee said as he turned the blade over. *"And the sheath must be Zilazen glass too?"*

"Um..." Misaki hesitated but realized that it would be hard to lie to the boy while he was holding the sheath in his hands. "Yes, on the inside."

"So, what happened to it?" Chul-hee asked, resting his fingertips on the ice Misaki had used to repair the sheath. He might not be a Takayubi warrior, but he was still a competent jijaka; he could almost certainly feel that the sheath had been severed.

She glanced at Takeru. *"Unfortunately, it got damaged,"* she said.

Chul-hee's fingers were still resting over the ice on the sheath, his brow creased in confusion. *"It feels like it was cut in two."*

"Isn't that interesting." Misaki smiled, taking the sword from him and sliding it back into the belt of her hakama.

"But it's cut!" Chul-hee said in confusion. *"Nothing can cut Zilazen..."* he trailed off, looking up at Takeru. His eyes flicked again to the cuts on Takeru's neck, then to Misaki's disheveled hair and clothing, and back to Takeru. His mouth worked soundlessly for a moment, but all the questions on his tongue were undoubtedly inappropriate to voice.

"We should get back to the village." Takeru motioned Chul-hee and Misaki after him and they continued up the mountain. "Let's find the other one and head back."

"Other one?" Chul-hee repeated.

"There were two of you who came down the mountain to look for us, were there not?"

Chul-hee shook his head. "I came alone."

"No..." Takeru stopped in his tracks, suddenly wary. "There was someone behind you."

"Are you sure, Takeru-sama?" Misaki asked. Sometimes an exhaustive use of jiya like a fight affected a theonite's senses.

"Maybe..."

Her words trailed off as movement caught her attention on the path ahead. A figure stood blocking their way, Matsuda blue kimono blowing gently in the wind, a teal-wrapped sword at his hip.

Mamoru.

Misaki screamed, her hands flying to her mouth. Terrified that something had made her start hallucinating, she looked to Takeru and Chul-hee, but they were also frozen where they stood, disbelieving eyes fixed on the apparition.

"H-h-how?" Chul-hee stuttered, shaking. "Why is he here?"

Mamoru drew his katana—and that was the giveaway. Just for a moment, brightness flickered across him, like dappled light across a forest floor. Misaki had seen bright ripples like that before and knew exactly what they meant.

That was not Mamoru, nor was it his ghost.

As the imitation Mamoru came at them, Takeru took an uncertain step back, an arm out to shield the other two. But Misaki stepped forward, gathering her jiya into an ice spear. Even knowing it wasn't really him, she couldn't shoot ice directly into her son's heart. She couldn't kill his image.

Chul-hee let out a cry of alarm as she fired her projectile. The ice struck the pretender in the shoulder, knocking him backward and shattering the illusion. Freckles scattered across Mamoru's cheeks, black hair turned brown and the blue kimono turned into a flapping gray cloak. The katana spun out of his hand and hit the snow as a long Hadean-style knife.

Even in his shock, Takeru reacted prudently, raising ice to freeze the stranger's arms and legs in place where he lay.

"What *is* that thing?" he demanded, more shaken than Misaki had ever seen him. He would be, having never met Elleen Elden. "Some kind of demon?"

"That's no demon." Misaki was striding toward the fallen creature. "It's a littigi."

"A what?"

"A type of sub-theonite," Misaki explained as she came to stand over the man. "They look like powerless adyns but they have the ability to manipulate light to create illusions. I knew a few in Carytha." But what the Hell was one of them doing here?

The man glared silently up at Misaki, but they both knew there was nothing he could do against her now. Littigiwu like himself were dangerous only in what they could make a person see; he would not have the physical strength to break himself out of Takeru's ice. An intense flash of light might leave Misaki temporarily blind, but she fought better without the use of her eyes anyway.

Secure in her safety, Misaki took a moment to survey the man. He appeared to be in his twenties or thirties—she had always found it difficult to place white people's ages—with dull green eyes and brown hair cut in a short Hadean style. The lines of a tattoo made a strange, swirling pattern through his smattering of brown freckles. She searched her memory for someone like this man, but she couldn't recall ever encountering a green-eyed littigi, let alone one with such strange tattoos. Even the tattoo ink was unlike anything Misaki had ever seen—shiny and metallic.

With a sweep of her hand, Misaki cleared the snow that had fallen on his face, just to be sure she wasn't imagining the silvery glint. He had something in his skin. It looked like metal threaded through his tattoos but when Misaki reached out with her jiya, the shining substance felt almost like liquid.

"You're very skilled," she said. That replication of Mamoru had been on par with one of Elleen's illusions. Nearly perfect. "Who are you?"

Takeru, who had most likely never seen a white person, approached more cautiously, Chul-hee trailing just behind him.

"It's alright, Takeru-sama," Misaki said. "He's just a human, like you or me—only weaker. Watch."

Putting a tabi to the man's arm, she applied a bit of pressure, and the bone snapped. The white man's body went rigid and his face contorted, but he didn't cry out. The only noise he made was a valiantly smothered grunt. Misaki raised her eyebrows. That sort of ironclad composure spoke of intense training, though she could feel his heart pounding rapidly in distress.

"Alright, I don't know how good your Shirojima Dialect is, so let's try Yammaninke," Misaki said. *"Who are you and who sent you here?"*

Normally, she wouldn't have taken any pleasure in torturing someone weaker than herself, even one who had tried to kill her. But this man had stolen her son's face. She would happily break every bone in his body.

"Don't speak Yammaninke, you piece of xuro? That's fine." She switched languages again. *"I speak Lindish too. Now, talk to me. Who are you? Did you come here from Carytha?"*

Robin had always worried about his old enemies pursuing him, but Misaki had never personally made many enemies in Livingston. Sure, she had sliced quite a few people, but that had mostly been as backup to Robin and Elleen. Most people thought of Firebird and didn't recall his Shadow.

The hooded gray cloak immediately brought to mind Kalleyso and his followers, but for all Kalleyso's bizarre and horrific gimmicks, Misaki had never known the gang lord to give his followers facial tattoos. Maybe that was a new practice? Or maybe the markings were some sort of native Hadean adornment that had nothing to do with the man's other affiliations?

"Is this about Livingston?" She ground her foot down, extracting another pained grunt from the supine littigi. *"Had a run in with Sirawu fifteen or sixteen years ago? You don't look like you're missing any appendages... though I'm happy to fix that for you."*

"Do you recognize him?" Takeru asked, unable to understand Misaki's Lindish.

"No, Takeru-sama. Do you?"

Takeru shook his head and then turned to Chul-hee. "Kwang?"

"D-don't look at me, Matsuda-dono," Chul-hee stammered. "I've never even met a littigi before."

"Well, this one must have been here for some time, spying." Misaki narrowed her eyes at the restrained intruder.

"What do you mean?"

"Littigiwu aren't magic. They have photographic memories, but they can't just pull faces out of the ether. They can only reproduce what they have observed, which means..."

"This man watched Mamoru when he was alive," Takeru said in quiet horror, "*weeks* ago. Why?"

"That's what he's going to tell us." Misaki looked down at the foreigner and switched back to Yammaninke, the language an international spy was most likely to understand. *"Isn't that right, littigi? You're going to tell us everything we want to know while you still have four limbs and a tongue."*

"Oh," Chul-hee said warily. "M-Matsuda-dono, I'm pretty sure that's against the international codes of—"

"Good thing those only apply to military operatives," Misaki said. "I'm a civilian."

"But—"

"Quiet, Kwang," Takeru ordered shortly.

"So?" Misaki prompted, glaring down at the littigi. *"Do you want to talk or do you want me to cut you?"*

Light flickered. The man's hair turned black and for a moment, Mamoru's face overlaid his, a pleading expression in his eyes. Agony lanced through Misaki and she stomped down hard. Her heel broke through the man's femur and his cruel illusion in a single crunch.

This time he *did* scream.

"No, no," she said sweetly as Chul-hee cringed. *"You don't want to waste your concentration on manipulative illusions right now. No, you're going to want to concentrate very hard on telling me what I want to know before this gets* really *unpleasant."*

The man set his jaw, agonized breaths coming fast through clenched teeth. His heart was racing, but he didn't answer.

"Now, don't be like that." Misaki drew Siradenyaa and Chul-hee covered his eyes. *"If you won't talk to me, you can't tell me which body parts you'd rather part with first. I'll just have to guess..."*

The man *did* speak then—in the most bizarrely accented

Yammaninke Misaki had ever heard.

"Voice activation."

Misaki's heart dropped. "Get back!" she cried.

"Detonate."

The reflexive ice wall Misaki formed between herself and the littigi never would have held against the blast, nor would her legs have propelled her far enough to escape. But Takeru's jiya surged up alongside hers, tripling the size of the wall and an arm around her waist swept her back. They crashed to the snow together as the explosion shook the mountain.

When the ringing in Misaki's ears faded enough that she could think straight, she lifted herself up onto her elbows and shook her head. Her back bumped into something colder than the snow beneath her and she realized that she was under Takeru's arm. He had braced his body just above hers to protect her from the falling debris.

"Are you alright?" she asked, her voice sounding warped and distant.

Takeru responded with something that sounded affirmative. Under his other arm, Chul-hee was groaning, his hands over his head. Worried that the boy was injured, Misaki reached out with her jiya to see if she could sense any bleeding.

"He's fine," Takeru said in exasperation, just as Chul-hee's groans solidified into words the words *'So loud!'*

Leaving Chul-hee curled up on the ground, Takeru stood and helped Misaki to her feet.

"What in all the realms was that?" Misaki asked, turning back to where the littigi had lain in the snow.

"I was hoping you might tell me."

Nothing remained of the man except a crater and a few shreds of flesh and gray fabric flung across the mountainside.

Misaki shook her head. "I've never encountered anyone like him. Other littigiwu, yes. Other people in gray cloaks, yes, but never anyone with tattoos or an accent like his." She went to retrieve Siradenyaa where it had stuck in the snow after flying from her hand.

"Were you really going to cut him?" Takeru asked, pulling a shaking Chul-hee to his feet.

"Only if he kept being uncooperative," Misaki said and carefully returned her sword to its sheath.

There was a pause.

"You enjoyed that." It wasn't a judgment; Takeru just seemed to be making an observation.

Misaki shrugged. "This is the sort of thing I used to do with my friends back in Livingston."

"At school?" Takeru looked confused.

"Well, *after* school," Misaki said, "at night. We didn't get much sleep."

"Matsuda-dono!" a voice called and Misaki and Takeru looked up to find Kazu's men and some of the Ameno koronu running down the slope toward them.

"We heard a sound like a bomb. What happened?"

"There has been an attempt on our lives," Takeru said as the men came to a stop at the site of the explosion. "My wife's and my own."

"What?"

Calmly, Takeru told the men what had happened, which of course sounded ridiculous.

"So, you think it was an assassin?" one of the Ameno koronu asked.

"It was *definitely* an assassin," Misaki said.

A littigi didn't put himself up against two powerful theonites unless he had a plan to end the fight quickly. This one had most likely hoped that his illusion of Mamoru would immobilize his targets for the moment he needed to kill them with that knife of his, which might have allowed him to escape with his life. The bomb had been his backup plan.

"Who do you think sent him?" one of Kazu's men asked. "The Ranganese, or..." he couldn't say it aloud, but everyone was thinking it: the Empire.

"This man was not from Namindugu," Takeru said. "He was white."

"There are white people who live in Namindugu, in the Ranganese Union," Chul-hee pointed out. It was something most Dunians didn't even know.

"Really?" Hakuyu said in surprise.

"They live far in the west," Misaki said, "near the border with Hades. They have their origins in a Hadean tribe called the Malikovish, but politically, they count as part of the Ranganese Union. I've never heard of any littigiwu among them, but it's possible."

Then again, it was equally possible for an organization to hire a foreign assassin to throw someone off their trail. But if the man *had* been sent by the Ranganese...

"Who is with my family?" Takeru voiced the question that had just leaped to the forefront of Misaki's mind.

"Your sister-in-law is with the children," the head Ameno said. "I have a few of my men helping work on the house. They should be safe."

Misaki was already running up the slope.

"Stay on the alert," Takeru told the men. "Report back to the village as soon as you've investigated to your satisfaction." And he was running alongside her.

Everything seemed normal when they reached the village, and they shared a breath of relief to find Setsuko and all the children safe in the Matsuda courtyard. Setsuko stood and rushed to meet them immediately.

"Is everything alright?" she asked urgently. "We heard a sound like an explosion and—Takeru—Matsuda-sama, you're injured!"

"We're fine," Takeru said. "Ameno-san," he addressed one of the men working on the house, a volunteer named Ameno Kentaro. "Run to the rest of the houses. Tell everyone to check that every person in their household is safe and accounted for. Have each volunteer leader do the same with his group. If anyone has spotted a suspicious person, have them report here immediately."

"What—"

"There will be time to ask questions later," Takeru cut him off. "Go!"

"Yes, Matsuda-dono." The man set down the beam he had been lifting and ran.

"What is going on?" Setsuko asked as Misaki took Izumo from her sister-in-law and bounced him gently on her hip.

"There was an attempt on our lives," Takeru said as Hiroshi and Nagasa gathered near the adults to listen curiously. "Neither of us is seriously hurt but we need to confirm that no one else in the village has been targeted."

"What? Who tried to kill you?" Setsuko asked.

"The details are unimportant for the time being," Takeru said. "For now, I'm just relieved that my family is safe."

Misaki would have expected Setsuko to ask more questions, but the other woman had stopped, staring at Takeru. Evidently, she had noticed the change in him, the way his voice carried a modicum of emotion. Her expression of confusion turned to one of shock when Takeru stooped and picked up Nagasa.

To Misaki's memory, Takeru had never held one of his children. Nagasa himself looked disoriented at suddenly finding himself so far from the ground.

"I've just been to see your brother, Nagasa-kun," Takeru said.

"Mamoru?" Nagasa said in a small voice.

"Yes."

Nagasa still looked profoundly confused. "Tou-sama... see Mamoru?"

"I did."

"Where is he?" Nagasa asked, his hands clutching his father's shoulder. "Where is Mamoru?"

"He's in the Laaxara now," Takeru said. "He promised that he wouldn't come to bother you anymore. He wants his little brother to be able to sleep."

"I can sleep?" It wasn't clear if Nagasa completely grasped his father's meaning, but the words seemed to calm him.

"You can sleep," Takeru said and placed Nagasa back on his feet. "He also wanted me to remind you one other thing." He took Nagasa's little chin between his thumb and forefinger. "A warrior doesn't cry."

Nagasa nodded.

"Mamoru doesn't want you to cry." Takeru rested a hand on Nagasa's head, ruffling the boy's hair before turning to his second son.

"Hiroshi..."

"Yes, Tou-sama?"

Takeru studied his secondborn for a moment, the little boy who stood with enough tension in his shoulders to break an adult. He didn't take Hiroshi into his arms—even as a little baby, Hiroshi had never much liked being held—but he knelt down to his eye level.

"I refused to teach Mamoru when he was your age. Did you know that?"

"No, Tou-sama."

"I regret that now," Takeru said evenly. "He was powerful, like only a Matsuda can be, and he needed a Matsuda to train him. You are the same, aren't you?"

Hiroshi stared at his father for a moment and then, as if a terrible pain were bleeding out of him, breathed, "Yes, Tou-sama."

"I can teach you to control this." Takeru put his fingertips to Hiroshi's chest. "This cold power that seems too big for your body. I can train you to control it and use it if you are ready. Your brother, Mamoru, your Uncle Takashi, and myself—we did not get proper training as small children. You are strong as we were, but I will make you stronger, if you are ready to learn from me. I will make you the strongest Matsuda who ever lived. Are you ready, Matsuda Hiroshi?"

"Yes, Tou-sama."

"Then I will see you in the dojo tomorrow morning before the sun rises."

Misaki watched in astonishment as the tension melted from Hiroshi's shoulders. He still stood unnaturally straight for such a young boy, but he no longer looked like something in him might snap.

"Great Nagi, Misaki," Setsuko whispered in Misaki's ear, her eyes wide. "What did you do to that man?"

"It's hard to explain," Misaki said with a smile.

Setsuko's eyes passed over Misaki's tangled hair, her borrowed hakama, and the black sword at her hip. If she was able to infer what had happened, she didn't pry. Instead, she lifted a hand and poked a finger into Misaki's cheek—into her dimple.

"Welcome back, pretty girl."

The men who had responded to the explosion returned shortly after. If they had thought that Takeru's story was crazy, their doubt had disappeared as they discovered the bloody chunks of the littigi scattered across the mountainside, and they were now eager to hear the story recounted in more detail.

However, before Takeru could respond to their barrage of questions, Ameno Kentaro came scrambling back into the courtyard.

"Matsuda-dono!" he said and Misaki could see on his face that something was wrong.

"What is it?"

"We're missing someone."

"What? Who?"

"A child," the man said, "a five-year-old girl named Ginkawa Yukimi."

Yukimi was one of the children orphaned in the Ranganese attack. Her young father and younger uncles had died trying to hold the northern pass. Her mother, one of Yukino Dai's cousins, had been hit by one of the bombs during the airstrike.

"Have everyone search their dwelling," Takeru said. "Mobilize the men to fan out and search the mountain—only the men," he added, "and only fighters. Blacksmiths, monks, and women are to remain in or near their own homes until we have confirmed that our assassin has no allies lurking on this mountain."

"What about the girl's parents?" one of the newer volunteers asked. "Where are they?"

"She has no parents," Takeru said, "but she is family to all of us. Ginkawa Yukimi's father died defending this village. Her mother was one of Lightning Dai's cousins, from the same branch of the Yukino family as my own mother. This child is our blood. She belongs to all of us, and it is our responsibility to find her safe."

"Do you think she was taken by the same person who set off the bomb?" one of the Ameno men asked. "Or do you think he had associates who took her?"

"I can't say." Takeru glanced for a moment toward Misaki, possibly thinking that she might have some idea, but she was as lost as he was.

What if the bomber *hadn't* come alone? What if there were more littigiwu? She had a sudden, sickening image of a stranger putting on the face of Ginkawa Yukimi's mother or father. If the tattooed man had watched and memorized Mamoru's features, he had almost certainly done the same to other residents of Takayubi. Takeru and Misaki had nearly fallen for their attacker's illusion; a traumatized five-year-old wouldn't stand a chance.

"The person my wife and I encountered earlier used illusions to take the form of our son," Takeru said. "My wife has experience with his type of sub-theonite. She will explain how to see through one of these illusions."

Misaki told the men to watch for flickering or ripples of light, like those on the surface of water. "Be wary of anyone who doesn't speak," she added. "Littigiwu can't imitate voices. As long as members of your search parties exchange words every time you cross paths, you should all be fine."

As the men scrambled to organize a search, Takeru sent Setsuko to gather the women and children so that he could conduct a second count and Misaki could instruct all of them on seeing through a littigi's illusions.

When all the men were gone, Takeru knelt outside the Matsuda compound and put his palms to the snow.

"What are you doing?" one of the women asked.

Takeru closed his eyes. "I'm going to find Ginkawa Yukimi."

He stayed there, perfectly still, for nearly a waati, leaving Misaki to try to explain to confused villagers and volunteers what he was doing. Some of them looked skeptical, but none of them were willing to question Takeru's abilities, however bizarre they might seem. When his eyes finally opened, he was frowning.

"Call the men back," he said quietly.

"What? Why Matsuda-dono?"

"The intruders are no longer on the mountain, and neither is Ginkawa Yukimi."

"What do you mean? Is she dead?"

Takeru shook his head. "I didn't sense any bodies in the snow or in the lake, and if she was exposed—up on rocks—our scouts would have found her. She is no longer on the mountain."

"So, someone just took her away?" one of the women asked, clutching her own little girl closer to her chest. "Why would anyone do that?"

Theories raced like flurries through the village through the rest of the evening. In the past week, the people of Takayubi had begun consolidating their food supplies in the wrecked remains of what had once been the Matsuda sitting room. Come spring, the half-room would not be structurally sound enough for occupation, but for the moment, Takeru's ice reinforcements made it a decent cafeteria, with the icier half serving as a refrigeration unit while the wooden half, open to the rest of the village, became a cooking area.

Every night, Misaki would gather a handful of women and they would cook together in a few large pots. With no electricity to run a grill or the single remaining rice cooker, it was more efficient to prepare the food for the whole village at once. Tonight an unprecedented number of women showed up to help with dinner, nearly half the women in Takayubi. Some came to talk. Some came for companionship. All made their hands busy helping.

"Do you think this is the government's way of trying to intimidate us?" Mayumi asked, passing Misaki the ladle she had asked for.

"First, it's dangerous to say things like that," Misaki said. "You want to be careful about who hears you. And second, I really doubt it."

"But Matsuda-dono, you were the one who suggested that the Emperor might send assassins—"

"I know," Misaki said, "but there are certain tactics a tyrannical government uses to intimidate its subjects. For one thing, they like to make themselves known for what they are—soldiers in uniform, not foreigners in weird costumes. I also think that if this was an attempt at intimidation, the kidnappers would have taken a child with living parents. That's what..." That was what the Yammankalu used to do to the Native Baxarians to keep them in line, but Misaki decided that she had spoken enough treason against the Empire without dragging their closest allies through the mud as well.

She shook her head. "If they wanted to maximize the psychological impact, they wouldn't have chosen an orphan."

"But she wasn't just any orphan," Fuyuhi protested, looking wounded. "She was a child of Takayubi, our blood. It's as your husband said: she belonged to all of us."

"But the government wouldn't understand that," Misaki said. She paused, midway through stirring the soup, a handful of spices poised above the bubbles. With the heat from the boiling water rushing over her skin, she remembered something Robin had said to her a long time ago, on that rooftop, when she had questioned whether the North Enders of Livingston were worth saving.

Everyone in this part of town has been oppressed or abandoned by theonite powers the rest of the world depends on. But they don't give up. Instead, they've made a life and a culture here for themselves. It's not perfect, but it's worth protecting, even if the ruling theonites, and the politicians, and the police have all decided otherwise.

She had never expected to understand that part of Robin, never thought those words would make so much sense to her.

"Matsuda-dono?" Fuyuhi said. "Are you alright?"

"Fine." Misaki opened her hand, dropping the spices into the soup. "Just remembering something..." She shook her head. "It doesn't matter. The point is, you saw what Colonel Song and his men were like. The way our village works, the way we care for each other, is something they wouldn't understand. This just doesn't have the hallmarks of a government trying to scare its people into obedience."

"Then do you think it's the Ranganese?" Fuyuko asked.

"I don't know," Misaki said, "and I really don't know why you ladies expect me to have all these answers. You know I'm a housewife, not a spy, right?"

Fuyuko shrugged. "You talk like one sometimes."

"And a lot of the time, you're right," Hyori said.

Misaki shook her head. "My husband and the other men will keep doing everything in their power to find out. In the meantime, all we can do is keep each other safe."

Yukimi's disappearance had the effect of making the village pull closer together. In another town, a missing orphan might have gone unnoticed, but this was Takayubi, and the loss reverberated through every parent and every home. Kotetsu Katashi and his children fashioned a set of standing torches, which the koronu then placed throughout the village to keep the space illuminated through the night, hopefully discouraging intruders. Mizumaki Fuyuko and two volunteers moved into the orphanage to make sure there were extra eyes on the children, a pair of Ameno men climbed to the Kumono temple to guard the monks who had taken up residence there, and sleep schedules were rearranged to ensure that at least three people were on watch at different stations throughout the village at all times. Except for the few men Takeru sent to inquire after Yukimi in the nearest fishing towns, everyone—residents and volunteers alike—stayed in or near the village.

Misaki had not known Ginkawa Yukimi or her parents, but she still felt an ache for the little girl as she put her own children to bed. Everyone in the village felt it—like the failure belonged to all of them.

When Misaki slid open the door to the bedroom, she found Takeru kneeling on the tatami, his back to her.

"Sorry," she whispered, recognizing the stillness of meditation. "I didn't mean to disturb you."

"It's alright," he said. "She's gone." He shook his head and turned to Misaki, his face looking hollow and tired in the lantern light. "There's no point."

"You've kept trying to find her this whole time?"

"I promised you that I would keep all of us safe."

"You did everything you could," Misaki said softly. "No one could have predicted this."

Kneeling before the wooden plank that now served as her dressing table, Misaki pulled the pins from her hair and let it down over her shoulders.

"So, you haven't had any ideas about what might have happened?" Takeru asked as she ran her fingers back through her hair, easing the tension from her scalp.

She shook her head. "I'm sorry, Takeru-sama."

"Who is Kalleyso?"

That question made Misaki pause, her fingers still in her hair. "Sorry?"

"You asked the littigi about someone called Kalleyso," Takeru said. "The name sounds familiar."

"You probably heard it on the TV at some point. He's a Livingston crime lord. He was well known in Carytha when I was— when I was a teenager. His followers wore gray robes, but they never had facial tattoos... or voice-activated bombs."

"But you thought to ask about him almost immediately," Takeru said. "What business would a local crime lord from the other side of the world have with Takayubi?"

"Well, it's possible that it's not Takayubi he has business with." Misaki's fingers slid to the end of her hair to fiddle with a knot there. "It's me."

"Why?" Takeru asked. "What is your relationship to this crime lord?"

Gathering a breath, Misaki turned from her makeshift dressing table to face her husband. "I spent my final year at Daybreak

Academy fighting him."

"What?"

"Well—not directly fighting," she amended, fingers working at the knot in her hair. "I think we only had the one physical confrontation. Mostly, my school friends and I fought his followers and tried to prevent him from overrunning Livingston's other gangs."

Takeru blinked at her with the blank look of a man absolutely oversaturated with new experiences for the day. He had been assaulted by his own subconscious, his wife, an illusionist, and a bomb all within the past twenty waatinu—that was to say nothing of all the talking he had done, which had to be taxing for a person who was most comfortable in the silence of his study or dojo. He was probably at the end of strange things he could absorb.

"It's probably not important," Misaki sighed. "Kalleyso was the first suspect who came to mind when I saw the gray cloak, but the rest doesn't add up. Sekhmet—Kalleyso—shouldn't even know my real identity. The only time we fought, we were both masked."

"You fought this person?"

"Not very successfully. He threw me off a building."

"You were... a crime-fighter?" Takeru said.

"Assistant crime-fighter," Misaki said. "My friends did most of the work."

"Your friends."

"Yes. Um… you've met one of them actually." Misaki looked into her lap, not meeting Takeru's eyes.

"The boy who came here for you," Takeru said. "Robin Thundyil."

Misaki winced. "Yes." Her shoulders tensed but Takeru didn't comment further on Robin.

"I thought you had just trained in the sword with your father," he said instead. "I didn't realize your practical experience went so far."

"Of course, you didn't," Misaki said, too tired to hide her annoyance but also too tired to muster genuine anger. "You told me never to speak about my time at Daybreak Academy."

"Ah, yes. I think… given the circumstances, we might revisit that order."

"Why did you do that?" she asked before she could stop herself. She wasn't sure if she was pushing her luck. She was unfamiliar with this new Takeru and how far his patience with her would extend, but it hurt, and she had to ask. "Why wouldn't you let me talk about my past?"

"I don't know," he murmured, stern eyes studying her in the lantern light. "Perhaps I was afraid."

"Afraid of what?"

"I don't know. My mother… whenever she talked about her life before us, it would make her sad… or angry."

Misaki didn't think she had ever heard Takeru speak about his mother. He looked troubled.

"Are you alright, Takeru-sama?"

"Just tired."

"You should get to sleep then," she said. "Remember, you promised to train Hiroshi before dawn."

"Oh." A vaguely miserable expression crossed Takeru's face. "That's right." He paused for a moment, frowning at the opposite wall. "He really killed a man with your sword?"

"Yes." Misaki looked at the floor. "I wish he hadn't—things had gotten out of hand. I'm sorry—"

"You're not the one who should be sorry. I should have been there to protect all of you. And even without me there, you had no reason to think a five-year-old would leave the safety of his hiding place to join the killing. No normal five-year-old would attempt that, let alone succeed. It's not your fault that boy turned out too much like me."

"Like you?"

"Not completely human. I think it can be dangerous, mixing powerful bloodlines the way we do in this family. Breed too strong and offspring start to become less like humans, more like gods."

"Isn't that the point?" Misaki asked. "To bring out that precious gods' blood, make the strongest offspring we can?"

"Yes, but that doesn't change the fact that it's dangerous—for the children and their mothers. I'm only thankful that Hiroshi didn't kill you."

"What?"

"Not with the sword," Takeru clarified. "Before that..."

"Takeru-sama, what are you talking about?"

He stared off somewhere she couldn't see, the ripples of lantern light accentuating the circles under his eyes. "You know. Even a strong woman doesn't fare well trying to birth a god."

"I'm not following, Takeru-sama."

"My mother, Yukino Tatsuki, was an uncannily powerful jijaka. Of course, as a woman, she did not have much occasion to use her jiya on a large scale, but... I do remember that she could clear the courtyard of snow with barely the wave of her hand. The women talked about a time a small child fell in the river and was pulled under by the current. Before the boy's mother could dive in after him, my own mother *lifted* the river, placing him back on the bank."

"Great Nami, Takeru-sama," Misaki said jokingly. "You're making me feel very inadequate."

"No." Takeru shook his head. "It can be a mistake, I think, to marry Matsudas and Yukinos. Creatures of such great power—the same sort of power—can have disastrous results."

"But your father wasn't—" Misaki stopped herself before the disrespectful comment could pass her lips. This new practice of conversing honestly with her husband might have confused her sense of propriety, but she had to remember that this was Takeru she was talking to. She couldn't speak ill of Matsuda Susumu.

"My father was not a master of the Whispering Blade," Takeru conceded, clearly knowing what she had meant to say, but he didn't seem angry, "nor did he ever achieve greatness as a jijaka, but he still carried the blood of the Matsuda line. Paired with my mother's power, that produced offspring so unnaturally powerful that even she struggled to carry them—carry *us*."

Takeru looked down, a shadow of guilt touching his features. "It almost seems that human limitation resists our existence, that maybe… the Gods are the sort of parents who do not wish their descendants to exceed them."

Misaki studied her husband for a moment. She had traced the lines of his perfect face so many times, wondering if there was really human flesh and blood to him, when he seemed like a creature sculpted by the Gods from pure winter. She had never thought to wonder how strange it would feel to *be* that creature, to know what a bizarre creation you were.

"I'm told that Takashi-nii-sama's birth left my mother weakened and sick. *My* birth nearly killed her, leaving her bedridden for a year. She miscarried late in her third pregnancy, while I was still very young. She might have been alright after that, but my father insisted they try again. She died a few months into that fourth pregnancy."

"I'm sorry, Takeru-sama. I didn't know any of that."

All anyone had told Misaki of her mother-in-law was that she had died of a persistent illness. She hadn't realized that miscarriages and death were commonplace in the Matsuda household. She wondered if her father had known. If he had known, would he have married her to this house? She shoved those thoughts away. It didn't matter. It was all done now. It had been done many years ago. And Misaki was still alive in this moment with her husband. That was all that mattered.

"We didn't talk about it," Takeru said. "If Takashi or I mentioned it—if we talked about our mother—Tou-sama would beat us."

This too was a new thought to Misaki. For years, she had viewed Matsuda Susumu as her tyrant; she never really considered what Takeru and Takashi would have suffered as his sons. And she had never thought to be thankful that neither of the brothers had carried on their father's violent tendencies.

The instances in which Takeru had raised a hand to Mamoru were few. Perhaps there had just been the once—that strange day Mamoru had called into question his Empire and everything he lived by. Of course, there was the dojo, where Takeru would hit Mamoru's side or his knuckles in training, when he left an opening, when there was a lesson to be learned. But Takashi and Takeru had learned their superior swordplay from their grandfather, Matsuda Mizudori. Susumu had never had any lessons for them. Only resentment.

"I think," Takeru said very slowly, "he was not a good father. He was *certainly* not a good husband."

Misaki looked at Takeru in complete shock.

"What is it?" he asked, seeing her eyes go wide.

"I just... I don't think I've ever heard you criticize your father."

She hadn't intended the look of shame that crossed his face. "I shouldn't disrespect him. I know. But..."

"But?"

"He hurt my mother."

That was no surprise to Misaki, especially if Takeru's mother had been as powerful as he described. If there was one thing Susumu had hated over anything else, it was being reminded of his own inadequacy.

"She hit him as well," Takeru continued slowly, as if reaching far back into his memory for things he had probably never articulated, things he had probably tried to forget. "They were always fighting. With other people, my mother was alright, she was a kind person, but she and my father could never agree on anything, and they made each other miserable. If he spoke to her, he was yelling. If she spoke to him, she was crying. Takashi-nii-sama told me much later that she had a wonderful smile." He shook his head. "I have no memory of her smiling."

"I'm sorry," Misaki said quietly. "I didn't know." But why was he telling her this now? He seemed so tired. Surely, he had dredged up enough pain for one day.

"It was obvious when you married me that you didn't want to be here," Takeru said, "so I tried to keep a respectful distance from you. I was certain that if you spoke about your life before coming here and all you left behind, that we would fight."

He was right. If Misaki had let herself dwell on Livingston and Robin, let herself speak about it, she *would* have fought him. But would that really have been such a bad thing? Would it have been worse than fifteen years of utter loneliness?

"I didn't want things between us to be like they were between my parents," Takeru said. "I didn't want our sons to grow up as I did… not quite human."

As Misaki looked at her husband in the lantern light, everything started to make sense. Takeru had never witnessed a marriage without violence. He had been trying to keep them from that the only way he knew how. With silence. In a twisted way, it all made sense.

"When you first miscarried, I was worried that you were heading toward the same fate as my mother. I thought that I was killing you."

"But you didn't," Misaki said, at once touched and confused by the idea that Takeru would blame himself for the weakness of *her* body. "That was my failure, not yours."

"Not a failure," Takeru said. "You're still alive."

"I…" Misaki blinked. "I lost your children."

"As I explained, that is common among Matsuda wives. It is less common for a woman to miscarry even once and survive. You must have been protected by the Gods… or perhaps by the blood magic that gives your family such strength. Perhaps your subconscious blood manipulation purged your dangerous offspring before the pregnancy could kill you both."

"You think I killed your children," Misaki said, "like your father always said."

"I think I saved my wife," Takeru said. "Your Tsusano blood helped you survive where my mother could not. In that way, I suppose, our fathers made us a good match."

Misaki breathed out with a twisted smile. "That's a bit morbid, Takeru-sama."

Takeru didn't return the smile. He was still wearing the pained, repentant expression that was so new to Misaki, so hard to look at, even if it was long overdue.

"I knew you were in pain after losing those children," he said, "the way my mother was in pain before she died. But I admit, to my shame, that I didn't know what to do. I still don't..."

"You're speaking to me," Misaki said. "All I wanted then was for you to speak to me, so I wouldn't be alone."

Takeru shook his head. "I thought that if I tried to put myself close to you, you would push me away. I thought that if I spoke to you, it would turn into a fight."

"But there are worse things than fighting," Misaki said. "I *like* a bit of fighting. It's silence I can't stand."

"Then I am the worst husband in Kaigen."

"No..." Misaki said softly, "I could have broken the silence too." She just hadn't had the courage.

So much of her anger had spawned from Takeru treating her like a doll, but she hadn't been much better. She had treated him like a human-shaped mass of ice without considering that there might be entirely human reasons that ice had formed.

"I'm sorry I left you in silence all this time," Takeru said. "I don't know if I understand it... but I am glad we fought today."

Misaki nodded. "Me too."

Men like Matsuda Takeru the First existed only in legends, because of course, there were no real men who could end the troubles of a kingdom with a stroke of the sword. Misaki and Takeru's fight hadn't magically imbued them with love and understanding. It didn't heal the pain of Mamoru's absence. But it was something, like the beginnings of a scab. It was the first sign that things could get better.

When Misaki and Takeru lay down on their futon together, a wave of their cold extinguished the flame in the lantern, leaving only the gray-blue mix of moonlight and shadows. The darkness didn't threaten nightmares now that Misaki was no longer alone in it. It seemed like the most natural thing in the world when Takeru moved to touch her—then he paused.

"What is it?" she whispered.

"You hate it when I touch you," he said—not an accusation but a simple fact. "You've always hated it."

Misaki didn't try to deny it.

She didn't know if she could *make* herself like his touch, but she leaned in and brushed her cheek against his fingers. Then she reached out and held him. Cold. But what did that matter? So was she. Nestling closer, she rested her head on his shoulder. He would never have that hot spark that set her desire to a boil, but when she closed her eyes, no nightmares came.

In her husband's embrace, wrapped in the sound of his steady breathing, she slept soundly for the first time in a month.

29

THE APPRENTICE

The next week, Colonel Song was back, this time accompanied by his superiors, Shirojima's provincial governor, and representatives from the Yammanka military. Song's idiot translator, Chou Kyung-tek, was there to introduce all of them in clumsy Shirojima Dialect.

"I present to you General Chun Chang-ho, Lieutenant Bek Jin-kyu, and your Prefectural Governor Lo Dong-soo. I believe you have already met Colonel Song Byung-woo."

Takeru bowed politely to each of the men.

"I also ask you to please welcome the representatives of our Yammanka allies, General Burema Kende, Lieutenant General Lansana Wagadu, and their translator and counselor, Jali Seydu Tirama." There was a second jaseli with the Yammankalu, younger than the first, wearing simpler robes. Misaki could only guess that he was the real jaseli's apprentice—a fairly new apprentice, judging by his age and nervousness—but he didn't get an introduction.

"It's a pleasure to meet you." Takeru spoke to the Yammankalu in Kaigengua, and Jali Tirama translated his words smoothly to Yammaninke. *"Thank you for being here."* Then, in Yammanka fashion, Takeru reached out and took General Kende's hand in his.

Misaki had gone over the tajaka greeting gesture with Takeru, convincing him to practice with her until it started to feel natural. The practice was only partially to make Takeru appear better informed before the foreign visitors. More than anything, Misaki wanted the Yammankalu to *feel* who they were dealing with. It worked. She noted subtle expressions of surprise on the tajakalu's faces as their fingers touched Takeru's and their lips touched his knuckles. Takeru was colder and palpably more powerful than the representatives of the Emperor, and Yammankalu, if nothing else, respected power.

"You will, of course, quarter us in your house, Matsuda," General Chun said.

"Yes," Takeru said stiffly. *"Of course."*

Fantastic, Misaki thought. With each of the important officials put up in their own room, there would not actually be space in the half-destroyed Matsuda compound for the Matsudas themselves. Misaki and Setsuko would, of course, be expected to be available to serve tea and food that they couldn't actually afford to give up, but the family would have to find a different place to sleep.

"Did you have something to add, Manga—I mean— Koroyaa?" the younger jaseli asked.

Koroyaa. Misaki blinked in surprise as she realized the question had been directed at her. It was a respectful address for a female member of the warrior class. The out-of-place question spoke of the jaseli's innocence; in Yamma, a married man and woman were equals, managing all important affairs together. This must have been his first time in Kaigen if the gender dynamics made him so uncomfortable.

Not only that, he had very nearly called Misaki *Manga* Koroyaa—a title for a woman of a ruling clan. In another country, a noble family like the Matsudas *would* have held manga koro status, but in Kaigen, the only official manga koro family was the Imperial house. Kaigen wasn't like Yamma, where many powerful families were allowed to flex their strength and vie for the throne if they wished. The Emperor of Kaigen didn't want any line other than his own claiming the inherent right to rule over any piece of his Empire, however small.

"Oh, don't mind me, Jalike," Misaki returned, equally respectful.

"I'm only here to support my husband."

It was demeaning, but Misaki found herself smiling. She had learned from her days spying that an inexperienced jaseli was like a poorly guarded treasury. Only the thing jaseliwu guarded was far more valuable than money; it was *information*.

"Setsuko, I need to ask a favor," Misaki said once the military officials and their translators were comfortably settled in the Matsuda compound.

"Sure thing."

"I need you to play hostess for a while in my stead."

"Where are you going?"

"Just on a little adventure," Misaki said, cracking her neck. "Going to see if I'm as smart as I used to think I was."

"Shall I get my niece?" It was what Setsuko had started calling Siradenyaa, since Misaki had explained the little sword's origins and the name 'Shadow's Daughter.'

"No," Misaki laughed, "but I am going to take this nephew of yours." She lifted Izumo out of his drawer—they were going to have to relinquish this room to their guests anyway—and bundled him into a sling.

"On an adventure?" Setsuko said, looking curious.

"He's cuter than I am," Misaki said, "makes me seem sympathetic and unthreatening. Isn't that right, little buddy?" She tapped Izumo on the nose.

"What—"

"I'll tell you how it goes when I get back... if there's anything to tell. Hopefully, there will be a lot."

Misaki waited in the shadows behind Hyori's shack, out of sight of the footpath through the village. Apprentices almost always got sent out on errands for their masters. The young jaseli was sure to emerge eventually, alone, and she would have her chance.

When she heard his shuffling footsteps and his teeth chattering in the perfectly pleasant spring air, she stepped out from behind the shack and 'accidentally' ran into him.

"Oh," the boy said in surprise. Then, hilariously, he tried to speak

Kaigengua: *"I... the truth of it is... I was making the way of... of walking in the direction of the place for to speak with one's lover—"*

"I nyuman, Jaliden," Misaki said, trying hard not to laugh. *"N'ye Yammaninke muku."*

"Oh." The jaseli's shoulders relaxed in relief. *"I forgot you could speak my language. As I was saying—or trying to—I was just on my way to deliver this message to your husband."* He pulled a piece of kayiri from the front of his robe.

"My husband is busy right now," Misaki said, *"but I would be happy to deliver it for you."*

"Oh..." the boy hesitated and then handed her the letter. *"Alright. Thank you."*

"It's no trouble. And I'm sorry. I didn't get your name, jaseli."

"Oh—sorry, Koroyaa. I'm Moriba Gesseke."

Gesseke. The boy was from a prestigious family. That was probably how he had secured an apprenticeship with such a skilled jaseli despite his lack of wit and charm. If he stumbled over his words this much back home in Yamma, his clan might have deliberately sent him to apprentice overseas to avoid embarrassment. Misaki would have placed him in his late teens or early twenties, the right age to be taking on his first serious apprenticeship.

"I'm actually very glad you're here," Misaki said. "I was going to ask your master about a few things, but since you're a Gesseke and you seem very competent, I wonder if you can help me."

"I can try, Koroyaa," the boy said, clearly flattered. *"What is it?"*

"It's just that, I've gotten some conflicting information from the Kaigenese soldiers I've spoken to. I wondered if you could offer me some clarity, from your uniquely informed position."

"Oh—um..." Gesseke looked apprehensive. *"I don't know if I can do that."*

"Really?" Misaki put on a crestfallen face. *"I just thought that, as the apprentice to the Yammankalu's main jaseli here, you might know what actually happened to this village."*

"I do, Koroyaa. I'm just not sure if I can tell you. Not without permission from my superiors."

"You need permission from your superiors to help a grieving woman put her doubts to rest?"

"It's not that I don't want you to know. I'm just not sure your Empire would want me to... I can't risk it."

"You can't risk it?" Misaki said with a calculated tremor of incredulous fear.

"Sorry?"

"I have a family, jaseli," Misaki let her voice shake, sounding vulnerable. Not out of control. Just vulnerable enough. *"A little baby. You think I want to get them all killed?"*

"I... that's not what I was trying to insinuate—"

"If you are worried about displeasing the Kaigenese Empire, I'm not someone you need to fear. All I want is to keep my family safe. And here in Kaigen, safe means being in line with the Empire's plan. You don't seem to understand; the only way I can do that is if I know the whole story."

"I don't know, Koroyaa..."

"If you never want me to repeat what you tell me to anyone, I won't. I just need to know."

"But..."

"You belong to a great line of wordsmiths, Moriba Gesseke," Misaki said, deciding to try out a jaseli tactic herself, *"singers and confidants to kings and queens."* The Daybreak jaseliwu always said a man was more malleable when his head was swelled with praise. *"For generations, members of your family have aided the Yammanka elite, cooling their anger, stoking their strength, guiding them through so many times of trouble. You, of all people, would understand how important it is for a leader to have good counsel."*

"Yes," Gesseke agreed, though he looked confused.

"You understand the danger of a powerful koro without a loyal confidant to rein him in."

"Of course."

"Well, this village has no jaseliwu," Misaki pressed toward the

point before the young man could get too lost. *"Our only jaseliwu were the Hibikis, and their entire family was wiped out in the attack. My husband has no advisors. He just has me. Surely you felt the nyama coming off my husband. His temper is not to be underestimated."*

"Koro Matsuda, are you threatening me?"

"No." Misaki let herself sound scandalized and hurt. *"Never, jaseli! I am... imploring you. If my husband can't put his rage to rest, if he lashes out, my whole family will be in danger. Please. Help me save my family."*

The boy looked torn.

"My husband is a great man, but he is also a traditional one. He can't negotiate between Kaigenese, Yammanka, and Ranganese culture and ideas the way that I can. Now, I can keep him working in line with your superiors' plans, but in order to do that, I need to know what those plans are. I need to understand what is really going on."

Gesseke still seemed uncertain. *"I'm not sure I'm supposed to talk about these things with the locals..."*

Misaki was surprised that he hadn't been explicitly told not to reveal secrets to the people of Takayubi until she realized that they were probably not expecting anyone in Takayubi to speak proficient enough Yammaninke to communicate with him.

"I understand," she said quickly, *"but believe me, I don't intend to misuse your knowledge. I swear it."* She adopted a solemn tone. *"Jali Gesseke, I swear on the Falleke that I will never repeat a word of this to anyone."* Over ninety percent of Duna's population worshipped the Falleke. Unsurprisingly, it didn't occur to this Yammanka-born jaseli that Misaki might not be one of them. He glanced around and then motioned her out of the open. Safely behind Hyori's shack, he met Misaki's eyes.

"You mustn't tell my jakama I spoke so openly to you."

"Of course," Misaki assured him. *"I would never meddle between jaseliwu."*

"As I'm sure you have noticed from this attack, the Ranganese

military has made great strides since the Keleba in terms of their troops' training."

"We did notice."

"Despite that, Ranga is still a relatively young power on the world stage. They still have the goal of eventually engaging Kaigen in another war and destroying the Empire completely, but they don't have a lot of confidence in their military. Our Ranganese spies have determined that these attacks were a sort of test."

"A test?" Misaki asked, feeling sick.

"You seem like a smart woman; I'm sure you've noted the commonality between all the areas Ranga attacked?"

Misaki nodded. *"They're the old fighting powers, the places where the Ranganese suffered the heaviest casualties during the Keleba."*

Gesseke nodded. *"What happened to your village and the other targeted areas was an experiment, to see if Ranga had become powerful enough to declare open war on Kaigen."*

"And what did they find?" Misaki's stomach knotted in dread and she clutched Izumo close. If Kaigen had to fight another war, then they were all dead. She understood that now with a cold certainty she had never been able to accept before. There would be no running away. She had married onto Kaigen's blade edge and made her family here. *"Is there going to be war, jaseli?"*

"No, but it was a close thing, Koro Matsuda. The Ranganese tested their strength on eight targets in total."

"Eight?" Misaki said in surprise. There had only been news of storms in Heibando, Yongseom, and Ishihama before Takayubi was attacked.

"Four great houses and four military strongholds," Gesseke said.

"I see." It was easier to cover up an attack in which few civilians had been involved. *"And what happened to the military strongholds?"*

"All of them were completely overrun," the jaseli said. *"In three cases, the Kaigenese military was able to hold off Ranga's rank and file soldiers, but those elite forces... they were no match for them."*

537

Misaki could hardly blame the Kaigenese soldiers. It took more than a few years of military training to face fighters as good as those Ranganese in black.

"I don't know if you realize," the jaseli said, *"what you did here was* extraordinary."

"No," Misaki said innocently, although of course, she realized how extraordinary it had been. It was why having to take orders from Kaigen's incompetent military officials was so insulting. *"I mean, we were just trying to stay alive."*

"Well, you may have kept your whole empire alive in the process," Gesseke said. *"The Ranganese Union still fears the warriors of these old houses like yours, with good reason. I suppose it must be frightening to consider that a small handful of civilians could do away with hundreds of your best fighters. It is that fear that your Emperor and we Yammankalu brought to bear on Ranga, to pressure them into a truce."*

So, the Emperor will use us to intimidate his enemies, but won't support us? Misaki thought bitterly.

"We... didn't mention to the Ranganese how many of yours they managed to take with them."

Misaki watched the shadow of a torch flame lap at the snow as she turned this new information over in her head.

"That explains why the Ranganese didn't use bombs, or assassins, or more covert tactics," she mused. *"They wanted to pit their strongest fighters directly against ours..."*

"That is correct. I doubt they had any idea there were theonites here who could diffuse their tornadoes or face their Sheng and Tian fighters in a melee. From what we can tell, some of their best fighters were sent here."

"After the tornado broke," Misaki said, *"they sent their soldiers against us in waves. Was the intention to keep count? How many it took to destroy us?"*

"We think so."

"I see. So, the Ranganese soldiers were just game pieces too."

"Not exactly."

"What do you mean?"

"According to the Jamuttaana my fankama has been working with, most of the Ranganese soldiers involved in this attack were not forced to come here. They volunteered."

"What? Why?"

"The Jamuttaana seemed to think some of them wanted revenge for what their parents and grandparents suffered under the Kaigenese Empire. Some of them believed they were freeing you. Most of them wanted the glory of bringing down Kaigen's greatest warrior houses.

"When we gathered the bodies, the Empire's military physicians did a rough survey of how many were killed by our bombs and bullets, and how many died of jiya-inflicted injuries. We've sent the Ranganese extensive photo evidence—hundreds of pictures—proving that jijakalu had killed most of their men before the Yammanka air support ever got here."

"And they took your word for it?"

"The whole affair was mediated by agents of the Jamu Kurankite for transparency. This has been an ongoing discussion between Yamma, Kaigen, and Ranga. I wish there was some way your husband and the others could be allowed to know... You people should be incredibly proud of what you've done here. In fighting so hard, you truly have protected your Empire. Any jaseli would be proud to sing of your deeds for the next generation."

"But it will have to stay quiet," Misaki said.

The young jaseli nodded. *"Koro Matsuda... I am so sorry about your son."*

Misaki just shook her head. She had done a good job controlling the interaction. If she let herself think about Mamoru, she would lose that control.

"Thank you, jaseli. I appreciate this."

"Truly, I wish your people could know."

"It's alright," she said softly. *"Thank you for speaking to me."*

The jaseli looked like he wanted to say more but before he got the chance, Misaki gathered Izumo close to her chest and melted into the shadows.

....

Later that night, Misaki took Takeru outside in the dark—with two whole families squeezed into the Mizumaki house, it was the only privacy they would get—and told him what she had learned from the jaseli. He listened with a faint frown until she had finished.

"So, there is no immediate danger from the Ranganese," he said. "We have time to rebuild."

"Yes."

"Good. I'm glad we have this information. That being said, you should not have done this thing without consulting me."

Misaki frowned, annoyed. Did he know how difficult it could be to get information out of a jaseli, who couldn't be threatened with force? And this was how thanked her?

"Well, no disrespect, Takeru-sama, but your Yammaninke isn't very good. I don't know that you would have been able to—"

"I am your husband, Misaki. Don't act without my permission again."

Misaki should have been angry. She *was* angry. After all he had seen her do, Takeru still couldn't outgrow decades of sexism and arrogance in the space of a week. He still talked down to her casually. He still expected her to obey. Like nothing had changed.

She drew in a deep breath, ready to tell him that she didn't need his permission to do as she pleased—but it was in that moment that she realized that something *had* changed. Her anger wasn't tied up in silence now, smothering her. The defiant breath filled her lungs easily and she had already opened her mouth with a barb to throw back at him, unafraid. And that—the simple fact that she was not afraid to argue—felt wonderful.

She felt a grin spread across her face as she realized that they *were* going to end up arguing. If not today, then the next day, or the next, they were going to fight again. To most people, that might not have seemed like the sign of a happy marriage, but Misaki never felt so viscerally connected with someone as she did in the middle of a confrontation. She had fought with her father and brothers, with Koli, Elleen, and Robin, with everyone she had ever really loved.

Like a madwoman, she beamed up at her husband.

"Why are you smiling?" Takeru looked unsettled.

"It's complicated."

"It's scary."

Misaki chuckled, then did her best to look contrite. Takeru had enough to worry about today without her attacking him again. Some other time. In a future that no longer seemed so cold and empty.

"I'm sorry." She meant it, but the lingering smile on her lips might not have done much to project honesty. "Truly, I didn't mean to disrespect you."

"I'm not displeased that you spoke to the jaseli," Takeru said. "I'm displeased that you acted alone."

"I said I was sorry. I'll obey you next time."

"Obey me? Misaki, that's not what I..." Takeru let out an agitated huff, and even in the dead of winter, his breath was so frozen that it misted and sank in the darkness.

"You what?" Misaki prompted when the tension had stretched too thin between them.

"I would like you to be honest with me and to trust me to protect you."

"I do trust you," she said earnestly. "I'm sorry."

"That was a dangerous thing for you to do. What if you had been found out?"

"It wasn't that much of a gamble, Takeru-sama. The boy wasn't a real jaseli, just an apprentice far out of his depth. I knew I could handle him."

"How could you know that?"

Misaki shrugged. "I hung out with some Yammanka jaseliwu at Daybreak. I learned to spot the weak ones."

"Like you learned to spot fonyaka tornadoes?"

"Sure."

Takeru's frown had deepened, but he didn't look angry. "Do we seem blind to you?"

"What?"

"Those of us who grew up in this village, believing firmly in everything the government told us," Takeru said. "We must seem so blind to you."

"Takeru-sama..." Misaki wanted to say 'no' but hadn't she just finished apologizing for being dishonest? "It's not your fault," she sighed. "I was lucky. My parents let me turn my education into a weird overseas adventure, knowing all I had to do was marry well out of school and, by chance, it ended up paying off in useful knowledge. When you've been around the world and seen all different kinds of lies, it gets easier to see through them. I don't fault you for being misinformed."

"You don't?"

"My father chose you over anyone else because he thought that I wouldn't marry a stupid man. And he was right." She looked up, meeting Takeru's eyes. "I wouldn't."

Takeru's frown had not faded. "I punished Mamoru for questioning the Empire," he said after a long moment and Misaki paused. Was that what was bothering him?

"You demanded that he stand by his words, think about what came out of his mouth," she said. "I don't think you were wrong to do that."

"But I *was* wrong about the Empire. I understand why you wouldn't trust me—"

"I *do* trust you," Misaki insisted. "Now, stand by your words, Matsuda Takeru. Protect us."

Misaki was not invited to the meeting between Takeru and the military representatives from the capital. However, as the wife of the new Matsuda patriarch, she was allowed in the room to serve the men their tea.

The Kaigenese military officials did most of the talking while the jaseli translator murmured quietly to the Yammanka officials, keeping them abreast of the conversation. Takeru, for the most part, was expected to simply listen and agree. As Misaki came in to pour the second round of tea, he *did* manage to find space in the conversation to ask Takayubi's most pressing question:

"When can we expect aid?"

"When the Emperor has the men available," General Chun said. It wasn't a real answer. *"I know you wouldn't understand this, being a civilian and not a true military man, but the Emperor cannot spare troops to distribute food and supplies when they are busy protecting his provinces from foreign invaders."*

"Respectfully, General, the Emperor's troops didn't protect this province," Takeru said. *"We did."*

It had probably been the wrong thing to say, but Misaki found herself struggling not to smile. She wondered if Takeru was aware that he had never been more attractive. It had never properly occurred to her before that moment, but perhaps the thing she found most attractive in men had never been power. It had never been danger. It was bravery. And her husband, facing these liars in a language that was not his own, was braver than any Matsuda facing an army on the battlefield.

Her eyes flicked to the other side of the table and she couldn't help feeling a surge of satisfaction at the uncomfortable looks on the officials' faces. General Chun, who had done the best job maintaining his composure, leaned forward and folded his hands on the table before him, his eyes narrowed.

"I will have you know that the Kaigenese military is as strong as it has ever been and more than competent to protect the Empire. While the attacks were not made public to avoid unrest, several military bases were targeted by the Ranganese."

"Oh?" Takeru raised his eyebrows and proved himself a flawlessly smooth liar when he said, "I wasn't aware."

"Yes. At all these military strongholds, the Ranganese and their tornadoes were decisively repelled with minimal casualties. I know this must seem incomprehensible when you and your fellow civilians struggled so much against the Ranganese here, but this is why the military is here to protect you."

As Jali Tirama translated for the Yammanka representatives, Misaki noticed Gesseke glance nervously at her and then at Takeru. He was probably wondering if she had violated their agreement and passed the truth on to her husband. Fortunately for everyone, Takeru took General Chun's lies in stride.

"I see. It seems I have spoken out of turn then. I apologize." Takeru's monotone was so blandly sincere that the general seemed to be having trouble deciding if he was being mocked or not.

Takeru might have called the general's lie, even without the intel Misaki had collected from their naïve jaseli friend. A theonite like Takeru could sense another's power and skill, and none of them were on his level—or Misaki's for that matter. A dragon knew when he was looking at worms and snakes. These were men who looked very good in their uniforms but would buckle before real jiya. They wore divine power on their clothing but carried none inside them. These men were empty.

"I want to make something clear to you, Matsuda. Your family name, whatever power you think it holds in this area, means nothing to the Empire. You and your family are valued citizens of the Empire—no more, no less. Do we understand each other?"

Takeru stared at the table before him. His jiya had gone still, completely calm. *When it's too much to be a man, I become the mountain.* Dread twisted Misaki's stomach. Takeru had only two choices: he could cave and bow beneath this man's heel, or he could kill every man in the room. Either way, Takayubi was doomed. Either way, he failed.

"Matsuda." General Chun prompted. *"Do we understand each other?"*

Takeru lifted his head. His voice was more than calm when he spoke again. It was strong. *"Perfectly."*

The general smiled. *"Excellent."*

"I do have one more request," Takeru said, *"if I may."*

General Chun nodded for him to continue.

"Please tell the Emperor not to provide any aid to Takayubi— now or at any time in the future."

The military men exchanged confused glances. *"Excuse me?"*

"If the Empire's troops are in the process of fighting a secret war, I would never want them to waste their efforts where they are not needed."

"But, Matsuda," Governor Lo cut in, looking stunned. *"This village has been almost completely destroyed. Without government aid—"*

"We will survive, Governor," Takeru said, *"as we have through hundreds of wars in the past. As General Chun says, we are loyal citizens of the Empire. We could never in good conscience take resources from the Imperial army when we are perfectly capable of taking care of ourselves."*

"You seem awfully confident," Colonel Song said with a disdainful frown.

"We are warriors here, not beggars, and we will be back on our feet by the next time you come. In fact, I urge you to visit again, when you have the time. Speaking of which, I want to apologize again for the lacking accommodations. They will be up to our high standards on your return."

"Well..." General Chun hesitated, looking suspicious but didn't seem to find anything wrong with Takeru's words. *"I suppose I can't argue with that. We will have to return to install a new mayor."*

"That won't be necessary."

"Sorry?"

"I am not just the successor to the Matsuda line after my brother. I also spent years serving in the late mayor's office, budgeting and planning projects like the construction of the info-com towers that allowed us to contact the capital so quickly during the attack. If you were to dig through the wreckage of the mayor's office right now, you would find my handwriting on every piece of important paperwork dating back six years."

"Oh..."

"Of course, if the Emperor feels the need to install his own mayor, I wouldn't think of objecting. I am, however, quite confident

that I can run this village to his satisfaction. If on your return, you can find any fault with my leadership, I will happily step down in favor of a candidate of your choosing."

"You really think that you can put this village back together?" Colonel Song sneered.

Takeru looked calmly into Colonel Song's eyes. *"I've promised that I will."*

"And you believe yourself qualified to deliver on those promises?"

"I explained my qualifications—"

"Forgive me for interrupting, Koro Matsuda, Koro Song," General Kende said in Yammaninke. It was the first time the imposing tajaka had spoken. His jaseli was quicker off the mark than Chou, smoothly translating the words to Kaigengua.

"I'm confused," General Kende addressed General Chun and Colonel Song. *"You were just complaining that you lack the resources and manpower to offer these people aid. I like this man."* He pointed to Takeru. *"He seems like a competent person. If he is confident that he can look after his village, why not let him do it?"*

They argued for a while, but the Yammanka General and his jaseli strangely seemed to hold more power in the situation than any of the Kaigenese. It was a disturbing sign of weakness on the Empire's part. Evidently, the Kaigenese Empire had deteriorated to a point where it was so much weaker than its hostile neighbor that Yamma was now calling all the shots. It made Misaki doubly glad that she had taken the time to teach Takeru the Yammanka handshake. A Yammanka could almost always be relied on to recognize and respect the most powerful theonite in the room.

Before Misaki could observe any more, Colonel Song dismissed her to go get more tea. When she returned with a fresh pot, the conversation had turned to the matter of Takayubi's discretion. This was all old news: no one was to speak of the attack, inside or outside their homes, the mass grave would not be marked in any way.

It was dark by the time the Matsudas were finally dismissed from their own home—though Misaki, of course, would have to be back early in the morning to serve the oppressors a nice breakfast.

Takeru did not speak as they made their way back to the Mizumaki house. They had needed those supplies, but Takeru had done everything he could. Had he pushed harder, the general would simply have ground the Empire's heel down harder in kind, humiliating him. If he had raised his voice or his jiya, or done anything that could be construed as a threat, he may well have doomed himself and what remained of his family. He had kept Takayubi safe, and saved what little face he could in the process. It was the best anyone could have done.

Walking a respectful pace behind her husband, Misaki peered up at him in the moonlight. The night was clear, white light illuminating his face well enough for Misaki to see that he was not angry. She might have thought that he was away in his meditative state, avoiding all emotion, except that his brows were pinched together just slightly. He was thinking.

"Is everything alright?" she asked softly.

"It will be," he said, "once I have the chance to write up a plan."

"A plan?"

"I can make one now," Takeru said, "now that I'm not so blind."

A few moments passed and he fell back two steps so that he and Misaki were walking side by side. Misaki had spent so many years pining after sun and firelight. She hadn't looked closely enough to see that Takeru had his own light about him. Subtle but clear. Something of the moonlit snow that seemed to live in his skin.

"This village no longer has a good theonite academy," he said. "Even in the unlikely event that the government has a change of heart in the coming years and helps us restore Kumono Academy in some form, it will not be the same without all the instructors we have lost."

"Mmm," Misaki agreed politely.

"When Hiroshi is old enough, he will go to your Daybreak Academy in Carytha. If he does well there, I think perhaps all three boys should go."

Misaki's mouth had fallen open. "Are you serious, Takeru-sama?"

"I won't raise another generation as blind as my own."

Because it was nighttime and no one was around to see, Misaki reached out and found her husband's sword-calloused fingers. They had been married fifteen years. It was the first time they had ever held hands.

30

THE FUTURE

The military retinue departed the next day, leaving the assembled villagers with a few veiled threats and empty words of encouragement. Takeru spoke to the crowd next, mounting an ice platform of his own making to give some equally empty words of thanks to General Chun.

Takeru's words meant little, but he had calculated the platform's placement carefully. To the government officials, it meant nothing. The villagers of Takayubi and the surrounding areas, however, knew that this was the place where Matsuda Takeru the First had faced Yukino Izumi a thousand years ago. This was the place where the founder of their society had declared a new order.

"Now to some announcements," he said when he had finished addressing the military officials. "Beginning tomorrow, this village will be implementing some new practices that will be essential to our survival. Today, all food is to be brought to the Matsuda compound, all building material brought to Kotetsu Katashi's shack. No exceptions."

"Are these your orders or the Empire's?" someone asked brazenly.

"These are my orders," Takeru said. "I have promised General Chun that, on his return, we would have the village fully rebuilt. That process begins today. You will all assemble here tomorrow morning for further instructions. Glory to Kaigen," he finished. "Long live the Emperor."

"Long live the Emperor," the village returned without enthusiasm.

Misaki and Setsuko oversaw the collection of the food while Takeru went over plans with Kotetsu Katashi and Kwang Tae-min. It was evening by the time Misaki went to Takeru's study.

"We've collected all the food in one place," she told him. With any other group of people, Misaki would have suspected families or individuals of withholding supplies, but not here.

"Good," Takeru said. "I'm going to need you and Setsuko to go through the supplies and give me a complete inventory of everything we have."

"Alright."

"I need the inventory divided into items that must be consumed within the week, within the month, and those that will keep until the ice melts."

"Yes, sir."

The task took Misaki and Setsuko the rest of the day, and they had to finish by lantern light, rocking the babies to sleep as they reviewed their last count.

"You're sure this is complete and accurate?" Takeru asked when Misaki brought him the results in his study.

"Yes." Misaki had checked carefully.

"Good."

"I also brought you some tea."

"Good," he said, though he didn't really seem to hear her. His eyes were already flicking over the inventory, though judging by the circles beneath them, he needed the caffeine.

"I'll just leave it right..." Misaki had to search the desk for a moment before she found a surface space that wasn't covered in lists and notes. "Right here."

She was already partway to the door when there a stiff, "Thank you."

"You're welcome."

"And could you close the door? The wind is noisy and I'm trying to concentrate."

"Um..." Misaki looked at the door, which was no more than a few clinging splinters after Takeru had broken it down... after *she* had attacked him and sealed him inside the room.

"Oh—" Takeru blinked, looking uncharacteristically flustered. "Never mind."

"I'm sorry," Misaki said because she felt that she should.

Takeru shook his head. "I'm the one who kicked it down." Looking away from her, he tossed back his cup of hot tea with the same desperation with which his brother used to down sake. "Go. Get some sleep."

"Yes, sir," Misaki murmured and withdrew to the bedroom.

Mamoru no longer invaded her dreams, but that night, she found that sleep wouldn't come. The room felt... too hot? That couldn't be right. It was winter. Slinging an arm out, she found the futon empty beside her. Still? Getting up, she arranged her kimono around her to make sure she was decent and then padded down the hall. Lantern light spilled out of Takeru's study to lap gently at the wood floor of the hallway.

"You're still awake?" she murmured, stepping into the doorway.

"I'm still busy," Takeru returned, not looking up from his desk. His desk had accumulated several more layers of kayiri—each sheaf crammed with some combination of text, diagrams, and equations.

His eyes flicked from one page to another with the feverish speed and ferocity of a warrior's sword flashing from one kill to another. She had always thought of her husband's angular face as something ageless and pristine, but here in the lantern light, he truly looked like a man in his forties.

"Leave me," he said shortly. "I'm concentrating."

Misaki was tempted to obey. That was what she would have done, back when she was still telling herself that her husband wasn't her responsibility.

"You have to speak in front of your people tomorrow," she reminded him. "Do you really want to do that on no sleep?"

Takeru's resting face was cross enough without frightening

circles around his eyes. If he didn't sleep, she worried he might just scare the remaining population of Takayubi off the mountainside. He looked up at her, haggard, his eyes narrowed, and for a moment she was sure he was about to snap at her not to question him.

"I don't want to do it without a plan in place," he said evenly. "You can understand that, can't you?"

Misaki nodded. Then she reached out and slid a hand over his shoulders and down his back, passing over the four-diamond Matsuda insignia and the coiled muscle beneath. He stiffened for a moment, his shoulders drawing back as if to shrug the hand off. Then he seemed to reconsider and stilled under the touch. Was he always this tense? This cold? Like cables of freezing steel wrapped in human skin... She pressed fingers into a pressure point.

For a moment, it was no more effective than trying to push her fingers into solid stone. Then she sent a pulse of jiya through her fingertips and smiled as she felt the smallest measure of tension leave his shoulders.

"Is there anything I can help with?" she asked.

"Are you very good with numbers?"

"No," she said honestly.

"Mmm." He frowned. "In that case, I'll have Kwang look over my work in the morning."

He rolled his shoulders, nudging Misaki's hand back. She took the small movement as rejection and was about to withdraw when Takeru reached across the desk and picked up a few sheets of kayiri.

"Look over this for me."

Misaki took the kayiri from him and was surprised to find that these pages did not bear numbers, but columns upon columns of words. Takeru's brushwork was as elegant and flawless as any calligrapher's, but many lines had been crossed out and rewritten.

"My brother... was good at inspiring others," Takeru explained. "I've never been good with people the way he was. If I don't plan the words, I won't know what to say."

"And... you want me to...?"

"Look over it for me. You know people. Please?"

"Of course." Misaki knelt at the desk opposite Takeru and started reading over the speech.

Takeru had the most space-efficient writing she had ever seen, substituting in compact Ranji for sprawling phonetic characters wherever possible. Embarrassingly, Misaki found it a bit difficult to read. While her spoken Kaigengua was much better than Takeru's, he was clearly more versed in the use of ancient characters.

As dawn colored the sky, she handed the kayiri back to him.

"You think this is what I should say?" he asked.

"Yes."

"Then I will memorize it. I..." He looked down at the kayiri and paused. "You crossed this whole page out." Confused, he leafed through the rest of the sheets. "You... crossed all of it out."

"I did," Misaki said. "Initially, I made notes and additions. Then I changed my mind."

"I don't understand."

"I don't think you need to say any of this."

"Well..." Takeru blinked, rubbed one eye with the heel of his hand, "Then... what—"

"Do you have a plan for them, Takeru-sama?"

"Yes."

"A good one?"

"I think so."

"Then that's all that matters," Misaki said firmly. "They've heard enough of 'Glory to the Empire' and empty words of comfort—not that yours weren't beautiful. You don't have to pretend to be your brother."

"So... what am I supposed to tell them?"

"Your plan," Misaki said. "No more, no less. You're a koro, Takeru-sama; your actions will always speak louder than your words. Everyone in this village already knows how long you worked for the mayor, they know that you care about them, and they've witnessed your strength. All they need to know now is that everything is going to be alright."

She looked up as she picked up the sound of Izumo crying from down the hall.

"I should go take care of that." She stood to leave, but paused, staring down at her husband. Without thinking, she leaned in and kissed him on the head—right on the crease between his brows.

"What?" He looked up in confusion—

And she kissed him on the mouth. He didn't pull away, so she slid her fingers into his hair, gripped the back of his neck, and pressed him closer.

His mouth was as icy as the rest of him, but somehow, the kiss wasn't hard. It didn't grate. In that freezing cold kiss, Misaki found a subtlety she had never known in her husband. He was not a single slab of rigid ice. Beneath the frozen mountain, there was the swell of tides. Beneath the snow, there was the bubbling of the Kumono spring and the rivers it sent racing beneath the ice and deep underground. Beneath the shiver of pines, their roots reached like fingers into the soil to grasp at the spring-warmed core of the mountain.

No pop and hiss of steam here, no flame to set the darkness jumping in aimless excitement. But where there was light, there was always room for shadow. Entwined with the snow-white light of Takeru's cold, she found herself seeping in and rooting deep.

When she broke the kiss Takeru was quiet, but he no longer looked confused. He seemed to understand what it had meant.

"I look forward to your plan," she said and hurried off to take care of Izumo.

As the people gathered before the ice platform to hear Takeru, Misaki and Setsuko sought out Hyori and stood beside her. The younger woman, now visibly pregnant, looked as though she had gotten about as much sleep as Takeru.

"Morning, Hyori-chan."

"Oh." Hyori blinked at Misaki with hollow eyes, ringed with darkness. "M-morning."

"How are you feeling?" Misaki asked.

"Fine," Hyori said shakily. "I'm feeling fine. Thank you."

"Don't be ridiculous, Hyori," Setsuko said more bluntly. "Your face has as much color in it as this snow, and your eyes look like a raccoon's."

"You don't have to put it like that, Setsuko," Misaki said.

"It's okay." Hyori grimaced, her lip trembling. "I know I've gotten ugly."

"Hey, hey!" That is not what I said!" Setsuko protested.

"You called me a raccoon."

"Yeah. The cutest little raccoon that ever lived." Setsuko pinched Hyori's cheek—the little of it there was to pinch. "Obviously."

"Oh, Setsuko," Misaki sighed.

"Have you been eating?" Setsuko asked Hyori, prodding the hollow in her cheek.

"I.... haven't been very hungry." Hyori had fisted her hands in the sleeves of her kimono to conceal the fact that they were shaking.

"Hyori-chan, you have to eat," Misaki said.

"You'll have lunch with us today," Setsuko declared brightly.

"That's alright, Setsuko-san. I don't—"

"We insist," Misaki said, just as Takeru mounted the platform and cleared his throat.

"People of Takayubi." While his voice was monotone as ever, it came out clear and strong. "Good morning. I have called all of you here because I have devised a plan to ensure our survival." He hadn't brought any of his notes with him. He didn't need to. The man could keep numbers in his head like a computer.

"Please, listen closely, as we will all have to adhere to this plan strictly if we hope to survive the coming months. Thanks to the tireless efforts of my wife and sister-in-law, I have inventoried and rationed all the food we currently have in the village. In addition to what we have here, our neighbors have agreed to contribute a generous amount of rice, fresh fish, and produce each month for as long as we need it. According to my calculations, this supply will support the entire village and a limited number of volunteer visitors for the next eleven months, until Sokolokalo of 5370.

"Food distribution and preparation will be overseen by my wife,

Misaki, and whomever she appoints to assist her. All requests for extra food must be processed through her."

Misaki eyed the crowd nervously, but no one objected. They trusted her. The realization created a warm feeling in her chest as Takeru continued.

"I want everyone to understand that from this day moving forward, I am considering all outside contributions of food and labor to be borrowed not donated."

"What?" a few voices said.

"What does that mean, Matsuda-dono?"

"It means," Takeru said calmly, "that we will be paying these good people back for their service in the future. I recognize that all of you are busy recovering and rebuilding at the moment, but we are not going to stay this way. I expect each family to have found a reliable source of income within the next eleven months."

"How?" someone demanded.

"We're all housewives," one of the Ikeno women pointed out. "How are we supposed to get the money to support a family, let alone pay the volunteers back for everything they've done?"

"Thank you for asking, Ikeno-san," Takeru said. "Your question brings me to the next part of my plan. I recognize that we don't seem to have much at the moment, but there is one resource that we have overlooked."

"What is that, Matsuda-dono?" one of the Ginkawa men asked.

"The pine forests," Takeru said. Most of the ancient forest that surrounded the western village had been leveled by the tornado, with the rest of it severely damaged. The desolation of the natural wonder was its own tragedy, though no one had given it much thought in the midst of so much human loss. After the villagers and volunteers had combed the fallen trees for bodies, no one had been back to the forest.

"All of you know that that forest has stood since the days of Yukino Hayase and Matsuda Takeru the First," Takeru said. "Its roots go deeper than you might think, making it an integral part of this mountainside. The collapsed trees will need to be removed to allow regrowth if we wish to avoid landslides, soil degradation, and other dangerous ecological changes to our mountain. While this will require a tremendous amount of work, it also presents an opportunity for us to bring some much-needed money to Takayubi in the short term.

"Kotetsu Katashi has estimated that we can gather several thousand guli's-worth of lumber from the fallen and damaged trees if we strip and treat the wood properly. Governor Lo has granted us a license to sell this lumber to building companies in the provincial capital in the spring. The rest of the supply will be set aside for our ongoing construction projects. Eventually, I intend to have everyone's family home rebuilt, but our first project will be a simple school building to replace the Takayubi public elementary, middle, and high schools destroyed in the storm. Numu Kotetsu has drawn up blueprints, and construction will begin immediately."

"What?" Someone said in confusion.

"Why would we build a school? We barely have enough houses to hold all of us."

"We cannot allow our children to fall behind in their education," Takeru said. "Also, the Takayubi public schools in the western village were a vital source of income for many families. The government may not be offering us direct aid, but they are required to pay the salaries of public school staff. Any citizens with the ability to read and teach the Empire standard curriculum may serve as teachers and administrative staff—including women."

It was a good idea. Most of Takayubi's population had enough education to read Kaigengua.

"For those who are not able to read as well, the school will require cleaning and maintenance staff, whose salaries will also be covered by the government. With everything proceeding according to Numu Kotetsu's plan, the school should be constructed and open to students in two months—sooner if there are koronu willing to assist our numuwu. Provincial Governor Lo has agreed to keep Takayubi's public school licenses active if we can have new facilities open for classes within that time. When the school building is finished, we will begin construction on a new village hall, which should open up at least four more government jobs."

Looking up at Takeru, Misaki realized that she was holding Izumo rather tightly and biting her lip in nervousness. A single school and government office couldn't employ a whole town, and many of Takayubi's adult women were now single parents who didn't have the time to work a proper job, but Takeru wasn't finished.

"I would now like to address all those volunteers who have assisted us these past weeks. In addition to paying your generosity back in the future, I would like to extend an invitation to all of you to stay."

Murmurs of confusion rippled through the crowd.

"I cannot offer monetary compensation at this time, but I am reopening the Matsuda dojo for training."

That sent a second, more excited ripple of whispers and exclamations.

"If any men are willing to relocate to Takayubi to support their widowed female relatives here—or even bring their own families to settle here with them—I will train them."

A few months ago, it would not have been an enticing offer. The sword seemed like an impractical, purely ceremonial pursuit in peacetime. But with the realization that Ranga could come knocking at their door any day and the Imperial army would do nothing to protect them, training with the greatest fighter on the Sword of Kaigen suddenly looked very appealing.

"Numu Kotetsu Katashi is also seeking partners and apprentices, if any craftsmen are interested in joining us here." Another nearly irresistible offer. "Two fishing families have moved to the foot of the mountain to fish the waters here, but all of us know that Takayubi's coast once supported over twenty fishing families— nyama to their souls." Takeru inclined his head toward Setsuko. "I have spoken to my sister-in-law, who is the sole surviving member of one of those families, and to the Chibas from the neighboring areas. They have agreed that this coast should be open to any fishing people wishing to settle there. Any fishermen who move to the base of this mountain will have our aid in constructing a new home and anything else they might need to get started."

"Respectfully, Matsuda-dono, what about aid from the Imperial army?"

"Well... that is irrelevant," Takeru said. "As I have just explained, we won't be needing it."

The whole village seemed reenergized after Takeru spoke and eagerly went to work collecting lumber from the lower slopes to construct the new school building.

The notable exception was Hyori. While others had pushed through their grief, Hyori never seemed to have moved past the horrors of the attack. There was an emptiness in her eyes that left Misaki feeling haunted, as if her friend had died somewhere in that night of wind and bullets.

One night, Misaki woke to the sound of tiny bare feet on the tatami.

"Kaa-chan?" a voice said and she sat up to find Nagasa standing in the doorway.

"Naga-kun? What is it?"

"There's a ghost outside."

"What?" Misaki murmured, rubbing her eyes. Nagasa had gotten better at articulating his thoughts in the past month; that didn't mean they always made sense, but it had been months since he had woken with a nightmare.

"There's a ghost outside," Nagasa repeated, eyes wide in the dark. "I can hear it."

Beside Misaki, Takeru slept soundly. He had worked himself to such exhaustion that he wasn't likely to wake unless the mountain started falling apart beneath them. Careful not to disturb him, Misaki slid out from under the covers and went to Nagasa.

"Come on, Naga-kun. Let's get you back to—"

She paused as she caught the sound that had woken her son.

"Ghost," Nagasa insisted solemnly.

The plaintive wail was distorted by the wind, but no mother could mistake it...

"That's not a ghost, Naga-kun," Misaki said. "That's a baby."

"A baby?"

"Yes." The sound was coming from Hyori's house. "Naga-kun, stay here. Get back in bed. Kaa-chan will be back soon."

Misaki rushed to the genkan, put on her tabi, fastened them with quick fingers, and grabbed her coat on her way out. When she stepped out the front doors, she found Setsuko already standing outside.

"Misaki," she said. "Did you hear—?"

"Yes," Misaki said, finishing pulling her coat on over bedclothes. The infant's cries were issuing from Hyori's shack. "Do you think she's already given birth? Isn't it early?"

Setsuko was counting the months and weeks on her fingers, mouthing to herself in thought. "Yeah, a bit." She perked up. "Maybe that's a good sign. "You know... maybe..."

Maybe the baby was Dai's.

Misaki nodded. "Let's go."

The Matsuda women were joined by Fuyuko, Fuyuhi, and a few men from the neighboring houses, who had awakened to the sound. The Mizumaki women carried lanterns, and Misaki noticed that two of the men—Ginkawa Aoki and the volunteer named Ameno Kentaro—had their swords. It seemed odd to bring weapons to check on a new mother and her baby, but there was something unsettling about that squalling. The shack's walls creaked as the group gathered around the door.

"Hyori-chan?" Setsuko knocked eagerly. "May we come in?"

There was no response, only the frantically repetitive cries of the infant, uninterrupted, as though no one else was there.

"Yukino-san!" Ginkawa Aoki tried, a bit louder. "Are you in there?"

"Hyori!" Setsuko's tone had grown more urgent. "Hyori, please answer us! Are you alright?"

"Apologies for the intrusion, Yukino-san," Aoki said finally, "we're coming in." And he broke down the door.

Setsuko was the first to rush in, followed closely by Misaki and the Mizumaki women with their lanterns.

Hyori lay on her side atop one of Yukino Dai's kimono that she had recovered from her old home, one hand curled into the fabric. Takenagi stuck through her body, its silvery blade protruding from her back.

She was dead.

"No! No!" Setsuko fell on Hyori's body, sobbing, as Fuyuko crumpled to her knees in shock and Fuyuhi turned her face away. "Hyori, come on!" Setsuko begged, tears running down her cheeks. "Come on, sweetheart, open those pretty eyes. Hyori! No! No!"

Misaki didn't go to the body. There were no tears left in her. She couldn't explain it; somehow, she had known before they broke the door down that Hyori was gone. She had been gone for a long time.

"Misaki, do something!" Setsuko sobbed, cradling Hyori's head in her lap. "Stop the bleeding!"

Misaki only shook her head. Even if Hyori's heart had still been beating, there was no way to save a person from a wound like that. Hyori must have braced Takenagi against something and thrown her full weight onto the blade—a decisive end.

"I'm sorry, Setsuko," Misaki whispered. "She's gone."

Stepping softly past Setsuko, Misaki went to the cradle, where the crying had not stopped. The baby was a girl, lying tangled in the blankets, her eyes screwed shut and her head thrown back as she bawled. She was the smallest infant Misaki had ever seen, but as her tiny hands moved, the air inside the shack stirred, brushing Misaki's hair and sleeves.

Great Nami. No child, not even a Matsuda, manifested powers the day they were born. It was unheard of. Shaken, Misaki remembered the terrifying death fonya of Hyori's rapist—so overwhelming it had thrown Misaki into the wall and destroyed the room.

"That is not Yukino-dono's child," Ameno Kentaro said in a fearful whisper. "It's not one of ours."

The baby was bleeding from a razor-thin cut on her neck that could only have come from a Kotetsu blade. With a chill, Misaki realized that Hyori must have held Takenagi to her baby's throat... but she had not dealt the finishing cut. In the end, she hadn't had it in her to kill her own child.

Ameno Kentaro's hand went to his katana.

"No." Misaki moved quickly around the cradle, placing herself in between the warrior and the infant.

"Move aside, Matsuda-dono." Kentaro started to draw his sword.

Her blood rising, Misaki grabbed his arm and forcibly slammed the weapon back into its sheath.

"Don't."

Kentaro's eyes widened at her strength. "M-Matsuda-dono..." He stared, uncomprehending, at the dainty hand clamped around his wrist. "Wh-what—"

"You will not harm this child," Misaki hissed.

"It's a fonyaka," he protested, trying and failing to pull his arm from Misaki's grip. "Look at that cut. Yukino herself was ready to kill it."

"But she didn't!" Misaki returned fiercely. "She held the blade and she made her choice. Her last decision in this world was that this child would live. Who are we to take that away from her?"

"But... it's a Ranganese child—"

"It is *Hyori's* child," Misaki hissed, shoving him back, "which means that it belongs to all of us. You will step away."

"Matsuda-dono," Ginkawa Aoki started. "I don't think—"

"Step *away*, Ginkawa-san."

Leaning over the cradle, Misaki put a hand to the baby's neck and healed the cut as best she could. Though thin, it was deep. Even with the best scabbing, it would almost certainly scar. When Misaki felt confident that the scab would hold, she carefully swaddled the tiny girl, stopping her squirming and the accompanying breeze.

"Matsuda-dono," Aoki tried again. "I know you're a woman and you're subject to your maternal instincts, but we need to think about this rationally. That thing is a fonyaka."

Ignoring Ginkawa's protests, Misaki lifted the infant in her arms and held her close, stroking her soft head. She was so tiny, and both men still had their hands on their swords.

"You will want to leave now, gentlemen."

"We're not leaving, Matsuda-dono."

"I think you are."

"But—"

"The child needs to nurse," Misaki said, and that shut them up.

Ginkawa Aoki, who had climbed over corpses in the dark and tourniqueted his comrade's arm with the tie of his sword, looked at his feet in embarrassment. Ameno Kentaro had gone rather red in the cheeks.

"Get out," she said, and this time neither of them protested.

In the end, Hyori's baby wouldn't take Misaki's breast, but she did eventually stop crying. When morning came, Misaki took the newborn to the orphanage.

"You will raise her along with all the other children orphaned in the attack," she told the finawu there. "I can't take her in, but this child is under my protection. I don't want to hear that any harm has come to her. Do you understand?"

"Yes, Matsuda-dono."

Hyori was cremated the next day. The house, tainted by the unspeakable act of suicide, had to be burned down too. With that, the Yukinos of Takayubi were truly gone. The baby, after all, was not a Yukino.

Though they were not allowed to speak of it, everyone silently understood that the child had come in with the wind that had taken so much away. As she grew, it became apparent that she did not have a drop of jiya in her, though the air around her was always restless. It almost seemed like her mother's grief had been born into her. Her eyes were huge, ancient, and haunted.

No one officially named her, but the village, in their whispers, called her Kazeko, Wind Child, for the terrible thing that had brought her into their midst. Perhaps that was the reason Takayubi tolerated her presence: she was walking memory. Bodies could be burned and buried. The blood of the dead could be washed from a blade. But this creature, with the eyes of Yukino Hyori and the power of a fonyaka, was irrefutable. They might fear and hate her, but she was living testament to everything the Empire had tried to erase.

As long she walked the Duna, no one could forget what had happened on the Sword of Kaigen.

31

ROBIN

Come spring the next year, Takayubi was a village again. Smaller and poorer than it had been, but recognizably a village, with houses, shops, and people waking each morning to go about their work.

The rich soil where the bodies had been burned had sprouted long grass and the beginnings of a grove of trees, lusher than any other place on the mountain. It gave Misaki a sense of peace and satisfaction to watch the vibrant greenery grow. The Empire may have refused to let the people of Takayubi mark the graves of the dead, but the mountain didn't forget.

Misaki paused there to pray, as she did every day on her way back up the mountain from the morning market. She set aside her baskets of fish and vegetables and waded through the waves of grass, realizing that a subtle footpath was forming there—a break in the grass, where her feet, Takeru's, Hiroshi's, and Nagasa's had walked the same way so many times in the past months. Today, for the first time, Misaki took Izumo from the sling across her chest and set him on his feet to walk with her.

Her youngest son wasn't quite two yet, and he looked at the grass with wide eyes, clearly unsure what to make of the bright green world suddenly towering all around him. Mamoru, Hiroshi, and Nagasa had all displayed shards of their forefathers' greatness by the time they started to walk—Mamoru in his ferocious spirit, Hiroshi in his ice-clad calm, Nagasa in his energy and vocabulary.

Izumo had none of those.

He was softer than his brothers somehow. Though born to a pair of killers—his mother, the underhanded ambush predator and his father an unquestioned alpha predator—he had a nervous air about him that was more characteristic of prey. Water moved but never frosted at his touch, and there was a constant wariness in his eyes, which were so much rounder and wider than those of any Matsuda Misaki had known. Without taking his gaze off the grass, he subconsciously tipped closer to his mother and reached a tiny hand out for her. She offered him her index finger and he held on tight as they made their way to the center of the greenery.

A black pine grew here, young like everything else in the grove, but wiry and strong. It was here that Misaki knelt and put her palms to the ground. Other people had their own special markers in the grove where they chose to pray. Obedient to the will of the Emperor, no one in Takayubi spoke about where they prayed and why, but there was an understanding among these people that ran deeper than spoken words.

Everyone in Takayubi knew that when Matsuda Takeru the First redesigned his family sign and seal for the new age, he chose characters meaning 'waiting field'—"To give the name a sense of promise," he had explained to his descendants. Everyone knew that prior to that, the name Matsuda had been written with more ancient characters meaning 'field of pines.'

Like the blood of gods, the things Takayubi knew went back thousands of years, and they would echo, wordlessly, in the tolling of the temple bell, for a thousand more. They would remain like roots, no matter what wind or bombs came upon the mountain. Yammankalu might need jaseliwu to sing their history aloud for them to weather the centuries. Hadeans might need theirs written in books. The truth of Takayubi was something one felt, from the depths of the ocean and the roots of trees.

Gathering water vapor to liquid in her hands, Misaki formed two rectangular blocks of ice. She etched characters into both—into the first, the incantation for purification, into the second the incantation of a mother's love.

Most Kaigenese wrote their prayers on pieces of cloth and kayiri, which they then tied to trees or temple posts at their holy sites. Since such prayers would have violated the Emperor's orders not to mark the area, the people of Takayubi had returned to a different way of honoring their dead, an ancient form of prayer that predated modern Falleya.

Misaki softly spoke the incantations with her eyes closed. Then she held out her ice talismans and let them melt between her fingers into the soil, watering the young pine and the surrounding green.

Nyama to you, Mamoru.

When she stood to go, Misaki found Izumo on his hands and knees watching an ant creep from a tree root onto a blade of grass. The whole time she had prayed, he hadn't made a sound. Aside from Hiroshi, Misaki had never known such a quiet child.

Unlike Hiroshi, however, Izumo gave her the impression that his head was alive with a clamor of thoughts. No matter what was going on around him, he always seemed to find some small thing to fascinate him—the drip from the end of an icicle, the stitches holding his own sleeves together, the slow progress of an ant following its fellows' scent trail up a blade of grass. Unlike Nagasa, he would not immediately voice half a dozen questions when he found something he didn't understand. Instead, he would sit and watch, and watch, and watch...

"Izu-kun?" Misaki said gently—and perhaps he was not quite like prey. Prey looked up when there was a noise, but Izumo seemed too absorbed to hear her. He reached out a single finger, delicately controlled for such a small child, and brushed the ant's twiddling antennae.

"Izu-kun," Misaki said again, and he blinked up at her.

"Water?" He asked, pointing down at the ant perched atop the blade of grass. "Water in it?"

"In the grass, yes," Misaki said. "The bug has different stuff inside it."

"Blood?"

"Not exactly," she said. "Not like yours and mine. Its body is filled with a different substance..." she struggled for the word for a moment, trying to think back to the chemical jiya classes of her school days. "*Hemolymph*, I think."

In practice, this information was useless to most jijakalu, who did not have the ability to manipulate substances other than fresh or salt water. But if Izumo already had the ability to sense the minuscule speck of unfamiliar fluid contained in an ant's body, he might be one of the exceptional few, like Misaki, who could manipulate a wide range of substances.

"Time to go." She held out her hand and he took her first two fingers in a grip so much weaker and softer than his brothers'.

Normally, Misaki had nothing but disdain for weakness—in herself or others. That was normal in a Shirojima koro. Already, Takeru was starting to look at his youngest son with displeasure, his frown deepening with each week that passed without Izumo displaying any of his brothers' power. Strangely, Misaki found herself feeling just the opposite about her Izumo. She had never seen anyone inspect their physical surroundings as closely as her fourth son—no one, except perhaps Koli Kuruma, the greatest inventor of his generation. She was beginning to suspect that Izumo had something none of his brothers had. She suspected that he might be a genius. And the more ridiculously he behaved, the more she seemed to love him.

Izumo stood, the branches of the young pine brushing his hair, and Misaki beamed. No matter what he grew into, she was excited to see it. This time she wouldn't miss a moment of it. Holding Izumo's hand, she bowed toward the black pine a last time.

Until tomorrow, Mamoru.

Once out of the grove, she strapped Izumo back into place on her chest, picked up her baskets, and headed up the path to the Matsuda compound. Everything seemed normal when she reached the house. The silence that had pervaded the Matsuda estate had retreated in the past months, giving way to the sounds that filled the air this morning—the laughter of Nagasa and Ayumi chasing each other through the halls, the thwack of wooden blades as Takeru's students warmed up in the dojo, the thudding hammers of numuwu working on the new addition to the front of the house.

She was slipping out of her tabi when she noticed an unfamiliar pair of shoes sitting in the genkan—black, with Yammanka-style magnetic fastenings. Not the shoes of a Shirojima native. Her stomach clenched in anxiety. Was a representative from the government here? Maybe the Empire had decided to come back and meddle after all? At the sound of footsteps, she looked up to find Setsuko rushing around the corner to meet her.

"Misaki!" Setsuko was wearing a strange expression, somewhere between excitement and anxiety. "You're back!"

"Yes." Misaki eyed her sister-in-law in confusion. "What's going on? Is something wrong?"

"I'm... not sure," Setsuko said, still breathless. Despite being flustered, she didn't seem upset.

"What—"

"Just come." Setsuko motioned Misaki inside, taking the heavy baskets from her shoulders. "Come see for yourself."

"Who's here?" Misaki said with a glance back at the black shoes.

"Just... just go see." Setsuko nodded toward the doorway to the recently reconstructed sitting room.

"But—"

"Your man has been struggling a bit. You know his Yammaninke isn't very good."

"His Yammaninke? What—"

"Go." Setsuko nudged her ample hip into Misaki's smaller one, sending her stumbling toward the sitting room.

Thoroughly confused but curious, Misaki threw one last look back at Setsuko, who gave her an encouraging nod. Then she straightened up and stepped into the sitting room doorway. Setsuko's strange behavior had her ready to expect the worst— Colonel Song or some other representative of the Empire here to ruin everything they had built. What she found was so, so much stranger.

Robin Thundyil knelt on a cushion at the low sitting room table opposite Takeru.

They were having tea.

Misaki's world simultaneously tore apart and crashed in on itself.

A dizzying, rending tear opened between her most vivid memories and the breathing reality of the scene before her. Robin was here, in the middle of her sitting room, his familiar face visibly aged fifteen years, drinking tea.

She put a hand to the doorframe to steady herself. The other hand clutched at Izumo, pressing the boy into her chest to feel his beating heart—to confirm that she was still in the real world.

Takeru noticed her first.

"Misaki," he said, his voice as neutrally placid as ever. "I'm glad you're back."

Robin lowered his teacup and turned to look at her, burning black eyes as warm as they had been sixteen years ago. Those eyes had seared themselves a place in her memory, making it entirely too disorienting to meet them in reality. Unable to process Robin's gaze, she sought out Takeru instead.

"Forgive my rudeness, Thundyil-san. I have to get back to training my students." Takeru stood. "Excuse me." He gave Robin a short bow and crossed to the doorway where his wife was still frozen in shock.

"Wh-what—what... what is this?" Misaki whispered, looking up at Takeru. "What is happening?"

"Your old friend came a long way to see you."

"But—what—"

"My students are waiting for me. Make sure you prepare our guest more tea. He's almost finished the pot Setsuko made." That was all Takeru said before sweeping away down the hall, leaving Misaki in her confusion.

Robin stood, smiling—merciful Nami, that smile. So familiar. Yet it was also the smile of a stranger, deepened with lines and angles that didn't quite belong to the Robin from her memories.

"Look at you," he said and the sound of his Lindish tugged at a long-forgotten feeling in her chest. *"You went and turned into a lady."*

Misaki let out a weak laugh. Her faded kimono, one of only three she still owned, had been washed so many times that it was starting to wear through. Between the rebuilding and her usual housework, she had all but given up on keeping her hair neat. She had never looked less like a lady in her life.

"And look at you," she returned with an amused glance over Robin's black and red kimono and the cloth bundle on his back. *"Don't you look sharp."*

"Shut up."

She made fun, but Robin had actually always been good at looking perfectly at home in any clothes, with any people he met. His willingness to change his appearance was just part of his particular brand of openness. If Robin sat down with a person, there was always a sense that they belonged to him and he belonged to them. As an orphan, he had learned to make family wherever he went.

Knowing she had been staring at his clothes to the point of rudeness, Misaki forced her gaze upward, to his face, to that open smile. It was still like seeing a ghost—he had been as good as one after she had resigned herself to the idea that she would never see him again.

Part of her wanted to back away. An equally powerful part of her wanted to fall forward and run to him. Caught between them, she swayed, toes curling on the threshold. She couldn't touch him. They both knew that. A simple pat on the shoulder would be considered improper, and if she touched his skin... she might come undone.

Izumo broke the silence with a confused burble and Robin turned his smile to the child.

"I met your two older sons when I arrived. Who is this?"

"Oh," Misaki breathed out, thankful for the break in the tension. *"This is Izumo."* Untying the cloth, she turned her youngest so that he was facing Robin and set him on his feet. *"He's—"* She paused with a fond roll of her eyes as Izumo scooted behind her and clamped his arms around her knee. *"He's shy around strangers."*

She was almost glad of Izumo's little body clinging to her leg. It kept her from teetering. She was so busy trying to regain her bearings that she didn't realize that the bundle on Robin's back had started moving until a little brown hand popped out. The hand found a grip on Robin's shoulder and was soon followed by a head of sleep-tousled hair and a pair of coal black eyes.

He had a child too.

The boy was unmistakably Robin's son. They had the same eyes, the same hair, and the child's skin, despite being a shade darker than Robin's, exuded the same fiery glow. Robin beamed as the sleepy toddler rubbed his eyes.

"Daniel," he said, *"this is Auntie Misaki."*

"What..." Misaki's voice had gotten unusually high and breathy. *"That's... When did this happen?"*

"It's a long story," Robin said.

Misaki might not have been able to touch Robin, but...

"May I?" She held out her arms.

"Of course." Robin unslung the cloth wrap from his back with as much grace as any Kaigenese housewife. *"I should warn you,"* he said, perching the tiny boy on his shoulder while he folded up the blue speckled fabric, *"he's at the age where he'll just randomly combust."*

"Right." Misaki remembered that about tajaka children.

"Feel free to drop him if he gets too hot."

"What?"

"It's what Elleen does. He usually lands on his feet."

Misaki laughed as she reached out and took Robin's son. An achingly evocative scent of smoke and spice washed over her as the boy's warmth filled her arms.

"Hello, Daniel," she said, her voice soft to conceal the emotion that had suddenly overcome her.

"I'm Daniel," the little tajaka said brightly.

"That's what I heard."

"Now you can say 'what's your name'?" Robin suggested gently.

Instead, Daniel grabbed onto one of Misaki's hairpins and said, *"What's that?"*

"That's my hairpin." Misaki reached behind her head and nudged his hand away from the accessory. *"I wouldn't touch it. It's a bit sharp."*

"What's sharp?"

"Nukeela," Robin translated to a language Misaki didn't know.

"It might hurt you. Ouch."

"Ouch," Daniel repeated happily and put his finger in his mouth.

"Your nyama feels just like your dad's," Misaki couldn't help but comment.

"That's my dad." Daniel took his finger out of his mouth and pointed at Robin.

"I know," Misaki laughed.

"I'm Daniel."

"Yes, you told me. It's an interesting name." Certainly not Disanka. She glanced at Robin. *"Where did it come from?"*

Robin's smile didn't disappear, but it lost some of its brightness. *"His mother chose it."*

"Oh." Misaki paused. *"And, um... his mother?"*

"She's gone."

"Oh, Robin, I... I'm sorry. I had no idea—"

"Well, I had no idea what had happened here until your old roommate, Guang Ya-li, tracked me down and suggested I check on you. Let's just agree that we need to do a better job keeping in touch."

"Yeah." Misaki tried to smile, but it proved to be a little too hard. *"I..."* She tried to think of something to say. *"I, um..."* Daniel spared her by grabbing a handful of her bangs and trying to clamber onto her shoulders. *"You like climbing?"* she giggled as Robin scolded his son in that language she didn't recognize.

"I'm a good climber," Daniel told her.

"My Mamoru was the same when he was your age."

"I also heard about your first son," Robin said. *"I'm so sorry. I wish I could have been here in time to... I wish I could have met him."*

"Oh, I don't know that that would have been a good idea," Misaki said, sweeping aside the threatening swell of emotion with another laugh. *"You two were dangerously alike. You could have gotten him into all kinds of trouble."* She found, once again, that she couldn't meet Robin's eyes. *"So, um..."* She bent to set Daniel on his feet. *"Has anyone shown you around the house?"*

"Not yet."

"Great," Misaki said. *"Let me give you the tour."* She turned to lead Robin out of the room and, in her distracted state, nearly tripped over Izumo who had shifted around her to cling to the other side of her kimono.

"Ara—!" She exclaimed, catching herself on the doorframe. " Izu-kun! What are you doing?"

Izumo appeared to be shying away from Daniel, who was determinedly trying to say 'hello.'

"I'm Daniel," the tiny tajaka said in Lindish, which Izumo of course, did not understand. *"Do you want to play with me?"*

Izumo just buried his face in Misaki's thigh, smothering a terrified sound.

"I don't think Izumo wants to play, Daniel," Robin said, pinching the back of Daniel's shirt between two fingers and pulling his son back a few steps. *"Let's leave him alone for now."*

"Why?" Daniel asked as Misaki set about prying Izumo from her leg.

"Because he doesn't want to play."

"Why?"

"I don't know. That's his business. Maybe we'll ask him later."

Izumo didn't willingly let go of his mother's leg until Robin picked Daniel up and put him on his shoulders. When he was sure that the terrifyingly friendly boy couldn't get to him, he detached and settled for holding Misaki's finger.

"Watch your head," Robin warned Daniel as he carefully ducked the two of them through the sitting room doorway to follow Misaki into the hall.

"On your *head,"* Daniel said as if that meant something.

"No, 'watch your head,'" Robin said. *"Kisee bhee cheez par apana sir mat maaro. Don't hit your head on anything."*

"Hit your head! Hit your head!" Daniel chanted happily, smacking his open palm on top of Robin's head as if it were a drum.

Misaki laughed and realized how thankful she was that Daniel was here. The idea of Robin having a child—of him being here with *her* children—was still difficult to wrap her head around, but there was something about a happy two-year-old that made everything simple.

"Does he always have this much energy?" Misaki asked as the little tajaka broke into a garbled song that didn't seem to be in any discernible language.

Robin gave her a tortured look as Daniel continued to use his head as a drum. *"You have no idea."*

She might have been embarrassed about the diminished state of the once-grand Matsuda compound, but if there was one person she knew would never judge a person by their material possessions, it was Robin.

"And through here is the dojo," she said in a low voice.

They stood quietly watching for a while as Takeru called instructions and his students responded, their wooden bokken clacking together. Even Daniel had fallen silent in fascination, leaning over the top of his father's head to watch the training jijakalu move through their drills in perfect unison—well, not quite perfect. Kwang Chul-hee still lagged behind the others by a half dinma here and there, but he was getting better.

Takeru's thirty-some students were all paired off by size except one, who drilled alone. Hiroshi's movements were as sharp and clean as any of the adults', but he was far too small to partner with any of the grown men or teenagers.

"We shouldn't disturb the class," Misaki whispered and motioned for Robin to follow her down the hall. *"We can come back for a better look when it's not full of students."*

Robin hesitated at the dojo doorway for a moment before following her. *"Was that your son, Hiroshi, in there?"*

"Yeah."

"I thought he was only six."

"He is."

"And he trains with the grown men?" Robin said in astonishment.

"Well, he's not a normal six."

Their last stop was the addition that Kotetsu's new apprentices had started to build onto the side of the Matsuda compound. The numuwu were taking a break but Misaki was pleased to see that they had started on the exterior wall.

"And what is this?" Robin asked, staring up at the naked structure.

"This," Misaki said, touching one of the beams, *"is going to be my restaurant."*

"Your what?"

"I'm opening a restaurant."

Takeru had vehemently opposed the idea of his wife working a normal job like a peasant, but after she had pointed out that she could employ some of the other villagers, and they had gone over a business plan, he had given in. In the end, it seemed that even Takeru's Matsuda pride could not overrule his financial sensibilities.

With Governor Lo's glowing recommendation, Takeru had stayed on as mayor of Takayubi. Between that modest government salary and the small amount of income he collected from his sword students, he had kept the family afloat through the recent months, but afloat wasn't enough. If they wanted to maintain their property and make a good future for the boys and Ayumi, they needed more.

As Robin looked around the space, a wide grin spread across his face. Shirojima men just didn't smile like that. *"Misaki, this is fantastic!"*

"You don't think it's a stupid idea?"

"It's an amazing idea! Although it might be a little small."

"What do you mean?"

"Well, after the province tastes your food, do you think the five or six tables you can fit in here are going to be enough to seat all your customers?"

Misaki folded her arms, unable to hold back a smile. *"I think you're misremembering how good my cooking was."*

"Nah," Robin said confidently, *"I'm not. Where did you get this idea anyway?"*

"After the storm, Takeru put me in charge of rationing our food supply. I found out I wasn't just good at cooking food for lots of people; I turn out to be pretty good at distributing it efficiently and directing a kitchen. Setsuko and I miss having our girls around. We figured employing a few might be a good way to keep them."

"Pita! Pita!" Daniel said, smacking the sides of his father's head.

"Ow. What is it, Daniel?" Robin asked.

"Fly!"

"Okay." Reaching back to grab a handful of Daniel's little red kimono, Robin threw him through the open roof, high into the air. The tiny tajaka shrieked with laughter even as Misaki yelped in alarm. She had forgotten how good Robin's reflexes were. He caught the boy neatly by his ankle on his way down.

"What now, kiddo?" he asked as his dangling son giggled. *"Up? Down?"*

"Down!"

"You got it." Robin lowered an upside-down Daniel to the floor and let go of his ankle.

As Misaki watched, the toddler walked a few steps forward on his hands before tumbling onto his feet and continuing on his way.

"Don't run too far now," Robin said.

Daniel blinked up at him, looking confused. Kneeling down, Robin switched languages. *"Bahut door bhaago mat, okay?"*

"Okay, Pita."

Misaki realized that the beautiful, rolling language Robin and Daniel spoke with each other must be Disaninke—a language Robin had not had much occasion to use since being forced to flee his homeland of Disa as a small child. Despite spending the majority of his life in the Lindish and Yammaninke-speaking country of Carytha, Robin was raising Daniel to be fluent in his mother tongue. It might not be particularly practical, but it was sweet.

"This really looks great, Misaki," Robin said when Daniel had toddled off to explore the space. *"You know I'm willing to help any way I can."*

"I'll ask the numuwu if they've got a job for you."

"I meant—"

"I know what you meant," Misaki cut him off. *"It's kind of you, but it's unnecessary. Also out of the question. The Matsuda house has its pride."*

"It wouldn't have to be a donation," Robin said. *"I can invest—"*

Misaki shook her head. *"We're going to be alright."*

The irony of the situation was not lost on Misaki: when she and Robin had first met, she had come from a rich family and he had had nothing...

"Robin?"

"Hmm?"

"I need to say something to you." It had been itching at her mind since she saw him in her sitting room.

His smile dimmed. He probably recognized the tension in her voice and braced himself.

"I'm sorry—"

"Don't." His voice had grown strained. *"Misaki, please. Don't apologize—"*

"Not for that." Even she wasn't cruel enough to bring *that* up. *"Or... not just for that anyway. It's more complicated. I just need to say that I'm sorry for... vacationing in your life."*

"What?" Robin looked genuinely surprised. *"What are you talking about?"*

"When we were younger, I came into your country with no understanding of what you, or Elleen—or anyone in Carytha, really—had suffered, and I was so disrespectful."

"I don't think you were disrespectful."

"But I was," Misaki said sadly. *"I was a rich, self-centered girl with no concept of what you were trying to do and why it was important. I used you and your work to satisfy my lust for danger, and that was wrong. I was despicable."*

"I never would have called you despicable," he said with entirely more compassion than she deserved. *"Overzealous, maybe."*

"How can you say that? I treated your peoples' lives as less than mine. I saw their suffering and it just... didn't matter to me. I'm such a cold person, it didn't matter until I was the one... until it was my home, my neighbors, my..." She pressed her lips together and rested a hand atop Izumo's head, pressing the clinging boy close against her hip.

"Your son?" Robin said gently.

"Now, as often as I think of him, I have to think of all those bodies Kalleyso left behind... peoples' sons and daughters. I just

never acknowledged that." She had been as bad as Colonel Song and his soldiers, who regarded Takayubi's fallen warriors as no more than lost game pieces. *"So I need to say sorry. I'm sorry for treating your life like a game."*

"I never held that against you, Misaki."

"How?" she demanded in disbelief. *"How can you be so forgiving?"*

"There was no way you could have understood. You can't until it's you. I know that."

"That doesn't make it right."

"No, but that's what humans are like. I knew as soon as I started forming the idea of Firebird that no one was going to understand. That didn't matter. I had to do it. You had enough faith in me to follow me into danger, even without understanding why. I'll always be grateful for that."

"You know it wasn't just faith," Misaki said quietly.

"Well then, I'm flattered anyway."

It was as close as either of them dared go in reference to what had happened between them, what they had been.

"Misaki, while we're exchanging apologies, I'm sorry that I didn't..." but of course Robin couldn't say it. He couldn't say that he should have taken her away. He sighed. *"For someone who tries to help people as a full-time job, sometimes... I can be very bad at figuring out the best way to do it. I'm sorry if I failed you, in any way."*

Misaki didn't know what to say. She couldn't repeat the things she had said to Robin the last time they had met—that she didn't want him, that he was beneath her, that he had misunderstood their relationship. She couldn't be that cruel to him all over again, especially when none of it was true. And yet, wouldn't it be just as cruel to tell him the truth? That she had wanted him more than her next breath, that she would have given anything to have him take her away, that she had held onto the agony for years? Instead, she said nothing at all.

"Daniel," Robin said, noticing his son climbing one of the beams. *"I think you should get down from there."*

"Up," Daniel said with a mischievous smile and continued shimmying upward.

"Down," Robin said firmly and crossed the space to pry the stubborn toddler from the beam.

"He's already a better climber than you ever were," Misaki said, impressed. None of her boys had ever been able to climb like that, not even Mamoru, who had loved climbing.

"Yeah," Robin said, setting Daniel on his feet and trying to steer him away from the network of naked beams. *"He gets it from his mom."*

Misaki pursed her lips, then tried to smile. *"Well, that should come in handy when he has to chase you across the rooftops of Livingston."*

"Maybe." A note of bitterness had tainted Robin's voice.

"What do you mean 'maybe'?"

"Well, let's not pretend that the ability to jump across rooftops is a guarantee of survival."

For the first time in their conversation, Misaki was overcome with the feeling that she was speaking to a stranger.

"Hey now," she said in confusion. *"What happened to the fearless optimist I knew?"*

Robin shrugged. *"He grew up."*

Something about his tone—the utter defeat in his voice—shook her to the core. *"Robin... What happened to you?"*

He just shook his head. *"It's such a long story. Long and sad. And it seems like you've had enough sadness of your own since I've seen you."*

"Hey," Misaki was surprised at the fiercely defensive note in her voice. *"It hasn't all been bad."*

Robin raised his eyebrows and she lifted her chin in response. *"Excuse me, but have you seen this boy?"* Misaki took Izumo's face between her thumb and forefinger. *"You see how cute he is?"*

Robin smiled, but it didn't reach his eyes.

With a sigh, Misaki ran a hand through Izumo's hair and said more seriously, *"Horrible things have happened, yes. My father-in-law hated me, I miscarried twice, one of my closest friends committed suicide, and I lost my first son."* She held Robin's gaze, unflinching. *"But if I learned one thing from Firebird, it's that a person's tragedy doesn't define them or cancel all the good in their life. I've had four wonderful children, whom I love. I still have three of them, and now, after all these years, it turns out, I have a good husband."* Misaki had never thought she would say those words, especially not to Robin Thundyil. *"I know, given what you know of him, it probably seems unbelievable—"*

"I believe it."

"I suppose you must have hoped," Misaki said, *"if you came all this way on the off chance he'd let you see me."*

"I didn't," Robin said.

"What do you mean?"

"He invited me."

"He what?"

"He said we might enjoy catching up, now that we're both parents, and that he would be grateful if I could spare some time to come see you. He told me there was some kind of incident, after the Rang—" He caught himself. *"After the storm."*

"Yeah," Misaki said. *"It was really strange. We were attacked by a littigi assassin."*

Some of the color drained from Robin's face. She had never seen the glow flee his skin like that, leaving him ashen. *"A littigi?"*

"I thought you said my husband discussed this with you."

"All he said was that he wanted to consult about an 'incident' after the 'storm' you had, and that his Yammaninke was too limited to elaborate. He wanted me to come and talk to you about it directly."

"I see." So, Takeru had practical reason for asking Robin to visit. Of course, he did. He was Takeru. *"Let's talk then."*

Misaki led Robin back to the sitting room, where they knelt at the table. He had her go back over the visual description of the assassin three times. On the third time through, he took a sketchpad from his bag and began drawing.

"You said the tattoos were in a pattern you had never seen before?" Robin said, his firepen scratching feverishly across the

kayiri. *"Describe them again. Exactly what did they look like?"*

"I don't know," Misaki shrugged. *"Swirly. Not angular like Yammanka designs, but not really wavy like Kaigenese art either. They were... curlier, I guess. I don't know. I'm not an artist."*

"Like this?" Robin held up his sketch.

"Yes," Misaki said in surprise. *"I don't think I'd have been able to draw it so nicely, but yes, that's* exactly *what it looked like."*

"You're sure?"

"Pretty sure."

"And he wore a gray cloak with a hood?"

"Yeah. I said that three times."

"Gods..."

"What is it Robin? What does this mean?"

"Well... It might *mean that all my insane fears aren't actually insane. It's all connected. He's behind all of it."*

"Who is?"

"He's gone by different names. I'm still trying to figure out the real one." He turned to Misaki. *"The littigi who attacked you... Around the time he was here, were there any other strange incidents? Did any children disappear? Any orphans?"*

"Yes," Misaki said in surprise, *"a little girl. How did you know?"*

"This is the kind of hunting ground his gray cloaks favor," Robin said, looking ill, *"full of strong theonites but secluded from the net of modern society. He likes to pick through warzones, where he can find powerful orphans wandering around, unprotected."*

"Wait, so, this man who sends the gray cloaks," Misaki said. *"Is he someone you met when you and Rakesh were in Disa?"*

"In a way."

"Okay. Good to see you haven't lost your ability to be cryptic and annoying."

"I'm not trying to be cryptic. I'm just... I'm not entirely sure who we're dealing with. All I really know is that he's planning carefully for the long term, building himself an army."

"An army?"

"Yes," Robin said, *"or what will be an army in thirteen years or so."*

"He's not just gathering soldiers. He's going to raise them." Misaki could hardly think of anything more terrifying.

Robin nodded. *"That's why he only takes children, never older than six."*

"So, he kidnaps these young jijakalu to raise as his own personal army?"

"Not just jijakalu," Robin said. *"Theonite and sub-theonite children have gone missing from warzones, slums, and little villages in Hades, Disa, the Taiyang Islands, and probably too many other places to count. Like I said, the gray cloaks target areas that aren't protected by their governments."*

"Gods!" So, this mysterious army, when it came of age, would be multi-powered? Depending on how it was executed, that could potentially make it the most dangerous fighting force in the world.

"The only commonality between all the children they take is their above-average power," Robin said. *"I assume the girl who went missing was powerful for her age?"*

"She was," Misaki said.

Now that she thought about it, Ginkawa Yukimi was a perfect candidate for the horrible thing Robin was describing. If someone had heard the littigi's bomb go off—if they needed to quickly snatch one child and get out unnoticed—she would have been the one. She was smaller than the other orphans, easy to physically overpower, but the blood of two powerful clans ran through her veins.

"From what I can tell, they try to pick out the most promising children they can whisk away without anyone noticing," Robin said. *"Thank the Gods they didn't come after your sons or your niece. I'm sure they would have liked that. It may be the reason that littigi tried to kill you and your husband."*

"Really?" Misaki said in horror.

"That or it may have been a more general attempt to destabilize the community. The more chaos the cloaks can generate, the easier it is for them to take the children they want without getting caught. They'll disappear as soon as someone comes close to finding them out."

"But you're going to stop them," Misaki said. *"You're going to save these children?"*

Robin looked away from her, toward the floor, seeming simultaneously older and smaller than she had ever seen him. *"I don't think I can."*

"What?" Who was this man behind the gray cloaks? What had he done with Robin Thundyil? *"What do you mean?"*

"You don't understand, Misaki. This man has abilities beyond me... beyond any of us. There are forces in this world—theonites— more powerful than anything you and I could have imagined when we were at Daybreak."

"I know that, Robin," Misaki said, exasperated. *"I did recently see a group of fonyakalu make a tornado big enough to blow a town away."*

"Right," Robin said. *"Now, imagine that instead of a group, that was one person."*

"What? Robin, that sounds impossible."

"It should be."

"So, you're not even going to try to stop this person?"

"I did try," Robin said with a flare of anger, *"and now Daniel doesn't have a mother."*

That made Misaki fall silent. *"Robin, I..."* She started to apologize, but he beat her to it.

"Sorry. I didn't mean to snap at you. I'm just... at a bit of a loss. There's so much information that isn't fitting together. If I can, I'd like to discuss all this with you and your husband together."

Misaki nodded. *"I'll talk to him and see when he has time. I hope there's something we can do to help."*

"I hope so too," Robin said grimly. *"At least this is good."* He gestured between the two of them. *"It's nice to have someone to bounce ideas off of."*

"You have a lot of people back home who are good for that. Like, does the Thundyil Firm still employ that professional jaseli you and Rakesh were so excited about?"

"Yeah."

"Well, surely he's the person to 'bounce ideas off.' Why haven't

you spoken to him?"

"I haven't seen him in almost four years."

"What?"

"Misaki, I haven't been in Carytha. Elleen and I were in Hades for three years, from '66 to '69."

"Oh." Misaki had always known that Elleen intended to go back to her wartorn homeland to see if she could use her powers to help her people. Robin had talked idly about going with her, but Misaki had never really thought he would do it. Firebird, she had thought, belonged in Livingston. He would never leave the city to fend for itself.

"Three years?" she said in disbelief.

"It wasn't supposed to be that long. Things got very complicated very fast and then..." He sighed. *"Well, like I said, it's a long story, but after we lost Daniel's mother, Elleen and I had to flee the country with our kids."*

"Wait, what!?" Misaki exclaimed. *"Elleen has kids too?"*

"Yeah. Didn't I mention that? She has twins, a boy and a girl."

"What—but—who with?" Misaki had trouble imagining what sort of person would be brave enough to woo someone as aloof and intimidating as Elleen—and she was married to Matsuda Takeru.

"His name is Uther," Robin said, *"the only other littigi we ever met as skilled as Elleen. Unfortunately, we had to leave him behind when the Jamu Kurankite snuck us out of the country. He was involved in too much rebel activity. Even a Jamuttaana never would have been able to get him across the border."*

"So, you and Elleen spent a bunch of time in Hades and made babies," Misaki said. *"What about Koli? How has he been?"*

"Oh, Koli went to Hades with us."

"What?" That was even more jarring than the news of Elleen having children. *"That doesn't sound like him!"* Hades was known to be the most dangerous country in the world for travelers. Why would a numu want to put himself in that kind of peril, especially one who so valued his head, his fingers, and his time undisturbed in his high-tech workshop?

"I know it seems weird," Robin said. *"He got restless and*

impulsive after his parents disinherited him."

"Wait—After what?" Misaki exclaimed, unsure if she could deal with any more jarring news about her old classmates. The Kurumas had disinherited Koli? That didn't make even a little bit of sense. He had always been his parents' spoiled favorite son, a prodigy whose ingenuity put all his siblings to shame. *"What did he do?"*

"He got married," Robin said. *"His parents did not approve his choice."*

"Why?" Misaki asked, her eyes wide in curiosity. *"What was wrong with her?"* What sort of woman would be so bad that she prompted Yamma's greatest numu family to cast out their most promising heir in generations? *"Was she a jaseli? A koro? An adyn?"*

"No, no." Robin smiled. *"None of those things. He married a nice, successful numu by the name of Nyeru Dumbaya."*

"Nyeru? But... isn't that a man's name?"

"Well, that was the part his parents didn't like."

Misaki gasped, both hands flying to her mouth. *"No!"*

"Did you not know that Koli was gay?" Robin looked amused.

"No!" Misaki said. *"You did?"*

"Of course."

"Since when?"

"I don't know." Robin shrugged. *"Our second year, maybe. I'm surprised he didn't mention it to you. You two always talked so much."*

"About weapons, not boys!" Misaki said, her voice shrill. *"Oh my Gods! So, his parents disinherited him because he married a man?"*

"Unfortunately, yes."

Misaki supposed that made sense. An upstanding numu family in the heart of Yamma couldn't reasonably be expected to react any other way.

"He acted like it didn't bother him," Robin said thoughtfully. *"He's weird like that, but I imagine it would be hard not to care. I mean, they were his parents—but I suppose you understand that better than I..."* Robin cleared his throat, clearly regretting having started the sentence.

"Yeah..."

It came as no surprise to Misaki that Koli had been defiant where she had not—but *marrying a man*? That didn't just cut him off from his parents. It cut him off from his clan, his religion, and his entire community. Yammanka Falleya was as deeply rooted in bloodlines and reproduction as the Ryuhon Falleya practiced in Shirojima. Koli would never be welcome among his own people again.

"He would have inherited his parents' company," Misaki said, a strange pain rising in her throat. *"He could have changed the world."*

Robin chuckled. *"I think Koli would resent the insinuation that he needs his parents' company or approval to change the world."*

"You're right." Misaki smiled. *"That was a stupid thing to say. But still..."*

When Misaki had considered running off with Robin, she had risked losing the acceptance of her family and the people of Shirojima. Koli had given up a multi-billion-walla inheritance, control of one of Yamma's biggest companies, his family, his friends, his network of craftsmen, even his religion... Just the thought made her shudder.

"They really do love each other," Robin said.

"Is that enough?" Misaki wondered aloud.

"Well, that's the question, isn't it?"

Despite any lingering regrets surrounding Robin, she knew she could never have cut herself off from her own roots so completely. Her strength was with these people. Her blood was of Shirojima's ocean. She experienced a strange moment of clarity as, for the first time in her life, she admired Koli's freedom from a distance, without envying it. He was Koli. She was Misaki, and just recently, she had become content with that.

"I can see why he might have wanted to get away from everything after that," Misaki said.

"In the end, it might not have been such a great idea for him to come to Hades with us," Robin said, *"seeing how we lost him."*

"You what?" Misaki exclaimed so loudly that Izumo started in her lap, and Setsuko stuck her head into room to check that

everything was okay.

"Oh, he's not dead," Robin said quickly. *"We've had communication from him since he disappeared, assuring us that he's fine. Of course, we combed his communications for any coded messages saying 'I'm not fine, come help me.' There was a hidden message in the last letter he sent—based on our old crime-fighting code system. It said: 'I actually am fine, idiots. Leave me alone.'"*

Misaki smiled. *"That does sound like him. Guess you'd better leave him alone."*

"That's what Elleen and I thought," Robin said. Vanishing into thin air in the middle of a foreign country wasn't even the weirdest thing Koli had ever done. *"Shockingly, his husband isn't very happy with us."*

"So, all three *of you went and got married while I was away?"* Misaki mused, rocking Izumo.

She wasn't surprised that Robin had found someone, but she had never pictured the other two members of their little group in romantic relationships. Koli especially was always so wrapped up in his work that she never would have thought he would find time for a girl—or a *boy*, as the case might be.

"That's the funny thing," Robin said. *"None of us are actually married in a technical sense."*

"What do you mean?"

"In Koli and Nyeru's case, it's not legal. They went through all the ceremonies, but their union isn't recognized by Yamma or Carytha. The time Elleen had with Uther was so chaotic that they never got around to an official marriage."

"And Daniel's mother?"

He sighed. *"Telling people we were married makes it easier, raises fewer questions. It was just a local ceremony in the village where we happened to be hiding at the time. I didn't understand half the words. I don't even know if it was legally binding."* He shook his head as if trying to clear it of memories. *"But I have to say... it's such a relief to be here and see that you're getting along with your husband."*

"I'm sorry," Misaki said. *"I'm sorry you didn't get a chance at*

that."

Robin let out a painful approximation of his usual laugh. *"I talk like I had plans to make a life with Daniel's mother, but I don't think there was ever much of a chance of that with her. She was... quite the character, not really the type to settle down and have a family."*

"I see." Sensing the pain in Robin, Misaki tried to shift the topic. *"So, if you left Hades last year, where have you been since then?"*

Robin shrugged. *"Around."*

He tried to explain, saying vague things about keeping people off his trail and needing to investigate this or that in Yamma, in Disa, in the Taiyang Islands. It was clear that he had been flitting around since Daniel had been born, like a bird that had just encountered a dangerous land predator and was now unwilling to touch down anywhere. He was afraid.

"I feel bad," he said. *"Your husband had been trying to contact me for a while before I actually got one of his messages. He's probably not the only one—"*

"Robin, you need to go home," Misaki said.

"Really?" Robin raised his eyebrows. *"I came here expecting to be thrown out before long, but not by you."*

"Don't be a child," Misaki snapped more harshly than she meant to. *"I didn't mean right this instant. As far as I'm concerned, you're always welcome here and you can stay as long as you want, but this isn't your home. Livingston is your home."*

"Technically, Disa is my homeland."

"But you were made new—made whole—in Livingston, like I was made new here."

"And are you whole?" There was no challenge or resentment in the question, only concern.

"Yes," Misaki said and it was true. It was true, for the first time ever, the moment she looked Robin directly in the eyes and said, *"I am whole."*

Wholeness, she had learned, was not the absence of pain but the ability to hold it.

"Livingston made you who you are. You'll never be more you

than you are on those streets. I don't know what you're doing running all over the world like you expect to find your strength somewhere else."

"You're probably right," he sighed. *"I never should have gone to Hades. There's only so much lasting good you can do in a place that doesn't really belong to you."*

"Tell you what," Misaki said. *"I'll talk to my husband and we'll let you ask all the questions you want on one condition."*

"Yeah?"

"That after this is done, you go home to Livingston and collect yourself."

Robin didn't say anything but he nodded in agreement. The two of them were quiet for a time. Izumo had gone to sleep in Misaki's lap.

"Do you want to tell me about her?" The words were easier for Misaki to say than she thought they would be.

"I wish I could."

"What do you mean?"

"I wish I had a hundred stories to tell about her." Robin's voice was quiet and far away. *"But I barely knew her. I was going to. At least, I was going to try..."*

"So, what happened?" Misaki asked. *"Was she sick with something?"*

"No. She died a koro's death."

Misaki found herself letting out a sigh. *"Damn it, Robin."*

"What?"

"It's just that I... all these years, I had a few things that comforted me. I would look out there." She nodded to the horizon visible through sitting room's open door. *"At the sun. And I would imagine that somewhere, you were happy. You made it work somehow. You found a girl who was nice enough to be gentle with your heart and tough enough to keep up with everything in it, and you had the family you always wanted."*

"Oh." Robin looked touched for a moment, then gave Misaki an amused smile. *"Well, that wasn't a very reasonable assumption."*

"But it made me happy."

Robin let out a laugh. *"Great Falleke, Misaki. What happened to my friend, the brutal cynic?"*

Misaki raised her chin stubbornly. *"She grew up."*

"Ha, ha. I see what you did there."

"Misaki!" Setsuko called from the hallway and then appeared in the doorway to the sitting room. "Hey, sorry to interrupt, but can you help me with dinner? I'd do it myself, but we have company and I don't want it to be terrible."

"Sure." Excusing herself, Misaki shifted Izumo onto her hip, and stood.

As she left the sitting room, Daniel scampered by, and she caught him by the back of his little red kimono. *"Daniel,"* she whispered, leaning in close, *"I have an important job for you."*

"What?"

"Go hug your dad."

Daniel looked confused for a moment but went and draped his arms around Robin's shoulders.

....

Misaki went to her bedroom that night eager to ask Takeru what in the world he had been thinking inviting Robin to their home. Unsurprisingly, he wasn't there. Training students in the dojo meant that he had to push his clerical work late into the night. Misaki couldn't remember the last time he had slept before she did.

He would be in his study now, hard at work. Knowing an interruption would be unwelcome, she resolved to wait up for him so they could talk. Drawing the lantern close, she pulled out her sewing and started stitching for something to keep her awake. It didn't work. Waatinu later, she was vaguely conscious of cool hands taking the needle and thread from her fingers and setting them aside before extinguishing the lantern. Darkness fell and familiar coolness covered her like a blanket of snow. When she woke to the light of dawn, Takeru was sound asleep beside her.

Birdsong echoed through the mist outside as she pulled herself onto her knees to consider her sleeping husband. Takeru was an intelligent person, but he tended to have a blind spot where human emotions were concerned. Could he really not know how she felt about Robin? She rested a hand over his steadily beating heart and decided he must know. He had seen the way she and Robin looked at each other that day, sixteen years ago, and he wasn't stupid.

Her mind spun back to that heart-stopping moment when he had lowered his Whispering Blade, exposing his neck. Was that what this was? Some sort of test?

"What are you doing, love?" she murmured into the morning stillness.

Her husband, still deeply asleep, had no answer.

....

Takeru remained overwhelmed with his dojo and administrative work for three days. Robin spent a good amount of that time attempting to help the numu men with the construction. Being a koro, he wasn't very good at using his taya to weld, and there was the language barrier to contend with. When he sensed that he was getting in the way, he took to following Misaki and Setsuko around, asking for housework he could help with, which amused Setsuko to no end.

"I'm a single parent," he said when Misaki gave him some green onions to slice and Setsuko went into a fit of laughter. *"And if Daniel is anything like me, he's going to be a bottomless pit when he gets bigger. I'll have to learn to cook competently sooner or later."*

Misaki translated for Setsuko, which just made her laugh harder. "Kare ippai kane ga aru jyanai ka?"

"What did she say now?"

"Aren't you super rich?" Misaki translated.

"Are rich people not allowed to cook?"

"Well, rich men *aren't."*

"He doesn't even know how to hold the knife!" Setsuko cackled.

"Don't mind Setsuko," Misaki said reassuringly. *"Your food can't possibly be as bad as hers."*

When they had mixed the vegetables, egg, flour, and meat into batter, Setsuko was still shaking her head. "I never thought I'd see a nobleman cook."

"Well, you've been missing out," Misaki said as she poured the batter into a pan. "Watch this." She handed the pan to Robin, who placed his open palm on the metal underside and carefully began to cook the okonomiyaki.

"Whaaaaat?" Setsuko exclaimed in astonishment, then slapped Robin's arm, heedless of the now sizzling pan in his hands. "You should stay forever, Thundyil-san! We'll save a fortune on gas!"

Setsuko flirting with Robin was one of the weirder things that Misaki had had to process in recent memory. Then again, Setsuko flirted with a lot of people, so Misaki decided she wouldn't dwell on it.

"Keep that at forty-six degrees Koumbia," she told Robin. *"I'm going to go call in the children. Be right back."*

Nagasa, now four years old, had been tasked with watching Daniel closely and dousing him if he caught fire, but so far that hadn't proved necessary. Currently, the little tajaka was kicking a ball back and forth with Ayumi.

Despite the fire hazard, Daniel turned to be a delight to have around. Most children spent at least a little time being wary and uncomfortable in a strange place full of foreigners, but it seemed that a life with Robin had accustomed Daniel to strange places and people. By the end of day one, the little tajaka was already playing with Nagasa and Ayumi as if he were one of the cousins. It took painfully shy Izumo another day to warm up to him, but Daniel was so persistently friendly—continuously babbling to him in a combination of Lindish and Disaninke that Izumo didn't understand—that Izumo eventually relented and crept out of his shell.

Hiroshi was the only one of the children who didn't warm to Robin's effervescent son. He didn't speak to Daniel, instead regarding him like some kind of strange stray animal he was being forced to tolerate in his home.

"You could try being friendly to him," Misaki suggested over breakfast one morning. "He's just a boy, like you."

"He smells weird," Hiroshi said flatly, "like an unwashed numu."

"That's how all tajakalu smell," Misaki said. "It's just smoke."

"*Weird* smoke," Hiroshi said. "I don't like him."

"That's no reason to be rude, Hiro-kun."

Hiroshi's frown deepened. "He looks like a fonyaka."

Misaki laughed. "*We* look like fonyakalu, Hiro-kun. Daniel has dark skin like a tajaka, and straight, short hair like a Carythian. There's nothing fonyaka about him."

"*What are we talking about?*" Robin asked, having heard his son's name in the conversation.

"*Nothing important,*" Misaki said with a dismissive wave. "*Hiroshi just thinks your son looks like a fonyaka for some reason.*"

"*Oh.*" Robin raised his eyebrows at Hiroshi. "*Smart boy.*"

"*What?*"

"*I wasn't going to bring it up... for obvious reasons,*" he said apologetically, "*but...*" He lowered his voice. "*Daniel is a fonyaka—or a quarter of one, anyway. His mother was half... and he does have her nose.*" He offered Hiroshi a smile that the frigid six-year-old did not return. "*Well-spotted, kiddo.*"

"I don't like *him* either," Hiroshi said bluntly, aware enough to realize that Robin could not understand him.

Robin's smile dimmed as he looked into Hiroshi's eyes but his gentleness did not. Misaki didn't get the chance to properly apologize for her son's behavior until later that evening, after the children had gone to bed.

"*He's not a particularly friendly child, but he's usually well-mannered around his elders,*" she said, gathering the dirty chopsticks, pans, and rice bowls into a pile. "*I don't know what got into him today.*"

"*I don't mind,*" Robin assured her, setting down the washtub she had told him to retrieve.

"*Well, I do.*" Misaki tied her sleeves back, yanking the cloth strips hard in her annoyance. "*I'm not trying to raise brats.*"

"*Harsh,*" Robin said as Misaki opened the kitchen window and streamed water from the raindrum into the tub. While Takeru, Kwang Tae-min and Kotetsu Katashi were working hard on restoring Takayubi's running water, the Matsudas' kitchen sink was still too temperamental for washing dishes.

When the tub was full, Robin had heated the water with one hand. With the other, he took one dish at a time from the stack and put it in the tub. Misaki kept the hot water swirling with her right hand. When she sensed that a dish in the bottom of the tub was clean, she retrieved it with her left hand, shook the water from it, and set it in the stack of clean dishes.

"Tell me if it gets too hot," Robin said as steam rose in curls from the tub. *"I don't want to burn you."*

"Please," Misaki said in exasperation. *"Don't flatter yourself."*

Those brief moments, when she darted a hand in for a dish, brought them as close to touching as they had come in fifteen years. It was almost too close. Misaki would have worried about the flush rising in her cheeks, but it was dim enough that it probably wasn't visible. Besides, it was a normal reaction to heat.

When Robin had been quiet for a time, she glanced up at his face and found him staring at her forearms. Normally, her kimono covered the scars, but her sleeves were tied back.

"Pretty scary, right?" She smirked, snatching a rice bowl from the tub. *"Don't I look dangerous?"*

"Knives?" he asked, cocking his head at the crisscrossing lines.

"Bladed fans," Misaki tossed the bowl into the air, spinning the water droplets into vapor as it flipped over. *"If you can believe it."* She caught the rice bowl and stacked it with the others. For a moment the only sound was the quiet rush of the water swirling between them.

"How much did he see?" Robin asked at length.

"What?"

"Hiroshi. During the 'storm'... did he see the fighting?"

"Worse," Misaki said, and she told Robin what Hiroshi had done during the attack.

"I don't understand that boy," she admitted wearily. *"I never have, from the time he was an infant. All Matsudas are raised to be warriors, but it's like he came out of the womb already sharpened for the kill. You know me; I've always had a violent streak—this*

little sliver of darkness in me that wants to kill. With Hiroshi... I don't know what else there is in him. I worry that hard, violent impulse might be all of him."

"You really think so?"

"How else does a five-year-old boy kill a man?"

"To protect his mother?" Robin suggested in that tone of voice of his—as if believing the best of people were obvious and simple.

"I don't know..."

"You remember my brother, Rakesh, right?"

"Of course." Robin's surly identical twin had never been part of their friend group, but he had been in several of Misaki's classes.

"He did unimaginable things to keep the two of us alive in Disa, when we were little. I don't think you can judge a child too harshly, when they're so young and under that much stress—"

"I never said I blamed him," Misaki said. *"By all accounts, he did the right thing—an action any adult koro would be proud to claim. It just... it scares me, Robin. I can't help but feel like I've failed him somehow."*

"What do you mean? Knowing you, I'm sure you did everything you could to protect him."

"No, that's not—I mean—of course, I regret my weakness. What fighter doesn't? But it's more than that. My husband is a formidable fighter, but I don't think he relishes violence. Not the way I do—or... did, back when I was younger. If Hiroshi has some kind of deep-seated tendency toward violence, it's something he inherited from me. It should be down to me to help him master it. But then, he's also emotionless and distant, like his father, so I've never really been able to connect with him. Now he's killed a man, and I don't know what to do about that. I look at him and I might as well still be pinned down under that fonyaka... I still can't do anything to save him."

"Have you told him that you forgive him?" Robin said, *"That you love him anyway?"*

"Why would he need my forgiveness? He protected me. With how much of a little Matsuda he is, my forgiveness might be an insult to him."

"Maybe. But he needs to know that he has it."

"You really think so?"

"You know he does."

In the silence that followed, Misaki realized that Robin was right. When she had thought of herself as a murderer, it was Setsuko's simple belief in her goodness that had pulled her out of the darkness. Surely every person had that need, on some level.

"Just keep loving him," Robin said. *"That's what I did with my brother, and he turned out ok—well..."* He cocked his head, *"mostly okay."*

Misaki let out a laugh, remembering how ferociously the Thundyil twins used to argue about everything—from money, to politics, to fighting techniques. *"You can't pretend that you approve of the way he turned out."*

"But I do owe him my life," Robin said seriously, *"in every sense. He's not just the reason I got to grow up... He's the reason I got to grow up with clean hands. No matter how insufferable he was, no matter how we fought, he knew that I was grateful to him. I have to think that helped."*

"Well, we're Matsudas," Misaki said, retrieving another dish. *"None of us got out of this with clean hands."*

"How many of them did you kill?"

"Nine, by the time the night was done." She glanced up at Robin, and the water in the tub slowed its swirling. *"What? No lecture?"*

"You had to protect your family."

Misaki nodded stiffly. She wondered if he knew how much it meant to her to hear him say that... to know he didn't look down on her. Nami, he was right, wasn't he? The forgiveness did help.

"I actually think I should thank you."

"Thank me?" Misaki said, caught off guard.

"You always insisted you would have killed someone to protect me—and now I know you weren't kidding. I appreciate you controlling the impulse during all our work in Livingston. That must have been difficult, considering the position I put you in."

"You're so weird, Robin." Misaki shook the water from her hands and let her sleeves back down. *"How can you just.. forgive*

people you disagree with so fundamentally."

"Easily," Robin said. *"If you, and my brother, and Elleen weren't precisely the way you are, I wouldn't be alive to disagree with any of you."*

....

It was on the third day that Misaki and Takeru finally carved out time to sit down and speak with Robin in private. Takeru's students had all gone home, and Setsuko was watching the children in the courtyard, ready to douse Daniel if his powers threatened to set anything on fire.

"Thundyil-san has some questions he needs to ask both of us," Misaki explained to her husband, "in connection with one of his investigations, if that's alright with you?"

"He is our guest. Of course."

"Go ahead." Misaki nodded to Robin.

"I'm interested in learning more about the powers of Shirojima's great houses."

Misaki translated, and if there was anyone attuned enough to read Takeru's minutely differing expressions, it was Robin. He picked up on the older man's apprehension before Takeru even spoke.

"I don't mean to infringe on your secrets," he said quickly. *"I would never try to steal information that belongs to your bloodline, or Misaki's. In truth, my investigation is geared more toward determining if someone has already stolen that information."*

Misaki explained and Takeru agreed to hear their guest's questions. When she had translated her husband's response to Lindish, Robin produced two parcels from his bag and unwrapped them to reveal that each contained a small slab of metal. As he laid them on the table, Misaki realized that they were the halves of a crude axe head that appeared to have been broken in two.

"The first technique I wanted to ask you about is the Whispering Blade," Robin said. *"Has there ever been anyone outside your family able to make ice like that—ice that can cut through metal?"*

598

Misaki knew the answer was 'no,' but she translated for Takeru anyway, out of courtesy.

"Of course not," Takeru said. "What a stupid question."

"No," Misaki said, not translating the second part. *"Metal-cutting ice is exclusive to the Matsuda line."*

"Ask him why he's taken out those pieces of metal."

"He's curious what your questions have to do with those." She nodded toward the halved axe head.

"This axe belonged to a man I knew," Robin said. *"I know it's made of inferior metal, a far cry from Kuruma or Kotetsu steel, but it was cut by ice. I saw it with my own eyes."*

Misaki translated to Dialect as Robin slid the two pieces of metal across the table for Takeru to examine.

"The man holding it was cut in half too, if that's relevant," Robin said as Takeru ran his fingers over the steel, *"a big hulking fankatigi. Good man. Good fighter."*

After translating, Misaki added that in her experience, fankatigi muscle was often harder to cut through than steel.

Takeru was frowning at the metal in his hands. "Kore wa Sasayaiba no shiwaza jyanai desu."

Misaki looked at her husband for a moment, then turned to Robin. *"He says that cut is not the work of a Whispering Blade."*

"Are you sure?" Robin asked.

"Honki desuka?" Misaki translated.

In response, Takeru gave Robin a faintly indignant look. Then he threw one piece of the axe head into the air. As it came down, the Whispering Blade flashed from his hand, striking it in two.

"Oh!" Robin exclaimed in surprise.

As the Whispering Blade sublimated, one piece of the axe head landed neatly in Takeru's hand. The other flew toward Robin, who managed to snatch it out of the air without cutting himself on the sharp edge.

With a dry look, Takeru held up his piece to show Robin the flawlessly smooth surface where his Whispering Blade had sheared through.

"Oh..." Robin looked from the hunk of metal in Takeru's hand to

the one in his own. The stroke of Takeru's Whispering Blade had created a mirror-like surface much cleaner than the original break. *"I see."*

"Aru jutsu," Takeru said, "kono mura de futsuu ni tsukawanai…"

"There is a jijaka technique not often practiced in this village," Misaki translated for her husband as he continued, *"wherein the fighter uses water or ice to propel metal blades. Could your killer have been employing something like that?"*

"Maybe…"

"You would have to go much further south to find experts in that technique. My husband recommends the towns of Sabaisu and Nadamui."

"Thank you," Robin said. *"I'll look into that. There's one more technique I need to ask about."*

"Sure. What is it?"

"Tell me about Blood Puppetry."

Misaki looked at Robin in shock. *"What?"*

"Kare ima donna kettou-jutsu kikimashita?" Takeru asked, noticing the expression on his wife's face. *What has he asked about now?*

"Tsusano Kettou-jutsu… Chiningyo," Misaki answered.

"Sou desuka?" Takeru looked amused before suggesting that Misaki explain to her friend the difference between a bloodline technique and a ghost story.

"Hai," Misaki said hesitantly and then turned to Robin. *"The Blood Puppeteers are a myth."*

"I know," Robin said, *"but for the sake of argument, just humor me, okay? If it was possible, would it work on a tajaka?"* He had started absently massaging his arm. *"Or a fonyaka?"*

"Oh, yes." Misaki didn't have to consult Takeru on this technique; she was the blood manipulator. *"I have to assume, it would work like any other blood-based technique. Those work best on non-jijakalu, who have limited control of the liquid in their own bodies."*

"Delightful."

"But like Takeru said, it isn't possible. My father is the most

accomplished blood manipulator in generations, and even he says it's just a tall tale. There's never been a documented case, only rumors."

"I know..."

"There's a 'but' coming, isn't there?" Misaki said. *"Robin, what did you see?"*

"It's not something I saw or heard," he said, *"or I wouldn't be bothering you with these questions. I know that ears and eyes can be tricked, but it* happened *to me, Misaki. I felt it."*

"Kare nanto iimashita?" Takeru asked, and Misaki caught him up on the conversation. Unsurprisingly, he shared her skepticism, but Robin was not one to make up stories. She told Takeru as much.

"This is going to sound weird..." Robin looked between the two jijakalu. *"Could one of you give me your best shot?"*

"Excuse me?"

"Please," Robin said. *"I need one of you to try to control my blood. I need to feel it again, to be sure that was what happened to me before."*

"I... don't..." Unsettled and uncertain, Misaki turned and translated to Takeru, to see what he thought of the request.

"Sonna koto suru to wa sugoku abundai desu. Shinakute ga iinjyanai desune," Takeru said, frowning deeply. "Aku no jutsu desu."

"My husband says this is not something to trifle with," Misaki translated, *"and... Robin, I'm inclined to agree. There is evil in that kind of technique."*

"Please," Robin said. *"I think..."* He took a breath. *"I think this is how he killed my wife."*

Misaki was silent, staring at Robin until Takeru prompted her to speak. When she translated haltingly, Takeru asked for elaboration.

"She was one of the fastest fighters I've ever seen," Robin explained. *"He wouldn't have been able to hit her unless somehow she was immobilized. I should have been able to get up and do something, but I couldn't move. Please. I need to know why I couldn't move."*

"Oh..." Misaki had to swallow hard before translating.

Takeru looked at Robin for a long moment and then shortly said, "Help him."

Misaki felt her eyes widen. "What?"

"If it's somewhere in your power, if there is a bit of Blood Puppeteer in you, I think you should do as he asks."

"But—you just said—"

"I would never force you to do this," Takeru added, "but if he is your friend, I think you should try. Your ability to manipulate blood is on par with that of any historical Tsusano. If you don't help him, there may not be anyone who can."

"You're right," she said.

"So?" Robin looked from Misaki to Takeru.

"I still think this is a bad idea," Misaki said, *"but my husband thinks I should help you."*

"Oh—you're going to do it?" Robin said in surprise.

"Takeru is more powerful than I am, but he isn't a blood manipulator. If we're going to do this, it has to be me."

Robin looked apprehensive.

"Do you still want to try?" Misaki asked.

Robin appeared to steel himself and answered, *"Yes, if it's possible."*

"To be perfectly honest, I'm not sure if it is," Misaki said. *"You'll need to give me time to work up to it, and I'm going to need you to be very still."*

She decided to try on a body part with a small amount of blood, where she could easily take control of the circulation. It had to be at an extremity, far from the beating heart where Robin's nyama was at its strongest.

"Put your hand on the table."

Robin lifted his right arm.

"Your left," Misaki said. *"I don't know how safe this is. I don't want to do permanent damage to your dominant hand."*

The warning was a last-ditch effort to make Robin lose his nerve, but of course, it didn't work. He nodded and rested his left hand on the table, palm up. Misaki didn't touch him; she simply held her hand over his and reached out with her jiya. She wasn't sure if the sound came from her or Robin—but there was a sharp gasp as her ice met his inner heat.

It was here, in the depths of their interlocked power, that she fully realized how much he had changed. In youth, Robin's nyama had leapt and crackled against hers, painful but joyful at the same time. Somewhere on his path, Robin had encountered suffering he couldn't turn to energy, something that had broken him. That something sat deep inside him, heavy, like molten metal, hotter than fire but lacking the jubilant brilliance of flame.

The Robin Thundyil she had known was gone.

Of course, Misaki had changed too. Her power, which used to dance along the surface of the world, shallow and free, now sank deep into Robin's molten veins, matching its intensity. Most jijakalu couldn't control liquid as hot as a tajaka's blood, but Misaki had always embraced the heat, and she forced her jiya into Robin's circulation, making his veins her own.

"Now..." Misaki found her voice shaking. *"Try to close your fist."*

Robin did, and she pulled against his pinky with all her strength. In a horrible moment, she felt his muscles strain against her, and then convulse, the little finger contorted—and she released his blood with a gasp.

As Robin snatched his hand back, Misaki found herself slumping forward. The effort had exhausted her, but she could see on Robin's face that it had worked. As she caught herself on the edge of the table with shaking arms, Takeru put a hand on her shoulder. The touch steadied her, easing the flamelike spasms of pain from her body, but her eyes were still on Robin's face.

"That was it," he said. *"That was what he did to me... my whole body."*

"Your whole body?" Misaki said in disbelief. She had only taken control of Robin's smallest finger and it had left her spent.

Robin looked up at Misaki and Takeru. *"I thought that your houses were as close as theonites could get to gods."*

"We are," Misaki said.

"Then I think..." Robin stared down at his hand. *"I think I might*

have gotten on the wrong side of a god." He looked like he might be sick.

"Robin..." Misaki's voice was timid, almost imploring, as if she could call back the boy she had known, who had never looked so scared. She wanted to apologize for pulling that horror to the surface. He had asked her to, yes, but she was still sorry. *"Robin, I—"*

"Excuse me." Robin stood too quickly, his usually graceful movements unsteady. *"Thank you for your help, Koro Matsuda."* He bowed, still clutching the hand Misaki had manipulated. *"I just need to... Excuse me."* He left the room.

"Your friend is very odd," Takeru said, looking after him.

"He is."

"You should go after him."

"Takeru-sama?"

"We don't know the effects that technique will have on him. Please, see that he isn't damaged."

Misaki nodded and rose to follow Robin.

She found him in the sitting room, kneeling before the family shrine, the printed photos of Mamoru and Takashi staring down at him. Takashi's picture was an old one, from the day he married Setsuko. He held himself in a stately fashion, but Misaki suspected he had been a bit tipsy when it was taken, an un-Matsuda-like hint of a smile curling the corner of his mouth.

The picture of Mamoru was recent, taken during what no one realized would be Kumono Academy's last school picture day. He sat straight in his school uniform, trying far too hard to appear serious. To Misaki, it perfectly captured her son--a boy with enough talent to never have to try hard at anything, who had tried harder than everyone at everything, until the very end.

Robin had never met Mamoru or Takashi. That, in itself, created a strange hole in the universe—a ghost in its own right. He had already visited the shrine and prayed on his first day in Takayubi. There was no reason for him to be kneeling here, staring at the photos now. He hadn't even known them. But he stared at the photos with burning intensity as he clutched his left hand in his right to rub the finger Misaki had manipulated.

"What if it all happens again?" he asked in a low voice. *"What if I can't protect Daniel?"*

Misaki pressed her lips together for a moment before answering. *"Maybe you can't."*

"How do I live with that?" Robin looked up at her. *"How did you do it? All of you... how did you do it?"*

"There is no 'how,' Robin," Misaki sighed. *"It's not a duel or a street fight. There's no winning technique to get through it okay, no ice that can protect you from it, no fire that can burn it away. You know that. You've lost family before."*

"Not like you..." Robin shook his head. *"I've been a bad friend. I should have asked about him earlier. Even if you didn't want to talk about it, I could have at least asked—like you asked about my wife. I should have asked what he was like."*

The oversight hadn't bothered Misaki. It wasn't that she *couldn't* talk about Mamoru, but it still hurt. It would always hurt.

"If you feel so bad about not asking, why haven't you?" she asked, placing her hands on her hips.

"I'm afraid," Robin said, turning back to look at Mamoru's picture. *"I'm afraid he was wonderful. I'm afraid he was brilliant like you, and powerful, and brave, and everything he possibly could have been."*

"He was," Misaki said softly.

"And it didn't matter?" Robin said.

"It did *matter,"* Misaki said fiercely. *"At the end, he* made *it matter. There are people in this village now who are only alive because he was everything he could be, but..."*

But he's still gone.

She didn't need to say it aloud. The thought hung in the air all around them. Misaki had learned to live with the weight of it, to go about her day, cook, clean, and play with her living children while it hung there, quiet but ever present. Robin seemed to be buckling beneath it.

"Misaki..." When he turned to her, his warm eyes were clouded with tears. *"I'm so sorry."*

"Come now, Robin." She tried to smile. *"You're a grown man. Don't cry."*

"This should not have happened to you."

Misaki shook her head. *"This shouldn't happen to anyone."*

"What have I done, Misaki?" Robin asked, a single tear sliding down his cheek. *"What have I done?"*

"I don't know," she said, trying to keep her tone light. *"You don't seem willing to elaborate. All I've heard is some nonsense about a blood puppeteer god. But you always knew you were going to face danger in your line of work. You even understood, to an extent, that it was going to affect the people around you. This is—"*

"I didn't mean to have a child," Robin said. *"I had decided I wasn't going to."*

"What are you talking about? You always wanted kids." Even at sixteen, Robin had talked about wanting children.

"It's not about what I want. Misaki, my life—my responsibilities—have gotten way too dangerous for a child."

"Wasn't it always that way?" Misaki asked. He had just been blind to it. They had both been blind to it.

"Maybe," he sighed, *"but until recently—ironically, until Daniel was actually born—I thought I could become strong enough to protect the people I cared about from anything. I understand now that that's not true. And it's too late."* He put his head in his hands and dug his fingers into his short hair, fists clenching.

"It was a mistake. I didn't mean to get her pregnant. I didn't mean for there to be a child. This was all a mistake."

"Don't say that."

"But—"

"I'm serious!" Misaki said, genuinely angry. *"Don't ever say that again. Not in front of me, and certainly not in front of Daniel."*

Robin looked up at her in surprise as she continued.

"Maybe everything you say is true. Maybe you have made all the worst possible decisions up to this point, but that's not going to change the fact that you're here now and so is your son. Do you really think treating his existence like a mistake is going to do either of you any good?"

"I..."

"Get up," Misaki sighed.

"What—"

"Come with me." She grabbed the front of his kimono.

She had never been strong enough to haul Robin around, but in the past few months, she had learned to send her jiya through her blood on command. She lifted him to his feet as if he were no bigger than Izumo and pulled him from the room. She didn't release him until they had stopped on the deck overlooking the courtyard. While numuwu worked on the restaurant addition, Nagasa, Ayumi, and Daniel were playing in the spring grass.

"Look." Misaki pointed across the courtyard at Daniel. *"Look at him."*

Robin did.

"That's your son," Misaki said, her voice suddenly harsh with emotion. *"Now, I don't know how unfortunate the circumstances of his birth were, and I don't know what kind of evil is after you, but it doesn't matter. Even if his life is hard, if this all turns out just as horribly as you imagine, you won't regret him. You'll never regret him."*

Robin stared across the courtyard without responding. Nagasa was manipulating a snowball to zigzag around while Ayumi and Daniel raced to catch it, tripping on each other and shrieking with laughter.

"I can't tell you everything is going to be alright," Misaki said. *"Neither of us is that naïve anymore, but I can tell you to live the time you have with that boy instead of spending it on worry and regret. You might have twenty years with him. You might only have two. If you waste that time, if you miss it, then when it ends, you're going to feel like the biggest idiot who ever lived."*

A moment had passed before Misaki realized that she was crying. It had been a long time since she had cried for Mamoru. Seeing Robin here with his son brought all the emotion back to the surface. He didn't reach for her physically. This new adult Robin was not so forward, but she felt his heat tug at her skin.

"Is—um—" She gulped, drawing her sleeve across her eyes. *"Is*

your finger alright?"

"What?"

"Let me see." She snatched his hand before she could think better of it.

"Oh—" Robin said as their skin touched. *"Y-you don't have to—"*

"My husband told me to check for damage," Misaki said thickly.

They were barely touching—Misaki holding his smallest finger between her thumb and forefinger—but it burned.

"Well?" Robin said. *"Are my blood vessels all okay?"*

"Seems like," Misaki said, but she didn't let go.

Her index finger curled around his pinky and they knotted together—dark and light, hot and cold. She knew in that moment that this was one more thing that would never go away. She would always love Robin, the same way she would always miss Mamoru. For everything that had changed, this hadn't. It hurt. Gods in the Deep, it hurt, but it didn't consume her. After so long, she had learned to carry it like a woman.

"I spent a lot of time regretting," she admitted. *"I had a brilliant son, loving friends, and a whole family growing up all around me. And I was too wrapped up in my own regret to cherish it. I didn't take ownership of that life until it was all slipping through my fingers and it was too late."*

"I'm so sorry," Robin said. *"I wish there was something I could—"*

"Don't be sorry," Misaki said firmly. *"Just promise me that you won't make the same mistake. That's what you can do for me. That's all I want from you, Robin Thundyil."* Across the courtyard, Daniel was yipping in delight as Nagasa threw another snowball and he ran to get it. *"If that boy missed out on having you as a father, that really would be the biggest waste in the universe."*

Robin left Takayubi the next day.

Watching Daniel say goodbye to the Matsuda children provided a thoroughly entertaining distraction from the confusion of emotions tangling inside Misaki. One of the things she had forgotten about tajaka children was how much they liked hugging. Nagasa, Izumo, and Ayumi all took it reasonably well, only freezing in surprise for a moment before managing to smile and pat Daniel on the back. Hiroshi went rigid, his lips parted in utter indignation, as the little tajaka squeezed him tight. For a moment, Misaki worried that Daniel was about to get an ice spike through the chest but Setsuko eventually rescued Hiroshi, scooping Daniel up into an enthusiastic embrace.

"Goodbye, weird little thing!" She tousled Daniel's hair, making it stick up off his head at an abundance of silly angles. "Come again soon, ne?"

Depositing Daniel at his father's feet, Setsuko gave Robin a more reserved farewell, then herded Ayumi and the brothers away to give Misaki and Robin a moment.

"*I* will *be back to visit,*" Robin said as he tried to wrestle a squirming Daniel into his cloth sling. "*If you'll still have me... and if I'm still in the realm of the living.*"

"*What do you mean 'if'?*" Misaki said sharply. "*You made me a promise, remember?*"

"*What?*"

"*Years ago, in Livingston, the day we fought Yaotl Texca, you promised that you wouldn't get yourself killed. Now, I don't care what you've gotten yourself into, I'm holding you to that. Are we clear, Thundyil?*"

"*Crystal clear.*" Robin gave her a smile, but it faded after a moment. "*I wish I was clear on what to do next.*"

"*I'll tell you what you're going to do. You're going to go back home, use those Thundyil Firm millions to set up a nice stable life for your son, and get to work.*"

"*Work?*"

"*Yeah. I imagine there's a lot of crime-fighting to catch up on.*"

"*And you're sure that's the answer?*"

"*No,*" she admitted, "*but I once saw the idea of Firebird turn a boy into a man. When you get back to those streets and the reason you started down this path in the first place, I think you'll find your strength again.*"

"*Thank you,*" he said softly.

The familiar ache rose between them—the burning urge to rush into an embrace, contained in the knowledge that they never could. It strained there between them as their eyes met. They didn't shake, or shout, or cry as they had when they were teenagers. They bore its weight like the man and the woman they had become.

"Let's be older when we meet again," Misaki said resolutely.

"What?"

"Not just in years. Let's be better, and wiser, and brighter next time."

Robin nodded and made another attempt to get Daniel into the baby sling.

"No, Pita!" Daniel whined, trying to swat Robin's hands away. *"No, no!"*

"Yah jaand ka samay hai," Robin spoke sternly to Daniel in Disaninke. *"You little dummy, it's too far for you to walk."*

Daniel pouted and reached his hands up to his father. *"Ride,"* he said.

"You gonna hold on?"

"Yeah." Daniel nodded.

"Okay then." Robin stowed the cloth wrap in his bag and swung Daniel up onto his shoulders instead. *"Hold tight, kiddo,"* he reminded him and Daniel promptly took hold of Robin's hair. *"Nyama to you, Matsuda Misaki."*

"And to you, Firebird."

"Say 'bye-bye,' Daniel," Robin said and made a show of waving.

"Bye-bye!" Daniel said, flapping his hand around in something like a wave. *"Bye-bye!"* he kept repeating as Robin left the Matsuda compound and walked down the village path into the reddening sky. *"Bye-bye!"*

Last time, she had left Robin wounded. It had felt rather like breaking his wings and pushing him off a cliff to fall into the mists of memory. This time, with Daniel on his shoulders, it felt like sending him into the future. Like sending him off with wings.

Misaki watched until Robin and his son had disappeared down the mountainside. When she had watched him leave sixteen years ago, she had been knotted, fists clenched, rigid with pain. There had been a sense that once he was gone, she would be utterly alone. This time, bare feet toddled across the deck toward her, and a soft hand grasped her index finger.

"Thanks, Izumo," she murmured.

Her youngest son reached for her and she picked him up, resting her cheek against his head as the sky turned red. Izumo was dozing with a thumb in his mouth by the time a colder aura materialized behind Misaki.

"Has he gone already?" Takeru asked.

Misaki managed a small nod, her eyes still resting on the sinking sun.

"I apologize. I meant to be here to see him off."

"Usually you're home earlier," she said. "Where were you?"

"I was visiting Kwang Tae-min. Did you know that Robin Thundyil just paid Geomijul Communications for the replacement of all the info-com towers that were destroyed?"

"He what?"

"He also asked Kwang Tae-min which construction companies he would recommend to put down good roads and build a new orphanage. Then he hired them as well."

Misaki sighed. "I guess that doesn't surprise me."

"Doesn't it?"

"He's always had a soft spot for orphans. We refused his money, so he had to do something with it."

"I knew he was wealthy," Takeru said, "but it seems I underestimated him."

"This isn't actually an unusual thing for him to do," Misaki said. "Even before he could afford it, he was generous to a fault."

Takeru shook his head. "Not just generous. He's clever. In the short term, the construction will provide jobs to numuwu and koronu who have none. In the long term, the towers and roads will be a great help in bringing customers and supplies to the new businesses we are trying to start."

"That's good," Misaki said. "We'll be able to pay him back in the future."

She wasn't surprised that Robin had found a way to help behind her back, but they were still Matsudas. They still had their pride.

"Of course," Takeru said. "I..." He seemed to be choosing his words carefully. "I felt that it was important that we speak to Robin Thundyil in person about what happened after the storm. I apologize if having him here was uncomfortable for you."

"No," Misaki said earnestly. "No, he's an old friend. It wasn't uncomfortable. I'm just surprised that you would ever allow him here again after what he... after the last time we saw him."

"That was a long time ago," Takeru said. "Still, I am sorry if it was painful."

Misaki looked at her husband in surprise. "Wh-why would it—"

"I'm not stupid," he said mildly.

She pressed her lips together, feeling a guilty blush color her cheeks. "And you let him come here anyway?"

"I trust you."

With the last of the sun touching her skin on one side and Takeru's cold on the other, Misaki found herself fascinated by the sheer scope of her emotions. She hadn't been surprised to realize that she still loved Robin. What was strange was that she could love him and love Takeru at the same time. In the last year, she had been astonished by how much pain she could hold in her, but until she stood on that front deck with Takeru beside her and Izumo in her arms, she had never held this much love.

Maybe that was the 'how' Robin had been looking for, the simple magic by which she held herself together. Love for what she had and what was gone. Love no matter the pain.

"You two... enjoyed catching up?" Takeru asked.

"We did. Sorry he didn't end up having more concrete information on our assassin."

"That wasn't the only reason I asked him here."

"It wasn't?"

"I... didn't want to leave you in your silence." Takeru seemed to choose his words carefully. "Sixteen years. You never got to say goodbye."

Misaki turned to her husband with a smile. It was different from the manic fighter's smile that used to light her face when she raced down alleys chasing Robin's flames. Back then, all she had wanted was to seethe, and burn, and fight, and feel. That was before she knew pain, before she had seen her son's body on fire. Now she found herself appreciating the cool steadiness of Takeru's power.

"I have some work to finish," Takeru said and made to withdraw. "I'll leave you to—" Misaki caught his sleeve between her thumb and forefinger.

"Stay," she said softly and tugged him in until their bodies leaned together. "Stay and watch the sun set with me."

Red seeped from the sky like blood washed out to sea, leaving only the blue waves of evening. Shadows nestled into the contours of the mountainside, and instead of stiffening against Takeru's nyama, Misaki sank into it, letting it cool her, as daylight turned to dusk.

She breathed out and the last of the ghosts lifted. Not just Mamoru's. There had been other ghosts trapped here: the spirit of a ferocious teenage girl and the boy she loved. They were gone now too, passed into the realm of memory where they belonged, where they could rest. As the spirits faded, so did the last of the ties that had bound Misaki to the horizon for so many years, dissolving like threads of blood in water.

As Izumo blinked awake in her arms, Misaki turned inward, toward her home and her husband. Her little boy smiled up at her, and the future was no longer at the burning edge of the sea. It was here, in a softly beating heart and black eyes, bright with promise.

The adventures of the Matsudas and the Thundyils continue in M. L. Wang's

Theonite Series

CAST OF CHARACTERS

FAMILIES OF SHIROJIMA

(named characters only)

Names are listed in Kaigenese order: family name followed by given name (i. e. Matsuda Mamoru). Characters who are not Kaigenese or Ranganese have a comma between their family and given name (i. e. Thundyil, Robin). Shirojima names are grouped according to household and ordered by male hierarchy.

MATSUDA 待つ田

Takayubi's leading warrior house, masters of the Whispering Blade (also called Sasayaiba), traditional allies of the Yukino family, with a unique cross-kafo apprenticeship relationship with the Kotetsus.

TAKERU the First 岳瑠 the mythical founder of the Matsuda line, the first master of the Whispering Blade, husband of Mitsuki.
MITSUKI 美月 (née Yukino) oldest daughter of Tukino Izumi, wife of Takeru the First, older sister of Yukino Hayase.

MIZUDORI 水同 father of Susumu and several daughters, grandfather and swordmaster to Takashi and Takeru, master of the

Whispering Blade.

SUSUMU 進 only son of Mizudori, husband of Tatsuki, father of Takashi and Takeru.

TATSUKI 龍貴 (née Yukino) wife of Susumu, mother of Takashi and Takeru.

TAKASHI 傑 first son of Susumu and Tatsuki, husband of Setsuko, father of Ayumi, wielder of the swords Nagimaru and Namimaru, master of the Whispering Blade.

SETSUKO 節子 (née Chiba) wife of Takashi, mother of Ayumi.

AYUMI 歩海 only child of Takashi and Setsuko.

TAKERU 岳瑠 second son of Susumu and Tatsuki, husband of Misaki, father of Mamoru, Hiroshi, Nagasa, and Izumo, wielder of the sword Kyougetsu Yari (also called the Moon Spire), master of the Whispering Blade.

MISAKI 海咲 (née Tsusano, alias: Sirawu, the Shadow) oldest child of Tsusano Koya, wife of Takeru, mother of Mamoru, Hiroshi, Nagasa, and Izumo.

MAMORU 真守 first son of Takeru and Misaki, a student at Kumono Academy, close friends with Yukino Yuuta and Mizumaki Itsuki.

HIROSHI 洋 second son of Takeru and Misaki.

NAGASA 永佐 third son of Takeru and Misaki, close friends with Yukino Ryota.

IZUMO 出雲 fourth son of Takeru and Misaki.

YUKINO 雪之

Takayubi's second greatest warrior house, known for their skill in traditional swordplay, ancient allies of the Matsuda family, keepers of the ancestral sword Takenagi (the Bamboo Cutter).

IZUMI 泉 an early convert to Falleya from mythic times, who ruled Takayubi for two decades and dueled Matsuda Takeru the First.

HAYASE 早瀬 Izumi's son, Mitsuki's younger brother, credited with saving Falleya in Takayubi.

RYOSUKE 涼介 father of Dai and two other sons, resident of Takayubi's old village.

DAI 大 (nickname: Lightning Dai) second son of Ryosuke, husband of Hyori, father of Ryota, wielder of the sword Takenagi, swordmaster at Kumono Academy.

HYORI 孝利 (née Ikeno) wife of Dai, mother of Ryota.

RYOTA 涼大 only son of Dai and Hyori.

YUUTA 勇太 a student at Kumono Academy, close friends with Matsuda Mamoru and Mizumaki Itsuki, younger cousin of Dai, a resident of Takayubi's western village.

HITOMU 一夢 father of Kiyomu and Shiro, younger cousin of Ryosuke, a resident of Takayubi's old village.

KIYOMU 清 first son of Hitomu.

SHIRO 白 second son of Hitomu.

TSUSANO 津佐之

Ishihama's leading warrior house, residents of the Arashiki (also called the Stormfort), keepers of the ancestral sword Anryuu (also called the Riptide or the Undertaker), known for their skill in blood manipulation.

RAIDEN 雷電 (nickname: the Giant) a mythical hero, the first wielder of Anryuu.

KOYA 功也 father of Misaki, Kazu, Kaito, and Raiki.

KAZU 和 first son of Koya, husband of Aicha, father of Kaida and two younger children.

AICHA 愛子 (née Mizumaki) wife of Kazu, mother of Kaida and two younger children.

KAIDA 海田 daughter of Kazu and Aicha.

KAITO 海翔 second son of Koya.

RAIKI 雷貴 third son of Koya.

GINKAWA 銀川

An ancient warrior house with branches throughout Shirojima.

AOKI 青木 a swordsman from Takayubi's old village.

YUKIMI 雪美 a five-year-old girl from Takayubi's old village.

AMENO 雨之

An ancient warrior house with powerful branches across the Kusanagi Peninsula. Their main stronghold is in Tatsuyama, Shirojima, where they are the ruling family. Members of their Takayubi branch are vassals to the Matsuda house.

KENTARO 健太郎 a volunteer from Tatsuyama.

SAMUSA 寒さ a sword instructor at Takayubi's elementary school, a resident of Takayubi's old village.

IKENO 池之

An ancient Shirojima warrior house, traditional vassals of the Matsuda and Ameno houses.

TSUYOSA 強さ first son of the current Ikeno patriarch, a resident of Takayubi's old village.

SHUN 俊 a resident of Takayubi's old village, Tsuyosa's cousin.

KATAKOURI 硬氷

A lesser Takayubi warrior house notable for specializing in archery over swordplay, traditional vassals of the Matsuda house.

HAKUZORA 白空 a student at Kumono Academy, a resident of Takayubi's old village.

HISATO 壽人 father of Mayumi, a resident of Takayubi's old village, born with a twisted leg.

   MAYUMI 雅弓 daughter and caregiver to Hisato.

MIZUMAKI 水卷

An ancient lesser warrior house, traditional vassals of the Matsudas, the Yukinos, and the Ginkawas, with many other branches throughout Shirojima.

ITSUKI 樹 a student at Kumono Academy and resident of Takayubi's western village, close friends with Matsuda Mamoru and Yukino Yuuta.

TOKI 土岐 family patriarch, older brother of Hyousuke, a resident of Takayubi's old village.

FUYUHI 冬日 wife of Toki, mother of Fuyuko.

   FUYUKO 冬子 daughter of Toki and Fuyuko.

HYOUSUKE 兵介 younger brother of Toki.

CHIBA 千波

A family of common fishermen, merchants, and farmers with branches throughout Shirojima.

MIZUIRO 水色 a fisherman from a village near Takayubi.

KOTETSU 鋼鉄

Takayubi's leading blacksmith house, traditional smiths of the Matsudas, the Yukinos, and their vassals, with a unique cross-kafo mentor relationship with the Matsuda house, credited with the creation of many great swords, including Takenagi, Kurokouri, Kumokei, and Kyougetsu.

KENZOU 建造 the mythical blacksmith who saved Matsuda Takeru the First from the Yukino invaders and began the special relationship between their families.

CHIZUE 千壽恵 mother of Katashi.

KATASHI 堅 son of Chizue, husband of Tamami, father of Atsushi, Hotaru, Naoko, and Kyoko, Takayubi's best swordsmith.

TAMAMI 珠実 wife of Katashi, mother of Atsushi, Hotaru, Naoko, and Kyoko.

ATSUSHI 敦 first son of Katashi and Tamami, close friends with Matsuda Mamoru.

HOTARU 螢 second son of Katashi and Tamami.

NAOKO 直子 daughter of Katashi and Tamami.

KYOKO 鏡 daughter of Katashi and Tamami.

SAORI 沙織 a lacquer specialist in Takayubi's numu village, Katashi's cousin, mother of Kasumi and several children.

KASUMI 霞 Saori's oldest daughter, mother of her own small baby.

OTHER SHIROJIMA FAMILIES

HAKUYU 白水 a lesser Ishihama warrior house, traditional vassals of the Tsusano family.

UMIIRO 海色 a lesser Ishihama fishing and warrior house, traditional vassals of the Tsusano family.

TETSUKAI 鉄火 a Kusanagi blacksmith house, ancient relatives of the Kotetsu family.

ISHINO 石之 an Ishihama blacksmith house, traditional smiths of the Tsusanos and their vassals, credited with forging the Tsusanos' ancestral sword Anryuu.

HIBIKI 響き a minor jaseli house with branches throughout Shirojima and Hakudao.

OTHER CHARACTERS

BEK JIN-KYU a lieutenant in the Imperial Kaigenese Army

CHOU KYUNG-TEK a translator jaseli in the Imperial Kaigenese Army.

CHUN CHANG-HO a general in the Imperial Kaigenese Army.

ELDEN, ELLEEN (alias: Whitewing) a Hadean-Carythian koro, littigi, student at Daybreak Academy, classmate and close friend of Robin Thundyil and Tsusano Misaki.

GESSEKE, MORIBA a Yammanka jaseli working as an apprentice under Seydu Tirama.

GUANG YA-LI a Ranganese koro, a student at Daybreak Academy, Misaki's former roommate.

KALLEYSO (real name: Shumba Sekhmet) a Livingston crime lord.

KENDE, BUREMA a general in the Yamrmanka army.

KURUMA, KOLI a prolific Yammanka inventor, Misaki's former classmate from Daybreak Academy.

KWANG CHUL-HEE a northern Kaigenese transfer student at

Takayubi's Kumono Academy, son of Tae-min.

KWANG TAE-MIN a northern Kaigenese representative of Geomijul Communications, father of Chul-hee.

LO DONG-SOO the provincial governor of Shirojima, Kaigen.

MATHABA, KOLONKA a Livingston criminal allied with Yaotl Texca and Mecatl Silangwe.

SILANGWE, MECATL a Livingston criminal allied with Yaotl Texca and Kolonka Mathaba.

SONG BYUNG-WOO a colonel in the Imperial Kaigenese Army.

TARORE, AZAR a student at Daybreak Academy.

TEXCA, YAOTL a Livingston criminal allied with Kolonka Mathaba and Mecatl Silangwe.

TIRAMA, SEYDU a translator jaseli in the Yammanka army.

THUNDYIL, ROBIN (alias: Firebird) a Disanka-Carythian koro, classmate and close friend to Tsusano Misaki.

WAGADU, LANSANA a lieutenant general in the Yammanka army.

WANGARA, KINORO a Yammanka-Sizwean swordsman and former Daybreak Academy student, son of Makan, former upperclassman and friend to Tsusano Misaki.

WANGARA, MAKAN a Yammanka swordsman and Daybreak Academy instructor, father of Kinoro, swordmaster to Tsusano Misaki.

GLOSSARY

Abiria a country occupying the southern part of the continent of North Baxaria, a former Yammanka colony populated by the descendants of indigenous Abirians, Yammanka colonizers, and the Hadean slaves they brought with them.

adyn a person with no telekinetic abilities or enhanced strength (by Earth standards, a regular human being).

Appa an informal Kaigengua noun and term of address meaning 'Dad' or 'Papa.'

Arashiki the ancestral castle of the Tsusano family in Ishihama, Shirojima, Kaigen, also called the 'Stormfort.'

awa a Yammaninke word meaning 'so,' 'well,' 'okay,' 'good,' or 'um.'

ano a Shirojima Dialect word meaning 'that,' 'um,' or 'so.'

Ba or **-ba** a respectful Yammaninke suffix for an important person.

Baba the Sizwean word for 'Father.'

Baxaria the two continents encompassing the former Yammanka colonies of Carytha and Abiria, and the former Sizwean colonies of Malusia and Zandile, meaning 'New World' in Yammaninke.

bloodline technique a fighting maneuver or trade secret (usually necessitating specific powers) that is passed down through a single family line and kept secret from outsiders.

Blood Needle a jijaka bloodline technique unique to the Tsusano family, wherein the practicioner takes control of a small amount of the blood inside their victim's body and freezes it in the shape of needle, which is used to strike pressure points or pierce vital organs, called 'Chihari' in Shirojima Dialect.

Blood Puppeteer a jijaka powerful enough to control another person's entire body by manipulating their blood, thought to exist only in legends and ghost stories.

bogolan a traditional type of Yammanka fabric associated with wealth, status, and professionalism.

bokken a blunt practice sword with the approximate weight and dimensions of a katana, usually made of wood.

bound a Dunian measure of distance (roughly equivalent to 26.4 feet or 7.74 meters).

Carytha a country occupying the northern part of the continent of North Baxaria, a former Yammanka colony populated by the descendants of various indigenous peoples, Yammanka colonizers, and Hadean slaves.

-chan an informal Shirojima Dialect suffix used to address a close female friend and/or a female person of lower status than the speaker.

click a Dunian measure of distance based on how far the sound of a clicked tongue can carry (roughly equivalent to 1.75 miles).

Daybreak Academy a theonite academy in Livingston, Carytha.

dinma (pl: **dinmanu**) a Dunian measure of time (roughly equivalent to 0.43 seconds).

Disa a country on the continent of Namindugu, a former Yammanka colony populated by the primarily tajaka descendants of native Disankalu and Yammanka colonizers.

Disanka (pl: **Disankalu**) a person from Disa; an adjective describing a person or thing originating from the nation of Disa or its culture.

Disaninke the main language spoken in the country of Disa (similar to Earth's Hindi).

dojo a training space in Shirojima fighting tradition.

Donkili a song performed by finawu to teach others about the history of the world and its relationship to the religion of Falleya.

-dono a deeply formal Shirojima Dialect suffix (used to address a member of a high koro family).

Duna a planet that closely resembles Earth in a dimension that parallels ours, also used more generally to refer to the realm of the present and the living.

jakama (**pl. jakamanu**) a Yammaninke word meaning 'teacher,' 'mentor,' or 'master,' a formal address used by an apprentice to address their mentor.

fankatigi (pl. **fankatigiwu** or **fankatiwu**) a sub-theonite with physical strength equal to or surpassing that of the average theonite.

Falleke the holy union of God, Kiye, and Goddess, Nyaare, in the Yammanka-originating religion of Falleya.

Falleka a practitioner of Falleya.

Falleya a Yammanka religion centered on the Falleke (the marriage between God, Kiye and Goddess, Nyaare) practiced throughout Duna.

fina (pl: **finawu**) a member of the fina kafo; a prefix for a member of the fina kafo, similar to the English 'Mr.' or 'Ms.'

Firebird the crime-fighting alter ego Robin Thundyil.

fonya a shortened form of **fonyoya** the ability to control air.

fonyaka a shortened form of **fonyojaka** (pl: **fonyakalu**) a theonite with the ability to control air.

genkan the entryway of a traditional Shirojima house, typically where one takes off or puts on shoes.

Geomijul a Kaigenese tech company specializing in info-com device technology.

guli a Kaigenese unit of currency (roughly equivalent to 50 American cents).

gbaati a shortened form of **kewaati** or **kettewaati** (pl: **gbaatinu**) a Yammanka measure of time (36 minutes in Earth time).

Hades the westernmost country on the continent of Namindugu, a former Yammanka colony, the original homeland of most of Duna's adyns.

Haijing a coastal city in the modern Ranganese Union, a major military stronghold of the Kaigenese Empire prior to the Keleba, meaning 'Sea Capital' in Rangagua.

hakama a traditional type of loose pants worn by swordsmen, archers, and other martial artists in Shirojima, Kaigen.

haori a traditional long coat, worn by men of status in Shirojima, Kaigen.

Heibandao a coastal city in Holangoku, Kaigen.

Ishihama a town in Shirojima, Kaigen, ancestral home of the Tsusano family.

Jali a prefix for a member of the jaseli kafo, similar to the English 'Mr.' or 'Ms.'

Jaliden a diminutive address for a young member of the jaseli kafo.

Jalike a respectful address for a male member of the jaseli kafo, roughly equivalent to the English 'Sir.'

Jamu Kurankite a global peace-keeping and humanitarian aid force of highly trained theonites based in Yamma, meaning literally the 'Peace Army.'

Jamuttaana (pl: **Jamuttaananu**) an agent of the Jamu Kurankite.

jaseli (pl: **jaseliwu**) a member of the endogamous Yammanka social class that specializes in speech, music, and dance.

jijaka (pl: **jijakalu**) a theonite with the ability to control water.

jiya the ability to control water.

Jungsan the capital city of the Kaigenese Empire, meaning 'Middle Mountain' in Kaigengua.

Kaa- a Shirojima Dialect prefix used when addressing one's mother (typically combined with –chan or the more formal –san).

kafo (pl. **kafonu**) an endogamous occupation-based social class.

kafoka (pl. **kafokalu**) a Yammaninke word used to refer to people of a kafo other than the koro kafo and/or individuals outside one's own kafo.

Kaigen a country occupying the easternmost part of the continent of Namindugu, the center of the Kaigenese Empire, home to most of Duna's jijakalu.

Kaigengua the primary language spoken in the country of Kaigen and the Kaigenese Empire (similar to Earth's Korean).

kallaana a racial slur used to refer to white adyns, meaning 'corpse' in Yammaninke.

Kama a respectful address for the head of the household (one's fankama), one's mentor (one's jakama), or someone in a position of authority over the speaker, roughly equivalent to the English 'Master,' can be used as a suffix to a first or last name.

kamaya a term referring to traditional Yammanka social hierarchy, including but not limited to the practice of powerful koronu providing for members of other kafonu in exchange for their services, and young people serving and apprenticing with more experienced members of their own kafo.

katana a traditional Kaigenese sword.

kayiri synthetic material similar to paper but fireproof and sturdier.

Keleba the first and only open war fought between Duna's theonite superpowers, precipitated in 5291 when Daybreak Academy principal Oyeda Biida was assassinated along with several students, meaning 'Great War' in Yammaninke.

Kiye God in the Yammanka religion of Falleya, typically associated with soul, vitality, and the sun.

Kolunjara the capital city of Yamma.

koro (pl: **koronu**) a member of the warrior or commoner class, also called 'kele koro.'

Koro a prefix for a member of the manga koro or kele koro kafo, similar to the English 'Mr.' or 'Ms.'

Koroden a diminutive address for a young member of the manga koro or the kele koro kafo.

Koronkalo the fifth month of the twelve-month Dunian calendar, named for Queen Koronkan Wagadu, the third queen of Yamma (roughly coincides with Earth's November).

koroyaa a respectful address for a female member of the kele koro or manga koro kafo, roughly equivalent to the English 'ma'am.'

koyin (pl. **koyinu**) a Dunian unit of measure about the width of a grown man's thumb (roughly equivalent to three Earth centimeters).

Kri a mythical figure in the religion of Falleya, the first female human ancestor and the mother of all tajakalu.

Kribakalo the last month of the twelve-month Dunian calendar, named for the mythical human ancestor Kri from the Donkili (roughly coincides with Earth's June).

Kudazwe a Dunian continent divided between two nations—the independent country of Kudazwe and Kaigenese Kudazwe, belonging to the Kaigenese Empire.

Kumono Academy a private high school for koro boys in an old temple on Mt. Takayubi in Shirojima, Kaigen, traditionally headed by the Matsuda family.

Kumono Lake a spring-fed lake on Mt. Takayubi in Shirojima, Kaigen.

-kun an informal Shirojima Dialect suffix, used to address a close male friend and/or a male person of lower status than the speaker.

Kusanagi a peninsula in Shirojima, Kaigen, called the 'Sword of Kaigen' for its history of cutting down would-be invaders.

Kyougetsu Yari the name of the white-lacquered katana forged by Kotetsu Katashi and wielded by Matsuda Takeru, meaning literally 'Spear of the Mirror Moon' in Shirojima Dialect, also called the 'Moon Spire.'

Laaxara the realm of the afterlife in the religion of Falleya.

langa or **lanya** (pl: **langana**) a Yammaninke swear word meaning 'curse' or 'malediction.'

Lazou Linghun a fonyaka bloodline technique, wherein the fighter vacuums the air from their victim's body through the mouth, collapsing their lungs, meaning 'Soul Pull' in Rangagua.

Lindish a language originating on the western islands of Hades and spoken in some parts of Carytha and Abiria (nearly identical to Earth's English).

littigi (pl: **littigiwu** or **littiwu**) a sub-theonite with the ability to control light.

Livingston the largest city in the country of Carytha.

The Longhouse Confederacy a coalition of Native Abirian tribes that banded together in an attempt to oust the Yammanka colonizers from Abiria and establish an independent nation once in 5135 and again in 5290.

manga koro (pl. **manga koronu**) a member of the ruling kafo.

Manga Koro a Yammaninke prefix for a member of the manga koro kafo, similar to English 'Lord,' or 'Lady.'

mattaku a Shirojima Dialect expression of exasperation.

The Moon Spire the name of the white-lacquered katana wielded by Matsuda Takeru, called 'Kyougetsu Yari' or 'Kyougetsu' in Shirojima Dialect.

Na the Yammaninke word for 'Mom' or 'Mother.'

Nadamui a town on one of the farthest southern islands of Shirojima, meaning 'Hill of Tears' in the local dialect.

Nagi a mythical deity from the Donkili, the founding male ancestor in Namindugu, conflated with God, Kiye, in Ryuhon Falleya.

Nagidon the first day of the eight-day Dunian week, named for the mythical human ancestor Nagi from the Donkili, a day of work.

nagiji a word used to refer to written characters of Kaigenese and/or Ranganese origin.

Nagimaru the name of the Kotetsu-forged katana wielded by the ambidextrous Matsuda Takashi (usually in his right hand), companion to the shorter wakizashi, Namimaru.

Nagino Falleya the prevailing denomination of Falleya in the Kaigenese Empire, which subscribes to all the main beats of the Yammanka creation myth.

Nami a mythical deity from the Donkili, the founding female ancestor in Namindugu, conflated with Goddess, Nyaare, in Ryuhon Falleya.

Namimaru the name of the Kotetsu-forged wakizashi wielded by the ambidextrous Matsuda Takashi (usually in his left hand), companion to the longer katana, Nagimaru.

Na-Nyaare or **Na-Nyaxare** a reverent address for Goddess, Nyaare, in the Yammanka religion of Falleya, meaning literally 'Mother Nyaare,' sometimes used as a mild oath.

ne a Shirojima Dialect particle indicating a request for confirmation, similar to English 'no?' 'isn't it?' or 'okay?'

nenneko a Shirojima Dialect nonsense word used as a soothing filler sound in lullabies.

Nii- a Shirojima Dialect address for one's older brother (typically combined with the suffix –san or the more deferent –sama).

numu (pl: **numuwu**) a member of the endogamous Yammanka social class that specializes in the creation of tools, weapons, clayware, and machinery.

Numu a prefix for a member of the numu kafo, similar to the English 'Mr.' or 'Ms.'

Numuden a diminutive address for a young member of the numu kafo.

Nyaare or **Nyaxare** Goddess in the Yammanka religion of Falleya.

nyama any active or potential energy in the universe.

Ranga a country on the continent of Namindugu, a former colony of the Kaigenese Empire, the current center of the Ranganese Union, home to most of Duna's fonyakalu.

The Ranganese Union a collective of nation-states occupying most of the continent of Namindugu, populated by a mix of fonyakalu and jijakalu.

Rangagua the primary language spoken in the country of Ranga and most of the Ranganese Union (similar to Earth's Mandarin Chinese).

Ryuhon Falleya the oldest Kaigenese denomination of Falleya based in the idea that all life originates from the ocean, defined by a belief that Nagi and Nami are the true form of the two founding gods of the world.

Ryuhon Falleka (pl. **Ryuhon Fallekalu**) a practitioner of Ryuhon Falleya.

Sabaisu a town on one of the farthest southern islands of Shirojima, meaning 'Shark Coast' in the local dialect.

-sama a formal Shirojima Dialect suffix, used to address someone of higher status than the speaker.

-san a somewhat formal Shirojima Dialect suffix, a polite way to address an acquaintance, friend, or someone of similar to or slightly higher status than the speaker.

Sasayaiba a jijaka bloodline technique, unique to the Matsuda family, wherein the practicioner turns ice into a bladed weapon hard enough for use in combat against steel weapons and theoretically able to cut through anything, meaning 'Whispering Blade' in Shirojima Dialect.

senkuli (pl. **senkuliwu**) a member of the endogamous Yammanka glass-working class that specializes in glasswork.

Senpai a Shirojima Dialect noun, suffix, and term of address meaning 'upperclassman' or 'senior.'

Sensei a Shirojima Dialect noun, suffix, and term of address meaning 'teacher.'

shimatta a Shirojima Dialect exclamatory curse word.

Shirojima a province in the Kaigenese Empire, comprised of a cluster of large and small islands.

Shirojima Dialect the native language of Shirojima, Kaigen (similar to Earth's Japanese).

Sibikalo the sixth month of the twelve-month Dunian calendar, named for the mythical human ancestor Sibi from the Donkili (roughly coincides with Earth's December).

siira (pl. **siiranu**) a Dunian measure of time (roughly equivalent to 0.72

Earth minutes).

Sizwe the southernmost country on the continent of Kelendugu, populated mostly by tajakalu, a former imperial power and old rival of Yamma's.

Sokolokalo the fourth month of the twelve-month Dunian calendar, named for Queen Sokolo Wagadu, the second queen of Yamma (roughly coincides with Earth's October).

sondatigi (pl. **sondatigiwu** or **sondatiwu**) a sub-theonite with the ability to control sound.

sub-theonite a person who has special abilities but does not qualify as one of the original types of theonite (tajaka, jijaka, fonyaka, or the now extinct senjaka and kabaka) such as littigiwu, sondatigiwu, and fankatigiwu.

stride a Dunian measure of distance (roughly equivalent to a meter or 3.3 feet).

Suradon the seventh day of the eight-day Dunian week, named for the mythical human ancestor Sura from the Donkili, a day of rest and reflection.

tabi two-toed cloth shoes worn in Shirojima, Kaigen.

tajaka (pl: **tajakalu**) a theonite with the ability to control fire.

Takayubi a mountain on the tip of the Kusanagi Peninsula in Shirojima, Kaigen, home to a small cluster of villages that share its name.

Takayubi High School the public co-ed high school on Mt. Takayubi in Shirojima, Kaigen.

Takenagi the name of the ancestral Kotetsu-forged katana wielded by generations of Yukino swordsmen (the most recent being Yukino Dai), meaning 'Bamboo Cutter' in Shirojima Dialect.

tanto a traditional Kaigenese dagger.

taya the ability to control fire.

theonite a person with the ability to remotely manipulate their physical surroundings in the form of air, water, fire, or solid substances.

Thulanism an anti-imperialist ideology originating in Sizwe.

Tou- a Shirojima Dialect prefix used to address and refer to one's father, usually combined with the suffix '-san' or the more deferent '-sama.'

waati (pl. **waatinu**) a Dunian measure of time (one hour and 12 minutes in Earth time).

walla (pl: **wallanu**) a Yammanka unit of currency used throughout most of the world (roughly equivalent to two dollars).

wakizashi a traditional Kaigenese sword, shorter than a full-sized katana but significantly longer than a dagger, good for close-quarters combat where a katana is too long.

The Whispering Blade a jijaka bloodline technique, unique to the Matsuda family, wherein the jijaka turns ice into a bladed weapon strong enough for use in combat against steel and glass weapons, called 'Sasayaiba' in Shirojima Dialect.

xuro a strong Yammaninke swear word, similar in meaning and application to English 'shit.'

Yamma a country occupying the central and northwestern part of the continent of Kelendugu, populated mainly by tajakalu.

Yammanka (pl: **Yammankalu**) a person from Yamma; an adjective describing a person or thing originating from the nation of Yamma or its culture.

Yammanka obsidian refers to a set of particularly sturdy types of glass developed by Yamma's senkuliwu, including the industrial jonjo glass and the nearly impervious Zilazen glass.

Yammaninke the main language spoken in Yamma, the most widely-spoken language on the Planet Duna (similar to Earth's West African languages of Maninka, Bambara, and Soninke).

Read more from the world of Duna at
mlwangbooks.com

And don't miss M. L. Wang's ongoing
Theonite Series!

ABOUT THE AUTHOR

M. L. Wang was born in Wisconsin in 1992, decided she wanted to be an author at the age of nine, and never grew up. She received her Bachelor of Arts in history from Knox College in 2015 and currently splits her time between writing and working at a martial arts school in her home city of Madison.

www.mlwangbooks.com